Anne of the Island and Tales of Avonlea

Anne of the Island and Tales of Avonlea

Anne of the Island

Chronicles of Avonlea

Further Chronicles of Avonlea

By Lucy Maud Montgomery

Illustrated

GRAMERCY BOOKS
NEW YORK • AVENEL

The works in this collection were originally published in three separate volumes: *Anne of the Island, Chronicles of Avonlea,* and *Further Chronicles of Avonlea.* This volume contains the complete and unabridged texts of the original editions. They have been completely reset for this volume.

This edition is published by Gramercy Books, distributed by Random House Value Publishing, Inc. 40 Engelhard Avenue, Avenel, New Jersey 07001.

Random House
New York • Toronto • London • Sydney • Auckland

Printed and bound in the United States of America.

Library of Congress Cataloging-in-Publication Data
Montgomery, L. M. (Lucy Maud), 1874–1942.
    [Anne of the island]
    Anne of the island and tales of Avonlea / by Lucy Maud
    Montgomery.
    p.   cm.
    Contents: Anne of the island—Chronicles of Avonlea—Further
chronicles of Avonlea.
    ISBN 0–517–03705–X
    [1. Orphans—Fiction. 2. Country life—Fiction. 3. Prince
Edward Island—Fiction.] I. Montgomery, L.M. (Lucy Maud),
1874–1942. Chronicles of Avonlea. 1991. II. Montgomery, L.M.
(Lucy Maud) 1874–1942. Further chronicles of Avonlea. 1991.
III. Title.
PZ7.M768Ann   1991
[Fic]—dc20   90–49344
                                       CIP
                                       AC

ISBN 0–517–03705–X
9 8 7 6 5

CONTENTS

INTRODUCTION

INDULGE YOURSELF! Turn on the lamp, curl up in a blanket and stay up till dawn reading tale after tale of love lost and love regained, of society's outcasts finding their own special kinds of love, of exasperating village eccentrics acceding to the demands of love. For here, in this collection of works by Lucy Maud Montgomery, the author of *Anne of Green Gables,* we have the unique chance to read not only one of the most romantic of the novels about Anne, *Anne of the Island,* but also the short stories that are, in a sense, the rich ores from which the author formed her vision—a vision that was to be fully realized in the Anne novels. These short stories, collected in *Chronicles of Avonlea* and *Further Chronicles of Avonlea,* are devilishly funny and also overpoweringly romantic.

Just as the characters in her short stories are often intriguingly self-contradictory, the author herself, Lucy Maud Montgomery, was a complex person. Mollie Gillen, in her biography of Montgomery, *The Wheel of Things* (Fitzhenry & Whiteside Limited, Canada, 1975), sums up Maud, as she preferred to be called, as having:

> . . . a tempestuous, contradictory personality that
> was at once critical and warm-hearted, forgiving and

yet not a little spiteful, courageous and fearful, and
perhaps above all else, loyal to her own personal
code; . . .

As a young woman, Maud fell deeply in love with a farmer
she felt was not suited to her, while she was engaged to another
man she did not love, and she finally broke the engagement.
Interestingly, in "The Education of Betty," in *Further Chronicles,*
Maud put into young Betty's mouth the declaration, "It could
not have made me a happy woman to marry one man, loving
another." At the death of her grandfather in 1898, Maud
returned from "boarding out" as a "village schoolma'am" to
spend many years caring for her stern grandmother, which
caused her to feel herself to be emotionally isolated. In January,
1907, she wrote in her diary (*The Selected Journals of L. M.
Montgomery, Volume I: 1889–1910,* Mary Rubio and Elizabeth
Waterston, editors, Oxford University Press, Toronto, 1985):

> There are times when I hate life! Other times again
> when I love it fiercely with an agonized realization
> of how beautiful I *could* make it if I had only half
> a chance. It seems to me that every instinct of my
> nature is thwarted except that which urges me to
> literature. . . . Everything else is denied me. I can-
> not garden. I cannot have any social life, I cannot
> have friends visit me . . .

In her stories, Maud created comedy out of her own pain.
Her story, "The Materializing of Cecil," opens with the pro-
tagonist ruminating:

> It had never worried me in the least that I wasn't
> married, although everybody in Avonlea pitied old
> maids: but it *did* worry me, and I frankly confess
> it, that I never had a chance to be.

In 1919, after her grandmother's death, Maud married Ewan
MacDonald, a Presbyterian minister. She wrote in her diary:

> Perfect and rapturous happiness, such as marriage
> with a man I loved intensely would give me, I have
> ceased to hope for. I would be content with a
> workaday, bread-and-butter happiness . . .

Maud filled her days with the many duties and social respon-
sibilities of being a minister's wife, often squeezing her writing
into snatches of time. She appeared in public as a highly
competent wife, a skilled homemaker and cook, and a merry
and empathic conversationalist. But what Maud herself did not
know when she married MacDonald was that he was subject
to what she called "recurrent constitutional melancholia." After
eight years of marriage, the full force of his despair broke upon
their marriage. Maud spent agonized months guarding his secret
while trying to find both a correct diagnosis and care for him.
She wrote in her diary, (*The Selected Journals, Volume II:
1910–1921,* Rubio and Waterston, editors, Oxford University
Press, Toronto, 1987):

> [Religious melancholia] was one of the things I had
> always had the most deeply rooted horror of. Every
> trouble in my life seemed as nothing beside this.

Indeed, Maud's life was the stuff of the melodrama to be found
in the short stories she had already written.

In "The Little Brown Book of Miss Emily," Maud quoted
the poet Whittier:

> The outward, wayward life we see
> The hidden springs we may not know.

Hidden behind the workaday lives of the Avonlea inhabitants
are heroism and depths of passion not to be guessed at. Maud
became a master at what she described as the "mingling of
comedy and tragedy." And what fun it is to immerse ourselves
in her short stories! In *Chronicles* and *Further Chronicles,* we
read not only of a man-hating woman and a woman-hating
man quarantined together, but also of a woman forced by a
cat to make up her mind about marriage. And in another story,
the ghost of a dead woman returns to counsel her sister:

Nothing matters in all God's universe except love. There is no pride where I have been and no false ideals.

And, of course, it is in *Anne of the Island*, which tells of Anne's four years at college, that Anne must make her own choices about love, separating her infatuation with one suitor from the quiet, abiding love she finds with another.

In fact, Anne takes the first steps toward understanding the complexities of love when she contends with her friends' reactions to a melodramatic tale that she has written. She is dismayed when everyone who reads her story, "Averil's Atonement," likes her villain better than her hero:

> "Anyhow," resumed the merciless Mr. Harrison, "I don't see why *Maurice Lennox* didn't get her. He was twice the man the other is. He did bad things, but he *did* them. *Perceval* hadn't time for anything but mooning."
>
> . . . "*Maurice Lennox* was the villain," said Anne indignantly. "I don't see why every one likes him better than *Perceval*."
>
> "Perceval is too good. He's aggravating. Next time you write about a hero put a little spice of human nature in him."

Maud here pokes sly fun at the overblown tales she first wrote as a beginning writer—though it is easy to guess how those stories evolved into the more polished ones that would eventually appear collected in *Chronicles* and *Further Chonicles*. Yet Maud only reluctantly introduced romance into Anne's life. Before beginning *Anne of the Island*, Maud knew that her public was champing at the bit for Anne to be romantically involved, but she felt herself unequal to the task. She confided in her diary *(Selected Journals, Volume II)*:

> My forte is in humor. Only childhood and elderly people can be treated humorously in books. Young women in the bloom of youth and romance should

be sacred from humor. It is the time of sentiment
and I am not good at depicting sentiment . . .

Maud, writing with sly wit, wickedly transformed her own
dismay at having to initiate Anne into love's mysteries into
Anne's indignation at her readers' reactions to "Averil's Atonement." And we can imagine the roguish delight with which
Maud made Anne's best friend, Diana, secretly alter the ending
of Anne's story in order to submit it to a contest sponsored
by a baking powder company. When finally published, Anne's
bland hero, Perceval, clasping Averil in his arms, ends his
staunch declaration that "the beautiful coming years will bring
us the fulfillment of our home of dreams" by adding, "in which
we will never use any baking powder except Rollings Reliable."
Maud's revenge?

Anne of the Island was published a few years after *Chronicles
of Avonlea.* The latter volume was composed of tales originally
published in various magazines in the new century's first decade.
Because the public demand for stories about Anne was so great,
Maud's publisher, L. C. Page and Company of Boston, urged
her to rewrite some of her short stories and to introduce Anne
into several of them—thus was born *Chronicles of Avonlea.*
Although Maud did not want *Further Chronicles of Avonlea*
published as an "Avonlea" or "Anne book," it was also put
together from some of Maud's many stories which had previously appeared in magazines, as *Chronicles* was. However, by
whatever name it is called, Maud's "Avonlea" was molded from
her shrewd observations of daily life on Prince Edward Island.
Further Chronicles has become part of the recognized Montgomery oeuvre, and today provides insights into Maud's development as a writer.

Maud delighted in her island's individualists, who staunchly
remain true to themselves, whatever the cost. In "Each In His
Own Tongue," we read of the conflict faced by Felix, a natural
violinist, whose grandfather tries to prevent him from following
his musical gift. Felix remembers playing his instrument while
watching a storm:

"I played something that was terrible—it just
played itself—it seemed as if something was lost

that could never be found again. . . . I couldn't
help playing it . . ."
"What on earth did you play, child?"
"I don't know." Felix shivered. "It was awful—
it was dreadful. It was fit to break your heart. But
it *had* to be played, if I played anything at all."

Readers of Maud's other works are reminded of mute, beautiful Kilmeny who, unable to speak, also expresses herself through her violin (in Maud's novel *Kilmeny of the Orchard,* published by Avenel Books, in the collection *Days of Dreams and Laughter*).

We remember that in *Anne of Green Gables,* Anne leads her friends in attempting to act out Tennyson's famous poem, *The Lady of Shalott.* This was no accidental choice by Maud: in that poem, Tennyson's heroine, the beautiful Elaine, steps out of the isolated, protected life she has spent devoted to artistic pursuits, to become a player in the game of love. So, too, does Anne, in *Anne of the Island.* And, in their various hidden ways, Maud's heroes and heroines in *Chronicles* and *Further Chronicles* step out of themselves to face the world. In writing of these diverse, endearing, eccentric, and vulnerable individuals, Maud created a testament to her own courage.

Ellen S. Shapiro

Brooklyn, New York
1991

ABOUT THE AUTHOR

LUCY MAUD MONTGOMERY is best known for her novels about Anne of Green Gables, but she was a prolific writer who also regularly wrote short storeis and poems. By the second decade of the twentieth century, when her publisher asked to reprint some of her short stories as *Chronicles of Avonlea,* she had almost four hundred published stories, which had already appeared in various periodicals, from which to choose.

Born in 1874 in a small village in Prince Edward Island, Canada, and sent to live nearby with her strict, duty-bound maternal grandparents when her mother died less than two years later, Maud (as she preferred to be called) did not have consistent contact with her father.

All her life, Maud juggled the demands of her sense of duty with her desire to write. She spent three years as an Island schoolteacher, and also worked for nearly a year on a newspaper in Halifax, Nova Scotia. But she returned to her grandmother's home upon the death of her grandfather in 1898 and lived alone with her grandmother for most of the next thirteen years. Out of this period came *Anne of Green Gables,* her first novel, published in 1908, which was an immediate and lasting success. After her grandmother died, Maud married a Presbyterian minister; they had two sons. She found taking Anne into adulthood a burden, but wrote *Anne of the Island* at the insistence of her publisher. By the end of her life, she was to write eight novels about Anne and her family.

Maud died in 1942, deeply discouraged by both World War II and family problems, but her spunky heroines have been cherished by generations of readers.

NOTES ON THE
ART AND THE TEXT

The illustrations appearing on the title pages before each of the selections in this collection show Anne of Green Gables at different periods in her life and in varying moods. The paintings for *Anne of the Island* and *Chronicles of Avonlea* were created originally for the first editions of those books, early in the twentieth century. The illustration which precedes *Further Chronicles of Avonlea* was originally commissioned as a frontispiece for *Anne's House of Dreams,* (a later book in the series about Anne of Green Gables), but it is included here because it captures so well the charming flavor of quaint and well-loved Avonlea.

* * *

In another dimension, the publisher notes that the modern reader may be surprised to discover old-fashioned styles of punctuation and spelling in this edition, but these have been retained in order to convey the flavor of the original works, which were published early in the twentieth century.

CLAIRE BOOSS
Editor

1991

XV

Anne of the Island and Tales of Avonlea

Anne
of the
Island

TO
ALL THE GIRLS ALL OVER THE WORLD
WHO HAVE "WANTED MORE" ABOUT
ANNE

CHAPTER 1

THE SHADOW OF CHANGE

"HARVEST IS ended and summer is gone," quoted Anne Shirley, gazing across the shorn fields dreamily. She and Diana Barry had been picking apples in the Green Gables orchard, but were now resting from their labours in a sunny corner, where airy fleets of thistledown drifted by on the wings of a wind that was still summer-sweet with the incense of ferns in the Haunted Wood.

But everything in the landscape around them spoke of autumn. The sea was roaring hollowly in the distance, the fields were bare and sere, scarfed with golden rod, the brook valley below Green Gables overflowed with asters of ethereal purple, and the Lake of Shining Waters was blue—blue—blue; not the changeful blue of spring, nor the pale azure of summer, but a clear, steadfast, serene blue, as if the water were past all moods and tenses of emotion and had settled down to a tranquillity unbroken by fickle dreams.

"It has been a nice summer," said Diana, twisting the new ring on her left hand with a smile. "And Miss Lavendar's wedding seemed to come as a sort of crown to it. I suppose Mr. and Mrs. Irving are on the Pacific coast now."

"It seems to me they have been gone long enough to go around the world," sighed Anne. "I can't believe it is only a week since they were married. Everything has changed. Miss Lavendar and Mr. and Mrs. Allan gone—how lonely the manse looks with the shutters all closed! I went past it last night, and it made me feel as if everybody in it had died."

"We'll never get another minister as nice as Mr. Allan," said Diana, with gloomy conviction. "I suppose we'll have all kinds of supplies this winter, and half the Sundays no preaching at all. And you and Gilbert gone—it will be awfully dull."

"Fred will be here," insinuated Anne slyly.

"When is Mrs. Lynde going to move up?" asked Diana, as if she had not heard Anne's remark.

"Tomorrow. I'm glad she's coming—but it will be another change. Marilla and I cleared everything out of the spare room yesterday. Do you know, I hated to do it? Of course, it was silly—but it did seem as if we were committing sacrilege. That old spare room has always seemed like a shrine to me. When I was a child I thought it the most wonderful apartment in the world. You remember what a consuming desire I had to sleep in a spare room bed—but not the Green Gables spare room. Oh, no, never there! It would have been too terrible—I couldn't have slept a wink from awe. I never *walked* through that room when Marilla sent me in on an errand—no, indeed, I tiptoed through it and held my breath, as if I were in church, and felt relieved when I got out of it. The pictures of George Whitefield and the Duke of Wellington hung there, one on each side of the mirror, and frowned so sternly at me all the time I was in, especially if I dared peep in the mirror, which was the only one in the house that didn't twist my face a little. I always wondered how Marilla dared houseclean that room. And now it's not only cleaned but stripped bare. George Whitefield and the Duke have been relegated to the up-stairs hall. 'So passes the glory of this world,'" concluded Anne, with a laugh in which there was a little note of regret. It is never pleasant to have our old shrines desecrated, even when we have outgrown them.

"I'll be so lonesome when you go," moaned Diana for the hundredth time. "And to think you go next week!"

"But we're together still," said Anne cheerily. "We mustn't let next week rob us of this week's joy. I hate the thought of going myself—home and I are such good friends. Talk of being lonesome! It's I who should groan. *You'll* be here with any number of your old friends—*and* Fred! While I shall be alone among strangers, not knowing a soul!"

"*Except* Gilbert—*and* Charlie Sloane," said Diana, imitating Anne's italics and slyness.

"Charlie Sloane will be a great comfort, of course," agreed Anne sarcastically; whereupon both those irresponsible damsels laughed. Diana knew exactly what Anne thought of Charlie Sloane; but, despite sundry confidential talks, she did *not* know just what Anne thought of Gilbert Blythe. To be sure, Anne herself did not know that.

"The boys may be boarding at the other end of Kingsport, for all I know," Anne went on. "I am glad I'm going to Redmond, and I am sure I shall like it after a while. But for the first few weeks I know I won't. I shan't even have the comfort of looking forward to the weekend visit home, as I had when I went to Queen's. Christmas will seem like a thousand years away."

"Everything is changing—or going to change," said Diana sadly. "I have a feeling that things will never be the same again, Anne."

"We have come to a parting of the ways, I suppose," said Anne thoughtfully. "We had to come to it. Do you think, Diana, that being grown-up is really as nice as we used to imagine it would be when we were children?"

"I don't know—there are *some* nice things about it," answered Diana, again caressing her ring with that little smile which always had the effect of making Anne feel suddenly left out and inexperienced. "But there are so many puzzling things, too. Sometimes I feel as if being grown-up just frightened me— and then I would give anything to be a little girl again."

"I suppose we'll get used to being grown-up in time," said Anne cheerfully. "There won't be so many unexpected things about it by and by—though, after all, I fancy it's the unexpected things that give spice to life. We're eighteen, Diana. In two more years we'll be twenty. When I was ten I thought twenty was a green old age. In no time you'll be a staid, middle-aged matron, and I shall be nice, old maid Aunt Anne, coming to visit you in vacations. You'll always keep a corner for me, won't you, Di darling? Not the spare room, of course—old

maids can't aspire to spare rooms, and I shall be as 'umble as
Uriah Heep, and quite content with a little over-the-porch or
off-the-parlour cubby hole."

"What nonsense you do talk, Anne," laughed Diana. "You'll
marry somebody splendid and handsome and rich—and no
spare room in Avonlea will be half gorgeous enough for you—
and you'll turn up your nose at all the friends of your youth."

"That would be a pity; my nose is quite nice, but I fear
turning it up would spoil it," said Anne, patting that shapely
organ. "I haven't so many good features that I could afford to
spoil those I have; so, even if I should marry the King of the
Cannibal Islands, I promise you I won't turn up my nose at
you, Diana."

With another gay laugh the girls separated, Diana to return
to Orchard Slope, Anne to walk to the Post Office. She found
a letter awaiting her there, and when Gilbert Blythe overtook
her on the bridge over the Lake of Shining Waters she was
sparkling with the excitement of it.

"Priscilla Grant is going to Redmond, too," she exclaimed.
"Isn't that splendid? I hoped she would, but she didn't think
her father would consent. He has, however, and we're to board
together. I feel that I can face an army with banners—or all
the professors of Redmond in one fell phalanx—with a chum
like Priscilla by my side."

"I think we'll like Kingsport," said Gilbert. "It's a nice old
burg, they tell me, and has the finest natural park in the world.
I've heard that the scenery in it is magnificent."

"I wonder if it will be—can be—any more beautiful than
this," murmured Anne, looking around her with the loving,
enraptured eyes of those to whom "home" must always be the
loveliest spot in the world, no matter what fairer lands may
lie under alien stars.

They were leaning on the bridge of the old pond, drinking
deep of the enchantment of the dusk, just at the spot where
Anne had climbed from her sinking dory on the day Elaine
floated down to Camelot. The fine, empurpling dye of sunset
still stained the western skies, but the moon was rising and the
water lay like a great, silver dream in her light. Remembrance
wove a sweet and subtle spell over the two young creatures.

"You are very quiet, Anne," said Gilbert at last.

"I'm afraid to speak or move for fear all this wonderful beauty will vanish just like a broken silence," breathed Anne.

Gilbert suddenly laid his hand over the slender white one lying on the rail of the bridge. His hazel eyes deepened into darkness, his still boyish lips opened to say something of the dream and hope that thrilled his soul. But Anne snatched her hand away and turned quickly. The spell of the dusk was broken for her.

"I must go home," she exclaimed, with a rather overdone carelessness. "Marilla had a headache this afternoon, and I'm sure the twins will be in some dreadful mischief by this time. I really shouldn't have stayed away so long."

She chattered ceaselessly and inconsequentially until they reached the Green Gables lane. Poor Gilbert hardly had a chance to get a word in edgewise. Anne felt rather relieved when they parted. There had been a new, secret self-consciousness in her heart with regard to Gilbert, ever since that fleeting moment of revelation in the garden of Echo Lodge. Something alien had intruded into the old, perfect, school-day comradeship—something that threatened to mar it.

"I never felt glad to see Gilbert go before," she thought, half-resentfully, half-sorrowfully, as she walked alone up the lane. "Our friendship will be spoiled if he goes on with this nonsense. It mustn't be spoiled—I won't let it. Oh, *why* can't boys be just sensible!"

Anne had an uneasy doubt that it was not strictly "sensible" that she should still feel on her hand the warm pressure of Gilbert's, as distinctly as she had felt it for the swift second his had rested there; and still less sensible that the sensation was far from being an unpleasant one—very different from that which had attended a similar demonstration on Charlie Sloane's part, when she had been sitting out a dance with him at a White Sands party three nights before. Anne shivered over the disagreeable recollection. But all problems connected with infatuated swains vanished from her mind when she entered the homely, unsentimental atmosphere of the Green Gables kitchen where an eight-year-old boy was crying grievously on the sofa.

"What is the matter, Davy?" asked Anne, taking him up in her arms. "Where are Marilla and Dora?"

"Marilla's putting Dora to bed," sobbed Davy, "and I'm

crying 'cause Dora fell down the outside cellar steps, heels over head, and scraped all the skin off her nose, and—"

"Oh, well, don't cry about it, dear. Of course, you are sorry for her, but crying won't help her any. She'll be all right tomorrow. Crying never helps any one, Davy-boy, and—"

"I ain't crying 'cause Dora fell down cellar," said Davy, cutting short Anne's well-meant preachment with increasing bitterness. "I'm crying 'cause I wasn't there to see her fall. I'm always missing some fun or other, seems to me."

"Oh, Davy!" Anne choked back an unholy shriek of laughter. "Would you call it fun to see poor little Dora fall down the steps and get hurt?"

"She wasn't *much* hurt," said Davy defiantly.

"'Course, if she'd been killed I'd have been real sorry, Anne. But the Keiths ain't so easy killed. They're like the Blewetts, I guess. Herb Blewett fell off the hayloft last Wednesday, and rolled right down through the turnip chute into the box stall, where they had a fearful wild, cross horse, and rolled right under his heels. And still he got out alive, with only three bones broke. Mrs. Lynde says there are some folks you can't kill with a meat-axe. Is Mrs. Lynde coming here tomorrow, Anne?"

"Yes, Davy, and I hope you'll be always very nice and good to her."

"I'll be nice and good. But will she ever put me to bed at nights, Anne?"

"Perhaps. Why?"

"'Cause," said Davy very decidedly, "if she does I won't say my prayers before her like I do before you, Anne."

"Why not?"

"'Cause I don't think it would be nice to talk to God before strangers, Anne. Dora can say hers to Mrs. Lynde if she likes, but *I* won't. I'll wait till she's gone and then say 'em. Won't that be all right, Anne?"

"Yes, if you are sure you won't forget to say them, Davy-boy."

"Oh, I won't forget, you bet. I think saying my prayers is great fun. But it won't be as good fun saying them alone as saying them to you. I wish you'd stay home, Anne. I don't see what you want to go away and leave us for."

"I don't exactly *want* to, Davy, but I feel I ought to go."

"If you don't want to go you needn't. You're grown up. When *I'm* grown up I'm not going to do one single thing I don't want to do, Anne."

"All your life, Davy, you'll find yourself doing things you don't want to do."

"I won't," said Davy flatly. "Catch me! I have to do things I don't want to now, 'cause you and Marilla'll send me to bed if I don't. But when I grow up you can't do that, and there'll be nobody to tell me not to do things. Won't I have the time! Say, Anne, Milty Boulter says his mother says you're going to college to see if you can catch a man. Are you, Anne? I want to know."

For a second Anne burned with resentment. Then she laughed, reminding herself that Mrs. Boulter's crude vulgarity of thought and speech could not harm her.

"No, Davy, I'm not. I'm going to study and grow and learn about many things."

"What things?"

> " 'Shoes and ships and sealing wax
>   And cabbages and kings.' "

quoted Anne.

"But if you *did* want to catch a man how would you go about it? I want to know," persisted Davy, for whom the subject evidently possessed a certain fascination.

"You'd better ask Mrs. Boulter," said Anne thoughtlessly. "I think it's likely she knows more about the process than I do."

"I will, the next time I see her," said Davy gravely.

"Davy! If you do!" cried Anne, realizing her mistake.

"But you just told me to," protested Davy aggrieved.

"It's time you went to bed," decreed Anne, by way of getting out of the scrape.

After Davy had gone to bed Anne wandered down to Victoria Island and sat there alone, curtained with fine-spun, moonlit gloom, while the water laughed around her in a duet of brook and wind. Anne had always loved that brook. Many a dream had she spun over its sparkling water in days gone by. She forgot love-lorn youths, and the cayenne speeches of malicious neighbours, and all the problems of her girlish existence. In imagination she sailed over storied seas that wash the distant shining shores of "faëry lands forlorn," where lost Atlantis and Elysium lie, with the evening star for pilot, to the land of Heart's Desire. And she was richer in those dreams than in realities; for things seen pass away, but the things that are unseen are eternal.

CHAPTER 2

GARLANDS OF AUTUMN

THE FOLLOWING week sped swiftly, crowded with innumerable "last things," as Anne called them. Goodbye calls had to be made and received, being pleasant or otherwise, according to whether callers and called-upon were heartily in sympathy with Anne's hopes, or thought she was too much puffed-up over going to college and that it was their duty to "take her down a peg or two."

The A.V.I.S. gave a farewell party in honour of Anne and Gilbert one evening at the home of Josie Pye, choosing that place, partly because Mr. Pye's house was large and convenient, partly because it was strongly suspected that the Pye girls would have nothing to do with the affair if their offer of the house for the party was not accepted. It was a very pleasant little time, for the Pye girls were gracious, and said and did nothing to mar the harmony of the occasion—which was not according to their wont. Josie was unusually amiable—so much so that she even remarked condescendingly to Anne,

"Your new dress is rather becoming to you, Anne. Really, you look *almost pretty* in it."

"How kind of you to say so," responded Anne, with dancing eyes. Her sense of humour was developing, and the speeches that would have hurt her at fourteen were becoming merely food for amusement now. Josie suspected that Anne was laughing at her behind those wicked eyes; but she contented herself with whispering to Gertie, as they went down-stairs, that Anne Shirley would put on more airs than ever now that she was going to college—you'd see!

All the "old crowd" was there, full of mirth and zest and youthful light-heartedness. Diana Barry, rosy and dimpled, shadowed by the faithful Fred; Jane Andrews, neat and sensible and plain; Ruby Gillis, looking her handsomest and brightest in a cream silk blouse, with red geraniums in her golden hair; Gilbert Blythe and Charlie Sloane, both trying to keep as near the elusive Anne as possible; Carrie Sloane, looking pale and melancholy because, so it was reported, her father would not allow Oliver Kimball to come near the place; Moody Spurgeon MacPherson, whose round face and objectionable ears were as round and objectionable as ever; and Billy Andrews, who sat in a corner all the evening, chuckled when any one spoke to him, and watched Anne Shirley with a grin of pleasure on his broad, freckled countenance.

Anne had known beforehand of the party, but she had not known that she and Gilbert were, as the founders of the Society, to be presented with a very complimentary "address" and "tokens of respect"—in her case a volume of Shakespeare's plays, in Gilbert's a fountain pen. She was so taken by surprise and pleased by the nice things said in the address, read in Moody Spurgeon's most solemn and ministerial tones, that the tears quite drowned the sparkle of her big gray eyes. She had worked hard and faithfully for the A.V.I.S., and it warmed the cockles of her heart that the members appreciated her efforts so sincerely. And they were all so nice and friendly and jolly—even the Pye girls had their merits; at that moment Anne loved all the world.

She enjoyed the evening tremendously, but the end of it rather spoiled all. Gilbert again made the mistake of saying something sentimental to her as they ate their supper on the moonlit verandah; and Anne, to punish him, was gracious to Charlie Sloane and allowed the latter to walk home with her. She found, however, that revenge hurts nobody quite so much as the one who tries to inflict it. Gilbert walked airily off with Ruby Gillis, and Anne could hear them laughing and talking gaily as they loitered along in the still, crisp autumn air. They were evidently having the best of good times, while she was horribly bored by Charlie Sloane, who talked unbrokenly on, and never, even by accident, said one thing that was worth listening to. Anne gave an occasional absent "yes" or "no," and thought how beautiful Ruby had looked that night, how very goggly Charlie's eyes were in the moonlight—worse even than by daylight—and that the world, somehow, wasn't quite such a nice place as she had believed it to be earlier in the evening.

"I'm just tired out—that is what is the matter with me," she said, when she thankfully found herself alone in her own room. And she honestly believed it was. But a certain little gush of joy, as from some secret, unknown spring, bubbled up in her heart the next evening, when she saw Gilbert striding down through the Haunted Wood and crossing the old log bridge with that firm, quick step of his. So Gilbert was not going to spend this last evening with Ruby Gillis after all!

"You look tired, Anne," he said.

"I am tired, and, worse than that, I'm disgruntled. I'm tired because I've been packing my trunk and sewing all day. But I'm disgruntled because six women have been here to say goodbye to me, and every one of the six managed to say something that seemed to take the colour right out of life and leave it as gray and dismal and cheerless as a November morning."

"Spiteful old cats!" was Gilbert's elegant comment.

"Oh, no, they weren't," said Anne seriously. "That is just the trouble. If they had been spiteful cats I wouldn't have minded them. But they are all nice, kind, motherly souls, who like me and whom I like, and that is why what they said, or hinted, had such undue weight with me. They let me see they thought I was crazy going to Redmond and trying to take a B.A., and ever since I've been wondering if I am. Mrs. Peter Sloane sighed and said she hoped my strength would hold out till I got through; and at once I saw myself a hopeless victim of nervous prostration at the end of my third year; Mrs. Eben Wright said it must cost an awful lot to put in four years at Redmond; and I felt all over me that it was unpardonable in me to squander Marilla's money and my own on such a folly;

Mrs. Jasper Bell said she hoped I wouldn't let college spoil me, as it did some people; and I felt in my bones that the end of my four Redmond years would see me a most insufferable creature, thinking I knew it all, and looking down on everything and everybody in Avonlea; Mrs. Elisha Wright said she understood that Redmond girls, especially those who belonged to Kingsport, were 'dreadful dressy and stuck-up,' and she guessed I wouldn't feel much at home among them; and I saw myself, a snubbed, dowdy, humiliated country girl, shuffling through Redmond's classic halls in copper-toed boots."

Anne ended with a laugh and a sigh commingled. With her sensitive nature all disapproval had weight, even the disapproval of those for whose opinions she had scant respect. For the time being life was savourless, and ambition had gone out like a snuffed candle.

"You surely don't care for what they said," protested Gilbert. "You know exactly how narrow their outlook on life is, excellent creatures though they are. To do anything *they* have never done is anathema maranatha. You are the first Avonlea girl who has ever gone to college; and you know that all pioneers are considered to be afflicted with moonstruck madness."

"Oh, I know. But *feeling* is so different from *knowing*. My common sense tells me all you can say, but there are times when common sense has no power over me. Common nonsense takes possession of my soul. Really, after Mrs. Elisha went away I hardly had the heart to finish packing."

"You're just tired, Anne. Come, forget it all and take a walk with me—a ramble back through the woods beyond the marsh. There should be something there I want to show you."

"Should be! Don't you know if it is there?"

"No. I only know it should be, from something I saw there in spring. Come on. We'll pretend we are two children again and we'll go the way of the wind."

They started gaily off. Anne, remembering the unpleasantness of the preceding evening, was very nice to Gilbert; and Gilbert, who was learning wisdom, took care to be nothing save the schoolboy comrade again. Mrs. Lynde and Marilla watched them from the kitchen window.

"That'll be a match some day," Mrs. Lynde said approvingly.

Marilla winced slightly. In her heart she hoped it would, but it went against her grain to hear the matter spoken of in Mrs. Lynde's gossipy matter-of-fact way.

"They're only children yet," she said shortly.

Mrs. Lynde laughed good-naturedly.

"Anne is eighteen; I was married when I was that age. We old folks, Marilla, are too much given to thinking children never grow up, that's what. Anne is a young woman and Gilbert's a man, and he worships the ground she walks on, as any one can see. He's a fine fellow, and Anne can't do better. I hope she won't get any romantic nonsense into her head at Redmond. I don't approve of them co-educational places and never did, that's what. I don't believe," concluded Mrs. Lynde solemnly, "that the students at such colleges ever do much else than flirt."

"They must study a little," said Marilla, with a smile.

"Precious little," sniffed Mrs. Rachel. "However, I think Anne will. She never was flirtatious. But she doesn't appreciate Gilbert at his full value, that's what. Oh, I know girls! Charlie Sloane is wild about her, too, but I'd never advise her to marry a Sloane. The Sloanes are good, honest, respectable people, of course. But when all's said and done, they're *Sloanes*."

Marilla nodded. To an outsider, the statement that Sloanes were Sloanes might not be very illuminating, but she understood. Every village has such a family; good, honest, respectable people they may be, but *Sloanes* they are and must ever remain, though they speak with the tongues of men and angels.

Gilbert and Anne, happily unconscious that their future was thus being settled by Mrs. Rachel, were sauntering through the shadows of the Haunted Wood. Beyond, the harvest hills were basking in an amber sunset radiance, under a pale, aerial sky of rose and blue. The distant spruce groves were burnished bronze, and their long shadows barred the upland meadows. But around them a little wind sang among the fir tassels, and in it there was the note of autumn.

"This wood really is haunted now—by old memories," said Anne, stooping to gather a spray of ferns, bleached to waxen whiteness by frost. "It seems to me that the little girls Diana and I used to be play here still, and sit by the Dryad's Bubble in the twilights, trysting with the ghosts. Do you know, I can never go up this path in the dusk without feeling a bit of the old fright and shiver? There was one especially horrifying phantom which we created—the ghost of the murdered child that crept up behind you and laid cold fingers on yours. I confess that, to this day, I cannot help fancying its little, furtive footsteps behind me when I come here after nightfall. I'm not afraid of the White Lady or the headless man or the skeletons, but I wish I had never imagined that baby's ghost into existence. How angry Marilla and Mrs. Barry were over that affair," concluded Anne, with reminiscent laughter.

The woods around the head of the marsh were full of purple vistas, threaded with gossamers. Past a dour plantation of gnarled spruces and a maple-fringed, sun-warm valley they found the "something" Gilbert was looking for.

"Ah, here it is," he said with satisfaction.

"An apple tree—and away back here!" exclaimed Anne delightedly.

"Yes, a veritable apple-bearing apple tree, too, here in the very midst of pines and beeches, a mile away from any orchard. I was here one day last spring and found it, all white with blossom. So I resolved I'd come again in the fall and see if it had been apples. See, it's loaded. They look good, too—tawny as russets but with a dusky red cheek. Most wild seedlings are green and uninviting."

"I suppose it sprang years ago from some chance-sown seed," said Anne dreamily. "And how it has grown and flourished and held its own here all alone among aliens, the brave determined thing!"

"Here's a fallen tree with a cushion of moss. Sit down, Anne— it will serve for a woodland throne. I'll climb for some apples. They all grow high—the tree had to reach up to the sunlight."

The apples proved to be delicious. Under the tawny skin was a white, white flesh, faintly veined with red; and, besides their own proper apple taste, they had a certain wild, delightful tang no orchard-grown apple ever possessed.

"The fatal apple of Eden couldn't have had a rarer flavour," commented Anne. "But it's time we were going home. See, it was twilight three minutes ago and now it's moonlight. What a pity we couldn't have caught the moment of transformation. But such moments never are caught, I suppose."

"Let's go back around the marsh and home by way of Lover's Lane. Do you feel as disgruntled now as when you started out, Anne?"

"Not I. Those apples have been as manna to a hungry soul. I feel that I shall love Redmond and have a splendid four years there."

"And after those four years—what?"

"Oh, there's another bend in the road at their end," answered Anne lightly. "I've no idea what may be around it—I don't want to have. It's nicer not to know."

Lover's Lane was a dear place that night, still and mysteriously dim in the pale radiance of the moonlight. They loitered through it in a pleasant chummy silence, neither caring to talk.

"If Gilbert were always as he has been this evening how nice and simple everything would be," reflected Anne.

Gilbert was looking at Anne, as she walked along. In her light dress, with her slender delicacy, she made him think of a white iris.

"I wonder if I can ever make her care for me," he thought, with a pang of self-distrust.

CHAPTER 3

GREETING AND FAREWELL

CHARLIE SLOANE, Gilbert Blythe and Anne Shirley left Avonlea the following Monday morning. Anne had hoped for a fine day. Diana was to drive her to the station and they wanted this, their last drive together for some time, to be a pleasant one. But when Anne went to bed Sunday night the east wind was moaning around Green Gables with an ominous prophecy which was fulfilled in the morning. Anne awoke to find rain-drops pattering against her window and shadowing the pond's gray surface with widening rings; hills and sea were hidden in mist, and the whole world seemed dim and dreary. Anne dressed in the cheerless gray dawn, for an early start was necessary to catch the boat train; she struggled against the tears that *would* well up in her eyes in spite of herself. She was leaving the home that was so dear to her, and something told her that she was leaving it forever, save as a holiday refuge. Things would never be the same again; coming back for vacations would not be living there. And oh, how dear and beloved everything was— that little white porch room, sacred to the dreams of girlhood, the old Snow Queen at the window, the brook in the hollow, the Dryad's Bubble, the Haunted Wood, and Lover's Lane— all the thousand and one dear spots where memories of the old years bided. Could she ever be really happy anywhere else?

Breakfast at Green Gables that morning was a rather doleful meal. Davy, for the first time in his life probably, could not eat, but blubbered shamelessly over his porridge. Nobody else seemed to have much appetite, save Dora, who tucked away her rations comfortably. Dora, like the immortal and most prudent Charlotte, who "went on cutting bread and butter" when her frenzied lover's body had been carried past on a shutter, was one of those fortunate creatures who are seldom disturbed by anything. Even at eight it took a great deal to ruffle Dora's placidity. She was sorry Anne was going away, of course, but was that any reason why she should fail to appreciate a poached egg on toast? Not at all. And, seeing that Davy could not eat his, Dora ate it for him.

Promptly on time Diana appeared with horse and buggy, her rosy face glowing above her raincoat. The goodbyes had to be said then somehow. Mrs. Lynde came in from her quarters to give Anne a hearty embrace and warn her to be careful of her health, whatever she did. Marilla, brusque and tearless, pecked Anne's cheek and said she supposed they'd hear from her when she got settled. A casual observer might have concluded that Anne's going mattered very little to her—unless said observer had happened to get a good look in her eyes. Dora kissed Anne primly and squeezed out two decorous little tears; but Davy, who had been crying on the back porch step ever since they rose from the table, refused to say goodbye at all. When he saw Anne coming towards him he sprang to his feet, bolted up the back stairs and hid in a clothes closet, out of which he would not come. His muffled howls were the last sounds Anne heard as she left Green Gables.

It rained heavily all the way to Bright River, to which station they had to go, since the branch line train from Carmody did not connect with the boat train. Charlie and Gilbert were on the station platform when they reached it, and the train was whistling. Anne had just time to get her ticket and trunk check, say a hurried farewell to Diana, and hasten on board. She wished she were going back with Diana to Avonlea; she knew she was going to die of homesickness. And oh, if only that dismal rain would stop pouring down as if the whole world were weeping over summer vanished and joys departed! Even Gilbert's presence brought her no comfort, for Charlie Sloane was there, too, and Sloanishness could be tolerated only in fine weather. It was absolutely insufferable in rain.

But when the boat steamed out of Charlottetown harbour things took a turn for the better. The rain ceased and the sun began to burst out goldenly now and again between the rents in the clouds, burnishing the gray seas with copper-hued radiance, and lighting up the mists that curtained the Island's red shores with gleams of gold foretokening a fine day after all. Besides, Charlie Sloane promptly became so seasick that he had to go below, and Anne and Gilbert were left alone on deck.

"I am very glad that all the Sloanes get seasick as soon as they go on water," thought Anne mercilessly. "I am sure I couldn't take my farewell look at the 'ould sod' with Charlie standing there pretending to look sentimentally at it, too."

"Well, we're off," remarked Gilbert unsentimentally.

"Yes, I feel like Byron's 'Childe Harold'—only it isn't really my 'native shore' that I'm watching," said Anne, winking her gray eyes vigorously. "Nova Scotia is that, I suppose. But one's native shore is the land one loves the best, and that's good old P.E.I. for me. I can't believe I didn't always live here. Those eleven years before I came seem like a bad dream. It's seven years since I crossed on this boat—the evening Mrs. Spencer brought me over from Hopetown. I can see myself, in that dreadful old wincey dress and faded sailor hat, exploring decks and cabins with enraptured curiosity. It was a fine evening;

and how those red Island shores did gleam in the sunshine. Now I'm crossing the strait again. Oh, Gilbert, I do hope I'll like Redmond and Kingsport, but I'm sure I won't!"

"Where's all your philosophy gone, Anne?"

"It's all submerged under a great, swamping wave of loneliness and homesickness. I've longed for three years to go to Redmond—and now I'm going—and I wish I weren't! Never mind! I shall be cheerful and philosophical again after I have just one good cry. I *must* have that, 'as a went'—and I'll have to wait until I get into my boarding-house bed tonight, wherever it may be, before I can have it. Then Anne will be herself again. I wonder if Davy has come out of the closet yet."

It was nine that night when their train reached Kingsport, and they found themselves in the blue-white glare of the crowded station. Anne felt horribly bewildered, but a moment later she was seized by Priscilla Grant, who had come to Kingsport on Saturday.

"Here you are, beloved! And I suppose you're as tired as I was when I got here Saturday night."

"Tired! Priscilla, don't talk of it. I'm tired, and green, and provincial, and only about ten years old. For pity's sake take your poor, broken-down chum to some place where she can hear herself think."

"I'll take you right up to our boarding-house. I've a cab ready outside."

"It's such a blessing you're here, Prissy. If you weren't I think I should just sit down on my suit-case, here and now, and weep bitter tears. What a comfort one familiar face is in a howling wilderness of strangers!"

"Is that Gilbert Blythe over there, Anne? How he has grown up this past year! He was only a schoolboy when I taught in Carmody. And of course that's Charlie Sloane. *He* hasn't changed—couldn't! He looked just like that when he was born, and he'll look like that when he's eighty. This way, dear. We'll be home in twenty minutes."

"Home!" groaned Anne. "You mean we'll be in some horrible boarding-house, in a still more horrible hall bedroom, looking out on a dingy back yard."

"It isn't a horrible boarding-house, Anne-girl. Here's our cab. Hop in—the driver will get your trunk. Oh, yes, the boarding-house—it's really a very nice place of its kind, as you'll admit tomorrow morning when a good night's sleep has turned your blues rosy pink. It's a big, old fashioned, gray stone house on St. John Street, just a nice little constitutional from Redmond. It used to be the 'residence' of great folk, but fashion has deserted St. John Street and its houses only dream now of better days. They're so big that the people living in them have to take boarders just to fill up. At least, that is the reason our landladies are very anxious to impress on us. They're delicious, Anne—our landladies, I mean."

"How many are there?"

"Two. Miss Hannah Harvey and Miss Ada Harvey. They were born twins about fifty years ago."

"I can't get away from twins, it seems," smiled Anne. "Wherever I go they confront me."

"Oh, they're not twins now, dear. After they reached the age of thirty they never were twins again. Miss Hannah has grown old, not too gracefully, and Miss Ada has stayed thirty, less gracefully still. I don't know whether Miss Hannah can smile or not; I've never caught her at it so far, but Miss Ada smiles all the time and that's worse. However, they're nice, kind souls, and they take two boarders every year because Miss Hannah's economical soul cannot bear to 'waste room space'—not because they need to or have to, as Miss Ada has told me seven times since Saturday night. As for our rooms, I admit they are hall bedrooms, and mine does look out on the back yard. Your room is a front one and looks out on Old St. John's graveyard, which is just across the street."

"That sounds gruesome," shivered Anne. "I think I'd rather have the back yard view."

"Oh, no, you wouldn't. Wait and see. Old St. John's is a darling place. It's been a graveyard so long that it's ceased to be one and has become one of the sights of Kingsport. I was all through it yesterday for a pleasure exertion. There's a big stone wall and a row of enormous trees all round it, and rows of trees all through it, and the queerest old tombstones, with the queerest and quaintest inscriptions. You'll go there to study, Anne, see if you don't. Of course, nobody is ever buried there now. But a few years ago they put up a beautiful monument to the memory of Nova Scotian soldiers who fell in the Crimean

War. It is just opposite the entrance gates and there's 'scope for imagination' in it, as you used to say. Here's your trunk at last—and the boys coming to say good-night. Must I really shake hands with Charlie Sloane, Anne? His hands are always so cold and fishy-feeling. We must ask them to call occasionally. Miss Hannah gravely told me we could have 'young gentlemen callers' two evenings in the week, if they went away at a reasonable hour; and Miss Ada asked me, smiling, please to be sure they didn't sit on her beautiful cushions. I promised to see to it; but goodness knows where else they *can* sit, unless they sit on the floor, for there are cushions on *everything*. Miss Ada even has an elaborate Battenburg one on top of the piano."

Anne was laughing by this time. Priscilla's gay chatter had the intended effect of cheering her up; homesickness vanished for the time being, and did not even return in full force when she finally found herself alone in her little bedroom. She went to her window and looked out. The street below was dim and quiet. Across it the moon was shining above the trees in Old St. John's, just behind the great dark head of the lion on the monument. Anne wondered if it could have been only that morning that she had left Green Gables. She had the sense of a long passage of time which one day of change and travel gives.

"I suppose that very moon is looking down on Green Gables now," she mused. "But I won't think about it—that way homesickness lies. I'm not even going to have my good cry. I'll put that off to a more convenient season, and just now I'll go calmly and sensibly to bed and to sleep."

CHAPTER 4

APRIL'S LADY

KINGSPORT IS a quaint old town, hearking back to early Colonial days, and wrapped in its ancient atmosphere, as some fine old dame in garments fashioned like those of her youth. Here and there it sprouts out into modernity, but at heart it is still unspoiled; it is full of curious relics, and haloed by the romance of many legends of the past. Once it was a mere frontier station on the fringe of the wilderness, and those were the days when Indians kept life from being monotonous to the settlers. Then it grew to be a bone of contention between the British and the French, being occupied now by the one and now by the other, emerging from each occupation with some fresh scar of battling nations branded on it.

It has in its park a martello tower, autographed all over by tourists, a dismantled old French fort on the hills beyond the town, and several antiquated cannon in its public squares. It has other historic spots also, which may be hunted out by the curious, and none is more quaint and delightful than Old St. John's Cemetery at the very core of the town, with streets of quiet, old-time houses on two sides, and busy, bustling, modern thoroughfares on the others. Every citizen of Kingsport feels a thrill of possessive pride in Old St. John's, for, if he be of any pretensions at all, he has an ancestor buried there, with a queer, crooked slab at his head, or else sprawling protectively over the grave, on which all the main facts of his history are recorded. For the most part no great art or skill was lavished on those old tombstones. The larger number are of roughly chiselled brown or gray native stone, and only in a few cases is there any attempt at ornamentation. Some are adorned with skull and cross-bones, and this grizzly decoration is frequently coupled with a cherub's head. Many are prostrate and in ruins. Into almost all Time's tooth has been gnawing, until some inscriptions have been completely effaced, and others can only be deciphered with difficulty. The graveyard is very full and very bowery, for it is surrounded and intersected by rows of elms

22

and willows, beneath whose shade the sleepers must lie very dreamlessly, forever crooned to by the winds and leaves over them, and quite undisturbed by the clamour of traffic just beyond.

Anne took the first of many rambles in Old St. John's the next afternoon. She and Priscilla had gone to Redmond in the forenoon and registered as students, after which there was nothing more to do that day. The girls gladly made their escape, for it was not exhilarating to be surrounded by crowds of strangers, most of whom had a rather alien appearance, as if not quite sure where they belonged.

The "freshettes" stood about in detached groups of two or three, looking askance at each other; the "freshies," wiser in their day and generation, had banded themselves together on the big staircase of the entrance hall, where they were shouting out glees with all the vigour of youthful lungs, as a species of defiance to their traditional enemies, the Sophomores, a few of whom were prowling loftily about, looking properly disdainful of the "unlicked cubs" on the stairs. Gilbert and Charlie were nowhere to be seen.

"Little did I think the day would ever come when I'd be glad of the sight of a Sloane," said Priscilla, as they crossed the campus, "but I'd welcome Charlie's goggle eyes almost ecstatically. At least, they'd be familiar eyes."

"Oh," sighed Anne. "I can't describe how I felt when I was standing there, waiting my turn to be registered—as insignificant as the teeniest drop in a most enormous bucket. It's bad enough to feel insignificant, but it's unbearable to have it grained into your soul that you will never, *can* never, be anything but insignificant, and that is how I did feel—as if I were invisible to the naked eye and some of those Sophs might step on me. I knew I would go down to my grave unwept, unhonoured and unsung."

"Wait till next year," comforted Priscilla. "Then we'll be able to look as bored and sophisticated as any Sophomore of them all. No doubt it is rather dreadful to feel insignificant; but I think it's better than to feel as big and awkward as I did—as if I were sprawled all over Redmond. That's how I felt—I suppose because I was a good two inches taller than any one

else in the crowd. *I* wasn't afraid a Soph might walk over me;
I was afraid they'd take me for an elephant, or an overgrown
sample of a potato-fed Islander."

"I suppose the trouble is we can't forgive big Redmond for
not being little Queen's," said Anne, gathering about her the
shreds of her old cheerful philosophy to cover her nakedness
of spirit. "When we left Queen's we knew everybody and had
a place of our own. I suppose we have been unconsciously
expecting to take life up at Redmond just where we left off at
Queen's, and now we feel as if the ground had slipped from
under our feet. I'm thankful that neither Mrs. Lynde nor Mrs.
Elisha Wright know, or ever will know, my state of mind at
present. They would exult in saying 'I told you so,' and be
convinced it was the beginning of the end. Whereas it is just
the end of the beginning."

"Exactly. That sounds more Anneish. In a little while we'll
be acclimated and acquainted, and all will be well. Anne, did
you notice the girl who stood alone just outside the door of
the co-eds' dressing room all the morning—the pretty one with
the brown eyes and crooked mouth?"

"Yes, I did. I noticed her particularly because she seemed
the only creature there who *looked* as lonely and friendless as
I *felt*. I had *you,* but she had no one."

"I think she felt pretty all-by-herselfish, too. Several times I
saw her make a motion as if to cross over to us, but she never
did it—too shy, I suppose. I wished she would come. If I hadn't
felt so much like the aforesaid elephant I'd have gone to her.
But I couldn't lumber across that big hall with all those boys
howling on the stairs. She was the prettiest freshette I saw today,
but probably favour is deceitful and even beauty is vain on
your first day at Redmond," concluded Priscilla with a laugh.

"I'm going across to Old St. John's after lunch," said Anne.
"I don't know that a graveyard is a very good place to go to
get cheered up, but it seems the only get-at-able place where
there are trees, and trees I must have. I'll sit on one of those
old slabs and shut my eyes and imagine I'm in the Avonlea
woods."

Anne did not do that, however, for she found enough of
interest in Old St. John's to keep her eyes wide open. They
went in by the entrance gates, past the simple, massive, stone

arch surmounted by the great lion of England.

> " 'And on Inkerman yet the wild bramble is gory,
> And those bleak heights henceforth shall be famous
>   in story,' "

quoted Anne, looking at it with a thrill. They found themselves in a dim, cool, green place where winds were fond of purring. Up and down the long grassy aisles they wandered, reading the quaint, voluminous epitaphs, carved in an age that had more leisure than our own.

" 'Here lieth the body of Albert Crawford, Esq.,' " read Anne from a worn, gray slab, " 'for many years Keeper of His Majesty's Ordnance at Kingsport. He served in the army till the peace of 1763, when he retired from bad health. He was a brave officer, the best of husbands, the best of fathers, the best of friends. He died October 29th, 1792, aged 84 years.' There's an epitaph for you, Prissy. There is certainly some 'scope for imagination' in it. How full such a life must have been of adventure! And as for his personal qualities, I'm sure human eulogy couldn't go further. I wonder if they told him he was all those best things while he was alive."

"Here's another," said Priscilla. "Listen—'To the memory of Alexander Ross, who died on the 22nd of September, 1840, aged 43 years. This is raised as a tribute of affection by one whom he served so faithfully for 27 years that he was regarded as a friend, deserving the fullest confidence and attachment.' "

"A very good epitaph," commented Anne thoughtfully. "I wouldn't wish a better. We are all servants of some sort, and if the fact that we are faithful can be truthfully inscribed on our tombstones nothing more need be added. Here's a sorrowful little gray stone, Prissy—'to the memory of a favourite child.' And here is another 'erected to the memory of one who is buried elsewhere.' I wonder where that unknown grave is. Really, Pris, the graveyards of today will never be as interesting as this. You were right—I shall come here often. I love it already. I see we're not alone here—there's a girl down at the end of this avenue."

"Yes, and I believe it's the very girl we saw at Redmond this morning. I've been watching her for five minutes. She has started to come up the avenue exactly half a dozen times, and half a dozen times has she turned and gone back. Either she's dreadfully shy or she has got something on her conscience. Let's go and meet her. It's easier to get acquainted in a graveyard than at Redmond, I believe."

They walked down the long grassy arcade towards the stranger, who was sitting on a gray slab under an enormous willow. She was certainly very pretty, with a vivid, irregular, bewitching type of prettiness. There was a gloss as of brown nuts on her satin-smooth hair and a soft, ripe glow on her round cheeks. Her eyes were big and brown and velvety, under oddly-pointed black brows, and her crooked mouth was rose-red. She wore a smart brown suit, with two very modish little shoes peeping from beneath it; and her hat of dull pink straw, wreathed with golden-brown poppies, had the indefinable, unmistakable air which pertains to the "creation" of an artist in millinery. Priscilla had a sudden stinging consciousness that her own hat had been trimmed by her village store milliner, and Anne wondered uncomfortably if the blouse she had made herself, and which Mrs. Lynde had fitted, looked *very* countrified and home-made besides the stranger's smart attire. For a moment both girls felt like turning back.

But they had already stopped and turned towards the gray slab. It was too late to retreat, for the brown-eyed girl had evidently concluded that they were coming to speak to her. Instantly she sprang up and came forward with outstretched hand and a gay, friendly smile in which there seemed not a shadow of either shyness or burdened conscience.

"Oh, I want to know who you two girls are," she exclaimed eagerly. "I've been *dying* to know. I saw you at Redmond this morning. Say, wasn't it *awful* there? For the time I wished I had stayed home and got married."

Anne and Priscilla both broke into unconstrained laughter at this unexpected conclusion. The brown-eyed girl laughed, too.

"I really did. I *could* have, you know. Come, let's all sit down on this gravestone and get acquainted. It won't be hard. I know we're going to adore each other—I knew it as soon as I saw you at Redmond this morning. I wanted so much to go right over and hug you both."

"Why didn't you?" asked Priscilla.

"Because I simply couldn't make up my mind to do it. I never can make up my mind about anything myself—I'm always afflicted with indecision. Just as soon as I decide to do something I feel in my bones that another course would be the correct one. It's a dreadful misfortune, but I was born that way, and there is no use in blaming me for it, as some people do. So I couldn't make up my mind to go and speak to you, much as I wanted to."

"We thought you were too shy," said Anne.

"No, no, dear. Shyness isn't among the many failings—or virtues—of Philippa Gordon—Phil for short. Do call me Phil right off. Now, what are your handles?"

"She's Priscilla Grant," said Anne, pointing.

"And *she's* Anne Shirley," said Priscilla, pointing in turn.

"And we're from the Island," said both together.

"I hail from Bolingbroke, Nova Scotia," said Philippa.

"Bolingbroke!" exclaimed Anne. "Why, that is where I was born."

"Do you really mean it? Why, that makes you a Bluenose after all."

"No, it doesn't," retorted Anne. "Wasn't it Dan O'Connell who said that if a man was born in a stable it didn't make him a horse? I'm Island to the core."

"Well, I'm glad you were born in Bolingbroke anyway. It makes us kind of neighbours, doesn't it? And I like that, because when I tell you secrets it won't be as if I were telling them to a stranger. I *have* to tell them. I can't keep secrets—it's no use to try. That's my worst failing—that, and indecision, as aforesaid. Would you believe it?—it took me half an hour to decide what hat to wear when I was coming here—*here,* to a graveyard! At first I inclined to my brown one with the feather; but as soon as I put it on I thought this pink one with the floppy brim would be more becoming. When I got *it* pinned in place I liked the brown one better. At last I put them close together on the bed, shut my eyes, and jabbed with a hat pin. The pin speared the pink one, so I put it on. It is becoming, isn't it? Tell me, what do you think of my looks?"

At this naïve demand, made in a perfectly serious tone,

Priscilla laughed again. But Anne said, impulsively squeezing Philippa's hand,

"We thought this morning that you were the prettiest girl we saw at Redmond."

Philippa's crooked mouth flashed into a bewitching, crooked smile over very white little teeth.

"I thought that myself," was her next astounding statement, "but I wanted some one else's opinion to bolster mine up. I can't decide even on my own appearance. Just as soon as I've decided that I'm pretty I begin to feel miserably that I'm not. Besides, I have a horrible old great-aunt who is always saying to me, with a mournful sigh, 'You were such a pretty baby. It's strange how children change when they grow up.' I adore aunts, but I detest great-aunts. Please tell me quite often that I am pretty, if you don't mind. I feel so much more comfortable when I can believe I'm pretty. And I'll be just as obliging to you if you want me to—I *can* be, with a clear conscience."

"Thanks," laughed Anne, "but Priscilla and I are so firmly convinced of our own good looks that we don't need any assurance about them, so you needn't trouble."

"Oh, you're laughing at me. I know you think I'm abominably vain, but I'm not. There really isn't one spark of vanity in me. And I'm never a bit grudging about paying compliments to other girls when they deserve them. I'm so glad I know you folks. I came up on Saturday and I've nearly died of home-sickness ever since. It's a horrible feeling, isn't it? In Bolingbroke I'm an important personage, and in Kingsport I'm just nobody! There were times when I could feel my soul turning a delicate blue. Where do you hang out?"

"Thirty-eight St. John's Street."

"Better and better. Why, I'm just around the corner on Wallace Street. I don't like my boarding-house, though. It's bleak and lonesome, and my room looks out on such an unholy back yard. It's the ugliest place in the world. As for cats—well, surely *all* the Kingsport cats can't congregate there at night, but half of them must. I adore cats on hearth rugs, snoozing before nice, friendly fires, but cats in back yards at midnight are totally different animals. The first night I was here I cried all night, and so did the cats. You should have seen my nose in the morning. How I wished I had never left home!"

"I don't know how you managed to make up your mind to come to Redmond at all, if you are really such an undecided person," said amused Priscilla.

"Bless your heart, honey, I didn't. It was father who wanted me to come here. His heart was set on it—why, I don't know. It seems perfectly ridiculous to think of *me* studying for a B.A. degree, doesn't it? Not but what I can do it, all right. I have heaps of brains."

"Oh!" said Priscilla vaguely.

"Yes. But it's such hard work to use them. And B.A.'s are such learned, dignified, wise, solemn creatures—they must be. No, *I* didn't want to come to Redmond. I did it just to oblige father. He *is* such a duck. Besides, I knew if I stayed home I'd have to get married. Mother wanted that—wanted it decidedly. Mother has plenty of decision. But I really hated the thought of being married for a few years yet. I want to have heaps of fun before I settle down. And, ridiculous as the idea of my being a B.A. is, the idea of my being an old married woman is still more absurd, isn't it? I'm only eighteen. No, I concluded I would rather come to Redmond than be married. Besides, how could I ever have made up my mind which man to marry?"

"Were there so many?" laughed Anne.

"Heaps. The boys like me awfully—they really do. But there were only two that mattered. The rest were all too young and too poor. I must marry a rich man, you know."

"Why must you?"

"Honey, you couldn't imagine *me* being a poor man's wife, could you? I can't do a single useful thing, and I am *very* extravagant. Oh, no, my husband must have heaps of money. So that narrowed them down to two. But I couldn't decide between two any easier than between two hundred. I knew perfectly well that whichever one I chose I'd regret all my life that I hadn't married the other."

"Didn't you—love—either of them? " asked Anne, a little hesitatingly. It was not easy for her to speak to a stranger of the great mystery and transformation of life.

"Goodness, no. *I* couldn't love anybody. It isn't in me. Besides I wouldn't want to. Being in love makes you a perfect slave, *I* think. And it would give a man such power to hurt you. I'd be afraid. No, no, Alec and Alonzo are two dear boys, and I like them both so much that I really don't know which I like the better. That is the trouble. Alec is the best looking, of course, and I simply couldn't marry a man who wasn't handsome. He is good-tempered, too, and has lovely, curly, black hair. He's rather too perfect—I don't believe I'd like a perfect husband—somebody I could never find fault with."

"Then why not marry Alonzo?" asked Priscilla gravely.

"Think of marrying a name like Alonzo!" said Phil dolefully. "I don't believe I could endure it. But he has a classic nose, and it *would* be a comfort to have a nose in the family that could be depended on. I can't depend on mine. So far, it takes after the Gordon pattern, but I'm so afraid it will develop Byrne tendencies as I grow older. I examine it every day anxiously to make sure it's still Gordon. Mother was a Byrne and has the Byrne nose in the Byrnest degree. Wait till you see it. I adore nice noses. Your nose is awfully nice, Anne Shirley. Alonzo's nose nearly turned the balance in his favour. But *Alonzo!* No, I couldn't decide. If I could have done as I did with the hats—stood them both up together, shut my eyes, and jabbed with a hatpin—it would have been quite easy."

"What did Alec and Alonzo feel like when you came away?" queried Priscilla.

"Oh, they still have hope. I told them they'd have to wait till I could make up my mind. They're quite willing to wait. They both worship me, you know. Meanwhile, I intend to have a good time. I expect I shall have heaps of beaux at Redmond. I can't be happy unless I have, you know. But don't you think the freshmen are fearfully homely? I saw only one really handsome fellow among them. He went away before you came. I heard his chum call him Gilbert. His chum had eyes that stuck out *that far*. But you're not going yet, girls? Don't go yet."

"I think we must," said Anne, rather coldly. "It's getting late, and I've some work to do."

"But you'll both come to see me, won't you?" asked Philippa, getting up and putting an arm around each. "And let me come to see you. I want to be chummy with you. I've taken such a fancy to you both. And I haven't quite disgusted you with my frivolity, have I?"

"Not quite," laughed Anne, responding to Phil's squeeze, with a return of cordiality.

"Because I'm not half so silly as I seem on the surface, you know. You just accept Philippa Gordon, as the Lord made her, with all her faults, and I believe you'll come to like her. Isn't this graveyard a sweet place? I'd love to be buried here. Here's a grave I didn't see before—this one in the iron railing—oh, girls, look, see—the stone says it's the grave of a middy who was killed in the fight between the *Shannon* and the *Chesapeake*. Just fancy!"

Anne paused by the railing and looked at the worn stone, her pulses thrilling with sudden excitement. The old graveyard, with its over-arching trees and long aisles of shadows, faded from her sight. Instead, she saw the Kingsport Harbor of nearly a century agone. Out of the mist came slowly a great frigate, brilliant with "the meteor flag of England." Behind her was another, with a still, heroic form, wrapped in his own starry flag, lying on the quarter deck—the gallant Lawrence. Time's finger had turned back his pages, and that was the *Shannon* sailing triumphant up the bay with the *Chesapeake* as her prize.

"Come back, Anne Shirley—come back," laughed Philippa, pulling her arm. "You're a hundred years away from us. Come back."

Anne came back with a sigh; her eyes were shining softly.

"I've always loved that old story," she said, "and although the English won that victory, I think it was because of the brave, defeated commander I love it. This grave seems to bring it so near and make it so real. This poor little middy was only eighteen. He 'died of desperate wounds received in gallant action'—so reads his epitaph. It is such as a soldier might wish for."

Before she turned away, Anne unpinned the little cluster of purple pansies she wore and dropped it softly on the grave of the boy who had perished in the great sea-duel.

"Well, what do you think of our new friend?" asked Priscilla, when Phil had left them.

"I like her. There is something very lovable about her, in spite of all her nonsense. I believe, as she says herself, that she isn't half as silly as she sounds. She's a dear, kissable baby—

and I don't know that she'll ever really grow up."

"I like her, too," said Priscilla decidedly. "She talks as much about boys as Ruby Gillis does. But it always enrages or sickens me to hear Ruby, whereas I just wanted to laugh good-naturedly at Phil. Now, what is the why of that?"

"There is a difference," said Anne meditatively. "I think it's because Ruby is really so *conscious* of boys. She plays at love and love-making. Besides, you feel, when she is boasting of her beaux that she is doing it to rub it well into you that you haven't half so many. Now, when Phil talks of her beaux it sounds as if she was just speaking of chums. She really looks upon boys as good comrades, and she is pleased when she has dozens of them tagging round, simply because she likes to be popular and to be thought popular. Even Alec and Alonzo—I'll never be able to think of those two names separately after this—are to her just two playfellows who want her to play with them all their lives. I'm glad we met her, and I'm glad we went to Old St. John's. I believe I've put forth a tiny soul-root into Kingsport soil this afternoon. I hope so. I hate to feel transplanted."

CHAPTER 5

LETTERS FROM HOME

FOR THE next three weeks Anne and Priscilla continued to feel as strangers in a strange land. Then, suddenly, everything seemed to fall into focus—Redmond, professors, classes, students, studies, social doings. Life became homogeneous again, instead of being made up of detached fragments. The Freshmen, instead of being a collection of unrelated individuals, found themselves a class, with a class spirit, a class yell, class interests, class antipathies and class ambitions. They won the day in the annual "Arts Rush" against the Sophomores, and thereby gained the respect of all the classes, and an enormous, confidence-giving opinion of themselves. For three years the Sophomores had won in the "rush"; that the victory of this year perched upon the Freshman's banner was attributed to the strategic generalship of Gilbert Blythe, who marshalled the campaign and originated certain new tactics, which demoralized the Sophs and swept the Freshmen to triumph. As a reward of merit he was elected president of the Freshman Class, a position of honour and responsibility—from a Fresh point of view, at least—coveted by many. He was also invited to join the "Lambs"—Redmondese for Lamba Theta—a compliment rarely paid to a Freshman. As a preparatory initiation ordeal he had to parade the principal business streets of Kingsport for a whole day wearing a sunbonnet and a voluminous kitchen apron of gaudily flowered calico. This he did cheerfully, doffing his sunbonnet with courtly grace when he met ladies of his acquaintance. Charlie Sloane, who had not been asked to join the Lambs, told Anne he did not see how Blythe could do it, and *he*, for his part, could never humiliate himself so.

"Fancy Charlie Sloane in a 'caliker' apron and a 'sun bunnit,'" giggled Priscilla. "He'd look exactly like his old Grandmother Sloane. Gilbert, now, looked as much like a man in them as in his own proper habiliments."

Anne and Priscilla found themselves in the thick of the social life of Redmond. That this came about so speedily was due in great measure to Philippa Gordon. Philippa was the daughter of a rich and well-known man, and belonged to an old and exclusive "Bluenose" family. This, combined with her beauty and charm—a charm acknowledged by all who met her—promptly opened the gates of all cliques, clubs and classes in Redmond to her; and where she went Anne and Priscilla went, too. Phil "adored" Anne and Priscilla, especially Anne. She was a loyal little soul, crystal-free from any form of snobbishness. "Love me, love my friends" seemed to be her unconscious motto. Without effort, she took them with her into her ever widening circle of acquaintanceship, and the two Avonlea girls found their social pathway at Redmond made very easy and pleasant for them, to the envy and wonderment of the other freshettes, who, lacking Philippa's sponsorship, were doomed to remain rather on the fringe of things during their first college year.

To Anne and Priscilla, with their more serious views of life, Phil remained the amusing, lovable baby she had seemed on their first meeting. Yet, as she said herself, she had "heaps" of brains. When or where she found time to study was a mystery, for she seemed always in demand for some kind of "fun," and her home evenings were crowded with callers. She had all the "beaux" that heart could desire, for nine-tenths of the Freshmen and a big fraction of all the other classes were rivals for her smiles. She was naïvely delighted over this, and gleefully recounted each new conquest to Anne and Priscilla, with comments that might have made the unlucky lover's ears burn fiercely.

"Alec and Alonzo don't seem to have any serious rival yet," remarked Anne, teasingly.

"Not one," agreed Philippa. "I write them both every week and tell them all about my young men here. I'm sure it must amuse them. But, of course, the one I like best I can't get. Gilbert Blythe won't take any notice of me, except to look at me as if I were a nice little kitten he'd like to pat. Too well I know the reason. I owe you a grudge, Queen Anne. I really ought to hate you and instead I love you madly, and I'm miserable if I don't see you every day. You're different from any girl I ever knew before. When you look at me in a certain way I feel what an insignificant, frivolous little beast I am, and I long to be better and wiser and stronger. And then I make good resolutions; but the first nice-looking mannie who comes my way knocks them all out of my head. Isn't college life magnificent? It's so funny to think I hated it that first day. But if I hadn't I might never got really acquainted with you. Anne, please tell me over again that you like me a little bit. I yearn to hear it."

"I like you a big bit—and I think you're a dear, sweet, adorable, velvety, clawless, little—kitten," laughed Anne, "but I don't see when you ever get time to learn your lessons."

Phil must have found time for she held her own in every class of her year. Even the grumpy old professor of Mathematics, who detested co-eds, and had bitterly opposed their admission to Redmond, couldn't floor her. She led the freshettes everywhere, except in English, where Anne Shirley left her far behind. Anne herself found the studies of her Freshman year very easy, thanks in great part to the steady work she and Gilbert had put in during those two past years in Avonlea. This left her more time for a social life which she thoroughly enjoyed. But never for a moment did she forget Avonlea and the friends there. To her, the happiest moments in each week were those in which letters came from home. It was not until she had got her first letters that she began to think she could ever like Kingsport or feel at home there. Before they came, Avonlea had seemed thousands of miles away; those letters brought it near and linked the old life to the new so closely that they began to seem one and the same, instead of two hopelessly segregated existences. The first batch contained six letters, from Jane Andrews, Ruby Gillis, Diana Barry, Marilla, Mrs. Lynde and Davy. Jane's was a copper-plate production, with every "t" nicely crossed and every "i" precisely dotted, and not an interesting sentence in it. She never mentioned the school, concerning which Anne was avid to hear; she never answered one of the questions Anne had asked in her letter. But she told Anne how many yards of lace she had recently crocheted, and the kind of weather they were having in Avonlea, and how she intended to have her new dress made, and the way she felt when her head ached. Ruby Gillis wrote a gushing epistle deploring Anne's absence, assuring her she was horribly missed in everything, asking what the Redmond "fellows" were like, and filling the rest with accounts of her own harrowing experiences with her numerous admirers. It was a silly, harmless letter, and Anne would have laughed over it had it not been for the postscript. "Gilbert seems to be enjoying Redmond, judging from his letters," wrote Ruby. "I don't think Charlie is so struck on it."

So Gilbert was writing to Ruby! Very well. He had a perfect right to, of course. Only—!! Anne did not know that Ruby had written the first letter and that Gilbert had answered it from mere courtesy. She tossed Ruby's letter aside contemptuously. But it took all Diana's breezy, newsy, delightful epistle to banish the sting of Ruby's postscript. Diana's letter contained a little too much Fred, but was otherwise crowded and crossed with items of interest, and Anne almost felt herself back in Avonlea while reading it. Marilla's was a rather prim and colourless epistle, severely innocent of gossip or emotion. Yet somehow it conveyed to Anne a whiff of the wholesome, simple life at Green Gables, with its savour of ancient peace, and the steadfast abiding love that was there for her. Mrs. Lynde's letter was full of church news. Having broken up housekeeping, Mrs. Lynde had more time than ever to devote to church affairs and had flung herself into them heart and soul. She was at present much worked up over the poor "supplies" they were having in the vacant Avonlea pulpit.

"I don't believe any but fools enter the ministry nowadays," she wrote bitterly. "Such candidates as they have sent us, and such stuff as they preach! Half of it ain't true, and, what's worse, it ain't sound doctrine. The one we have now is the worst of the lot. He mostly takes a text and preaches about something else. And he says he doesn't believe all the heathen will be eternally lost. The idea! If they won't all the money we've been giving to Foreign Missions will be clean wasted, that's what! Last Sunday night he announced that next Sunday he'd preach on the axe-head that swam. I think he'd better confine himself to the Bible and leave sensational subjects alone. Things have come to a pretty pass if a minister can't find enough in Holy Writ to preach about, that's what. What church do you attend, Anne? I hope you go regularly. People are apt to get so careless about church-going away from home, and I understand college students are great sinners in this respect. I'm told many of them actually study their lessons on Sunday. I hope you'll never sink that low, Anne. Remember how you were brought up. And be very careful what friends you make. You never know what sort of creatures are in them colleges. Outwardly they may be as whited sepulchers and inwardly as ravening wolves, that's what. You'd better not have anything to say to any young man who isn't from the Island.

"I forgot to tell you what happened the day the minister called here. It was the funniest thing I ever saw. I said to Marilla, 'If Anne had been here wouldn't she have had a laugh?' Even Marilla laughed. You know he's a very short, fat little man with bow legs. Well, that old pig of Mr. Harrison's—the big, tall one—had wandered over here that day again and broke into the yard, and it got into the back porch, unbeknowns to us, and it was there when the minister appeared in the doorway. It made one wild bolt to get out, but there was nowhere to bolt to except between them bow legs. So there it went, and, being as it was so big and the minister so little, it took him clean off his feet and carried him away. His hat went one way and his cane another, just as Marilla and I got to the door. I'll never forget the look of him. And that poor pig was near scared to death. I'll never be able to read that account in the Bible of the swine that rushed madly down the steep place into the sea without seeing Mr. Harrison's pig careering down the hill with that minister. I guess the pig thought he had the Old Boy on his back instead of inside of him. I was thankful the twins weren't about. It wouldn't have been the right thing for them to have seen a minister in such an undignified predicament. Just before they got to the brook the minister jumped off or fell off. The pig rushed through the brook like mad and up through the woods. Marilla and I run down and helped the minister get up and brush his coat. He wasn't hurt, but he was mad. He seemed to hold Marilla and me responsible for it all, though we told him the pig didn't belong to us, and had been pestering us all summer. Besides, what did he come to the back door for? You'd never have caught Mr. Allan doing that. It'll be a long time before we get a man like Mr. Allan. But it's an ill wind that blows no good. We've never seen hoof or hair of that pig since, and it's my belief we never will.

"Things is pretty quiet in Avonlea. I don't find Green Gables as lonesome as I expected. I think I'll start another cotton warp quilt this winter. Mrs. Silas Sloane has a handsome new apple-leaf pattern.

"When I feel that I must have some excitement I read the murder trials in that Boston paper my niece sends me. I never used to do it, but they're real interesting. The States must be an awful place. I hope you'll never go there, Anne. But the way girls roam over the earth now is something terrible. It always makes me think of Satan in the Book of Job, going to and fro and walking up and down. I don't believe the Lord ever intended it, that's what.

"Davy has been pretty good since you went away. One day he was bad and Marilla punished him by making him wear Dora's apron all day, and then he went and cut all Dora's aprons up. I spanked him for that and then he went and chased my rooster to death.

"The MacPhersons have moved down to my place. She's a great housekeeper and very particular. She's rooted all my June lilies up because she says they make a garden look so untidy. Thomas set them lilies out when we were married. Her husband seems a nice sort of a man, but she can't get over being an old maid, that's what.

"Don't study too hard, and be sure and put your winter underclothes on as soon as the weather gets cool. Marilla worries a lot about you, but I tell her you've got a lot more sense than I ever thought you would have at one time, and that you'll be all right."

Davy's letter plunged into a grievance at the start.

"Dear anne, please write and tell marilla not to tie me to the rale of the bridge when I go fishing the boys make fun of me when she does. Its awful lonesome here without you but grate fun in school. Jane andrews is crosser than you. I scared mrs. lynde with a jacky lantern last nite. She was offel mad and she was mad cause I chased her old rooster round the yard till he fell down ded. I didn't mean to make him fall down ded. What made him die, anne, I want to know. Mrs. lynde threw him into the pig pen she mite of sold him to mr. blair. mr. blair is giving 50 sense apeace for good ded roosters now. I herd mrs. lynde asking the minister to pray for her. What did she do that was so bad, anne, I want to know. I've got a kite with a magnificent tail, anne. Milty bolter told me a grate story in school yesterday. it is troo. old Joe Mosey and Leon were playing cards one nite last week in the woods. The cards were on a stump and a big black man bigger than the trees come along and grabbed the cards and the stump and disapered with a noys like thunder. Ill bet they were skared. Milty says the black man was the old harry. was he, anne, I want to know. Mr. kimball over at spenservale is very sick and will have to go to the hospitable. please excuse me while I ask marilla if thats spelled rite. Marilla says its the silem he has to go to not the other place. He thinks he has a snake inside of him. whats it like to have a snake inside of you, anne. I want to know. mrs. lawrence bell is sick to. mrs. lynde says that all that is the matter with her is that she thinks too much about her insides."

"I wonder," said Anne, as she folded up her letters, "what Mrs. Lynde would think of Philippa."

CHAPTER 6

IN THE PARK

"WHAT ARE you going to do with yourselves today, girls?" asked Philippa, popping into Anne's room one Saturday afternoon.

"We are going for a walk in the park," answered Anne. "I ought to stay in and finish my blouse. But I couldn't sew on a day like this. There's something in the air that gets into my blood and makes a sort of glory in my soul. My fingers would twitch and I'd sew a crooked seam. So it's ho for the park and the pines."

"Does 'we' include any one but yourself and Priscilla?"

"Yes, it includes Gilbert and Charlie, and we'll be very glad if it will include you, also."

"But," said Philippa dolefully, "if I go I'll have to be gooseberry, and that will be a new experience for Philippa Gordon."

"Well, new experiences are broadening. Come along, and you'll be able to sympathize with all poor souls who have to play gooseberry often. But where are all the victims?"

"Oh, I was tired of them all and simply couldn't be bothered with any of them today. Besides, I've been feeling a little blue— just a pale, elusive azure. It isn't serious enough for anything darker. I wrote Alec and Alonzo last week. I put the letters into envelopes and addressed them, but I didn't seal them up. That evening something funny happened. That is, Alec would think it funny, but Alonzo wouldn't be likely to. I was in a hurry, so I snatched Alec's letter—as I thought—out of the envelope and scribbled down a postscript. Then I mailed both letters. I got Alonzo's reply this morning. Girls, I had put that postscript to *his* letter and he was furious. Of course he'll get over it—and I don't care if he doesn't—but it spoiled my day. So I thought I'd come to you darlings to get cheered up. After the football season opens I won't have any spare Saturday afternoons. I adore football. I've got the most gorgeous cap and sweater striped in Redmond colours to wear to the games. To be sure, a little way off I'll look like a walking barber's pole. Do you know that that Gilbert of yours has been elected Captain of the Freshman football team?"

"Yes, he told us so last evening," said Priscilla, seeing that

39

outraged Anne would not answer. "He and Charlie were down. We knew they were coming, so we painstakingly put out of sight or out of reach all Miss Ada's cushions. That very elaborate one with the raised embroidery I dropped on the floor in the corner behind the chair it was on. I thought it would be safe there. But would you believe it? Charlie Sloane made for that chair, noticed the cushion behind it, solemnly fished it up, and sat on it the whole evening. Such a wreck of a cushion as it was! Poor Miss Ada asked me today, still smiling, but oh, so reproachfully, why I had allowed it to be sat upon. I told her I hadn't—that it was a matter of predestination coupled with inveterate Sloanishness and I wasn't a match for both combined."

"Miss Ada's cushions are really getting on my nerves," said Anne. "She finished two new ones last week, stuffed and embroidered within an inch of their lives. There being absolutely no other cushionless place to put them she stood them up against the wall on the stair landing. They topple over half the time and if we come up or down the stairs in the dark we fall over them. Last Sunday, when Dr. Davis prayed for all those exposed to the perils of the sea, I added in thought 'and for all those who live in houses where cushions are loved not wisely but too well!' There! we're ready, and I see the boys coming through Old St. John's. Do you cast in your lot with us, Phil?"

"I'll go, if I can walk with Priscilla and Charlie. That will be a bearable degree of gooseberry. That Gilbert of yours is a darling, Anne, but why *does* he go around so much with Goggle-eyes?"

Anne stiffened. She had no great liking for Charlie Sloane; but he was of Avonlea, so no outsider had any business to laugh at him.

"Charlie and Gilbert have always been friends," she said coldly. "Charlie is a nice boy. He's not to blame for his eyes."

"Don't tell me that! He is! He must have done something dreadful in a previous existence to be punished with such eyes. Pris and I are going to have such sport with him this afternoon. We'll make fun of him to his face and he'll never know it."

Doubtless, "the abandoned P's," as Anne called them, did carry out their amiable intentions. But Sloane was blissfully ignorant; he thought he was quite a fine fellow to be walking with two such co-eds, especially Philippa Gordon, the class beauty and belle. It must surely impress Anne. She would see that some people appreciated him at his real value.

Gilbert and Anne loitered a little behind the others, enjoying the calm, still beauty of the autumn afternoon under the pines of the park, on the road that climbed and twisted around the harbour shore.

"The silence here is like a prayer, isn't it?" said Anne, her face upturned to the shining sky. "How I love the pines! They seem to strike their roots deep into the romance of all the ages. It is so comforting to creep away now and then for a good talk with them. I always feel so happy out here."

> " 'And so in mountain solitudes o'ertaken
> As by some spell divine,
> Their cares drop from them like the needles shaken
> From out the gusty pine,' "

quoted Gilbert.

"They make our little ambitions seem rather petty, don't they, Anne?"

"I think, if ever any great sorrow came to me, I would come to the pines for comfort," said Anne dreamily.

"I hope no great sorrow ever will come to you, Anne," said Gilbert, who could not connect the idea of sorrow with the vivid, joyous creature beside him, unwitting that those who can soar to the highest heights can also plunge to the deepest depths, and that the natures which enjoy most keenly are those which also suffer most sharply.

"But there must—sometime," mused Anne. "Life seems like a cup of glory held to my lips just now. But there must be some bitterness in it—there is in every cup. I shall taste mine some day. Well, I hope I shall be strong and brave to meet it. And I hope it won't be through my own fault that it will come. Do you remember what Dr. Davis said last Sunday evening— that the sorrows God sent us brought comfort and strength with them, while the sorrows we brought on ourselves, through folly or wickedness, were by far the hardest to bear? But we mustn't talk of sorrow on an afternoon like this. It's meant for the sheer joy of living, isn't it?"

"If I had my way I'd shut everything out of your life but happiness and pleasure, Anne," said Gilbert in the tone that meant "danger ahead."

"Then you would be very unwise," rejoined Anne hastily. "I'm sure no life can be properly developed and rounded out without some trial and sorrow—though I suppose it is only when we are pretty comfortable that we admit it. Come—the others have got to the pavilion and are beckoning to us."

They all sat down in the little pavilion to watch an autumn sunset of deep red fire and pallid gold. To their left lay Kingsport, its roofs and spires dim in their shroud of violet smoke. To their right lay the harbour, taking on tints of rose and copper as it stretched out into the sunset. Before them the water shimmered, satin smooth and silver gray, and beyond, clean shaven William's Island loomed out of the mist, guarding the town like a sturdy bull-dog. Its lighthouse beacon flared through the mist like a baleful star, and was answered by another in the far horizon.

"Did you ever see such a strong-looking place?" asked Philippa. "I don't want William's Island especially, but I'm sure I couldn't get it if I did. Look at that sentry on the summit of the fort, right beside the flag. Doesn't he look as if he had stepped out of a romance?"

"Speaking of romance," said Priscilla, "we've been looking for heather—but, of course, we couldn't find any. It's too late in the season, I suppose."

"Heather!" exclaimed Anne. "Heather doesn't grow in America, does it?"

"There are just two patches of it in the whole continent," said Phil, "one right here in the park, and one somewhere else in Nova Scotia, I forget where. The famous Highland Regiment, the Black Watch, camped here one year, and, when the men shook out the straw of their beds in the spring, some seeds of heather took root."

"Oh, how delightful!" said enchanted Anne.

"Let's go home around by Spofford Avenue," suggested Gilbert. "We can see all 'the handsome houses where the wealthy nobles dwell.' Spofford Avenue is the finest residential street in Kingsport. Nobody can build on it unless he's a millionaire."

"Oh, do," said Phil. "There's a perfectly killing little place

I want to show you, Anne. *It* wasn't built by a millionaire. It's the first place after you leave the park, and must have grown while Spofford Avenue was still a country road. It *did* grow— it wasn't built! I don't care for the houses on the Avenue. They're too brand new and plate-glassy. But this little spot is a dream—and its name—but wait till you see it."

They saw it as they walked up the pine-fringed hill from the park. Just on the crest, where Spofford Avenue petered out into a plain road, was a little white frame house with groups of pines on either side of it, stretching their arms protectingly over its low roof. It was covered with red and gold vines, through which its green-shuttered windows peeped. Before it was a tiny garden, surrounded by a low stone wall. October though it was, the garden was still very sweet with dear, old-fashioned, unworldly flowers and shrubs—sweet may, southern-wood, lemon verbena, alyssum, petunias, marigolds and chrysanthemums. A tiny brick wall, in herring-bone pattern, led from the gate to the front porch. The whole place might have been transplanted from some remote country village; yet there was something about it that made its nearest neighbour, the big lawn-encircled palace of a tobacco king, look exceedingly crude and showy and ill-bred by contrast. As Phil said, it was the difference between being born and being made.

"It's the dearest place I ever saw," said Anne delightedly. "It gives me one of my old, delightful, funny aches. It's dearer and quainter than even Miss Lavendar's stone house."

"It's the name I want you to notice especially," said Phil. "Look—in white letters, around the archway over the gate. 'Patty's Place.' Isn't that killing? Especially on this Avenue of Pinehursts and Elmwolds and Cedarcrofts? 'Patty's Place,' if you please! I adore it."

"Have you any idea who Patty is?" asked Priscilla.

"Patty Spofford is the name of the old lady who owns it, I've discovered. She lives there with her niece, and they've lived there for hundreds of years, more or less—maybe a little less, Anne. Exaggeration is merely a flight of poetic fancy. I understand that wealthy folk have tried to buy the lot time and again—it's really worth a small fortune now, you know—but 'Patty' won't sell upon any consideration. And there's an apple orchard behind the house in place of a back yard—you'll see it when we get a little past—a real apple orchard on Spofford Avenue!"

"I'm going to dream about 'Patty's Place' tonight," said Anne. "Why, I feel as if I belonged to it. I wonder if, by any chance, we'll ever see the inside of it."

"It isn't likely," said Priscilla.

Anne smiled mysteriously.

"No, it isn't likely. But I believe it will happen. I have a queer, creepy, crawly feeling—you can call it a presentiment, if you like—that 'Patty's Place' and I are going to be better acquainted yet."

CHAPTER 7

HOME AGAIN

THOSE FIRST three weeks at Redmond had seemed long; but the rest of the term flew by on wings of wind. Before they realized it the Redmond students found themselves in the grind of Christmas examinations, emerging therefrom more or less triumphantly. The honour of leading in the Freshman classes fluctuated between Anne, Gilbert and Philippa; Priscilla did very well; Charlie Sloane scraped through respectably, and comported himself as complacently as if he had led in everything.

"I can't really believe that this time tomorrow I'll be in Green Gables," said Anne on the night before departure. "But I shall be. And you, Phil, will be in Bolingbroke with Alec and Alonzo."

"I'm longing to see them," admitted Phil, between the chocolates she was nibbling. "They really are such dear boys, you know. Oh, I'm going to have a splendid time in the holidays. There's to be no end of dances and drives and general jamborees. I shall never forgive you, Queen Anne, for not coming home with me for the holidays."

" 'Never' means three days with you, Phil. It was dear of you to ask me.—and I'd love to go to Bolingbroke some day.

But I can't go this year—I *must* go home. You don't know how my heart longs for it."

"You won't have much of a time," said Phil scornfully. "There'll be one or two quilting parties, I suppose; and all the old gossips will talk you over to your face and behind your back. You'll die of lonesomeness, child."

"In Avonlea?" said Anne, highly amused.

"Now, if you'd come with me you'd have a perfectly gorgeous time. Bolingbroke would go wild over you, Queen Anne—your hair and your style and, oh, everything! You're so *different*. You'd be such a success—and I would bask in reflected glory—'not the rose but near the rose.' *Do* come, after all, Anne."

"Your picture of social triumphs is quite fascinating, Phil, but I'll paint one to off-set it. I'm going home to an old country farmhouse, once green, rather faded now, set among leafless apple orchards. There is a brook below and a December fir wood beyond, where I've heard harps swept by the fingers of rain and wind. There is a pond near by that will be gray and brooding now. There will be two oldish ladies in the house, one tall and thin, one short and fat; and there will be two twins, one a perfect model, the other what Mrs. Lynde calls a 'holy terror.' There will be a little room up-stairs over the porch, where old dreams hang thick, and a big, fat, glorious feather bed which will almost seem the height of luxury after a boarding-house mattress. How do you like my picture, Phil?"

"It seems a very dull one," said Phil, with a grimace.

"Oh, but I've left out the transforming thing," said Anne softly. "There'll be love there, Phil—faithful, tender love, such as I'll never find anywhere else in the world—love that's waiting for *me*. That makes my picture a masterpiece, doesn't it, even if the colours are not very brilliant?"

Phil silently got up, tossed her box of chocolates away, went up to Anne, and put her arms about her.

"Anne, I wish I was like you," she said soberly.

Diana met Anne at the Carmody station the next night, and they drove home together under silent, star-sown depths of sky. Green Gables had a very festal appearance as they drove up the lane. There was a light in every window, the glow breaking out through the darkness like flame-red blossoms swung against the dark background of the Haunted Wood. And in the yard was a brave bonfire with two gay little figures dancing around it, one of which gave an unearthly yell as the buggy turned in under the poplars.

"Davy means that for an Indian war-whoop," said Diana. "Mr. Harrison's hired boy taught it to him, and he's been practising it up to welcome you with. Mrs. Lynde says it has worn her nerves to a frazzle. He creeps up behind her, you know, and then lets go. He was determined to have a bonfire for you, too. He's been piling up dry branches for a fortnight and pestering Marilla to be let pour some kerosene oil over it before setting it on fire. I guess she did, by the smell, though Mrs. Lynde said up to the last that Davy would blow himself and everybody else up if he was let."

Anne was out of the buggy by this time, and Davy was rapturously hugging her knees, while even Dora was clinging to her hand.

"Isn't that a bully bonfire, Anne? Just let me show you how to poke it—see the sparks? I did it for you, Anne, 'cause I was so glad you were coming home."

The kitchen door opened and Marilla's spare form darkened against the inner light. She preferred to meet Anne in the shadows, for she was horribly afraid that she was going to cry with joy,—she, stern, repressed Marilla, who thought all display of deep emotion unseemly. Mrs. Lynde was behind her, sonsy, kindly, matronly, as of yore. The love that Anne had told Phil was waiting for her surrounded her and enfolded her with its blessing and its sweetness. Nothing, after all, could compare with old ties, old friends, and old Green Gables! How starry Anne's eyes were as they sat down to the loaded supper table, how pink her cheeks, how silver-clear her laughter! And Diana was going to stay all night, too. How like the dear old times it was! And the rose-bud tea-set graced the table! With Marilla the force of nature could no further go.

"I suppose you and Diana will now proceed to talk all night," said Marilla sarcastically, as the girls went up-stairs. Marilla was always sarcastic after any self-betrayal.

"Yes," agreed Anne gaily, "but I'm going to put Davy to bed first. He insists on that."

"You bet," said Davy, as they went along the hall. "I want somebody to say my prayers to again. It's no fun saying them alone."

"You don't say them alone, Davy. God is always with you to hear you."

"Well, I can't see Him," objected Davy. "I want to pray to somebody I can see, but I *won't* say them to Mrs. Lynde or Marilla, there now!"

Nevertheless, when Davy was garbed in his gray flannel nighty, he did not seem in a hurry to begin. He stood before Anne, shuffling one bare foot over the other, and looked undecided.

"Come, dear, kneel down," said Anne.

Davy came and buried his head in Anne's lap, but he did not kneel down.

"Anne," he said in a muffled voice, "I don't feel like praying after all. I haven't felt like it for a week now. I—I *didn't* pray last night nor the night before."

"Why not, Davy?" asked Anne gently.

"You—you won't be mad if I tell you?" implored Davy.

Anne lifted the little gray-flannelled body on her knee and cuddled his head on her arm.

"Do I ever get 'mad' when you tell me things, Davy?"

"No-o-o, you never do. But you get sorry, and that's worse. You'll be awful sorry when I tell you this, Anne—and you'll be 'shamed of me, I s'pose."

"Have you done something naughty, Davy, and is that why you can't say your prayers?"

"No, I haven't done anything naughty—yet. But I want to do it."

"What is it, Davy?"

"I—I want to say a bad word, Anne," blurted out Davy, with a desperate effort. "I heard Mr. Harrison's hired boy say it one day last week, and ever since I've been wanting to say it *all* the time—even when I'm saying my prayers."

"Say it then, Davy."

Davy lifted his flushed face in amazement.

"But, Anne, it's an *awful* bad word."

"Say it!"

Davy gave her another incredulous look, then in a low voice he said the dreadful word. The next minute his face was burrowing against her.

"Oh, Anne, I'll never say it again—never. I'll never *want* to say it again. I knew it was bad, but I didn't s'pose it was so— so—I didn't s'pose it was like *that.*"

"No, I don't think you'll ever want to say it again, Davy— or think it, either. And I wouldn't go about much with Mr. Harrison's hired boy if I were you."

"He can make bully war-whoops," said Davy a little regretfully.

"But you don't want your mind filled with bad words, do you, Davy—words that will poison it and drive out all that is good and manly?"

"No," said Davy, owl-eyed with introspection.

"Then don't go with those people who use them. And now do you feel as if you could say your prayers, Davy?"

"Oh, yes," said Davy, eagerly wriggling down on his knees, "I can say them now all right. I ain't scared now to say 'if I should die before I wake,' like I was when I was wanting to say that word."

Probably Anne and Diana did empty out their souls to each other that night, but no record of their confidences has been preserved. They both looked as fresh and bright-eyed at breakfast as only youth can look after unlawful hours of revelry and confession. There had been no snow up to this time, but as Diana crossed the old log bridge on her homeward way the white flakes were beginning to flutter down over the fields and woods, russet and gray in their dreamless sleep. Soon the faraway slopes and hills were dim and wraith-like through their gauzy scarfing, as if pale autumn had flung a misty bridal veil over her hair and was waiting for her wintry bridegroom. So they had a white Christmas after all, and a very pleasant day it was. In the forenoon letters and gifts came from Miss Lavendar and Paul; Anne opened them in the cheerful Green Gables kitchen, which was filled with what Davy, sniffing in ecstasy, called "pretty smells."

"Miss Lavendar and Mr. Irving are settled in their new home now." reported Anne. "I am sure Miss Lavendar is perfectly happy—I know it by the general tone of her letter—but there's a note from Charlotta the Fourth. She doesn't like Boston at all, and she is fearfully homesick. Miss Lavendar wants me to go through to Echo Lodge some day while I'm home and light a fire to air it, and see that the cushions aren't getting mouldy. I think I'll get Diana to go over with me next week, and we can spend the evening with Theodora Dix. I want to see

Theodora. By the way, is Ludovic Speed still going to see her?"

"They say so," said Marilla, "and he's likely to continue it. Folks have given up expecting that that courtship will ever arrive anywhere."

"I'd hurry him up a bit, if I was Theodora, that's what," said Mrs. Lynde. And there is not the slightest doubt but that she would.

There was also a characteristic scrawl from Philippa, full of Alec and Alonzo, what they said and what they did, and how they looked when they saw her.

"But I can't make up my mind yet which to marry," wrote Phil. "I do wish you had come with me to decide for me. Some one will have to. When I saw Alec my heart gave a great thump and I thought, 'He must be the right one.' And then, when Alonzo came, thump went my heart again. So that's no guide, though it should be, according to all the novels I've ever read. Now, Anne, *your* heart wouldn't thump for anybody but the genuine Prince Charming, would it? There must be something radically wrong with mine. But I'm having a perfectly gorgeous time. How I wish you were here! It's snowing today, and I'm rapturous. I was so afraid we'd have a green Christmas and I loathe them. You know, when Christmas is a dirty grayey-browney affair, looking as if it had been left over a hundred years ago and had been in soak ever since, it is called a *green* Christmas! Don't ask me why. As Lord Dundreary says 'there are thome thingth no fellow can underthtand.'

"Anne, did you ever get on a street car and then discover that you hadn't any money with you to pay your fare? I did, the other day. It's quite awful. I had a nickel with me when I got on the car. I thought it was in the left pocket of my coat. When I got settled down comfortably I felt for it. It wasn't there. I had a cold chill. I felt in the other pocket. Not there. I had another chill. Then I felt in a little inside pocket. All in vain. I had two chills at once.

"I took off my gloves, laid them on the seat, and went over all my pockets again. It was not there. I stood up and shook myself, and then looked on the floor. The car was full of people, who were going home from the opera, and they all stared at me, but I was past caring for a little thing like that.

"But I could not find my fare. I concluded I must have put

it in my mouth and swallowed it inadvertently.

"I didn't know what to do. Would the conductor, I wondered, stop the car and put me off in ignominy and shame? Was it possible that I could convince him that I was merely the victim of my own absent-mindedness, and not an unprincipled creature trying to obtain a ride upon false pretences? How I wished that Alec or Alonzo were there. But they weren't because I wanted them. If I *hadn't* wanted them they would have been there by the dozen. And I couldn't decide what to say to the conductor when he came around. As soon as I got one sentence of explanation mapped out in my mind I felt nobody could believe it and I must compose another. It seemed there was nothing to do but trust in Providence, and for all the comfort that gave me I might as well have been the old lady who, when told by the captain during a storm that she must put her trust in the Almighty exclaimed, 'Oh, Captain, is it as bad as that?'

"Just at the conventional moment, when all hope had fled, and the conductor was holding out his box to the passenger next to me, I suddenly remembered where I had put that wretched coin of the realm. I hadn't swallowed it after all. I meekly fished it out of the index finger of my glove and poked it in the box. I smiled at everybody and felt that it was a beautiful world."

The visit to Echo Lodge was not the least pleasant of many pleasant holiday outings. Anne and Diana went back to it by the old way of the beech woods, carrying a lunch basket with them. Echo Lodge, which had been closed ever since Miss Lavendar's wedding, was briefly thrown open to wind and sunshine once more, and firelight glimmered again in the little rooms. The perfume of Miss Lavendar's rose bowl still filled the air. It was hardly possible to believe that Miss Lavendar would not come tripping in presently, with her brown eyes a-star with welcome, and that Charlotta the Fourth, blue of bow and wide of smile, would not pop through the door. Paul, too, seemed hovering around, with his fairy fancies.

"It really makes me feel a little bit like a ghost revisiting the old time glimpses of the moon," laughed Anne. "Let's go out and see if the echoes are at home. Bring the old horn. It is still behind the kitchen door."

The echoes were at home, over the white river, as silver-clear and multitudinous as ever; and when they had ceased to answer the girls locked up Echo Lodge again and went away in the perfect half hour that follows the rose and saffron of a winter sunset.

CHAPTER 8

ANNE'S FIRST PROPOSAL

THE OLD year did not slip away in a green twilight, with a pinky-yellow sunset. Instead, it went out with a wild, white bluster and blow. It was one of the nights when the storm-wind hurtles over the frozen meadows and black hollows, and moans around the eaves like a lost creature, and drives the snow sharply against the shaking panes.

"Just the sort of night people like to cuddle down between their blankets and count their mercies," said Anne to Jane Andrews, who had come up to spend the afternoon and stay all night. But when they were cuddled between their blankets, in Anne's little porch room, it was not her mercies of which Jane was thinking.

"Anne," she said very solemnly, "I want to tell you something. May I?"

Anne was feeling rather sleepy after the party Ruby Gillis had given the night before. She would much rather have gone to sleep than listen to Jane's confidences, which she was sure would bore her. She had no prophetic inkling of what was coming. Probably Jane was engaged, too; rumour averred that Ruby Gillis was engaged to the Spencervale school-teacher, about whom all the girls were said to be quite wild.

"I'll soon be the only fancy-free maiden of our old quartette," thought Anne, drowsily. Aloud she said, "Of course."

"Anne," said Jane, still more solemnly, "what do you think of my brother Billy?"

Anne gasped over this unexpected question, and floundered

helplessly in her thoughts. Goodness, what *did* she think of Billy Andrews? She had never thought *anything* about him—round-faced, stupid, perpetually smiling, good-natured Billy Andrews. Did *anybody* ever think about Billy Andrews?

"I—I don't understand, Jane," she stammered. "What do you mean—exactly?"

"Do you like Billy?" asked Jane bluntly.

"Why—why—yes, I like him, of course," gasped Anne, wondering if she were telling the literal truth. Certainly she did not *dis*like Billy. But could the indifferent tolerance with which she regarded him, when he happened to be in her range of vision, be considered positive enough for liking? *What* was Jane trying to elucidate?

"Would you like him for a husband?" asked Jane calmly.

"A husband!" Anne had been sitting up in bed, the better to wrestle with the problem of her exact opinion of Billy Andrews. Now she fell flatly back on her pillows, the very breath gone out of her. "*Whose* husband?"

"Yours, of course," answered Jane. "Billy wants to marry you. He's always been crazy about you—and now father has given him the upper farm in his own name and there's nothing to prevent him from getting married. But he's so shy he couldn't ask you himself if you'd have him, so he got me to do it. I'd rather not have, but he gave me no peace till I said I would, if I got a good chance. What do you think about it, Anne?"

Was it a dream? Was it one of those nightmare things in which you find yourself engaged or married to some one you hate or don't know, without the slightest idea how it ever came about? No, she, Anne Shirley, was lying there, wide awake, in her own bed, and Jane Andrews was beside her, calmly proposing for her brother Billy. Anne did not know whether she wanted to writhe or laugh; but she could do neither, for Jane's feelings must not be hurt.

"I—I couldn't marry Billy, you know, Jane," she managed to gasp. "Why, such an idea never occurred to me—never!"

"I don't suppose it did," agreed Jane. "Billy has always been far too shy to think of courting. But you might think it over, Anne. Billy is a good fellow. I must say that, if he *is* my brother. He has no bad habits and he's a great worker, and you can depend on him. 'A bird in the hand is worth two in the bush.' He told me to tell you he'd be quite willing to wait till you got through college, if you insisted, though he *rather* get married this spring before the planting begins. He's always be very good to you, I'm sure, and you know, Anne, I'd love to have you for a sister."

"I can't marry Billy," said Anne decidedly. She had recovered her wits, and was even feeling a little angry. It was all so ridiculous. "There is no use thinking of it, Jane. I don't care anything for him in that way, and you must tell him so."

"Well, I didn't suppose you would," said Jane with a resigned sigh, feeling that she had done her best. "I told Billy I didn't believe it was a bit of use to ask you, but he insisted. Well, you've made your decision, Anne, and I hope you won't regret it."

Jane spoke rather coldly. She had been perfectly sure that the enamoured Billy had no chance at all of inducing Anne to marry him. Nevertheless, she felt a little resentment that Anne Shirley, who was, after all, merely an adopted orphan, without kith or kin, should refuse *her* brother—one of the Avonlea Andrews. Well, pride sometimes goes before a fall, Jane reflected ominously.

Anne permitted herself to smile in the darkness over the idea that she might ever regret not marrying Billy Andrews.

"I hope Billy won't feel very badly over it," she said nicely.

Jane made a movement as if she were tossing her head on her pillow.

"Oh, he won't break his heart. Billy has too much good sense for that. He likes Nettie Blewett pretty well, too, and mother would rather he married her than any one. She's such a good manager and saver. I think, when Billy is once sure you won't have him, he'll take Nettie. Please don't mention this to any one, will you, Anne?"

"Certainly not," said Anne, who had no desire whatever to publish abroad the fact that Billy Andrews wanted to marry her, preferring her, when all was said and done, to Nettie Blewett. Nettie Blewett!

"And now I suppose we'd better go to sleep," suggested Jane.

To sleep went Jane easily and speedily; but, though very unlike MacBeth in most respects, she had certainly contrived to murder sleep for Anne. That proposed-to damsel lay on a wakeful pillow until the wee sma's, but her meditations were far from being romantic. It was not, however, until the next morning that she had an opportunity to indulge in a good laugh over the whole affair. When Jane had gone home—still with a hint of frost in voice and manner because Anne had declined so ungratefully and decidedly the honour of an alliance with the House of Andrews—Anne retreated to the porch room, shut the door, and had her laugh out at last.

"If I could only share the joke with some one!" she thought. "But I can't. Diana is the only one I'd want to tell, and, even if I hadn't sworn secrecy to Jane, I can't tell Diana things now. She tells everything to Fred—I know she does. Well, I've had my first proposal. I supposed it would come some day—but I certainly never thought it would be by proxy. It's awfully funny—and yet there's a sting in it, too, somehow."

Anne knew quite well wherein the sting consisted, though she did not put it into words. She had had her secret dreams of the first time some one should ask her the great question. And it had, in those dreams, always been very romantic and beautiful: and the "some one" was to be very handsome and dark-eyed and distinguished-looking and eloquent, whether he were Prince Charming to be enraptured with "yes," or one to whom a regretful, beautifully worded, but hopeless refusal must be given. If the latter, the refusal was to be expressed so delicately that it would be next best thing to acceptance, and he would go away, after kissing her hand, assuring her of his unalterable, lifelong devotion. And it would always be a beautiful memory, to be proud of and a little sad about, also.

And now, this thrilling experience had turned out to be merely grotesque. Billy Andrews had got his sister to propose for him because his father had given him the upper farm; and if Anne wouldn't "have him" Nettie Blewett would. There was romance for you, with a vengeance! Anne laughed—and then sighed. The bloom had been brushed from one little maiden dream. Would the painful process go on until everything became prosaic and hum-drum?

CHAPTER 9

AN UNWELCOME LOVER AND A WELCOME FRIEND

THE SECOND term at Redmond sped as quickly as had the first—"actually whizzed away," Philippa said. Anne enjoyed it thoroughly in all its phases—the stimulating class rivalry, the making and deepening of new and helpful friendships, the gay little social stunts, the doings of the various societies of which she was a member, the widening of horizons and interests. She studied hard, for she had made up her mind to win the Thorburn Scholarship in English. This being won, meant that she could come back to Redmond the next year without trenching on Marilla's small savings—something Anne was determined she would not do.

Gilbert, too, was in full chase after a scholarship, but found plenty of time for frequent calls at Thirty-eight, St. John's. He was Anne's escort at nearly all the college affairs, and she knew that their names were coupled in Redmond gossip. Anne raged over this but was helpless; she could not cast an old friend like Gilbert aside, especially when he had grown suddenly wise and wary, as behooved him in the dangerous proximity of more than one Redmond youth who would gladly have taken his place by the side of the slender, red-haired co-ed, whose gray eyes were as alluring as stars of evening. Anne was never attended by the crowd of willing victims who hovered around Philippa's conquering march through her Freshman year; but there was a lanky, brainy Freshie, a jolly, little, round Sophomore, and a tall, learned Junior who all liked to call at Thirty-eight, St. John's, and talk over 'ologies and 'isms, as well as lighter subjects, with Anne, in the be-cushioned parlour of that domicile. Gilbert did not love any of them, and he was exceedingly careful to give none of them the advantage over him by any untimely display of his real feelings Anne-ward. To her he had become again the boy-comrade of Avonlea days, and as such could hold his own against any smitten swain who had so far entered the lists against him. As a companion, Anne honestly acknowledged nobody could be so satisfactory as Gilbert; she was very glad, so she told herself, that he had evidently dropped all nonsensical ideas—though she spent considerable time secretly wondering why.

Only one disagreeable incident marred that winter. Charlie Sloane, sitting bolt upright on Miss Ada's most dearly beloved cushion, asked Anne one night if she would promise "to become Mrs. Charlie Sloane some day." Coming after Billy Andrews' proxy effort, this was not quite the shock to Anne's romantic sensibilities that it would otherwise have been; but it was certainly another heart-rending disillusion. She was angry, too, for she felt that she had never given Charlie the slightest encouragement to suppose such a thing possible. But what could you expect of a Sloane, as Mrs. Rachel Lynde would ask scornfully? Charlie's whole attitude, tone, air, words, fairly reeked with Sloanishness. He was conferring a great honour— no doubt whatever about that. And when Anne, utterly insensible to the honour, refused him, as delicately and considerately as she could—for even a Sloane had feelings which ought not to be unduly lacerated—Sloanishness still further betrayed itself. Charlie certainly did not take his dismissal as Anne's imaginary rejected suitors did. Instead, he became angry, and showed it; he said two or three quite nasty things; Anne's temper flashed up mutinously and she retorted with a cutting little speech whose keenness pierced even Charlie's protective Sloanishness and reached the quick; he caught up his hat and flung himself out of the house with a very red face; Anne rushed up-stairs, falling twice over Miss Ada's cushions on the way, and threw herself on her bed, in tears of humiliation and rage. Had she actually stooped to quarrel with a Sloane? Was it possible anything Charlie Sloane could say had power to make her angry? Oh, this was degradation, indeed—worse even than being the rival of Nettie Blewett!

"I wish I need never see the horrible creature again," she sobbed vindictively into her pillows.

She could not avoid seeing him again, but the outraged Charlie took care that it should not be at very close quarters. Miss Ada's cushions were henceforth safe from his depredations, and when he met Anne on the street, or in Redmond's halls, his bow was icy in the extreme. Relations between these two old schoolmates continued to be thus strained for nearly a year! Then Charlie transferred his blighted affections to a round, rosy, snub-nosed, blue-eyed, little Sophomore who appreciated them as they deserved, whereupon he forgave Anne and condescended to be civil to her again; in a patronizing manner intended to show her just what she had lost.

One day Anne scurried excitedly into Priscilla's room.

"Read that," she cried, tossing Priscilla a letter. "It's from Stella—and she's coming to Redmond next year—and what do you think of her idea? I think it's a perfectly splendid one, if we can only carry it out. Do you suppose we can, Pris?"

"I'll be better able to tell you when I find out what it is," said Priscilla, casting aside a Greek lexicon and taking up Stella's letter. Stella Maynard had been one of their chums at Queen's Academy and had been teaching school ever since.

"But I'm going to give it up, Anne dear," she wrote, "and go to college next year. As I took the third year at Queen's I can enter the Sophomore year. I'm tired of teaching in a back country school. Some day I'm going to write a treatise on 'The Trials of a Country Schoolmarm.' It will be a harrowing bit of realism. It seems to be the prevailing impression that we live in clover, and have nothing to do but draw our quarter's salary. My treatise shall tell the truth about us. Why, if a week should pass without some one telling me that I am doing easy work for big pay I would conclude that I might as well order my ascension robe 'immediately and to onct.' 'Well, you get your money easy,' some rate-payer will tell me, condescendingly. 'All you have to do is to sit there and hear lessons.' I used to argue the matter at first, but I'm wiser now. Facts are stubborn things, but, as some one has wisely said, not half so stubborn as fallacies. So I only smile loftily now in eloquent silence. Why, I have nine grades in my school and I have to teach a little of everything, from investigating the interiors of earthworms to the study of the solar system. My youngest pupil is four—his mother sends him to school to 'get him out of the way'—and my oldest twenty—it 'suddenly struck him' that it would be easier to go to school and get an education than follow the plough any longer. In the wild effort to cram all sorts of research into six hours a day I don't wonder if the children feel like the little boy who was taken to see the biograph. 'I have to look for what's coming next before I know what went last,' he complained. I feel like that myself.

"And the letters I get, Anne! Tommy's mother writes me that Tommy is not coming on in arithmetic as fast as she would like. He is only in simple reduction yet, and Johnny Johnson is in fractions, and Johnny isn't half as smart as her Tommy, and she can't understand it. And Susy's father wants to know why Susy can't write a letter without mis-spelling half the words, and Dick's aunt wants me to change his seat, because that bad Brown boy he is sitting with is teaching him to say naughty words.

"As to the financial part—but I'll not begin on *that*. Those whom the gods wish to destroy they first make country schoolmarms!

"There, I feel better, after that growl. After all, I've enjoyed these past two years. But I'm coming to Redmond.

"And now, Anne, I've a little plan. You know how I loathe boarding. I've boarded for four years and I'm so tired of it. I don't feel like enduring three years more of it. Now, why can't you and Priscilla and I club together, rent a little house somewhere in Kingsport, and board ourselves? It would be cheaper than any other way. Of course, we would have to have a housekeeper and I have one ready on the spot. You've heard me speak of Aunt Jamesina? She's the sweetest aunt that ever lived, in spite of her name. She can't help that! She was called Jamesina because her father, whose name was James, was drowned at sea a month before she was born. I always call her Aunt Jimsie. Well, her only daughter has recently married and gone to the foreign mission field. Aunt Jamesina is left alone in a great big house, and she is horribly lonesome. She will come to Kingsport and keep house for us if we want her, and I know you'll both love her. The more I think of the plan the more I like it. We could have such good, independent times.

"Now, if you and Priscilla agree to it, wouldn't it be a good idea for you, who are on the spot, to look around and see if you can find a suitable house this spring? That would be better than leaving it till the fall. If you could get a furnished one so much the better, but if not, we can scare up a few sticks of furniture between us and old family friends with attics. Anyhow, decide as soon as you can and write me, so that Aunt Jamesina will know what plans to make for next year."

"I think it's a good idea," said Priscilla.

"So do I," agreed Anne delightedly. "Of course, we have a nice boarding-house here, but, when all's said and done, a boarding house isn't home. So let's go house-hunting at once, before exams come on."

"I'm afraid it will be hard enough to get a really suitable house," warned Priscilla. "Don't expect too much, Anne. Nice houses in nice localities will probably be away beyond our means. We'll likely have to content ourselves with a shabby little place on some street whereon live people whom to know is to be unknown, and make life inside compensate for the outside."

Accordingly they went house-hunting, but to find just what they wanted proved even harder than Priscilla had feared. Houses there were galore, furnished and unfurnished; but one was too big, another too small; this one too expensive, that one too far from Redmond. Exams were on and over; the last week of the term came and still their "house o' dreams," as Anne called it, remained a castle in the air.

"We shall have to give up and wait till the fall, I suppose," said Priscilla wearily, as they rambled through the park on one of April's darling days of breeze and blue, when the harbour was creaming and shimmering beneath the pearl-hued mists floating over it. "We may find some shack to shelter us then; and if not, boarding-houses we shall have always with us."

"I'm not going to worry about it just now, anyway, and spoil this lovely afternoon," said Anne, gazing around her with delight. The fresh chill air was faintly charged with the aroma of pine balsam, and the sky above was crystal clear and blue—a great inverted cup of blessing. "Spring is singing in my blood today, and the lure of April is abroad on the air. I'm seeing visions and dreaming dreams, Pris. That's because the wind is from the west. I do love the west wind. It sings of hope and gladness, doesn't it? When the east wind blows I always think of sorrowful rain on the eaves and sad waves on a gray shore. When I get old I shall have rheumatism when the wind is east."

"And isn't it jolly when you discard furs and winter garments for the first time and sally forth, like this, in spring attire?" laughed Priscilla. "Don't you feel as if you had been made over new?"

"Everything is new in the spring," said Anne. "Springs them-selves are always so new, too. No spring is ever just like any other spring. It always has something of its own to be its own peculiar sweetness. See how green the grass is around that little pond, and how the willow buds are bursting."

"And exams are over and gone—the time of Convocation will soon come—next Wednesday. This day week we'll be home."

"I'm glad," said Anne dreamily. "There are so many things I want to do. I want to sit on the back porch steps and feel the breeze blowing down over Mr. Harrison's fields. I want to hunt ferns in the Haunted Wood and gather violets in Violet Vale. Do you remember the day of our golden picnic, Priscilla? I want to hear the frogs singing and the poplars whispering. But I've learned to love Kingsport, too, and I'm glad I'm coming back next fall. If I hadn't won the Thorburn I don't believe I could have. I *couldn't* take any of Marilla's little hoard."

"If we could only find a house!" sighed Priscilla. "Look over there at Kingsport, Anne—houses, houses everywhere, and not one for us."

"Stop it, Pris. 'The best is yet to be.' Like the old Roman, we'll find a house or build one. On a day like this there's no such word as fail in my bright lexicon."

They lingered in the park until sunset, living in the amazing miracle and glory and wonder of the springtide; and they went home as usual, by way of Spofford Avenue, that they might have the delight of looking at Patty's Place.

"I feel as if something mysterious were going to happen right away—'by the pricking of my thumbs,'" said Anne, as they went up the slope. "It's a nice story-bookish feeling. Why—why—why! Priscilla Grant, look over there and tell me if it's true, or am I seein' things?"

Priscilla looked. Anne's thumbs and eyes had not deceived her. Over the arched gateway of Patty's Place dangled a little, modest sign. It said "To Let, Furnished. Inquire Within."

"Priscilla," said Anne, in a whisper, "do you suppose it's possible that we could rent Patty's Place?"

"No, I don't," averred Priscilla. "It would be too good to be true. Fairy tales don't happen nowadays. I *won't* hope, Anne.

The disappointment would be too awful to bear. They're sure to want more for it than we can afford. Remember, it's on Spofford Avenue."

"We must find out anyhow," said Anne resolutely. "It's too late to call this evening, but we'll come tomorrow. Oh, Pris, if we can get this darling spot! I've always felt that my fortunes were linked with Patty's Place, ever since I saw it first."

CHAPTER 10

PATTY'S PLACE

THE NEXT evening found them treading resolutely the herringbone walk through the tiny garden. The April wind was filling the pine trees with its roundelay, and the grove was alive with robins—great, plump, saucy fellows, strutting along the paths. The girls rang rather timidly, and were admitted by a grim and ancient handmaiden. The door opened directly into a large living-room, where by a cheery little fire sat two other ladies, both of whom were also grim and ancient. Except that one looked to be about seventy and the other fifty, there seemed little difference between them. Each had amazingly big, light-blue eyes behind steel-rimmed spectacles; each wore a cap and a gray shawl; each was knitting without haste and without rest; each rocked placidly and looked at the girls without speaking; and just behind each sat a large white china dog, with round green spots all over it, a green nose and green ears. Those dogs captured Anne's fancy on the spot; they seemed like the twin guardian deities of Patty's Place.

For a few minutes nobody spoke. The girls were too nervous to find words, and neither the ancient ladies nor the china dogs seemed conversationally inclined. Anne glanced about the room. What a dear place it was! Another door opened out of it directly into the pine grove and the robins came boldly up on the very step. The floor was spotted with round, braided mats, such as

Marilla made at Green Gables, but which were considered out of date everywhere else, even in Avonlea. And yet here they were on Spofford Avenue! A big, polished grandfather's clock ticked loudly and solemnly in a corner. There were delightful little cupboards over the mantel-piece, behind whose glass doors gleamed quaint bits of china. The walls were hung with old prints and silhouettes. In one corner the stairs went up, and at the first low turn was a long window with an inviting seat. It was all just as Anne had known it must be.

By this time the silence had grown too dreadful, and Priscilla nudged Anne to intimate that she *must* speak.

"We—we—saw by your sign that this house is to let," said Anne faintly, addressing the older lady, who was evidently Miss Patty Spofford.

"Oh, yes," said Miss Patty. "I intended to take that sign down today."

"Then—then we are too late," said Anne sorrowfully. "You've let it to some one else?"

"No, but we have decided not to let it at all."

"Oh, I'm so sorry," exclaimed Anne impulsively. "I love this place so. I did hope we could have got it."

Then did Miss Patty lay down her knitting, take off her specs, rub them, put them on again, and for the first time look at Anne as at a human being. The other lady followed her example so perfectly that she might as well have been a reflection in a mirror.

"You *love* it," said Miss Patty with emphasis. "Does that mean that you really *love* it? Or that you merely like the looks of it? The girls nowadays indulge in such exaggerated statements that one never can tell what they *do* mean. It wasn't so in my young days. *Then* a girl did not say she *loved* turnips, in just the same tone as she might have said she loved her mother or her Saviour."

Anne's conscience bore her up.

"I really do love it," she said gently. "I've loved it ever since I saw it last fall. My two college chums and I want to keep house next year instead of boarding, so we are looking for a little place to rent; and when I saw that this house was to let I was so happy."

"If you love it, you can have it," said Miss Patty. "Maria

and I decided today that we would not let it after all, because we did not like any of the people who have wanted it. We don't *have* to let it. We can afford to go to Europe even if we don't let it. It would help us out, but not for gold will I let my home pass into the possession of such people as have come here and looked at it. *You* are different. I believe you do love it and will be good to it. You can have it."

"If—if we can afford to pay what you ask for it," hesitated Anne.

Miss Patty named the amount required. Anne and Priscilla looked at each other. Priscilla shook her head.

"I'm afraid we can't afford quite so much," said Anne, choking back her disappointment. "You see, we are only college girls and we are poor."

"What were you thinking you could afford?" demanded Miss Patty, ceasing not to knit.

Anne named her amount. Miss Patty nodded gravely.

"That will do. As I told you, it is not strictly necessary that we should let it at all. We are not rich, but we have enough to go to Europe on. I have never been in Europe in my life, and never expected or wanted to go. But my niece there, Maria Spofford, has taken a fancy to go. Now, you know a young person like Maria can't go globe-trotting alone."

"No—I—I suppose not," murmured Anne, seeing that Miss Patty was quite solemnly in earnest.

"Of course not. So I have to go along to look after her. I expect to enjoy it, too; I'm seventy years old, but I'm not tired of living yet. I daresay I'd have gone to Europe before if the idea had occurred to me. We shall be away for two years, perhaps three. We sail in June and we shall send you the key, and leave all in order for you to take possession when you choose. We shall pack away a few things we prize especially, but all the rest will be left."

"Will you leave the china dogs?" asked Anne timidly.

"Would you like me to?"

"Oh, indeed, yes. They are delightful."

A pleased expression came into Miss Patty's face.

"I think a great deal of those dogs," she said proudly. "They are over a hundred years old, and they have sat on either side of this fireplace ever since my brother Aaron brought them

from London fifty years ago. Spofford Avenue was called after
my brother Aaron."

"A fine man he was," said Miss Maria, speaking for the first
time. "Ah, you don't see the like of him nowadays."

"He was a good uncle to you, Maria," said Miss Patty, with
evident emotion. "You do well to remember him."

"I shall always remember him," said Miss Maria solemnly.
"I can see him, this minute, standing there before that fire,
with his hands under his coat-tails, beaming on us."

Miss Maria took out her handkerchief and wiped her eyes;
but Miss Patty came resolutely back from the regions of sentiment to those of business.

"I shall leave the dogs where they are, if you will promise
to be very careful of them," she said. "Their names are Gog
and Magog. Gog looks to the right and Magog to the left. And
there's just one thing more. You don't object, I hope, to this
house being called Patty's Place?"

"No, indeed. We think that is one of the nicest things about
it."

"You have sense, I see," said Miss Patty in a tone of great
satisfaction. "Would you believe it? All the people who came
here to rent the house wanted to know if they couldn't take
the name off the gate during their occupation of it. I told them
roundly that the name went with the house. This has been
Patty's Place ever since my brother Aaron left it to me in his
will, and Patty's Place it shall remain until I die and Maria
dies. After that happens the next possessor can call it any fool
name he likes," concluded Miss Patty, much as she might have
said, "After that—the deluge." "And now, wouldn't you like
to go over the house and see it all before we consider the
bargain made?"

Further exploration still further delighted the girls. Besides
the big living-room, there was a kitchen and a small bedroom
down-stairs. Up-stairs were three rooms, one large and two
small. Anne took an especial fancy to one of the small ones,
looking out into the big pines, and hoped it would be hers. It
was papered in pale blue and had a little, old-timey toilet table
with sconces for candles. There was a diamond-paned window
with a seat under the blue muslin frills that would be a satisfying
spot for studying or dreaming.

"It's all so delicious that I know we are going to wake up and find it a fleeting vision of the night," said Priscilla as they went away.

"Miss Patty and Miss Maria are hardly such stuff as dreams are made of," laughed Anne. "Can you fancy them 'globe-trotting'—especially in those shawls and caps?"

"I suppose they'll take them off when they really begin to trot," said Priscilla, "but I know they'll take their knitting with them everywhere. They simply couldn't be parted from it. They will walk about Westminster Abbey and knit, I feel sure. Meanwhile, Anne, we shall be living in Patty's Place—*and* on Spofford Avenue. I feel like a millionairess even now."

"I feel like one of the morning stars that sang for joy," said Anne.

Phil Gordon crept into Thirty-eight, St. John's, that night and flung herself on Anne's bed.

"Girls, dear, I'm tired to death. I feel like the man without a country—or was it without a shadow? I forget which. Anyway, I've been packing up."

"And I suppose you are worn out because you couldn't decide which things to pack first, or where to put them," laughed Priscilla.

"E-zackly. And when I had got everything jammed in somehow, and my landlady and her maid had both sat on it while I locked it, I discovered I had packed a whole lot of things I wanted for Convocation at the very bottom. I had to unlock the old thing and poke and dive into it for an hour before I fished out what I wanted. I would get hold of something that felt like what I was looking for, and I'd yank it up, and it would be something else. No, Anne, I did NOT swear."

"I didn't say you did."

"Well, you looked it. But I admit my thoughts verged on the profane. And I have such a cold in the head—I can do nothing but sniffle, sigh and sneeze. Isn't that alliterative agony for you? Queen Anne, do say something to cheer me up."

"Remember that next Thursday night you'll be back in the land of Alec and Alonzo," suggested Anne.

Phil shook her head dolefully.

"More alliteration. No, I don't want Alec and Alonzo when I have a cold in the head. But what has happened you two?

Now that I look at you closely you seem all lighted up with an internal iridescence. Why, you're actually *shining!* What's up?"

"We are going to live in Patty's Place next winter," said Anne triumphantly. "*Live,* mark you, not board! We've rented it, and Stella Maynard is coming, and her aunt is going to keep house for us."

Phil bounced up, wiped her nose, and fell on her knees before Anne.

"Girls—girls—let me come, too. Oh, I'll be so good. If there's no room for me I'll sleep in the little dog-house in the orchard— I've seen it. Only let me come."

"Get up, you goose."

"I won't stir off my marrow bones till you tell me I can live with you next winter."

Anne and Priscilla looked at each other. Then Anne said slowly.

"Phil dear, we'd love to have you. But we may as well speak plainly. I'm poor—Pris is poor—Stella Maynard is poor—our housekeeping will have to be very simple and our table plain. You'd have to live as we would. Now, you are rich and your boarding-house fare attests the fact."

"Oh, what do I care for that?" demanded Phil tragically. "Better a dinner of herbs where your chums are than a stalled ox in a lonely boarding-house. Don't think I'm *all* stomach, girls. I'll be willing to live on bread and water—with just a *leetle* jam—if you'll let me come."

"And then," continued Anne, "there will be a good deal of work to be done. Stella's aunt can't do it all. We all expect to have our chores to do. Now, you—"

"Toil not, neither do I spin," finished Philippa. "But I'll learn to do things. You'll only have to show me once. I *can* make my own bed to begin with. And remember that, though I can't cook, I *can* keep my temper. That's something. And I *never* growl about the weather. That's more. Oh, please, please! I never wanted anything so much in my life—and this floor is awfully hard."

"There's just one more thing," said Priscilla resolutely. "You, Phil, as all Redmond knows, entertain callers almost every evening. Now, at Patty's Place we can't do that. We have decided that we shall be at home to our friends on Friday evenings only. If you come with us you'll have to abide by that rule."

"Well, you don't think I'll mind that, do you? Why, I'm glad of it. I knew I should have had some such rule myself, but I hadn't enough decision to make it or stick to it. When I can shuffle off the responsibility on you it will be a real relief. If you won't let me cast in my lot with you I'll die of the disappointment and then I'll come back and haunt you. I'll camp on the very doorstep of Patty's Place and you won't be able to go out or come in without falling over my spook."

Again Anne and Priscilla exchanged eloquent looks.

"Well," said Anne, "of course we can't promise to take you until we've consulted with Stella; but I don't think she'll object, and, as far as we are concerned, you may come and glad welcome."

"If you get tired of our simple life you can leave us, and no questions asked," added Priscilla.

Phil sprang up, hugged them both jubilantly, and went on her way rejoicing.

"I hope things will go right," said Priscilla soberly.

"We must *make* them go right," avowed Anne. "I think Phil will fit into our 'appy little 'ome very well."

"Oh, Phil's a dear to rattle round with and be chums. And, of course, the more there are of us the easier it will be on our slim purses. But how will she be to live with? You have to summer and winter with any one before you know if she's *livable* or not."

"Oh, well, we'll all be put to the test, as far as that goes. And we must quit us like sensible folk, living and let live. Phil isn't selfish, though she's a little thoughtless, and I believe we will all get on beautifully in Patty's Place."

CHAPTER 11

THE ROUND OF LIFE

ANNE WAS back in Avonlea with the luster of the Thorburn Scholarship on her brow. People told her she hadn't changed much, in a tone which hinted they were surprised and a little disappointed she hadn't. Avonlea had not changed, either. At least, so it seemed at first. But as Anne sat in the Green Gables pew, on the first Sunday after her return, and looked over the congregation, she saw several little changes which, all coming home to her at once, made her realize that time did not quite stand still, even in Avonlea. A new minister was in the pulpit. In the pews more than one familiar face was missing forever. Old "Uncle Abe," his prophesying over and done with, Mrs. Peter Sloane, who had sighed, it was to be hoped, for the last time, Timothy Cotton, who, as Mrs. Rachel Lynde said "had actually managed to die at last after practising at it for twenty years," and old Josiah Sloane, whom nobody knew in his coffin because he had his whiskers neatly trimmed, were all sleeping in the little graveyard behind the church. And Billy Andrews was married to Nettie Blewett! They "appeared out" that Sunday. When Billy, beaming with pride and happiness, showed his be-plumed and be-silked bride into the Harmon Andrews' pew, Anne dropped her lids to hide her dancing eyes. She recalled the stormy winter night of the Christmas holidays when Jane had proposed for Billy. He certainly had not broken his heart over his rejection. Anne wondered if Jane had also proposed to Nettie for him, or if he had mustered enough spunk to ask the fateful question himself. All the Andrews family seemed to share in his pride and pleasure, from Mrs. Harmon in the pew to Jane in the choir. Jane had resigned from the Avonlea school and intended to go West in the fall.

"Can't get a beau in Avonlea, that's what," said Mrs. Rachel Lynde scornfully. "*Says* she thinks she'll have better health out West. I never heard her health was poor before."

"Jane is a nice girl," Anne had said loyally. "She never tried to attract attention, as some did."

"Oh, she never chased the boys, if that's what you mean,"

said Mrs. Rachel. "But she'd like to be married, just as much as anybody, that's what. What else would take her out West to some forsaken place whose only recommendation is that men are plenty and women scarce? Don't you tell me!"

But it was not at Jane Anne gazed that day in dismay and surprise. It was at Ruby Gillis, who sat beside her in the choir. What had happened to Ruby? She was even handsomer than ever; but her blue eyes were too bright and lustrous, and the colour of her cheeks was hectically brilliant; besides, she was very thin; the hands that held her hymn-book were almost transparent in their delicacy.

"Is Ruby Gillis ill?" Anne asked of Mrs. Lynde, as they went home from church.

"Ruby Gillis is dying of galloping consumption," said Mrs. Lynde bluntly. "Everybody knows it except herself and her family. *They* won't give in. If you ask *them,* she's perfectly well. She hasn't been able to teach since she had that attack of congestion in the winter, but she says she's going to teach again in the fall, and she's after the White Sands school. She'll be in her grave, poor girl, when White Sands school opens, that's what."

Anne listened in shocked silence. Ruby Gillis, her old school-chum, dying? Could it be possible? Of late years they had grown apart; but the old tie of school-girl intimacy was there, and made itself felt sharply in the tug the news gave at Anne's heart-strings. Ruby, the brilliant, the merry, the coquettish! It was impossible to associate the thought of her with anything like death. She had greeted Anne with gay cordiality after church, and urged her to come up the next evening.

"I'll be away Tuesday and Wednesday evenings," she had whispered triumphantly. "There's a concert at Carmody and a party at White Sands. Herb Spencer's going to take me. He's my *latest.* Be sure to come up tomorrow. I'm dying for a good talk with you. I want to hear all about your doings at Redmond."

Anne knew that Ruby meant that she wanted to tell Anne all about her own recent flirtations, but she promised to go, and Diana offered to go with her.

"I've been wanting to go to see Ruby for a long while," she told Anne, when they left Green Gables the next evening, "but I really couldn't go alone. It's so awful to hear Ruby rattling on as she does, and pretending there is nothing the matter with her, even when she can hardly speak for coughing. She's fighting so hard for her life, and yet she hasn't any chance at all, they say."

The girls walked silently down the red, twilit road. The robins were singing vespers in the high tree-tops, filling the golden air with their jubilant voices. The silver fluting of the frogs came from marshes and ponds, over fields where seeds were beginning to stir with life and thrill to the sunshine and rain that had drifted over them. The air was fragrant with the wild, sweet, wholesome smell of young raspberry copses. White mists were hovering in the silent hollows and violet stars were shining bluely on the brooklands.

"What a beautiful sunset," said Diana. "Look, Anne, it's just like a land in itself, isn't it? That long, low bank of purple cloud is the shore, and the clear sky further on is like a golden sea."

"If we could sail to it in the moonshine boat Paul wrote of in his old composition—you remember?—how nice it would be," said Anne, rousing from her reverie. "Do you think we could find all our yesterdays there, Diana—all our old springs and blossoms? The beds of flowers that Paul saw there are the roses that have bloomed for us in the past?"

"Don't!" said Diana. "You make me feel as if we were old women with everything in life behind us."

"I think I've almost felt as if we were since I heard about poor Ruby," said Anne. "If it is true that she is dying any other sad thing might be true, too."

"You don't mind calling in at Elisha Wright's for a moment, do you?" asked Diana. "Mother asked me to leave this little dish of jelly for Aunt Atossa."

"Who is Aunt Atossa?"

"Oh, haven't you heard? She's Mrs. Samson Coates of Spencervale—Mrs. Elisha Wright's aunt. She's father's aunt, too. Her husband died last winter and she was left very poor and lonely, so the Wrights took her to live with them. Mother thought we ought to take her, but father put his foot down. Live with Aunt Atossa he would not."

"Is she so terrible?" asked Anne absently.

"You'll probably see what she's like before we can get away," said Diana significantly. "Father says she has a face like a hatchet—it cuts the air. But her tongue is sharper still."

Late as it was Aunt Atossa was cutting potato sets in the Wright kitchen. She wore a faded old wrapper, and her gray hair was decidedly untidy. Aunt Atossa did not like being "caught in a kilter," so she went out of her way to be disagreeable.

"Oh, so you're Anne Shirley?" she said, when Diana introduced Anne. "I've heard of you." Her tone implied that she had heard nothing good. "Mrs. Andrews was telling me you were home. She said you had improved a good deal."

There was no doubt Aunt Atossa thought there was plenty of room for further improvement. She ceased not from cutting sets with much energy.

"Is it any use to ask you to sit down?" she inquired sarcastically. "Of course, there's nothing very entertaining here for you. The rest are all away."

"Mother sent you this little pot of rhubarb jelly," said Diana pleasantly. "She made it today and thought you might like some."

"Oh, thanks," said Aunt Atossa sourly. "I never fancy your mother's jelly—she always makes it too sweet. However, I'll try to worry some down. My appetite's been dreadful poor this spring. I'm far from well," continued Aunt Atossa solemnly, "but still I keep a-doing. People who can't work aren't wanted *here*. If it isn't too much trouble will you be condescending enough to set the jelly in the pantry? I'm in a hurry to get these spuds done tonight. I suppose you two *ladies* never do anything like this. You'd be afraid of spoiling your hands."

"I used to cut potato sets before we rented the farm," smiled Anne.

"I do it yet," laughed Diana. "I cut sets three days last week. Of course," she added teasingly, "I did my hands up in lemon juice and kid gloves every night after it."

Aunt Atossa sniffed.

"I suppose you got that notion out of some of those silly magazines you read so many of. I wonder your mother allows you. But she always spoiled you. We all thought when George married her she wouldn't be a suitable wife for him."

Aunt Atossa sighed heavily, as if all forebodings upon the

occasion of George Barry's marriage had been amply and darkly fulfilled.

"Going, are you?" she inquired, as the girls rose. "Well, I suppose you can't find much amusement talking to an old woman like me. It's such a pity the boys ain't home."

"We want to run in and see Ruby Gillis a little while," explained Diana.

"Oh, anything does for an excuse, of course," said Aunt Atossa, amiably. "Just whip in and whip out before you have time to say how-do decently. It's college airs, I s'pose. You'd be wiser to keep away from Ruby Gillis. The doctors say consumption's catching. I always knew Ruby'd get something, gadding off to Boston last fall for a visit. People who ain't content to stay home always catch something."

"People who don't go visiting catch things, too. Sometimes they even die," said Diana solemnly.

"Then they don't have themselves to blame for it," retorted Aunt Atossa triumphantly. "I hear you are to be married in June, Diana."

"There is no truth in that report," said Diana, blushing.

"Well, don't put it off too long," said Aunt Atossa significantly. "You'll fade soon—you're all complexion and hair. And the Wrights are terrible fickle. You ought to wear a hat, *Miss Shirley*. Your nose is freckling scandalous. My, but you *are* redheaded! Well, I s'pose we're all as the Lord made us! Give Marilla Cuthbert my respects. She's never been to see me since I come to Avonlea, but I s'pose I oughtn't to complain. The Cuthberts always did think themselves a cut higher than any one else round here."

"Oh, isn't she dreadful?" gasped Diana, as they escaped down the lane.

"She's worse than Miss Eliza Andrews," said Anne. "But then think of living all your life with a name like Atossa! Wouldn't it sour almost any one? She should have tried to imagine her name was Cordelia. It might have helped her a great deal. It certainly helped me in the days when I didn't like *Anne*."

"Josie Pye will be just like her when she grows up," said Diana. "Josie's mother and Aunt Atossa are cousins, you know. Oh, dear, I'm glad that's over. She's so malicious—she seems to put a bad flavour in everything. Father tells such a funny story about her. One time they had a minister in Spencervale who was a very good, spiritual man but very deaf. He couldn't hear any ordinary conversation at all. Well, they used to have a prayer meeting on Sunday evenings, and all the church members present would get up and pray in turn, or say a few words on some Bible verse. But one evening Aunt Atossa bounced up. She didn't either pray or preach. Instead, she lit into everybody else in the church and gave them a fearful raking down, calling them right out by name and telling them how they all had behaved, and casting up all the quarrels and scandals of the past ten years. Finally she wound up by saying that she was disgusted with Spencervale church and she never meant to darken its door again, and she hoped a fearful judgment would come upon it. Then she sat down out of breath, and the minister, who hadn't heard a word she said, immediately remarked, in a very devout voice, 'Amen! The Lord grant our dear sister's prayer!' You ought to hear father tell the story."

"Speaking of stories, Diana," remarked Anne, in a significant, confidential tone, "do you know that lately I have been wondering if I could write a short story—a story that would be good enough to be published?"

"Why, of course you could," said Diana, after she had grasped the amazing suggestion. "You used to write perfectly thrilling stories years ago in our old Story Club."

"Well, I hardly meant one of that kind of stories," smiled Anne. "I've been thinking about it a little of late, but I'm almost afraid to try, for, if I should fail, it would be too humiliating."

"I heard Priscilla say once that all Mrs. Morgan's first stories were rejected. But I'm sure yours wouldn't be, Anne, for it's likely editors have more sense nowadays."

"Margaret Burton, one of the Junior girls at Redmond, wrote a story last winter and it was published in the *Canadian Woman.* I really do think I could write one at least as good."

"And will you have it published in the *Canadian Woman?*"

"I might try one of the bigger magazines first. It all depends on what kind of a story I write."

"What is it to be about?"

"I don't know yet. I want to get hold of a good plot. I believe that is very necessary from an editor's point of view. The only thing I've settled on is the heroine's name. It is to be *Averil Lester*. Rather pretty, don't you think? Don't mention this to any one, Diana. I haven't told anybody but you and Mr. Harrison. *He* wasn't very encouraging—he said there was far too much trash written nowadays as it was, and he'd expected something better of me, after a year at college."

"What does Mr. Harrison know about it?" demanded Diana scornfully.

They found the Gillis home gay with lights and callers. Leonard Kimball, of Spencervale, and Morgan Bell, of Carmody, were glaring at each other across the parlour. Several merry girls had dropped in. Ruby was dressed in white and her eyes and cheeks were very brilliant. She laughed and chattered incessantly, and after the other girls had gone she took Anne up-stairs to display her new summer dresses.

"I've a blue silk to make up yet, but it's a little heavy for summer wear. I think I'll leave it until the fall. I'm going to teach in White Sands, you know. How do you like my hat? That one you had on in church yesterday was real dinky. But I like something brighter for myself. Did you notice those two ridiculous boys down-stairs? They've both come determined to sit each other out. I don't care a single bit about either of them, you know. Herb Spencer is the one I like. Sometimes I really do think's he's *Mr. Right*. At Christmas I thought the Spencervale schoolmaster was that. But I found out something about him that turned me against him. He nearly went insane when I turned him down. I wish those two boys hadn't come tonight. I wanted to have a nice good talk with you, Anne, and tell you such heaps of things. You and I were always good chums, weren't we?"

Ruby slipped her arm about Anne's waist with a shallow little laugh. But just for a moment their eyes met, and, behind all the luster of Ruby's, Anne saw something that made her heart ache.

"Come up often, won't you, Anne?" whispered Ruby. "Come alone—I want you."

"Are you feeling quite well, Ruby?"

"Me! Why, I'm perfectly well. I never felt better in my life. Of course, that congestion last winter pulled me down a little.

But just see my colour. I don't look much like an invalid, I'm sure."

Ruby's voice was almost sharp. She pulled her arm away from Anne, as if in resentment, and ran down-stairs, where she was gayer than ever, apparently so much absorbed in bantering her two swains that Diana and Anne felt rather out of it and soon went away.

—————— CHAPTER 12 ——————

"AVERIL'S ATONEMENT"

"WHAT ARE you dreaming of, Anne?"

The two girls were loitering one evening in a fairy hollow of the brook. Ferns nodded in it, and little grasses were green, and wild pears hung finely-scented, white curtains around it.

Anne roused herself from her reverie with a happy sigh.

"I was thinking out my story, Diana."

"Oh, have you really begun it?" cried Diana, all alight with eager interest in a moment.

"Yes, I have only a few pages written, but I have it all pretty well thought out. I've had such a time to get a suitable plot. None of the plots that suggested themselves suited a girl named *Averil*."

"Couldn't you have changed her name?"

"No, the thing was impossible. I tried to, but I couldn't do it, any more than I could change yours. *Averil* was so real to me that no matter what other name I tried to give her I just thought of her as *Averil* behind it all. But finally I got a plot that matched her. Then came the excitement of choosing names for all my characters. You have no idea how fascinating that is. I've lain awake for hours thinking over those names. The hero's name is *Perceval Dalrymple.*"

"Have you named *all* the characters?" asked Diana wistfully. "If you hadn't I was going to ask you to let me name *one*—

just some unimportant person. I'd feel as if I had a share in the story then."

"You may name the little hired boy who lived with the *Lesters*," conceded Anne. "He is not very important, but he is the only one left unnamed."

"Call him *Raymond Fitzosborne*," suggested Diana, who had a store of such names laid away in her memory, relics of the old "Story Club," which she and Anne and Jane Andrews and Ruby Gillis had had in their schooldays.

Anne shook her head doubtfully.

"I'm afraid that is too aristocratic a name for a chore boy, Diana. I couldn't imagine a Fitzosborne feeding pigs and picking up chips, could you?"

Diana didn't see why, if you had an imagination at all, you couldn't stretch it to that extent; but probably Anne knew best, and the chore boy was finally christened *Robert Ray,* to be called *Bobby* should occasion require.

"How much do you suppose you'll get for it?" asked Diana.

But Anne had not thought about this at all. She was in pursuit of fame, not filthy lucre, and her literary dreams were as yet untainted by mercenary considerations.

"You'll let me read it, won't you?" pleaded Diana.

"When it is finished I'll read it to you and Mr. Harrison, and I shall want you to criticise it *severely*. No one else shall see it until it is published."

"How are you going to end it—happily or unhappily?"

"I'm not sure. I'd like it to end unhappily, because that would be so much more romantic. But I understand editors have a prejudice against sad endings. I heard Professor Hamilton say once that nobody but a genius should try to write an unhappy ending. And," concluded Anne modestly, "I'm anything but a genius."

"Oh, I like happy endings best. You'd better let him marry her," said Diana, who, especially since her engagement to Fred, thought this was how every story should end.

"But you like to cry over stories?"

"Oh, yes, in the middle of them. But I like everything to come right at last."

"I must have *one* pathetic scene in it," said Anne thoughtfully.

"I might let *Robert Ray* be injured in an accident and have a death scene."

"No, you mustn't kill *Bobby* off," declared Diana, laughing. "He belongs to me and I want him to live and flourish. Kill somebody else if you have to."

For the next fortnight Anne writhed or revelled, according to mood, in her literary pursuits. Now she would be jubilant over a brilliant idea, now despairing because some contrary character would *not* behave properly. Diana could not understand this.

"*Make* them do as you want them to," she said.

"I can't," mourned Anne. "Averil is such an unmanagable heroine. She *will* do and say things I never meant her to. Then that spoils everything that went before and I have to write it all over again."

Finally, however, the story was finished, and Anne read it to Diana in the seclusion of the porch gable. She had achieved her "pathetic scene" without sacrificing *Robert Ray,* and she kept a watchful eye on Diana as she read it. Diana rose to the occasion and cried properly; but, when the end came, she looked a little disappointed.

"Why did you kill *Maurice Lennox?*" she asked reproachfully.

"He was the villain," protested Anne. "He had to be punished."

"I like him best of them all," said unreasonable Diana.

"Well, he's dead, and he'll have to stay dead," said Anne, rather resentfully. "If I had let him live he'd have gone on persecuting *Averil* and *Perceval.*"

"Yes—unless you had reformed him."

"That wouldn't have been romantic, and, besides, it would have made the story too long."

"Well, anyway, it's a perfectly elegant story, Anne, and will make you famous, of that I'm sure. Have you got a title for it?"

"Oh, I decided on the title long ago. I call it *Averil's Atonement.* Doesn't that sound nice and alliterative? Now, Diana, tell me candidly, do you see any faults in my story?"

"Well," hesitated Diana, "that part where *Averil* makes the cake doesn't seem to me quite romantic enough to match the rest. It's just what anybody might do. Heroines shouldn't do cooking, *I* think."

"Why, that is where the humour comes in, and it's one of the best parts of the whole story," said Anne. And it may be stated that in this she was quite right.

Diana prudently refrained from any further criticism, but Mr. Harrison was much harder to please. First he told her there was entirely too much description in the story.

"Cut out all those flowery passages," he said unfeelingly.

Anne had an uncomfortable conviction that Mr. Harrison was right, and she forced herself to expunge most of her beloved descriptions, though it took three re-writings before the story could be pruned down to please the fastidious Mr. Harrison.

"I've left out *all* the descriptions but the sunset," she said at last. "I simply *couldn't* let it go. It was the best of them all."

"It hasn't anything to do with the story," said Mr. Harrison, "and you shouldn't have laid the scene among rich city people. What do you know of them? Why didn't you lay it right here in Avonlea—changing the name, of course, or else Mrs. Rachel Lynde would probably think she was the heroine."

"Oh, that would never have done," protested Anne. "Avonlea is the dearest place in the world, but it isn't quite romantic enough for the scene of a story."

"I daresay there's been many a romance in Avonlea—and many a tragedy, too," said Mr. Harrison drily. "But your folks ain't like real folks anywhere. They talk too much and use too high-flown language. There's one place where that *Dalrymple* chap talks even on for two pages, and never lets the girl get a word in edgewise. If he'd done that in real life she'd have pitched him."

"I don't believe it," said Anne flatly. In her secret soul she thought that the beautiful, poetical things said to *Averil* would win any girl's heart completely. Besides, it was gruesome to hear of *Averil,* the stately, queen-like *Averil,* "pitching" any one. *Averil* "declined her suitors."

"Anyhow," resumed the merciless Mr. Harrison, "I don't see why *Maurice Lennox* didn't get her. He was twice the man the other is. He did bad things, but he *did* them. *Perceval* hadn't time for anything but mooning."

"Mooning." That was even worse than "pitching!"

"*Maurice Lennox* was the villain," said Anne indignantly. "I don't see why every one likes him better than *Perceval.*"

"Perceval is too good. He's aggravating. Next time you write about a hero put a little spice of human nature in him."

"*Averil* couldn't have married *Maurice.* He was bad."

"She'd have reformed him. You *can* reform a man; you can't reform a jelly-fish, of course. Your story isn't bad—it's kind of interesting, I'll admit. But you're too young to write a story that would be worth while. Wait ten years."

Anne made up her mind that the next time she wrote a story she wouldn't ask anybody to criticise it. It was too discouraging. She would not read the story to Gilbert, although she told him about it.

"If it is a success you'll see it when it is published, Gilbert, but if it is a failure nobody shall ever see it."

Marilla knew nothing about the venture. In imagination Anne saw herself reading a story out of a magazine to Marilla, entrapping her into praise of it—for in imagination all things are possible—and then triumphantly announcing herself the author.

One day Anne took to the Post Office a long, bulky envelope, addressed, with the delightful confidence of youth and inexperience, to the very biggest of the "big" magazines. Diana was as excited over it as Anne herself.

"How long do you suppose it will be before you hear from it?" she asked.

"It shouldn't be longer than a fortnight. Oh, how happy and proud I shall be if it is accepted!"

"Of course it will be accepted, and they will likely ask you to send them more. You may be as famous as Mrs. Morgan some day, Anne, and then how proud I'll be of knowing you," said Diana, who possessed, at least, the striking merit of an unselfish admiration of the gifts and graces of her friends.

A week of delightful dreaming followed, and then came a bitter awakening. One evening Diana found Anne in the porch gable, with suspicious-looking eyes. On the table lay a long envelope and a crumpled manuscript.

"Anne, your story hasn't come back?" cried Diana incredulously.

"Yes, it has," said Anne shortly.

"Well, that editor must be crazy. What reason did he give?"

"No reason at all. There is just a printed slip saying that it wasn't found available."

"I never thought much of that magazine, anyway," said Diana hotly. "The stories in it are not half as interesting as those in the *Canadian Woman,* although it costs so much more. I suppose the editor is prejudiced against any one who isn't a Yankee. Don't be discouraged, Anne. Remember how Mrs. Morgan's stories came back. Send yours to the *Canadian Woman.*"

"I believe I will," said Anne, plucking up heart. "And if it is published I'll send that American editor a marked copy. But I'll cut the sunset out. I believe Mr. Harrison was right."

Out came the sunset; but in spite of this heroic mutilation the editor of the *Canadian Woman* sent *Averil's Atonement* back so promptly that the indignant Diana declared that it couldn't have been read at all, and vowed she was going to stop her subscription immediately. Anne took this second rejection with the calmness of despair. She locked the story away in the garret trunk where the old Story Club tales reposed; but first she yielded to Diana's entreaties and gave her a copy.

"This is the end of my literary ambitions," she said bitterly.

She never mentioned the matter to Mr. Harrison, but one evening he asked her bluntly if her story had been accepted.

"No, the editor wouldn't take it," she answered briefly.

Mr. Harrison looked sidewise at the flushed, delicate profile.

"Well, I suppose you'll keep on writing them," he said encouragingly.

"No, I shall never try to write a story again," declared Anne, with the hopeless finality of nineteen when a door is shut in its face.

"I wouldn't give up altogether," said Mr. Harrison reflectively. "I'd write a story once in a while, but I wouldn't pester editors with it. I'd write of people and places like I knew, and I'd make my characters talk everyday English; and I'd let the sun rise and set in the usual quiet way without much fuss over the fact. If I had to have villains at all, I'd give them a chance, Anne—I'd give them a chance. There *are* some terrible bad men in the world, I suppose, but you'd have to go a long piece to find them—though Mrs. Lynde believes we're all bad. But most of us have got a little decency somewhere in us. Keep on writing, Anne."

"No. It was very foolish of me to attempt it. When I'm through Redmond I'll stick to teaching. I *can* teach. I can't write stories."

"It'll be time for you to be getting a husband when you're through Redmond," said Mr. Harrison. "I don't believe in putting marrying off too long—like I did."

Anne got up and marched home. There were times when Mr. Harrison was really intolerable. "Pitching," "mooning," and "getting a husband." Ow!!

CHAPTER 13

THE WAY OF TRANSGRESSORS

DAVY AND DORA were ready for Sunday School. They were going alone, which did not often happen, for Mrs. Lynde always attended Sunday School. But Mrs. Lynde had twisted her ankle and was lame, so she was staying home this morning. The twins were also to represent the family at church, for Anne had gone away the evening before to spend Sunday with friends in Carmody, and Marilla had one of her headaches.

Davy came down-stairs slowly. Dora was waiting in the hall for him, having been made ready by Mrs. Lynde. Davy had attended to his own preparations. He had a cent in his pocket for the Sunday School collection, and a five-cent piece for the church collection; he carried his Bible in one hand and his Sunday School quarterly in the other; he knew his lesson and his Golden Text and his catechism question perfectly. Had he not studied them—perforce—in Mrs. Lynde's kitchen, all last Sunday afternoon? Davy, therefore, should have been in a placid frame of mind. As a matter of fact, despite text and catechism, he was inwardly as a ravening wolf.

Mrs. Lynde limped out of her kitchen as he joined Dora.

"Are you clean?" she demanded severely.

"Yes—all of me that shows," Davy answered with a defiant scowl.

Mrs. Rachel sighed. She had her suspicions about Davy's neck and ears. But she knew that if she attempted to make a personal examination Davy would likely take to his heels and she could not pursue him today.

"Well, be sure you behave yourselves," she warned them. "Don't walk in the dust. Don't stop in the porch to talk to the other children. Don't squirm or wriggle in your places. Don't forget the Golden Text. Don't lose your collection or forget to put it in. Don't whisper at prayer time, and don't forget to pay attention to the sermon."

Davy deigned no response. He marched away down the lane, followed by the meek Dora. But his soul seethed within him. Davy had suffered, or thought he had suffered, many things at the hands and tongue of Mrs. Rachel Lynde since she had come to Green Gables, for Mrs. Lynde could not live with anybody, whether they were nine or ninety, without trying to bring them up properly. And it was only the preceding afternoon that she had interfered to influence Marilla against allowing Davy to go fishing with the Timothy Cottons. Davy was still boiling over this.

As soon as he was out of the lane Davy stopped and twisted his countenance into such an unearthly and terrific contortion that Dora, although she knew his gifts in that respect, was honestly alarmed lest he should never in the world be able to get it straightened out again.

"Darn her," exploded Davy.

"Oh, Davy, don't swear," gasped Dora in dismay.

" 'Darn' isn't swearing—not real swearing. And I don't care if it is," retorted Davy recklessly.

"Well, if you *must* say dreadful words don't say them on Sunday," pleaded Dora.

Davy was as yet far from repentance, but in his secret soul he felt that, perhaps, he had gone a little too far.

"I'm going to invent a swear word of my own," he declared.

"God will punish you if you do," said Dora solemnly.

"Then I think God is a mean old scamp," retorted Davy.

"Doesn't He know a fellow must have some way of 'spressing his feelings?"

"Davy!!!" said Dora. She expected that Davy would be struck down dead on the spot. But nothing happened.

"Anyway, I ain't going to stand any more of Mrs. Lynde's bossing," spluttered Davy. "Anne and Marilla may have the right to boss me, but *she* hasn't. I'm going to do every single thing she told me not to do. You watch me."

In grim, deliberate silence, while Dora watched him with the fascination of horror, Davy stepped off the green grass of the roadside, ankle deep into the fine dust which four weeks of rainless weather had made on the road, and marched along in it, shuffling his feet viciously until he was enveloped in a hazy cloud.

"That's the beginning," he announced triumphantly. "And I'm going to stop in the porch and talk as long as there's anybody there to talk to. I'm going to squirm and wriggle and whisper, and I'm going to say I don't know the Golden Text. And I'm going to throw away both of my collections *right now.*"

And Davy hurled cent and nickel over Mr. Barry's fence with fierce delight.

"Satan made you do that," said Dora reproachfully.

"He didn't," cried Davy indignantly. "I just thought it out for myself. And I've thought of something else. I'm not going to Sunday School or church at all. I'm going up to play with the Cottons. They told me yesterday they weren't going to Sunday School today, 'cause their mother was away and there was nobody to make them. Come along, Dora, we'll have a great time."

"I don't want to go," protested Dora.

"You've got to," said Davy. "If you don't come I'll tell Marilla that Frank Bell kissed you in school last Monday."

"I couldn't help it. I didn't know he was going to," cried Dora, blushing scarlet.

"Well, you didn't slap him or seem a bit cross," retorted Davy. "I'll tell her *that,* too, if you don't come. We'll take the short cut up this field."

"I'm afraid of those cows," protested poor Dora, seeing a prospect of escape.

"The very idea of your being scared of those cows," scoffed
Davy. "Why, they're both younger than you."

"They're bigger," said Dora.

"They won't hurt you. Come along, now. This is great. When
I grow up I ain't going to bother going to church at all. I
believe I can get to heaven by myself."

"You'll go to the other place if you break the Sabbath day,"
said unhappy Dora, following him sorely against her will.

But Davy was not scared—yet. Hell was very far off, and
the delights of a fishing expedition with the Cottons were very
near. He wished Dora had more spunk. She kept looking back
as if she were going to cry every minute, and that spoiled a
fellow's fun. Hang girls, anyway. Davy did not say "darn" this
time, even in thought. He was not sorry—yet—that he had
said it once, but it might be as well not to tempt the Unknown
Powers too far on one day.

The small Cottons were playing in their back yard, and hailed
Davy's appearance with whoops of delight. Pete, Tommy, Adolphus, and Mirabel Cotton were all alone. Their mother and
older sisters were away. Dora was thankful Mirabel was there,
at least. She had been afraid she would be alone in a crowd
of boys. Mirabel was almost as bad as a boy—she was so noisy
and sunburned and reckless. But at least she wore dresses.

"We've come to go fishing," announced Davy.

"Whoop," yelled the Cottons. They rushed away to dig worms
at once, Mirabel leading the van with a tin can. Dora could
have sat down and cried. Oh, if only that hateful Frank Bell
had never kissed her! Then she could have defied Davy, and
gone to her beloved Sunday School.

They dared not, of course, go fishing on the pond, where
they would be seen by people going to church. They had to
resort to the brook in the woods behind the Cotton house. But
it was full of trout, and they had a glorious time that morning—
at least the Cottons certainly had, and Davy seemed to have
it. Not being entirely bereft of prudence, he had discarded boots
and stockings and borrowed Tommy Cotton's overalls. Thus
accoutered, bog and marsh and undergrowth had no terrors for
him. Dora was frankly and manifestly miserable. She followed
the others in their peregrinations from pool to pool, clasping
her Bible and quarterly tightly and thinking with bitterness of

soul of her beloved class where she should be sitting that very moment, before a teacher she adored. Instead, here she was roaming the woods with those half-wild Cottons, trying to keep her boots clean and her pretty white dress free from rents and stains. Mirabel had offered the loan of an apron but Dora had scornfully refused.

The trout bit as they always do on Sundays. In an hour the transgressors had all the fish they wanted, so they returned to the house, much to Dora's relief. She sat primly on a hencoop in the yard while the others played an uproarious game of tag; and then they all climbed to the top of the pig-house roof and cut their initials on the saddle-board. The flat-roofed henhouse and a pile of straw beneath gave Davy another inspiration. They spent a splendid half hour climbing on the roof and diving off into the straw with whoops and yells.

But even unlawful pleasures must come to an end. When the rumble of wheels over the pond bridge told that people were going home from church Davy knew they must go. He discarded Tommy's overalls, resumed his own rightful attire, and turned away from his string of trout with a sigh. No use to think of taking them home.

"Well, hadn't we a splendid time?" he demanded defiantly, as they went down the hill field.

"I hadn't," said Dora flatly. "And I don't believe you had—really—either," she added, with a flash of insight that was not to be expected of her.

"I had so," cried Davy, but in the voice of one who doth protest too much. "No wonder *you* hadn't—just sitting there like a—like a mule."

"I ain't going to 'sociate with the Cottons," said Dora loftily.

"The Cottons are all right," retorted Davy. "And they have far better times than we have. They do just as they please and say just what they like before everybody. *I*'m going to do that, too, after this."

"There are lots of things you wouldn't dare say before everybody," averred Dora.

"No, there isn't."

"There is, too. Would you," demanded Dora gravely, "would you say 'tomcat' before the minister?"

This was a staggerer. Davy was not prepared for such a

concrete example of the freedom of speech. But one did not have to be consistent with Dora.

"Of course not," he admitted sulkily. " 'Tomcat' isn't a holy word. I wouldn't mention such an animal before a minister at all."

"But if you had to?" persisted Dora.

"I'd call it a Thomas pussy," said Davy.

"*I* think 'gentleman cat' would be more polite," reflected Dora.

"*You* thinking!" retorted Davy with withering scorn.

Davy was not feeling comfortable, though he would have died before he admitted it to Dora. Now that the exhilaration of truant delights had died away, his conscience was beginning to give him salutary twinges. After all, perhaps it would have been better to have gone to Sunday School and church. Mrs. Lynde might be bossy; but there was always a box of cookies in her kitchen cupboard and she was not stingy. At this inconvenient moment Davy remembered that when he had torn his new school pants the week before, Mrs. Lynde had mended them beautifully and never said a word to Marilla about them.

But Davy's cup of iniquity was not yet full. He was to discover that one sin demands another to cover it. They had dinner with Mrs. Lynde that day, and the first thing she asked Davy was,

"Were all your class in Sunday School today?"

"Yes'm," said Davy with a gulp. "All were there—'cept one."

"Did you say your Golden Text and catechism?"

"Yes'm."

"Did you put your collection in?"

"Yes'm."

"Was Mrs. Malcolm MacPherson in church?"

"I don't know." This, at least, was the truth, thought wretched Davy.

"Was the Ladies' Aid announced for next week?"

"Yes'm"—quakingly.

"Was prayer-meeting?"

"I—I don't know."

"You *should* know. You should listen more attentively to the announcements. What was Mr. Harvey's text?"

Davy took a frantic gulp of water and swallowed it and the

last protest of conscience together. He glibly recited an old Golden Text learned several weeks ago. Fortunately Mrs. Lynde now stopped questioning him; but Davy did not enjoy his dinner. He could only eat one helping of pudding.

"What's the matter with you?" demanded justly astonished Mrs. Lynde. "Are you sick?"

"No," muttered Davy.

"You look pale. You'd better keep out of the sun this afternoon," admonished Mrs. Lynde.

"Do you know how many lies you told Mrs. Lynde?" asked Dora reproachfully, as soon as they were alone after dinner.

Davy, goaded to desperation, turned fiercely.

"I don't know and I don't care," he said. "You just shut up, Dora Keith."

Then poor Davy betook himself to a secluded retreat behind the wood-pile to think over the way of transgressors.

Green Gables was wrapped in darkness and silence when Anne reached home. She lost no time going to bed, for she was very tired and sleepy. There had been several Avonlea jollifications the preceding week, involving rather late hours. Anne's head was hardly on her pillow before she was half asleep; but just then her door was softly opened and a pleading voice said, "Anne."

Anne sat up drowsily.

"Davy, is that you? What is the matter?"

A white-clad figure flung itself across the floor and on to the bed.

"Anne," sobbed Davy, getting his arms about her neck. "I'm awful glad you're home. I couldn't go to sleep till I'd told somebody."

"Told somebody what?"

"How mis'rubul I am."

"Why are you miserable, dear?"

"'Cause I was so bad today, Anne. Oh, I was awful bad— badder'n I've ever been yet."

"What did you do?"

"Oh, I'm afraid to tell you. You'll never like me again, Anne. I couldn't say my prayers tonight. I couldn't tell God what I'd done. I was 'shamed to have Him know."

"But He knew anyway, Davy."

"That's what Dora said. But I thought p'raps He mightn't have noticed just at the time. Anyway, I'd rather tell you first."

"*What* is it you did?"

Out it all came in a rush.

"I run away from Sunday School—and went fishing with the Cottons—and I told ever so many whoppers to Mrs. Lynde—oh! 'most half a dozen—and—and—I—I said a swear word, Anne—a pretty near swear word, anyhow—and I called God names."

There was a silence. Davy didn't know what to make of it. Was Anne so shocked that she never would speak to him again?

"Anne, what are you going to do to me?" he whispered.

"Nothing, dear. You've been punished already, I think."

"No, I haven't. Nothing's been done to me."

"You've been very unhappy ever since you did wrong, haven't you?"

"You bet!" said Davy emphatically.

"That was your conscience punishing you, Davy."

"What's my conscience? I want to know."

"It's something in you, Davy, that always tells you when you are doing wrong and makes you unhappy if you persist in doing it. Haven't you noticed that?"

"Yes, but I didn't know what it was. I wish I didn't have it. I'd have lots more fun. Where is my conscience, Anne? I want to know. Is it in my stomach?"

"No, it's in your soul," answered Anne, thankful for the darkness, since gravity must be preserved in serious matters.

"I s'pose I can't get clear of it then," said Davy with a sigh. "Are you going to tell Marilla and Mrs. Lynde on me, Anne?"

"No, dear, I'm not going to tell any one. You are sorry you were naughty, aren't you?"

"You bet!"

"And you'll never be bad like that again."

"No, but—" added Davy cautiously, "I might be bad some other way."

"You won't say naughty words, or run away on Sundays, or tell falsehoods to cover up your sins?"

"No. It doesn't pay," said Davy.

"Well, Davy, just tell God you are sorry and ask Him to forgive you."

"Have *you* forgive me, Anne?"

"Yes, dear."

"Then," said Davy joyously, "I don't care much whether God does or not."

"Davy!"

"Oh—I'll ask Him—I'll ask Him," said Davy quickly, scrambling off the bed, convinced by Anne's tone that he must have said something dreadful. "I don't mind asking Him, Anne— Please, God, I'm awful sorry I behaved bad today and I'll try to be good on Sundays always and please forgive me—There now, Anne."

"Well, now, run off to bed like a good boy."

"All right. Say, I don't feel mis'rubul any more. I feel fine. Good-night."

"Good-night."

Anne slipped down on her pillows with a sigh of relief. Oh— how sleepy—she was! In another second—

"Anne!"

Davy was back again by her bed. Anne dragged her eyes open.

"What is it now, dear?" she asked, trying to keep a note of impatience out of her voice.

"Anne, have you ever noticed how Mr. Harrison spits? Do you s'pose, if I practise hard, I can learn to spit just like him?"

Anne sat up.

"Davy Keith," she said, "go straight to your bed and don't let me catch you out of it again tonight! Go, now!"

Davy went, and stood not upon the order of his going.

CHAPTER 14

THE SUMMONS

ANNE was sitting with Ruby Gillis in the Gillis' garden after the day had crept lingeringly through it and was gone. It had been a warm, smoky summer afternoon. The world was in a splendour of out-flowering. The idle valleys were full of hazes. The woodways were pranked with shadows and the fields with the purple of the asters.

Anne had given up a moonlight drive to the White Sands beach that she might spend the evening with Ruby. She had so spent many evenings that summer, although she often wondered what good it did any one, and sometimes went home deciding that she could not go again.

Ruby grew paler as the summer waned; the White Sands school was given up—"her father thought it better that she shouldn't teach till New Year's"—and the fancy work she loved oftener and oftener fell from hands grown too weary for it. But she was always gay, always hopeful, always chattering and whispering of her beaux, and their rivalries and despairs. It was this that made Anne's visits hard for her. What had once been silly or amusing was gruesome now; it was death peering through a wilful mask of life. Yet Ruby seemed to cling to her, and never let her go until she had promised to come again soon. Mrs. Lynde grumbled about Anne's frequent visits, and declared she would catch consumption; even Marilla was dubious.

"Every time you go to see Ruby you come home looking tired out," she said.

"It's so very sad and dreadful," said Anne in a low tone. "Ruby doesn't seem to realize her condition in the least. And yet I somehow feel she needs help—craves it—and I want to give it to her and can't. All the time I'm with her I feel as if I were watching her struggle with an invisible foe—trying to push it back with such feeble resistance as she has. That is why I come home tired."

But tonight Anne did not feel this so keenly. Ruby was strangely quiet. She said not a word about parties and drives and dresses and "fellows." She lay in the hammock, with her untouched work beside her, and a white shawl wrapped about her thin shoulders. Her long yellow braids of hair—how Anne had envied those beautiful braids in old schooldays!—lay on either side of her. She had taken the pins out—they made her head ache, she said. The hectic flush was gone for the time, leaving her pale and childlike.

The moon rose in the silvery sky, empearling the clouds around her. Below, the pond shimmered in its hazy radiance. Just beyond the Gillis homestead was the church, with the old graveyard beside it. The moonlight shone on the white stones, bringing them out in clear-cut relief against the dark trees behind.

"How strange the graveyard looks by moonlight!" said Ruby suddenly. "How ghostly!" she shuddered. "Anne, it won't be long now before I'll be lying over there. You and Diana and all the rest will be going about, full of life—and I'll be there—in the old graveyard—dead!"

The surprise of it bewildered Anne. For a few moments she could not speak.

"You know it's so, don't you?" said Ruby insistently.

"Yes, I know," answered Anne in a low tone. "Dear Ruby, I know."

"Everybody knows it," said Ruby bitterly. "I know it—I've known it all summer, though I wouldn't give in. And, oh, Anne"—she reached out and caught Anne's hand pleadingly, impulsively—"I don't want to die. I'm *afraid* to die."

"Why should you be afraid, Ruby?" asked Anne quietly.

"Because—because—oh, I'm not afraid but that I'll go to heaven, Anne. I'm a church member. But—it'll be all so different. I think—and think—and I get so frightened—and—and—homesick. Heaven must be very beautiful, of course, the Bible says so—but, Anne, *it won't be what I've been used to.*"

Through Anne's mind drifted an intrusive recollection of a funny story she had heard Philippa Gordon tell—the story of some old man who had said very much the same thing about the world to come. It *had* sounded funny then—she remembered how she and Priscilla had laughed over it. But it did not seem in the least humorous now, coming from Ruby's pale, trembling lips. It was sad, tragic—and *true!* Heaven could not be what Ruby had been used to. There had been nothing in her gay, frivolous life, her shallow ideals and aspirations, to fit her for that great change, or make the life to come seem to her anything but alien and unreal and undesirable. Anne wondered helplessly what she could say that would help her. Could she say anything? "I think, Ruby," she began hesitatingly—for it was difficult for Anne to speak to any one of the deepest thoughts of her heart, or the new ideas that had vaguely begun to shape themselves in her mind, concerning the great mysteries of life here and hereafter, superseding her old childish conceptions, and it was hardest of all to speak of them to such as Ruby Gillis—"I think, perhaps, we have very mistaken ideas about heaven— what it is and what it holds for us. I don't think it can be so very different from life here as most people seem to think. I believe we'll just go on living, a good deal as we live here— and be *ourselves* just the same—only it will be easier to be good and to—follow the highest. All the hindrances and perplexities will be taken away, and we shall see clearly. Don't be afraid, Ruby."

"I can't help it," said Ruby pitifully. "Even if what you say about heaven is true—and you can't be sure—it may be only that imagination of yours—it won't be *just* the same. It *can't* be. I want to go on living *here*. I'm so young, Anne. I haven't had my life. I've fought so hard to live—and it isn't any use— I have to die—and leave *everything* I care for."

Anne sat in a pain that was almost intolerable. She could not tell comforting falsehoods; and all that Ruby said was so horribly true. She *was* leaving everything she cared for. She had laid up her treasures on earth only; she had lived solely for the little things of life—the things that pass—forgetting the great things that go onward into eternity, bridging the gulf between the two lives and making of death a mere passing from one dwelling to the other—from twilight to unclouded day. God would take care of her there—Anne believed—she would learn—but now it was no wonder her soul clung, in blind helplessness, to the only things she knew and loved.

Ruby raised herself on her arm and lifted up her bright, beautiful blue eyes to the moonlit skies.

"I want to live," she said, in a trembling voice. "I want to live like other girls. I—I want to be married, Anne—and— and—have little children. You know I always loved babies,

Anne. I couldn't say this to any one but you. I know you understand. And then poor Herb—he—he loves me and I love him, Anne. The others meant nothing to me, but *he* does— and if I could live I would be his wife and be so happy. Oh, Anne, it's hard."

Ruby sank back on her pillows and sobbed convulsively. Anne pressed her hand in an agony of sympathy—silent sympathy, which perhaps helped Ruby more than broken, imperfect words could have done; for presently she grew calmer and her sobs ceased.

"I'm glad I've told you this, Anne," she whispered. "It has helped me just to say it all out. I've wanted to all summer— every time you came I wanted to talk it over with you—but I *couldn't*. It seemed as if it would make death so *sure* if I *said* I was going to die, or if any one else said it or hinted it. I wouldn't say it, or even think it. In the daytime, when people were around me and everything was cheerful, it wasn't so hard to keep from thinking of it. But in the night, when I couldn't sleep—it was so dreadful, Anne. I couldn't get away from it then. Death just came and stared me in the face, until I got so frightened I could have screamed."

"But you won't be frightened any more, Ruby, will you? You'll be brave, and believe that all is going to be well with you."

"I'll try. I'll think over what you have said, and try to believe it. And you'll come up as often as you can, won't you, Anne?"

"Yes, dear."

"It—it won't be very long now, Anne. I feel sure of that. And I'd rather have you than any one else. I always liked you best of all the girls I went to school with. You were never jealous, or mean, like some of them were. Poor Em White was up to see me yesterday. You remember Em and I were such chums for three years when we went to school? And then we quarrelled the time of the school concert. We've never spoken to each other since. Wasn't it silly? Anything like that seems silly *now*. But Em and I made up the old quarrel yesterday. She said she'd have spoken years ago, only she thought I wouldn't. And I never spoke to her because I was sure she wouldn't speak to me. Isn't it strange how people misunderstand each other, Anne?"

"Most of the trouble in life comes from misunderstanding, I think," said Anne. "I must go now, Ruby. It's getting late—and you shouldn't be out in the damp."

"You'll come up soon again."

"Yes, very soon. And if there's anything I can do to help you I'll be so glad."

"I know. You *have* helped me already. Nothing seems quite so dreadful now. Good-night, Anne."

"Good-night, dear."

Anne walked home very slowly in the moonlight. The evening had changed something for her. Life held a different meaning, a deeper purpose. On the surface it would go on just the same; but the deeps had been stirred. It must not be with her as with poor butterfly Ruby. When she came to the end of one life it must not be to face the next with the shrinking terror of something wholly different—something for which accustomed thought and ideal and aspiration had unfitted her. The little things of life, sweet and excellent in their place, must not be the things lived for; the highest must be sought and followed; the life of heaven must be begun here on earth.

That good-night in the garden was for all time. Anne never saw Ruby in life again. The next night the A.V.I.S. gave a farewell party to Jane Andrews before her departure for the West. And, while light feet danced and bright eyes laughed and merry tongues chattered, there came a summons to a soul in Avonlea that might not be disregarded or evaded. The next morning the word went from house to house that Ruby Gillis was dead. She had died in her sleep, painlessly and calmly, and on her face was a smile—as if, after all, death had come as a kindly friend to lead her over the threshold, instead of the grisly phantom she had dreaded.

Mrs. Rachel Lynde said emphatically after the funeral that Ruby Gillis was the handsomest corpse she ever laid eyes on. Her loveliness, as she lay, white-clad, among the delicate flowers that Anne had placed about her, was remembered and talked of for years in Avonlea. Ruby had always been beautiful; but her beauty had been of the earth, earthy; it had had a certain insolent quality in it, as if it flaunted itself in the beholder's eye; spirit had never shone through it, intellect had never refined it. But death had touched it and consecrated it, bringing out

delicate modellings and purity of outline never seen before—
doing what life and love and great sorrow and deep womanhood
joys might have done for Ruby. Anne, looking down through
a mist of tears, at her old playfellow, thought she saw the face
God had meant Ruby to have, and remembered it so always.

Mrs. Gillis called Anne aside into a vacant room before the
funeral procession left the house, and gave her a small packet.

"I want you to have this," she sobbed. "Ruby would have
liked you to have it. It's the embroidered centerpiece she was
working at. It isn't quite finished—the needle is sticking in it
just where her poor little fingers put it the last time she laid
it down, the afternoon before she died."

"There's always a piece of unfinished work left," said Mrs.
Lynde, with tears in her eyes. "But I suppose there's always
some one to finish it."

"How difficult it is to realize that one we have always known
can really be dead," said Anne, as she and Diana walked home.
"Ruby is the first of our schoolmates to go. One by one, sooner
or later, all the rest of us must follow."

"Yes, I suppose so," said Diana uncomfortably. She did not
want to talk of that. She would have preferred to have discussed
the details of the funeral—the splendid white velvet casket Mr.
Gillis had insisted on having for Ruby—"the Gillises must
always make a splurge, even at funerals," quoth Mrs. Rachel
Lynde—Herb Spencer's sad face, the uncontrolled, hysteric grief
of one of Ruby's sisters—but Anne would not talk of these
things. She seemed wrapped in a reverie in which Diana felt
lonesomely that she had neither lot nor part.

"Ruby Gillis was a great girl to laugh," said Davy suddenly.
"Will she laugh as much in heaven as she did in Avonlea,
Anne? I want to know."

"Yes, I think she will," said Anne.

"Oh, Anne," protested Diana, with a rather shocked smile.

"Well, why not, Diana?" asked Anne seriously. "Do you
think we'll never laugh in heaven?"

"Oh—I—I don't know," floundered Diana. "It doesn't seem
just right, somehow. You know it's rather dreadful to laugh in
church."

"But heaven won't be like church—all the time," said Anne.

"I hope it ain't," said Davy emphatically. "If it is *I* don't want to go. Church is awful dull. Anyway, I don't mean to go for ever so long. I mean to live to be a hundred years old, like Mr. Thomas Blewett of White Sands. He says he's lived so long 'cause he always smoked tobacco and it killed all the germs. Can I smoke tobacco pretty soon, Anne?"

"No, Davy, I hope you'll never use tobacco," said Anne absently.

"What'll you feel like if the germs kill me then?" demanded Davy.

CHAPTER 15

A DREAM TURNED UPSIDE DOWN

"JUST ONE more week and we go back to Redmond," said Anne. She was happy at the thought of returning to work, classes and Redmond friends. Pleasing visions were also being woven around Patty's Place. There was a warm pleasant sense of home in the thought of it, even though she had never lived there.

But the summer had been a very happy one, too—a time of glad living with summer suns and skies, a time of keen delight in wholesome things; a time of renewing and deepening of old friendships; a time in which she had learned to live more nobly, to work more patiently, to play more heartily.

"All life lessons are not learned at college," she thought. "Life teaches them everywhere."

But alas, the final week of that pleasant vacation was spoiled for Anne, by one of those impish happenings which are like a dream turned upside down.

"Been writing any more stories lately?" inquired Mr. Harrison genially one evening when Anne was taking tea with him and Mrs. Harrison.

"No," answered Anne, rather crisply.

"Well, no offence meant. Mrs. Hiram Sloane told me the

other day that a big envelope addressed to the Rollings Reliable
Baking Powder Company of Montreal had been dropped into
the post office box a month ago, and she suspicioned that
somebody was trying for the prize they'd offered for the best
story that introduced the name of their baking powder. She
said it wasn't addressed in your writing, but I thought maybe
it was you."

"Indeed, no! I saw the prize offer, but I'd never dream of
competing for it. I think it would be perfectly disgraceful to
write a story to advertise a baking powder. It would be almost
as bad as Judson Parker's patent medicine fence."

So spake Anne loftily, little dreaming of the valley of humiliation awaiting her. That very evening Diana popped into
the porch gable, bright-eyed and rosy cheeked, carrying a letter.

"Oh, Anne, here's a letter for you. I was at the office, so I
thought I'd bring it along. Do open it quick. If it is what I
believe it is I shall just be wild with delight."

Anne, puzzled, opened the letter and glanced over the type-
written contents.

"Miss Anne Shirley,
    "Green Gables,
       "Avonlea, P.E. Island.
"DEAR MADAM: We have much pleasure in informing you
that your charming story *'Averil's Atonement'* has won the prize
of twenty-five dollars offered in our recent competition. We
enclose the check herewith. We are arranging for the publication
of the story in several prominent Canadian newspapers, and
we also intend to have it printed in pamphlet form for distri-
bution among our patrons. Thanking you for the interest you
have shown in our enterprise,
                            "We remain,
                        "Yours very truly,
            "THE ROLLINGS RELIABLE BAKING POWDER CO."

"I don't understand," said Anne, blankly.
Diana clapped her hands.
"Oh, I *knew* it would win the prize—I was sure of it. *I* sent
your story into the competition, Anne."
"Diana—Barry!"

"Yes, I did," said Diana gleefully, perching herself on the bed. "When I saw the offer I thought of your story in a minute, and at first I thought I'd ask you to send it in. But then I was afraid you wouldn't—you had so little faith left in it. So I just decided I'd send the copy you gave me, and say nothing about it. Then, if it didn't win the prize, you'd never know and you wouldn't feel badly over it, because the stories that failed were not to be returned, and if it did you'd have such a delightful surprise."

Diana was not the most discerning of mortals, but just at this moment it struck her that Anne was not looking exactly over-joyed. The surprise was there, beyond doubt—but where was the delight?

"Why, Anne, you don't seem a bit pleased!" she exclaimed.

Anne instantly manufactured a smile and put it on.

"Of course I couldn't be anything but pleased over your unselfish wish to give me pleasure," she said slowly. "But you know—I'm so amazed—I can't realize it—and I don't understand. There wasn't a word in my story about—about—" Anne choked a little over the word—"baking powder."

"Oh, I put that in," said Diana, reassured. "It was as easy as wink—and of course my experience in our old Story Club helped me. You know the scene where Averil makes the cake? Well, I just stated that she used the Rollings Reliable in it, and that was why it turned out so well; and then, in the last paragraph, where *Perceval* clasps *Averil* in his arms and says, 'Sweetheart, the beautiful coming years will bring us the fulfilment of our home of dreams,' I added, 'in which we will never use any baking powder except Rollings Reliable.'"

"Oh," gasped poor Anne, as if some one had dashed cold water on her.

"And you've won the twenty-five dollars," continued Diana jubilantly. "Why, I heard Priscilla say once that the *Canadian Woman* only pays five dollars for a story!"

Anne held out the hateful pink slip in shaking fingers.

"I can't take it—it's yours by right, Diana. You sent the story in and made the alterations. I—I would certainly never have sent it. So you must take the check."

"I'd like to see myself," said Diana scornfully. "Why, what I did wasn't any trouble. The honour of being a friend of the prize-winner is enough for me. Well, I must go. I should have gone straight home from the post office for we have company. But I simply had to come and hear the news. I'm *so* glad for your sake, Anne."

Anne suddenly bent forward, put her arms about Diana, and kissed her cheek.

"I think you are the sweetest and truest friend in the world, Diana," she said, with a little tremble in her voice, "and I assure you I appreciate the motive of what you've done."

Diana, pleased and embarrassed, got herself away, and poor Anne, after flinging the innocent check into her bureau drawer as if it were blood-money, cast herself on her bed and wept tears of shame and outraged sensibility. Oh, she could never live this down—never!

Gilbert arrived at dusk, brimming over with congratulations, for he had called at Orchard Slope and heard the news. But his congratulations died on his lips at sight of Anne's face.

"Why, Anne, what is the matter? I expected to find you radiant over winning Rollings Reliable prize. Good for you!"

"Oh, Gilbert, not you," implored Anne, in an *et-tu Brute* tone. "I thought *you* would understand. Can't you see how awful it is?"

"I must confess I can't. *What* is wrong?"

"Everything," moaned Anne. "I feel as if I were disgraced forever. What do you think a mother would feel like if she found her child tattooed over with a baking powder advertisement? I feel just the same. I loved my poor little story, and I wrote it out of the best that was in me. And it is *sacrilege* to have it degraded to the level of a baking powder advertisement. Don't you remember what Professor Hamilton used to tell us in the literature class at Queen's? He said we were never to write a word for a low or unworthy motive, but always to cling to the very highest ideals. What will he think when he hears I've written a story to advertise Rollings Reliable? And, oh, when it gets out at Redmond! Think how I'll be teased and laughed at!"

"That you won't," said Gilbert, wondering uneasily if it were that confounded Junior's opinion in particular over which Anne was worried. "The Reds will think just as I thought—that you, being like nine out of ten of us, not over-burdened with worldly wealth, had taken this way of earning an honest penny to help yourself through the year. I don't see that there's anything low or unworthy about that, or anything ridiculous either. One would rather write masterpieces of literature no doubt—but meanwhile board and tuition fees have to be paid."

This common-sense, matter-of-fact view of the case cheered Anne a little. At least it removed her dread of being laughed at, though the deeper hurt of an outraged ideal remained.

CHAPTER 16

ADJUSTED RELATIONSHIPS

"IT'S THE homiest spot I ever saw—it's homier than home," avowed Philippa Gordon, looking about her with delighted eyes. They were all assembled at twilight in the big living-room at Patty's Place—Anne and Priscilla, Phil and Stella, Aunt Jamesina, Rusty, Joseph, the Sarah-Cat, and Gog and Magog. The firelight shadows were dancing over the walls; the cats were purring; and a huge bowl of hot-house chrysanthemums, sent to Phil by one of the victims, shone through the golden gloom like creamy moons.

It was three weeks since they had considered themselves settled, and already all believed the experiment would be a success. The first fortnight after their return had been a pleasantly exciting one; they had been busy setting up their household gods, organizing their little establishment, and adjusting different opinions.

Anne was not over-sorry to leave Avonlea when the time came to return to college. The last few days of her vacation had not been pleasant. Her prize story had been published in the Island papers; and Mr. William Blair had, upon the counter of his store, a huge pile of pink, green and yellow pamphlets, containing it, one of which he gave to every customer. He sent a complimentary bundle to Anne, who promptly dropped them all in the kitchen stove. Her humiliation was the consequence of her own ideals only, for Avonlea folks thought it quite splendid that she should have won the prize. Her many friends regarded her with honest admiration; her few foes with scornful envy. Josie Pye said she believed Anne Shirley had just copied the story; she was sure she remembered reading it in a paper years before. The Sloanes, who had found out or guessed that Charlie had been "turned down," said they didn't think it was much to be proud of; almost any one could have done it, if she tried. Aunt Atossa told Anne she was very sorry to hear she had taken to writing novels; nobody born and bred in Avonlea would do it; that was what came of adopting orphans from goodness knew where, with goodness knew what kind of parents. Even Mrs. Rachel Lynde was darkly dubious about the propriety of writing fiction, though she was almost reconciled to it by that twenty-five dollar check.

"It is perfectly amazing, the price they pay for such lies, that's what," she said, half-proudly, half-severely.

All things considered, it was a relief when going-away time came. And it was very jolly to be back at Redmond, a wise, experienced Soph with hosts of friends to greet on the merry opening day. Pris and Stella and Gilbert were there, Charlie Sloane, looking more important than ever Sophomore looked before, Phil, with the Alec-and-Alonzo question still unsettled, and Moody Spurgeon MacPherson. Moody Spurgeon had been teaching school ever since leaving Queen's, but his mother had concluded it was high time he gave it up and turned his attention to learning how to be a minister. Poor Moody Spurgeon fell on hard luck at the very beginning of his college career. Half a dozen ruthless Sophs, who were among his fellow-boarders, swooped down upon him one night and shaved half of his head. In this guise the luckless Moody Spurgeon had to go about until his hair grew again. He told Anne bitterly that there were times when he had his doubts as to whether he was really called to be a minister.

Aunt Jamesina did not come until the girls had Patty's Place ready for her. Miss Patty had sent the key to Anne, with a letter in which she said Gog and Magog were packed in a box under the spare-room bed, but might be taken out when wanted; in a postscript she added that she hoped the girls would be careful about putting up pictures. The living room had been newly papered five years before and she and Miss Maria did not want any more holes made in that new paper than was absolutely necessary. For the rest she trusted everything to Anne.

How those girls enjoyed putting their nest in order! As Phil said, it was almost as good as getting married. You had the fun of home-making without the bother of a husband. All brought something with them to adorn or make comfortable the little house. Pris and Phil and Stella had nick-nacks and pictures galore, which latter they proceeded to hang according to taste, in reckless disregard of Miss Patty's new paper.

"We'll putty the holes up when we leave, dear—she'll never know," they said to protesting Anne.

Diana had given Anne a pine needle cushion and Miss Ada had given both her and Priscilla a fearfully and wonderfully embroidered one. Marilla had sent a big box of preserves, and darkly hinted at a hamper for Thanksgiving, and Mrs. Lynde gave Anne a patch work quilt and loaned her five more.

"You take them," she said authoritatively. "They might as well be in use as packed away in that trunk in the garret for moths to gnaw."

No moths would ever have ventured near those quilts, for they reeked of moth-balls to such an extent that they had to be hung in the orchard of Patty's Place a full fortnight before they could be endured indoors. Verily, aristocratic Spofford Avenue had rarely beheld such a display. The gruff old millionaire who lived "next door" came over and wanted to buy the gorgeous red and yellow "tulip-pattern" one which Mrs. Rachel had given Anne. He said his mother used to make quilts like that, and by Jove, he wanted one to remind him of her. Anne would not sell it, much to his disappointment, but she wrote all about it to Mrs. Lynde. That highly-gratified lady sent word back that she had one just like it to spare, so the tobacco king got his quilt after all, and insisted on having it spread on his bed, to the disgust of his fashionable wife.

Mrs. Lynde's quilts served a very useful purpose that winter. Patty's Place for all its many virtues, had its faults also. It was really a rather cold house; and when the frosty nights came the girls were very glad to snuggle down under Mrs. Lynde's quilts, and hoped that the loan of them might be accounted unto her for righteousness. Anne had the blue room she had coveted at sight. Priscilla and Stella had the large one. Phil was blissfully content with the little one over the kitchen; and Aunt Jamesina was to have the down-stairs one off the living-room. Rusty at first slept on the doorstep.

Anne, walking home from Redmond a few days after her return, became aware that the people that she met surveyed her with a covert, indulgent smile. Anne wondered uneasily what was the matter with her. Was her hat crooked? Was her belt loose? Craning her head to investigate, Anne, for the first time, saw Rusty.

Trotting along behind her, close to her heels, was quite the most forlorn specimen of the cat-tribe she had ever beheld. The animal was well past kittenhood, lank, thin, disreputable-looking. Pieces of both ears were lacking, one eye was temporarily out of repair, and one jowl ludicrously swollen. As for colour, if a once black cat had been well and thoroughly singed the result would have resembled the hue of this waif's thin, draggled, unsightly fur.

Anne "shooed," but the cat would not "shoo." As long as she stood he sat back on his haunches and gazed at her reproachfully out of his one good eye; when she resumed her walk he followed. Anne resigned herself to his company until she reached the gate of Patty's Place, which she coldly shut in his face, fondly supposing she had seen the last of him. But when, fifteen minutes later, Phil opened the door, there sat the rusty-brown cat on the step. More, he promptly darted in and sprang upon Anne's lap with a half-pleading, half-triumphant "miaow."

"Anne," said Stella severely, "do you own that animal?"

"No, I do *not,*" protested disgusted Anne. "The creature followed me home from somewhere. I couldn't get rid of him. Ugh, get down. I like decent cats reasonably well; but I don't like beasties of your complexion."

Pussy, however, refused to get down. He coolly curled up in Anne's lap and began to purr.

"He has evidently adopted you," laughed Priscilla.

"I won't *be* adopted," said Anne stubbornly.

"The poor creature is starving," said Phil pityingly. "Why, his bones are almost coming through his skin."

"Well, I'll give him a square meal and then he must return to whence he came," said Anne resolutely.

The cat was fed and put out. In the morning he was still on the doorstep. On the doorstep he continued to sit, bolting in whenever the door was opened. No coolness of welcome had the least effect on him; of nobody save Anne did he take the least notice. Out of compassion the girls fed him; but when a week had passed they decided that something must be done. The cat's appearance had improved. His eye and cheek had resumed their normal appearance; he was not quite so thin; and he had been seen washing his face.

"But for all that we can't keep him," said Stella. "Aunt Jimsie is coming next week and she will bring the Sarah-cat with her. We can't keep two cats; and if we did this Rusty Coat would fight all the time with the Sarah-cat. He's a fighter by nature. He had a pitched battle last evening with the tobacco-king's cat and routed him, horse, foot and artillery."

"We must get rid of him," agreed Anne, looking darkly at the subject of their discussion, who was purring on the hearth-rug with an air of lamb-like meekness. "But the question is—how? How can four unprotected females get rid of a cat who *won't* be got rid of?"

"We must chloroform him," said Phil briskly. "That is the most humane way."

"Who of us knows anything about chloroforming a cat?" demanded Anne gloomily.

"I do, honey. It's one of my few—sadly few—useful accomplishments. I've disposed of several at home. You take the cat in the morning and give him a good breakfast. Then you take an old burlap bag—there's one in the back porch—put the cat on it and turn over him a wooden box. Then take a two-ounce bottle of chloroform, uncork it, and slip it under the edge of the box. Put a heavy weight on top of the box and leave it till evening. The cat will be dead, curled up peacefully as if he were asleep. No pain—no struggle."

"It sounds easy," said Anne dubiously.

"It *is* easy. Just leave it to me. I'll see to it," said Phil reassuringly.

Accordingly the chloroform was procured, and the next morning Rusty was lured to his doom. He ate his breakfast, licked his chops, and climbed into Anne's lap. Anne's heart misgave her. This poor creature loved her—trusted her. How could she be a party to his destruction?

"Here, take him," she said hastily to Phil. "I feel like a murderess."

"He won't suffer, you know," comforted Phil, but Anne had fled.

The fatal deed was done in the back porch. Nobody went near it that day. But at dusk Phil declared that Rusty must be buried.

"Pris and Stella must dig his grave in the orchard," decreed Phil, "and Anne must come with me to lift the box off. That's the part I always hate."

The two conspirators tip-toed reluctantly to the back porch. Phil gingerly lifted the stone she had put on the box. Suddenly, faint but distinct, sounded an unmistakable mew under the box.

"He—he isn't dead," gasped Anne, sitting blankly down on the kitchen door-step.

"He must be," said Phil incredulously.

Another tiny mew proved that he wasn't. The two girls stared at each other.

"What will we do?" questioned Anne.

"Why in the world don't you come?" demanded Stella, appearing in the doorway. "We've got the grave ready. 'What, silent still and silent all?' " she quoted teasingly.

" 'Oh, no, the voices of the dead
Sound like the distant torrent's fall,' "
promptly counter-quoted Anne, pointing solemnly to the box.

A burst of laughter broke the tension.

"We must leave him here till morning," said Phil, replacing the stone. "He hasn't mewed for five minutes. Perhaps the mews we heard were his dying groan. Or perhaps we merely imagined them, under the strain of our guilty consciences."

But, when the box was lifted in the morning, Rusty bounded at one gay leap to Anne's shoulder where he began to lick her face affectionately. Never was there a cat more decidedly alive.

"Here's a knot hole in the box," groaned Phil. "I never saw it. That's why he didn't die. Now, we've got to do it all over again."

"No, we haven't," declared Anne suddenly. "Rusty isn't going to be killed again. He's my cat—and you've just got to make the best of it."

"Oh, well, if you'll settle with Aunt Jimsie and the Sarah-cat," said Stella, with the air of one washing her hands of the whole affair.

From that time Rusty was one of the family. He slept o' nights on the scrubbing cushion in the back porch and lived on the fat of the land. By the time Aunt Jamesina came he was plump and glossy and tolerably respectable. But, like Kipling's cat, he "walked by himself." His paw was against every cat, and every cat's paw against him. One by one he vanquished the aristocratic felines of Spofford Avenue. As for human beings, he loved Anne and Anne alone. Nobody else even dared stroke him. An angry spit and something that sounded much like very improper language greeted any one who did.

"The airs that cat puts on are perfectly intolerable," declared Stella.

"Him was a nice old pussens, him was," vowed Anne, cuddling her pet defiantly.

"Well, I don't know how he and the Sarah-cat will ever make out to live together," said Stella pessimistically. "Cat-fights in the orchard o' nights are bad enough. But cat-fights here in the living-room are unthinkable."

In due time Aunt Jamesina arrived. Anne and Priscilla and Phil had awaited her advent rather dubiously; but when Aunt Jamesina was enthroned in the rocking chair before the open fire they figuratively bowed down and worshipped her.

Aunt Jamesina was a tiny old woman with a little, softly-triangular face, and large, soft blue eyes that were alight with unquenchable youth, and as full of hopes as a girl's. She had pink cheeks and snow-white hair which she wore in quaint little puffs over her ears.

"It's a very old-fashioned way," she said, knitting industriously at something as dainty and pink as a sunset cloud. "But *I* am old-fashioned. My clothes are, and it stands to reason my opinions are, too. I don't say they're any the better of that, mind you. In fact, I daresay they're a good deal the worse. But they've worn nice and easy. New shoes are smarter than old ones, but the old ones are more comfortable. I'm old enough to indulge myself in the matter of shoes and opinions. I mean to take it real easy here. I know you expect me to look after you and keep you proper, but I'm not going to do it. You're old enough to know how to behave if you're ever going to be. So, as far as I am concerned," concluded Aunt Jamesina, with a twinkle in her young eyes, "you can all go to destruction in your own way."

"Oh, will somebody separate those cats?" pleaded Stella, shudderingly.

Aunt Jamesina had brought with her not only the Sarah-cat but Joseph. Joseph, she explained, had belonged to a dear friend of hers who had gone to live in Vancouver.

"She couldn't take Joseph with her so she begged me to take him. I really couldn't refuse. He's a beautiful cat—that is, his disposition is beautiful. She called him Joseph because his coat is of many colours."

It certainly was. Joseph, as the disgusted Stella said, looked like a walking rag-bag. It was impossible to say what his ground colour was. His legs were white with black spots on them. His back was gray with a huge patch of yellow on one side and a black patch on the other. His tail was yellow with a gray tip. One ear was black and one yellow. A black patch over one eye gave him a fearfully rakish look. In reality he was meek and inoffensive, of a sociable disposition. In one respect, if in no other, Joseph was like a lily of the field. He toiled not neither did he spin or catch mice. Yet Solomon in all his glory slept not on softer cushions, or feasted more fully on fat things.

Joseph and the Sarah-cat arrived by express in separate boxes. After they had been released and fed, Joseph selected the cushion and corner which appealed to him, and the Sarah-cat gravely sat her down before the fire and proceeded to wash her face. She was a large, sleek, gray-and-white cat, with an enormous dignity which was not at all impaired by any consciousness of her plebeian origin. She had been given to Aunt Jamesina by her washerwoman.

"Her name was Sarah, so my husband always called puss the Sarah-cat," explained Aunt Jamesina. "She is eight years old, and a remarkable mouser. Don't worry, Stella. The Sarah-cat *never* fights and Joseph rarely."

"They'll have to fight here in self-defence," said Stella.

At this juncture Rusty arrived on the scene. He bounded joyously half way across the room before he saw the intruders. Then he stopped short; his tail expanded until it was as big as three tails. The fur on his back rose up in a defiant arch; Rusty lowered his head, uttered a fearful shriek of hatred and defiance, and launched himself at the Sarah-cat.

That stately animal had stopped washing her face and was looking at him curiously. She met his onslaught with one contemptuous sweep of her capable paw. Rusty went rolling helplessly over on the rug; he picked himself up dazedly. What sort of a cat was this who had boxed his ears? He looked dubiously at the Sarah-cat. Would he or would he not? The Sarah-cat deliberately turned her back on him and resumed her toilet operations. Rusty decided that he would not. He never did. From that time on the Sarah-cat ruled the roost. Rusty never again interfered with her.

But Joseph rashly sat up and yawned. Rusty, burning to avenge his disgrace, swooped down upon him. Joseph, pacific by nature, could fight upon occasion and fight well. The result was a series of drawn battles. Every day Rusty and Joseph fought at sight. Anne took Rusty's part and detested Joseph. Stella was in despair. But Aunt Jamesina only laughed.

"Let them fight it out," she said tolerantly. "They'll make friends after a bit. Joseph needs some exercise—he was getting too fat. And Rusty has to learn he isn't the only cat in the world."

Eventually Joseph and Rusty accepted the situation and from sworn enemies became sworn friends. They slept on the same cushion with their paws about each other, and gravely washed each other's faces.

"We've all got used to each other," said Phil. "And I've learned how to wash dishes and sweep a floor."

"But you needn't try to make us believe you can chloroform a cat," laughed Anne.

"It was all the fault of the knot-hole," protested Phil.

"It was a good thing the knot-hole was there," said Aunt Jamesina rather severely. "Kittens *have* to be drowned, I admit, or the world would be over-run. But no decent, grown-up cat should be done to death—unless he sucks eggs."

"You wouldn't have thought Rusty very decent if you'd seen

him when he came here," said Stella. "He positively looked like the Old Nick."

"I don't believe Old Nick can be so very ugly," said Aunt Jamesina reflectively. "He wouldn't do so much harm if he was. *I* always think of him as a rather handsome gentleman."

CHAPTER 17

A LETTER FROM DAVY

"IT'S BEGINNING to snow, girls," said Phil, coming in one November evening, "and there are the loveliest little stars and crosses all over the garden walk. I never noticed before what exquisite things snowflakes really are. One has time to notice things like that in the simple life. Bless you all for permitting me to live it. It's really delightful to feel worried because butter has gone up five cents a pound."

"Has it?" demanded Stella, who kept the household accounts.

"It has—and here's your butter. I'm getting quite expert at marketing. It's better fun than flirting," concluded Phil gravely.

"Everything is going up scandalously," sighed Stella.

"Never mind. Thank goodness air and salvation are still free," said Aunt Jamesina.

"And so is laughter," added Anne. "There's no tax on it yet and that is well, because you're all going to laugh presently. I'm going to read you Davy's letter. His spelling has improved immensely this past year, though he is not strong on apostrophes, and he certainly possesses the gift of writing an interesting letter. Listen and laugh, before we settle down to the evening's study-grind."

"Dear Anne," ran Davy's letter, "I take my pen to tell you that we are all pretty well and hope this will find you the same. It's snowing some today and Marilla says the old woman in the sky is shaking her feather beds. Is the old woman in the sky God's wife, Anne? I want to know.

"Mrs. Lynde has been real sick but she is better now. She fell down the cellar stairs last week. When she fell she grabbed hold of the shelf with all the milk pails and stewpans on it, and it gave way and went down with her and made a splendid crash. Marilla thought it was an earthquake at first. One of the stewpans was all dinged up and Mrs. Lynde straned her ribs. The doctor come and give her medicine to rub on her ribs but she didn't understand him and took it all inside instead. The doctor said it was a wonder it dident kill her but it dident and it cured her ribs and Mrs. Lynde says doctors dont know much anyhow. But we couldent fix up the stewpan. Marilla had to throw it out. Thanksgiving was last week. There was no school and we had a great dinner. I et mince pie and rost turkey and frut cake and donuts and cheese and jam and choklut cake. Marilla said Id die but I dident. Dora had earake after it, only it wasent in her ears it was in her stummick. I dident have earake anywhere.

"Our new teacher is a man. He does things for jokes. Last week he made all us third-class boys write a composishun on what kind of a wife we'd like to have and the girls what kind of a husband. He laughed fit to kill when he read them. This was mine. I thought youd like to see it.

" 'The kind of a wife Id like to Have.

" 'She must have good manners and get my meals on time and do what I tell her and always be very polite to me. She must be fifteen years old. She must be good to the poor and keep her house tidy and be good tempered and go to church reglarly. She must be very handsome and have curly hair. If I get a wife that is just what I like Ill be an awful good husband to her. I think a woman ought to be awful good to her husband. Some poor women havent any husbands.

" 'THE END.'

"I was at Mrs. Isaac Wrights funeral at White Sands last week. The husband of the corpse felt real sorry. Mrs. Lynde says Mrs. Wrights grandfather stole a sheep but Marilla says we mustent speak ill of the dead. Why mustent we, Anne? I want to know. It's pretty safe, ain't it?

"Mrs. Lynde was awful mad the other day because I asked her if she was alive in Noah's time. I dident mean to hurt her feelings. I just wanted to know. Was she, Anne?

"Mr. Harrison wanted to get rid of his dog. So he hunged him once but he come to life and scooted for the barn while Mr. Harrison was digging the grave, so he hunged him again and he stayed dead that time. Mr. Harrison has a new man working for him. He's awful okward. Mr. Harrison says he is left handed in both his feet. Mr. Barry's hired man is lazy. Mrs. Barry says that but Mr. Barry says he aint lazy exactly only he thinks it easier to pray for things than to work for them.

"Mrs. Harmon Andrews prize pig that she talked so much of died in a fit. Mrs. Lynde says it was a judgment on her for pride. But I think it was hard on the pig. Milty Boulter has been sick. The doctor gave him medecine and it tasted horrid. I offered to take it for him for a quarter but the Boulters are so mean. Milty says he'd rather take it himself and save his money. I asked Mrs. Boulter how a person would go about catching a man and she got awful mad and said she dident know, shed never chased men.

"The A.V.I.S. is going to paint the hall again. They're tired of having it blue.

"The new minister was here to tea last night. He took three pieces of pie. If I did that Mrs. Lynde would call me piggy. And he et fast and took big bites and Marilla is always telling me not to do that. Why can ministers do what boys can't? I want to know.

"I havent any more news. Here are six kisses. xxxxxx. Dora sends one. Heres hers. x.

"Your loving friend
"DAVID KEITH"

"P.S. Anne, who was the devils father? I want to know."

CHAPTER 18

MISS JOSEPHINE REMEMBERS THE ANNE-GIRL

WHEN CHRISTMAS holidays came the girls of Patty's Place scattered to their respective homes, but Aunt Jamesina elected to stay where she was.

"I couldn't go to any of the places I've been invited and take those three cats," she said. "And I'm not going to leave the poor creatures here alone for nearly three weeks. If we had any decent neighbours who would feed them I might, but there's nothing except millionaires on this street. So I'll stay here and keep Patty's Place warm for you."

Anne went home with the usual joyous anticipations—which were not wholly fulfilled. She found Avonlea in the grip of such an early, cold, and stormy winter as even the "oldest inhabitant" could not recall. Green Gables was literally hemmed in by huge drifts. Almost every day of that ill-starred vacation it stormed fiercely; and even on fine days it drifted unceasingly. No sooner were the roads broken than they filled in again. It was almost impossible to stir out. The A.V.I.S. tried, on three evenings, to have a party in honour of the college students, and on each evening the storm was so wild that nobody could go, so they gave up the attempt in despair. Anne, despite her love of and loyalty to Green Gables, could not help thinking longingly of Patty's Place, its cosy open fire, Aunt Jamesina's mirthful eyes, the three cats, the merry chatter of the girls, the pleasantness of Friday evenings when college friends dropped in to talk of grave and gay.

Anne was lonely; Diana, during the whole of the holidays, was imprisoned at home with a bad attack of bronchitis. She could not come to Green Gables and it was rarely Anne could get to Orchard Slope, for the old way through the Haunted Wood was impassable with drifts, and the long way over the frozen Lake of Shining Waters was almost as bad. Ruby Gillis was sleeping in the white-heaped graveyard; Jane Andrews was teaching a school on western prairies. Gilbert, to be sure, was still faithful, and waded up to Green Gables every possible evening. But Gilbert's visits were not what they once were.

Anne almost dreaded them. It was very disconcerting to look up in the midst of a sudden silence and find Gilbert's hazel eyes fixed upon her with a quite unmistakable expression in their grave depths; and it was still more disconcerting to find herself blushing hotly and uncomfortably under his gaze, just as if—just as if—well, it was very embarrassing. Anne wished herself back at Patty's Place, where there was always somebody else about to take the edge off a delicate situation. At Green Gables Marilla went promptly to Mrs. Lynde's domain when Gilbert came and insisted on taking the twins with her. The significance of this was unmistakable and Anne was in a helpless fury over it.

Davy, however, was perfectly happy. He revelled in getting out in the morning and shovelling out the paths to the well and henhouse. He gloried in the Christmas-tide delicacies which Marilla and Mrs. Lynde vied with each other in preparing for Anne, and he was reading an enthralling tale, in a school library book, of a wonderful hero who seemed blessed with a miraculous faculty for getting into scrapes from which he was usually delivered by an earthquake or a volcanic explosion, which blew him high and dry out of his troubles, landed him in a fortune, and closed the story with proper *éclat*.

"I tell you it's a bully story, Anne," he said ecstatically. "I'd ever so much rather read it than the Bible."

"Would you?" smiled Anne.

Davy peered curiously at her.

"You don't seem a bit shocked, Anne. Mrs. Lynde was awful shocked when I said it to her."

"No, I'm not shocked, Davy. I think it's quite natural that a nine-year-old boy would sooner read an adventure story than the Bible. But when you are older I hope and think that you will realize what a wonderful book the Bible is."

"Oh, I think some parts of it are fine," conceded Davy. "That story about Joseph now—it's bully. But if I'd been Joseph *I* wouldn't have forgive the brothers. No, siree, Anne. I'd have cut all their heads off. Mrs. Lynde was awful mad when I said that and shut the Bible up and said she'd never read me any more of it if I talked like that. So I don't talk now when she reads it Sunday afternoons; I just think things and say them to Milty Boulter next day in school. I told Milty the story

about Elisha and the bears and it scared him so he's never
made fun of Mr. Harrison's bald head since. Are there any
bears on P.E. Island, Anne? I want to know."

"Not nowadays," said Anne, absently, as the wind blew a
scud of snow against the window. "Oh, dear, will it ever stop
storming."

"God knows," said Davy airily, preparing to resume his
reading.

Anne *was* shocked this time.

"Davy!" she exclaimed reproachfully.

"Mrs. Lynde says that," protested Davy. "One night last week
Marilla said 'Will Ludovic Speed and Theodora Dix *ever* get
married,' and Mrs. Lynde said, 'God knows'—just like that."

"Well, it wasn't right for her to say it," said Anne, promptly
deciding upon which horn of this dilemma to empale herself.
"It isn't right for anybody to take that name in vain or speak
it lightly, Davy. Don't ever do it again."

"Not if I say it slow and solemn, like the minister?" queried
Davy gravely.

"No, not even then."

"Well, I won't. Ludovic Speed and Theodora Dix live in
Middle Grafton and Mrs. Rachel says he has been courting her
for a hundred years. Won't they soon be too old to get married,
Anne? I hope Gilbert won't court *you* that long. When are you
going to be married, Anne? Mrs. Lynde says it's a sure thing."

"Mrs. Lynde is a—" began Anne hotly; then stopped.

"Awful old gossip," completed Davy calmly. "That's what
every one calls her. But *is* it a sure thing, Anne? I want to
know."

"You're a very silly little boy, Davy," said Anne, stalking
haughtily out of the room. The kitchen was deserted and she
sat down by the window in the fast falling wintry twilight. The
sun had set and the wind had died down. A pale chilly moon
looked out behind a bank of purple clouds in the west. The
sky faded out, but the strip of yellow along the western horizon
grew brighter and fiercer, as if all the stray gleams of light were
concentrating in one spot; the distant hills, rimmed with priest-
like firs, stood out in dark distinctness against it. Anne looked
across the still, white fields, cold and lifeless in the harsh light
of that grim sunset, and sighed. She was very lonely; and she

was sad at heart; for she was wondering if she would be able to return to Redmond next year. It did not seem likely. The only scholarship possible in the Sophomore year was a very small affair. She would not take Marilla's money; and there seemed little prospect of being able to earn enough in the summer vacation.

"I suppose I'll just have to drop out next year," she thought drearily, "and teach a district school again until I earn enough to finish my course. And by that time all my old class will have graduated and Patty's Place will be out of the question. But there! I'm not going to be a coward. I'm thankful I can earn my way through if necessary."

"Here's Mr. Harrison wading up the lane," announced Davy, running out. "I hope he's brought the mail. It's three days since we got it. I want to see what them pesky Grits are doing. I'm a Coservative, Anne. And I tell you, you have to keep your eye on them Grits."

Mr. Harrison had brought the mail, and merry letters from Stella and Priscilla and Phil soon dissipated Anne's blues. Aunt Jamesina, too, had written, saying that she was keeping the hearth-fire alight, and that the cats were all well, and the house plants doing fine.

"The weather has been real cold," she wrote, "so I let the cats sleep in the house—Rusty and Joseph on the sofa in the living-room, and the Sarah-cat on the foot of my bed. It's real company to hear her purring when I wake up in the night and think of my poor daughter in the foreign field. If it was anywhere but in India I wouldn't worry, but they say the snakes out there are terrible. It takes all the Sarah-cat's purring to drive away the thought of those snakes. I have enough faith for everything but the snakes. I can't think why Providence ever made them. Sometimes I don't think He did. I'm inclined to believe the Old Harry had a hand in making *them*."

Anne had left a thin, typewritten communication till the last, thinking it unimportant. When she had read it she sat very still, with tears in her eyes.

"What is the matter, Anne?" asked Marilla.

"Miss Josephine Barry is dead," said Anne, in a low tone.

"So she has gone at last," said Marilla. "Well, she has been sick for over a year, and the Barrys have been expecting to hear of her death any time. It is well she is at rest for she has suffered dreadfully, Anne. She was always kind to you."

"She has been kind to the last, Marilla. This letter is from her lawyer. She has left me a thousand dollars in her will."

"Gracious, ain't that an awful lot of money," exclaimed Davy. "She's the woman you and Diana lit on when you jumped into the spare room bed, ain't she? Diana told me that story. Is that why she left you so much?"

"Hush, Davy," said Anne gently. She slipped away to the porch gable with a full heart, leaving Marilla and Mrs. Lynde to talk over the news to their hearts' content.

"Do you s'pose Anne will ever get married now?" speculated Davy anxiously. "When Dorcas Sloane got married last summer she said if she'd had enough money to live on she'd never have been bothered with a man, but even a widower with eight children was better'n living with a sister-in-law."

"Davy Keith, do hold your tongue," said Mrs. Rachel severely. "The way you talk is scandalous for a small boy, that's what."

CHAPTER 19

AN INTERLUDE

"To think that this is my twentieth birthday, and that I've left my teens behind me forever," said Anne, who was curled up on the hearth-rug with Rusty in her lap, to Aunt Jamesina who was reading in her pet chair. They were alone in the living room. Stella and Priscilla had gone to a committee meeting and Phil was up-stairs adorning herself for a party.

"I suppose you feel kind of sorry," said Aunt Jamesina. "The teens are such a nice part of life. I'm glad I've never gone out of them myself."

Anne laughed.

"You never will, Aunty. You'll be eighteen when you should

be a hundred. Yes, I'm sorry, and a little dissatisfied as well. Miss Stacy told me long ago that by the time I was twenty my character would be formed, for good or evil. I don't feel that it's what it should be. It's full of flaws."

"So's everybody's," said Aunt Jamesina cheerfully. "Mine's cracked in a hundred places. Your Miss Stacy likely meant that when you were twenty your character would have got its permanent bent in one direction or 'tother, and would go on developing in that line. Don't worry over it, Anne. Do your duty by God and your neighbour and yourself, and have a good time. That's my philosophy and it's always worked pretty well. Where's Phil off to tonight?"

"She's going to a dance, and she's got the sweetest dress for it—creamy yellow silk and cobwebby lace. It just suits those brown tints of hers."

"There's magic in the words 'silk' and 'lace,' isn't there?" said Aunt Jamesina. "The very sound of them makes me feel like skipping off to a dance. And *yellow* silk. It makes one think of a dress of sunshine. I always wanted a yellow silk dress, but first my mother and then my husband wouldn't hear of it. The very first thing I'm going to do when I get to heaven is to get a yellow silk dress."

Amid Anne's peal of laughter Phil came down-stairs, trailing clouds of glory, and surveyed herself in the long oval mirror on the wall.

"A flattering looking-glass is a promoter of amiability," she said. "The one in my room does certainly make me green. Do I look pretty nice, Anne?"

"Do you really know how pretty you are, Phil?" asked Anne, in honest admiration.

"Of course I do. What are looking-glasses and men for? That wasn't what I meant. Are all my ends tucked in? Is my skirt straight? And would this rose look better lower down? I'm afraid it's too high—it will make me look lop-sided. But I hate things tickling my ears."

"Everything is just right, and that southwest dimple of yours is lovely."

"Anne, there's one thing in particular I like about you,— you're so ungrudging. There isn't a particle of envy in you."

"Why should she be envious?" demanded Aunt Jamesina.

"She's not quite as good-looking as you, maybe, but she's got a far handsomer nose."

"I know it," conceded Phil.

"My nose always has been a great comfort to me," confessed Anne.

"And I love the way your hair grows on your forehead, Anne. And that one wee curl, always looking as if it were going to drop, but never dropping, is delicious. But as for noses, mine is a dreadful worry to me. I know by the time I'm forty it will be Byrney. What do you think I'll look like when I'm forty, Anne?"

"Like an old, matronly, married woman," teased Anne.

"I won't," said Phil, sitting down comfortably to wait for her escort. "Joseph, you calico beastie, don't you dare jump on my lap. I won't go to a dance all over cat-hairs. No, Anne, I *won't* look matronly. But no doubt I'll be married."

"To Alec or Alonzo?" asked Anne.

"To one of them, I suppose," sighed Phil, "if I can ever decide which."

"It shouldn't be hard to decide," scolded Aunt Jamesina.

"I was born a see-saw, Aunty, and nothing can ever prevent me from teetering."

"You ought to be more level-headed, Philippa."

"It's best to be level-headed, of course," agreed Philippa, "but you miss lots of fun. As for Alec and Alonzo, if you knew them you'd understand why it's difficult to choose between them. They're equally nice."

"Then take somebody who is nicer," suggested Aunt Jamesina. "There's that Senior who is so devoted to you—Will Leslie. He has such nice, large, mild eyes."

"They're a little bit too large and too mild—like a cow's," said Phil cruelly.

"What do you say about George Parker?"

"There's nothing to say about him except that he always looks as if he had just been starched and ironed."

"Marr Holworthy then. You can't find a fault with him."

"No, he would do if he wasn't poor. I must marry a rich man, Aunt Jamesina. That—and good looks—is an indispensable qualification. I'd marry Gilbert Blythe if he were rich."

"Oh, would you?" said Anne, rather viciously.

"We don't like that idea a little bit, although we don't want Gilbert ourselves, oh, no," mocked Phil. "But don't let's talk of disagreeable subjects. I'll have to marry sometime, I suppose, but I shall put off the evil day as long as I can."

"You mustn't marry anybody you don't love, Phil, when all's said and done," said Aunt Jamesina.

> " 'Oh, hearts that loved in the good old way,
> Have been out o' the fashion this many a day.' "

trilled Phil mockingly. "There's the carriage. I fly—Bi-bi, you two old-fashioned darlings."

When Phil had gone Aunt Jamesina looked solemnly at Anne.

"That girl is pretty and sweet and good-hearted, but do you think she is quite right in her mind, by spells, Anne?"

"Oh, I don't think there's anything the matter with Phil's mind," said Anne, hiding a smile. "It's just her way of talking."

Aunt Jamesina shook her head.

"Well, I hope so, Anne. I do hope so, because I love her. But *I* can't understand her—she beats me. She isn't like any of the girls I ever knew, or any of the girls I was myself."

"How many girls were you, Aunt Jimsie?"

"About half a dozen, my dear."

CHAPTER 20

GILBERT SPEAKS

"This has been a dull, prosy day," yawned Phil, stretching herself idly on the sofa, having previously dispossessed two exceedingly indignant cats.

Anne looked up from *Pickwick Papers*. Now that spring examinations were over she was treating herself to Dickens.

"It has been a prosy day for us," she said thoughtfully, "but to some people it has been a wonderful day. Some one has

been rapturously happy in it. Perhaps a great deed has been
done somewhere today—or a great poem written—or a great
man born. And some heart has been broken, Phil."

"Why did you spoil your pretty thought by tagging that last
sentence on, honey?" grumbled Phil. "I don't like to think of
broken hearts—or anything unpleasant."

"Do you think you'll be able to shirk unpleasant things all
your life, Phil?"

"Dear me, no. Am I not up against them now? You don't
call Alec and Alonzo pleasant things, do you, when they simply
plague my life out?"

"You never take anything seriously, Phil."

"Why should I? There are enough folks who do. The world
needs people like me, Anne, just to amuse it. It would be a
terrible place if *everybody* were intellectual and serious and in
deep, deadly earnest. *My* mission is, as *Josiah Allen* says, 'to
charm and allure.' Confess now. Hasn't life at Patty's Place
been really much brighter and pleasanter this past winter because
I've been here to leaven you?"

"Yes, it has," owned Anne.

"And you all love me—even Aunt Jamesina, who thinks I'm
stark mad. So why should I try to be different? Oh, dear, I'm
so sleepy. I was awake until one last night, reading a harrowing
ghost story. I read it in bed, and after I had finished it do you
suppose I could get out of bed to put the light out? No! And
if Stella had not fortunately come in late that lamp would have
burned good and bright till morning. When I heard Stella I
called her in, explained my predicament, and got her to put
out the light. If I had got out myself to do it I knew something
would grab me by the feet when I was getting in again. By the
way, Anne, has Aunt Jamesina decided what to do this summer?"

"Yes, she's going to stay here. I know she's doing it for the
sake of those blessed cats, although she says it's too much
trouble to open her own house, and she hates visiting."

"What are you reading?"

"Pickwick."

"That's a book that always makes me hungry," said Phil.
"There's so much good eating in it. The characters seem always

to be revelling on ham and eggs and milk punch. I generally
go on a cupboard rummage after reading *Pickwick*. The mere
thought reminds me that I'm starving. Is there any tidbit in
the pantry, Queen Anne?"

"I made a lemon pie this morning. You may have a piece
of it."

Phil dashed out to the pantry and Anne betook herself to
the orchard in company with Rusty. It was a moist, pleasantly-
odorous night in early spring. The snow was not quite all gone
from the park; a little dingy bank of it yet lay under the pines
of the harbour road, screened from the influence of April suns.
It kept the harbour road muddy, and chilled the evening air.
But grass was growing green in sheltered spots and Gilbert had
found some pale, sweet arbutus in a hidden corner. He came
up from the park, his hands full of it.

Anne was sitting on the big gray boulder in the orchard
looking at the poem of a bare, birchen bough hanging against
the pale red sunset with the very perfection of grace. She was
building a castle in air—a wondrous mansion whose sunlit
courts and stately halls were steeped in Araby's perfume, and
where she reigned queen and chatelaine. She frowned as she
saw Gilbert coming through the orchard. Of late she had managed not to be left alone with Gilbert. But he had caught her
fairly now; and even Rusty had deserted her.

Gilbert sat down beside her on the boulder and held out his
Mayflowers.

"Don't these remind you of home and our old school-day
picnics, Anne?"

Anne took them and buried her face in them.

"I'm in Mr. Silas Sloane's barrens this very minute," she
said rapturously.

"I suppose you will be there in reality in a few days?"

"No, not for a fortnight. I'm going to visit with Phil in
Bolingbroke before I go home. You'll be in Avonlea before I
will."

"No, I shall not be in Avonlea at all this summer, Anne.
I've been offered a job in the *Daily News* office and I'm going
to take it."

"Oh," said Anne vaguely. She wondered what a whole Avon-

lea summer would be like without Gilbert. Somehow she did
not like the prospect. "Well," she concluded flatly, "it is a
good thing for you, of course."

"Yes, I've been hoping I would get it. It will help me out
next year."

"You mustn't work *too* hard," said Anne, without any very
clear idea of what she was saying. She wished desperately that
Phil would come out. "You've studied very constantly this
winter. Isn't this a delightful evening? Do you know, I found
a cluster of white violets under that old twisted tree over there
today? I felt as if I had discovered a gold mine."

"You are always discovering gold mines," said Gilbert—also
absently.

"Let us go and see if we can find some more," suggested
Anne eagerly. "I'll call Phil and—"

"Never mind Phil and the violets just now, Anne," said
Gilbert quietly, taking her hand in a clasp from which she
could not free it. "There is something I want to say to you."

"Oh, don't say it," cried Anne, pleadingly. "Don't—*please,*
Gilbert."

"I must. Things can't go on like this any longer. Anne, I
love you. You know I do. I—I can't tell you how much. Will
you promise me that some day you'll be my wife?"

"I—I can't," said Anne miserably. "Oh, Gilbert—you—you've
spoiled everything."

"Don't you care for me at all?" Gilbert asked after a very
dreadful pause, during which Anne had not dared to look up.

"Not—not in that way. I do care a great deal for you as a
friend. But I don't love you, Gilbert."

"But can't you give me some hope that you will—yet?"

"No, I can't," exclaimed Anne desperately. "I never, never
can love you—in that way—Gilbert. You must never speak of
this to me again."

There was another pause—so long and so dreadful that Anne
was driven at last to look up. Gilbert's face was white to the
lips. And his eyes—but Anne shuddered and looked away.
There was nothing romantic about this. Must proposals be
either grotesque or—horrible? Could she ever forget Gilbert's
face?

"Is there anybody else?" he asked at last in a low voice.

"No—no," said Anne eagerly. "I don't care for any one like *that*—and I *like* you better than anybody else in the world, Gilbert. And we must—we *must* go on being friends, Gilbert."

Gilbert gave a bitter little laugh.

"Friends! Your friendship can't satisfy me, Anne. I want your love—and you tell me I can never have that."

"I'm sorry. Forgive me, Gilbert," was all Anne could say. Where, oh, where were all the gracious and graceful speeches wherewith, in imagination, she had been wont to dismiss rejected suitors?

Gilbert released her hand gently.

"There isn't anything to forgive. There have been times when I thought you did care. I've deceived myself, that's all. Goodbye, Anne."

Anne got herself to her room, sat down on her window seat behind the pines, and cried bitterly. She felt as if something incalculably precious had gone out of her life. It was Gilbert's friendship, of course. Oh, why must she lose it after this fashion?

"What is the matter, honey?" asked Phil, coming in through the moonlit gloom.

Anne did not answer. At that moment she wished Phil were a thousand miles away.

"I suppose you've gone and refused Gilbert Blythe. You are an idiot, Anne Shirley!"

"Do you call it idiotic to refuse to marry a man I don't love?" said Anne coldly, goaded to reply.

"You don't know love when you see it. You've tricked something out with your imagination that you think love, and you expect the real thing to look like that. There, that's the first sensible thing I've ever said in my life. I wonder how I managed it?"

"Phil," pleaded Anne, "please go away and leave me alone for a little while. My world has tumbled into pieces. I want to reconstruct it."

"Without any Gilbert in it?" said Phil, going.

A world without any Gilbert in it! Anne repeated the words drearily. Would it not be a very lonely, forlorn place? Well, it was all Gilbert's fault. He had spoiled their beautiful comradeship. She must just learn to live without it.

CHAPTER 21

ROSES OF YESTERDAY

THE FORTNIGHT Anne spent in Bolingbroke was a very pleasant one, with a little undercurrent of vague pain and dissatisfaction running through it whenever she thought about Gilbert. There was not, however, much time to think about him. "Mount Holly," the beautiful old Gordon homestead, was a very gay place, overrun by Phil's friends of both sexes. There was quite a bewildering succession of drives, dances, picnics and boating parties, all expressively lumped together by Phil under the head of "jamborees"; Alec and Alonzo were so constantly on hand that Anne wondered if they ever did anything but dance attendance on that will-o'-the-wisp of a Phil. They were both nice, manly fellows, but Anne would not be drawn into any opinion as to which was the nicer.

"And I depended so on you to help me make up my mind which of them I should promise to marry," mourned Phil.

"You must do that for yourself. You are quite expert at making up your mind as to whom other people should marry," retorted Anne, rather caustically.

"Oh, that's a very different thing," said Phil truly.

But the sweetest incident of Anne's sojourn in Bolingbroke was the visit to her birthplace—the little shabby yellow house in an out-of-the-way street she had so often dreamed about. She looked at it with delighted eyes, as she and Phil turned in at the gate.

"It's almost exactly as I've pictured it," she said. "There is no honeysuckle over the windows, but there *is* a lilac tree by the gate, and—yes, there are the muslin curtains in the windows. How glad I am it is still painted yellow."

A very tall, very thin woman opened the door.

"Yes, the Shirleys lived here twenty years ago," she said, in answer to Anne's question. "They had it rented. I remember 'em. They both died of fever at onct. It was turrible sad. They left a baby. I guess it's dead long ago. It was a sickly thing. Old Thomas and his wife took it—as if they hadn't enough of their own."

124

"It didn't die," said Anne, smiling. "I was that baby."

"You don't say so! Why, you *have* grown," exclaimed the woman, as if she were much surprised that Anne was not still a baby. "Come to look at you, I see the resemblance. You're complected like your pa. He had red hair. But you favour your ma in your eyes and mouth. She was a nice little thing. My darter went to school to her and was nigh crazy about her. They was buried in the one grave and the School Board put up a tombstone to them as a reward for faithful service. Will you come in?"

"Will you let me go all over the house?" asked Anne eagerly.

"Laws, yes, you can if you like. 'Twon't take you long— there ain't much of it. I keep at my man to build a new kitchen, but he ain't one of your hustlers. The parlour's in there and there's two rooms up-stairs. Just prowl about your-selves. I've got to see to the baby. The east room was the one you were born in. I remember your ma saying she loved to see the sunrise; and I mind hearing that you was born just as the sun was rising and its light on your face was the first thing your ma saw."

Anne went up the narrow stairs and into that little east room with a full heart. It was as a shrine to her. Here her mother had dreamed the exquisite, happy dreams of anticipated moth-erhood; here that red sunrise light had fallen over them both in the sacred hour of birth; here her mother had died. Anne looked about her reverently, her eyes dim with tears. It was for her one of the jewelled hours of life that gleam out radiantly forever in memory.

"Just to think of it—mother was younger than I am now when I was born," she whispered.

When Anne went down-stairs the lady of the house met her in the hall. She held out a dusty little packet tied with faded blue ribbon.

"Here's a bundle of old letters I found in that closet up-stairs when I came here," she said. "I dunno what they are— I never bothered to look in 'em, but the address on the top one is 'Miss Bertha Willis,' and that was your ma's maiden name. You can take 'em if you'd keer to have 'em."

"Oh, thank you—thank you," cried Anne, clasping the packet rapturously.

"That was all that was in the house," said her hostess. "The furniture was all sold to pay the doctor bills, and Mrs. Thomas got your ma's clothes and little things. I reckon they didn't last long among that drove of Thomas youngsters. They was destructive young animals, as I mind 'em."

"I haven't one thing that belonged to my mother," said Anne, chokily. "I—I can never thank you enough for these letters."

"You're quite welcome. Law's, but your eyes is like your ma's. She could just about talk with hers. Your father was sorter homely but awful nice. I mind hearing folks say when they was married that there never was two people more in love with each other—Pore creetures, they didn't live much longer; but they was awful happy while they was alive, and I s'pose that counts for a good deal."

Anne longed to get home to read her precious letters; but she made one little pilgrimage first. She went alone to the green corner of the "old" Bolingbroke cemetery where her father and mother were buried, and left on their grave the white flowers she carried. Then she hastened back to Mount Holly, shut herself up in her room, and read the letters. Some were written by her father, some by her mother. There were not many—only a dozen in all—for Walter and Bertha Shirley had not been often separated during their courtship. The letters were yellow and faded and dim, blurred with the touch of passing years. No profound words of wisdom were traced on the stained and wrinkled pages, but only lines of love and trust. The sweetness of forgotten things clung to them—the far-off, fond imaginings of those long-dead lovers. Bertha Shirley had possessed the gift of writing letters which embodied the charming personality of the writer in words and thoughts that retained their beauty and fragrance after the lapse of time. The letters were tender, intimate, sacred. To Anne, the sweetest of all was the one written after her birth to the father on a brief absence. It was full of a proud young mother's accounts of "baby"— her cleverness, her brightness, her thousand sweetnesses.

"I love her best when she is asleep and better still when she is awake," Bertha Shirley had written in the postscript. Probably it was the last sentence she had ever penned. The end was very near for her.

"This has been the most beautiful day of my life," Anne

said to Phil that night. "I've *found* my father and mother. Those letters have made them *real* to me. I'm not an orphan any longer. I feel as if I had opened a book and found roses of yesterday, sweet and beloved, between its leaves."

CHAPTER 22

SPRING AND ANNE RETURN TO GREEN GABLES

THE FIRELIGHT shadows were dancing over the kitchen walls at Green Gables, for the spring evening was chilly; through the open east window drifted in the subtly sweet voices of the night. Marilla was sitting by the fire—at least, in body. In spirit she was roaming olden ways, with feet grown young. Of late Marilla had thus spent many an hour, when she thought she should have been knitting for the twins.

"I suppose I'm growing old," she said.

Yet Marilla had changed but little in the past nine years, save to grow something thinner, and even more angular; there was a little more gray in the hair that was still twisted up in the same hard knot, with two hairpins—*were* they the same hairpins?—still stuck through it. But her expression was very different; the something about the mouth which had hinted at a sense of humour had developed wonderfully; her eyes were gentler and milder, her smile more frequent and tender.

Marilla was thinking of her whole past life, her cramped but not unhappy childhood, the jealously hidden dreams and the blighted hopes of her girlhood, the long, gray, narrow, monotonous years of dull middle life that followed. And the coming of Anne—the vivid, imaginative, impetuous child with her heart of love, and her world of fancy, bringing with her colour and warmth and radiance, until the wilderness of existence had blossomed like the rose. Marilla felt that out of her sixty years she had *lived* only the nine that had followed the advent of Anne. And Anne would be home tomorrow night.

The kitchen door opened. Marilla looked up expecting to see Mrs. Lynde. Anne stood before her, tall and starry-eyed, with her hands full of Mayflowers and violets.

"Anne Shirley!" exclaimed Marilla. For once in her life she was surprised out of her reserve; she caught her girl in her arms and crushed her and her flowers against her heart, kissing the bright hair and sweet face warmly. "I never looked for you till tomorrow night. How did you get from Carmody?"

"Walked, dearest of Marillas. Haven't I done it a score of times in the Queen's days? The mailman is to bring my trunk tomorrow; I just got homesick all at once, and came a day earlier. And oh! I've had such a lovely walk in the May twilight; I stopped by the barrens and picked these Mayflowers; I came through Violet-Vale; it's just a big bowlful of violets now—the dear, sky-tinted things. Smell them, Marilla—drink them in."

Marilla sniffed obligingly, but she was more interested in Anne than in drinking violets.

"Sit down, child. You must be real tired. I'm going to get you some supper."

"There's a darling moonrise behind the hills tonight, Marilla, and oh, how the frogs sang me home from Carmody! I do love the music of the frogs. It seems bound up with all my happiest recollections of old spring evenings. And it always reminds me of the night I came here first. Do you remember it, Marilla?"

"Well, yes," said Marilla with emphasis. "I'm not likely to forget it ever."

"They used to sing so madly in the marsh and brook that year. I would listen to them at my window in the dusk, and wonder how they could seem so glad and so sad at the same time. Oh, but it's good to be home again! Redmond was splendid and Bolingbroke delightful—but Green Gables is *home.*"

"Gilbert isn't coming home this summer, I hear," said Marilla.

"No." Something in Anne's tone made Marilla glance at her sharply, but Anne was apparently absorbed in arranging her violets in a bowl. "See, aren't they sweet?" she went on hurriedly. "The year is a book, isn't it, Marilla? Spring's pages are written in Mayflowers and violets, summer's in roses, autumn's in red maple leaves, and winter in holly and evergreen."

"Did Gilbert do well in his examinations?" persisted Marilla.

"Excellently well. He led his class. But where are the twins and Mrs. Lynde?"

"Rachel and Dora are over at Mr. Harrison's. Davy is down at Boulters'. I think I hear him coming now."

Davy burst in, saw Anne, stopped, and then hurled himself upon her with a joyful yell.

"Oh, Anne, ain't I glad to see you! Say, Anne, I've grown two inches since last fall. Mrs. Lynde measured me with her tape today, and say, Anne, see my front tooth. It's gone. Mrs. Lynde tied one end of a string to it and the other end to the door, and then shut the door. I sold it to Milty for two cents. Milty's collecting teeth."

"What in the world does he want teeth for?" asked Marilla.

"To make a necklace for playing Indian Chief," explained Davy, climbing upon Anne's lap. "He's got fifteen already, and everybody else's promised, so there's no use in the rest of us starting to collect, too. I tell you the Boulters are great business people."

"Were you a good boy at Mrs. Boulter's?" asked Marilla severely.

"Yes; but say, Marilla, I'm tired of being good."

"You'd get tired of being bad much sooner, Davy-boy," said Anne.

"Well, it'd be fun while it lasted, wouldn't it?" persisted Davy. "I could be sorry for it afterwards, couldn't I?"

"Being sorry wouldn't do away with the consequences of being bad, Davy. Don't you remember the Sunday last summer when you ran away from Sunday School? You told me then that being bad wasn't worth while. What were you and Milty doing today?"

"Oh, we fished and chased the cat, and hunted for eggs, and yelled at the echo. There's a great echo in the bush behind the Boulter barn. Say, what is echo, Anne; I want to know."

"Echo is a beautiful nymph, Davy, living far away in the woods, and laughing at the world from among the hills."

"What does she look like?"

"Her hair and eyes are dark, but her neck and arms are white as snow. No mortal can ever see how fair she is. She is fleeter than a deer, and that mocking voice of hers is all we can know of her. You can hear her calling at night; you can hear her laughing under the stars. But you can never see her. She flies afar if you follow her, and laughs at you always just over the next hill."

"Is that all true, Anne? Or is it a whopper?" demanded Davy staring.

"Davy," said Anne despairingly, "haven't you sense enough to distinguish between a fairy-tale and a falsehood?"

"Then *what* is it that sasses back from the Boulter bush? I want to know," insisted Davy.

"When you are a little older, Davy, I'll explain it all to you."

The mention of age evidently gave a new turn to Davy's thoughts for after a few moments of reflection, he whispered solemnly:

"Anne, I'm going to be married."

"When?" asked Anne with equal solemnity.

"Oh, not until I'm grown-up, of course."

"Well, that's a relief, Davy. Who is the lady?"

"Stella Fletcher; she's in my class at school. And say, Anne, she's the prettiest girl you ever saw. If I die before I grow up you'll keep an eye on her, won't you?"

"Davy Keith, do stop talking such nonsense," said Marilla severely.

"'Tisn't nonsense," protested Davy in an injured tone. "She's my promised wife, and if I was to die she'd be my promised widow, wouldn't she? And she hasn't got a soul to look after her except her old grandmother."

"Come and have your supper, Anne," said Marilla, "and don't encourage that child in his absurd talk."

CHAPTER 23

PAUL CANNOT FIND THE ROCK PEOPLE

LIFE WAS very pleasant in Avonlea that summer, although Anne, amid all her vacation joys, was haunted by a sense of "something gone which should be there." She would not admit, even in her inmost reflections, that this was caused by Gilbert's absence. But when she had to walk home alone from prayer meetings and A.V.I.S. pow-wows, while Diana and Fred, and many other gay couples, loitered along the dusky, starlit country roads, there was a queer, lonely ache in her heart which she could not explain away. Gilbert did not even write to her, as she thought he might have done. She knew he wrote to Diana occasionally, but she would not inquire about him; and Diana, supposing that Anne heard from him, volunteered no information. Gilbert's mother, who was a gay, frank, light-hearted lady, but not over-burdened with tact, had a very embarrassing habit of asking Anne, always in a painfully distinct voice and always in the presence of a crowd, if she had heard from Gilbert lately. Poor Anne could only blush horribly and murmur, "not very lately," which was taken by all, Mrs. Blythe included, to be merely a maidenly evasion.

Apart from this, Anne enjoyed her summer. Priscilla came for a merry visit in June; and, when she had gone, Mr. and Mrs. Irving, Paul and Charlotta the Fourth came "home" for July and August.

Echo Lodge was the scene of gaieties once more, and the echoes over the river were kept busy mimicking the laughter that rang in the old garden behind the spruces.

"Miss Lavendar" had not changed, except to grow even sweeter and prettier. Paul adored her, and the companionship between them was beautiful to see.

"But I don't call her 'mother' just by itself," he explained to Anne. "You see, *that* name belongs just to my own little mother, and I can't give it to any one else. *You* know, teacher. But I call her 'Mother Lavendar' and I love her next best to father. I—I even love her a *little* better than you, teacher."

"Which is just as it ought to be," answered Anne.

Paul was thirteen now and very tall for his years. His face and eyes were as beautiful as ever, and his fancy was still like a prism, separating everything that fell upon it into rainbows. He and Anne had delightful rambles to wood and field and shore. Never were there two more thoroughly "kindred spirits."

Charlotta the Fourth had blossomed out into young ladyhood. She wore her hair now in an enormous pompadour and had discarded the blue ribbon bows of auld lang syne, but her face was as freckled, her nose as snubbed, and her mouth and smiles as wide as ever.

"You don't think I talk with a Yankee accent, do you, Miss Shirley, ma'am?" she demanded anxiously.

"I don't notice it, Charlotta."

"I'm real glad of that. They said I did at home, but I thought likely they just wanted to aggravate me. I don't want no Yankee accent. Not that I've a word to say against the Yankees, Miss Shirley, ma'am. They're real civilized. But give me old P.E. Island every time."

Paul spent his first fortnight with his grandmother Irving in Avonlea. Anne was there to meet him when he came, and found him wild with eagerness to get to the shore—Nora and the Golden Lady and the Twin Sailors would be there. He could hardly wait to eat his supper. Could he not see Nora's elfin face peering around the point, watching for him wistfully? But it was a very sober Paul who came back from the shore in the twilight.

"Didn't you find your Rock People?" asked Anne.

Paul shook his chestnut curls sorrowfully.

"The Twin Sailors and the Golden Lady never came at all," he said. "Nora was there—but Nora is not the same, teacher. She is changed."

"Oh, Paul, it is you who are changed," said Anne. "You have grown too old for the Rock People. They like only children for playfellows. I am afraid the Twin Sailors will never again come to you in the pearly, enchanted boat with the sail of moonshine; and the Golden Lady will play no more for you on her golden harp. Even Nora will not meet you much longer. You must pay the penalty of growing-up, Paul. You must leave fairyland behind you."

"You two talk as much foolishness as ever you did," said old Mrs. Irving, half-indulgently, half-reprovingly.

"Oh, no, we don't," said Anne, shaking her head gravely. "We are getting very, very wise, and it is such a pity. We are never half so interesting when we have learned that language is given us to enable us to conceal our thoughts."

"But it isn't—it is given us to exchange our thoughts," said Mrs. Irving seriously. She had never heard of Tallyrand and did not understand epigrams.

Anne spent a fortnight of halcyon days at Echo Lodge in the golden prime of August. While there she incidentally contrived to hurry Ludovic Speed in his leisurely courting of Theodora Dix, as related duly in another chronicle of her history.[1] Arnold Sherman, an elderly friend of the Irvings, was there at the same time, and added not a little to the general pleasantness of life.

"What a nice play-time this has been," said Anne. "I feel like a giant refreshed. And it's only a fortnight more till I go back to Kingsport, and Redmond and Patty's Place. Patty's Place is the dearest spot, Miss Lavendar. I feel as if I had two homes—one at Green Gables and one at Patty's Place. But where has the summer gone? It doesn't seem a day since I came home that spring evening with the Mayflowers. When I was little I couldn't see from one end of the summer to the other. It stretched before me like an unending season. Now 'tis a handbreadth, 'tis a tale.' "

"Anne, are you and Gilbert Blythe as good friends as you used to be?" asked Miss Lavendar quietly.

"I am just as much Gilbert's friend as ever I was, Miss Lavendar."

Miss Lavendar shook her head.

"I see something's gone wrong, Anne. I'm going to be impertinent and ask what. Have you quarrelled?"

"No; it's only that Gilbert wants more than friendship and I can't give him more."

"Are you sure of that, Anne?"

"Perfectly sure."

---

[1] *Chronicles of Avonlea.*

"I'm very, very sorry."

"I wonder why everybody seems to think I ought to marry Gilbert Blythe," said Anne petulantly.

"Because you were made and meant for each other, Anne— that is why. You needn't toss that young head of yours. It's a fact."

CHAPTER 24

ENTER JONAS

"Prospect Point,
"August 20th.

"Dear Anne—spelled—with—an—E," wrote Phil, "I must prop my eyelids open long enough to write you. I've neglected you shamefully this summer, honey, but all my other correspondents have been neglected, too. I have a huge pile of letters to answer, so I must gird up the loins of my mind and hoe in. Excuse my mixed metaphors. I'm fearfully sleepy. Last night Cousin Emily and I were calling at a neighbour's. There were several other callers there, and, as soon as those unfortunate creatures left, our hostess and her three daughters picked them all to pieces. I knew they would begin on Cousin Emily and me as soon as the door shut behind us. When we came home Mrs. Lilly informed us that the aforesaid neighbour's hired boy was supposed to be down with scarlet fever. You can always trust Mrs. Lilly to tell you cheerful things like that. I have a horror of scarlet fever. I couldn't sleep when I went to bed for thinking of it. I tossed and tumbled about, dreaming fearful dreams when I did snooze for a minute; and at three I wakened up with a high fever, a sore throat, and a raging headache. I knew I had scarlet fever; I got up in a panic and hunted up Cousin Emily's 'doctor book' to read up the symptoms. Anne, I had them all. So I went back to bed, and knowing the worst, slept like a top the rest of the night. Though why a top should sleep sounder than anything else I never could understand. But this morning I was quite well, so it couldn't have been the fever. I suppose if I did catch it last night it couldn't have developed so soon. I can remember that in day-time, but at three o'clock at night I never can be logical.

"I suppose you wonder what I'm doing at Prospect Point. Well, I always like to spend a month of summer at the shore, and father insists that I come to his second-cousin Emily's 'select boarding-house' at Prospect Point. So a fortnight ago I came as usual. And as usual old 'Uncle Mark Miller' brought me from the station with his ancient buggy and what he calls his 'generous purpose' horse. He is a nice old man and gave me a handful of pink peppermints. Peppermints always seem to me such a religious sort of candy.—I suppose because when I was a little girl Grandmother Gordon always gave them to me in church. Once I asked, referring to the smell of peppermints, 'Is that the odour of sanctity?' I didn't like to eat Uncle Mark's peppermints because he just fished them loose out of his pocket, and had to pick some rusty nails and other things from among them before he gave them to me. But I wouldn't hurt his dear old feelings for anything, so I carefully sowed them along the road at intervals. When the last one was gone, Uncle Mark said, a little rebukingly, 'Ye shouldn't a'et all them candies to onct, Miss Phil. You'll likely have the stummick-ache.'

"Cousin Emily has only five boarders besides myself—four old ladies and one young man. My right-hand neighbour is Mrs. Lilly. She is one of those people who seem to take a gruesome pleasure in detailing all their many aches and pains and sicknesses. You cannot mention any ailment but she says, shaking her head, 'Ah, I know too well what that is'—and then you get all the details. Jonas declares he once spoke of locomotor ataxia in her hearing and she said she knew too well what that was. She suffered from it for ten years and was finally cured by a travelling doctor.

"Who is Jonas? Just wait, Anne Shirley. You'll hear all about Jonas in the proper time and place. He is not to be mixed up with estimable old ladies.

"My left-hand neighbour at the table is Mrs. Phinney. She always speaks with a wailing, dolorous voice—you are nervously expecting her to burst into tears every moment. She gives you the impression that life to her is indeed a vale of tears, and that a smile, never to speak of a laugh, is a frivolity truly reprehensible. She has a worse opinion of me than Aunt Jamesina, and she doesn't love me hard to atone for it, as Aunty J. does, either.

"Miss Maria Grimsby sits cati-corner from me. The first day I came I remarked to Miss Maria that it looked a little like rain—and Miss Maria laughed. I said the road from the station was very pretty—and Miss Maria laughed. I said there seemed to be a few mosquitoes left yet—and Miss Maria laughed. I said that Prospect Point was as beautiful as ever—and Miss Maria laughed. If I were to say to Miss Maria, 'My father has hanged himself, my mother has taken poison, my brother is in the penitentiary, and I am in the last stages of consumption,' Miss Maria would laugh. She can't help it—she was born so; but it's very sad and awful.

"The fifth old lady is Mrs. Grant. She is a sweet old thing; but she never says anything but good of anybody and so she is a very uninteresting conversationalist.

"And now for Jonas, Anne.

"That first day I came I saw a young man sitting opposite to me at the table, smiling at me as if he had known me from my cradle. I knew, for Uncle Mark had told me, that his name was Jonas Blake, that he was a Theological Student from St. Columba, and that he had taken charge of the Point Prospect Mission Church for the summer.

"He is a very ugly young man—really, the ugliest young man I've ever seen. He has a big, loose-jointed figure with absurdly long legs. His hair is tow-colour and lank, his eyes are green, and his mouth is big, and his ears—but I never think about his ears if I can help it.

"He has a lovely voice—if you shut your eyes he is adorable—and he certainly has a beautiful soul and disposition.

"We were good chums right away. Of course he is a graduate of Redmond, and that is a link between us. We fished and boated together; and we walked on the sands by moonlight. He didn't look so homely by moonlight and oh, he was nice. Niceness fairly exhaled from him. The old ladies—except Mrs. Grant—don't approve of Jonas, because he laughs and jokes—

and because he evidently likes the society of frivolous me better than theirs.

"Somehow, Anne, I don't want him to think me frivolous. This is ridiculous. Why should I care what a tow-haired person called Jonas, whom I never saw before, thinks of me?

"Last Sunday Jonas preached in the village church. I went, of course, but I couldn't realize that Jonas was going to preach. The fact that he was a minister—or going to be one—persisted in seeming a huge joke to me.

"Well, Jonas preached. And, by the time he had preached ten minutes, I felt so small and insignificant that I thought I must be invisible to the naked eye. Jonas never said a word about women and he never looked at me. But I realized then and there what a pitiful, frivolous, small-souled little butterfly I was, and how horribly different I must be from Jonas' ideal woman. *She* would be grand and strong and noble. He was so earnest and tender and true. He was everything a minister ought to be. I wondered how I could ever have thought him ugly— but he really is!—with those inspired eyes and that intellectual brow which the roughly-falling hair hid on week days.

"It was a splendid sermon and I could have listened to it forever, and it made me feel utterly wretched. Oh, I wish I was like *you*, Anne.

"He caught up with me on the road home, and grinned as cheerfully as usual. But his grin could never deceive me again. I had seen the *real* Jonas. I wondered if he could ever see the *real* Phil—whom *nobody*, not even you, Anne, has ever seen yet.

" 'Jonas,' I said—I forgot to call him Mr. Blake. Wasn't it dreadful? But there are times when things like that don't matter— 'Jonas, you were born to be a minister. You *couldn't* be anything else.'

" 'No, I couldn't,' he said soberly. 'I tried to be something else for a long time—I didn't want to be a minister. But I came to see at last that it was the work given me to do—and God helping me, I shall try to do it.'

"His voice was low and reverent. I thought that he would do his work and do it well and nobly; and happy the woman fitted by nature and training to help him do it. *She* would be no feather, blown about by every fickle wind of fancy. *She*

would always know what hat to put on. Probably she would
have only one. Ministers never have much money. But she
wouldn't mind having one hat or none at all, because she would
have Jonas.

"Anne Shirley, don't you dare to say or hint or think that
I've fallen in love with Mr. Blake. Could *I* care for a lank,
poor, ugly theologue—named Jonas? As Uncle Mark says, 'It's
impossible, and what's more it's improbable.'

"Good-night,

"PHIL

"P.S. It is impossible—but I am horribly afraid it's true. I'm
happy and wretched and scared. *He* can *never* care for me, I
know. Do you think I could ever develop into a passable
minister's wife, Anne? And *would* they expect me to lead in
prayer? P.G."

--------------- CHAPTER 25 ---------------

ENTER PRINCE CHARMING

"I'M CONTRASTING the claims of indoors and out," said Anne,
looking from the window of Patty's Place to the distant pines
of the park.

"I've an afternoon to spend in sweet doing nothing, Aunt
Jimsie. Shall I spend it here where there is a cosy fire, a plateful
of delicious russets, three purring and harmonious cats, and
two impeccable china dogs with green noses? Or shall I go to
the park, where there is the lure of gray woods and of gray
water lapping on the harbour rocks?"

"If I was as young as you, I'd decide in favour of the park,"
said Aunt Jamesina, tickling Joseph's yellow ear with a knitting
needle.

"I thought that you claimed to be as young as any of us,
Aunty," teased Anne.

"Yes, in my soul. But I'll admit my legs aren't as young as

yours. You go and get some fresh air, Anne. You look pale lately."

"I think I will go to the park," said Anne restlessly. "I don't feel like tame domestic joys today. I want to feel alone and free and wild. The park will be empty, for every one will be at the foot-ball match."

"Why didn't you go to it?"

" 'Nobody axed me, sir, she said,'—at least, nobody but that horrid little Dan Ranger. I wouldn't go anywhere with him; but rather than hurt his poor little tender feelings I said I wasn't going to the game at all. I don't mind. I'm not in the mood for foot-ball today somehow."

"You go and get some fresh air," repeated Aunt Jamesina, "but take your umbrella, for I believe it's going to rain. I've rheumatism in my leg."

"Only old people should have rheumatism, Aunty."

"Anybody is liable to rheumatism in her legs, Anne. It's only old people who should have rheumatism in their souls, though. Thank goodness, I never have. When you get rheumatism in your soul you might as well go and pick out your coffin."

It was November—the month of crimson sunsets, parting birds, deep, sad hymns of the sea, passionate wind-songs in the pines. Anne roamed through the pineland alleys in the park and, as she said, let that great sweeping wind blow the fogs out of her soul. Anne was not wont to be troubled with soul fog. But, somehow, since her return to Redmond for this third year, life had not mirrored her spirit back to her with its old, perfect, sparkling clearness.

Outwardly, existence at Patty's Place was the same pleasant round of work and study and recreation that it had always been. On Friday evenings the big, firelighted living-room was crowded by callers and echoed to endless jest and laughter, while Aunt Jamesina smiled beamingly on them all. The "Jonas" of Phil's letter came often, running up from St. Columba on the early train and departing on the late. He was a general favourite at Patty's Place, though Aunt Jamesina shook her head and opined that divinity students were not what they used to be.

"He's *very* nice, my dear," she told Phil, "but ministers ought to be graver and more dignified."

"Can't a man laugh and laugh and be a Christian still?" demanded Phil.

"Oh, *men*—yes. But I was speaking of *ministers,* my dear," said Aunt Jamesina rebukingly. "And you shouldn't flirt so with Mr. Blake—you really shouldn't."

"I'm not flirting with him," protested Phil.

Nobody believed her, except Anne. The others thought she was amusing herself as usual, and told her roundly that she was behaving very badly.

"Mr. Blake isn't of the Alec-and-Alonzo type, Phil," said Stella severely. "He takes things seriously. You may break his heart."

"Do you really think I could?" asked Phil. "I'd love to think so."

"Philippa Gordon! I never thought you were utterly unfeeling. The idea of you saying you'd love to break a man's heart!"

"I didn't say so, honey. Quote me correctly. I said I'd like to think I *could* break it. I would like to know I had the *power* to do it."

"I don't understand you, Phil. You are leading that man on deliberately—and you know you don't mean anything by it."

"I mean to make him ask me to marry him if I can," said Phil calmly.

"I give you up," said Stella hopelessly.

Gilbert came occasionally on Friday evenings. He seemed always in good spirits, and held his own in the jests and repartee that flew about. He neither sought nor avoided Anne. When circumstances brought them in contact he talked to her pleasantly and courteously, as to any newly-made acquaintance. The old camaraderie was gone entirely. Anne felt it keenly; but she told herself she was very glad and thankful that Gilbert had got so completely over his disappointment in regard to her. She had really been afraid, that April evening in the orchard, that she had hurt him terribly and that the wound would be long in healing. Now she saw that she need not have worried. Men have died and the worms have eaten them but not for love. Gilbert evidently was in no danger of immediate dissolution. He was enjoying life, and he was full of ambition and zest. For him there was to be no wasting in despair because a woman was fair and cold. Anne, as she listened to the ceaseless badinage that went on between him and Phil, wondered if she had only imagined that look in his eyes when she had told him she could never care for him.

There were not lacking those who would gladly have stepped into Gilbert's vacant place. But Anne snubbed them without fear and without reproach. If the real Prince Charming was never to come she would none of a substitute. So she sternly told herself that gray day in the windy park.

Suddenly the rain of Aunt Jamesina's prophecy came with a swish and rush. Anne put up her umbrella and hurried down the slope. As she turned out on the harbour road a savage gust of wind tore along it. Instantly her umbrella turned wrong side out. Anne clutched at it in despair. And then—there came a voice close to her:

"Pardon me—may I offer you the shelter of my umbrella?"

Anne looked up. Tall and handsome and distinguished-looking—dark, melancholy, inscrutable eyes—melting, musical, sympathetic voice—yes, the very hero of her dreams stood before her in the flesh. He could not have more closely resembled her ideal if he had been made to order.

"Thank you," she said confusedly.

"We'd better hurry over to that little pavilion on the point," suggested the unknown. "We can wait there until this shower is over. It is not likely to rain so heavily very long."

The words were very commonplace, but oh, the tone! And the smile which accompanied them! Anne felt her heart beating strangely.

Together they scurried to the pavilion and sat breathlessly down under its friendly roof. Anne laughingly held up her false umbrella.

"It is when my umbrella turns inside out that I am convinced of the total depravity of inanimate things," she said gaily.

The rain drops sparkled on her shining hair; its loosened rings curled around her neck and forehead. Her cheeks were flushed, her eyes big and starry. Her companion looked down at her admiringly. She felt herself blushing under his gaze. Who could he be? Why, there was a bit of the Redmond white and scarlet pinned to his coat-lapel. Yet she had thought she knew, by sight at least, all the Redmond students except the Freshmen. And this courtly youth surely was no Freshman.

"We are schoolmates, I see," he said, smiling at Anne's colours. "That ought to be sufficient introduction. My name is Royal Gardner. And you are the Miss Shirley who read the Tennyson paper at the Philomathic the other evening, aren't you?"

"Yes; but I cannot place you at all," said Anne, frankly. "Please, where *do* you belong?"

"*I* feel as if I didn't belong anywhere yet. I put in my Freshman and Sophomore years at Redmond two years ago. I've been in Europe ever since. Now I've come back to finish my Arts course."

"This is my Junior year, too," said Anne.

"So we are classmates as well as college-mates. I am reconciled to the loss of the years that the locust has eaten," said her companion, with a world of meaning in those wonderful eyes of his.

The rain came steadily down for the best part of an hour. But the time seemed really very short. When the clouds parted and a burst of pale November sunshine fell athwart the harbour and the pines Anne and her companion walked home together. By the time they had reached the gate of Patty's Place he had asked permission to call, and had received it. Anne went in with cheeks of flame and her heart beating to her finger-tips. Rusty, who climbed into her lap and tried to kiss her, found a very absent welcome. Anne, with her soul full of romantic thrills, had no attention to spare just then for a crop-eared pussy cat.

That evening a parcel was left at Patty's Place for Miss Shirley. It was a box containing a dozen magnificent roses. Phil pounced impertinently on the card that fell from it, read the name and the poetical quotation written on the back.

"Royal Gardner!" she exclaimed. "Why, Anne, I didn't know you were acquainted with Roy Gardner!"

"I met him in the park this afternoon in the rain," explained Anne hurriedly. "My umbrella turned inside out and he came to my rescue with his."

"Oh!" Phil peered curiously at Anne. "And is that exceedingly common-place incident any reason why he should send us long-stemmed roses by the dozen, with a very sentimental rhyme?

Or why we should blush divinest rosy-red when we look at his card? Anne, thy face betrayeth thee."

"Don't talk nonsense, Phil. Do you know Mr. Gardner?"

"I've met his two sisters, and I know of him. So does everybody worth while in Kingsport. The Gardners are among the richest, bluest, of Bluenoses. Roy is adorably handsome and clever. Two years ago his mother's health failed and he had to leave college and go abroad with her—his father is dead. He must have been greatly disappointed to have to give up his class, but they say he was perfectly sweet about it. Fee—fi—fo—fum, Anne. I smell romance. Almost do I envy you, but not quite. After all, Roy Gardner isn't Jonas."

"You goose!" said Anne loftily. But she lay long awake that night, nor did she wish for sleep. Her waking fancies were more alluring than any vision of dreamland. Had the real Prince come at last? Recalling those glorious dark eyes which had gazed so deeply into her own, Anne was very strongly inclined to think he had.

CHAPTER 26

ENTER CHRISTINE

THE GIRLS at Patty's Place were dressing for the reception which the Juniors were giving for the Seniors in February. Anne surveyed herself in the mirror of the blue room with girlish satisfaction. She had a particularly pretty gown on. Originally it had been only a simple little slip of cream silk with a chiffon over-dress. But Phil had insisted on taking it home with her in the Christmas holidays and embroidering tiny rosebuds all over the chiffon. Phil's fingers were deft, and the result was a dress which was the envy of every Redmond girl. Even Allie Boone, whose frocks came from Paris, was wont to look with longing eyes on that rosebud concoction as Anne trailed up the main staircase at Redmond in it.

Anne was trying the effect of a white orchid in her hair. Roy Gardner had sent her white orchids for the reception, and she knew no other Redmond girl would have them that night—when Phil came in with admiring gaze.

"Anne, this is certainly your night for looking handsome. Nine nights out of ten I can easily outshine you. The tenth you blossom out suddenly into something that eclipses me altogether. How do you manage it?"

"It's the dress, dear. Fine feathers."

"Tisn't. The last evening you flamed out into beauty you wore your old blue flannel shirtwaist that Mrs. Lynde made you. If Roy hadn't already lost head and heart about you he certainly would tonight. But I don't like orchids on you, Anne. No; it isn't jealousy. Orchids don't seem to *belong* to you. They're too exotic—too tropical—too insolent. Don't put them in your hair, anyway."

"Well, I won't. I admit I'm not fond of orchids myself. I don't think they're related to me. Roy doesn't often send them—he knows I like flowers I can live with. Orchids are only things you can visit with."

"Jonas sent me some dear pink rosebuds for the evening—but—he isn't coming himself. He said he had to lead a prayer-meeting in the slums! I don't believe he wanted to come. Anne, I'm horribly afraid Jonas doesn't really care anything about me. And I'm trying to decide whether I'll pine away and die, or go on and get my B.A. and be sensible and useful."

"You couldn't possibly be sensible and useful, Phil, so you'd better pine away and die," said Anne cruelly.

"Heartless Anne!"

"Silly Phil! You know quite well that Jonas loves you."

"But—he won't *tell* me so. And I can't *make* him. He *looks* it, I'll admit. But speak-to-me-only-with-thine-eyes isn't a really reliable reason for embroidering doilies and hemstitching table-cloths. I don't want to begin such work until I'm really engaged. It would be tempting Fate."

"Mr. Blake is afraid to ask you to marry him, Phil. He is poor and can't offer you a home such as you've always had. You know that is the only reason he hasn't spoken long ago."

"I suppose so," agreed Phil dolefully. "Well"—brightening up—"if he *won't* ask me to marry him I'll ask him, that's all.

So it's bound to come right. I won't worry. By the way, Gilbert Blythe is going about constantly with Christine Stuart. Did you know?"

Anne was trying to fasten a little gold chain about her throat. She suddenly found the clasp difficult to manage. *What* was the matter with it—or with her fingers?

"No," she said carelessly. "Who is Christine Stuart?"

"Ronald Stuart's sister. She's in Kingsport this winter studying music. I haven't seen her, but they say she's very pretty and that Gilbert is quite crazy over her. How angry I was when you refused Gilbert, Anne. But Roy Gardner was fore-ordained for you. I can see that now. You were right, after all."

Anne did not blush, as she usually did when the girls assumed that her eventual marriage to Roy Gardner was a settled thing. All at once she felt rather dull. Phil's chatter seemed trivial and the reception a bore. She boxed poor Rusty's ears.

"Get off that cushion instantly, you cat, you! Why don't you stay down where you belong?"

Anne picked up her orchids and went down-stairs, where Aunt Jamesina was presiding over a row of coats hung before the fire to warm. Roy Gardner was waiting for Anne and teasing the Sarah-cat while he waited. The Sarah-cat did not approve of him. She always turned her back on him. But everybody else at Patty's Place liked him very much. Aunt Jamesina, carried away by his unfailing and deferential courtesy, and the pleading tones of his delightful voice, declared he was the nicest young man she ever knew, and that Anne was a very fortunate girl. Such remarks made Anne restive. Roy's wooing had certainly been as romantic as girlish heart could desire, but—she wished Aunt Jamesina and the girls would not take things so for granted. When Roy murmured a poetical compliment as he helped her on with her coat, she did not blush and thrill as usual; and he found her rather silent in their brief walk to Redmond. He thought she looked a little pale when she came out of the co-eds' dressing-room; but as they entered the reception-room her colour and sparkle suddenly returned to her. She turned to Roy with her gayest expression. He smiled back at her with what Phil called "his deep, black, velvety smile." Yet she really did not see Roy at all. She was acutely conscious that Gilbert was standing under the palms just across the room talking to a girl who must be Christine Stuart.

She was very handsome, in the stately style destined to become rather massive in middle life. A tall girl, with large dark-blue eyes, ivory outlines, and a gloss of darkness on her smooth hair.

"She looks just as I've always wanted to look," thought Anne miserably. "Rose-leaf complexion—starry violet eyes—raven hair—yes, she has them all. It's a wonder her name isn't Cordelia Fitzgerald into the bargain! But I don't believe her figure is as good as mine, and her nose certainly isn't."

Anne felt a little comforted by this conclusion.

CHAPTER 27

MUTUAL CONFIDENCES

March came in that winter like the meekest and mildest of lambs, bringing days that were crisp and golden and tingling, each followed by a frosty pink twilight which gradually lost itself in an elfland of moonshine.

Over the girls at Patty's Place was falling the shadow of April examinations. They were studying hard; even Phil had settled down to text and notebooks with a doggedness not to be expected of her.

"I'm going to take the Johnson Scholarship in Mathematics," she announced calmly. "I could take the one in Greek easily, but I'd rather take the mathematical one because I want to prove to Jonas that I'm really enormously clever."

"Jonas likes you better for your big brown eyes and your crooked smile than for all the brains you carry under your curls," said Anne.

"When I was a girl it wasn't considered lady-like to know anything about Mathematics," said Aunt Jamesina. "But times have changed. I don't know that it's all for the better. Can you cook, Phil?"

"No, I never cooked anything in my life except a ginger-bread and it was a failure—flat in the middle and hilly round the edges. You know the kind. But, Aunty, when I begin in good earnest to learn to cook don't you think the brains that enable me to win a mathematical scholarship will also enable me to learn cooking just as well?"

"Maybe," said Aunt Jamesina cautiously. "I am not decrying the higher education of women. My daughter is an M.A. She can cook, too. But I taught her to cook *before* I let a college professor teach her Mathematics."

In mid-March came a letter from Miss Patty Spofford, saying that she and Miss Maria had decided to remain abroad for another year.

"So you may have Patty's Place next winter, too," she wrote. "Maria and I are going to run over Egypt. I want to see the Sphinx once before I die."

"Fancy those two dames 'running over Egypt'! I wonder if they'll look up at the Sphinx and knit," laughed Priscilla.

"I'm so glad we can keep Patty's Place for another year," said Stella. "I was afraid they'd come back. And then our jolly little nest here would be broken up—and we poor callow nestlings thrown out on the cruel world of boarding-houses again."

"I'm off for a tramp in the park," announced Phil, tossing her book aside. "I think when I am eighty I'll be glad I went for a walk in the park tonight."

"What do you mean?" asked Anne.

"Come with me and I'll tell you, honey."

They captured in their ramble all the mysteries and magics of a March evening. Very still and mild it was, wrapped in a great, white, brooding silence—a silence which was yet threaded through with many little silvery sounds which you could hear if you hearkened as much with your soul as your ears. The girls wandered down a long pineland aisle that seemed to lead right out into the heart of a deep-red, overflowing winter sunset.

"I'd go home and write a poem this blessed minute if I only knew how," declared Phil, pausing in an open space where a rosy light was staining the green tips of the pines. "It's all so wonderful here—this great, white stillness, and those dark trees that always seem to be thinking."

" 'The woods were God's first temples,' " quoted Anne softly. "One can't help feeling reverent and adoring in such a place. I always feel so near Him when I walk among the pines."

"Anne, I'm the happiest girl in the world," confessed Phil suddenly.

"So Mr. Blake has asked you to marry him at last?" said Anne calmly.

"Yes. And I sneezed three times while he was asking me. Wasn't that horrid? But I said 'yes' almost before he finished— I was so afraid he might change his mind and stop. I'm besottedly happy. I couldn't really believe before that Jonas would ever care for frivolous me."

"Phil, you're not really frivolous," said Anne gravely. " 'Way down underneath that frivolous exterior of yours you've got a dear, loyal, womanly little soul. Why do you hide it so?"

"I can't help it, Queen Anne. You are right—I'm not frivolous at heart. But there's a sort of frivolous skin over my soul and I can't take it off. As *Mrs. Poyser* says, I'd have to be hatched over again and hatched different before I could change it. But Jonas knows the real me and loves me, frivolity and all. And I love him. I never was so surprised in my life as I was when I found out I loved him. I'd never thought it possible to fall in love with an ugly man. Fancy me coming down to one solitary beau. And one named Jonas! But I mean to call him Jo. That's such a nice, crisp little name. I couldn't nickname Alonzo."

"What about Alec and Alonzo?"

"Oh, I told them at Christmas that I never could marry either of them. It seems so funny now to remember that I ever thought it possible that I might. They felt so badly I just cried over both of them—howled. But I knew there was only one man in the world I could ever marry. I had made up my own mind for once and it was real easy, too. It's very delightful to feel so sure, and know it's your own sureness and not somebody else's."

"Do you suppose you'll be able to keep it up?"

"Making up my mind, you mean? I don't know, but Jo has given me a splendid rule. He says, when I'm perplexed, just to do what I would wish I had done when I shall be eighty. Anyhow, Jo can make up his mind quickly enough, and it would be uncomfortable to have too much mind in the same house."

"What will your father and mother say?"

"Father won't say much. He thinks everything I do right. But mother *will* talk. Oh, her tongue will be as Byrney as her nose. But in the end it will be all right."

"You'll have to give up a good many things you've always had, when you marry Mr. Blake, Phil."

"But I'll have *him*. I won't miss the other things. We're to be married a year from next June. Jo graduates from St. Columba this spring, you know. Then he's going to take a little mission church down on Patterson Street in the slums. Fancy me in the slums! But I'd go there or to Greenland's icy mountains with him."

"And this is the girl who would *never* marry a man who wasn't rich," commented Anne to a young pine tree.

"Oh, don't cast up the follies of my youth to me. I shall be poor as gaily as I've been rich. You'll see. I'm going to learn how to cook and make over dresses. I've learned how to market since I've lived at Patty's Place; and once I taught a Sunday School class for a whole summer. Aunt Jamesina says I'll ruin Jo's career if I marry him. But I won't. I know I haven't much sense or sobriety, but I've got what is ever so much better— the knack of making people like me. There is a man in Bolingbroke who lisps and always testifies in prayer-meeting. He says, 'If you can't thine like an electric thtar thine like a candle-thtick.' I'll be Jo's little candlestick."

"Phil, you're incorrigible. Well, I love you so much that I can't make nice, light, congratulatory little speeches. But I'm heart-glad of your happiness."

"I know. Those big gray eyes of yours are brimming over with real friendship, Anne. Some day I'll look the same way at you. You're going to marry Roy, aren't you, Anne?"

"My dear Philippa, did you ever hear of the famous Betty Baxter, who 'refused a man before he'd axed her'? I am not going to emulate that celebrated lady by either refusing or accepting any one before he 'axes' me."

"All Redmond knows that Roy is crazy about you," said

Phil candidly. "And you *do* love him, don't you, Anne?"

"I—I suppose so," said Anne reluctantly. She felt that she ought to be blushing while making such a confession; but she was not; on the other hand, she always blushed hotly when any one said anything about Gilbert Blythe or Christine Stuart in her hearing. Gilbert Blythe and Christine Stuart were nothing to her—absolutely nothing. But Anne had given up trying to analyze the reason of her blushes. As for Roy, of course she was in love with him—madly so. How could she help it? Was he not her ideal? Who could resist those glorious dark eyes, and that pleading voice? Were not half the Redmond girls wildly envious? And what a charming sonnet he had sent her, with a box of violets, on her birthday! Anne knew every word of it by heart. It was very good stuff of its kind, too. Not exactly up to the level of Keats or Shakespeare—even Anne was not so deeply in love as to think that. But it was very tolerable magazine verse. And it was addressed to *her*—not to Laura or Beatrice or the Maid of Athens, but to her, Anne Shirley. To be told in rhythmical cadences that her eyes were stars of the morning—that her cheek had the flush it stole from the sunrise—that her lips were redder than the roses of Paradise, was thrillingly romantic. Gilbert would never have dreamed of writing a sonnet to her eyebrows. But then, Gilbert could see a joke. She had once told Roy a funny story—and he had not seen the point of it. She recalled the chummy laugh she and Gilbert had had together over it, and wondered uneasily if life with a man who had no sense of humour might not be somewhat uninteresting in the long run. But who could expect a melancholy, inscrutable hero to see the humourous side of things? It would be flatly unreasonable.

CHAPTER 28

A JUNE EVENING

"I WONDER what it would be like to live in a world where it was always June," said Anne, as she came through the spice and bloom of the twilit orchard to the front-door steps, where Marilla and Mrs. Rachel were sitting, talking over Mrs. Samson Coates' funeral, which they had attended that day. Dora sat between them, diligently studying her lessons; but Davy was sitting tailor-fashion on the grass, looking as gloomy and depressed as his single dimple would let him.

"You'd get tired of it," said Marilla, with a sigh.

"I darsay; but just now I feel that it would take me a long time to get tired of it, if it were all as charming as today. Everything loves June. Davy-boy, why this melancholy November face in blossom-time?"

"I'm just sick and tired of living," said the youthful pessimist.

"At ten years? Dear me, how sad!"

"I'm not making fun," said Davy with dignity. "I'm dis— dis—discouraged"—bringing out the big word with a valiant effort.

"Why and wherefore?" asked Anne, sitting down beside him.

" 'Cause the new teacher that come when Mr. Holmes got sick give me ten sums to do for Monday. It'll take me all day tomorrow to do them. It isn't fair to have to work Saturdays. Milty Boulter said he wouldn't do them, but Marilla says I've got to. I don't like Miss Carson a bit."

"Don't talk like that about your teacher, Davy Keith," said Mrs. Rachel severely. "Miss Carson is a very fine girl. There is no nonsense about her."

"That doesn't sound very attractive," laughed Anne. "I like people to have a little nonsense about them. But I'm inclined to have a better opinion of Miss Carson than you have. I saw her in prayer-meeting last night, and she has a pair of eyes that can't always look sensible. Now, Davy-boy, take heart of grace. 'To-morrow will bring another day' and I'll help you with the sums as far as in me lies. Don't waste this lovely hour 'twixt light and dark worrying over arithmetic."

"Well, I won't," said Davy, brightening up. "If you help me with the sums I'll have 'em done in time to go fishing with Milty. I wish old Aunt Atossa's funeral was tomorrow instead of today. I wanted to go to it 'cause Milty said his mother said Aunt Atossa would be sure to rise up in her coffin and say sarcastic things to the folks that come to see her buried. But Marilla said she didn't."

"Poor Atossa laid in her coffin peaceful enough," said Mrs. Lynde solemnly. "I never saw her look so pleasant before, that's what. Well, there weren't many tears shed over her, poor old soul. The Elisha Wrights are thankful to be rid of her, and I can't say I blame them a mite."

"It seems to me a most dreadful thing to go out of the world and not leave one person behind you who is sorry you are gone," said Anne, shuddering.

"Nobody except her parents ever loved poor Atossa, that's certain, not even her husband," averred Mrs. Lynde. "She was his fourth wife. He'd sort of got into the habit of marrying. He only lived a few years after he married her. The doctor said he died of dyspepsia, but I shall always maintain that he died of Atossa's tongue, that's what. Poor soul, she always knew everything about her neighbours, but she never was very well acquainted with herself. Well, she's gone anyhow; and I suppose the next excitement will be Diana's wedding."

"It seems so funny and horrible to think of Diana's being married," sighed Anne, hugging her knees and looking through the gap in the Haunted Wood to the light that was shining in Diana's room.

"I don't see what's horrible about it, when she's doing so well," said Mrs. Lynde emphatically. "Fred Wright has a fine farm and he is a model young man."

"He certainly isn't the wild, dashing, wicked, young man Diana once wanted to marry," smiled Anne. "Fred is extremely good."

"That's just what he ought to be. Would you want Diana to marry a wicked man? Or marry one yourself?"

"Oh, no. I wouldn't want to marry anybody who was wicked, but I think I'd like it if he *could* be wicked and *wouldn't*. Now, Fred is *hopelessly* good."

"You'll have more sense some day, I hope," said Marilla.

Marilla spoke rather bitterly. She was grievously disappointed. She knew Anne had refused Gilbert Blythe. Avonlea gossip buzzed over the fact, which had leaked out, nobody knew how. Perhaps Charlie Sloane had guessed and told his guesses for truth. Perhaps Diana had betrayed it to Fred and Fred had been indiscreet. At all events it was known; Mrs. Blythe no longer asked Anne, in public or private, if she had heard lately from Gilbert, but passed her by with a frosty bow. Anne, who had always liked Gilbert's merry, young-hearted mother, was grieved in secret over this. Marilla said nothing; but Mrs. Lynde gave Anne many exasperated digs about it, until fresh gossip reached that worthy lady, through the medium of Moody Spurgeon MacPherson's mother, that Anne had another "beau" at college, who was rich and handsome and good all in one. After that Mrs. Rachel held her tongue, though she still wished in her inmost heart that Anne had accepted Gilbert. Riches were all very well; but even Mrs. Rachel, practical soul though she was, did not consider them the one essential. If Anne "liked" the Handsome Unknown better than Gilbert there was nothing more to be said; but Mrs. Rachel was dreadfully afraid that Anne was going to make the mistake of marrying for money. Marilla knew Anne too well to fear this; but she felt that something in the universal scheme of things had gone sadly awry.

"What is to be, will be," said Mrs. Rachel gloomily, "and what isn't to be happens sometimes. I can't help believing it's going to happen in Anne's case, if Providence doesn't interfere, that's what."

Mrs. Rachel sighed. She was afraid Providence wouldn't interfere; and she didn't dare to.

Anne had wandered down to the Dryad's Bubble and was curled up among the ferns at the root of the big white birch where she and Gilbert had so often sat in summers gone by. He had gone into the newspaper office again when college closed, and Avonlea seemed very dull without him. He never wrote to her, and Anne missed the letters that never came. To be sure, Roy wrote twice a week; his letters were exquisite compositions which would have read beautifully in a memoir or biography. Anne felt herself more deeply in love with him than ever when she read them; but her heart never gave the

queer, quick, painful bound at sight of his letters which it had
given one day when Mrs. Hiram Sloane had handed her out
an envelope addressed in Gilbert's black, upright handwriting.
Anne had hurried home to the east-gable and opened it eagerly—to find a typewritten copy of some college society report—"only that and nothing more." Anne flung the harmless
screed across her room and sat down to write an especially
nice epistle to Roy.

Diana was to be married in five more days. The gray house
at Orchard Slope was in a turmoil of baking and brewing and
boiling and stewing, for there was to be a big, old-timey wedding.
Anne, of course, was to be bridesmaid, as had been arranged
when they were twelve years old, and Gilbert was coming from
Kingsport to be best-man. Anne was enjoying the excitement
of the various preparations, but under it all she carried a little
heartache. She was, in a sense, losing her dear old chum; Diana's
new home would be two miles from Green Gables, and the
old constant companionship could never be theirs again. Anne
looked up at Diana's light and thought how it had beaconed
to her for many years; but soon it would shine through the
summer twilights no more. Two big, painful tears welled up
in her gray eyes.

"Oh," she thought, "how horrible it is that people have to
grow up—and marry—and *change!*"

CHAPTER 29

DIANA'S WEDDING

"AFTER ALL, the only real roses are the pink ones," said Anne,
as she tied white ribbon around Diana's bouquet in the west-
ward-looking gable at Orchard Slope. "They are the flowers of
love and faith."

Diana was standing nervously in the middle of the room,
arrayed in her bridal white, her black curls frosted over with

the film of her wedding veil. Anne had draped that veil, in accordance with the sentimental compact of years before.

"It's all pretty much as I used to imagine it long ago, when I wept over your inevitable marriage and our consequent parting," she laughed. "You are the bride of my dreams, Diana, with the 'lovely misty veil'; and I am your bridesmaid. But, alas! I haven't the puffed sleeves—though these short lace ones are even prettier. Neither is my heart wholly breaking nor do I exactly hate Fred."

"We are not really parting, Anne," protested Diana. "I'm not going far away. We'll love each other just as much as ever. We've always kept that 'oath' of friendship we swore long ago, haven't we?"

"Yes. We've kept it faithfully. We've had a beautiful friendship, Diana. We've never marred it by one quarrel or coolness or unkind word; and I hope it will always be so. But things can't be quite the same after this. You'll have other interests. I'll just be on the outside. But 'such is life' as Mrs. Rachel says. Mrs. Rachel has given you one of her beloved knitted quilts of the 'tobacco stripe' pattern, and she says when I am married she'll give me one, too."

"The mean thing about your getting married is that I won't be able to be *your* bridesmaid," lamented Diana.

"I'm to be Phil's bridesmaid next June, when she marries Mr. Blake, and then I must stop, for you know the proverb 'three times a bridesmaid, never a bride,'" said Anne, peeping through the window over the pink and snow of the blossoming orchard beneath. "Here comes the minister, Diana."

"Oh, Anne," gasped Diana, suddenly turning very pale and beginning to tremble. "Oh, Anne—I'm so nervous—I can't go through with it—Anne, I know I'm going to faint."

"If you do I'll drag you down to the rain-water hogshead and drop you in," said Anne unsympathetically. "Cheer up, dearest. Getting married can't be so very terrible when so many people survive the ceremony. See how cool and composed *I* am, and take courage."

"Wait till your turn comes, Miss Anne. Oh, Anne, I hear father coming up-stairs. Give me my bouquet. Is my veil right? Am I very pale?"

"You look just lovely. Di, darling, kiss me goodbye for the

last time. Diana Barry will never kiss me again."

"Diana Wright will, though. There, mother's calling. Come."

Following the simple, old-fashioned way in vogue then, Anne went down to the parlour on Gilbert's arm. They met at the top of the stairs for the first time since they had left Kingsport, for Gilbert had arrived only that day. Gilbert shook hands courteously. He was looking very well, though, as Anne instantly noted, rather thin. He was not pale; there was a flush on his cheek that had burned into it as Anne came along the dim hall towards him, in her soft, white dress with lilies-of-the-valley in the shining masses of her hair. As they entered the crowded parlour together a little murmur of admiration ran around the room. "What a fine-looking pair they are," whispered the impressible Mrs. Rachel to Marilla.

Fred ambled in alone, with a very red face, and then Diana swept in on her father's arm. She did not faint, and nothing untoward occurred to interrupt the ceremony. Feasting and merry-making followed; then, as the evening waned, Fred and Diana drove away through the moonlight to their new home, and Gilbert walked with Anne to Green Gables.

Something of their old comradeship had returned during the informal mirth of the evening. Oh, it was nice to be walking over that well-known road with Gilbert again!

The night was so very still that one should have been able to hear the whisper of roses in blossom—the laughter of daisies—the piping of grasses—many sweet sounds, all tangled up together. The beauty of moonlight on familiar fields irradiated the world.

"Can't we take a ramble up Lovers' Lane before you go in?" asked Gilbert as they crossed the bridge over the Lake of Shining Waters, in which the moon lay like a great, drowned blossom of gold.

Anne assented readily. Lovers' Lane was a veritable path in fairyland that night—a shimmering, mysterious place, full of wizardry in the white-woven enchantment of moonlight. There had been a time when such a walk with Gilbert through Lovers' Lane would have been far too dangerous. But Roy and Christine had made it very safe now. Anne found herself thinking a good deal about Christine as she chatted lightly to Gilbert. She had met her several times before leaving Kingsport, and had been charmingly sweet to her. Christine had also been charmingly sweet. Indeed, they were a most cordial pair. But for all that, their acquaintance had not ripened into friendship. Evidently Christine was not a kindred spirit.

"Are you going to be in Avonlea all summer?" asked Gilbert.

"No. I'm going down east to Valley Road next week. Esther Haythorne wants me to teach for her through July and August. They have a summer term in that school, and Esther isn't feeling well. So I'm going to substitute for her. In one way I don't mind. Do you know, I'm beginning to feel a little bit like a stranger in Avonlea now? It makes me sorry—but it's true. It's quite appalling to see the number of children who have shot up into big boys and girls—really young men and women—these past two years. Half of my pupils are grown up. It makes me feel awfully old to see them in the places you and I and our mates used to fill."

Anne laughed and sighed. She felt very old and mature and wise—which showed how young she was. She told herself that she longed greatly to go back to those dear merry days when life was seen through a rosy mist of hope and illusion, and possessed an indefinable something that had passed away forever. Where was it now—the glory and the dream?

" 'So wags the world away,' " quoted Gilbert practically, and a trifle absently. Anne wondered if he were thinking of Christine. Oh, Avonlea was going to be so lonely now—with Diana gone!

CHAPTER 30

MRS. SKINNER'S ROMANCE

ANNE STEPPED off the train at Valley Road station and looked about to see if any one had come to meet her. She was to board with a certain Miss Janet Sweet, but she saw no one who answered in the least to her preconception of that lady, as formed from Esther's letter. The only person in sight was an elderly woman, sitting in a wagon with mail bags piled around her. Two hundred would have been a charitable guess at her weight; her face was as round and red as a harvest-moon and almost as featureless. She wore a tight, black, cashmere dress, made in the fashion of ten years ago, a little dusty black straw hat trimmed with bows of yellow ribbon, and faded black lace mits.

"Here, you," she called, waving her whip at Anne. "Are you the new Valley Road schoolma'am?"

"Yes."

"Well, I thought so. Valley Road is noted for its good-looking schoolma'ams, just as Millersville is noted for its humly ones. Janet Sweet asked me this morning if I could bring you out. I said, 'Sartin I kin, if she don't mind being scrunched up some. This rig of mine's kinder small for the mail bags and I'm some heftier than Thomas!' Just wait, miss, till I shift these bags a bit and I'll tuck you in somehow. It's only two miles to Janet's. Her next-door neighbour's hired boy is coming for your trunk tonight. My name is Skinner—Amelia Skinner."

Anne was eventually tucked in, exchanging amused smiles with herself during the process.

"Jog along, black mare," commanded Mrs. Skinner, gathering up the reins in her pudgy hands. "This is my first trip on the mail rowte. Thomas wanted to hoe his turnips today so he asked me to come. So I jest sot down and took a standing-up snack and started. I sorter like it. O'course it's rather tejus. Part of the time I sits and thinks and the rest I jest sits. Jog along, black mare. I want to git home airly. Thomas is terrible lonesome when I'm away. You see, we haven't been married very long."

"Oh!" said Anne politely.

"Just a month. Thomas courted me for quite a spell, though. It was real romantic."

Anne tried to picture Mrs. Skinner on speaking terms with romance and failed.

"Oh?" she said again.

"Yes. Y'see, there was another man after me. Jog along, black mare. I'd been a widder so long folks had given up expecting me to marry again. But when my darter—she's a schoolma'am like you—went out West to teach I felt real lonesome and wasn't nowise sot against the idea. Bime-by Thomas began to come up and so did the other feller—William Obadiah Seaman, *his* name was. For a long time I couldn't make up my mind which of them to take, and they kep' coming and coming, and I kep' worrying. Y'see, W. O. was rich—he had a fine place and carried considerable style. He was by far the best match. Jog along, black mare."

"Why didn't you marry him?" asked Anne.

"Well, y'see, he didn't love me," answered Mrs. Skinner, solemnly.

Anne opened her eyes widely and looked at Mrs. Skinner. But there was not a glint of humour on that lady's face. Evidently Mrs. Skinner saw nothing amusing in her own case.

"He'd been a widder-man for three years, and his sister kept house for him. Then she got married and he just wanted some one to look after his house. It was worth looking after, too, mind you that. It's a handsome house. Jog along, black mare. As for Thomas, he was poor, and if his house didn't leak in dry weather it was about all that could be said for it, though it looks kind of pictureaskew. But, y'see, I loved Thomas, and I didn't care one red cent for W. O. So I argued it out with myself. 'Sarah Crowe,' says I—my first was a Crowe—'you can marry your rich man if you like but you won't be happy. Folks can't get along together in this world without a little bit of love. You'd just better tie up to Thomas, for he loves you and you love him and nothing else ain't going to do you.' Jog along, black mare. So I told Thomas I'd take him. All the time I was getting ready I never dared drive past W. O.'s place for fear the sight of that fine house of his would put me in the swithers again. But now I never think of it at all, and I'm just that comfortable and happy with Thomas. Jog along, black mare."

"How did William Obadiah take it?" queried Anne.

"Oh, he rumpussed a bit. But he's going to see a skinny old maid in Millersville now, and I guess she'll take him fast enough. She'll make him a better wife than his first did. W. O. never wanter to marry *her*. He just asked her to marry him 'cause his father wanted him to, never dreaming but that she'd say 'no.' But mind you, she said 'yes.' There was a predicament for you. Jog along, black mare. She was a great housekeeper, but most awful mean. She wore the same bonnet for eighteen years. Then she got a new one and W. O. met her on the road and didn't know her. Jog along, black mare. I feel that I'd a narrer escape. I might have married him and been most awful miserable, like my poor cousin, Jane Ann. Jane Ann married a rich man she didn't care anything about, and she hasn't the life of a dog. She come to see me last week and says, says she, 'Sarah Skinner, I envy you. I'd rather live in a little hut on the side of the road with a man I was fond of than in my big house with the one I've got.' Jane Ann's man ain't such a bad sort, nuther, though he's so contrary that he wears his fur coat when the thermometer's at ninety. The only way to git him to do anything is to coax him to do the opposite. But there ain't any love to smooth things down and it's a poor way of living. Jog along, black mare. There's Janet's place in the hollow— 'Wayside,' she calls it. Quite pictureaskew, ain't it? I guess you'll be glad to git out of this, with all them mail bags jamming round you."

"Yes, but I have enjoyed my drive with you very much," said Anne sincerely.

"Git away now!" said Mrs. Skinner, highly flattered. "Wait till I tell Thomas that. He always feels dretful tickled when I git a compliment. Jog along, black mare. Well, here we are. I hope you'll git on well in the school, miss. There's a short cut to it through the ma'sh back of Janet's. If you take that way be awful keerful. If you once got stuck in that black mud you'd be sucked right down and never seen or heard tell of again till the day of judgment, like Adam Palmer's cow. Jog along, black mare."

CHAPTER 31

ANNE TO PHILIPPA

"ANNE SHIRLEY to Philippa Gordon, greeting.

"Well-beloved, it's high time I was writing you. Here am I, installed once more as a country 'schoolma'am' at Valley Road, boarding at 'Wayside,' the home of Miss Janet Sweet. Janet is a dear soul and very nice-looking; tall, but not over-tall; stoutish, yet with a certain restraint of outline suggestive of a thrifty soul who is not going to be over-lavish even in the matter of avoirdupois. She has a knot of soft, crimpy, brown hair with a thread of gray in it, a sunny face with rosy cheeks, and big, kind eyes as blue as forget-me-nots. Moreover, she is one of those delightful, old-fashioned cooks who don't care a bit if they ruin your digestion as long as they can give you feasts of fat things.

"I like her; and she likes me—principally, it seems, because she had a sister named Anne who died young.

" 'I'm real glad to see you,' she said briskly, when I landed in her yard. 'My, you don't look a mite like I expected. I was sure you'd be dark—my sister Anne was dark. And here you're red-headed!'

"For a few minutes I thought I wasn't going to like Janet as much as I had expected at first sight. Then I reminded myself that I really must be more sensible than to be prejudiced against any one simply because she called my hair red. Probably the word 'auburn' was not in Janet's vocabulary at all.

" 'Wayside' is a dear sort of little spot. The house is small and white, set down in a delightful little hollow that drops away from the road. Between road and house is an orchard and flower-garden all mixed up together. The front door walk is bordered with quahog clam-shells—'cow-hawks,' Janet calls them; there is Virginia Creeper over the porch and moss on the roof. My room is a neat little spot 'off the parlour'—just big enough for the bed and me. Over the head of my bed there is a picture of Robby Burns standing at Highland Mary's grave, shadowed by an enormous weeping willow tree. Robby's face is so lugubrious that it is no wonder I have bad dreams. Why,

161

the first night I was here I dreamed I *couldn't laugh.*

"The parlour is tiny and neat. Its one window is so shaded by a huge willow that the room has a grotto-like effect of emerald gloom. There are wonderful tidies on the chairs, and gay mats on the floor, and books and cards carefully arranged on a round table, and vases of dried grass on the mantel-piece. Between the vases is a cheerful decoration of preserved coffin plates—five in all, pertaining respectively to Janet's father and mother, a brother, her sister Anne, and a hired man who died here once! If I go suddenly insane some of these days 'know all men by these presents' that those coffin-plates have caused it.

"But it's all delightful and I said so. Janet loved me for it, just as she detested poor Esther because Esther had said so much shade was unhygienic and had objected to sleeping on a feather bed. Now, I glory in feather-beds, and the more unhygienic and feathery they are the more I glory. Janet says it is such a comfort to see me eat; she had been so afraid I would be like Miss Haythorne, who wouldn't eat anything but fruit and hot water for breakfast and tried to make Janet give up frying things. Esther is really a dear girl, but she is rather given to fads. The trouble is that she hasn't enough imagination and *has* a tendency to indigestion.

"Janet told me I could have the use of the parlour when any young men called! I don't think there are many to call. I haven't seen a young man in Valley Road yet, except the next-door hired boy—Sam Tolliver, a very tall, lank, tow-haired youth. He came over one evening recently and sat for an hour on the garden fence, near the front porch where Janet and I were doing fancy-work. The only remarks he volunteered in all that time were, 'Hev a peppermint, miss! *Dew* now—fine thing for cat*arrh,* peppermints,' and, 'Powerful lot o' jump-grasses round here ter-night. Yep.'

"But there *is* a love affair going on here. It seems to be my fortune to be mixed up, more or less actively, with elderly love affairs. Mr. and Mrs. Irving always say that I brought about their marriage. Mrs. Stephen Clark of Carmody persists in being most grateful to me for a suggestion which somebody else would probably have made if I hadn't. I do really think, though, that Ludovic Speed would never have got any further along than placid courtship if I had not helped him and Theodora Dix out.

"In the present affair I am only a passive spectator. I've tried once to help things along and made an awful mess of it. So I shall not meddle again. I'll tell you all about it when we meet."

CHAPTER 32

TEA WITH MRS. DOUGLAS

ON THE first Thursday night of Anne's sojourn in Valley Road Janet asked her to go to prayer-meeting. Janet blossomed out like a rose to attend that prayer-meeting. She wore a pale-blue, pansy-sprinkled muslin dress with more ruffles than one would ever have supposed economical Janet could be guilty of, and a white leghorn hat with pink roses and three ostrich feathers on it. Anne felt quite amazed. Later on she found out Janet's motive in so arraying herself—a motive as old as Eden.

Valley Road prayer-meetings seemed to be essentially feminine. There were thirty-two women present, two half-grown boys, and one solitary man, beside the minister. Anne found herself studying this man. He was not handsome or young or graceful; he had remarkably long legs—so long that he had to keep them coiled up under his chair to dispose of them—and he was stoop-shouldered. His hands were big, his hair wanted barbering, and his moustache was unkempt. But Anne thought she liked his face; it was kind and honest and tender; there was something else in it, too—just what, Anne found it hard to define. She finally concluded that this man had suffered and been strong, and it had been made manifest in his face. There was a sort of patient, humorous endurance in his expression which indicated that he would go to the stake if need be, but would keep on looking pleasant until he really had to begin squirming.

When prayer-meeting was over this man came up to Janet and said,

"May I see you home, Janet?"

Janet took his arm—"as primly and shyly as if she were no more than sixteen, having her first escort home," Anne told the girls at Patty's Place later on.

"Miss Shirley, permit me to introduce Mr. Douglas," she said stiffly.

Mr. Douglas nodded and said,

"I was looking at you in prayer-meeting, miss, and thinking what a nice little girl you were."

Such a speech from ninety-nine people out of a hundred would have annoyed Anne bitterly; but the way in which Mr. Douglas said it made her feel that she had received a very real and pleasing compliment. She smiled appreciatively at him and dropped obligingly behind on the moonlit road.

So Janet had a beau! Anne was delighted. Janet would make a paragon of a wife—cheery, economical, tolerant, and a very queen of cooks. It would be a flagrant waste on Nature's part to keep her a permanent old maid.

"John Douglas asked me to take you up to see his mother," said Janet the next day. "She's bed-rid a lot of the time and never goes out of the house. But she's powerful fond of company and always wants to see my boarders. Can you go up this evening?"

Anne assented; but later in the day Mr. Douglas called on his mother's behalf to invite them up to tea on Saturday evening.

"Oh, why didn't you put on your pretty pansy dress?" asked Anne, when they left home. It was a hot day, and poor Janet, between her excitement and her heavy black cashmere dress, looked as if she were being broiled alive.

"Old Mrs. Douglas would think it terrible frivolous and unsuitable, I'm afraid. John likes that dress, though," she added wistfully.

The old Douglas homestead was half a mile from "Wayside" cresting a windy hill. The house itself was large and comfortable, old enough to be dignified, and girdled with maple groves and orchards. There were big, trim barns behind it, and everything bespoke prosperity. Whatever the patient endurance in Mr. Douglas' face had meant it hadn't, so Anne reflected, meant debts and duns.

John Douglas met them at the door and took them into the sitting-room, where his mother was enthroned in an arm-chair.

Anne had expected old Mrs. Douglas to be tall and thin, because Mr. Douglas was. Instead, she was a tiny scrap of a woman, with soft pink cheeks, mild blue eyes, and a mouth like a baby's. Dressed in a beautiful, fashionably-made black silk dress, with a fluffy white shawl over her shoulders, and her snowy hair surmounted by a dainty lace cap, she might have posed as a grandmother doll.

"How do you do, Janet dear?" she said sweetly. "I am *so* glad to see you again, dear." She put up her pretty old face to be kissed. "And this is our new teacher. I'm delighted to meet you. My son has been singing your praises until I'm half jealous, and I'm sure Janet ought to be wholly so."

Poor Janet blushed, Anne said something polite and conventional, and then everybody sat down and made talk. It was hard work, even for Anne, for nobody seemed at ease except old Mrs. Douglas, who certainly did not find any difficulty in talking. She made Janet sit by her and stroked her hand occasionally. Janet sat and smiled, looking horribly uncomfortable in her hideous dress, and John Douglas sat without smiling.

At the tea-table Mrs. Douglas gracefully asked Janet to pour the tea. Janet turned redder than ever but did it. Anne wrote a description of that meal to Stella.

"We had cold tongue and chicken and strawberry preserves, lemon pie and tarts and chocolate cake and raisin cookies and pound cake and fruit cake—and a few other things, including more pie—caramel pie, I think it was. After I had eaten twice as much as was good for me, Mrs. Douglas sighed and said she feared she had nothing to tempt my appetite.

" 'I'm afraid dear Janet's cooking has spoiled you for any other,' she said sweetly. 'Of course nobody in Valley Road aspires to rival *her*. Won't you have another piece of pie, Miss Shirley? You haven't eaten *anything*.'

"Stella, I had eaten a helping of tongue and one of chicken, three biscuits, a generous allowance of preserves, a piece of pie, a tart, and a square of chocolate cake!"

After tea Mrs. Douglas smiled benevolently and told John to take "dear Janet" out into the garden and get her some roses. "Miss Shirley will keep me company while you are out—

won't you?" she said plaintively. She settled down in her armchair with a sigh.

"I am a very frail old woman, Miss Shirley. For over twenty years I've been a great sufferer. For twenty long, weary years I've been dying by inches."

"How painful!" said Anne, trying to be sympathetic and succeeding only in feeling idiotic.

"There have been scores of nights when they've thought I could never live to see the dawn," went on Mrs. Douglas solemnly. "Nobody knows what I've gone through—nobody can know but myself. Well, it can't last very much longer now. My weary pilgrimage will soon be over, Miss Shirley. It is a great comfort to me that John will have such a good wife to look after him when his mother is gone—a great comfort, Miss Shirley."

"Janet is a lovely woman," said Anne warmly.

"Lovely! A beautiful character," assented Mrs. Douglas "And a perfect housekeeper—something *I* never was. My health would not permit it, Miss Shirley. I am indeed thankful that John has made such a wise choice. I hope and believe that he will be happy. He is my only son, Miss Shirley, and his happiness lies very near my heart."

"Of course," said Anne stupidly. For the first time in her life she was stupid. Yet she could not imagine why. She seemed to have absolutely nothing to say to this sweet, smiling, angelic old lady who was patting her hand so kindly.

"Come and see me soon again, dear Janet," said Mrs. Douglas lovingly, when they left. "You don't come half often enough. But then I suppose John will be bringing you here to stay all the time one of these days."

Anne, happening to glance at John Douglas, as his mother spoke, gave a positive start of dismay. He looked as a tortured man might look when his tormentors gave the rack the last turn of possible endurance. She felt sure he must be ill and hurried poor blushing Janet away.

"Isn't old Mrs. Douglas a sweet woman?" asked Janet, as they went down the road.

"M—m," answered Anne absently. She was wondering why John Douglas had looked so.

"She's been a terrible sufferer," said Janet feelingly. "She takes terrible spells. It keeps John all worried up. He's scared to leave home for fear his mother will take a spell and nobody there but the hired girl."

CHAPTER 33

"HE JUST KEPT COMING AND COMING"

THREE DAYS later Anne came home from school and found Janet crying. Tears and Janet seemed so incongruous that Anne was honestly alarmed.

"Oh, what is the matter?" she cried anxiously.

"I'm—I'm forty today," sobbed Janet.

"Well, you were nearly that yesterday and it didn't hurt," comforted Anne, trying not to smile.

"But—but," went on Janet with a big gulp, "John Douglas won't ask me to marry him."

"Oh, but he will," said Anne lamely. "You must give him time, Janet."

"Time!" said Janet with indescribable scorn. "He has had twenty years. How much time does he want?"

"Do you mean that John Douglas has been coming to see you for twenty years?"

"He has. And he has never so much as mentioned marriage to me. And I don't believe he ever will now. I've never said a word to a mortal about it, but it seems to me I've just got to talk it out with some one at last or go crazy. John Douglas begun to go with me twenty years ago, before mother died. Well, he kept coming and coming, and after a spell I begun making quilts and things; but he never said anything about getting married, only just kept coming and coming. There wasn't anything I could do. Mother died when we'd been going together for eight years. I thought he maybe would speak out then, seeing as I was left alone in the world. He was real kind and feeling, and did everything he could for me, but he never said marry. And that's the way it has been going on ever since. People blame *me* for it. They say I won't marry him because his mother is so sickly and I don't want the bother of waiting on her. Why, I'd *love* to wait on John's mother! But I let them think so. I'd rather they'd blame me than pity me! It's so dreadful humiliating that John won't ask me. And *why* won't he? Seems to me if I only knew his reason I wouldn't mind it so much."

"Perhaps his mother doesn't want him to marry anybody," suggested Anne.

"Oh, she does. She's told me time and again that she'd love to see John settled before her time comes. She's always giving him hints—you heard her yourself the other day. I thought I'd ha' gone through the floor."

"It's beyond me," said Anne helplessly. She thought of Ludovic Speed. But the cases were not parallel. John Douglas was not a man of Ludovic's type.

"You should show more spirit, Janet," she went on resolutely. "Why didn't you send him about his business long ago?"

"I couldn't," said poor Janet pathetically. "You see, Anne, I've always been awful fond of John. He might just as well keep coming as not, for there was never anybody else I'd want, so it didn't matter."

"But it might have made him speak out like a man," urged Anne.

Janet shook her head.

"No, I guess not. I was afraid to try, anyway, for fear he'd think I meant it and just go. I suppose I'm a poor-spirited creature, but that is how I feel. And I can't help it."

"Oh, you *could* help it, Janet. It isn't too late yet. Take a firm stand. Let that man know you are not going to endure his shilly-shallying any longer. I'll back you up."

"I dunno," said Janet hopelessly. "I dunno if I could ever get up enough spunk. Things have drifted so long. But I'll think it over."

Anne felt that she was disappointed in John Douglas. She had liked him so well, and she had not thought him the sort of man who would play fast and loose with a woman's feelings for twenty years. He certainly should be taught a lesson, and Anne felt vindictively that she would enjoy seeing the process.

Therefore she was delighted when Janet told her, as they were going to prayer-meeting the next night, that she meant to show some "sperrit."

"I'll let John Douglas see I'm not going to be trodden on any longer."

"You are perfectly right," said Anne emphatically.

When prayer-meeting was over John Douglas came up with his usual request. Janet looked frightened but resolute.

"No, thank you," she said icily. "I know the road home pretty well alone. I ought to, seeing I've been travelling it for forty years. So you needn't trouble yourself, *Mr.* Douglas."

Anne was looking at John Douglas; and, in that brilliant moonlight, she saw the last twist of the rack again. Without a word he turned and strode down the road.

"Stop! Stop!" Anne called wildly after him, not caring in the least for the other dumbfoundered onlookers. "Mr. Douglas, stop! Come back."

John Douglas stopped but he did not come back. Anne flew down the road, caught his arm and fairly dragged him back to Janet.

"You must come back," she said imploringly. "It's all a mistake, Mr. Douglas—all my fault. I made Janet do it. She didn't want to—but it's all right now, isn't it, Janet?"

Without a word Janet took his arm and walked away. Anne followed them meekly home and slipped in by the back door.

"Well, you are a nice person to back one up," said Janet sarcastically.

"I couldn't help it, Janet," said Anne repentantly. "I just felt as if I had stood by and seen murder done. I *had* to run after him."

"Oh, I'm just as glad you did. When I saw John Douglas making off down that road I just felt as if every little bit of joy and happiness that was left in my life was going with him. It was an awful feeling."

"Did he ask you why you did it?" asked Anne.

"No, he never said a word about it," replied Janet, dully.

CHAPTER 34

JOHN DOUGLAS SPEAKS AT LAST

ANNE WAS not without a feeble hope that something might come of it after all. But nothing did. John Douglas came and took Janet driving, and walked home from prayer-meeting with her, as he had been doing for twenty years, and as he seemed likely to do for twenty years more. The summer waned. Anne taught her school and wrote letters and studied a little. Her walks to and from school were pleasant. She always went by way of the swamp; it was a lovely place—a boggy soil, green with the greenest of mossy hillocks; a silvery brook meandered through it and spruces stood erectly, their boughs a-trail with gray-green mosses, their roots overgrown with all sorts of woodland lovelinesses.

Nevertheless, Anne found life in Valley Road a little monotonous. To be sure, there was one diverting incident.

She had not seen the lank, tow-headed Samuel of the peppermints since the evening of his call, save for chance meetings on the road. But one warm August night he appeared, and solemnly seated himself on the rustic bench by the porch. He wore his usual working habiliments, consisting of vari-patched trousers, a blue jean shirt, out at the elbows, and a ragged straw hat. He was chewing a straw and he kept on chewing it while he looked solemnly at Anne. Anne laid her book aside with a sigh and took up her doily. Conversation with Sam was really out of the question.

After a long silence Sam suddenly spoke.

"I'm leaving over there," he said abruptly, waving his straw in the direction of the neighbouring house.

"Oh, are you?" said Anne politely.

"Yep."

"And where are you going now?"

"Wall, I've been thinking some of gitting a place of my own. There's one that'd suit me over at Millersville. But ef I rents it I'll want a woman."

"I suppose so," said Anne vaguely.

"Yep."

There was another long silence. Finally Sam removed his straw again and said,

"Will yeh hev me?"

"Wh—a—t!" gasped Anne.

"Will yeh hev me?"

"Do you mean—*marry* you?" queried poor Anne feebly.

"Yep."

"Why, I'm hardly acquainted with you," cried Anne indignantly.

"But yeh'd git acquainted with me after we was married," said Sam.

Anne gathered up her poor dignity.

"Certainly I won't marry you," she said haughtily.

"Wall, yeh might do worse," expostulated Sam. "I'm a good worker and I've got some money in the bank."

"Don't speak of this to me again. Whatever put such an idea into your head?" said Anne, her sense of humour getting the better of her wrath. It was such an absurd situation.

"Yeh're a likely-looking girl and hev a right-smart way o' stepping," said Sam. "I don't want no lazy woman. Think it over. I won't change my mind yit awhile. Wall, I must be gitting. Gotter milk the cows."

Anne's illusions concerning proposals had suffered so much of late years that there were few of them left. So she could laugh whole-heartedly over this one, not feeling any secret sting. She mimicked poor Sam to Janet that night, and both of them laughed immoderately over his plunge into sentiment.

One afternoon, when Anne's sojourn in Valley Road was drawing to a close, Alec Ward came driving down to "Wayside" in hot haste for Janet.

"They want you at the Douglas place quick," he said. "I really believe old Mrs. Douglas is going to die at last, after pretending to do it for twenty years."

Janet ran to get her hat. Anne asked if Mrs. Douglas was worse than usual.

"She's not half as bad," said Alec solemnly, "and that's what makes me think it's serious. Other times she'd be screaming and throwing herself all over the place. This time she's lying still and mum. When Mrs. Douglas is mum she is pretty sick, you bet."

"You don't like old Mrs. Douglas?" said Anne curiously.

"I like cats as *is* cats. I don't like cats as is women," was Alec's cryptic reply.

Janet came home in the twilight.

"Mrs. Douglas is dead," she said wearily. "She died soon after I got there. She just spoke to me once—'I suppose you'll marry John now?' she said. It cut me to the heart, Anne. To think John's own mother thought I wouldn't marry him because of her! I couldn't say a word either—there were other women there. I was thankful John had gone out."

Janet began to cry drearily. But Anne brewed her a hot drink of ginger tea to her comforting. To be sure, Anne discovered later on that she had used white pepper instead of ginger; but Janet never knew the difference.

The evening after the funeral Janet and Anne were sitting on the front porch steps at sunset. The wind had fallen asleep in the pinelands and lurid sheets of heat-lightning flickered across the northern skies. Janet wore her ugly black dress and looked her very worst, her eyes and nose red from crying. They talked little, for Janet seemed faintly to resent Anne's efforts to cheer her up. She plainly preferred to be miserable.

Suddenly the gate-latch clicked and John Douglas strode into the garden. He walked towards them straight over the geranium bed. Janet stood up. So did Anne. Anne was a tall girl and wore a white dress; but John Douglas did not see her.

"Janet," he said, "will you marry me?"

The words burst out as if they had been wanting to be said for twenty years and *must* be uttered now, before anything else.

Janet's face was so red from crying that it couldn't turn any redder, so it turned a most unbecoming purple.

"Why didn't you ask me before?" she said slowly.

"I couldn't. She made me promise not to—mother made me promise not to. Nineteen years ago she took a terrible spell. We thought she couldn't live through it. She implored me to promise not to ask you to marry me while she was alive. I didn't want to promise such a thing, even though we all thought she couldn't live very long—the doctor only gave her six months. But she begged it on her knees, sick and suffering. I had to promise."

"What had your mother against me?" cried Janet.

"Nothing—nothing. She just didn't want another woman—
any woman—there while she was living. She said if I didn't
promise she'd die right there and I'd have killed her. So I
promised. And she's held me to that promise ever since, though
I've gone on my knees to her in my turn to beg her to let me
off."

"Why didn't you tell me this?" asked Janet chokingly. "If
I'd only *known!* Why didn't you just tell me?"

"She made me promise I wouldn't tell a soul," said John
hoarsely. "She swore me to it on the Bible; Janet, I'd never
have done it if I'd dreamed it was to be for so long. Janet,
you'll never know what I've suffered these nineteen years. I
know I've made you suffer, too, but you'll marry me for all,
won't you, Janet? Oh, Janet, won't you? I've come as soon as
I could to ask you."

At this moment the stupified Anne came to her senses and
realized that she had no business to be there. She slipped away
and did not see Janet until the next morning, when the latter
told her the rest of the story.

"That cruel, relentless, deceitful old woman!" cried Anne.

"Hush—she's dead," said Janet solemnly. "If she wasn't—
but she *is.* So we mustn't speak evil of her. But I'm happy at
last, Anne. And I wouldn't have minded waiting so long a bit
if I'd only known why."

"When are you to be married?"

"Next month. Of course it will be very quiet. I suppose
people will talk terrible. They'll say I made enough haste to
snap John up as soon as his poor mother was out of the way.
John wanted to let them know the truth but I said, 'No, John;
after all she was your mother, and we'll keep the secret between
us, and not cast any shadow on her memory. I don't mind
what people say, now that I know the truth myself. It don't
matter a mite. Let it all be buried with the dead,' says I to
him. So I coaxed him round to agree with me."

"You're much more forgiving than I could ever be," Anne
said, rather crossly.

"You'll feel differently about a good many things when you
get to be my age," said Janet tolerantly. "That's one of the
things we learn as we grow older—how to forgive. It comes
easier at forty than it did at twenty."

CHAPTER 35

THE LAST REDMOND YEAR OPENS

"HERE WE are, all back again, nicely sunburned and rejoicing as a strong man to run a race," said Phil, sitting down on a suit-case with a sigh of pleasure. "Isn't it jolly to see this dear old Patty's Place again—and Aunty—and the cats? Rusty has lost another piece of ear, hasn't he?"

"Rusty would be the nicest cat in the world if he had no ears at all," declared Anne loyally from her trunk, while Rusty writhed about her lap in a frenzy of welcome.

"Aren't you glad to see us back, Aunty?" demanded Phil.

"Yes. But I wish you'd tidy things up," said Aunt Jamesina plaintively, looking at the wilderness of trunks and suit-cases by which the four laughing, chattering girls were surrounded. "You can talk just as well later on. Work first and then play used to be my motto when I was a girl."

"Oh, we've just reversed that in this generation, Aunty. *Our* motto is play your play and then dig in. You can do your work so much better if you've had a good bout of play first."

"If you are going to marry a minister," said Aunt Jamesina, picking up Joseph and her knitting and resigning herself to the inevitable with the charming grace that made her the queen of house-mothers, "you will have to give up such expressions as 'dig in.' "

"Why?" moaned Phil. "Oh, why must a minister's wife be supposed to utter only prunes and prisms? I shan't. Everybody on Patterson Street uses slang—that is to say, metaphorical language—and if I didn't they would think me insufferably proud and stuck up."

"Have you broken the news to your family?" asked Priscilla, feeding the Sarah-cat bits from her lunch-basket.

Phil nodded.

"How did they take it?"

"Oh, mother rampaged. But I stood rock-firm—even I, Philippa Gordon, who never before could hold fast to anything. Father was calmer. Father's own daddy was a minister, so you see he has a soft spot in his heart for the cloth. I had Jo up to Mount Holly, after mother grew calm, and they both loved him. But mother gave him some frightful hints in every conversation regarding what she had hoped for me. Oh, my vacation pathway hasn't been exactly strewn with roses, girls dear. But— I've won out and I've got Jo. Nothing else matters."

"To you," said Aunt Jamesina darkly.

"Nor to Jo, either," retorted Phil. "You keep on pitying him. Why, pray? *I* think he's to be envied. He's getting brains, beauty, and a heart of gold in *ME*."

"It's well we know how to take your speeches," said Aunt Jamesina patiently. "I hope you don't talk like that before strangers. What would they think?"

"Oh, I don't want to know what they think. *I* don't want to see myself as others see me. I'm sure it would be horribly uncomfortable most of the time. I don't believe Burns was really sincere in that prayer, either."

"Oh, I daresay we all pray for some things that we really don't want, if we were only honest enough to look into our hearts," owned Aunt Jamesina candidly. "I've a notion that such prayers don't rise very far. *I* used to pray that I might be enabled to forgive a certain person, but I know now I really didn't want to forgive her. When I finally got that I *did* want to I forgave her without having to pray about it."

"I can't picture you as being unforgiving for long," said Stella.

"Oh, I used to be. But holding spite doesn't seem worth while when you get along in years."

"That reminds me," said Anne, and told the tale of John and Janet.

"And now tell us about that romantic scene you hinted so darkly at in one of your letters," demanded Phil.

Anne acted out Samuel's proposal with great spirit. The girls shrieked with laughter and Aunt Jamesina smiled.

"It isn't in good taste to make fun of your beaux," she said severely; "but," she added calmly, "I always did it myself."

"Tell us about your beaux, Aunty," entreated Phil. "You must have had any number of them."

"They're not in the past tense," retorted Aunt Jamesina. "I've got them yet. There are three old widowers at home who have been casting sheep's eyes at me for some time. You children needn't think you own all the romance in the world."

"Widowers and sheep's eyes don't sound very romantic, Aunty."

"Well, no; but young folks aren't always romantic either. Some of my beaux certainly weren't. I used to laugh at them scandalous, poor boys. There was Jim Elwood—he was always in a sort of day-dream—never seemed to sense what was going on. He didn't wake up to the fact that I'd said 'no' till a year after I'd said it. When he did get married his wife fell out of the sleigh one night when they were driving home from church and he never missed her. Then there was Dan Winston. He knew too much. He knew everything in this world and most of what is in the next. He could give you an answer to any question, even if you asked him when the Judgment Day was to be. Milton Edwards was real nice and I liked him but I didn't marry him. For one thing, he took a week to get a joke through his head, and for another he never asked me. Horatio Reeve was the most interesting beau I ever had. But when he told a story he dressed it up so that you couldn't see it for frills. I never could decide whether he was lying or just letting his imagination run loose."

"And what about the others, Aunty?"

"Go away and unpack," said Aunt Jamesina, waving Joseph at them by mistake for a needle. "The others were too nice to make fun of. I shall respect their memory. There's a box of flowers in your room, Anne. They came about an hour ago."

After the first week the girls of Patty's Place settled down to a steady grind of study; for this was their last year at Redmond and graduation honours must be fought for persistently. Anne devoted herself to English, Priscilla pored over classics, and Philippa pounded away at Mathematics. Sometimes they grew tired, sometimes they felt discouraged, sometimes nothing seemed worth the struggle for it. In one such mood Stella wandered up to the blue room one rainy November evening. Anne sat on the floor in a little circle of light cast by the lamp beside her, amid a surrounding snow of crumpled manuscript.

"What in the world are you doing?"

"Just looking over some old Story Club yarns. I wanted something to cheer *and* inebriate. I'd studied until the world seemed azure. So I came up here and dug these out of my trunk. They are so drenched in tears and tragedy that they are excruciatingly funny."

"I'm blue and discouraged myself," said Stella, throwing herself on the couch. "Nothing seems worth while. My very thoughts are old. I've thought them all before. What is the use of living after all, Anne?"

"Honey, it's just brain fag that makes us feel that way, and the weather. A pouring rainy night like this, coming after a hard day's grind, would squelch any one but a *Mark Tapley*. You know it *is* worth while to live."

"Oh, I suppose so. But I can't prove it to myself just now."

"Just think of all the great and noble souls who have lived and worked in the world," said Anne dreamily. "Isn't it worth while to come after them and inherit what they won and taught? And think of all the great people in the world today! Isn't it worth while to think we can share their inspiration? And then, all the great souls that will come in the future? Isn't it worth while to work a little and prepare the way for them—make just one step in their path easier?"

"Oh, my mind agrees with you, Anne. But my soul remains doleful and uninspired. I'm always grubby and dingy on rainy nights."

"Some nights I like the rain—I like to lie in bed and hear it pattering on the roof and drifting through the pines."

"I like it when it stays on the roof," said Stella. "It doesn't always. I spent a gruesome night in an old country farm-house last summer. The roof leaked and the rain came pattering down on my bed. There was no poetry in *that*. I had to get up in the 'mirk midnight' and chivy round to pull the bedstead out of the drip—and it was one of those solid, old-fashioned beds that weigh a ton—more or less. And then that drip-drop, drip-drop kept up all night until my nerves just went to pieces. You've no idea what an eerie noise a great drop of rain falling with a mushy thud on a bare floor makes in the night. It sounds like ghostly footsteps and all that sort of thing. What are you laughing over, Anne?"

"These stories. As Phil would say they are killing—in more senses than one, for everybody died in them. What dazzlingly lovely heroines we had—and how we dressed them! Silks—

satins—velvets—jewels—laces—they never wore anything else. Here is one of Jane Andrews' stories depicting her heroine as sleeping in a beautiful white satin night-dress trimmed with seed pearls."

"Go on," said Stella. "I begin to feel that life *is* worth living as long as there's a laugh in it."

"Here's one I wrote. My heroine is disporting herself at a ball 'glittering from head to foot with large diamonds of the first water.' But what booted beauty or rich attire? 'The paths of glory lead but to the grave.' They must either be murdered or die of a broken heart. There was no escape for them."

"Let me read some of your stories."

"Well, here's my masterpiece. Note its cheerful title—'*My Graves.*' I shed quarts of tears while writing it, and the other girls shed gallons while I read it. Jane Andrews' mother scolded her frightfully because she had so many handkerchiefs in the wash that week. It's a harrowing tale of the wanderings of a Methodist minister's wife. I made her a Methodist because it was necessary that she should wander. She buried a child every place she lived in. There were nine of them and their graves were severed far apart, ranging from Newfoundland to Vancouver. I described the children, pictured their several death beds, and detailed their tombstones and epitaphs. I had intended to bury the whole nine but when I had disposed of eight my invention of horrors gave out and I permitted the tenth to live as a hopeless cripple."

While Stella read *My Graves,* punctuating its tragic paragraphs with chuckles, and Rusty slept the sleep of a just cat who has been out all night curled up on a Jane-Andrews tale of a beautiful maiden of fifteen who went to nurse in a leper colony—of course dying of the loathsome disease finally—Anne glanced over the other manuscripts and recalled the old days at Avonlea school when the members of the Story Club, sitting under the spruce trees or down among the ferns by the brook, had written them. What fun they had had! How the sunshine and mirth of those olden summers returned as she read. Not all the glory that was Greece or the grandeur that was Rome could weave such wizardry as those funny, tearful tales of the Story Club. Among the manuscripts Anne found one written on sheets of wrapping paper. A wave of laughter filled her gray eyes as she recalled the time and place of its genesis. It was a sketch she had written the day she fell through the roof of the Cobb duckhouse on the Tory Road.

Anne glanced over it, then fell to reading it intently. It was a little dialogue between asters and sweet-peas, wild canaries in the lilac bush, and the guardian spirit of the garden. After she had read it, she sat, staring into space; and when Stella had gone she smoothed out the crumpled manuscript.

"I believe I will," she said resolutely.

CHAPTER 36

THE GARDNERS' CALL

"HERE IS a letter with an Indian stamp for you, Aunt Jimsie," said Phil. "Here are three for Stella, and two for Pris, and a glorious fat one for me from Jo. There's nothing for you, Anne, except a circular."

Nobody noticed Anne's flush as she took the thin letter Phil tossed her carelessly. But a few minutes later Phil looked up to see a transfigured Anne.

"Honey, what good thing has happened?"

"The *Youth's Friend* has accepted a little sketch I sent them a fortnight ago," said Anne, trying hard to speak as if she were accustomed to having sketches accepted every mail, but not quite succeeding.

"Anne Shirley! How glorious! What was it? When is it to be published? Did they pay you for it?"

"Yes; they've sent a check for ten dollars, and the editor writes that he would like to see more of my work. Dear man, he shall. It was an old sketch I found in my box. I re-wrote it and sent it in–but I never really thought it could be accepted because it had no plot," said Anne, recalling the bitter experiences of *Averil's Atonement.*

"What are you going to do with that ten dollars, Anne? Let's all go up town and get drunk," suggested Phil.

"I *am* going to squander it in a wild soulless revel of some sort," declared Anne gaily. "At all events it isn't tainted money—like the check I got for that horrible Reliable Baking Powder story. I spent *it* usefully for clothes and hated them every time I put them on."

"Think of having a real live author at Patty's Place," said Priscilla.

"It's a great responsibility," said Aunt Jamesina solemnly.

"Indeed it is," agreed Pris with equal solemnity. "Authors are kittle cattle. You never know when or how they will break out. Anne may make copy of *us.*"

"I meant that the ability to write for the Press was a great responsibility," said Aunt Jamesina severely; "and I hope Anne realizes it. My daughter used to write stories before she went to the foreign field, but now she has turned her attention to higher things. She used to say her motto was 'Never write a line you would be ashamed to read at your own funeral.' You'd better take that for yours, Anne, if you are going to embark in literature. Though, to be sure," added Aunt Jamesina perplexedly, "Elizabeth always used to laugh when she said it. She always laughed so much that I don't know how she ever came to decide on being a missionary. I'm thankful she did—I prayed that she might—but—I wish she hadn't."

Then Aunt Jamesina wondered why those giddy girls all laughed.

Anne's eyes shone all that day; literary ambitions sprouted and budded in her brain; their exhilaration accompanied her to Jennie Cooper's walking party, and not even the sight of Gilbert and Christine, walking just ahead of her and Roy, could quite subdue the sparkle of her starry hopes. Nevertheless, she was not so rapt from things of earth as to be unable to notice that Christine's walk was decidedly ungraceful.

"But I suppose Gilbert looks only at her face. So like a man," thought Anne scornfully.

"Shall you be home Saturday afternoon?" asked Roy.

"Yes."

"My mother and sisters are coming to call on you," said Roy quietly.

Something went over Anne which might be described as a

thrill, but it was hardly a pleasant one. She had never met any of Roy's family; she realized the significance of his statement; and it had, somehow, an irrevocableness about it that chilled her.

"I shall be glad to see them," she said flatly; and then wondered if she really would be glad. She ought to be, of course. But would it not be something of an ordeal? Gossip had filtered to Anne regarding the light in which the Gardners viewed the "infatuation" of son and brother. Roy must have brought pressure to bear in the matter of this call. Anne knew she would be weighed in the balance. From the fact that they had consented to call she understood that, willingly or unwillingly, they regarded her as a possible member of their clan.

"I shall just be myself. I shall not *try* to make a good impression," thought Anne loftily. But she was wondering what dress she would better wear Saturday afternoon, and if the new style of high hair-dressing would suit her better than the old; and the walking party was rather spoiled for her. By night she had decided that she would wear her brown chiffon on Saturday, but would do her hair low.

Friday afternoon none of the girls had classes at Redmond. Stella took the opportunity to write a paper for the Philomathic Society, and was sitting at the table in the corner of the living-room with an untidy litter of notes and manuscript on the floor around her. Stella always vowed she never could write anything unless she threw each sheet down as she completed it. Anne, in her flannel blouse and serge skirt, with her hair rather blown from her windy walk home, was sitting squarely in the middle of the floor, teasing the Sarah-cat with a wishbone. Joseph and Rusty were both curled up in her lap. A warm plummy odour filled the whole house, for Priscilla was cooking in the kitchen. Presently she came in, enshrouded in a huge work-apron, with a smudge of flour on her nose, to show Aunt Jamesina the chocolate cake she had just iced.

At this auspicious moment the knocker sounded. Nobody paid any attention to it save Phil, who sprang up and opened it, expecting a boy with the hat she had bought that morning. On the doorstep stood Mrs. Gardner and her daughters.

Anne scrambled to her feet somehow, emptying two indignant cats out of her lap as she did so, and mechanically shifting her wish-bone from her right hand to her left. Priscilla, who would have had to cross the room to reach the kitchen door, lost her head, wildly plunged the chocolate cake under a cushion on the ingle-nook sofa, and dashed up-stairs. Stella began feverishly gathering up her manuscript. Only Aunt Jamesina and Phil remained normal. Thanks to them, everybody was soon sitting at ease, even Anne. Priscilla came down, apronless and smudge-less, Stella reduced her corner to decency, and Phil saved the situation by a stream of ready small talk.

Mrs. Gardner was tall and thin and handsome, exquisitely gowned, cordial with a cordiality that seemed a trifle forced. Aline Gardner was a younger edition of her mother, lacking the cordiality. She endeavoured to be nice, but succeeded only in being haughty and patronizing. Dorothy Gardner was slim and jolly and rather tomboyish. Anne knew she was Roy's favourite sister and warmed to her. She would have looked very much like Roy if she had had dreamy dark eyes instead of roguish hazel ones. Thanks to her and Phil, the call really went off very well, except for a slight sense of strain in the atmosphere and two rather untoward incidents. Rusty and Joseph, left to themselves, began a game of chase, and sprang madly into Mrs. Gardner's silken lap and out of it in their wild career. Mrs. Gardner lifted her lorgnette and gazed after their flying forms as if she had never seen cats before, and Anne, choking back slightly nervous laughter, apologized as best she could.

"You are fond of cats?" said Mrs. Gardner, with a slight intonation of tolerant wonder.

Anne, despite her affection for Rusty, was *not* especially fond of cats, but Mrs. Gardner's tone annoyed her. Inconsequently she remembered that Mrs. John Blythe was so fond of cats that she kept as many as her husband would allow.

"They *are* adorable animals, aren't they?" she said wickedly.

"I have never liked cats," said Mrs. Gardner remotely.

"I love them," said Dorothy. "They are so nice and selfish. Dogs are *too* good and unselfish. They make me feel uncomfortable. But cats are gloriously human."

"You have two delightful old china dogs there. May I look at them closely?" said Aline, crossing the room towards the fire-place and thereby becoming the unconscious cause of the other accident. Picking up Magog, she sat down on the cushion under which was secreted Priscilla's chocolate cake. Priscilla and Anne exchanged agonized glances but could do nothing. The stately Aline continued to sit on the cushion and discuss china dogs until the time of departure.

Dorothy lingered behind a moment to squeeze Anne's hand and whisper impulsively.

"I *know* you and I are going to be chums. Oh, Roy has told me all about you. I'm the only one of the family he tells things to, poor boy—nobody *could* confide in mamma and Aline, you know. What glorious times you girls must have here! Won't you let me come often and have a share in them?"

"Come as often as you like," Anne responded heartily, thankful that one of Roy's sisters was likable. She would never like Aline, so much was certain; and Aline would never like her, though Mrs. Gardner might be won. Altogether, Anne sighed with relief when the ordeal was over.

> " 'Of all sad words of tongue or pen
> The saddest are it might have been.' "

quoted Priscilla tragically, lifting the cushion. "This cake is now what you might call a flat failure. And the cushion is likewise ruined. Never tell me that Friday isn't unlucky."

"People who send word they are coming on Saturday shouldn't come on Friday," said Aunt Jamesina.

"I fancy it was Roy's mistake," said Phil. "That boy isn't really responsible for what he says when he talks to Anne. Where *is* Anne?"

Anne had gone up-stairs. She felt oddly like crying. But she made herself laugh instead. Rusty and Joseph had been *too* awful! And Dorothy *was* a dear.

CHAPTER 37

FULL-FLEDGED B.A.'S

"I WISH I were dead, or that it were tomorrow night," groaned Phil.

"If you live long enough both wishes will come true," said Anne calmly.

"It's easy for you to be serene. You're at home in Philosophy. I'm not—and when I think of that horrible paper tomorrow I quail. If I should fail in it what would Jo say?"

"You won't fail. How did you get on in Greek today?"

"I don't know. Perhaps it was a good paper and perhaps it was bad enough to make Homer turn over in his grave. I've studied and mulled over notebooks until I'm incapable of forming an opinion of anything. How thankful little Phil will be when all this examinating is over."

"Examinating? I never heard such a word."

"Well, haven't I as good a right to make a word as any one else?" demanded Phil.

"Words aren't made—they grow," said Anne.

"Never mind—I begin faintly to discern clear water ahead where no examination breakers loom. Girls, do you—can you realize that our Redmond life is almost over?"

"I can't," said Anne, sorrowfully. "It seems just yesterday that Pris and I were alone in that crowd of Freshmen at Redmond. And now we are Seniors in our final examinations."

"'Potent, wise, and reverend Seniors,'" quoted Phil. "Do you suppose we really are any wiser than when we came to Redmond?"

"You don't act as if you were at times," said Aunt Jamesina severely.

"Oh, Aunt Jimsie, haven't we been pretty good girls, take us by and large, these three winters you've mothered us?" pleaded Phil.

"You've been four of the dearest, sweetest, goodest girls that ever went together through college," averred Aunt Jamesina, who never spoiled a compliment by misplaced economy. "But I mistrust you haven't any too much sense yet. It's not to be

184

expected, of course. Experience teaches sense. You can't learn it in a college course. You've been to college four years and I never was, but I know heaps more than you do, young ladies."

" 'There are lots of things that never go by rule,
    There's a powerful pile o' knowledge
    That you never get at college,
    There are heaps of things you never learn at school,' "

quoted Stella.

"Have you learned anything at Redmond except dead languages and geometry and such trash?" queried Aunt Jamesina.

"Oh, yes. I think we have, Aunty," protested Anne.

"We've learned the truth of what Professor Woodleigh told us last Philomathic," said Phil. "He said, 'Humour is the spiciest condiment in the feast of existence. Laugh at your mistakes but learn from them, joke over your troubles but gather strength from them, make a jest of your difficulties but overcome them.' Isn't that worth learning, Aunt Jimsie?"

"Yes, it is, dearie. When you've learned to laugh at the things that should be laughed at, and *not* to laugh at those that shouldn't, you've got wisdom and understanding."

"What have you got out of your Redmond course, Anne?" murmured Priscilla aside.

"I think," said Anne slowly, "that I really have learned to look upon each little hindrance as a jest and each great one as the foreshadowing of victory. Summing up, I think that is what Redmond has given me."

"I shall have to fall back on another Professor Woodleigh quotation to express what it has done for me," said Priscilla. "You remember that he said in his address, 'There is so much in the world for us all if we only have the eyes to see it, and the heart to love it, and the hand to gather it to ourselves— so much in men and women, so much in art and literature, so much everywhere in which to delight, and for which to be thankful.' I think Redmond has taught me that in some measure, Anne."

"Judging from what you all say," remarked Aunt Jamesina, "the sum and substance is that you can learn—if you've got natural gumption enough—in four years at college what it would

take about twenty years of living to teach you. Well, that
justifies higher education in my opinion. It's a matter I was
always dubious about before."

"But what about people who haven't natural gumption, Aunt
Jimsie?"

"People who haven't natural gumption *never* learn," retorted
Aunt Jamesina, "neither in college or life. If they live to be a
hundred they really don't know anything more than when they
were born. It's their misfortune not their fault, poor souls. But
those of us who have some gumption should duly thank the
Lord for it."

"Will you please define what gumption is, Aunt Jimsie?"
asked Phil.

"No, I won't, young woman. Any one who has gumption
knows what it is, and any one who hasn't can never know
what it is. So there is no need of defining it."

The busy days flew by and examinations were over. Anne
took High Honours in English. Priscilla took Honours in Classics, and Phil in Mathematics. Stella obtained a good all-round
showing. Then came Convocation.

"This is what I would once have called an epoch in my life,"
said Anne, as she took Roy's violets out of their box and gazed
at them thoughtfully. She meant to carry them, of course, but
her eyes wandered to another box on her table. It was filled
with lilies-of-the-valley, as fresh and fragrant as those which
bloomed in the Green Gables yard when June came to Avonlea.
Gilbert Blythe's card lay beside it.

Anne wondered why Gilbert should have sent her flowers
for Convocation. She had seen very little of him during the
past winter. He had come to Patty's Place only one Friday
evening since the Christmas holidays, and they rarely met
elsewhere. She knew he was studying very hard, aiming at High
Honours and the Cooper Prize, and he took little part in the
social doings of Redmond. Anne's own winter had been quite
gay socially. She had seen a good deal of the Gardners; she
and Dorothy were very intimate; college circles expected the
announcement of her engagement to Roy any day. Anne expected it herself. Yet just before she left Patty's Place for
Convocation she flung Roy's violets aside and put Gilbert's
lilies-of-the-valley in their place. She could not have told why

she did it. Somehow, old Avonlea days and dreams and friend-ships seemed very close to her in this attainment of her long-cherished ambitions. She and Gilbert had once pictured out merrily the day on which they should be capped and gowned graduates in Arts. The wonderful day had come and Roy's violets had no place in it. Only her old friend's flowers seemed to belong to this fruition of old-blossoming hopes which he had once shared.

For years this day had beckoned and allured to her; but when it came the one single, keen, abiding memory it left with her was not that of the breathless moment when the stately president of Redmond gave her cap and diploma and hailed her B.A.; it was not of the flash in Gilbert's eyes when he saw her lilies, nor the puzzled pained glance Roy gave her as he passed her on the platform. It was not of Aline Gardner's condescending congratulations, or Dorothy's ardent, impulsive good wishes. It was of one strange, unaccountable pang that spoiled this long-expected day for her and left in it a certain faint but enduring flavour of bitterness.

The Arts graduates gave a graduation dance that night. When Anne dressed for it she tossed aside the pearl beads she usually wore and took from her trunk the small box that had come to Green Gables on Christmas day. In it was a thread-like gold chain with a tiny pink enamel heart as a pendant. On the accompanying card was written, "With all good wishes from your old chum, Gilbert." Anne, laughing over the memory the enamel heart conjured up of the fatal day when Gilbert had called her "Carrots" and vainly tried to make his peace with a pink candy heart, had written him a nice little note of thanks. But she had never worn the trinket. Tonight she fastened it about her white throat with a dreamy smile.

She and Phil walked to Redmond together. Anne walked in silence; Phil chattered of many things. Suddenly she said,

"I heard today that Gilbert Blythe's engagement to Christine Stuart was to be announced as soon as Convocation was over. Did you hear anything of it?"

"No," said Anne.

"I think it's true," said Phil lightly.

Anne did not speak. In the darkness she felt her face burning. She slipped her hand inside her collar and caught at the gold chain. One energetic twist and it gave way. Anne thrust the broken trinket into her pocket. Her hands were trembling and her eyes were smarting.

But she was the gayest of all the gay revellers that night, and told Gilbert unregretfully that her card was full when he came to ask her for a dance. Afterwards, when she sat with the girls before the dying embers at Patty's Place, removing the spring chilliness from their satin skins, none chatted more blithely than she of the day's events.

"Moody Spurgeon MacPherson called here tonight after you left," said Aunt Jamesina, who had sat up to keep the fire on. "He didn't know about the graduation dance. That boy ought to sleep with a rubber band around his head to train his ears not to stick out. I had a beau once who did that and it improved him immensely. It was I who suggested it to him and he took my advice, but he never forgave me for it."

"Moody Spurgeon is a very serious young man," yawned Priscilla. "He is concerned with graver matters than his ears. He is going to be a minister, you know."

"Well, I suppose the Lord doesn't regard the ears of a man," said Aunt Jamesina gravely, dropping all further criticism of Moody Spurgeon. Aunt Jamesina had a proper respect for the cloth even in the case of an unfledged parson.

CHAPTER 38

FALSE DAWN

"Just imagine—this night week I'll be in Avonlea—delightful thought!" said Anne, bending over the box in which she was packing Mrs. Rachel Lynde's quilts. "But just imagine—this night week I'll be gone forever from Patty's Place—horrible thought!"

"I wonder if the ghost of all our laughter will echo through

the maiden dreams of Miss Patty and Miss Maria," speculated
Phil.

Miss Patty and Miss Maria were coming home, after having
trotted over most of the habitable globe.

"We'll be back the second week in May," wrote Miss Patty.
"I expect Patty's Place will seem rather small after the Hall of
the Kings at Karnak, but I never did like big places to live in.
And I'll be glad enough to be home again. When you start
travelling late in life you're apt to do too much of it because
you know you haven't much time left, and it's a thing that
grows on you. I'm afraid Maria will never be contented again."

"I shall leave here my fancies and dreams to bless the next
comer," said Anne, looking around the blue room wistfully—
her pretty blue room where she had spent three such happy
years. She had knelt at its window to pray and had bent from
it to watch the sunset behind the pines. She had heard the
autumn raindrops beating against it and had welcomed the
spring robins at its sill. She wondered if old dreams could haunt
rooms—if, when one left forever the room where she had joyed
and suffered and laughed and wept, something of her, intangible
and invisible, yet none the less real, did not remain behind
like a voiceful memory.

"I think," said Phil, "that a room where one dreams and
grieves and rejoices and *lives* becomes inseparably connected
with those processes and acquires a personality of its own. I
am sure if I came into this room fifty years from now it would
say 'Anne, Anne' to me. What nice times we've had here,
honey! What chats and jokes and good chummy jamborees!
Oh, dear me! I'm to marry Jo in June and I know I will be
rapturously happy. But just now I feel as if I wanted this lovely
Redmond life to go on forever."

"I'm unreasonable enough just now to wish that, too," admitted Anne. "No matter what deeper joys may come to us
later on we'll never again have just the same delightful, irresponsible existence we've had here. It's over forever, Phil."

"What are you going to do with Rusty?" asked Phil, as that
privileged pussy padded into the room.

"*I* am going to take him home with me and Joseph and the
Sarah-cat," announced Aunt Jamesina, following Rusty. "It
would be a shame to separate those cats now that they have

learned to live together. It's a hard lesson for cats and humans to learn."

"I'm sorry to part with Rusty," said Anne regretfully, "but it would be no use to take him to Green Gables. Marilla detests cats, and Davy would tease his life out. Besides, I don't suppose I'll be home very long. I've been offered the principalship of the Summerside High School."

"Are you going to accept it?" asked Phil.

"I—I haven't decided yet," answered Anne, with a confused flush.

Phil nodded understandingly. Naturally Anne's plans could not be settled until Roy had spoken. He would soon—there was no doubt of that. And there was no doubt that Anne would say "yes" when he said "Will you, please?" Anne herself regarded the state of affairs with a seldom-ruffled complacency. She was deeply in love with Roy. True, it was not just what she had imagined love to be. But was anything in life, Anne asked herself wearily, like one's imagination of it? It was the old diamond disillusion of childhood repeated—the same disappointment she had felt when she had first seen the chill sparkle instead of the purple splendour she had anticipated. "That's not my idea of a diamond," she had said. But Roy was a dear fellow and they would be very happy together, even if some indefinable zest was missing out of life. When Roy came down that evening and asked Anne to walk in the park every one at Patty's Place knew what he had come to say; and every one knew, or thought they knew, what Anne's answer would be.

"Anne is a very fortunate girl," said Aunt Jamesina.

"I suppose so," said Stella, shrugging her shoulders. "Roy is a nice fellow and all that. But there's really nothing in him."

"That sounds very like a jealous remark, Stella Maynard," said Aunt Jamesina rebukingly.

"It does—but I am not jealous," said Stella calmly. "I love Anne and I like Roy. Everybody says she is making a brilliant match, and even Mrs. Gardner thinks her charming now. It all sounds as if it were made in heaven, but I have my doubts. Make the most of that, Aunt Jamesina."

Roy asked Anne to marry him in the little pavilion on the harbour shore where they had talked on the rainy day of their first meeting. Anne thought it very romantic that he should have chosen that spot. And his proposal was as beautifully worded as if he had copied it, as one of Ruby Gillis' lovers had done, out of a Deportment of Courtship and Marriage. The whole effect was quite flawless. And it was also sincere. There was no doubt that Roy meant what he said. There was no false note to jar the symphony. Anne felt that she ought to be thrilling from head to foot. But she wasn't; she was horribly cool. When Roy paused for his answer she opened her lips to say her fateful yes.

And then—she found herself trembling as if she were reeling back from a precipice. To her came one of those moments when we realize, as by a blinding flash of illumination, more than all our previous years have taught us. She pulled her hand from Roy's.

"Oh, I can't marry you—I can't—I can't," she cried, wildly.

Roy turned pale—and also looked rather foolish. He had—small blame to him—felt very sure.

"What do you mean?" he stammered.

"I mean that I can't marry you," repeated Anne desperately. "I thought I could—but I can't."

"Why can't you?" Roy asked more calmly.

"Because—I don't care enough for you."

A crimson streak came into Roy's face.

"So you've just been amusing yourself these two years?" he said slowly.

"No, no, I haven't," gasped poor Anne. Oh, how could she explain? She *couldn't* explain. There are some things that cannot be explained. "I did think I cared—truly I did—but I know now I don't."

"You have ruined my life," said Roy bitterly.

"Forgive me," pleaded Anne miserably, with hot cheeks and stinging eyes.

Roy turned away and stood for a few minutes looking out seaward. When he came back to Anne, he was very pale again.

"You can give me no hope?" he said.

Anne shook her head mutely.

"Then—goodbye," said Roy. "I can't understand it—I can't believe you are not the woman I've believed you to be. But reproaches are idle between us. You are the only woman I can ever love. I thank you for your friendship, at least. Goodbye, Anne."

"Goodbye," faltered Anne. When Roy had gone she sat for a long time in the pavilion, watching a white mist creeping subtly and remorselessly landward up the harbour. It was her hour of humiliation and self-contempt and shame. Their waves went over her. And yet, underneath it all, was a queer sense of recovered freedom.

She slipped into Patty's Place in the dusk and escaped to her room. But Phil was there on the window seat.

"Wait," said Anne, flushing to anticipate the scene. "Wait till you hear what I have to say. Phil, Roy asked me to marry him—and I refused."

"You—you *refused* him?" said Phil blankly.

"Yes."

"Anne Shirley, are you in your senses?"

"I think so," said Anne wearily. "Oh, Phil, don't scold me. You don't understand."

"I certainly don't understand. You've encouraged Roy Gardner in every way for two years—and now you tell me you've refused him. Then you've just been flirting scandalously with him. Anne, I couldn't have believed it of *you*."

"I *wasn't* flirting with him—I honestly thought I cared up to the last minute—and then—well, I just knew I *never* could marry him."

"I suppose," said Phil cruelly, "that you intended to marry him for his money, and then your better self rose up and prevented you."

"I *didn't*. I never thought about his money. Oh, I can't explain it to you any more than I could to him."

"Well, I certainly think you have treated Roy shamefully," said Phil in exasperation. "He's handsome and clever and rich and good. What more do you want?"

"I want some one who *belongs* in my life. He doesn't. I was swept off my feet at first by his good looks and knack of paying romantic compliments; and later on I thought I *must* be in love because he was my dark-eyed ideal."

"I am bad enough for not knowing my own mind, but you are worse," said Phil.

"*I do* know my own mind," protested Anne. "The trouble

is, my mind changes and then I have to get acquainted with it all over again."

"Well, I suppose there is no use in saying anything to you."

"There is no need, Phil. I'm in the dust. This has spoiled everything backwards. I can never think of Redmond days without recalling the humiliation of this evening. Roy despises me—and you despise me—and I despise myself."

"You poor darling," said Phil, melting. "Just come here and let me comfort you. I've no right to scold you. I'd have married Alec or Alonzo if I hadn't met Jo. Oh, Anne, things are so mixed-up in real life. They aren't clear-cut and trimmed off, as they are in novels."

"I hope that *no* one will ever again ask me to marry him as long as I live," sobbed poor Anne, devoutly believing that she meant it.

CHAPTER 39

DEALS WITH WEDDINGS

ANNE FELT that life partook of the nature of an anti-climax during the first few weeks after her return to Green Gables. She missed the merry comradeship of Patty's Place. She had dreamed some brilliant dreams during the past winter and now they lay in the dust around her. In her present mood of self-disgust, she could not immediately begin dreaming again. And she discovered that, while solitude with dreams is glorious, solitude without them has few charms.

She had not seen Roy again after their painful parting in the park pavilion; but Dorothy came to see her before she left Kingsport.

"I'm awfully sorry you won't marry Roy," she said. "I did want you for a sister. But you are quite right. He would bore you to death. I love him, and he is a dear sweet boy, but really he isn't a bit interesting. He looks as if he ought to be, but he isn't."

"This won't spoil *our* friendship, will it, Dorothy?" Anne had asked wistfully.

"No, indeed. You're too good to lose. If I can't have you for a sister I mean to keep you as a chum anyway. And don't fret over Roy. He *is* feeling terribly just now—I have to listen to his out-pourings every day—but he'll get over it. He always does."

"Oh—*always?*" said Anne with a slight change of voice. "So he has 'got over it' before?"

"Dear me, yes," said Dorothy frankly. "Twice before. And he raved to me just the same both times. Not that the others actually refused him—they simply announced their engagements to someone else. Of course, when he met you he vowed to me that he had never really loved before—that the previous affairs had been merely boyish fancies. But I don't think you need worry."

Anne decided not to worry. Her feelings were a mixture of relief and resentment. Roy had certainly told her she was the only one he had ever loved. No doubt he believed it. But it was a comfort to feel that she had not, in all likelihood, ruined his life. There were other goddesses, and Roy, according to Dorothy, must needs be worshipping at some shrine. Nevertheless, life was stripped of several more illusions, and Anne began to think drearily that it seemed rather bare.

She came down from the porch gable on the evening of her return with a sorrowful face.

"What has happened to the old Snow Queen, Marilla?"

"Oh, I knew you'd feel bad over that," said Marilla. "I felt bad myself. That tree was there ever since I was a young girl. It blew down in the big gale we had in March. It was rotten at the core."

"I'll miss it so," grieved Anne. "The porch gable doesn't seem the same room without it. I'll never look from its window again without a sense of loss. And oh, I never came home to Green Gables before that Diana wasn't here to welcome me."

"Diana has something else to think of just now," said Mrs. Lynde significantly.

"Well, tell me all the Avonlea news," said Anne, sitting down on the porch steps, where the evening sunshine fell over her hair in a fine golden rain.

"There isn't much news except what we've wrote you," said Mrs. Lynde. "I suppose you haven't heard that Simon Fletcher broke his leg last week. It's a great thing for his family. They're getting a hundred things done that they've always wanted to do but couldn't as long as he was about, the old crank."

"He came of an aggravating family," remarked Marilla.

"Aggravating? Well, rather! His mother used to get up in prayer-meeting and tell all her children's shortcomings and ask prayers for them. 'Course it made them mad, and worse than ever."

"You haven't told Anne the news about Jane," suggested Marilla.

"Oh, Jane," sniffed Mrs. Lynde. "Well," she conceded grudgingly, "Jane Andrews is home from the West—came last week—and she's going to be married to a Winnipeg millionaire. You may be sure Mrs. Harmon lost no time in telling it far and wide."

"Dear old Jane—I'm so glad," said Anne heartily. "She deserves the good things of life."

"Oh, I ain't saying anything against Jane. She's a nice enough girl. But she isn't in the millionaire class, and you'll find there's not much to recommend that man but his money, that's what. Mrs. Harmon says he's an Englishman who has made money in mines but *I* believe he'll turn out to be a Yankee. He certainly must have money, for he has just showered Jane with jewelry. Her engagement ring is a diamond cluster so big that it looks like a plaster on Jane's fat paw."

Mrs. Lynde could not keep some bitterness out of her tone. Here was Jane Andrews, that plain little plodder, engaged to a millionaire, while Anne, it seemed, was not yet bespoken by any one, rich or poor. And Mrs. Harmon Andrews did brag insufferably.

"What has Gilbert Blythe been doing to himself at college?" asked Marilla. "I saw him when he came home last week, and he is so pale and thin I hardly knew him."

"He studied very hard last winter," said Anne. "You know

he took High Honours in Classics and the Cooper Prize. It hasn't been taken for five years! So I think he's rather run down. We're all a little tired."

"Anyhow, you're a B.A. and Jane Andrews isn't and never will be," said Mrs. Lynde, with gloomy satisfaction.

A few evenings later Anne went down to see Jane, but the latter was away in Charlottetown—"getting sewing done," Mrs. Harmon informed Anne proudly. "Of course an Avonlea dressmaker wouldn't do for Jane under the circumstances."

"I've heard something very nice about Jane," said Anne.

"Yes, Jane has done pretty well, even if she isn't a B.A.," said Mrs. Harmon, with a slight toss of her head. "Mr. Inglis is worth millions, and they're going to Europe on their wedding tour. When they come back they'll live in a perfect mansion of marble in Winnipeg. Jane has only one trouble—she can cook so well and her husband won't let her cook. He is so rich he hires his cooking done. They're going to keep a cook and two other maids and a coachman and a man-of-all-work. But what about *you,* Anne? I don't hear anything of your being married, after all your college-going."

"Oh," laughed Anne, "I am going to be an old maid. I really can't find anyone to suit me."

It was rather wicked of her. She deliberately meant to remind Mrs. Andrews that if she became an old maid it was not because she had not had at least one chance of marriage. But Mrs. Harmon took swift revenge.

"Well, the over-particular girls generally get left, I notice. And what's this I hear about Gilbert Blythe being engaged to a Miss Stuart? Charlie Sloane tells me she is perfectly beautiful. Is it true?"

"I don't know if it is true that he is engaged to Miss Stuart," replied Anne, with Spartan composure, "but it is certainly true that she is very lovely."

"I once thought you and Gilbert would have made a match of it," said Mrs. Harmon. "If you don't take care, Anne, all your beaux will slip through your fingers."

Anne decided not to continue her duel with Mrs. Harmon. You could not fence with an antagonist who met rapier thrust with blow of battle axe.

"Since Jane is away," she said, rising haughtily, "I don't

think I can stay longer this morning. I'll come down when she comes home."

"Do," said Mrs. Harmon effusively. "Jane isn't a bit proud. She just means to associate with her old friends the same as ever. She'll be real glad to see you."

Jane's millionaire arrived the last of May and carried her off in a blaze of splendour. Mrs. Lynde was spitefully gratified to find that Mr. Inglis was every day of forty, and short and thin and grayish. Mrs. Lynde did not spare him in her enumeration of his shortcomings, you may be sure.

"It will take all his gold to gild a pill like him, that's what," said Mrs. Rachel solemnly.

"He looks kind and good-hearted," said Anne loyally, "and I'm sure he thinks the world of Jane."

"Humph!" said Mrs. Rachel.

Phil Gordon was married the next week and Anne went over to Bolingbroke to be her bridesmaid. Phil made a dainty fairy of a bride, and the Rev. Jo was so radiant in his happiness that nobody thought him plain.

"We're going for a lovers' saunter through the land of Evangeline," said Phil, "and then we'll settle down on Patterson Street. Mother thinks it is terrible—she thinks Jo might at least take a church in a decent place. But the wilderness of the Patterson slums will blossom like the rose for me if Jo is there. Oh, Anne, I'm so happy my heart aches with it."

Anne was always glad in the happiness of her friends; but it is sometimes a little lonely to be surrounded everywhere by a happiness that is not your own. And it was just the same when she went back to Avonlea. This time it was Diana who was bathed in the wonderful glory that comes to a woman when her first-born is laid beside her. Anne looked at the white young mother with a certain awe that had never entered into her feelings for Diana before. Could this pale woman with the rapture in her eyes be the little black-curled, rosy-cheeked Diana she had played with in vanished schooldays? It gave her a queer desolate feeling that she herself somehow belonged only in those past years and had no business in the present at all.

"Isn't he perfectly beautiful?" said Diana proudly.

The little fat fellow was absurdly like Fred—just as round, just as red. Anne really could not say conscientiously that she

thought him beautiful, but she vowed sincerely that he was
sweet and kissable and altogether delightful.

"Before he came I wanted a girl, so that I could call her
Anne," said Diana. "But now that little Fred is here I wouldn't
exchange him for a million girls. He just *couldn't* have been
anything but his own precious self."

" 'Every little baby is the sweetest and the best,' " quoted
Mrs. Allan gaily. "If little Anne *had* come you'd have felt just
the same about her."

Mrs. Allan was visiting in Avonlea, for the first time since
leaving it. She was as gay and sweet and sympathetic as ever.
Her old girl friends had welcomed her back rapturously. The
reigning minister's wife was an estimable lady, but she was not
exactly a kindred spirit.

"I can hardly wait till he gets old enough to talk," sighed
Diana. "I just long to hear him say 'mother.' And oh, I'm
determined that his first memory of me shall be a nice one.
The first memory I have of my mother is of her slapping me
for something I had done. I am sure I deserved it, and mother
was always a good mother and I love her dearly. But I do wish
my first memory of her was nicer."

"I have just one memory of my mother and it is the sweetest
of all my memories," said Mrs. Allan. "I was five years old,
and I had been allowed to go to school one day with my two
older sisters. When school came out my sisters went home in
different groups, each supposing I was with the other. Instead
I had run off with a little girl I had played with at recess. We
went to her home, which was near the school, and began making
mud pies. We were having a glorious time when my older sister
arrived, breathless and angry.

" 'You naughty girl,' she cried, snatching my reluctant hand
and dragging me along with her. 'Come home this minute. Oh,
you're going to catch it! Mother is awful cross. She is going to
give you a good whipping.'

"I had never been whipped. Dread and terror filled my poor
little heart. I have never been so miserable in my life as I was
on that walk home. I had not meant to be naughty. Phemy
Cameron had asked me to go home with her and I had not
known it was wrong to go. And now I was to be whipped for
it. When we got home my sister dragged me into the kitchen

where mother was sitting by the fire in the twilight. My poor
wee legs were trembling so that I could hardly stand. And
mother—mother just took me up in her arms, without one
word of rebuke or harshness, kissed me and held me close to
her heart. 'I was so frightened you were lost, darling,' she said
tenderly. I could see the love shining in her eyes as she looked
down on me. She never scolded or reproached me for what I
had done—only told me I must never go away again without
asking permission. She died very soon afterwards. That is the
only memory I have of her. Isn't it a beautiful one?"

Anne felt lonelier than ever as she walked home, going by
way of the Birch Path and Willowmere. She had not walked
that way for many moons. It was a darkly-purple bloomy night.
The air was heavy with blossom fragrance—almost too heavy.
The cloyed senses recoiled from it as from an overfull cup.
The birches of the path had grown from the fairy saplings of
old to big trees. Everything had changed. Anne felt that she
would be glad when the summer was over and she was away
at work again. Perhaps life would not seem so empty then.

> " 'I've tried the world—it wears no more
> The colouring of romance it wore,' "

sighed Anne—and was straightway much comforted by the
romance in the idea of the world being denuded of romance.

CHAPTER 40

A BOOK OF REVELATION

THE IRVINGS came back to Echo Lodge for the summer, and
Anne spent a happy three weeks there in July. Miss Lavendar
had not changed; Charlotta the Fourth was a very grown-up
young lady now, but still adored Anne sincerely.

"When all's said and done, Miss Shirley, ma'am, I haven't

seen any one in Boston that's equal to you," she said frankly.

Paul was almost grown-up, too. He was sixteen, his chestnut curls had given place to close-cropped brown locks, and he was more interested in foot-ball than fairies. But the bond between him and his old teacher still held. Kindred spirits alone do not change with changing years.

It was a wet, bleak, cruel evening in July when Anne came back to Green Gables. One of the fierce summer storms which sometimes sweep over the gulf was ravaging the sea. As Anne came in the first rain-drops dashed against the panes.

"Was that Paul who brought you home?" asked Marilla. "Why didn't you make him stay all night. It's going to be a wild evening."

"He'll reach Echo Lodge before the rain gets very heavy, I think. Anyway, he wanted to go back tonight. Well, I've had a splendid visit, but I'm glad to see you dear folks again. 'East, west, hame's best.' Davy, have you been growing again lately?"

"I've growed a whole inch since you left," said Davy proudly. "I'm as tall as Milty Boulter now. Ain't I glad. He'll have to stop crowing about being bigger. Say, Anne, did you know that Gilbert Blythe is dying?"

Anne stood quite silent and motionless, looking at Davy. Her face had gone so white that Marilla thought she was going to faint.

"Davy, hold your tongue," said Mrs. Rachel angrily. "Anne, don't look like that—*don't look like that!* We didn't mean to tell you so suddenly."

"Is—it—true?" asked Anne in a voice that was not hers.

"Gilbert is very ill," said Mrs. Lynde gravely. "He took down with typhoid fever just after you left for Echo Lodge. Did you never hear of it?"

"No," said that unknown voice.

"It was a very bad case from the start. The doctor said he'd been terribly run down. They've a trained nurse and everything's been done. *Don't* look like that, Anne. While there's life there's hope."

"Mr. Harrison was here this evening and he said they had no hope of him," reiterated Davy.

Marilla, looking old and worn and tired, got up and marched Davy grimly out of the kitchen.

"Oh, *don't* look so, dear," said Mrs. Rachel, putting her kind old arms about the pallid girl. "I haven't given up hope, indeed I haven't. He's got the Blythe constitution in his favour, that's what."

Anne gently put Mrs. Lynde's arms away from her, walked blindly across the kitchen, through the hall, up the stairs to her old room. At its window she knelt down, staring out unseeingly. It was very dark. The rain was beating down over the shivering fields. The Haunted Wood was full of the groans of mighty trees wrung in the tempest, and the air throbbed with the thunderous crash of billows on the distant shore. And Gilbert was dying!

There is a book of Revelation in everyone's life, as there is in the Bible. Anne read hers that bitter night, as she kept her agonized vigil through the hours of storm and darkness. She loved Gilbert—had always loved him! She knew that now. She knew that she could no more cast him out of her life without agony than she could have cut off her right hand and cast it from her. And the knowledge had come too late—too late even for the bitter solace of being with him at the last. If she had not been so blind—so foolish—she would have had the right to go to him now. But he would never know that she loved him—he would go away from this life thinking that she did not care. Oh, the black years of emptiness stretching before her! She could not live through them—she could not! She cowered down by her window and wished, for the first time in her gay young life, that she could die, too. If Gilbert went away from her, without one word or sign or message, she could not live. Nothing was of any value without him. She belonged to him and he to her. In her hour of supreme agony she had no doubt of that. He did not love Christine Stuart—never had loved Christine Stuart. Oh, what a fool she had been not to realize what the bond was that had held her to Gilbert—to think that the flattered fancy she had felt for Roy Gardner had been love. And now she must pay for her folly as for a crime.

Mrs. Lynde and Marilla crept to her door before they went to bed, shook their heads doubtfully at each other over the silence, and went away. The storm raged all night, but when the dawn came it was spent. Anne saw a fairy fringe of light on the skirts of darkness. Soon the eastern hill-tops had a fire-shot ruby rim. The clouds rolled themselves away into great, soft, white masses on the horizon; the sky gleamed blue and silvery. A hush fell over the world.

Anne rose from her knees and crept down-stairs. The freshness of the rain-wind blew against her white face as she went out into the yard, and cooled her dry, burning eyes. A merry rollicking whistle was lilting up the lane. A moment later Pacifique Buote came in sight.

Anne's physical strength suddenly failed her. If she had not clutched at a low willow bough she would have fallen. Pacifique was George Fletcher's hired man, and George Fletcher lived next door to the Blythes. Mrs. Fletcher was Gilbert's aunt. Pacifique would know if—if—Pacifique would know what there was to be known.

Pacifique strode sturdily on along the red lane, whistling. He did not see Anne. She made three futile attempts to call him. He was almost past before she succeeded in making her quivering lips call, "Pacifique!"

Pacifique turned with a grin and a cheerful good-morning.

"Pacifique," said Anne faintly, "did you come from George Fletcher's this morning?"

"Sure," said Pacifique amiably. "I got de word las' night dat my fader, he was seeck. It was so stormy dat I couldn't go den, so I start vair early dis mornin'. I'm goin' troo de woods for short cut."

"Did you hear how Gilbert Blythe was this morning?"

Anne's desperation drove her to the question. Even the worst would be more endurable than this hideous suspense.

"He's better," said Pacifique. "He got de turn las' night. De doctor say he'll be all right now dis soon while. Had close shave, dough! Dat boy, he jus' keel himself at colloge. Well, I mus' hurry. De old man, he'll be in hurry to see me."

Pacifique resumed his walk and his whistle. Anne gazed after him with eyes where joy was driving out the strained anguish of the night. He was a very lank, very ragged, very homely youth. But in her sight he was as beautiful as those who bring good tidings on the mountains. Never, as long as she lived, would Anne see Pacifique's brown, round, black-eyed face without a warm remembrance of the moment when he had given to her the oil of joy for mourning.

Long after Pacifique's gay whistle had faded into the phantom of music and then into silence far up under the maples of Lover's Lane Anne stood under the willows, tasting the poignant sweetness of life when some great dread has been removed from it. The morning was a cup filled with mist and glamour. In the corner near her was a rich surprise of new-blown, crystal-dewed roses. The trills and trickles of song from the birds in the big tree above her seemed in perfect accord with her mood. A sentence from a very old, very true, very wonderful Book came to her lips,

"Weeping may endure for a night but joy cometh in the morning."

CHAPTER 41

LOVE TAKES UP THE GLASS OF TIME

"I've come up to ask you to go for one of our old-time rambles through September woods and 'over hills where spices grow,' this afternoon," said Gilbert, coming suddenly around the porch corner. "Suppose we visit Hester Gray's garden."

Anne, sitting on the stone step with her lap full of a pale, filmy, green stuff, looked up rather blankly.

"Oh, I wish I could," she said slowly, "but I really can't, Gilbert. I'm going to Alice Penhallow's wedding this evening, you know. I've got to do something to this dress, and by the time it's finished I'll have to get ready. I'm so sorry. I'd love to go."

"Well, can you go tomorrow afternoon, then?" asked Gilbert, apparently not much disappointed.

"Yes, I think so."

"In that case I shall hie me home at once to do something I should otherwise have to do tomorrow. So Alice Penhallow is to be married tonight. Three weddings for you in one summer,

Anne—Phil's, Alice's, and Jane's. I'll never forgive Jane for not inviting me to her wedding."

"You really can't blame her when you think of the tremendous Andrews connection who had to be invited. The house could hardly hold them all. I was only bidden by grace of being Jane's old chum—at least on Jane's part. I think Mrs. Harmon's motive for inviting me was to let me see Jane's surpassing gorgeousness."

"Is it true that she wore so many diamonds that you couldn't tell where the diamonds left off and Jane began?"

Anne laughed.

"She certainly wore a good many. What with all the diamonds and white satin and tulle and lace and roses and orange-blossoms, prim little Jane was almost lost to sight. But she was *very* happy, and so was Mr. Inglis—and so was Mrs. Harmon."

"Is that the dress you're going to wear tonight?" asked Gilbert, looking down at the fluffs and frills.

"Yes. Isn't it pretty? And I shall wear star-flowers in my hair. The Haunted Wood is full of them this summer."

Gilbert had a sudden vision of Anne, arrayed in a frilly green gown, with the virginal curves of arms and throat slipping out of it, and white stars shining against the coils of her ruddy hair. The vision made him catch his breath. But he turned lightly away.

"Well, I'll be up tomorrow. Hope you'll have a nice time tonight."

Anne looked after him as he strode away, and sighed. Gilbert was friendly—very friendly—far too friendly. He had come quite often to Green Gables after his recovery, and something of their old comradeship had returned. But Anne no longer found it satisfying. The rose of love made the blossom of friendship pale and scentless by contrast. And Anne had again begun to doubt if Gilbert now felt anything for her but friendship. In the common light of common day her radiant certainty of that rapt morning had faded. She was haunted by a miserable fear that her mistake could never be rectified. It was quite likely that it was Christine whom Gilbert loved after all. Perhaps he was even engaged to her. Anne tried to put all unsettling hopes out of her heart, and reconcile herself to a future where work and ambition must take the place of love. She could do good, if not noble, work as a teacher; and the success her little sketches were beginning to meet with in certain editorial sanctums argued well for her budding literary dreams. But—but—Anne picked up her green dress and sighed again.

When Gilbert came the next afternoon he found Anne waiting for him, fresh as the dawn and fair as a star, after all the gaiety of the preceding night. She wore a green dress—not the one she had worn to the wedding, but an old one which Gilbert had told her at a Redmond reception he liked especially. It was just the shade of green that brought out the rich tints of her hair, and the starry gray of her eyes and the iris-like delicacy of her skin. Gilbert, glancing at her sideways as they walked along a shadowy wood-path, thought she had never looked so lovely. Anne, glancing sideways at Gilbert, now and then, thought how much older he looked since his illness. It was as if he had put boyhood behind him forever.

The day was beautiful and the way was beautiful. Anne was almost sorry when they reached Hester Gray's garden, and sat down on the old bench. But it was beautiful there, too—as beautiful as it had been on the far-away day of the Golden Picnic, when Diana and Jane and Priscilla and she had found it. Then it had been lovely with narcissus and violets; now golden rod had kindled its fairy torches in the corners and asters dotted it bluely. The call of the brook came up through the woods from the valley of birches with all its old allurement; the mellow air was full of the purr of the sea; beyond were fields rimmed by fences bleached silvery gray in the suns of many summers, and long hills scarfed with the shadows of autumnal clouds; with the blowing of the west wind old dreams returned.

"I think," said Anne softly, "that 'the land where dreams come true' is in the blue haze yonder, over that little valley."

"Have you any unfulfilled dreams, Anne?" asked Gilbert.

Something in his tone—something she had not heard since that miserable evening in the orchard at Patty's Place—made Anne's heart beat wildly. But she made answer lightly.

"Of course. Everybody has. It wouldn't do for us to have all our dreams fulfilled. We would be as good as dead if we had nothing left to dream about. What a delicious aroma that low-descending sun is extracting from the asters and ferns. I wish we could *see* perfumes as well as smell them. I'm sure they would be very beautiful."

Gilbert was not to be thus side-tracked.

"I have a dream," he said slowly. "I persist in dreaming it, although it has often seemed to me that it could never come true. I dream of a home with a hearth-fire in it, a cat and dog, the footsteps of friends—and *you!"*

Anne wanted to speak but she could find no words. Happiness was breaking over her like a wave. It almost frightened her.

"I asked you a question over two years ago, Anne. If I ask it again today will you give me a different answer?"

Still Anne could not speak. But she lifted her eyes, shining with all the love-rapture of countless generations, and looked into his for a moment. He wanted no other answer.

They lingered in the old garden until twilight, sweet as dusk in Eden must have been, crept over it. There was so much to talk over and recall—things said and done and heard and thought and felt and misunderstood.

"I thought you loved Christine Stuart," Anne told him, as reproachfully as if she had not given him every reason to suppose that she loved Roy Gardner.

Gilbert laughed boyishly.

"Christine was engaged to somebody in her home town. I knew it and she knew I knew it. When her brother graduated he told me his sister was coming to Kingsport the next winter to take music, and asked me if I would look after her a bit, as she knew no one and would be very lonely. So I did. And then I liked Christine for her own sake. She is one of the nicest girls I've ever known. I knew college gossip credited us with being in love with each other. I didn't care. Nothing mattered much to me for a time there, after you told me you could never love me, Anne. There was nobody else—there never could be anybody else for me but you. I've loved you ever since that day you broke your slate over my head in school."

"I don't see how you could keep on loving me when I was such a little fool," said Anne.

"Well, I tried to stop," said Gilbert frankly, "not because I thought you what you call yourself, but because I felt sure there was no chance for me after Gardner came on the scene. But I couldn't—and I can't tell you, either, what it's meant to me these two years to believe you were going to marry him, and be told every week by some busybody that your engagement was on the point of being announced. I believed it until one blessed day when I was sitting up after the fever. I got a letter from Phil Gordon—Phil Blake, rather—in which she told me there was really nothing between you and Roy, and advised me to 'try again.' Well, the doctor was amazed at my rapid recovery after that."

Anne laughed—then shivered.

"I can never forget the night I thought you were dying, Gilbert. Oh, I knew—I *knew* then—and I thought it was too late."

"But it wasn't, sweetheart. Oh, Anne, this makes up for everything, doesn't it? Let's resolve to keep this day sacred to perfect beauty all our lives for the gift it has given us."

"It's the birthday of our happiness," said Anne softly. "I've always loved this old garden of Hester Gray's, and now it will be dearer than ever."

"But I'll have to ask you to wait a long time, Anne," said Gilbert sadly. "It will be three years before I'll finish my medical course. And even then there will be no diamond sunbursts and marble halls."

Anne laughed.

"I don't want sunbursts and marble halls. I just want *you.* You see I'm quite as shameless as Phil about it. Sunbursts and marble halls may be all very well, but there is more 'scope for imagination' without them. And as for the waiting, that doesn't matter. We'll just be happy, waiting and working for each other—and dreaming. Oh, dreams will be very sweet now."

Gilbert drew her close to him and kissed her. Then they walked home together in the dusk, crowned king and queen in the bridal realm of love, along winding paths fringed with the sweetest flowers that ever bloomed, and over haunted meadows where winds of hope and memory blew.

Chronicles
of
Avonlea

TO THE MEMORY OF
MRS. WILLIAM A. HOUSTON,
A DEAR FRIEND, WHO HAS GONE BEYOND

THE HURRYING OF LUDOVIC

ANNE SHIRLEY was curled up on the window-seat of Theodora Dix's sitting-room one Saturday evening, looking dreamily afar at some fair starland beyond the hills of sunset. Anne was visiting for a fortnight of her vacation at Echo Lodge, where Mr. and Mrs. Stephen Irving were spending the summer, and she often ran over to the old Dix homestead to chat for awhile with Theodora. They had had their chat out, on this particular evening, and Anne was giving herself over to the delight of building an air-castle. She leaned her shapely head, with its braided coronet of dark red hair, against the window-casing, and her gray eyes were like the moonlight gleam of shadowy pools.

Then she saw Ludovic Speed coming down the lane. He was yet far from the house, for the Dix lane was a long one, but Ludovic could be recognized as far as he could be seen. No one else in Middle Grafton had such a tall, gently-stooping, placidly-moving figure. In every kink and turn of it there was an individuality all Ludovic's own.

Anne roused herself from her dreams, thinking it would only be tactful to take her departure. Ludovic was courting Theodora. Everyone in Grafton knew that, or, if anyone were in ignorance of the fact, it was not because he had not had time to find

211

out. Ludovic had been coming down that lane to see Theodora, in the same ruminating, unhastening fashion, for fifteen years!

When Anne, who was slim and girlish and romantic, rose to go, Theodora, who was plump and middle-aged, and practical, said, with a twinkle in her eye:

"There isn't any hurry, child. Sit down and have your call out. You've seen Ludovic coming down the lane, and, I suppose, you think you'll be a crowd. But you won't. Ludovic rather likes a third person around, and so do I. It spurs up the conversation as it were. When a man has been coming to see you straight along, twice a week for fifteen years, you get rather talked out by spells."

Theodora never pretended to bashfulness where Ludovic was concerned. She was not at all shy of referring to him and his dilatory courtship. Indeed, it seemed to amuse her.

Anne sat down again and together they watched Ludovic coming down the lane, gazing calmly about him at the lush clover fields and the blue loops of the river winding in and out of the misty valley below.

Anne looked at Theodora's placid, finely-moulded face and tried to imagine what she herself would feel like if she were sitting there, waiting for an elderly lover who had, seemingly, taken so long to make up his mind. But even Anne's imagination failed her for this.

"Anyway," she thought, impatiently, "if I wanted him I think I'd find some way of hurrying him up. Ludovic *Speed!* Was there ever such a misfit of a name? Such a name for such a man is a delusion and a snare."

Presently Ludovic got to the house, but stood so long on the doorstep in a brown study, gazing into the tangled green boskage of the cherry orchard, that Theodora finally went and opened the door before he knocked. As she brought him into the sitting-room she made a comical grimace at Anne over his shoulder.

Ludovic smiled pleasantly at Anne. He liked her; she was the only young girl he knew, for he generally avoided young girls—they made him feel awkward and out of place. But Anne did not affect him in this fashion. She had a way of getting on with all sorts of people, and, although they had not known her very long, both Ludovic and Theodora looked upon her as an old friend.

Ludovic was tall and somewhat ungainly, but his unhesitating placidity gave him the appearance of a dignity that did not otherwise pertain to him. He had a drooping, silky, brown moustache, and a little curly tuft of imperial—a fashion which was regarded as eccentric in Grafton, where men had clean-shaven chins or went full-bearded. His eyes were dreamy and pleasant, with a touch of melancholy in their blue depths.

He sat down in the big bulgy old armchair that had belonged to Theodora's father. Ludovic always sat there, and Anne declared that the chair had come to look like him.

The conversation soon grew animated enough. Ludovic was a good talker when he had somebody to draw him out. He was well read, and frequently surprised Anne by his shrewd comments on men and matters out in the world, of which only the faint echoes reached Deland River. He had also a liking for religious arguments with Theodora, who did not care much for politics or the making of history, but was avid of doctrines, and read everything pertaining thereto. When the conversation drifted into an eddy of friendly wrangling between Ludovic and Theodora over Christian Science, Anne understood that her usefulness was ended for the time being, and that she would not be missed.

"It's star time and good-night time," she said, and went away quietly.

But she had to stop to laugh when she was well out of sight of the house, in a green meadow be-starred with the white and gold of daisies. A wind, odour-freighted, blew daintily across it. Anne leaned against a white birch tree in the corner and laughed heartily, as she was apt to do whenever she thought of Ludovic and Theodora. To her eager youth this courtship of theirs seemed a very amusing thing. She liked Ludovic, but she allowed herself to be provoked with him.

"The dear, big, irritating goose!" she said aloud. "There never was such a lovable idiot before. He's just like the alligator in the old rhyme, who wouldn't go along, and wouldn't keep still, but just kept bobbing up and down."

Two evenings later, when Anne went over to the Dix place, she and Theodora drifted into a conversation about Ludovic. Theodora, who was the most industrious soul alive, and had a mania for fancy work into the bargain, was busying her smooth, plump fingers with a very elaborate Battenburg lace centrepiece. Anne was lying back in a little rocker, with her slim hands folded in her lap, watching Theodora. She realized that Theodora was very handsome, in a stately, Juno-like fashion of firm, white flesh, large clearly-chiselled outlines, and great, cowey, brown eyes. When Theodora was not smiling she looked very imposing. Anne thought it likely that Ludovic held her in awe.

"Did you and Ludovic talk about Christian Science *all* Saturday evening?" she asked.

Theodora overflowed into a smile.

"Yes, and we even quarrelled over it. At least *I* did. Ludovic wouldn't quarrel with anyone. You have to fight air when you spar with him. I hate to square up to a person who won't hit back."

"Theodora," said Anne coaxingly, "I am going to be curious and impertinent. You can snub me if you like. Why don't you and Ludovic get married?"

Theodora laughed comfortably.

"That's a question Grafton folks have been asking for quite a while, I reckon, Anne. Well, I'd have no objection to marrying Ludovic. That's frank enough for you, isn't it? But it's not easy to marry a man unless he asks you. And Ludovic has never asked me."

"Is he too shy?" persisted Anne. Since Theodora was in the mood, she meant to sift this puzzling affair to the bottom.

Theodora dropped her work and looked meditatively out over the green slopes of the summer world.

"No, I don't think it is that. Ludovic isn't shy. It's just his way—the Speed way. The Speeds are all dreadfully deliberate. They spend years thinking over a thing before they make up their minds to do it. Sometimes they get so much in the habit of thinking about it that they never get over it—like old Alder Speed, who was always talking of going to England to see his brother, but never went, though there was no earthly reason why he shouldn't. They're not lazy, you know, but they love to take their time."

"And Ludovic is just an aggravated case of Speedism," suggested Anne.

"Exactly. He never hurried in his life. Why, he has been

thinking for the last six years of getting his house painted. He talks it over with me every little while, and picks out the colour, and there the matter stays. He's fond of me, and he means to ask me to have him sometime. The only question is—will the time ever come?"

"Why don't you hurry him up?" asked Anne impatiently.

Theodora went back to her stitches with another laugh.

"If Ludovic could be hurried up I'm not the one to do it. I'm too shy. It sounds ridiculous to hear a woman of my age and inches say that, but it is true. Of course, I know it's the only way any Speed ever did make out to get married. For instance, there's a cousin of mine married to Ludovic's brother. I don't say she proposed to him out and out, but, mind you, Anne, it wasn't far from it. I couldn't do anything like that. I *did* try once. When I realized that I was getting sere and mellow, and all the girls of my generation were going off on either hand, I tried to give Ludovic a hint. But it stuck in my throat. And now I don't mind. If I don't change Dix to Speed until I take the initiative, it will be Dix to the end of life. Ludovic doesn't realize that we are growing old, you know. He thinks we are giddy young folks yet, with plenty of time before us. That's the Speed failing. They never find out they're alive until they're dead."

"You're fond of Ludovic, aren't you?" asked Anne, detecting a note of real bitterness among Theodora's paradoxes.

"Laws, yes," said Theodora candidly. She did not think it worth while to blush over so settled a fact. "I think the world and all of Ludovic. And he certainly does need somebody to look after him. He's neglected—he looks frayed. You can see that for yourself. That old aunt of his looks after his house in some fashion, but she doesn't look after *him*. And he's coming now to the age when a man needs to be looked after and coddled a bit. I'm lonesome here, and Ludovic is lonesome up there, and it does seem ridiculous, doesn't it? I don't wonder that we're the standing joke of Grafton. Goodness knows, I laugh at it enough myself. I've sometimes thought that if Ludovic could be made jealous it might spur him along. But I never could flirt and there's nobody to flirt with if I could. Everybody hereabouts looks upon me as Ludovic's property and nobody would dream of interfering with him."

"Theodora," cried Anne, "I have a plan!"

"Now, what are you going to do?" exclaimed Theodora.

Anne told her. At first Theodora laughed and protested. In the end, she yielded somewhat doubtfully, overborne by Anne's enthusiasm.

"Well, try it, then," she said, resignedly. "If Ludovic gets mad and leaves me I'll be worse off than ever. But nothing venture, nothing win. And there is a fighting chance, I suppose. Besides, I must admit I'm tired of his dilly-dallying."

Anne went back to Echo Lodge tingling with delight in her plot. She hunted up Arnold Sherman, and told him what was required of him. Arnold Sherman listened and laughed. He was an elderly widower, an intimate friend of Stephen Irving, and had come down to spend part of the summer with him and his wife in Prince Edward Island. He was handsome in a mature style, and he had a dash of mischief in him still, so that he entered readily enough into Anne's plan. It amused him to think of hurrying Ludovic Speed, and he knew that Theodora Dix could be depended on to do her part. The comedy would not be dull, whatever its outcome.

The curtain rose on the first act after prayer meeting on the next Thursday night. It was bright moonlight when the people came out of church, and everybody saw it plainly. Arnold Sherman stood upon the steps close to the door, and Ludovic Speed leaned up against a corner of the graveyard fence, as he had done for years. The boys said he had worn the paint off that particular place. Ludovic knew of no reason why he should paste himself up against the church door. Theodora would come out as usual, and he would join her as she went past the corner.

This was what happened; Theodora came down the steps, her stately figure outlined in its darkness against the gush of lamplight from the porch. Arnold Sherman asked her if he might see her home. Theodora took his arm calmly, and together they swept past the stupefied Ludovic, who stood helplessly gazing after them as if unable to believe his eyes.

For a few moments he stood there limply; then he started down the road after his fickle lady and her new admirer. The boys and irresponsible young men crowded after, expecting some excitement, but they were disappointed. Ludovic strode on until he overtook Theodora and Arnold Sherman, and then fell meekly in behind them.

Theodora hardly enjoyed her walk home, although Arnold Sherman laid himself out to be especially entertaining. Her heart yearned after Ludovic, whose shuffling footsteps she heard behind her. She feared that she had been very cruel, but she was in for it now. She steeled herself by the reflection that it was all for his own good, and she talked to Arnold Sherman as if he were the one man in the world. Poor, deserted Ludovic, following humbly behind, heard her, and if Theodora had known how bitter the cup she was holding to his lips really was, she would never have been resolute enough to present it, no matter for what ultimate good.

When she and Arnold turned in at her gate Ludovic had to stop. Theodora looked over her shoulder and saw him standing still on the road. His forlorn figure haunted her thoughts all night. If Anne had not run over the next day and bolstered up her convictions, she might have spoiled everything by prematurely relenting.

Ludovic, meanwhile, stood still on the road, quite oblivious to the hoots and comments of the vastly amused small boy contingent, until Theodora and his rival disappeared from his view under the firs in the hollow of her lane. Then he turned about and went home, not with his usual leisurely amble, but with a perturbed stride which proclaimed his inward disquiet.

He felt bewildered. If the world had come suddenly to an end or if the lazy, meandering Grafton River had turned about and flowed up hill, Ludovic could not have been more astonished. For fifteen years he had walked home from meetings with Theodora; and now this elderly stranger, with all the glamour of "the States" hanging about him, had coolly walked off with her under Ludovic's very nose. Worse—most unkindest cut of all—Theodora had gone with him willingly; nay, she had evidently enjoyed his company. Ludovic felt the stirring of a righteous anger in his easy-going soul.

When he reached the end of his lane, he paused at his gate, and looked at his house, set back from the lane in a crescent of birches. Even in the moonlight, its weather-worn aspect was plainly visible. He thought of the "palatial residence" rumour ascribed to Arnold Sherman in Boston, and stroked his chin nervously with his sunburnt fingers. Then he doubled up his fist and struck it smartly on the gate-post.

"Theodora needn't think she is going to jilt me in this fashion, after keeping company with me for fifteen years," he said. "*I'll* have something to say to it, Arnold Sherman or no Arnold Sherman. The impudence of the puppy!"

The next morning Ludovic drove to Carmody and engaged Joshua Pye to come and paint his house, and that evening, although he was not due till Saturday night, he went down to see Theodora.

Arnold Sherman was there before him, and was actually sitting in Ludovic's own prescriptive chair. Ludovic had to deposit himself in Theodora's new wicker rocker, where he looked and felt lamentably out of place.

If Theodora felt the situation to be awkward, she carried it off superbly. She had never looked handsomer, and Ludovic perceived that she wore her second best silk dress. He wondered miserably if she had donned it in expectation of his rival's call. She had never put on silk dresses for him. Ludovic had always been the meekest and mildest of mortals, but he felt quite murderous as he sat mutely there and listened to Arnold Sherman's polished conversation.

"You should just have been here to see him glowering," Theodora told the delighted Anne the next day. "It may be wicked of me, but I felt real glad. I was afraid he might stay away and sulk. So long as he comes here and sulks I don't worry. But he is feeling badly enough, poor soul, and I'm really eaten up by remorse. He tried to outstay Mr. Sherman last night, but he didn't manage it. You never saw a more depressed-looking creature than he was as he hurried down the lane. Yes, he actually hurried."

The following Sunday evening Arnold Sherman walked to church with Theodora, and sat with her. When they came in Ludovic Speed suddenly stood up in his pew under the gallery. He sat down again at once, but everybody in view had seen him, and that night folks in all the length and breadth of Grafton River discussed the dramatic occurrence with keen enjoyment.

"Yes, he jumped right up as if he was pulled to his feet, while the minister was reading the chapter," said his cousin,

Lorella Speed, who had been in church, to her sister, who had not. "His face was as white as a sheet, and his eyes were just glaring out of his head. I never felt so thrilled, I declare! I almost expected him to fly at them then and there. But he just gave a sort of gasp and set down again. I don't know whether Theodora Dix saw him or not. She looked as cool and unconcerned as you please."

Theodora had not seen Ludovic, but if she looked cool and unconcerned, her appearance belied her, for she felt miserably flustered. She could not prevent Arnold Sherman coming to church with her, but it seemed to her like going too far. People did not go to church and sit together in Grafton unless they were the next thing to being engaged. What if this filled Ludovic with the narcotic of despair instead of wakening him up! She sat through the service in misery and heard not one word of the sermon.

But Ludovic's spectacular performances were not yet over. The Speeds might be hard to get started, but once they were started their momentum was irresistible. When Theodora and Mr. Sherman came out Ludovic was waiting on the steps. He stood up straight and stern, with his head thrown back and his shoulders squared. There was open defiance in the look he cast on his rival, and masterfulness in the mere touch of the hand he laid on Theodora's arm.

"May I see you home, Miss Dix?" his words said. His tone said, "I am going to see you home whether or no."

Theodora, with a deprecating look at Arnold Sherman, took his arm, and Ludovic marched her across the green amid a silence which the very horses tied to the storm fence seemed to share. For Ludovic 'twas a crowded hour of glorious life.

Anne walked all the way over from Avonlea the next day to hear the news. Theodora smiled consciously.

"Yes, it is really settled at last, Anne. Coming home last night Ludovic asked me plump and plain to marry him,— Sunday and all as it was. It's to be right away—for Ludovic won't be put off a week longer than necessary."

"So Ludovic Speed has been hurried up to some purpose at last," said Mr. Sherman, when Anne called in at Echo Lodge, brimful with her news. "And you are delighted, of course, and my poor pride must be the scapegoat. I shall always be re-

membered in Grafton as the man from Boston who wanted
Theodora Dix and couldn't get her."

"But that won't be true, you know," said Anne comfortingly.

Arnold Sherman thought of Theodora's ripe beauty, and the
mellow companionableness she had revealed in their brief in-
tercourse.

"I'm not perfectly sure of that," he said, with a half sigh.

OLD LADY LLOYD

I. The May Chapter

SPENCERVALE GOSSIP always said that "Old Lady Lloyd" was rich and mean and proud. Gossip, as usual, was one-third right and two-thirds wrong. Old Lady Lloyd was neither rich nor mean; in reality she was pitifully poor—so poor that "Crooked Jack" Spencer, who dug her garden and chopped her wood for her, was opulent by contrast; for he, at least, never lacked three meals a day, and the Old Lady could sometimes achieve no more than one. But she *was* very proud—so proud that she would have died rather than let the Spencervale people, among whom she had queened it in her youth, suspect how poor she was and to what straits was sometimes reduced. She much preferred to have them think her miserly and odd—a queer old recluse who never went anywhere, even to church, and who paid the smallest subscription to the minister's salary of anyone in the congregation.

"And her just rolling in wealth!" they said indignantly. "Well, she didn't get her miserly ways from her parents. *They* were real generous and neighbourly. There never was a finer gentleman than old Doctor Lloyd. He was always doing kindnesses to everybody; and he had a way of doing them that made you feel as if you was doing the favour, not him. Well, well, let Old Lady Lloyd keep herself and her money to herself if she wants to. If she doesn't want our company, she doesn't have to suffer it, that's all. Reckon she isn't none too happy for all her money and pride."

No, the Old Lady was none too happy, that was unfortunately true. It is not easy to be happy when your life is eaten up with loneliness and emptiness on the spiritual side, and when, on the material side, all you have between you and starvation is the little money your hens bring you in.

The Old Lady lived "away back at the old Lloyd place," as it was always called. It was a quaint, low-eaved house, with big chimneys and square windows and with spruces growing thickly all around it. The Old Lady lived there all alone and there were weeks at a time when she never saw a human being except Crooked Jack. What the Old Lady did with herself and how she put in her time was a puzzle the Spencervale people could not solve. The children believed she amused herself counting the gold in the big black box under her bed. Spencervale children held the Old Lady in mortal terror; some of them—the "Spencer Road" fry—believed she was a witch; all of them would run if, when wandering about the woods in search of berries or spruce gum, they saw at a distance the spare, upright form of the Old Lady, gathering sticks for her fire. Mary Moore was the only one who was quite sure she was not a witch.

"Witches are always ugly," she said decisively, "and Old Lady Lloyd isn't ugly. She's real pretty—she's got such soft white hair and big black eyes and a little white face. Those Road children don't know what they're talking of. Mother says they're a very ignorant crowd."

"Well, she doesn't ever go to church, and she mutters and talks to herself all the time she's picking up sticks," maintained Jimmy Kimball stoutly.

The Old Lady talked to herself because she was really very fond of company and conversation. To be sure, when you have talked to nobody but yourself for nearly twenty years it is apt to grow somewhat monotonous; and there were times when the Old Lady would have sacrificed everything but her pride for a little human companionship. At such times she felt very bitter and resentful towards Fate for having taken everything from her. She had nothing to love, and that is about as unwholesome a condition as is possible to anyone.

It was always hardest in the spring. Once upon a time the Old Lady—when she had not been the Old Lady, but pretty, wilful, high-spirited Margaret Lloyd—had loved springs; now she hated them because they hurt her; and this particular spring of this particular May chapter hurt her more than any that had gone before. The Old Lady felt as if she could *not* endure the ache of it. Everything hurt her—the new green tips on the firs, the fairy mists down in the little beech hollow below the house, the fresh smell of the red earth Crooked Jack spaded up in her garden. The Old Lady lay awake all one moonlit night and cried for very heartache. She even forgot her body hunger in her soul hunger; and the Old Lady had been hungry, more or less, all that week. She was living on store biscuits and water, so that she might be able to pay Crooked Jack for digging her garden. When the pale, lovely dawn-colour came stealing up the sky behind the spruces the Old Lady buried her face in her pillow and refused to look at it.

"I hate the new day," she said rebelliously. "It will be just like all the other hard, common days. I don't want to get up and live it. And oh, to think that long ago I reached out my hands joyfully to every new day, as to a friend who was bringing me good tidings! I loved the mornings then—sunny or gray, they were as delightful as an unread book—and now I hate them—hate them—hate them!"

But the Old Lady got up nevertheless, for she knew Crooked Jack would be coming early to finish the garden. She arranged her beautiful, thick, white hair very carefully, and put on her purple silk dress with the little gold spots in it. The Old Lady always wore silk from motives of economy. It was much cheaper to wear a silk dress that had belonged to her mother than to buy new print at the store. The Old Lady had plenty of silk dresses which had belonged to her mother. She wore them morning, noon, and night, and Spencervale people considered it an additional evidence of her pride. As for the fashion of them, it was, of course, just because she was too mean to have them made over. They did not dream that the Old Lady never

put on one of the silk dresses without agonizing over its un-
fashionableness, and that even the eyes of Crooked Jack cast
on her antique flounces and overskirts were almost more than
her feminine vanity could endure.

In spite of the fact that the Old Lady had not welcomed the
new day, its beauty charmed her when she went out for a walk
after her dinner—or, rather, after her mid-day biscuit. It was
so fresh, so sweet, so virgin; and the spruce woods around the
old Lloyd place were athrill with busy spring doings and all
sprinkled through with young lights and shadows. Some of their
delight found its way into the Old Lady's bitter heart as she
wandered through them, and when she came out at the little
plank bridge over the brook down under the beeches she felt
almost gentle and tender once more. There was one big beech
there, in particular, which the Old Lady loved for reasons best
known to herself—a great, tall beech with a trunk like the shaft
of a gray marble column and a leafy spread of branches over
the still, golden-brown pool made beneath it by the brook. It
had been a young sapling in the days that were haloed by the
vanished glory of the Old Lady's life.

The Old Lady heard childish voices and laughter afar up the
lane which led to William Spencer's place just above the woods.
William Spencer's front lane ran out to the main road in a
different direction, but this "back lane" furnished a short cut
and his children always went to school that way.

The Old Lady shrank hastily back behind a clump of young
spruces. She did not like the Spencer children because they
always seemed so afraid of her. Through the spruce screen she
could see them coming gaily down the lane—the two older
ones in front, the twins behind, clinging to the hands of a tall,
slim, young girl—the new music teacher probably. The Old
Lady had heard from the egg pedlar that she was going to
board at William Spencer's, but she had not heard her name.

She looked at her with some curiosity as they drew near—
and then all at once the Old Lady's heart gave a great bound
and began to beat as it had not beaten for years, while her
breath came quickly and she trembled violently. Who—*who*
could this girl be?

Under the new music teacher's straw hat were masses of fine
chestnut hair of the very shade and wave that the Old Lady

remembered on another head in vanished years; from under those waves looked large, violet-blue eyes with very black lashes and brows—and the Old Lady knew those eyes as well as she knew her own; and the new music teacher's face, with all its beauty of delicate outline and dainty colouring and glad, buoyant youth, was a face from the Old Lady's past—a perfect resemblance in every respect save one; the face which the Old Lady remembered had been weak, with all its charm; but this girl's face possessed a fine, dominant strength compact of sweetness and womanliness. As she passed by the Old Lady's hiding place she laughed at something one of the children said; and oh, but the Old Lady knew that laughter well. She had heard it before under that very beech tree.

She watched them until they disappeared over the wooded hill beyond the bridge; and then she went back home as if she walked in a dream. Crooked Jack was delving vigorously in the garden; ordinarily the Old Lady did not talk much with Crooked Jack, for she disliked his weakness for gossip; but now she went into the garden, a stately old figure in her purple, gold-spotted silk, with the sunshine gleaming on her white hair.

Crooked Jack had seen her go out and had remarked to himself that the Old Lady was losing ground; she was pale and peaked-looking. He now concluded that he had been mistaken. The Old Lady's cheeks were pink and her eyes shining. Somewhere in her walk she had shed ten years at least. Crooked Jack leaned on his spade and decided that there weren't many finer looking women anywhere than Old Lady Lloyd. Pity she was such an old miser!

"Mr. Spencer," said the Old Lady graciously—she always spoke very graciously to her inferiors when she talked to them at all—"can you tell me the name of the new music teacher who is boarding at Mr. William Spencer's?"

"Sylvia Gray," said Crooked Jack.

The Old Lady's heart gave another great bound. But she had known it—she had known that girl with Leslie Gray's hair and eyes and laugh must be Leslie Gray's daughter.

Crooked Jack spat on his hand and resumed his work but his tongue went faster than his spade, and the Old Lady listened greedily. For the first time she enjoyed and blessed Crooked Jack's garrulity and gossip. Every word he uttered was as an apple of gold in a picture of silver to her.

He had been working at William Spencer's the day the new music teacher had come, and what Crooked Jack couldn't find out about any person in one whole day—at least as far as outward life went—was hardly worth finding out. Next to discovering things did he love telling them, and it would be hard to say which enjoyed that ensuing half-hour more—Crooked Jack or the Old Lady.

Crooked Jack's account, boiled down, amounted to this; both Miss Gray's parents had died when she was a baby; she had been brought up by an aunt; she was very poor and very ambitious.

"Wants a moosical eddication," finished up Crooked Jack, "and, by jingo, she orter have it, for anything like the voice of her I never heerd. She sung for us that evening after supper and I thought 'twas an angel singing. It just went through me like a shaft o' light. The Spencer young ones are crazy over her already. She's got twenty pupils around here and in Grafton and Avonlea."

When the Old Lady had found out everything Crooked Jack could tell her, she went into the house and sat down by the window of her little sitting-room to think it all over. She was tingling from head to foot with excitement.

Leslie's daughter! This Old Lady had had her romance once. Long ago—forty years ago—she had been engaged to Leslie Gray, a young college student who taught in Spencervale for the summer term one year—the golden summer of Margaret Lloyd's life. Leslie had been a shy, dreamy, handsome fellow with literary ambitions, which, as he and Margaret both firmly believed, would one day bring him fame and fortune.

Then there had been a foolish, bitter quarrel at the end of that golden summer. Leslie had gone away in anger; afterwards he had written; but Margaret Lloyd, still in the grasp of her pride and resentment, had sent a harsh answer. No more letters came; Leslie Gray never returned; and one day Margaret wakened to the realization that she had put love out of her life forever. She knew it would never be hers again; and from that moment her feet were turned from youth to walk down the valley of shadow to a lonely, eccentric age.

Many years later she heard of Leslie's marriage; then came

news of his death, after a life that had not fulfilled his dreams for him. Nothing more she had heard or known—nothing to this day, when she had seen his daughter pass her by unseeing in the beech hollow.

"His daughter! And she might have been *my* daughter," murmured the Old Lady. "Oh, if I could only know her and love her—and perhaps win her love in return! But I cannot. I could not have Leslie Gray's daughter know how poor I am— how low I have been brought. I could not bear that. And to think she is living so near me, the darling—just up the lane and over the hill. I can see her go by every day—I can have that dear pleasure, at least. But oh, if I could only do something for her—give her some little pleasure! It would be such a delight."

When the Old Lady happened to go into her spare room that evening she saw from it a light shining through a gap in the trees on the hill. She knew that it shone from the Spencer's spare room. So it was Sylvia's light. The Old Lady stood in the darkness and watched it until it went out—watched it with a great sweetness breathing in her heart, such as rises from old rose-leaves when they are stirred. She fancied Sylvia moving about her room, brushing and braiding her long, glistening hair—laying aside her little trinkets and girlish adornments— making her simple preparations for sleep. When the light went out the Old Lady pictured a slight white figure kneeling by the window in the soft starshine; and the Old Lady knelt down then and there and said her own prayers in fellowship. She said the simple form of words she had always used; but a new spirit seemed to inspire them; and she finished with a new petition—"Let me think of something I can do for her, dear Father—some little, little thing that I can do for her."

The Old Lady had slept in the same room all her life—the one looking north into the spruces—and loved it; but the next day she moved into the spare room without a regret. It was to be her room after this; she must be where she could see Sylvia's light; she put the bed where she could lie in it and look at the earth star which had suddenly shone across the twilight shadows of her heart. She felt very happy; she had not felt happy for many years; but now a strange, new, dream-like interest, remote from the harsh realities of her existence, but none the less comforting and alluring, had entered into her life. Besides, she had thought of something she could do for Sylvia—"a little, little thing" that might give her pleasure.

Spencervale people were wont to say regretfully that there were no Mayflowers in Spencervale; the Spencervale young fry, when they wanted Mayflowers, thought they had to go over to the barrens at Avonlea, six miles away, for them. Old Lady Lloyd knew better. In her many long, solitary rambles she had discovered a little clearing far back in the woods—a southward-sloping, sandy hill on a tract of woodland belonging to a man who lived in town—which in spring was starred over with the pink and white of arbutus.

To this clearing the Old Lady betook herself that afternoon, walking through wood lanes and under dim spruce arches like a woman with a glad purpose. All at once the spring was dear and beautiful to her once more; for love had entered again into her heart, and her starved soul was feasting on its divine nourishment.

Old Lady Lloyd found a wealth of Mayflowers on the sandy hill. She filled her basket with them, gloating over the loveliness which was to give pleasure to Sylvia. When she got home she wrote on a slip of paper, "For Sylvia." It was not likely anyone in Spencervale would know her handwriting, but, to make sure, she disguised it, writing in round, big letters like a child's. She carried her Mayflowers down to the hollow and heaped them in a recess between the big roots of the old beech, with the little note thrust through a stem on top.

Then the Old Lady deliberately hid behind the spruce clump. She had put on her dark green silk on purpose for hiding. She had not long to wait. Soon Sylvia Gray came down the hill with Mattie Spencer. When she reached the bridge she saw the Mayflowers and gave an exclamation of delight. Then she saw her name and her expression changed to wonder. The Old Lady, peering through the boughs, could have laughed for very pleasure over the success of her little plot.

"For me!" said Sylvia, lifting the flowers. "*Can* they really be for me, Mattie? Who could have left them here?"

Mattie giggled.

"I believe it was Chris Stewart," she said. "I know he was over at Avonlea last night. And ma says he's taken a notion to you—she knows by the way he looked at you when you were singing night before last. It would be just like him to do something queer like this—he's such a shy fellow with the girls."

Sylvia frowned a little. She did not like Mattie's expressions; but she did like Mayflowers, and she did not dislike Chris Stewart, who had seemed to her merely a nice, modest, country boy. She lifted the flowers and buried her face in them.

"Anyway, I'm much obliged to the giver, whoever he or she is," she said merrily. "There's nothing I love like Mayflowers. Oh, how sweet they are!"

When they had passed the Old Lady emerged from her lurking place, flushed with triumph. It did not vex her that Sylvia should think Chris Stewart had given her the flowers; nay, it was all the better, since she would be the less likely to suspect the real donor. The main thing was that Sylvia should have the delight of them. That quite satisfied the Old Lady, who went back to her lonely house with the cockles of her heart all in a glow.

It soon was a matter of gossip in Spencervale that Chris Stewart was leaving Mayflowers at the beech hollow for the music teacher every other day. Chris himself denied it, but he was not believed. Firstly, there were no Mayflowers in Spencervale; secondly, Chris had to go to Carmody every other day to haul milk to the butter factory and Mayflowers grew in Carmody; and, thirdly, the Stewarts always had a romantic streak in them. Was not that enough circumstantial evidence for anybody?

As for Sylvia, she did not mind if Chris had a boyish admiration for her and expressed it thus delicately. She thought it very nice of him, indeed, when he did not vex her with any other advances, and she was quite content to enjoy his May-flowers.

Old Lady Lloyd heard all the gossip about it from the egg pedlar, and listened to him with laughter glimmering far down in her eyes. The egg pedlar went away and vowed he'd never seen the Old Lady so spry as she was this spring; she seemed real interested in the young folk's doings.

The Old Lady kept her secret and grew young in it. She walked back to the Mayflower hill as long as the Mayflowers lasted; and she always hid in the spruces to see Sylvia Gray go by. Every day she loved her more, and yearned after her more deeply. All the long repressed tenderness of her nature overflowed to this girl who was unconscious of it. She was proud of Sylvia's grace and beauty, and sweetness of voice and laughter. She began to like the Spencer children because they worshipped Sylvia; she envied Mrs. Spencer because the latter could minister to Sylvia's needs. Even the egg pedlar seemed a delightful person because he brought news of Sylvia—her social popularity, her professional success, the love and admiration she had won already.

The Old Lady never dreamed of revealing herself to Sylvia. That, in her poverty, was not to be thought of for a moment. It would have been very sweet to know her—sweet to have her come to the old house—sweet to talk to her—to enter into her life. But it might not be. The Old Lady's pride was still far stronger than her love. It was the one thing she had never sacrificed and never—so she believed—could sacrifice.

--------------------- *II. The June Chapter* ---------------------

There were no Mayflowers in June; but now the Old Lady's garden was full of blossoms and every morning Sylvia found a bouquet of them by the beech—the perfumed ivory of white narcissus, the flame of tulips, the fairy branches of bleeding-heart, the pink-and-snow of little, thorny, single, sweet-breathed early roses. The Old Lady had no fear of discovery, for the flowers that grew in her garden grew in every other Spencervale garden as well, including the Stewart garden. Chris Stewart, when he was teased about the music teacher, merely smiled and held his peace. Chris knew perfectly well who was the real giver of those flowers. He had made it his business to find out when the Mayflower gossip started. But since it was evident Old Lady Lloyd did not wish it to be known Chris told no one. Chris had always liked Old Lady Lloyd ever since the day, ten years before, when she had found him crying in the woods with a cut foot and had taken him into her house, and bathed and bound the wound, and given him ten cents to buy candy at the store. The Old Lady went without her supper that night because of it, but Chris never knew that.

The Old Lady thought it a most beautiful June. She no longer hated the new days; on the contrary she welcomed them.

"Every day is an uncommon day now," she said jubilantly to herself—for did not almost every day bring her a glimpse of Sylvia? Even on rainy days the Old Lady gallantly braved rheumatism to hide behind her clump of dripping spruces and watch Sylvia pass. The only days she could not see her were Sundays; and no Sundays had ever seemed so long to Old Lady Lloyd as those June Sundays did.

One day the egg pedlar had news for her.

"The music teacher is going to sing a solo for a collection piece tomorrow," he told her.

The Old Lady's black eyes flashed with interest.

"I didn't know Miss Gray was a member of the choir," she said.

"Jined two Sundays ago. I tell you our music is something worth listening to now. The church'll be packed tomorrow, I reckon—her name's gone all over the country for singing. You ought to come and hear it, Miss Lloyd."

The pedlar said this out of bravado, merely to show he wasn't scared of the Old Lady, for all her grand airs. The Old Lady made no answer, and he thought he had offended her. He went away, wishing he hadn't said it. Had he but known it, the Old Lady had forgotten the existence of all and any egg pedlars. He had blotted himself and his insignificance out of her consciousness by his last sentence. All her thoughts, feelings, and wishes were submerged in a very whirlpool of desire to hear Sylvia sing that solo. She went into the house in a tumult and tried to conquer that desire. She could not do it, even though she summoned all her pride to her aid. Pride said:

"You will have to go to church to hear her. You haven't fit clothes to go to church in. Think what a figure you will make before them all."

But, for the first time, a more insistent voice than pride spoke to her soul—and, for the first time, the Old Lady listened to it. It was too true that she had never gone to church since the day on which she had to begin wearing her mother's silk dresses. The Old Lady herself thought that this was very wicked;

and she tried to atone by keeping Sunday very strictly, and always having a little service of her own, morning and evening. She sang three hymns in her cracked voice, prayed aloud, and read a sermon. But she could not bring herself to go to church in her out-of-date clothes—she, who had once set the fashions in Spencervale; and the longer she stayed away the more impossible it seemed that she should ever again go. Now the impossible had become, not only possible, but insistent. She must go to church and hear Sylvia sing, no matter how ridiculous she appeared, no matter how people talked and laughed at her.

Spencervale congregation had a mild sensation the next afternoon. Just before the opening of service Old Lady Lloyd walked up the aisle and sat down in the long-unoccupied Lloyd pew, in front of the pulpit.

The Old Lady's very soul was writhing within her. She recalled the reflection she had seen in her mirror before she left—the old black silk in the mode of thirty years agone and the queer little bonnet of shirred black satin. She thought how absurd she must look in the eyes of her world.

As a matter of fact, she did not look in the least absurd. Some women might have; but the Old Lady's stately distinction of carriage and figure was so subtly commanding that it did away with the consideration of garmenting altogether.

The Old Lady did not know this. But she did know that Mrs. Kimball, the storekeeper's wife, presently rustled into the next pew in the very latest fashion of fabric and mode; she and Mrs. Kimball were the same age, and there had been a time when the latter had been content to imitate Margaret Lloyd's costumes at a humble distance. But the storekeeper had proposed, and things were changed now; and there sat poor Old Lady Lloyd, feeling the change bitterly, and half wishing she had not come to church at all.

Then all at once the Angel of Love touched these foolish thoughts, born of vanity and morbid pride, and they melted away as if they had never been. Sylvia Gray had come into the choir, and was sitting just where the afternoon sunshine fell over her beautiful hair like a halo. The Old Lady looked at her in a rapture of satisfied longing and thenceforth the service was blessed to her, as anything is blessed which comes through the medium of unselfish love, whether human or divine. Nay, are they not one and the same, differing in degree only, not in kind?

The Old Lady had never had such a good, satisfying look at Sylvia before. All her former glimpses had been stolen and fleeting. Now she sat and gazed upon her to her hungry heart's content, lingering delightedly over every little charm and loveliness—the way Sylvia's shining hair rippled back from her forehead, the sweet little trick she had of dropping quickly her long-lashed eyelids when she encountered too bold or curious a glance, and the slender, beautifully modelled hands—so like Leslie Gray's hands—that held her hymn book. She was dressed very plainly in a black skirt and a white shirtwaist; but none of the other girls in the choir, with all their fine feathers, could hold a candle to her—as the egg pedlar said to his wife going home from church.

The Old Lady listened to the opening hymns with keen pleasure. Sylvia's voice thrilled through and dominated them all. But when the ushers got up to take the collection an undercurrent of subdued excitement flowed over the congregation. Sylvia rose and came forward to Janet Moore's side at the organ. The next moment her beautiful voice soared through the building like the very soul of melody—true, clear, powerful, sweet. Nobody in Spencervale had ever listened to such a voice, except Old Lady Lloyd herself, who in her youth had heard enough good singing to enable her to be a tolerable judge of it. She realized instantly that this girl of her heart had a great gift—a gift that would some day bring her fame and fortune if it could be duly trained and developed.

"Oh, I'm so glad I came to church," thought Old Lady Lloyd.

When the solo was ended the Old Lady's conscience compelled her to drag her eyes and thoughts from Sylvia, and fasten them on the minister, who had been flattering himself all through the opening portion of the service that Old Lady Lloyd had come to church on his account. He was newly settled, having been in charge of Spencervale congregation only a few months; he was a clever little fellow and he honestly thought it was the fame of his preaching that had brought Old Lady Lloyd out to church.

When the service was over all the Old Lady's neighbours

came to speak to her, with kindly smile and handshake. They thought they ought to encourage her, now that she had made a start in the right direction; the Old Lady liked their cordiality, and liked it none the less because she detected in it the same unconscious respect and deference she had been wont to receive in the old days—a respect and deference which her personality compelled from all who approached her. The Old Lady was surprised to find that she could command it still, in defiance of unfashionable bonnet and ancient attire.

Janet Moore and Sylvia Gray walked home from church together.

"Did you see Old Lady Lloyd out today?" asked Janet. "I was amazed when she walked in. She has never been to church in my recollection. What a quaint old figure she is! She's very rich, you know, but she wears her mother's old clothes and never gets a new thing. Some people think she is mean; but," concluded Janet charitably, "I believe it is simply eccentricity."

"I felt that was Miss Lloyd as soon as I saw her, although I had never seen her before," said Sylvia dreamily. "I have been wishing to see her—for a certain reason. She has a very striking face. I should like to meet her—to know her."

"I don't think it's likely you ever will," said Janet carelessly. "She doesn't like young people and she never goes anywhere. I don't think I'd like to know her. I'd be afraid of her—she has such stately ways and such strange, piercing eyes."

"*I* shouldn't be afraid of her," said Sylvia to herself, as she turned into the Spencer lane. "But I don't expect I'll ever become acquainted with her. If she knew who I am I suppose she would dislike me. I suppose she never suspects that I am Leslie Gray's daughter."

The minister, thinking it well to strike while the iron was hot, went up to call on Old Lady Lloyd the very next afternoon. He went in fear and trembling, for he had heard things about Old Lady Lloyd; but she made herself so agreeable in her high-bred fashion that he was delighted and told his wife when he went home that Spencervale people didn't understand Miss Lloyd. This was perfectly true; but it is by no means certain that the minister understood her either.

He made only one mistake in tact, but, as the Old Lady did not snub him for it, he never knew he made it. When he was leaving he said, "I hope we shall see you at church next Sunday, Miss Lloyd."

"Indeed, you will," said the Old Lady emphatically.

―――――――――― III. The July Chapter ――――――――――

The first day of July Sylvia found a little birch bark boat full of strawberries at the beech in the hollow. They were the earliest of the season; the Old Lady had found them in one of her secret haunts. They would have been a toothsome addition to the Old Lady's own slender bill of fare; but she never thought of eating them. She got far more pleasure out of the thought of Sylvia's enjoying them for her tea. Thereafter the strawberries alternated with the flowers as long as they lasted, and then came blueberries and raspberries. The blueberries grew far away and the Old Lady had many a tramp after them. Sometimes her bones ached at night because of it; but what cared the Old Lady for that? Bone ache is easier to endure than soul ache; and the Old Lady's soul had stopped aching for the first time in many a year. It was being nourished with heavenly manna.

One evening Crooked Jack came up to fix something that had gone wrong with the Old Lady's well. The Old Lady wandered affably out to him; for she knew he had been working at the Spencers' all day, and there might be crumbs of information about Sylvia to be picked up.

"I reckon the music teacher's feeling pretty blue this evening," Crooked Jack remarked, after straining the Old Lady's patience to the last verge of human endurance by expatiating on William Spencer's new pump, and Mrs. Spencer's new washing-machine, and Amelia Spencer's new young man.

"Why?" asked the Old Lady, turning very pale. Had anything happened to Sylvia?

"Well, she's been invited to a big party at Mrs. Moore's brother's in town, and she hasn't got a dress to go in," said Crooked Jack. "They're great swells and everybody will be got up regardless. Mrs. Spencer was telling me about it. She says Miss Gray can't afford a new dress because she's helping to pay her aunt's doctor bills. She says she's sure Miss Gray feels awful disappointed over it, though she doesn't let on. But Mrs. Spencer says she knows she was crying after she went to bed last night."

The Old Lady turned and went into the house abruptly. This was dreadful. Sylvia must go to that party—she *must*. But how was it to be managed? Through the Old Lady's brain passed wild thoughts of her mother's silk dresses. But none of them would be suitable, even if there were time to make one over. Never had the Old Lady so bitterly regretted her vanished wealth.

"I've only two dollars in the house," she said, "and I've got to live on that till the next day the egg pedlar comes round. Is there anything I can sell—*anything?* Yes, yes, the grape jug!"

Up to this time the Old Lady would as soon have thought of trying to sell her head as the grape jug. The grape jug was two hundred years old and had been in the Lloyd family ever since it was a jug at all. It was a big, pot-bellied affair, festooned with pink-gilt grapes, and with a verse of poetry printed on one side, and it had been given as a wedding present to the Old Lady's great-grandmother. As long as the Old Lady could remember it had sat on the top shelf in the cupboard in the sitting-room wall, far too precious ever to be used.

Two years before, a woman who collected old china had explored Spencervale, and, getting word of the grape jug, had boldly invaded the old Lloyd place and offered to buy it. She never, to her dying day, forgot the reception the Old Lady gave her; but, being wise in her day and generation, she left her card, saying that if Miss Lloyd ever changed her mind about selling the jug she would find that she, the aforesaid collector, had not changed hers about buying it. People who make a hobby of heirloom china must meekly overlook snubs, and this particular person had never seen anything she coveted so much as that grape jug.

The Old Lady had torn the card to pieces; but she remembered the name and address. She went to the cupboard and took down the beloved jug.

"I never thought to part with it," she said wistfully, "but Sylvia must have a dress, and there is no other way. And, after all, when I'm gone, who would there be to have it? Strangers would get it then—it might as well go to them now. I'll have to go to town tomorrow morning, for there's no time to lose if the party is Friday night. I haven't been to town for ten years. I dread the thought of going, more than parting with the jug. But for Sylvia's sake!"

It was all over Spencervale by the next morning that Old Lady Lloyd had gone to town, carrying a carefully guarded box. Everybody wondered why she went; most people supposed she had become too frightened to keep her money in a black box below her bed, when there had been two burglaries over at Carmody, and had taken it to the bank.

The Old Lady sought out the address of the china collector, trembling with fear that she might be dead or gone. But the collector was there, very much alive, and as keenly anxious to possess the grape jug as ever. The Old Lady, pallid with the pain of her trampled pride, sold the grape jug and went away, believing that her great-grandmother must have turned over in her grave at the moment of the transaction. Old Lady Lloyd felt like a traitor to her traditions.

But she went unflinchingly to a big store and, guided by that special Providence which looks after simple-minded old souls in their dangerous excursions into the world, found a sympathetic clerk who knew just what she wanted and got it for her. The Old Lady selected a very dainty muslin gown, with gloves and slippers in keeping; and she ordered it sent at once, expressage prepaid, to Miss Sylvia Gray, in care of William Spencer, Spencervale.

Then she paid down the money—the whole price of the jug, minus a dollar and a half for railroad fare—with a grand, careless air and departed. As she marched erectly down the aisle of the store, she encountered a sleek, portly, prosperous man coming in. As their eyes met the man started and his bland face flushed crimson; he lifted his hat and bowed confusedly. But the Old Lady looked through him as if he wasn't there, and passed on with not a sign of recognition about her. He took one step after her, then stopped and turned away, with a rather disagreeable smile and a shrug of his shoulders.

Nobody would have guessed, as the Old Lady swept out, how her heart was seething with abhorrence and scorn. She would not have had the courage to come to town, even for Sylvia's sake, if she had thought she would meet Andrew

Cameron. The mere sight of him opened up anew a sealed
fountain of bitterness in her soul; but the thought of Sylvia
somehow stemmed the torrent, and presently the Old Lady was
smiling rather triumphantly, thinking rightly that she had come
off best in that unwelcome encounter. *She,* at any rate, had
not faltered and coloured, and lost her presence of mind.

"It is little wonder *he* did," thought the Old Lady vindictively.
It pleased her that Andrew Cameron should lose, before her,
the front of adamant he presented to the world. He was her
cousin and the only living creature Old Lady Lloyd hated; and
she hated and despised him with all the intensity of her intense
nature. She and hers had sustained grievous wrong at his hands,
and the Old Lady was convinced that she would rather die
than take any notice of his existence.

Presently, she resolutely put Andrew Cameron out of her
mind. It was desecration to think of him and Sylvia together.
When she laid her weary head on her pillow that night she
was so happy that even the thought of the vacant shelf in the
room below, where the grape jug had always been, gave her
only a momentary pang.

"It's sweet to sacrifice for one we love—it's sweet to have
someone to sacrifice for," thought the Old Lady.

Desire grows by what it feeds on. The Old Lady thought she
was content; but Friday evening came and found her in a
perfect fever to see Sylvia in her party dress. It was not enough
to fancy her in it; nothing would do the Old Lady but seeing
her.

"And I *shall* see her," said the Old Lady resolutely, looking
out from her window at Sylvia's light gleaming through the
firs. She wrapped herself in a dark shawl and crept out, slipping
down to the hollow and up the wood lane. It was a misty,
moonlight night, and a wind, fragrant with the aroma of clover
fields, blew down the lane to meet her.

"I wish I could take your perfume—the soul of you—and
pour it into her life," said the Old Lady aloud to that wind.

Sylvia Gray was standing in her room, ready for the party.
Before her stood Mrs. Spencer and Amelia Spencer and all the
little Spencer girls, in an admiring semi-circle. There was another
spectator. Outside, under the lilac bush, Old Lady Lloyd was
standing. She could see Sylvia plainly, in her dainty dress, with

the pale pink roses Old Lady Lloyd had left at the beech that day for her in her hair. Pink as they were, they were not so pink as her cheeks, and her eyes shone like stars. Amelia Spencer put up her hand to push back a rose that had fallen a little out of place, and the Old Lady envied her fiercely.

"That dress couldn't have fitted better if it had been made for you," said Mrs. Spencer admiringly. "Ain't she lovely, Amelia? Who *could* have sent it?"

"Oh, I feel sure that Mrs. Moore was the fairy godmother," said Sylvia. "There is nobody else who would. It was dear of her—she knew I wished so much to go to the party with Janet. I wish Aunty could see me now." Sylvia gave a little sigh in spite of her joy. "There's nobody else to care very much."

Ah, Sylvia, you were wrong! There was somebody else— somebody who cared very much—an Old Lady, with eager, devouring eyes, who was standing under the lilac bush and who presently stole away through the moonlit orchard to the woods like a shadow, going home with a vision of you in your girlish beauty to companion her through the watches of that summer night.

--------------------- *IV. The August Chapter* ---------------------

One day the minister's wife rushed in where Spencervale people had feared to tread, went boldly to Old Lady Lloyd, and asked her if she wouldn't come to their Sewing Circle, which met fortnightly on Saturday afternoons.

"We are filling a box to send to our Trinidad missionary," said the minister's wife, "and we should be so pleased to have you come, Miss Lloyd."

The Old Lady was on the point of refusing rather haughtily. Not that she was opposed to missions—or sewing circles either— quite the contrary; but she knew that each member of the Circle was expected to pay ten cents a week for the purpose of procuring sewing materials; and the poor Old Lady really did not see how she could afford it. But a sudden thought checked her refusal before it reached her lips.

"I suppose some of the young girls go to the Circle?" she said craftily.

"Oh, they all go," said the minister's wife. "Janet Moore and Miss Gray are our most enthusiastic members. It is very lovely of Miss Gray to give her Saturday afternoons—the only ones she has free from pupils—to our work. But she really has the sweetest disposition."

"I'll join your Circle," said the Old Lady promptly. She was determined she would do it, if she had to live on two meals a day to save the necessary fee.

She went to the Sewing Circle at James Martin's the next Saturday, and did the most beautiful hand sewing for them. She was so expert at it that she didn't need to think about it at all, which was rather fortunate, for all her thoughts were taken up with Sylvia, who sat in the opposite corner with Janet Moore, her graceful hands busy with a little boy's coarse gingham shirt. Nobody thought of introducing Sylvia to Old Lady Lloyd, and the Old Lady was glad of it. She sewed finely away, and listened with all her ears to the girlish chatter which went on in the opposite corner. One thing she found out—Sylvia's birthday was the twentieth of August. And the Old Lady was straightaway fired with a consuming wish to give Sylvia a birthday present. She lay awake most of the night wondering if she could do it, and most sorrowfully concluded that it was utterly out of the question, no matter how she might pinch and contrive. Old Lady Lloyd worried quite absurdly over this, and it haunted her like a spectre until the next Sewing Circle day.

It met at Mrs. Moore's, and Mrs. Moore was especially gracious to Old Lady Lloyd, and insisted on her taking the wicker rocker in the parlour. The Old Lady would rather have been in the sitting-room with the young girls, but she submitted for courtesy's sake—and she had her reward. Her chair was just behind the parlour door, and presently Janet Moore and Sylvia Gray came and sat on the stairs in the hall outside, where a cool breeze blew in through the maples before the front door.

They were talking of their favourite poets. Janet, it appeared, adored Byron and Scott. Sylvia leaned to Tennyson and Browning.

"Do you know," said Sylvia softly, "my father was a poet? He published a little volume of verse once; and, Janet, I've never seen a copy of it, and oh, how I would love to! It was published when he was at college—just a small, private edition to give his friends. He never published any more—poor father! I think life disappointed him. But I have such a longing to see that little book of his verse. I haven't a scrap of his writings. If I had it would seem as if I possessed something of him— of his heart, his soul, his inner life. He would be something more than a mere name to me."

"Didn't he have a copy of his own—didn't your mother have one?" asked Janet.

"Mother hadn't. She died when I was born, you know, but Aunty says there was no copy of father's poems among mother's books. Mother didn't care for poetry, Aunty says—Aunty doesn't either. Father went to Europe after mother died, and he died there the next year. Nothing that he had with him was ever sent home to us. He had sold most of his books before he went, but he gave a few of his favourite ones to Aunty to keep for me. *His* book wasn't among them. I don't suppose I shall ever find a copy; but I should be so delighted if I only could."

When the Old Lady got home she took from her top bureau drawer an inlaid box of sandalwood. It held a little, slim, limp volume, wrapped in tissue paper—the Old Lady's most treasured possession. On the fly-leaf was written, "To Margaret, with the author's love."

The Old Lady turned the yellowed leaves with trembling fingers and, through eyes brimming with tears, read the verses, although she had known them all by heart for years. She meant to give the book to Sylvia for a birthday present—one of the most precious gifts ever given, if the value of gifts is gauged by the measure of self-sacrifice involved. In that little book was immortal love—old laughter—old tears—old beauty which had bloomed like a rose years ago, holding still its sweetness like old rose leaves.

She removed the telltale fly-leaf; and late on the night before Sylvia's birthday the Old Lady crept, under cover of the darkness, through by-ways and across fields, as if bent on some nefarious expedition, to the little Spencervale store where the post-office was kept. She slipped the thin parcel through the slit in the door, and then stole home again, feeling a strange sense of loss and loneliness. It was as if she had given away the last link between herself and her youth. But she did not regret it. It would give Sylvia pleasure, and that had come to be the overmastering passion of the Old Lady's heart.

The next night the light in Sylvia's room burned very late and the Old Lady watched it triumphantly, knowing the meaning of it. Sylvia was reading her father's poems and the Old Lady in her darkness read them too, murmuring the lines over and over to herself. After all, giving away the book had not mattered so very much. She had the soul of it still—and the fly-leaf with the name, in Leslie's writing, by which nobody ever called her now.

The Old Lady was sitting on the Marshall sofa the next Sewing Circle afternoon when Sylvia Gray came and sat down beside her. The Old Lady's hands trembled a little and one side of a handkerchief, which was afterwards given as a Christmas present to a little olive-skinned coolie in Trinidad, was not quite so exquisitely done as the other three sides.

Sylvia at first talked of the Circle, and Mrs. Marshall's dahlias, and the Old Lady was in the seventh heaven of delight, though she took care not to show it, and was even a little more stately and finely mannered than usual. When she asked Sylvia how she liked living in Spencervale, Sylvia said,

"Very much. Everybody is so kind to me. Besides"—Sylvia lowered her voice so that nobody but the Old Lady could hear it—"I have a fairy godmother here who does the most beautiful and wonderful things for me."

Sylvia, being a girl of fine instincts, did not look at Old Lady Lloyd as she said this. But she would not have seen anything if she had looked. The Old Lady was not a Lloyd for nothing.

"How very interesting," she said, indifferently.

"Isn't it? I am so grateful to her and I have wished so much she might know how much pleasure she has given me. I have found lovely flowers and delicious berries on my path all summer; I feel sure she sent me my party dress. But the dearest gift came last week on my birthday—a little volume of my father's poems. I can't express what I felt on receiving them. But I longed to meet my fairy godmother and thank her."

"Quite a fascinating mystery, isn't it? Have you really no idea who she is?"

The Old Lady asked this dangerous question with marked

success. She would not have been so successful if she had not been so sure that Sylvia had no idea of the old romance between her and Leslie Gray. As it was, she had a comfortable conviction that she herself was the very last person Sylvia would be likely to suspect.

Sylvia hesitated for an almost unnoticeable moment. Then she said, "I haven't tried to find out, because I don't think she wants me to know. At first, of course, in the matter of the flowers and dress, I did try to solve the mystery; but, since I received the book, I became convinced that it was my fairy godmother who was doing it all, and I have respected her wish for concealment and always shall. Perhaps some day she will reveal herself to me. I hope so, at least."

"I wouldn't hope it," said the Old Lady discouragingly. "Fairy godmothers—at least, in all the fairy tales I ever read—are somewhat apt to be queer, crochety people, much more agreeable when wrapped up in mystery than when met face to face."

"I'm convinced that mine is the very opposite, and that the better I became acquainted with her the more charming a personage I should find her," said Sylvia gaily.

Mrs. Marshall came up at this juncture and entreated Miss Gray to sing for them. Miss Gray consenting sweetly, the Old Lady was left alone and was rather glad of it. She enjoyed her conversation with Sylvia much more in thinking it over after she got home than while it was taking place. When an Old Lady has a guilty conscience it is apt to make her nervous and distract her thoughts from immediate pleasure. She wondered a little uneasily if Sylvia really did suspect her. Then she concluded that it was out of the question. Who would suspect a mean, unsociable Old Lady, who had no friends, and who gave only five cents to the Sewing Circle when everyone else gave ten or fifteen, to be a fairy godmother, the donor of beautiful party dresses, and the recipient of gifts from romantic, aspiring young poets?

─────────── *V. The September Chapter* ───────────

In September the Old Lady looked back on the summer and owned to herself that it had been a strangely happy one, with Sundays and Sewing Circle days standing out like golden punctuation marks in a poem of life. She felt like an utterly different woman; and other people thought her different also. The Sewing Circle women found her so pleasant, and even friendly, that they began to think they had misjudged her, and that perhaps it was eccentricity after all, and not meanness, which accounted for her peculiar mode of living. Sylvia Gray always came and talked to her on Circle afternoons now, and the Old Lady treasured every word she said in her heart and repeated them over and over to her lonely self in the watches of the night.

Sylvia never talked of herself or her plans, unless asked about them; and the Old Lady's self-consciousness prevented her from asking any personal questions; so their conversation kept to the surface of things, and it was not from Sylvia, but from the minister's wife that the Old Lady finally discovered what her darling's dearest ambition was.

The minister's wife had dropped in at the old Lloyd place one evening late in September, when a chilly wind was blowing up from the northeast and moaning about the eaves of the house, as if the burden of its lay were "harvest is ended and summer is gone." The Old Lady had been listening to it, as she plaited a little basket of sweet grass for Sylvia. She had walked all the way to Avonlea sand-hills for it the day before, and she was very tired. And her heart was sad. This summer, which had so enriched her life, was almost over; and she knew that Sylvia Gray talked of leaving Spencervale at the end of October. The Old Lady's heart felt like very lead within her at the thought, and she almost welcomed the advent of the minister's wife as a distraction, although she was desperately afraid that the minister's wife had called to ask for a subscription for the new vestry carpet, and the Old Lady simply could not afford to give one cent.

But the minister's wife had merely dropped in on her way home from the Spencers' and she did not make any embarrassing requests. Instead, she talked about Sylvia Gray, and her words fell on the Old Lady's ears like separate pearl notes of unutterably sweet music. The minister's wife had nothing but praise for Sylvia—she was so sweet and beautiful and winning.

"And with *such* a voice," said the minister's wife enthusiastically, adding with a sigh, "It's such a shame she can't have it properly trained. She would certainly become a great singer—competent critics have told her so. But she is so poor she doesn't think she can ever possibly manage it—unless she can get one of the Cameron scholarships, as they are called; and she has very little hope of that, although the professor of music who taught her has sent her name in."

"What are the Cameron scholarships?" asked the Old Lady.

"Well, I suppose you have heard of Andrew Cameron, the millionaire?" said the minister's wife, serenely unconscious that she was causing the very bones of the Old Lady's family skeleton to jangle in their closet.

Into the Old Lady's white face came a sudden faint stain of colour, as if a rough hand had struck her cheek.

"Yes, I've heard of him," she said.

"Well, it seems that he had a daughter, who was a very beautiful girl, and whom he idolized. She had a fine voice, and he was going to send her abroad to have it trained. And she died. It nearly broke his heart, I understand. But ever since he sends one young girl away to Europe every year for a thorough musical education under the best teachers—in memory of his daughter. He has sent nine or ten already; but I fear there isn't much chance for Sylvia Gray, and she doesn't think there is herself."

"Why not?" asked the Old Lady spiritedly. "I am sure that there can be few voices equal to Miss Gray's."

"Very true. But you see these so-called scholarships are private affairs, dependent solely on the whim and choice of Andrew Cameron himself. Of course, when a girl has friends who use their influence with him he will often send her on their recommendation. They say he sent a girl last year who hadn't much of a voice at all just because her father had been an old business crony of his. But Sylvia doesn't know anyone at all who would, to use a slang term, have any 'pull' with Andrew Cameron, and she is not acquainted with him herself. Well, I must be going; we'll see you at the Manse on Saturday, I hope, Miss Lloyd. The Circle meets there, you know."

"Yes, I know," said the Old Lady absently. When the minister's wife had gone she dropped her sweet-grass basket and sat for a long, long time with her hands lying idly in her lap, and her big black eyes staring unseeingly at the wall before her.

Old Lady Lloyd, so pitifully poor that she had to eat six crackers the less a week to pay her fee to the Sewing Circle, knew that it was in her power—*hers*—to send Leslie Gray's daughter to Europe for her musical education! If she chose to use her "pull" with Andrew Cameron—if she went to him and asked him to send Sylvia Gray abroad the next year—she had no doubt whatever that it would be done. It all lay with her— if—if—*if* she could so far crush and conquer her pride as to stoop to ask a favour of the man who had wronged her and hers so bitterly.

Years ago, her father, acting under the advice and urgency of Andrew Cameron, had invested all his little fortune in an enterprise that had turned out a failure. Abraham Lloyd lost every dollar he possessed and his family were reduced to utter poverty. Andrew Cameron might have been forgiven for a mistake; but there was a strong suspicion, amounting to almost certainty, that he had been guilty of something far worse than a mistake in regard to his uncle's investment. Nothing could be legally proved; but it was certain that Andrew Cameron, already noted for his "sharp practices," emerged with improved finances from an entanglement that had ruined many better men; and old Doctor Lloyd had died broken-hearted, believing that his nephew had deliberately victimized him.

Andrew Cameron had not quite done this; he had meant well enough by his uncle at first, and what he had finally done he tried to justify to himself by the doctrine that a man must look out for Number One.

Margaret Lloyd made no such excuses for him; she held him responsible, not only for her lost fortune, but for her father's death, and never forgave him for it. When Abraham Lloyd had died, Andrew Cameron, perhaps pricked by his conscience, had come to her, sleekly and smoothly, to offer her financial aid. He would see, he told her, that she never suffered want.

Margaret Lloyd flung his offer back in his face after a fashion that left nothing to be desired in the way of plain speaking.

She would die, she told him passionately, before she would accept a penny or a favour from him. He had preserved an unbroken show of good temper, expressed his heartfelt regret that she should cherish such an unjust opinion of him, and had left her with an oily assurance that he would always be her friend, and would always be delighted to render her any assistance in his power whenever she should choose to ask for it.

The Old Lady had lived for twenty years in the firm conviction that she would die in the poorhouse—as, indeed, seemed not unlikely—before she would ask a favour of Andrew Cameron. And so, in truth, she would have, had it been for herself. But for Sylvia! Could she so far humble herself for Sylvia's sake?

The question was not easily or speedily settled, as had been the case in the matters of the grape jug and the book of poems. For a whole week the Old Lady fought her pride and bitterness. Sometimes, in the hours of sleepless night, when all human resentments and rancours seemed petty and contemptible, she thought she had conquered it. But in the daytime, with the picture of her father looking down at her from the wall, and the rustle of her unfashionable dresses, worn because of Andrew Cameron's double dealing, in her ears, it got the better of her again.

But the Old Lady's love for Sylvia had grown so strong and deep and tender that no other feeling could endure finally against it. Love is a great miracle worker; and never had its power been more strongly made manifest than on the cold, dull, autumn morning when the Old Lady walked to Bright River railway station and took the train to Charlottetown, bent on an errand the very thought of which turned her soul sick within her. The station master who sold her her ticket thought Old Lady Lloyd looked uncommonly white and peaked—"as if she hadn't slept a wink or eaten a bite for a week," he told his wife at dinner time. "Guess there's something wrong in her business affairs. This is the second time she's gone to town this summer."

When the Old Lady reached the town she ate her slender little lunch and then walked out to the suburb where the Cameron factories and warehouses were. It was a long walk for her, but she could not afford to drive. She felt very tired when she was shown into the shining, luxurious office where Andrew Cameron sat at his desk.

After the first startled glance of surprise, he came forward beamingly, with outstretched hand.

"Why, Cousin Margaret! This is a pleasant surprise. Sit down—allow me, this is a much more comfortable chair. Did you come in this morning? And how is everybody out in Spencervale?"

The Old Lady had flushed at his first words. To hear the name by which her father and mother and lover had called her on Andrew Cameron's lips seemed like profanation. But, she told herself, the time was past for squeamishness. If she could ask a favour of Andrew Cameron she could bear lesser pangs. For Sylvia's sake she shook hands with him, for Sylvia's sake she sat down in the chair he offered. But for no living human being's sake could this determined Old Lady infuse any cordiality into her manner or her words. She went straight to the point with Lloyd simplicity.

"I have come to ask a favour of you," she said, looking him in the eye, not at all humbly or meekly, as became a suppliant, but challengingly and defiantly, as if she dared him to refuse.

"*De*-lighted to hear it, Cousin Margaret." Never was anything so bland and gracious as his tone. "Anything I can do for you I shall be only too pleased to do. I am afraid you have looked upon me as an enemy, Margaret, and I assure you I have felt your injustice keenly. I realize that some appearances were against me, but—"

The Old Lady lifted her hand and stemmed his eloquence by that one gesture.

"I did not come here to discuss that matter," she said. "We will not refer to the past, if you please. I came to ask a favour, not for myself, but for a very dear young friend of mine—a Miss Gray, who has a remarkably fine voice which she wishes to have trained. She is poor, so I came to ask you if you would give her one of your musical scholarships. I understand her name has already been suggested to you, with a recommendation from her teacher. I do not know what he has said of her voice, but I do know he could hardly overrate it. If you send her abroad for training you will not make any mistake."

The Old Lady stopped talking. She felt sure Andrew Cameron would grant her request; but she did hope he would grant it rather rudely or unwillingly. She could accept the favour so much more easily if it were flung to her like a bone to a dog. But not a bit of it, Andrew Cameron was suaver than ever. Nothing could give him greater pleasure than to grant his dear Cousin Margaret's request—he only wished it involved more trouble on his part. Her little protege should have her musical education assuredly—she should go abroad next year—and he was *de*-lighted—

"Thank you," said the Old Lady, cutting him short again. "I am much obliged to you—and I ask you not to let Miss Gray know anything of my interference. And I shall not take up any more of your valuable time. Good afternoon."

"Oh, you mustn't go so soon," he said, with some real kindness or clannishness permeating the hateful cordiality of his voice—for Andrew Cameron was not entirely without the homely virtues of the average man. He had been a good husband and father; he had once been very fond of his Cousin Margaret; and he was really very sorry that "circumstances" had "compelled" him to act as he had done in that old affair of her father's investment. "You must be my guest tonight."

"Thank you. I must return home tonight," said the Old Lady firmly, and there was that in her tone which told Andrew Cameron that it would be useless to urge her. But he insisted on telephoning for his carriage to drive her to the station. The Old Lady submitted to this, because she was secretly afraid her own legs would not suffice to carry her there; she even shook hands with him at parting, and thanked him a second time for granting her request.

"Not at all," he said. "Please try to think a little more kindly of me, Cousin Margaret."

When the Old Lady reached the station she found, to her dismay, that her train had just gone and that she would have to wait two hours for the evening one. She went into the waiting-room and sat down. She was very tired. All the excitement that had sustained her was gone and she felt weak and old. She had nothing to eat, having expected to get home in time for tea; the waiting-room was chilly, and she shivered in her thin, old, silk mantilla. Her head ached and her heart likewise. She had won Sylvia's desire for her; but Sylvia would go out of her life, and the Old Lady did not see how she was to go on living after that. Yet she sat there unflinchingly for two hours, an upright, indomitable old figure, silently fighting her losing battle with the forces of physical and mental pain, while happy people came and went, and laughed and talked before her.

At eight o'clock the Old Lady got off the train at Bright River station, and slipped off unnoticed into the darkness of the wet night. She had two miles to walk and a cold rain was falling. Soon the Old Lady was wet to the skin and chilled to the marrow. She felt as if she were walking in a bad dream. Blind instinct alone guided her over the last mile and up the lane to her own house. As she fumbled at her door she realized that a burning heat had suddenly taken the place of her chilliness. She stumbled in over her threshold and closed the door.

VI. The October Chapter

On the second morning after Old Lady Lloyd's journey to town Sylvia Gray was walking blithely down the wood lane. It was a beautiful autumn morning, clear and crisp and sunny; the frosted ferns, drenched and battered with the rain of yesterday, gave out a delicious fragrance; here and there in the woods a maple waved a gay crimson banner, or a branch of birch showed pale golden against the dark, unchanging spruces. The air was very pure and exhilarating. Sylvia walked with a joyous lightness of step and uplift of brow.

At the beech in the hollow she paused for an expectant moment, but there was nothing among the gray old roots for her. She was just turning away when little Teddy Kimball, who lived next door to the manse, came running down the slope from the direction of the old Lloyd place. Teddy's freckled face was very pale.

"Oh, Miss Gray!" he gasped. "I guess Old Lady Lloyd has gone clean crazy at last. The minister's wife asked me to run up to the Old Lady, with a message about the Sewing Circle—and I knocked—and knocked—and nobody came—so I thought

I'd just step in and leave the letter on the table. But when I opened the door I heard an awful queer laugh in the sitting-room, and next minute the Old Lady came to the sitting-room door. Oh, Miss Gray, she looked awful. Her face was red and her eyes awful wild—and she was muttering and talking to herself and laughing like mad. I was so scared I just turned and run."

Sylvia, without stopping for reflection, caught Teddy's hand and ran up the slope. It did not occur to her to be frightened, although she thought with Teddy, that the poor, lonely, eccentric Old Lady had really gone out of her mind at last.

The Old Lady was sitting on the kitchen sofa when Sylvia entered. Teddy, too frightened to go in, lurked on the step outside. The Old Lady still wore the damp black silk dress in which she had walked from the station. Her face was flushed, her eyes wild, her voice hoarse. But she knew Sylvia and cowered down.

"Don't look at me," she moaned. "Please go away—I can't bear that *you* should know how poor I am. You're to go to Europe—Andrew Cameron is going to send you—I asked him— he couldn't refuse *me*. But please go away."

Sylvia did not go away. At a glance she had seen that this was sickness and delirium, not insanity. She sent Teddy off in hot haste for Mrs. Spencer, and when Mrs. Spencer came they induced the Old Lady to go to bed, and sent for the doctor. By night everybody in Spencervale knew that Old Lady Lloyd had pneumonia.

Mrs. Spencer announced that she meant to stay and nurse the Old Lady. Several other women offered assistance. Everybody was kind and thoughtful. But the Old Lady did not know it. She was in a high fever and delirium. She did not even know Sylvia Gray, who came and sat by her every minute she could spare. Sylvia Gray now knew all that she had suspected— the Old Lady was her fairy godmother. The Old Lady babbled of Sylvia incessantly, revealing all her love for her, betraying all the sacrifices she had made. Sylvia's heart ached with love and tenderness, and she prayed earnestly that the Old Lady might recover.

"I want her to know that I give her love for love," she murmured.

Everybody knew now how poor the Old Lady really was.
She let slip all the jealously guarded secrets of her existence,
except her old love for Leslie Gray. Even in delirium something
sealed her lips as to that. But all else came out—her anguish
over her unfashionable attire, her pitiful makeshifts and con-
trivances, her humiliation over wearing unfashionable dresses
and paying only five cents where every other Sewing Circle
member paid ten. The kindly women who waited on her listened
to her with tear-filled eyes, and repented of their harsh judg-
ments in the past.

"But who would have thought it?" said Mrs. Spencer to the
minister's wife. "Nobody ever dreamed that her father had lost
all his money, though folks supposed he had lost some in that
old affair of the silver mine out west. It's shocking to think of
the way she has lived all these years, often with not enough
to eat—and going to bed in winter days to save fuel. Though
I suppose if we had known we couldn't have done much for
her, she's so desperate proud. But if she lives, and will let us
help her, things will be different after this. Crooked Jack says
he'll never forgive himself for taking pay for the few little jobs
he did for her. He says, if she'll only let him, he'll do everything
she wants done for her after this for nothing. Ain't it strange
what a fancy she's took to Miss Gray? Think of her doing all
those things for her all summer, and selling the grape jug and
all. Well, the Old Lady certainly isn't mean, but nobody made
a mistake in calling her queer. It all does seem desperate pitiful.
Miss Gray's taking it awful hard. She seems to think about as
much of the Old Lady as the Old Lady thinks of her. She's
so worked up she don't even seem to care about going to
Europe next year. She's really going—she's had word from
Andrew Cameron. I'm awful glad, for there never was a sweeter
girl in the world; but she says it will cost too much if the Old
Lady's life is to pay for it."

Andrew Cameron heard of the Old Lady's illness and came
out to Spencervale himself. He was not allowed to see the Old
Lady, of course; but he told all concerned that no expense or
trouble was to be spared, and the Spencervale doctor was
instructed to send his bill to Andrew Cameron and hold his
peace about it. Moreover, when Andrew Cameron went back
home he sent a trained nurse out to wait on the Old Lady, a

capable, kindly woman who contrived to take charge of the case without offending Mrs. Spencer—than which no higher tribute could be paid to her tact!

The Old Lady did not die—the Lloyd constitution brought her through. One day, when Sylvia came in, the Old Lady smiled up at her, with a weak, faint, sensible smile, and murmured her name, and the nurse said that the crisis was past.

The Old Lady made a marvellously patient and tractable invalid. She did just as she was told and accepted the presence of the nurse as a matter of course.

But one day, when she was strong enough to talk a little, she said to Sylvia,

"I suppose Andrew Cameron sent Miss Hayes here, did he?"

"Yes," said Sylvia rather timidly.

The old lady noticed the timidity and smiled, with something of her old humour and spirit in her black eyes.

"Time has been when I'd have packed off unceremoniously any person Andrew Cameron sent here," she said. "But, Sylvia, I have gone through the Valley of the Shadow of Death, and I have left pride and resentment behind me for ever, I hope. I no longer feel as I felt towards Andrew. I can even accept a personal favour from him now. At last I can forgive him for the wrong he did me and mine. Sylvia, I find that I have been letting no ends of cats out of bags in my illness. Everybody knows now how poor I am—but I don't seem to mind it a bit. I'm only sorry that I ever shut my neighbours out of my life because of my foolish pride. Everyone has been so kind to me, Sylvia. In the future, if my life is spared, it is going to be a very different sort of life. I'm going to open it to all the kindness and companionship I can find in young and old. I'm going to help them all I can and let them help me. I *can* help people—I've learned that money isn't the only power for helping people. Anyone who has sympathy and understanding to give has a treasure that is without money and without price. And oh, Sylvia, you've found out what I never meant you to know. But I don't mind that now, either."

Sylvia took the Old Lady's thin white hand and kissed it.

"I can never thank you enough for what you have done for me, dearest Miss Lloyd," she said earnestly. "And I am so glad that all mystery is done away with between us, and I can love you as much and as openly as I have longed to do. I am so glad and so thankful that you love me, dear fairy godmother."

"Do you know *why* I love you so?" said the Old Lady wistfully. "Did I let *that* out in my raving, too?"

"No. But I think I know. It is because I am Leslie Gray's daughter, isn't it? I know that father loved you—his brother, Uncle Willis, told me all about it."

"I spoiled my own life because of my wicked pride," said the Old Lady sadly. "But you will love me in spite of it all, won't you, Sylvia? And you will come to see me sometimes? And write me after you go away?"

"I am coming to see you every day," said Sylvia. "I am going to stay in Spencervale for a whole year yet, just to be near you. And next year when I go to Europe—thanks to you, fairy godmother—I'll write you every day. We are going to be the best of chums, and we are going to have a most beautiful year of comradeship!"

The Old Lady smiled contentedly. Out in the kitchen the minister's wife, who had brought up a dish of jelly, was talking to Mrs. Spencer about the Sewing Circle. Through the open window, where the red vines hung, came the pungent, sun-warm October air. The sunshine fell over Sylvia's chestnut hair like a crown of glory and youth.

"I do feel so perfectly happy," said the Old Lady, with a long, rapturous breath.

EACH IN HIS OWN TONGUE

THE HONEY-TINTED autumn sunshine was falling thickly over the crimson and amber maples around old Abel Blair's door. There was only one outer door in old Abel's house, and it almost always stood wide open. A little black dog, with one ear missing and a lame forepaw, almost always slept on the worn red sandstone slab which served old Abel for a doorstep; and on the still more worn sill above it a large gray cat almost always slept. Just inside the door, on a bandy-legged chair of elder days, old Abel almost always sat.

He was sitting there this afternoon—a little old man, sadly twisted with rheumatism; his head was abnormally large, thatched with long, wiry black hair; his face was heavily lined and swarthily sunburned; his eyes were deep-set and black, with occasional peculiar golden flashes in them. A strange looking man was old Abel Blair; and as strange was he as he looked, Lower Carmody people would have told you.

Old Abel was almost always sober in these, his later years. He was sober today. He liked to bask in that ripe sunlight as well as his dog and cat did; and in such baskings he almost always looked out of his doorway at the far, fine blue sky over the tops of the crowding maples. But today he was not looking at the sky; instead, he was staring at the black, dusty rafters

255

of his kitchen, where hung dried meats and strings of onions and bunches of herbs and fishing tackle and guns and skins.

But old Abel saw not these things; his face was the face of a man who beholds visions, compact of heavenly pleasure and hellish pain, for old Abel was seeing what he might have been—and what he was; as he always saw when Felix Moore played to him on the violin. And the awful joy of dreaming that he was young again, with unspoiled life before him, was so great and compelling that it counterbalanced the agony in the realization of a dishonoured old age, following years in which he had squandered the wealth of his soul in ways where Wisdom lifted not her voice.

Felix Moore was standing opposite to him, before an untidy stove, where the noon fire had died down into pallid, scattered ashes. Under his chin he held old Abel's brown, battered fiddle; his eyes, too, were fixed on the ceiling; and he, too, saw things not lawful to be uttered in any language save that of music; and of all music, only that given forth by the anguished, enraptured spirit of the violin. And yet this Felix was little more than twelve years old, and his face was still the face of a child who knows nothing of either sorrow or sin or failure or remorse. Only in his large, gray-black eyes was there something not of the child—something that spoke of an inheritance from many hearts, now ashes, which had aforetime grieved and joyed, and struggled and failed, and succeeded and grovelled. The inarticulate cries of their longings had passed into this child's soul, and transmuted themselves into the expression of his music.

Felix was a beautiful child. Carmody people, who stayed at home, thought so; and old Abel Blair, who had roamed afar in many lands, thought so; and even the Rev. Stephen Leonard, who taught, and tried to believe, that favour is deceitful and beauty is vain, thought so.

He was a slight lad, with sloping shoulders, a slim brown neck, and a head set on it with staglike grace and uplift. His hair, cut straight across his brow and falling over his ears, after some caprice of Janet Andrews, the minister's housekeeper, was a glossy blue-black. The skin of his face and hands was like ivory; his eyes were large and beautifully tinted—gray, with dilating pupils; his features had the outlines of a cameo. Carmody mothers considered him delicate, and had long foretold that the minister would never bring him up; but old Abel pulled his grizzled moustache when he heard such forebodings and smiled.

"Felix Moore will live," he said positively. "You can't kill that kind until their work is done. He's got a work to do—if the minister'll let him do it. And if the minister don't let him do it, then I wouldn't be in that minister's shoes when he comes to the judgment—no, I'd rather be in my own. It's an awful thing to cross the purposes of the Almighty, either in your own life or anybody else's. Sometimes I think it's what's meant by the unpardonable sin—ay, that I do!"

Carmody people never asked what old Abel meant. They had long ago given up such vain questioning. When a man had lived as old Abel had lived for the greater part of his life, was it any wonder he said crazy things? And as for hinting that Mr. Leonard, a man who was really almost too good to live, was guilty of any sin, much less an unpardonable one— well, there now! what use was it to be taking any account of old Abel's queer speeches? Though, to be sure, there was no great harm in a fiddle, and maybe Mr. Leonard was a mite too strict that way with the child. But then, could you wonder at it? There was his father, you see.

Felix finally lowered the violin, and came back to old Abel's kitchen with a long sigh. Old Abel smiled drearily at him— the smile of a man who has been in the hands of the tormentors.

"It's awful the way you play—it's awful," he said with a shudder. "I never heard anything like it—and you that never had any teaching since you were nine years old, and not much practice, except what you could get here now and then on my old, battered fiddle. And to think you make it up yourself as you go along! I suppose your grandfather would never hear to your studying music—would he now?"

Felix shook his head.

"I know he wouldn't, Abel. He wants me to be a minister. Ministers are good things to be, but I'm afraid I can't be a minister."

"Not a pulpit minister. There's different kinds of ministers, and each must talk to men in his own tongue if he's going to do 'em any real good," said old Abel meditatively. "*Your* tongue is music. Strange that your grandfather can't see that for himself, and him such a broad-minded man! He's the only minister I ever had much use for. He's God's own if ever a man was. And he loves you—yes, sir, he loves you like the apple of his eye."

"And I love him," said Felix warmly. "I love him so much that I'll even try to be a minister for his sake, though I don't want to be."

"What do you want to be?"

"A great violinist," answered the child, his ivory-hued face suddenly warming into living rose. "I want to play to thousands—and see their eyes look as yours do when I play. Sometimes your eyes frighten me, but oh, it's a splendid fright! If I had father's violin I could do better. I remember that he once said it had a soul that was doing purgatory for its sins when it had lived on earth. I don't know what he meant, but it did seem to me that *his* violin was alive. He taught me to play on it as soon as I was big enough to hold it."

"Did you love your father?" asked old Abel, with a keen look.

Again Felix crimsoned; but he looked straightly and steadily into his old friend's face.

"No," he said, "I didn't; but," he added, gravely and deliberately, "I don't think you should have asked me such a question."

It was old Abel's turn to blush. Carmody people would not have believed he could blush; and perhaps no living being could have called that deepening hue into his weather-beaten cheek save only this gray-eyed child of the rebuking face.

"No, I guess I shouldn't," he said. "But I'm always making mistakes. I've never made anything else. That's why I'm nothing more than 'Old Abel' to the Carmody people. Nobody but you and your grandfather ever calls me 'Mr. Blair.' Yet William Blair at the store up there, rich and respected as he is, wasn't half as clever a man as I was when we started in life: you mayn't believe that, but it's true. And the worst of it is, young Felix, that most of the time I don't care whether I'm Mr. Blair or old Abel. Only when you play I care. It makes me feel just as a look I saw in a little girl's eyes some years ago made me feel. Her name was Anne Shirley and she lived with the Cuthberts down at Avonlea. We got into a conversation at Blair's store. She could talk a blue streak to anyone, that girl could. I happened to say about something that it didn't matter to a battered old hulk of sixty odd like me. She looked at me with her big, innocent eyes, a little reproachful like, as if I'd said something awful heretical. 'Don't you think, Mr. Blair,' she says, 'that the older we get the more things ought to matter to us?'—as grave as if she'd been a hundred instead of eleven. 'Things matter *so* much to me now,' she says, clasping her hands thisaway, 'and I'm sure that when I'm sixty they'll matter just five times as much to me.' Well, the way she looked and the way she spoke made me feel downright ashamed of myself because things had stopped mattering with me. But never mind all that. My miserable old feelings don't count for much. What come of your father's fiddle?"

"Grandfather took it away when I came here. I think he burned it. And I long for it so often."

"Well, you've always got my old brown fiddle to come to when you must."

"Yes, I know. And I'm glad for that. But I'm hungry for a violin all the time. And I only come here when the hunger gets too much to bear. I feel as if I oughtn't to come even then—I'm always saying I won't do it again, because I know grandfather wouldn't like it, if he knew."

"He has never forbidden it, has he?"

"No, but that is because he doesn't know I come here for that. He never thinks of such a thing. I feel sure he *would* forbid it, if he knew. And that makes me very wretched. And yet I *have* to come. Mr. Blair, do you know why grandfather can't bear to have me play on the violin? He loves music, and he doesn't mind my playing on the organ, if I don't neglect other things. I can't understand it, can you?"

"I have a pretty good idea, but I can't tell you. It isn't my secret. Maybe he'll tell you himself some day. But, mark you, young Felix, he has got good reasons for it all. Knowing what I know, I can't blame him over much, though I think he's mistaken. Come now, play something more for me before you go—something that's bright and happy this time, so as to leave me with a good taste in my mouth. That last thing you played took me straight to heaven—but heaven's awful near to hell, and at the last you tipped me in."

"I don't understand you," said Felix, drawing his fine, narrow black brows together in a perplexed frown.

"No—and I wouldn't want you to. You couldn't understand unless you was an old man who had it in him once to do something and be a *man,* and just went and made himself a devilish fool. But there must be something in you that understands things—all kinds of things—or you couldn't put it all into music the way you do. How do you do it? How in—how *do* you do it, young Felix?"

"I don't know. But I play differently to different people. I don't know how that is. When I'm alone with you I have to play one way; and when Janet comes over here to listen I feel quite another way—not so thrilling, but happier and lonelier. And that day when Jessie Blair was here listening I felt as if I wanted to laugh and sing—as if the violin wanted to laugh and sing all the time."

The strange, golden gleam flashed through old Abel's sunken eyes.

"God," he muttered under his breath, "I believe the boy can get into other folk's souls somehow, and play out what *his* soul sees there."

"What's that you say?" inquired Felix, petting his fiddle.

"Nothing—never mind—go on. Something lively now, young Felix. Stop probing into my soul, where you haven't no business to be, you infant, and play me something out of your own— something sweet and happy and pure."

"I'll play the way I feel on sunshiny mornings, when the birds are singing and I forget I have to be a minister," said Felix simply.

A witching, gurgling, mirthful strain, like mingled bird and brook song, floated out on the still air, along the path where the red and golden maple leaves were falling very softly, one by one. The Reverend Stephen Leonard heard it, as he came along the way, and the Reverend Stephen Leonard smiled. Now, when Stephen Leonard smiled, children ran to him, and grown people felt as if they looked from Pisgah over to some fair land of promise beyond the fret and worry of their care-dimmed earthly lives.

Mr. Leonard loved music, as he loved all things beautiful, whether in the material or the spiritual world, though he did not realize how much he loved them for their beauty alone, or he would have been shocked and remorseful. He himself was beautiful. His figure was erect and youthful, despite seventy years. His face was as mobile and charming as a woman's, yet with all a man's tried strength and firmness in it, and his dark blue eyes flashed with the brilliance of one and twenty; even his silken silvery hair could not make an old man of him. He was worshipped by everyone who knew him, and he was, in so far as mortal man may be, worthy of that worship.

"Old Abel is amusing himself with his violin again," he thought. "What a delicious thing he is playing! He has quite a gift for the violin. But how can he play such a thing as that—a battered old hulk of a man who has, at one time or another, wallowed in almost every sin to which human nature can sink? He was on one of his sprees three days ago—the first one for over a year—lying dead-drunk in the market square in Charlottetown among the dogs; and now he is playing something that only a young archangel on the hills of heaven ought to be able to play. Well, it will make my task all the easier. Abel is always repentant by the time he is able to play on his fiddle."

Mr. Leonard was on the door-stone. The little black dog had frisked down to meet him, and the gray cat rubbed her head against his leg. Old Abel did not notice him; he was beating time with uplifted hand and smiling face to Felix's music, and his eyes were young again, glowing with laughter and sheer happiness.

"Felix! What does this mean?"

The violin bow clattered from Felix's hand upon the floor; he swung around and faced his grandfather. As he met the passion of grief and hurt in the old man's eyes his own clouded with an agony of repentance.

"Grandfather—I'm sorry," he cried brokenly.

"Now, now!" Old Abel had risen deprecatingly. "It's all my fault, Mr. Leonard. Don't you blame the boy. I coaxed him to play a bit for me. I didn't feel fit to touch the fiddle yet myself—too soon after Friday, you see. So I coaxed him on—wouldn't give him no peace till he played. It's all my fault."

"No," said Felix, throwing back his head. His face was as white as marble, yet it seemed ablaze with desparate truth and scorn of old Abel's shielding lie. "No, grandfather, it isn't Abel's fault. I came over here on purpose to play, because I thought you had gone to the harbour. I have come here often, ever since I have lived with you."

"Ever since you have lived with me you have been deceiving me like this, Felix?"

There was no anger in Mr. Leonard's tone—only measureless sorrow. The boy's sensitive lips quivered.

"Forgive me, grandfather," he whispered beseechingly.

"You never forbid him to come," old Abel broke in angrily. "Be just, Mr. Leonard—be just."

"I *am* just. Felix knows that he has disobeyed me, in the spirit if not in the letter. Do you not know it, Felix?"

"Yes, grandfather, I have done wrong—I've known that I was doing wrong every time I came. Forgive me, grandfather."

"Felix, I forgive you, but I ask you to promise me, here and now, that you will never again, as long as you live, touch a violin."

Dusky crimson rushed madly over the boy's face. He gave a cry as if he had been lashed with a whip. Old Abel sprang to his feet.

"Don't you ask such a promise of him, Mr. Leonard," he cried furiously. "It's a sin, that's what it is. Man, man, what blinds you? You *are* blind. Can't you see what is in the boy? His soul is full of music. It'll torture him to death—or to worse—if you don't let it have way."

"There is a devil in such music," said Mr. Leonard hotly.

"Ay, there may be, but don't forget that there's a Christ in it, too," retorted old Abel in a low tense tone.

Mr. Leonard looked shocked; he considered that old Abel had uttered blasphemy. He turned away from him rebukingly.

"Felix, promise me."

There was no relenting in his face or tone. He was merciless in the use of the power he possessed over that young, loving spirit. Felix understood that there was no escape; but his lips were very white as he said,

"I promise, grandfather."

Mr. Leonard drew a long breath of relief. He knew that promise would be kept. So did old Abel. The latter crossed the floor and sullenly took the violin from Felix's relaxed hand. Without a word or look he went into the little bedroom off the kitchen and shut the door with a slam of righteous indignation. But from its window he stealthily watched his visitors go away. Just as they entered on the maple path Mr. Leonard laid his hand on Felix's head and looked down at him. Instantly the boy flung his arm up over the old man's shoulder and smiled at him. In the look they exchanged there was boundless love and trust—ay, and good-fellowship. Old Abel's scornful eyes again held the golden flash.

"How those two love each other!" he muttered enviously. "And how they torture each other!"

Mr. Leonard went to his study to pray when he got home. He knew that Felix had run for comforting to Janet Andrews, the little thin, sweet-faced, rigid-lipped woman who kept house for them. Mr. Leonard knew that Janet would disapprove of his action as deeply as old Abel had done. She would say nothing, she would only look at him with reproachful eyes over the teacups at suppertime. But Mr. Leonard believed he had done what was best and his conscience did not trouble him, though his heart did.

Thirteen years before this, his daughter Margaret had almost broken that heart by marrying a man of whom he could not approve. Martin Moore was a professional violinist. He was a popular performer, though not in any sense a great one. He met the slim, golden-haired daughter of the manse at the house of a college friend she was visiting in Toronto, and fell straightaway in love with her. Margaret had loved him with all her virginal heart in return, and married him, despite her father's disapproval. It was not to Martin Moore's profession that Mr. Leonard objected, but to the man himself. He knew that the violinist's past life had not been such as became a suitor for Margaret Leonard; and his insight into character warned him that Martin Moore could never make any woman lastingly happy.

Margaret Leonard did not believe this. She married Martin

Moore and lived one year in paradise. Perhaps that atoned for
the three bitter years which followed—that, and her child. At
all events, she died as she had lived, loyal and uncomplaining.
She died alone, for her husband was away on a concert tour,
and her illness was so brief that her father had not time to
reach her before the end. Her body was taken home to be
buried beside her mother in the little Carmody churchyard.
Mr. Leonard wished to take the child, but Martin Moore refused
to give him up.

Six years later Moore, too, died, and at last Mr. Leonard
had his heart's desire—the possession of Margaret's son. The
grandfather awaited the child's coming with mingled feelings.
His heart yearned for him, yet he dreaded to meet a second
edition of Martin Moore. Suppose Margaret's son resembled
his handsome vagabond of a father! Or, worse still, suppose he
were cursed with his father's lack of principle, his instability,
his Bohemian instincts. Thus Mr. Leonard tortured himself
wretchedly before the coming of Felix.

The child did not look like either father or mother. Instead,
Mr. Leonard found himself looking into a face which he had
put away under the grasses thirty years before—the face of his
girl bride, who had died at Margaret's birth. Here again were
her lustrous gray-black eyes, her ivory outlines, her fine-traced
arch of brow; and here, looking out of those eyes, seemed her
very spirit again. From that moment the soul of the old man
was knit to the soul of the child, and they loved each other
with a love surpassing that of women.

Felix's only inheritance from his father was his love of music.
But the child had genius, where his father had possessed only
talent. To Martin Moore's outward mastery of the violin was
added the mystery and intensity of his mother's nature, with
some more subtle quality still, which had perhaps come to him
from the grandmother he so strongly resembled. Moore had
understood what a career was naturally before the child, and
he had trained him in the technique of his art from the time
the slight fingers could first grasp the bow. When nine-year-
old Felix came to the Carmody manse he had mastered as
much of the science of the violin as nine out of ten musicians
acquire in a lifetime; and he brought with him his father's
violin; it was all Martin Moore had to leave his son—but it

was an Amati, the commercial value of which nobody in Carmody suspected. Mr. Leonard had taken possession of it and Felix had never seen it since. He cried himself to sleep many a night for the loss of it. Mr. Leonard did not know this, and if Janet Andrews suspected it she held her tongue— an art in which she excelled. She "saw no harm in a fiddle," herself, and thought Mr. Leonard absurdly strict in the matter, though it would not have been well for the luckless outsider who might have ventured to say as much to her. She had connived at Felix's visits to old Abel Blair, squaring the matter with her Presbyterian conscience by some peculiar process known only to herself.

When Janet heard of the promise which Mr. Leonard had exacted from Felix she seethed with indignation; and, though she "knew her place" better than say anything to Mr. Leonard about it, she made her disapproval so plainly manifest in her bearing that the stern, gentle old man found the atmosphere of his hitherto peaceful manse unpleasantly chill and hostile for a time.

It was the wish of his heart that Felix should be a minister, as he would have wished his own son to be, had one been born to him. Mr. Leonard thought rightly that the highest work to which any man could be called was a life of service to his fellows; but he made the mistake of supposing the field of service much narrower than it is—of failing to see that a man may minister to the needs of humanity in many different but equally effective ways.

Janet hoped that Mr. Leonard might not exact the fulfillment of Felix's promise; but Felix himself, with the instinctive understanding of perfect love, knew that it was vain to hope for any change of viewpoint in his grandfather. He addressed himself to the keeping of his promise in letter and in spirit. He never went again to old Abel's; he did not even play on the organ, though this was not forbidden, because any music wakened in him a passion of longing and ecstasy which demanded expression with an intensity not to be borne. He flung himself grimly into his studies and conned Latin and Greek verbs with a persistency which soon placed him at the head of all competitors.

Only once in the long winter did he come near to breaking

his promise. One evening, when March was melting into April, and the pulses of spring were stirring under the lingering snow, he was walking home from school alone. As he descended into the little hollow below the manse a lively lilt of music drifted up to meet him. It was only the product of a mouth-organ, manipulated by a little black-eyed, French-Canadian hired boy, sitting on the fence by the brook; but there was music in the ragged urchin and it came out through his simple toy. It tingled over Felix from head to foot; and, when Leon held out the mouth-organ with a fraternal grin of invitation, he snatched at it as a famished creature might snatch at food.

Then, with it half way to his lips, he paused. True, it was only the violin he had promised never to touch; but he felt that if he gave way ever so little to the desire that was in him, it would sweep everything before it. If he played on Leon Boute's mouth-organ, there in that misty spring dale, he would go to old Abel's that evening; he *knew* he would go. To Leon's amazement, Felix threw the mouth-organ back at him and ran up the hill as if he were pursued. There was something in his boyish face that frightened Leon; and it frightened Janet Andrews as Felix rushed past her in the hall of the manse.

"Child, what's the matter with you?" she cried. "Are you sick? Have you been scared?"

"No, no. Leave me alone, Janet," said Felix chokingly, dashing up the stairs to his own room.

He was quite composed when he came down to tea, an hour later, though he was unusually pale and had purple shadows under his large eyes.

Mr. Leonard scrutinized him somewhat anxiously; it suddenly occurred to the old minister that Felix was looking more delicate than his wont this spring. Well, he had studied hard all winter, and he was certainly growing very fast. When vacation came he must be sent away for a visit.

"They tell me Naomi Clark is real sick," said Janet. "She has been ailing all winter, and now she's fast to her bed. Mrs. Murphy says she believes the woman is dying, but nobody dares tell her so. She won't give in she's sick, nor take medicine. And there's nobody to wait on her except that simple creature, Maggie Peterson."

"I wonder if I ought to go and see her," said Mr. Leonard uneasily.

"What use would it be to bother yourself? You know she wouldn't see you—she'd shut the door in your face like she did before. She's an awful wicked woman—but it's kind of terrible to think of her lying there sick, with no responsible person to tend her."

"Naomi Clark is a bad woman and she lived a life of shame, but I like her, for all that," remarked Felix, in the grave, meditative tone in which he occasionally said rather startling things.

Mr. Leonard looked somewhat reproachfully at Janet Andrews, as if to ask her why Felix should have attained to this dubious knowledge of good and evil under her care; and Janet shot a dour look back which, being interpreted, meant that if Felix went to the district school she could not and would not be held responsible if he learned more there than arithmetic and Latin.

"What do you know of Naomi Clark to like or dislike?" she asked curiously. "Did you ever see her?"

"Oh, yes," Felix replied, addressing himself to his cherry preserve with considerable gusto. "I was down at Spruce Cove one night last summer when a big thunderstorm came up. I went to Naomi's house for shelter. The door was open, so I walked right in, because nobody answered my knock. Naomi Clark was at the window, watching the cloud coming up over the sea. She just looked at me once, but didn't say anything, and then went on watching the cloud. I didn't like to sit down because she hadn't asked me to, so I went to the window by her and watched it, too. It was a dreadful sight—the cloud was so black and the water so green, and there was such a strange light between the cloud and the water; yet there was something splendid in it, too. Part of the time I watched the storm, and the other part I watched Naomi's face. It was dreadful to see, like the storm, and yet I liked to see it.

"After the thunder was over it rained a while longer, and Naomi sat down and talked to me. She asked me who I was, and when I told her she asked me to play something for her on her violin,"—Felix shot a deprecating glance at Mr.

Leonard—"because, she said, she'd heard I was a great hand at it. She wanted something lively, and I tried just as hard as I could to play something like that. But I couldn't. I played something that was terrible—it just played itself—it seemed as if something was lost that could never be found again. And before I got through Naomi came at me, and tore the violin from me, and—*swore*. And she said, 'You big-eyed brat, how did you know *that?*' Then she took me by the arm—and she hurt me, too, I can tell you—and she put me right out in the rain and slammed the door."

"The rude, unmannerly creature!" said Janet indignantly.

"Oh, no, she was quite in the right," said Felix composedly. "It served me right for what I played. You see, she didn't know I couldn't help playing it. I suppose she thought I did it on purpose."

"What on earth did you play, child?"

"I don't know." Felix shivered. "It was awful—it was dreadful. It was fit to break your heart. But it *had* to be played, if I played anything at all."

"I don't understand what you mean—I declare I don't," said Janet in bewilderment.

"I think we'll change the subject of conversation," said Mr. Leonard.

It was a month later when "the simple creature, Maggie" appeared at the manse door one evening and asked for the preacher.

"Naomi wants ter see yer," she mumbled. "Naomi sent Maggie ter tell yer ter come at onct."

"I shall go, certainly," said Mr. Leonard gently. "Is she very ill?"

"Her's dying," said Maggie with a broad grin. "And her's awful skeered of hell. Her just knew ter-day her was dying. Maggie told her—her wouldn't believe the harbour women, but her believed Maggie. Her yelled awful."

Maggie chuckled to herself over the gruesome remembrance. Mr. Leonard, his heart filled with pity, called Janet and told her to give the poor creature some refreshment. But Maggie shook her head.

"No, no, preacher, Maggie must get right back to Naomi. Maggie'll tell her the preacher's coming ter save her from hell."

She uttered an eerie cry, and ran at full speed shoreward through the spruce woods.

"The Lord save us!" said Janet in an awed tone. "I knew the poor girl was simple, but I didn't know she was like *that*. And are you going, sir?"

"Yes, of course. I pray God I may be able to help the poor soul," said Mr. Leonard sincerely. He was a man who never shirked what he believed to be his duty; but duty had sometimes presented itself to him in pleasanter guise than this summons to Naomi Clark's death-bed.

The woman had been the plague spot of Lower Carmody and Carmody Harbour for a generation. In the earlier days of his ministry to the congregation he had tried to reclaim her, and Naomi had mocked and flouted him to his face. Then, for the sake of those to whom she was a snare or a heart-break, he had endeavoured to set the law in motion against her, and Naomi had laughed the law to scorn. Finally, he had been compelled to let her alone.

Yet Naomi had not always been an outcast. Her girlhood had been innocent; but she was the possessor of a dangerous beauty, and her mother was dead. Her father was a man notorious for his harshness and violence of temper. When Naomi made the fatal mistake of trusting to a false love that betrayed and deserted, he drove her from his door with taunts and curses.

Naomi took up her quarters in a little deserted house at Spruce Cove. Had her child lived it might have saved her. But it died at birth, and with its little life went her last chance of worldly redemption. From that time forth her feet were set in the way that takes hold on hell.

For the past five years, however, Naomi had lived a tolerably respectable life. When Janet Peterson had died, her idiot daughter, Maggie, had been left with no kith or kin in the world. Nobody knew what was to be done with her, for nobody wanted to be bothered with her. Naomi Clark went to the girl and offered her a home. People said she was no fit person to have charge of Maggie, but everybody shirked the unpleasant task of interfering in the matter, except Mr. Leonard, who went to expostulate with Naomi, and, as Janet said, for his pains got her door shut in his face.

But from the day when Maggie Peterson went to live with her, Naomi ceased to be the harbour Magdalen.

The sun had set when Mr. Leonard reached Spruce Cove, and the harbour was veiling itself in a wondrous twilight splendour. Afar out, the sea lay throbbing and purple, and the moan of the bar came through the sweet, chill spring air with its burden of hopeless, endless longing and seeking. The sky was blossoming into stars above the afterglow; out to the east the moon was rising, and the sea beneath it was a thing of radiance and silver and glamour; and a little harbour boat that went sailing across it was transmuted into an elfin shallop from the coast of fairyland.

Mr. Leonard sighed as he turned from the sinless beauty of the sea and sky to the threshold of Naomi Clark's house. It was very small—one room below, and a sleeping-loft above; but a bed had been made up for the sick woman by the downstairs window looking out on the harbour; and Naomi lay on it, with a lamp burning at her head and another at her side, although it was not yet dark. A great dread of darkness had always been one of Naomi's peculiarities.

She was tossing restlessly on her poor couch, while Maggie crouched on a box at the foot. Mr. Leonard had not seen her for five years, and he was shocked at the change in her. She was much wasted; her clear-cut, aquiline features had been of the type which becomes indescribably witch-like in old age, and, though Naomi Clark was barely sixty, she looked as if she might be a hundred. Her hair streamed over the pillow in white, uncared-for tresses, and the hands that plucked at the bed-clothes were like wrinkled claws. Only her eyes were unchanged; they were as blue and brilliant as ever, but now filled with such agonized terror and appeal that Mr. Leonard's gentle heart almost stood still with the horror of them. They were the eyes of a creature driven wild with torture, hounded by furies, clutched by unutterable fear.

Naomi sat up and dragged at his arm.

"Can you help me? Can you help me?" she gasped imploringly. "Oh, I thought you'd never come! I was skeered I'd die before you got here—die and go to hell. I didn't know before today that I was dying. None of those cowards would tell me. Can you help me?"

"If I cannot, God can," said Mr. Leonard gently. He felt himself very helpless and inefficient before this awful terror and frenzy. He had seen sad death-beds—troubled death-beds—ay, and despairing death-beds, but never anything like this.

"God!" Naomi's voice shrilled terribly as she uttered the name. "I can't go to God for help. Oh, I'm skeered of hell, but I'm skeereder still of God. I'd rather go to hell a thousand times over than face God after the life I've lived. I tell you I'm sorry for living wicked—I was always sorry for it all the time. There ain't never been a moment I wasn't sorry, though nobody would believe it. I was driven on by fiends of hell. Oh, you don't understand—you *can't* understand—but I was always sorry!"

"If you repent, that is all that is necessary. God will forgive you if you ask Him."

"No, He can't! Sins like mine can't be forgiven. He can't—and He won't."

"He can and He will. He is a God of love, Naomi."

"No," said Naomi with stubborn conviction. "He isn't a God of love at all. That's why I'm skeered of him. No, no. He's a God of wrath and justice and punishment. Love! There ain't no such thing as love! I've never found it on earth, and I don't believe it's to be found in God."

"Naomi, God loves us like a father."

"Like *my* father?" Naomi's shrill laughter, pealing through the still room, was hideous to hear.

The old minister shuddered.

"No—no! As a kind, tender, all-wise father. Naomi—as you would have loved your little child if it had lived."

Naomi cowered and moaned.

"Oh, I wish I could believe *that.* I wouldn't be frightened if I could believe that. *Make* me believe it. Surely you can make me believe that there's love and forgiveness in God if you believe it yourself."

"Jesus Christ forgave and loved the Magdalen, Naomi."

"Jesus Christ? Oh, I ain't afraid of *Him.* Yes, *He* could

understand and forgive. He was half human. I tell you it's God I'm skeered of."

"They are one and the same," said Mr. Leonard helplessly. He knew he could not make Naomi realize it. This anguished death-bed was no place for a theological exposition on the mysteries of the Trinity.

"Christ died for you, Naomi. He bore your sins in His own body on the cross."

"We bear our own sins," said Naomi fiercely. "I've borne mine all my life—and I'll bear them for all eternity. I can't believe anything else. I *can't* believe God can forgive me. I've ruined people body and soul—I've broken hearts and poisoned homes—I'm worse than a murderess. No—no—no, there's no hope for me." Her voice rose again into that shrill, intolerable shriek. "I've got to go to hell. It ain't so much the fire I'm skeered of as the outer darkness. I've always been so skeered of darkness—it's so full of awful things and thoughts. Oh, there ain't nobody to help me! Man ain't no good and I'm too skeered of God."

She wrung her hands. Mr. Leonard walked up and down the room in the keenest anguish of spirit he had ever known. What could he do? What could he say? There was healing and peace in his religion for this woman as for all others, but he could express it in no language which this tortured soul could understand. He looked at her writhing face; he looked at the idiot girl chuckling to herself at the foot of the bed; he looked through the open door to the remote, starlit night—and a horrible sense of utter helplessness overcame him. He could do nothing—nothing! In all his life he had never known such bitterness of soul as the realization brought home to him.

"What is the good of you if you can't help me?" moaned the dying woman. "Pray—pray—pray!" she shrilled suddenly.

Mr. Leonard dropped on his knees by the bed. He did not know what to say. No prayer that he had ever prayed was of use here. The old, beautiful formulas, which had soothed and helped the passing of many a soul, were naught save idle, empty words to Naomi Clark. In his anguish of mind Stephen Leonard gasped out the briefest and sincerest prayer his lips had ever uttered.

"O, God, our Father! Help this woman. Speak to her in a tongue which she can understand."

A beautiful, white face appeared for a moment in the light that streamed out of the doorway into the darkness of the night. No one noticed it, and it quickly drew back into the shadow. Suddenly Naomi fell back on her pillow, her lips blue, her face horribly pinched, her eyes rolled up in her head. Maggie started up, pushed Mr. Leonard aside, and proceeded to administer some remedy with surprising skill and deftness. Mr. Leonard, believing Naomi to be dying, went to the door, feeling sick and bruised in soul.

Presently a figure stole out into the light.

"Felix, is that you?" said Mr. Leonard in a startled tone.

"Yes, sir." Felix came up to the stone step. "Janet got frightened that you might fall on that rough road after dark, so she made me come after you with a lantern. I've been waiting behind the point, but at last I thought I'd better come and see if you would be staying much longer. If you will be, I'll go back to Janet and leave the lantern here with you."

"Yes, that will be the best thing to do. I may not be ready to go home for some time yet," said Mr. Leonard, thinking that the death-bed of sin behind him was no sight for Felix's young eyes.

"Is that your grandson you're talking to?" Naomi spoke clearly and strongly. The spasm had passed. "If it is, bring him in. I want to see him."

Reluctantly Mr. Leonard signed Felix to enter. The boy stood by Naomi's bed and looked down at her with sympathetic eyes. But at first she did not look at him—she looked past him at the minister.

"I might have died in that spell," she said, with sullen reproach in her voice, "and if I had I'd been in hell now. You can't help me—I'm done with you. There ain't any hope for me, and I know it now."

She turned to Felix.

"Take down that fiddle on the wall and play something for me," she said imperiously. "I'm dying—and I'm going to hell—and I don't want to think of it. Play me something to take my thoughts off it—I don't care what you play. I was always fond of music—there was always something in it for me I never found anywhere else."

Felix looked at his grandfather. The old man nodded; he felt too ashamed to speak; he sat with his fine silver head in his hands, while Felix took down and tuned the old violin, on which so many godless lilts had been played in many a wild revel. Mr. Leonard felt that he had failed his religion. He could not give Naomi the help that was in it for her.

Felix drew the bow softly, perplexedly over the strings. He had no idea what he should play. Then his eyes were caught and held by Naomi's burning, mesmeric, blue gaze as she lay on her crumpled pillow. A strange, inspired look came over the boy's face. He began to play as if it were not he who played, but some mightier power, of which he was but the passive instrument.

Sweet and soft and wonderful was the music that stole through the room. Mr. Leonard forgot his heart-break and listened to it in puzzled amazement. He had never heard anything like it before. How could the child play like that? He looked at Naomi and marvelled at the change in her face. The fear and frenzy were going out of it; she listened breathlessly, never taking her eyes from Felix. At the foot of the bed the idiot girl sat with tears on her cheeks.

In that strange music was the joy of innocent, mirthful childhood, blent with the laughter of waves and the call of glad winds. Then it held the wild, wayward dreams of youth, sweet and pure in all their wildness and waywardness. They were followed by a rapture of young love—all-surrendering, all-sacrificing love.

The music changed. It held the torture of unshed tears, the anguish of a heart deceived and desolate. Mr. Leonard almost put his hands over his ears to shut out its intolerable poignancy. But on the dying woman's face was only a strange relief, as if some dumb, long-hidden pain had at last won to the healing of utterance.

The sullen indifference of despair came next, the bitterness of smouldering revolt and misery, the reckless casting away of all good. There was something indescribably evil in the music now—so evil that Mr. Leonard's white soul shuddered away in loathing, and Maggie cowered and whined like a frightened animal.

Again the music changed. And in it now there was agony and fear—and repentance and a cry for pardon. To Mr. Leonard there was something strangely familiar in it. He struggled to recall where he had heard it before; then he suddenly knew— he had heard it before Felix came in Naomi's terrible words! He looked at his grandson with something like awe. Here was a power of which he knew nothing—a strange and dreadful power. Was it of God! Or of Satan?

For the last time the music changed. And now it was not music at all—it was a great, infinite forgiveness, an all-comprehending love. It was healing for a sick soul; it was light and hope and peace. A Bible text, seemingly incongruous, came into Mr. Leonard's mind—"This is the house of God; this is the gate of heaven."

Felix lowered the violin and dropped wearily on a chair by the bed. The inspired light faded from his face; once more he was only a tired boy. But Stephen Leonard was on his knees, sobbing like a child; and Naomi Clark was lying still, with her hands clasped over her breast.

"I understand now," she said very softly. "I couldn't see it before—and now it's so plain. I just *feel* it. God *is* a God of love. He can forgive anybody—even me—even me. He knows all about it. I ain't skeered any more. He just loves me and forgives me as I'd have loved and forgiven my baby if she'd lived, no matter how bad she was, or what she did. The minister told me that but I couldn't believe it. I *know* it now. And He sent you here tonight, boy, to tell it to me in a way that I could feel it."

Naomi Clark died just as the dawn came up over the sea. Mr. Leonard rose from his watch at her bedside and went to the door. Before him spread the harbour, gray and austere in the faint light, but afar out the sun was rending asunder the milk-white mists in which the sea was scarfed, and under it was a virgin glow of sparkling water.

The fir trees on the point moved softly and whispered together. The whole world sang of spring and resurrection and life; and behind him Naomi Clark's dead face took on the peace that passes understanding.

The old minister and his grandson walked home together in a silence that neither wished to break. Janet Andrews gave them a good scolding and an excellent breakfast. Then she ordered them both to bed; but Mr. Leonard, smiling at her, said:

"Presently, Janet, presently. But now take this key, go up to the black chest in the garret, and bring me what you will find there."

When Janet had gone he turned to Felix.

"Felix, would you like to study music as your life-work?"

Felix looked up, with a transfiguring flush on his wan face.

"Oh, grandfather! Oh, grandfather!"

"You may do so, my child. After this night I dare not hinder you. Go with my blessing, and may God guide and keep you, and make you strong to do His work and tell His message to humanity in your own appointed way. It is not the way I desired for you—but I see that I was mistaken. Old Abel spoke truly when he said there was a Christ in your violin as well as a devil. I understand what he meant now."

He turned to meet Janet, who came into the study with a violin. Felix's heart throbbed; he recognized it. Mr. Leonard took it from Janet and held it out to the boy.

"This is your father's violin, Felix. See to it that you never make your music the servant of the power of evil—never debase it to unworthy ends. For your responsibility is as your gift, and God will exact the accounting of it from you. Speak to the world in your own tongue through it, with truth and sincerity; and all I have hoped for you will be abundantly fulfilled."

LITTLE JOSCELYN

"It simply isn't to be thought of, Aunty Nan," said Mrs. William Morrison decisively. Mrs. William Morrison was one of those people who always speak decisively. If they merely announce that they are going to peel the potatoes for dinner their hearers realize that there is no possible escape for the potatoes. Moreover, these people are always given their full title by everybody. William Morrison was called Billy oftener than not; but, if you had asked for Mrs. Billy Morrison, nobody in Avonlea would have known what you meant at first guess.

"You must see that for yourself, Aunty," went on Mrs. William, hulling strawberries nimbly with her large, firm, white fingers as she talked. Mrs. William always improved every shining moment. "It is ten miles to Kensington, and just think how late you would be getting back. You are not able for such a drive. You wouldn't get over it for a month. You know you are anything but strong this summer."

Aunty Nan sighed, and patted the tiny, furry, gray morsel of a kitten in her lap with trembling fingers. She knew, better than anyone else could know it, that she was not strong that summer. In her secret soul, Aunty Nan, sweet and frail and timid under the burden of her seventy years, felt with mysterious unmistakable prescience that it was to be her last summer at

277

the Gull Point Farm. But that was only the more reason why she should go to hear little Joscelyn sing; she would never have another chance. And oh, to hear little Joscelyn sing just once— Joscelyn, whose voice was delighting thousands out in the big world, just as in the years gone by it had delighted Aunty Nan and the dwellers at the Gull Point Farm for a whole golden summer with carols at dawn and dusk about the old place!

"Oh, I know I'm not very strong, Maria," said Aunty Nan pleadingly, "but I am strong enough for that. Indeed I am. I could stay at Kensington over night with George's folks, you know, and so it wouldn't tire me much. I do so want to hear Joscelyn sing. Oh, how I love little Joscelyn."

"It passes my understanding, the way you hanker after that child," cried Mrs. William impatiently. "Why, she was a perfect stranger to you when she came here, and she was here only one summer!"

"But oh, such a summer!" said Aunty Nan softly. "We all loved little Joscelyn. She just seemed like one of our own. She was one of God's children, carrying love with them everywhere. In some ways that little Anne Shirley the Cuthberts have got up there at Green Gables reminds me of her, though in other ways they're not a bit alike. Joscelyn was a beauty."

"Well, that Shirley snippet certainly isn't that," said Mrs. William sarcastically. "And if Joscelyn's tongue was one third as long as Anne Shirley's the wonder to me is that she didn't talk you all to death out of hand."

"Little Joscelyn wasn't much of a talker," said Aunty Nan dreamily. "She was kind of a quiet child. But you remembered what she did say. And I've never forgotten little Joscelyn."

Mrs. William shrugged her plump, shapely shoulders.

"Well, it was fifteen years ago, Aunty Nan, and Joscelyn can't be very 'little' now. She is a famous woman, and she has forgotten all about you, you can be sure of that."

"Joscelyn wasn't the kind that forgets," said Aunty Nan loyally. "And, anyway, the point is, *I* haven't forgotten *her*. Oh, Maria, I've longed for years and years just to hear her sing once more. It seems as if I *must* hear my little Joscelyn sing once again before I die. I've never had the chance before and I never will have it again. Do please ask William to take me to Kensington."

"Dear me, Aunty Nan, this is really childish," said Mrs. William, whisking her bowlful of berries into the pantry. "You must let other folks be the judge of what is best for you now. You aren't strong enough to drive to Kensington, and, even if you were, you know well enough that William couldn't go to Kensington tomorrow night. He has got to attend that political meeting at Newbridge. They can't do without him."

"Jordan could take me to Kensington," pleaded Aunty Nan, with very unusual persistence.

"Nonsense! You couldn't go to Kensington with the hired man. Now, Aunty Nan, do be reasonable. Aren't William and I kind to you? Don't we do everything for your comfort?"

"Yes, oh, yes," admitted Aunty Nan deprecatingly.

"Well, then, you ought to be guided by our opinion. And you must just give up thinking about the Kensington concert, Aunty, and not worry yourself and me about it any more. I am going down to the shore field now to call William to tea. Just keep an eye on the baby in chance he wakes up, and see that the teapot doesn't boil over."

Mrs. William whisked out of the kitchen, pretending not to see the tears that were falling over Aunty Nan's withered pink cheeks. Aunty Nan was really getting very childish, Mrs. William reflected, as she marched down to the shore field. Why, she cried now about every little thing! And such a notion—to want to go to the Old Timers' concert at Kensington and be so set on it! Really, it was hard to put up with her whims, Mrs. William sighed virtuously.

As for Aunty Nan, she sat alone in the kitchen, and cried bitterly, as only lonely old age can cry. It seemed to her that she could not bear it, that she *must* go to Kensington. But she knew that it was not to be, since Mrs. William had decided otherwise. Mrs. William's word was law at Gull Point Farm.

"What's the matter with my old Aunty Nan?" cried a hearty young voice from the doorway. Jordan Sloane stood there, his round, freckled face looking as anxious and sympathetic as it was possible for such a very round, very freckled face to look. Jordan was the Morrisons' hired boy that summer and he worshipped Aunty Nan.

"Oh, Jordan," sobbed Aunty Nan, who was not above telling her troubles to the hired help, although Mrs. William thought she ought to be, "I can't go to Kensington tomorrow night to hear little Joscelyn sing at the Old Timers' concert. Maria says I can't."

"That's too bad," said Jordan. "Old cat," he muttered after the retreating and serenely unconscious Mrs. William. Then he shambled in and sat down on the sofa beside Aunty Nan.

"There, there, don't cry," he said, patting her thin little shoulder with his big, sunburned paw. "You'll make yourself sick if you go on crying, and we can't get along without you at Gull Point Farm."

Aunty Nan smiled wanly.

"I'm afraid you'll soon have to get on without me, Jordan. I'm not going to be here very long now. No, I'm not, Jordan, I know it. Something tells me so very plainly. But I would be willing to go—glad to go, for I'm very tired, Jordan—if I could only have heard little Joscelyn sing once more."

"Why are you so set on hearing her?" asked Jordan. "She ain't no kin to you, is she?"

"No, but dearer to me—dearer to me than many of my own. Maria thinks that is silly, but you wouldn't if you'd known her, Jordan. Even Maria herself wouldn't, if she had known her. It is fifteen years since she came here one summer to board. She was a child of thirteen then, and hadn't any relations except an old uncle who sent her to school in winter and boarded her out in summer, and didn't care a rap about her. The child was just starving for love, Jordan, and she got it here. William and his brothers were just children then, and they hadn't any sister. We all just worshipped her. She was so sweet, Jordan. And pretty, oh my! like a little girl in a picture, with great long curls, all black and purply and fine as spun silk, and big dark eyes, and such pink cheeks—real wild rose cheeks. And sing! My land! But couldn't she sing! Always singing, every hour of the day that voice was ringing round the old place. I used to hold my breath to hear it. She always said that she meant to be a famous singer some day, and I never doubted it a mite. It was born in her. Sunday evening she used to sing hymns for us. Oh, Jordan, it makes my old heart young again to remember it. A sweet child she was, my little Joscelyn! She used to write me for three or four years after she went away, but I haven't heard a word from her for long and long. I daresay she has forgotten me, as Maria says. 'Twouldn't be any wonder. But I haven't forgotten her, and oh, I want to see and hear her terrible much. She is to sing at the Old Timers' concert tomorrow night at Kensington. The folks who are getting the concert up are friends of hers, or, of course, she'd never have come to a little country village. Only sixteen miles away—and I can't go."

Jordan couldn't think of anything to say. He reflected savagely that if he had a horse of his own he would take Aunty Nan to Kensington, Mrs. William or no Mrs. William. Though, to be sure, it *was* a long drive for her; and she was looking very frail this summer.

"Ain't going to last long," muttered Jordan, making his escape by the porch door as Mrs. William puffed in by the other. "The sweetest old creetur that ever was created'll go when she goes. Yah, ye old madam, I'd like to give you a piece of my mind, that I would!"

This last was for Mrs. William, but was delivered in a prudent undertone. Jordan detested Mrs. William, but she was a power to be reckoned with, all the same. Meek, easy-going Billy Morrison did just what his wife told him to.

So Aunty Nan did not get to Kensington to hear little Joscelyn sing. She said nothing more about it but after that night she seemed to fail very rapidly. Mrs. William said it was the hot weather, and that Aunty Nan gave way too easily. But Aunty Nan could not help giving way now; she was very, very tired. Even her knitting wearied her. She would sit for hours in her rocking chair with the gray kitten in her lap, looking out of the window with dreamy, unseeing eyes. She talked to herself a good deal, generally about little Joscelyn. Mrs. William told Avonlea folk that Aunty Nan had got terribly childish and always accompanied the remark with a sigh that intimated how much she, Mrs. William, had to contend with.

Justice must be done to Mrs. William, however. She was not unkind to Aunty Nan; on the contrary, she was very kind to her in the letter. Her comfort was scrupulously attended to, and Mrs. William had the grace to utter none of her complaints in the old woman's hearing. If Aunty Nan felt the absence of the spirit she never murmured at it.

One day, when the Avonlea slopes were golden-hued with

the ripened harvest, Aunty Nan did not get up. She complained of nothing but great weariness. Mrs. William remarked to her husband that if *she* lay in bed every day she felt tired there wouldn't be much done at Gull Point Farm. But she prepared an excellent breakfast and carried it patiently up to Aunty Nan, who ate little of it.

After dinner Jordan crept up by way of the back stairs to see her. Aunty Nan was lying with her eyes fixed on the pale pink climbing roses that nodded about the window. When she saw Jordan she smiled.

"Them roses put me so much in mind of little Joscelyn," she said softly. "She loved them so. If I could only see her! Oh, Jordan, if I could only see her! Maria says it's terrible childish to be always harping on that string, and mebbe it is. But—oh, Jordan, there's such a hunger in my heart for her, such a hunger!"

Jordan felt a queer sensation in his throat, and twisted his ragged straw hat about in his big hands. Just then a vague idea which had hovered in his brain all day crystallized into decision. But all he said was:

"I hope you'll feel better soon, Aunty Nan."

"Oh, yes, Jordan, dear, I'll be better soon," said Aunty Nan with her own sweet smile. " 'The inhabitant shall not say I am sick,' you know. But if I could only see little Joscelyn first!"

Jordan went out and hurried down-stairs. Billy Morrison was in the stable, when Jordan stuck his head over the half-door.

"Say, can I have the rest of the day off, sir? I want to go to Kensington."

"Well, I don't mind," said Billy Morrison amiably. "May's well get your jaunting done 'fore harvest comes on. And here, Jord; take this quarter and get some oranges for Aunty Nan. Needn't mention it to headquarters."

Billy Morrison's face was solemn, but Jordan winked as he pocketed the money.

"If I've any luck I'll bring her something that'll do her more good than the oranges," he muttered, as he hurried off to the pasture. Jordan had a horse of his own now, a rather bony nag, answering to the name of Dan. Billy Morrison had agreed to pasture the animal if Jordan used him in the farm work, an arrangement scoffed at by Mrs. William in no measured terms.

Jordan hitched Dan into the second best buggy, dressed himself in his Sunday clothes, and drove off. On the road he re-read a paragraph he had clipped from the *Charlottetown Daily Enterprise* of the previous day.

"Joscelyn Burnett, the famous contralto, is spending a few days in Kensington on her return from her Maritime concert tour. She is the guest of Mr. and Mrs. Bromley, of The Beeches."

"Now if I can get there in time," said Jordan emphatically.

Jordan got to Kensington, put Dan up in a livery stable, and inquired the way to The Beeches. He felt rather nervous when he found it, it was such a stately, imposing place, set back from the street in an emerald green seclusion of beautiful grounds.

"Fancy me stalking up to that front door and asking for Miss Joscelyn Burnett," grinned Jordan sheepishly. "Mebbe they'll tell me to go around to the back and inquire for the cook. But you're going just the same, Jordan Sloane, and no skulking. March right up now. Think of Aunty Nan and don't let style down you."

A pert-looking maid answered Jordan's ring, and stared at him when he asked for Miss Burnett.

"I don't think you can see her," she said shortly, scanning his country cut of hair and clothes rather superciliously. "What is your business with her?"

The maid's scorn roused Jordan's "dander," as he would have expressed it.

"I'll tell her that when I see her," he retorted coolly. "Just you tell her that I've a message for her from Aunty Nan Morrison of Gull Point Farm, Avonlea. If she hain't forgot, that'll fetch her. You might as well hurry up, if you please, I've not overly too much time."

The pert maid decided to be civil at least and invited Jordan to enter. But she left him standing in the hall while she went in search of Miss Burnett. Jordan gazed about him in amazement. He had never been in any place like this before. The hall was wonderful enough, and through the open doors on either hand stretched vistas of lovely rooms that, to Jordan's eyes, looked like those of a palace.

"Gee whiz! How do they ever move around without knocking things over?"

Then Joscelyn Burnett came, and Jordan forgot everything else. This tall, beautiful woman, in her silken draperies, with a face like nothing Jordan had ever seen, or even dreamed about—could this be Aunty Nan's little Joscelyn? Jordan's round, freckled countenance grew crimson. He felt horribly tongue-tied and embarrassed. What could he say to her? How could he say it?

Joscelyn Burnett looked at him with her large, dark eyes— the eyes of a woman who had suffered much, and learned much, and won through struggle to victory.

"You have come from Aunty Nan?" she said. "Oh, I am so glad to hear from her. Is she well? Come in here and tell me all about her."

She turned towards one of those fairy-like rooms, but Jordan interrupted her desperately.

"Oh, not in there, ma'am. I'd never get it out. Just let me blunder through it out here someways. Yes'm, Aunty Nan, she ain't very well. She's—she's dying, I guess. And she's longing for you night and day. Seems as if she couldn't die in peace without seeing you. She wanted to get to Kensington to hear you sing, but that old cat of a Mrs. William—begging your pardon, ma'am—wouldn't let her come. She's always talking of you. If you can come out to Gull Point Farm and see her, I'll be most awful obliged to you, ma'am."

Joscelyn Burnett looked troubled. She had not forgotten Gull Point Farm, nor Aunty Nan; but for years the memory had been dim, crowded into the background of consciousness by the more exciting events of her busy life. Now it came back with a rush. She recalled it all tenderly—the peace and beauty and love of that olden summer, and sweet Aunty Nan, so very wise in the lore of all things simple and good and true. For the moment Joscelyn Burnett was a lonely, hungry-hearted little girl again, seeking for love and finding it not, until Aunty Nan had taken her into her great mother-heart and taught her its meaning.

"Oh, I don't know," she said perplexedly. "If you had come sooner—I leave on the 11.30 train tonight. I *must* leave by then or I shall not reach Montreal in time to fill a very important engagement. And yet I must see Aunty Nan, too. I have been careless and neglectful. I might have gone to see her before. How can we manage it?"

"I'll bring you back to Kensington in time to catch that train," said Jordan eagerly. "There's nothing I wouldn't do for Aunty Nan—me and Dan. Yes, sir, you'll get back in time. Just think of Aunty Nan's face when she sees you!"

"I will come," said the great singer, gently.

It was sunset when they reached Gull Point Farm. An arc of warm gold was over the spruces behind the house. Mrs. William was out in the barn-yard, milking, and the house was deserted, save for the sleeping baby in the kitchen and the little old woman with the watchful eyes in the up-stairs room.

"This way, ma'am," said Jordan, inwardly congratulating himself that the coast was clear. "I'll take you right up to her room."

Up-stairs Joscelyn tapped at the half-open door and went in. Before it closed behind her Jordan heard Aunty Nan say, "Joscelyn! Little Joscelyn!" in a tone that made him choke again. He stumbled thankfully down-stairs, to be pounced upon by Mrs. William in the kitchen.

"Jordan Sloane, who was that stylish woman you drove into the yard with? And what have you done with her?"

"That was Miss Joscelyn Burnett," said Jordan, expanding himself. This was his hour of triumph over Mrs. William. "I went to Kensington and brung her out to see Aunty Nan. She's up with her now."

"Dear me," said Mrs. William helplessly. "And me in my milking rig! Jordan, for pity's sake hold the baby while I go and put on my black silk. You might have given a body some warning. I declare I don't know which is the greatest idiot, you or Aunty Nan!"

As Mrs. William flounced out of the kitchen Jordan took his satisfaction in a quiet laugh.

Up-stairs in the little room was a great glory of sunset and gladness of human hearts. Joscelyn was kneeling by the bed, with her arms about Aunty Nan; and Aunty Nan, with her face all irradiated, was stroking Joscelyn's dark hair fondly.

"O, little Joscelyn," she murmured, "it seems too good to be true. It seems like a beautiful dream. I knew you the minute you opened the door, my dearie. You haven't changed a bit. And you're a famous singer now, little Joscelyn! I always knew you would be. Oh, I want you to sing a piece for me—just one, won't you, dearie? Sing that piece people like to hear you sing best. I forget the name, but I've read about it in the papers. Sing it for me, little Joscelyn."

And Joscelyn, standing by Aunty Nan's bed, in the sunset light, sang the song she had sung to many a brilliant audience on many a noted concert-platform—sang it as even she had never sung before, while Aunty Nan lay and listened beatifically, and down-stairs even Mrs. William held her breath, entranced by the exquisite melody that floated through the old farmhouse.

"O, little Joscelyn!" breathed Aunty Nan in rapture, when the song ended.

Joscelyn knelt by her again and they had a long talk of old days. One by one they recalled the memories of that vanished summer. The past gave up its tears and its laughter. Heart and fancy alike went roaming through the ways of the long ago. Aunty Nan was perfectly happy. And then Joscelyn told her all the story of her struggles and triumphs since they had parted.

When the moonlight began to creep in through the low window Aunty Nan put out her hand and touched Joscelyn's bowed head.

"Little Joscelyn," she whispered, "if it ain't asking too much, I want you to sing just one other piece. Do you remember when you were here how we sung hymns in the parlour every Sunday night and my favourite always was 'The Sands of Time are Sinking?' I ain't never forgot how you used to sing that, and I want to hear it just once again, dearie. Sing it for me, little Joscelyn."

Joscelyn rose and went to the window. Lifting back the curtain she stood in the splendour of the moonlight, and sang the grand old hymn. At first Aunty Nan beat time to it feebly on the counterpane; but when Joscelyn came to the verse, "With mercy and with judgment," she folded her hands over her breast and smiled.

When the hymn ended Joscelyn came over to the bed.

"I am afraid I must say goodbye now, Aunty Nan," she said.

Then she saw that Aunty Nan had fallen asleep. She would

not waken her, but she took from her breast the cluster of crimson roses she wore and slipped them gently between the toil-worn fingers.

"Goodbye, dear, sweet mother-heart," she murmured.

Down-stairs she met Mrs. William splendid in rustling black silk, her broad, rubicund face smiling, overflowing with apologies and welcomes, which Joscelyn cut short coldly.

"Thank you, Mrs. Morrison, but I cannot possibly stay longer. No, thank you, I don't care for any refreshments. Jordan is going to take me back to Kensington at once. I came out to see Aunty Nan."

"I'm certain she'd be delighted," said Mrs. William effusively. "She's been talking about you for weeks."

"Yes, it has made her very happy," said Joscelyn gravely. "And it has made me happy, too. I love Aunty Nan, Mrs. Morrison, and I owe her much. In all my life I have never met a woman so purely, unselfishly good and noble and true."

"Fancy now," said Mrs. William, rather overcome at hearing this great singer pronounce such an encomium on quiet, timid old Aunty Nan.

Jordan drove Joscelyn back to Kensington; and up-stairs in her room Aunty Nan slept, with that rapt smile on her face and Joscelyn's red roses in her hands. Thus it was that Mrs. William found her, going in the next morning with her breakfast. The sunlight crept over the pillow, lighting up the sweet old face and silver hair, and stealing downward to the faded red roses on her breast. Smiling and peaceful and happy lay Aunty Nan, for she had fallen on the sleep that knows no earthly waking while little Joscelyn sang.

THE WINNING OF LUCINDA

THE MARRIAGE of a Penhallow was always the signal for a gathering of the Penhallows. From the uttermost parts of the earth they would come—Penhallows by birth, and Penhallows by marriage and Penhallows by ancestry. East Grafton was the ancient habitat of the race, and Penhallow Grange, where "old" John Penhallow lived, was a Mecca to them.

As for the family itself, the exact kinship of all its various branches and ramifications was a hard thing to define. Old Uncle Julius Penhallow was looked upon as a veritable wonder because he carried it all in his head and could tell on sight just what relation any one Penhallow was to any other Penhallow. The rest made a blind guess at it, for the most part, and the younger Penhallows let it go at loose cousinship.

In this instance it was Alice Penhallow, daughter of "young" John Penhallow, who was to be married. Alice was a nice girl, but she and her wedding only pertain to this story in so far as they furnish a background for Lucinda; hence nothing more need be said of her.

On the afternoon of her wedding day—the Penhallows held to the good, old-fashioned custom of evening weddings with a rousing dance afterwards—Penhallow Grange was filled to overflowing with guests who had come there to have tea and rest themselves before going down to "young" John's. Many of them had driven fifty miles. In the big autumnal orchard the younger fry foregathered and chatted and coquetted. Upstairs, in "old" Mrs. John's bedroom, she and her married daughters held high conclave. "Old" John had established himself with his sons and sons-in-law in the parlour, and the three daughters-in-law were making themselves at home in the blue sitting-room, ear-deep in harmless family gossip. Lucinda and Romney Penhallow were also there.

Thin Mrs. Nathaniel Penhallow sat in a rocking chair and toasted her toes at the grate, for the brilliant autumn afternoon was slightly chilly and Lucinda, as usual, had the window open. She and plump Mrs. Frederick Penhallow did most of the talking, Mrs. George Penhallow being rather out of it by reason of her newness. She was George Penhallow's second wife, married only a year. Hence, her contributions to the conversation were rather spasmodic, hurled in, as it were, by dead reckoning, being sometimes appropriate and sometimes savouring of a point of view not strictly Penhallowesque.

Romney Penhallow was sitting in a corner, listening to the chatter of the women, with the inscrutable smile that always vexed Mrs. Frederick. Mrs. George wondered within herself what he did there among the women. She also wondered just where he belonged on the family tree. He was not one of the uncles, yet he could not be much younger than George.

"Forty, if he is a day," was Mrs. George's mental dictum, "but a very handsome and fascinating man. I never saw such a splendid chin and dimple."

Lucinda, with bronze-coloured hair and the whitest of skins, defiant of merciless sunlight and revelling in the crisp air, sat on the sill of the open window behind the crimson vine leaves, looking out into the garden, where dahlias flamed and asters broke into waves of purple and snow. The ruddy light of the autumn afternoon gave a sheen to the waves of her hair and brought out the exceeding purity of her Greek outlines.

Mrs. George knew who Lucinda was—a cousin of the second generation, and, in spite of her thirty-five years, the acknowledged beauty of the whole Penhallow connection.

She was one of those rare women who keep their loveliness unmarred by the passage of years. She had ripened and matured but she had not grown old. The older Penhallows were still inclined, from sheer force of habit, to look upon her as a girl, and the younger Penhallows hailed her as one of themselves. Yet Lucinda never aped girlishness; good taste and a strong sense of humour preserved her amid many temptations thereto. She was simply a beautiful, fully developed woman, with whom Time had declared a truce, young with a mellow youth which had nothing to do with years.

Mrs. George liked and admired Lucinda. Now, when Mrs. George liked and admired any person, it was a matter of necessity with her to impart her opinions to the most convenient confidant. In this case it was Romney Penhallow to whom Mrs. George remarked sweetly:

"Really, don't you think our Lucinda is looking remarkably well this fall?"

It seemed a very harmless, inane, well-meant question. Poor Mrs. George might well be excused for feeling bewildered over the effect. Romney gathered his long legs together, stood up, and swept the unfortunate speaker a crushing Penhallow bow of state.

"Far be it from me to disagree with the opinion of a lady—especially when it concerns another lady," he said, as he left the blue room.

Overcome by the mordant satire in his tone, Mrs. George glanced speechlessly at Lucinda. Behold, Lucinda had squarely turned her back on the party and was gazing out into the garden, with a very decided flush on the snowy curves of her neck and cheek. Then Mrs. George looked at her sisters-in-law. They were regarding her with the tolerant amusement they might bestow on a blundering child. Mrs. George experienced that subtle prescience whereby it is given us to know that we have put our foot in it. She felt herself turning an uncomfortable brick-red. What Penhallow skeleton had she unwittingly jangled? Why, oh, why, was it such an evident breach of the proprieties to praise Lucinda?

Mrs. George was devoutly thankful that a summons to the tea-table rescued her from her mire of embarrassment. The meal was spoiled for her, however; the mortifying recollection of her mysterious blunder conspired with her curiosity to banish appetite. As soon as possible after tea she decoyed Mrs. Frederick

out into the garden and in the dahlia walk solemnly demanded
the reason of it all.

Mrs. Frederick indulged in a laugh which put the mettle of
her festal brown silk seams to the test.

"My dear Cecilia, it was *so* amusing," she said, a little
patronizingly.

"But *why!*" cried Mrs. George, resenting the patronage and
the mystery. "What was so dreadful in what I said? Or so
funny? And *who* is this Romney Penhallow who mustn't be
spoken to?"

"Oh, Romney is one of the Charlottetown Penhallows,"
explained Mrs. Frederick. "He is a lawyer there. He is a first
cousin of Lucinda's and a second of George's—or is he? Oh,
bother! You must go to Uncle John's if you want the genealogy.
I'm in a chronic muddle concerning Penhallow relationship.
And, as for Romney, of course you can speak to him about
anything you like except Lucinda. Oh, you innocent! To ask
him if he didn't think Lucinda was looking well! And right
before her, too! Of course he thought you did it on purpose
to tease him. That was what made him so savage and sarcastic."

"But *why?*" persisted Mrs. George, sticking tenaciously to
her point.

"Hasn't George told you?"

"No," said George's wife in mild exasperation. "George has
spent most of his time since we were married telling me odd
things about the Penhallows, but he hasn't got to that yet,
evidently."

"Why, my dear, it is our family romance. Lucinda and
Romney are in love with each other. They have been in love
with each other for fifteen years and in all that time they have
never spoken to each other once!"

"Dear me!" murmured Mrs. George, feeling the inadequacy
of mere language. Was this a Penhallow method of courtship?
"But *why?*"

"They had a quarrel fifteen years ago," said Mrs. Frederick
patiently. "Nobody knows how it originated or anything about
it except that Lucinda was in the wrong. We know that, because
Lucinda herself admitted it to us afterwards. But, in the first
flush of her rage, she told Romney that she would never speak
to him again as long as she lived. And *he* said he would never

speak to her until she spoke first—because, you see, as she was in the wrong she ought to make the first advance. And they never have spoken. Everybody in the connection, I suppose, has taken turns trying to reconcile them, but nobody has succeeded. I don't believe that Romney has ever so much as *thought* of any other woman in his whole life, and certainly Lucinda has never thought of any other man. You will notice she still wears Romney's ring. They're practically engaged still, of course. And Romney said once that if Lucinda would just say one word, no matter what it was, even if it were something insulting, he would speak, too, and beg her pardon for his share in the quarrel—because then, you see, he would not be breaking his word. He hasn't referred to the matter for years, but I presume that he is of the same mind still. And they are just as much in love with each other as they ever were. He's always hanging about where she is—when other people are there, too, that is. He avoids her like a plague when she is alone. That was why he was stuck out in the blue room with us today. There doesn't seem to be a particle of resentment between them. If Lucinda would only speak! But that Lucinda will not do."

"Don't you think she will yet?" said Mrs. George.

Mrs. Frederick shook her crimped head sagely.

"Not now. The whole thing has hardened too long. Her pride will never let her speak. We used to hope she would be tricked into it by forgetfulness or accident—we used to lay traps for her—but all to no effect. It is such a shame, too. They were made for each other. Do you know, I get cross when I begin to thrash the whole silly affair over like this. Doesn't it sound as if we were talking of the quarrel of two schoolchildren? Of late years we have learned that it does not do to speak of Lucinda to Romney, even in the most commonplace way. He seems to resent it."

"*He* ought to speak," cried Mrs. George warmly. "Even if she were in the wrong ten times over, he ought to overlook it and speak first."

"But he won't. And she won't. You never saw two such determined mortals. They get it from their grandfather on the mother's side—old Absalom Gordon. There is no such stubbornness on the Penhallow side. His obstinacy was a proverb, my dear—actually a proverb. What ever he said he would stick to if the skies fell. He was a terrible old man to swear, too," added Mrs. Frederick, dropping into irrelevant reminiscence. "He spent a long while in a mining camp in his younger days and he never got over it—the habit of swearing, I mean. It would have made your blood run cold, my dear, to have heard him go on at times. And yet he was a real good old man every other way. He couldn't help it someway. He tried to, but he used to say that profanity came as natural to him as breathing. It used to mortify his family terribly. Fortunately, none of them took after him in that respect. But he's dead—and one shouldn't speak ill of the dead. I must go and get Mattie Penhallow to do my hair. I would burst these sleeves clean out if I tried to do it myself and I don't want to dress over again. You won't be likely to talk to Romney about Lucinda again, my dear Cecilia?"

"Fifteen years!" murmured Mrs. George helplessly to the dahlias. "Engaged for fifteen years and never speaking to each other! Dear heart and soul, think of it! Oh, these Penhallows!"

Meanwhile, Lucinda, serenely unconscious that her love story was being mouthed over by Mrs. Frederick in the dahlia garden, was dressing for the wedding. Lucinda still enjoyed dressing for a festivity, since the mirror still dealt gently with her. Moreover, she had a new dress. Now, a new dress—and especially one as nice as this—was a rarity with Lucinda, who belonged to a branch of the Penhallows noted for being chronically hard up. Indeed, Lucinda and her widowed mother were positively poor, and hence a new dress was an event in Lucinda's existence. An uncle had given her this one—a beautiful, perishable thing, such as Lucinda would never have dared to choose for herself, but in which she revelled with feminine delight.

It was of pale green voile—a colour which brought out admirably the ruddy gloss of her hair and the clear brilliance of her skin. When she had finished dressing she looked at herself in the mirror with frank delight. Lucinda was not vain, but she was quite well aware of the fact of her beauty and took an impersonal pleasure in it, as if she were looking at some finely painted picture by a master hand.

The form and face reflected in the glass satisfied her. The puffs and draperies of the green voile displayed to perfection the full, but not over-full, curves of her fine figure. Lucinda lifted her arm and touched a red rose to her lips with the hand upon which shone the frosty glitter of Romney's diamond, looking at the graceful slope of her shoulder and the splendid line of chin and throat with critical approval.

She noted, too, how well the gown became her eyes, bringing out all the deeper colour in them. Lucinda had magnificent eyes. Once Romney had written a sonnet to them in which he compared their colour to ripe blueberries. This may not sound poetical to you unless you know or remember just what the tints of ripe blueberries are—dusky purple in some lights, clear slate in others, and yet again in others the misty hue of early meadow violets.

"You really look very well," remarked the real Lucinda to the mirrored Lucinda. "Nobody would think you were an old maid. But you are. Alice Penhallow, who is to be married tonight, was a child of five when you thought of being married fifteen years ago. That makes you an old maid, my dear. Well, it is your own fault, and it will continue to be your own fault, you stubborn offshoot of a stubborn breed!"

She flung her train out straight and pulled on her gloves.

"I do hope I won't get any spots on this dress tonight," she reflected. "It will have to do me for a gala dress for a year at least—and I have a creepy conviction that it is fearfully spottable. Bless Uncle Mark's good, uncalculating heart! How I would have detested it if he had given me something sensible and useful and ugly—as Aunt Emilia would have done."

They all went to "young" John Penhallow's at early moonrise. Lucinda drove over the two miles of hill and dale with a youthful second cousin, by name, Carey Penhallow. The wedding was quite a brilliant affair. Lucinda seemed to pervade the social atmosphere, and everywhere she went a little ripple of admiration trailed after her like a wave. She was undeniably a belle, yet she found herself feeling faintly bored and was rather glad than otherwise when the guests began to fray off.

"I'm afraid I'm losing my capacity for enjoyment," she thought, a little drearily. "Yes, I must be growing old. That is what it means when social functions begin to bore you."

It was that unlucky Mrs. George who blundered again. She

was standing on the veranda when Carey Penhallow dashed up.

"Tell Lucinda that I can't take her back to the Grange. I have to drive Mark and Cissy Penhallow to Bright River to catch the two o'clock express. There will be plenty of chances for her with the others."

At this moment George Penhallow, holding his rearing horse with difficulty, shouted for his wife. Mrs. George, all in a flurry, dashed back into the still crowded hall. Exactly to whom she gave her message was never known to any of the Penhallows. But a tall, ruddy-haired girl, dressed in pale green organdy—Anne Shirley from Avonlea—told Marilla Cuthbert and Rachel Lynde as a joke the next morning how a chubby little woman in a bright pink fascinator had clutched her by the arm, and gasped out:

"Carey Penhallow can't take you—he says you're to look out for someone else," and was gone before she could answer or turn around.

Thus it was that Lucinda, when she came out to the veranda step, found herself unaccountably deserted. All the Grange Penhallows were gone; Lucinda realized this after a few moments of bewildered seeking, and she understood that if she were to get to the Grange that night she must walk. Plainly there was nobody to take her.

Lucinda was angry. It is not pleasant to find yourself forgotten and neglected. It is still less pleasant to walk home alone along a country road, at one o'clock in the morning, wearing a pale green voile. Lucinda was not prepared for such a walk. She had nothing on her feet save thin-soled shoes, and her only wraps were a flimsy fascinator and a short coat.

"What a guy I shall look, stalking home alone in this rig," she thought crossly.

There was no help for it unless she confessed her plight to some of the stranger guests and begged a drive home. Lucinda's pride scorned such a request and the admission of neglect it involved. No, she would walk, since that was all there was to it; but she would not go by the main road to be stared at by all and sundry who might pass her. There was a short cut by way of a lane across the fields; she knew every inch of it although she had not traversed it for years.

She gathered up the green voile as trimly as possible, slipped around the house in the kindly shadows, picked her way across the side lawn, and found a gate which opened into a birch-bordered lane where the frosted trees shone with silvery-golden radiance in the moonlight. Lucinda flitted down the lane, growing angrier at every step as the realization of how shamefully she seemed to have been treated came home to her. She believed that nobody had thought about her at all, which was tenfold worse than premeditated neglect.

As she came to the gate at the lower end of the lane a man who was leaning over it started, with a quick intake of his breath, which, in any other man than Romney Penhallow, or for any other woman than Lucinda Penhallow, would have been an exclamation of surprise.

Lucinda recognized him with a great deal of annoyance and a little relief. She would not have to walk home alone. But with Romney Penhallow! Would he think she had contrived it so purposely?

Romney silently opened the gate for her, silently latched it behind her, and silently fell into step beside her. Down across a velvety sweep of field they went; the air was frosty, calm and still; over the world lay a haze of moonshine and mist that converted East Grafton's prosaic hills and fields into a shimmering fairyland.

At first Lucinda felt angrier than ever. What a ridiculous situation! How the Penhallows would laugh over it!

As for Romney, he, too, was angry with the trick impish chance had played him. He liked being the butt of an awkward situation as little as most men; and certainly to be obliged to walk home over moonlit fields at one o'clock in the morning with the woman he had loved and never spoken to for fifteen years was the irony of fate with a vengeance. Would she think he had schemed for it? And how the deuce did she come to be walking home from the wedding at all?

By the time they had crossed the field and reached the wild cherry lane beyond it, Lucinda's anger was mastered by her saving sense of humour. She was even smiling a little maliciously under her fascinator.

The lane was a place of enchantment—a long, moonlit colonnade adown which beguiling wood nymphs might have footed it featly. The moonshine fell through the arching boughs and made a mosaic of silver light and clear-cut shadow for the unfriendly lovers to walk in. On either side was the hovering gloom of the woods, and around them a great silence unstirred by wind or murmur.

Midway in the lane Lucinda was attacked by a sentimental recollection. She thought of the last time Romney and she had walked home together through this very lane, from a party at "young" John's. It had been moonlight then too, and—Lucinda checked a sigh—they had walked hand in hand. Just here, by the big gray beech, he had stopped her and kissed her. Lucinda wondered if he were thinking of it, too, and stole a look at him from under the lace border of her fascinator.

But he was striding moodily along with his hands in his pockets, and his hat pulled down over his eyes, passing the old beech without a glance at it. Lucinda checked another sigh, gathered up an escaped flutter of voile, and marched on.

Past the lane a range of three silvery harvest fields sloped down to Peter Penhallow's brook—a wide, shallow stream bridged over in the olden days by the mossy trunk of an ancient fallen tree. When Lucinda and Romney arrived at the brook they gazed at the brawling water blankly. Lucinda remembered that she must not speak to Romney just in time to prevent an exclamation of dismay. There was no tree! There was no bridge of any kind over the brook!

Here was a predicament! But before Lucinda could do more than despairingly ask herself what was to be done now Romney answered—not in words, but in deeds. He coolly picked Lucinda up in his arms, as if she had been a child instead of a full grown woman of no mean avoirdupois, and began to wade with her through the water.

Lucinda gasped helplessly. She could not forbid him and she was so choked with rage over his presumption that she could not have spoken in any case. Then came the catastrophe. Romney's foot slipped on a treacherous round stone—there was a tremendous splash—and Romney and Lucinda Penhallow were sitting down in the middle of Peter Penhallow's brook.

Lucinda was the first to regain her feet. About her clung in heart-breaking limpness the ruined voile. The remembrance of all her wrongs that night rushed over her soul, and her eyes blazed in the moonlight. Lucinda Penhallow had never been so angry in her life.

"You d—d idiot!" she said, in a voice that literally shook with rage.

Romney meekly scrambled up the bank after her.

"I'm awfully sorry, Lucinda," he said, striving with uncertain success to keep a suspicious quiver of laughter out of his tone. "It was wretchedly clumsy of me, but that pebble turned right under my foot. Please forgive me—for that—and for other things."

Lucinda deigned no answer. She stood on a flat stone and wrung the water from the poor green voile. Romney surveyed her apprehensively.

"Hurry, Lucinda," he entreated. "You will catch your death of cold."

"I never take cold," answered Lucinda, with chattering teeth. "And it is my dress I am thinking of—was thinking of. You have more need to hurry. You are sopping wet yourself and you know you are subject to colds. There—come."

Lucinda picked up the stringy train, which had been so brave and buoyant five minutes before, and started up the field at a brisk rate. Romney came up to her and slipped his arm through hers in the old way. For a time they walked along in silence. Then Lucinda began to shake with inward laughter. She laughed silently for the whole length of the field; and at the line fence between Peter Penhallow's land and the Grange acres she paused, threw back the fascinator from her face, and looked at Romney defiantly.

"You are thinking of—*that,*" she cried, "and I am thinking of it. And we will go on, thinking of it at intervals for the rest of our lives. But if you ever mention it to me I'll never forgive you, Romney Penhallow!"

"I never will," Romney promised. There was more than a suspicion of laughter in his voice this time, but Lucinda did not choose to resent it. She did not speak again until they reached the Grange gate. Then she faced him solemnly.

"It was a case of atavism," she said. "Old Grandfather Gordon was to blame for it."

At the Grange almost everybody was in bed. What with the

guests straggling home at intervals and hurrying sleepily off to
their rooms, nobody had missed Lucinda, each set supposing
she was with some other set. Mrs. Frederick, Mrs. Nathaniel
and Mrs. George alone were up. The perennially chilly Mrs.
Nathaniel had kindled a fire of chips in the blue room grate
to warm her feet before retiring, and the three women were
discussing the wedding in subdued tones when the door opened
and the stately form of Lucinda, stately even in the draggled
voile, appeared, with the damp Romney behind her.

"Lucinda Penhallow!" gasped they, one and all.

"I was left to walk home," said Lucinda coolly. "So Romney
and I came across the fields. There was no bridge over the
brook, and when he was carrying me over he slipped and we
fell in. That is all. No, Cecilia, I never take cold, so don't
worry. Yes, my dress is ruined, but that is of no consequence.
No, thank you, Cecilia, I do not care for a hot drink. Romney,
do go and take off those wet clothes of yours immediately. No,
Cecilia, I will *not* take a hot footbath. I am going straight to
bed. Good night."

When the door closed on the pair the three sisters-in-law
stared at each other. Mrs. Frederick, feeling herself incapable
of expressing her sensations originally, took refuge in a quotation:

" 'Do I sleep, do I dream, do I wonder and doubt?
   Is things what they seem, or is visions about?' "

"There will be another Penhallow wedding soon," said Mrs.
Nathaniel, with a long breath. "Lucinda has spoken to Romney
at last."

"Oh, *what* do you suppose she said to him?" cried Mrs.
George.

"My dear Cecilia," said Mrs. Frederick, "we shall never
know."

They never did know.

OLD MAN SHAW'S GIRL

"Day after tomorrow—day after tomorrow," said Old Man Shaw, rubbing his long slender hands together gleefully. "I have to keep saying it over and over, so as to really believe it. It seems far too good to be true that I'm to have Blossom again. And everything is ready. Yes, I think everything is ready, except a bit of cooking. And won't this orchard be a surprise to her! I'm just going to bring her out here as soon as I can, never saying a word. I'll fetch her through the spruce lane, and when we come to the end of the path I'll step back casual-like, and let her go out from under the trees alone, never suspecting. It'll be worth ten times the trouble to see her big, brown eyes open wide and hear her say, 'Oh, daddy! Why, daddy!' "

He rubbed his hands again and laughed softly to himself. He was a tall, bent old man, whose hair was snow white, but whose face was fresh and rosy. His eyes were a boy's eyes, large, blue and merry, and his mouth had never got over a youthful trick of smiling at any provocation—and, oft-times, at no provocation at all.

To be sure, White Sands people would not have given you the most favourable opinion in the world of Old Man Shaw. First and foremost, they would have told you that he was "shiftless," and had let his bit of a farm run out while he pottered with flowers and bugs, or rambled aimlessly about in the woods, or read books along the shore. Perhaps it was true; but the old farm yielded him a living, and further than that Old Man Shaw had no ambition. He was as blithe as a pilgrim on a pathway climbing to the west. He had learned the rare secret that you must take happiness when you find it—that there is no use in marking the place and coming back to it at a more convenient season, because it will not be there then. And it is very easy to be happy if you know, as Old Man Shaw most thoroughly knew, how to find pleasure in little things. He enjoyed life, he had always enjoyed life and helped others to enjoy it; consequently his life was a success, whatever White Sands people might think of it. What if he had not "improved" his farm? There are some people to whom life will never be anything more than a kitchen garden; and there are others to whom it will always be a royal palace with domes and minarets of rainbow fancy.

The orchard of which he was so proud was as yet little more than the substance of things hoped for—a flourishing plantation of young trees which would amount to something later on. Old Man Shaw's house was on the crest of a bare, sunny hill, with a few staunch old firs and spruces behind it—the only trees that could resist the full sweep of the winds that blew bitterly up from the sea at times. Fruit trees would never grow near it, and this had been a great grief to Sara.

"Oh, daddy, if we could just have an orchard!" she had been wont to say wistfully, when other farmhouses in White Sands were smothered whitely in apple bloom. And when she had gone away, and her father had nothing to look forward to save her return, he was determined she should find an orchard when she came back.

Over the southward hill, warmly sheltered by spruce woods and sloping to the sunshine, was a little field, so fertile that all the slack management of a life-time had not availed to exhaust it. Here Old Man Shaw set out his orchard and saw it flourish, watching and tending it until he came to know each tree as a child and loved it. His neighbours laughed at him, and said that the fruit of an orchard so far away from the house would all be stolen. But as yet there was no fruit, and when the time came for bearing there would be enough and to spare.

"Blossom and me'll get all we want, and the boys can have the rest, if they want 'em worse'n they want a good conscience," said that unworldly, unbusiness-like Old Man Shaw.

On his way back home from his darling orchard he found a rare fern in the woods and dug it up for Sara—she had loved ferns. He planted it at the shady, sheltered side of the house and then sat down on the old bench by the garden gate to read her last letter—the letter that was only a note, because she was coming home soon. He knew every word of it by heart, but that did not spoil the pleasure of re-reading it every half-hour.

Old Man Shaw had not married until late in life, and had, so White Sands people said, selected a wife with his usual judgment—which, being interpreted, meant no judgment at all; otherwise, he would never have married Sara Glover, a mere slip of a girl, with big brown eyes like a frightened wood creature's, and the delicate, fleeting bloom of a spring May-flower.

"The last woman in the world for a farmer's wife—no strength or get-up about her."

Neither could White Sands folk understand what on earth Sara Glover had married him for.

"Well, the fool crop was the only one that never failed."

Old Man Shaw—he was Old Man Shaw even then, although he was only forty—and his girl bride had troubled themselves not at all about White Sands opinions. They had one year of perfect happiness, which is always worth living for, even if the rest of life be a dreary pilgrimage, and then Old Man Shaw found himself alone again, except for little Blossom. She was christened Sara, after her dead mother, but she was always Blossom to her father—the precious little blossom whose plucking had cost the mother her life.

Sara Glover's people, especially a wealthy aunt in Montreal, had wanted to take the child, but Old Man Shaw grew almost fierce over the suggestion. He would give his baby to no one. A woman was hired to look after the house, but it was the father who cared for the baby in the main. He was as tender and faithful and deft as a woman. Sara never missed a mother's care, and she grew up into a creature of life and light and beauty, a constant delight to all who knew her. She had a way of embroidering life with stars. She was dowered with all the charming characteristics of both parents, with a resilient vitality and activity which had pertained to neither of them. When she was ten years old she had packed all hirelings off, and kept house for her father for six delightful years—years in which they were father and daughter, brother and sister, and "chums." Sara never went to school, but her father saw to her education after a fashion of his own. When their work was done they lived in the woods and fields, in the little garden they had made on the sheltered side of the house, or on the shore, where sunshine and storm were to them equally lovely and beloved. Never was comradeship more perfect or more wholly satisfactory.

"Just wrapped up in each other," said White Sands folk, half-enviously, half-disapprovingly.

When Sara was sixteen Mrs. Adair, the wealthy aunt aforesaid, pounced down on White Sands in a glamour of fashion and culture and outer worldliness. She bombarded Old Man Shaw with such arguments that he had to succumb. It was a shame that a girl like Sara should grow up in a place like White Sands, "with no advantages and no education," said Mrs. Adair scornfully, not understanding that wisdom and knowledge are two entirely different things.

"At least let me give my dear sister's child what I would have given my own daughter if I had had one," she pleaded tearfully. "Let me take her with me and send her to a good school for a few years. Then, if she wishes, she may come back to you, of course."

Privately, Mrs. Adair did not for a moment believe that Sara would want to come back to White Sands, and her queer old father, after three years of the life she would give her.

Old Man Shaw yielded, influenced thereto not at all by Mrs. Adair's readily flowing tears, but greatly by his conviction that justice to Sara demanded it. Sara herself did not want to go; she protested and pleaded; but her father, having become convinced that it was best for her to go, was inexorable. Everything, even her own feelings, must give way to that. But she was to come back to him without let or hindrance when her "schooling" was done. It was only on having this most clearly understood that Sara would consent to go at all. Her last words, called back to her father through her tears as she and her aunt drove down the lane, were,

"I'll be back, daddy. In three years I'll be back. Don't cry, but just look forward to that."

He had looked forward to it through the three long, lonely years that followed, in all of which he never saw his darling. Half a continent was between them and Mrs. Adair had vetoed vacation visits, under some specious pretence. But every week brought its letter from Sara. Old Man Shaw had every one of them, tied up with one of her old blue hair ribbons, and kept in her mother's little rosewood work-box in the parlour. He spent every Sunday afternoon re-reading them, with her photograph before him. He lived alone, refusing to be pestered with kind help, but he kept the house in beautiful order.

"A better housekeeper than farmer," said White Sands people. He would have nothing altered. When Sara came back she was not to be hurt by changes. It never occurred to him that she might be changed herself.

And now those three interminable years were gone, and Sara was coming home. She wrote him nothing of her aunt's pleadings and reproaches and ready, futile tears; she wrote only that she would graduate in June and start for home a week later. Thenceforth Old Man Shaw went about in a state of beatitude, making ready for her homecoming. As he sat on the bench in the sunshine, with the blue sea sparkling and crinkling down at the foot of the green slope, he reflected with satisfaction that all was in perfect order. There was nothing left to do save count the hours until that beautiful, longed-for day after to-morrow. He gave himself over to a reverie, as sweet as a daydream in a haunted valley.

The red roses were out in bloom. Sara had always loved those red roses—they were as vivid as herself, with all her own fulness of life and joy of living. And, besides these, a miracle had happened in Old Man Shaw's garden. In one corner was a rose-bush which had never bloomed, despite all the coaxing they had given it—"the sulky rose-bush," Sara had been wont to call it. Lo! this summer had flung the hoarded sweetness of years into plentiful white blossoms, like shallow ivory cups with a haunting, spicy fragrance. It was in honour of Sara's home-coming—so Old Man Shaw liked to fancy. All things, even the sulky rose-bush, knew she was coming back, and were making glad because of it.

He was gloating over Sara's letter when Mrs. Peter Blewett came. She told him she had run up to see how he was getting on, and if he wanted anything seen to before Sara came.

Old Man Shaw shook his head.

"No'm, thank you, ma'am. Everything is attended to. I couldn't let anyone else prepare for Blossom. Only to think, ma'am, she'll be home the day after tomorrow. I'm just filled clear through, body, soul, and spirit, with joy to think of having my little Blossom at home again."

Mrs. Blewett smiled sourly. When Mrs. Blewett smiled it foretokened trouble, and wise people had learned to have sudden business elsewhere before the smile could be translated into words. But Old Man Shaw had never learned to be wise where Mrs. Blewett was concerned, although she had been his nearest neighbour for years, and had pestered his life out with advice and "neighbourly turns."

Mrs. Blewett was one with whom life had gone awry. The effect on her was to render happiness in other people a personal insult. She resented Old Man Shaw's beaming delight in his daughter's return, and she "considered it her duty" to rub the bloom off straightway.

"Do you think Sary'll be contented in White Sands now?" she asked.

Old Man Shaw looked slightly bewildered.

"Of course she'll be contented," he said slowly. "Isn't it her home? And ain't I here?"

Mrs. Blewett smiled again, with double distilled contempt for such simplicity.

"Well, it's a good thing you're so sure of it, I suppose. If 'twas my daughter that was coming back to White Sands, after three years of fashionable life among rich, stylish folks and at a swell school, I wouldn't have a minute's peace of mind. I'd know perfectly well that she'd look down on everything here, and be discontented and miserable."

"*Your* daughter might," said Old Man Shaw, with more sarcasm than he had supposed he had possessed, "but Blossom won't."

Mrs. Blewett shrugged her sharp shoulders.

"Maybe not. It's to be hoped not, for both your sakes, I'm sure. But I'd be worried if 'twas me. Sary's been living among fine folks, and having a gay, exciting time, and it stands to reason she'll think White Sands fearful lonesome and dull. Look at Lauretta Bradley. She was up in Boston for just a month last winter and she's never been able to endure White Sands since."

"Lauretta Bradley and Sara Shaw are two different people," said Sara's father, trying to smile.

"And your house, too," pursued Mrs. Blewett ruthlessly. "It's such a queer, little, old place. What'll she think of it after her aunt's? I've heard tell Mrs. Adair lives in a perfect palace. I'll just warn you kindly that Sary'll probably look down on you, and you might as well be prepared for it. Of course, I suppose she kind of thinks she has to come back, seeing she promised you so solemn she would. But I'm certain she doesn't want to, and I don't blame her either."

Even Mrs. Blewett had to stop for breath, and Old Man Shaw found his opportunity. He had listened, dazed and shrinking, as if she were dealing him physical blows, but now a swift change swept over him. His blue eyes flashed ominously, straight into Mrs. Blewett's straggling, ferrety gray orbs.

"If you've said your say, Martha Blewett, you can go," he said passionately. "I'm not going to listen to another such word. Take yourself out of my sight, and your malicious tongue out of my hearing!"

Mrs. Blewett went, too dumfounded by such an unheard-of outburst in mild Old Man Shaw to say a word of defence or attack. When she had gone Old Man Shaw, the fire all faded from his eyes, sank back on his bench. His delight was dead; his heart was full of pain and bitterness. Martha Blewett was a warped and ill-natured woman, but he feared there was altogether too much truth in what she said. Why had he never thought of it before? Of course White Sands would seem dull and lonely to Blossom; of course the little gray house where she was born would seem a poor abode after the splendours of her aunt's home. Old Man Shaw walked through his garden and looked at everything with new eyes. How poor and simple everything was! How sagging and weather-beaten the old house! He went in, and up-stairs to Sara's room. It was neat and clean, just as she had left it three years ago. But it was small and dark; the ceiling was discoloured, the furniture old-fashioned and shabby; she would think it a poor, mean place. Even the orchard over the hill brought him no comfort now. Blossom would not care for orchards. She would be ashamed of her stupid old father and the barren farm. She would hate White Sands, and chafe at the dull existence, and look down on everything that went to make up his uneventful life.

Old Man Shaw was unhappy enough that night to have satisfied even Mrs. Blewett had she known. He saw himself as he thought White Sands folk must see him—a poor, shiftless, foolish old man, who had only one thing in the world worth while, his little girl, and had not been of enough account to keep her.

"Oh, Blossom, Blossom!" he said, and when he spoke her name it sounded as if he spoke the name of one dead.

After a little the worst sting passed away. He refused to believe long that Blossom would be ashamed of him; he knew she would not. Three years could not so alter her loyal nature— no, nor ten times three years. But she would be changed—she would have grown away from him in those three busy, brilliant years. His companionship could no longer satisfy her. How simple and childish he had been to expect it! She would be sweet and kind—Blossom could never be anything else. She would not show open discontent or dissatisfaction; she would not be like Lauretta Bradley; but it would be there, and he would divine it, and it would break his heart. Mrs. Blewett was right. When he had given Blossom up he should not have made a half-hearted thing of his sacrifice—he should not have bound her to come back to him.

He walked about in his little garden until late at night, under the stars, with the sea crooning and calling to him down the slope. When he finally went to bed he did not sleep, but lay until morning with tear-wet eyes and despair in his heart. All the forenoon he went about his usual daily work absently. Frequently he fell into long reveries, standing motionless wherever he happened to be, and looking dully before him. Only once did he show any animation. When he saw Mrs. Blewett coming up the lane he darted into the house, locked the door, and listened to her knocking in grim silence. After she had gone he went out, and found a plate of fresh doughnuts, covered with a napkin, placed on the bench at the door. Mrs. Blewett meant to indicate thus that she bore him no malice for her curt dismissal the day before; possibly her conscience gave her some twinges also. But her doughnuts could not minister to the mind she had diseased. Old Man Shaw took them up, carried them to the pig-pen, and fed them to the pigs. It was the first spiteful thing he had done in his life, and he felt a most immoral satisfaction in it.

In mid-afternoon he went out to the garden, finding the new loneliness of the little house unbearable. The old bench was warm in the sunshine. Old Man Shaw sat down with a long sigh, and dropped his white head wearily on his breast. He had decided what he must do. He would tell Blossom that she might go back to her aunt and never mind about him—he would do very well by himself and he did not blame her in the least.

He was still sitting broodingly there when a girl came up the lane. She was tall and straight, and walked with a kind of uplift in her motion, as if it would be rather easier to fly than not. She was dark, with a rich dusky sort of darkness, suggestive of the bloom on purple plums, or the glow of deep red apples among bronze leaves. Her big brown eyes lingered on everything in sight, and little gurgles of sound now and again came through her parted lips, as if inarticulate joy were thus expressing itself.

At the garden gate she saw the bent figure on the old bench, and the next minute she was flying along the rose walk.

"Daddy!" she called, "Daddy!"

Old Man Shaw stood up in hasty bewilderment; then a pair of girlish arms were about his neck, and a pair of warm red lips were on his; girlish eyes, full of love, were looking up into his, and a never-forgotten voice, tingling with laughter and tears blended into one delicious chord, was crying,

"Oh, daddy, is it really you? Oh, I can't tell you how good it is to see you again!"

Old Man Shaw held her tightly in a silence of amazement and joy too deep for wonder. Why, this was his Blossom—the very Blossom who had gone away three years ago! A little taller, a little more womanly, but his own dear Blossom, and no stranger. There was a new heaven and a new earth for him in the realization.

"Oh, Baby Blossom!" he murmured, "Little Baby Blossom!"

Sara rubbed her cheek against the faded coat sleeve.

"Daddy darling, this moment makes up for everything, doesn't it?"

"But—but—where did you come from?" he asked, his senses beginning to struggle out of their bewilderment of surprise. "I didn't expect you till tomorrow. You didn't have to walk from the station, did you? And your old daddy not there to welcome you!"

Sara laughed, swung herself back by the tips of her fingers and danced around him in the childish fashion of long ago.

"I found I could make an earlier connection with the C.P.A. yesterday and get to the Island last night. I was in such a fever to get home that I jumped at the chance. Of course I walked from the station—it's only two miles and every step was a benediction. My trunks are over there. We'll go after them tomorrow, daddy, but just now I want to go straight to every one of the dear old nooks and spots at once."

"You must get something to eat first," he urged fondly. "And there ain't much in the house, I'm afraid. I was going to bake tomorrow morning. But I guess I can forage you out something, darling."

He was sorely repenting having given Mrs. Blewett's doughnuts to the pigs, but Sara brushed all such considerations aside with a wave of her hand.

"I don't want anything to eat just now. By and by we'll have a snack; just as we used to get up for ourselves whenever we felt hungry. Don't you remember how scandalized White Sands folk used to be at our irregular hours? I'm hungry; but it's soul hunger, for a glimpse of all the dear old rooms and places. Come—there are four hours yet before sunset, and I want to cram into them all I've missed out of these three years. Let us begin right here with the garden. Oh, daddy, by what witchcraft have you coaxed the sulky rose-bush into bloom?"

"No witchcraft at all—it just bloomed because you were coming home, baby," said her father.

They had a glorious afternoon of it, those two children. They explored the garden and then the house. Sara danced through every room, and then up to her own, holding fast to her father's hand.

"Oh, it's lovely to see my little room again, daddy. I'm sure all my old hopes and dreams are waiting here for me."

She ran to the window and threw it open, leaning out.

"Daddy, there's no view in the world so beautiful as that curve of sea between the headlands. I've looked at magnificent scenery—and then I'd shut my eyes and conjure up that picture. Oh, listen to the wind keening in the trees! How I've longed for that music!"

He took her to the orchard and followed out his crafty plan of surprise perfectly. She rewarded him by doing exactly what he had dreamed of her doing, clapping her hands and crying out:

"Oh, daddy! Why, daddy!"

They finished up with the shore, and then at sunset they came back and sat down on the old garden bench. Before them a sea of splendour burning like a great jewel stretched to the gateways of the west. The long headlands on either side were darkly purple, and the sun left behind him a vast, cloudless arc of fiery daffodil and elusive rose. Back over the orchard in a cool, green sky glimmered a crystal planet, and the night poured over them a clear wine of dew from her airy chalice. The spruces were rejoicing in the wind, and even the battered firs were singing of the sea. Old memories trooped into their hearts like shining spirits.

"Baby Blossom," said Old Man Shaw falteringly, "are you quite sure you'll be contented here? Out there"—with a vague sweep of his hand towards horizons that shut out a world far removed from White Sands—"there's pleasure and excitement and all that. Won't you miss it? Won't you get tired of your old father and White Sands?"

Sara patted his hand gently.

"The world out there is a good place," she said thoughtfully. "I've had three splendid years and I hope they'll enrich my whole life. There are wonderful things out there to see and learn, fine, noble people to meet, beautiful deeds to admire; but," she wound her arm about his neck and laid her cheek against his—"there was no daddy!"

And Old Man Shaw looked silently at the sunset—or, rather, through the sunset to still grander and more radiant splendours beyond, of which the things seen were only the pale reflections, not worthy of attention from those who had the gift of further sight.

AUNT OLIVIA'S BEAU

AUNT OLIVIA told Peggy and me about him on the afternoon we went over to help her gather her late roses for pot-pourri. We found her strangely quiet and preoccupied. As a rule she was fond of mild fun, alert to hear East Grafton gossip, and given to sudden little trills of almost girlish laughter, which for the time being dispelled the atmosphere of gentle old-maidishness which seemed to hang about her as a garment. At such moments we did not find it hard to believe—as we did at other times—that Aunt Olivia had once been a girl herself.

This day she picked the roses absently, and shook the fairy petals into her little sweet-grass basket with the air of a woman whose thoughts were far away. We said nothing, knowing that Aunt Olivia's secrets always came our way in time. When the rose-leaves were picked we carried them in and upstairs in single file, Aunt Olivia bringing up the rear to pick up any stray rose-leaf we might drop. In the south-west room, where there was no carpet to fade, we spread them on newspapers on the floor. Then we put our sweet-grass baskets back in the proper place in the proper closet in the proper room. What would have happened to us, or to the sweet-grass baskets, if this had not been done I do not know. Nothing was ever permitted to remain an instant out of place in Aunt Olivia's house.

When we went downstairs Aunt Olivia asked us to go into the parlour. She had something to tell us, she said, and as she opened the door a delicate pink flush spread over her face. I noted it, with surprise, but no inkling of the truth came to me—for nobody ever connected the idea of possible lovers or marriage with this prim little old maid, Olivia Sterling.

Aunt Olivia's parlour was much like herself—painfully neat. Every article of furniture stood in exactly the same place it had always stood. Nothing was ever suffered to be disturbed. The tassels of the crazy cushion lay just so over the arm of the sofa, and the crochet antimacassar was always spread at precisely the same angle over the horsehair rocking chair. No speck of dust was ever visible; no fly ever invaded that sacred apartment.

Aunt Olivia pulled up a blind, to let in what light could sift finely through the vine leaves, and sat down in a high-backed old chair that had appertained to her great-grandmother. She folded her hands in her lap, and looked at us with shy appeal in her blue-gray eyes. Plainly she found it hard to tell us her secret, yet all the time there was an air of pride and exultation about her; somewhat, also, of a new dignity. Aunt Olivia could never be self-assertive, but if it had been possible that would have been her time for it.

"Have you ever heard me speak of Mr. Malcolm Mac-Pherson?" asked Aunt Olivia.

We had never heard her, or anybody else, speak of Mr. Malcolm MacPherson; but volumes of explanation could not have told us more about him than did Aunt Olivia's voice when she pronounced his name. We knew, as if it had been proclaimed to us in trumpet tones, that Mr. Malcolm Mac-Pherson must be Aunt Olivia's beau, and the knowledge took away our breath. We even forgot to be curious, so astonished were we.

And there sat Aunt Olivia, proud and shy and exulting and shamefaced, all at once!

"He is a brother of Mrs. John Seaman's across the bridge," explained Aunt Olivia with a little simper. "Of course you don't remember him. He went out to British Columbia twenty years ago. But he is coming home now—and—and—tell your father, won't you—I—I—don't like to tell him—Mr. Malcolm MacPherson and I are going to be married."

"Married!" gasped Peggy. And "married!" I echoed stupidly. Aunt Olivia bridled a little.

"There is nothing unsuitable in that, is there?" she asked, rather crisply.

"Oh, no, no," I hastened to assure her, giving Peggy a surreptitious kick to divert her thoughts from laughter. "Only you must realize, Aunt Olivia, that this is a very great surprise to us."

"I thought it would be so," said Aunt Olivia complacently. "But your father will know—he will remember. I do hope he won't think me foolish. He did not think Mr. Malcolm MacPherson was a fit person for me to marry once. But that was long ago, when Mr. Malcolm MacPherson was very poor. He is in very comfortable circumstances now."

"Tell us all about it, Aunt Olivia," said Peggy. She did not look at me, which was my salvation. Had I caught Peggy's eye when Aunt Olivia said "Mr. Malcolm MacPherson" in that tone I must have laughed, willy-nilly.

"When I was a girl the MacPhersons used to live across the road from here. Mr. Malcolm MacPherson was my beau then. But my family—and your father especially—dear me, I do hope he won't be very cross—were opposed to his attentions and were very cool to him. I think that was why he never said anything to me about getting married then. And after a time he went away, as I have said, and I never heard anything from him directly for many a year. Of course, his sister sometimes gave me news of him. But last June I had a letter from him. He said he was coming home to settle down for good on the old Island, and he asked me if I would marry him. I wrote back and said I would. Perhaps I ought to have consulted your father, but I was afraid he would think I ought to refuse Mr. Malcolm MacPherson."

"Oh, I don't think father will mind," said Peggy reassuringly.

"I hope not, because, of course, I would consider it my duty in any case to fulfil the promise I have given to Mr. Malcolm MacPherson. He will be in Grafton next week, the guest of his sister, Mrs. John Seaman, across the bridge."

Aunt Olivia said that exactly as if she were reading it from the personal column of the *Daily Enterprise.*

"When is the wedding to be?" I asked.

"Oh!" Aunt Olivia blushed distressfully. "I do not know the exact date. Nothing can be definitely settled until Mr. Malcolm MacPherson comes. But it will not be before September, at the earliest. There will be so much to do. You will tell your father, won't you?"

We promised that we would, and Aunt Olivia arose with an air of relief. Peggy and I hurried over home, stopping, when we were safely out of earshot, to laugh. The romances of the middle-aged may be to them as tender and sweet as those of youth, but they are apt to possess a good deal of humour for onlookers. Only youth can be sentimental without being mirth-provoking. We loved Aunt Olivia and were glad for her late, new-blossoming happiness; but we felt amused over it also. The recollection of her "Mr. Malcolm MacPherson" was too much for us every time we thought of it.

Father pooh-poohed incredulously at first, and, when we had convinced him, guffawed with laughter. Aunt Olivia need not have dreaded any more opposition from her cruel family.

"MacPherson was a good fellow enough, but horribly poor," said father. "I hear he has done very well out west, and if he and Olivia have a notion of each other they are welcome to marry as far as I am concerned. Tell Olivia she mustn't take a spasm if he tracks some mud into her house once in a while."

Thus it was all arranged, and, before we realized it at all, Aunt Olivia was mid-deep in marriage preparations, in all of which Peggy and I were quite indispensable. She consulted us in regard to everything, and we almost lived at her place in those days preceding the arrival of Mr. Malcolm MacPherson.

Aunt Olivia plainly felt very happy and important. She had always wished to be married; she was not in the least strong-minded and her old-maidenhood had always been a sore point with her. I think she looked upon it as somewhat of a disgrace. And yet she was a born old maid; looking at her, and taking all her primness and little set ways into consideration, it was quite impossible to picture her as the wife of Mr. Malcolm MacPherson, or anybody else.

We soon discovered that, to Aunt Olivia, Mr. Malcolm MacPherson represented a merely abstract proposition—the man who was to confer on her the long-withheld dignity of matronhood. Her romance began and ended there, although she was quite unconscious of this herself, and believed that she was deeply in love with him.

"What will be the result, Mary, when he arrives in the flesh and she is compelled to deal with 'Mr. Malcolm MacPherson' as a real, live man, instead of a nebulous 'party of the second part' in the marriage ceremony?" queried Peggy, as she hemmed table-napkins for Aunt Olivia, sitting on her well-scoured sandstone steps, and carefully putting all thread-clippings and ravellings into the little basket which Aunt Olivia had placed there for that purpose.

"It may transform her from a self-centered old maid into a woman for whom marriage does not seem such an incongruous thing," I said.

The day on which Mr. Malcolm MacPherson was expected Peggy and I went over. We had planned to remain away, thinking that the lovers would prefer their first meeting to be unwitnessed, but Aunt Olivia insisted on our being present. She was plainly nervous; the abstract was becoming concrete. Her little house was in spotless, speckless order from top to bottom. Aunt Olivia had herself scrubbed the garret floor and swept the cellar steps that very morning with as much painstaking care as if she expected that Mr. Malcolm MacPherson would hasten to inspect each at once and she must stand or fall by his opinion of them.

Peggy and I helped her to dress. She insisted on wearing her best black silk, in which she looked unnaturally fine. Her soft muslin became her much better, but we could not induce her to wear it. Anything more prim and bandboxy than Aunt Olivia when her toilet was finished it has never been my lot to see. Peggy and I watched her as she went downstairs, her skirt held stiffly up all around her that it might not brush the floor.

" 'Mr. Malcolm MacPherson' will be inspired with such awe that he will only be able to sit back and gaze at her," whispered Peggy. "I wish he would come and have it over. This is getting on my nerves."

Aunt Olivia went into the parlour, settled herself in the old

carved chair, and folded her hands. Peggy and I sat down on
the stairs to await his coming in a crisping suspense. Aunt
Olivia's kitten, a fat, bewhiskered creature, looking as if it were
cut out of black velvet, shared our vigil and purred in maddening
peace of mind.

We could see the garden path and gate through the hall
window, and therefore supposed we should have full warning
of the approach of Mr. Malcolm MacPherson. It was no wonder,
therefore, that we positively jumped when a thunderous knock
crashed against the front door and re-echoed through the house.
Had Mr. Malcolm MacPherson dropped from the skies?

We afterwards discovered that he had come across lots and
around the house from the back, but just then his sudden
advent was almost uncanny. I ran downstairs and opened the
door. On the step stood a man about six feet two in height,
and proportionately broad and sinewy. He had splendid shoulders, a great crop of curly black hair, big, twinkling blue eyes,
and a tremendous crinkly black beard that fell over his breast
in shining waves. In brief, Mr. Malcolm MacPherson was what
one would call instinctively, if somewhat tritely, "a magnificent
specimen of manhood."

In one hand he carried a bunch of early goldenrod and
smoke-blue asters.

"Good afternoon," he said in a resonant voice which seemed
to take possession of the drowsy summer afternoon. "Is Miss
Olivia Sterling in? And will you please tell her that Malcolm
MacPherson is here?"

I showed him into the parlour. Then Peggy and I peeped
through the crack of the door. Anyone would have done it.
We would have scorned to excuse ourselves. And, indeed, what
we saw would have been worth several conscience spasms if
we had felt any.

Aunt Olivia arose and advanced primly, with outstretched
hand.

"Mr. MacPherson, I am very glad to see you," she said
formally.

"It's yourself, Nillie!" Mr. Malcolm MacPherson gave two
strides.

He dropped his flowers on the floor, knocked over a small
table, and sent the ottoman spinning against the wall. Then he

had caught Aunt Olivia in his arms and—smack, smack, smack!
Peggy sank back upon the stair-step with her handkerchief
stuffed in her mouth. Aunt Olivia was being kissed!

Presently Mr. Malcolm MacPherson held her back at arm's
length in his big paws and looked her over. I saw Aunt Olivia's
eyes roam over his arm to the inverted table and the litter of
asters and goldenrod. Her sleek crimps were all ruffled up, and
her lace fichu twisted half around her neck. She looked distressed.

"It's not a bit changed you are, Nillie," said Mr. Malcolm
MacPherson admiringly. "And it's good I'm feeling to see you
again. Are you glad to see me, Nillie?"

"Oh, of course," said Aunt Olivia.

She twisted herself free and went to set up the table. Then
she turned to the flowers, but Mr. Malcolm MacPherson had
already gathered them up, leaving a goodly sprinkling of leaves
and stalks on the carpet.

"I picked these for you in the river field, Nillie," he said.
"Where will I be getting something to stick them in? Here, this
will do."

He grasped a frail, painted vase on the mantel, stuffed the
flowers in it, and set it on the table. The look on Aunt Olivia's
face was too much for me at last. I turned, caught Peggy by
the shoulder and dragged her out of the house.

"He will horrify the very soul out of Aunt Olivia's body if
he goes on like this," I gasped. "But he's splendid—and he
thinks the world of her—and, oh, Peggy, did you *ever* hear
such kisses? Fancy Aunt Olivia!"

It did not take us long to get well acquainted with Mr.
Malcolm MacPherson. He almost haunted Aunt Olivia's house,
and Aunt Olivia insisted on our staying with her most of the
time. She seemed to be very shy of finding herself alone with
him. He horrified her a dozen times in an hour; nevertheless,
she was very proud of him, and liked to be teased about him,
too. She was delighted that we admired him.

"Though, to be sure, he is very different in his looks from
what he used to be," she said. "He is so dreadfully big! And
I do not like a beard, but I have not the courage to ask him
to shave it off. He might be offended. He has bought the old
Lynde place in Avonlea and wants to be married in a month.

But, dear me, that is too soon. It—it would be hardly proper."

Peggy and I liked Mr. Malcolm MacPherson very much. So did father. We were glad that he seemed to think Aunt Olivia perfection. He was as happy as the day was long; but poor Aunt Olivia, under all her surface pride and importance, was not. Amid all the humour of the circumstances Peggy and I snuffed tragedy compounded with the humour.

Mr. Malcolm MacPherson could never be trained to old-maidishness, and even Aunt Olivia seemed to realize this. He never stopped to clean his boots when he came in, although she had an ostentatiously new scraper put at each door for his benefit. He seldom moved in the house without knocking some of Aunt Olivia's treasures over. He smoked cigars in her parlour and scattered the ashes over the floor. He brought her flowers every day and stuck them into whatever receptacle came handiest. He sat on her cushions and rolled her antimacassars up into balls. He put his feet on her chair rungs—and all with the most distracting unconsciousness of doing anything out of the way. He never noticed Aunt Olivia's fluttering nervousness at all. Peggy and I laughed more than was good for us those days. It was so funny to see Aunt Olivia hovering anxiously around, picking up flower stems, and smoothing out tidies, and generally following him about to straighten out things. Once she even got a wing and a dustpan and swept the cigar ashes under his very eyes.

"Now don't be worrying yourself over that, Nillie," he protested. "Why, I don't mind a litter, bless you!"

How good and jolly he was, that Mr. Malcolm MacPherson! Such songs as he sang, such stories as he told, such a breezy, unconventional atmosphere as he brought into that prim little house, where stagnant dulness had reigned for years! He worshipped Aunt Olivia, and his worship took the concrete form of presents galore. He brought her a present almost every visit—generally some article of jewelry. Bracelets, rings, chains, eardrops, lockets, bangles, were showered upon our precise little aunt; she accepted them deprecatingly, but never wore them. This hurt him a little, but she assured him she would wear them all sometime.

"I am not used to jewelry, Mr. MacPherson," she would tell him.

Her engagement ring she did wear—it was a rather "loud" combination of engraved gold and opals. Sometimes we caught her turning it on her finger with a very troubled face.

"I would be sorry for Mr. Malcolm MacPherson if he were not so much in love with her," said Peggy. "But as he thinks that she is perfection he doesn't need sympathy."

"I am sorry for Aunt Olivia," I said. "Yes, Peggy, I am. Mr. MacPherson is a splendid man, but Aunt Olivia is a born old maid, and it is outraging her very nature to be anything else. Don't you see how it's hurting her? His big, splendid man-ways are harrowing her very soul up—she can't get out of her little, narrow groove, and it is killing her to be pulled out."

"Nonsense!" said Peggy. Then she added with a laugh,

"Mary, did you ever see anything so funny as Aunt Olivia sitting on 'Mr. Malcolm MacPherson's' knee?"

It *was* funny. Aunt Olivia thought it very unbecoming to sit there before us, but he made her do it. He would say, with his big, jolly laugh, "Don't be minding the little girls," and pull her down on his knee and hold her there. To my dying day I shall never forget the expression on the poor little woman's face.

But, as the days went by and Mr. Malcolm MacPherson began to insist on a date being set for the wedding, Aunt Olivia grew to have a strangely disturbed look. She became very quiet, and never laughed except under protest. Also, she showed signs of petulance when any of us, but especially father, teased her about her beau. I pitied her, for I think I understood better than the others what her feelings really were. But even I was not prepared for what did happen. I would not have believed that Aunt Olivia could do it. I thought that her desire for marriage in the abstract would outweigh the disadvantages of the concrete. But one can never reckon with real, bred-in-the-bone old-maidism.

One morning Mr. Malcolm MacPherson told us all that he was coming up that evening to make Aunt Olivia set the day. Peggy and I laughingly approved, telling him that it was high time for him to assert his authority, and he went off in great good humour across the river field, whistling a Highland strath-spey. But Aunt Olivia looked like a martyr. She had a fierce attack of housecleaning that day, and put everything in flawless order, even to the corners.

"As if there was going to be a funeral in the house," sniffed Peggy.

Peggy and I were up in the south-west room at dusk that evening, piecing a quilt, when we heard Mr. Malcolm Mac-Pherson shouting out in the hall below to know if anyone was home. I ran out to the landing, but as I did so Aunt Olivia came out of her room, brushed past me, and flitted downstairs.

"Mr. MacPherson," I heard her say with double-distilled primness, "will you please come into the parlour? I have something to say to you."

They went in, and I returned to the south-west room.

"Peg, there's trouble brewing," I said. "I'm sure of it by Aunt Olivia's face—it was *gray*. And she has gone down *alone*—and shut the door."

"I am going to hear what she says to him," said Peggy resolutely. "It is her own fault—she has spoiled us by always insisting that we should be present at their interviews. That poor man has had to do his courting under our very eyes. Come on, Mary."

The south-west room was directly over the parlour and there was an open stovepipe-hole leading up therefrom. Peggy removed the hat box that was on it, and we both deliberately and shamelessly crouched down and listened with all our might.

It was easy enough to hear what Mr. Malcolm MacPherson was saying.

"I've come up to get the date settled, Nillie, as I told you. Come now, little woman, name the day."

Smack!

"Don't, Mr. MacPherson," said Aunt Olivia. She spoke as a woman who has keyed herself up to the doing of some very distasteful task and is anxious to have it over and done with as soon as possible. "There is something I must say to you. I cannot marry you, Mr. MacPherson."

There was a pause. I would have given much to have seen the pair of them. When Mr. Malcolm MacPherson spoke his voice was that of blank, uncomprehending amazement.

"Nillie, what is it you are meaning?" he said.

"I cannot marry you, Mr. MacPherson," repeated Aunt Olivia.

"Why not?" Surprise was giving way to dismay.

"I don't think you will understand, Mr. MacPherson," said Aunt Olivia, faintly. "You don't realize what it means for a woman to give up everything—her own home and friends and all her past life, so to speak, and go far away with a stranger."

"Why, I suppose it will be rather hard. But, Nillie, Avonlea isn't very far away—not more than twelve miles, if it will be that."

"Twelve miles! It might as well be at the other side of the world to all intents and purposes," said Aunt Olivia obstinately. "I don't know a living soul there, except Rachel Lynde."

"Why didn't you say so before I bought the place, then? But it's not too late. I can be selling it and buying right here in East Grafton if that will please you—though there isn't half as nice a place to be had. But I'll fix it up somehow!"

"No, Mr. MacPherson," said Aunt Olivia firmly, "that doesn't cover the difficulty. I knew you would not understand. My ways are not your ways and I cannot make them over. For— you track mud in—and—and—you don't care whether things are tidy or not."

Poor Aunt Olivia had to be Aunt Olivia; if she were being burned at the stake I verily believe she would have dragged some grotesqueness into the tragedy of the moment.

"The devil!" said Mr. Malcolm MacPherson—not profanely or angrily, but as in sheer bewilderment. Then he added, "Nillie, you must be joking. It's careless enough I am—the west isn't a good place to learn finicky ways—but you can teach me. You're not going to throw me over because I track mud in!"

"I cannot marry you, Mr. MacPherson," said Aunt Olivia again.

"You can't be meaning it!" he exclaimed, because he was beginning to understand that she did mean it, although it was impossible for his man mind to understand anything else about the puzzle. "Nillie, it's breaking my heart you are! I'll do anything—go anywhere—be anything you want—only don't be going back on me like this."

"I cannot marry you, Mr. MacPherson," said Aunt Olivia for the fourth time.

"Nillie!" exclaimed Mr. Malcolm MacPherson. There was such real agony in his tone that Peggy and I were suddenly stricken with contrition. What were we doing? We had no right to be listening to this pitiful interview. The pain and protest in his voice had suddenly banished all the humour from it, and left naught but the bare, stark tragedy. We rose and tiptoed out of the room, wholesomely ashamed of ourselves.

When Mr. Malcolm MacPherson had gone, after an hour of useless pleading, Aunt Olivia came up to us, pale and prim and determined, and told us that there was to be no wedding. We could not pretend surprise, but Peggy ventured a faint protest.

"Oh, Aunt Olivia, do you think you have done right?"

"It was the only thing I could do," said Aunt Olivia stonily. "I could not marry Mr. Malcolm MacPherson and I told him so. Please tell your father—and kindly say nothing more to me about the matter."

Then Aunt Olivia went downstairs, got a broom, and swept up the mud Mr. Malcolm MacPherson had tracked over the steps.

Peggy and I went home and told father. We felt very flat, but there was nothing to be done or said. Father laughed at the whole thing, but I could not laugh. I was sorry for Mr. Malcolm MacPherson and, though I was angry with her, I was sorry for Aunt Olivia, too. Plainly she felt badly enough over her vanished hopes and plans, but she had developed a strange and baffling reserve which nothing could pierce.

"It's nothing but a chronic case of old-maidism," said father impatiently.

Things were very dull for a week. We saw no more of Mr. Malcolm MacPherson and we missed him dreadfully. Aunt Olivia was inscrutable, and worked with fierceness at superfluous tasks.

One evening father came home with some news.

"Malcolm MacPherson is leaving on the 7:30 train for the west," he said. "He has rented the Avonlea place and he's off. They say he is mad as a hatter at the trick Olivia played on him."

After tea Peggy and I went over to see Aunt Olivia, who had asked our advice about a wrapper. She was sewing as for dear life, and her face was primmer and colder than ever. I wondered if she knew of Mr. Malcolm MacPherson's departure. Delicacy forbade me to mention it but Peggy had no such scruples.

"Well, Aunt Olivia, your beau is off," she announced cheerfully. "You won't be bothered with him again. He is leaving on the mail train for the west."

Aunt Olivia dropped her sewing and stood up. I have never seen anything like the transformation that came over her. It was so thorough and sudden as to be almost uncanny. The old maid vanished completely, and in her place was a woman, full to the lips with primitive emotion and pain.

"What shall I do?" she cried in a terrible voice. "Mary— Peggy—what shall I do?"

It was almost a shriek. Peggy turned pale.

"Do you care?" she said stupidly.

"Care! Girls, I shall *die* if Malcolm MacPherson goes away! I have been mad—I must have been mad. I have almost died of loneliness since I sent him away. But I thought he would come back! I must see him—there is time to reach the station before the train goes if I go by the fields."

She took a wild step towards the door, but I caught her back with a sudden mind-vision of Aunt Olivia flying bareheaded and distraught across the fields.

"Wait a moment, Aunt Olivia. Peggy, run home and get father to harness Dick in the buggy as quickly as he can. We'll drive Aunt Olivia to the station. We'll get you there in time, Aunty."

Peggy flew, and Aunt Olivia dashed upstairs. I lingered behind to pick up her sewing, and when I got to her room she had her hat and cape on. Spread out on the bed were all the boxes of gifts which Mr. Malcolm MacPherson had brought her, and Aunt Olivia was stringing their contents feverishly about her person. Rings, three brooches, a locket, three chains and a watch all went on—anyway and anyhow. A wonderful sight it was to see Aunt Olivia bedizened like that!

"I would never wear them before—but I'll put them all on now to show him I'm sorry," she gasped, with trembling lips.

When the three of us crowded into the buggy, Aunt Olivia grasped the whip before we could prevent her and, leaning out, gave poor Dick such a lash as he had never felt in his life before. He went tearing down the steep, stony, fast-darkening road in a fashion which made Peggy and me cry out in alarm. Aunt Olivia was usually the most timid of women, but now she didn't seem to know what fear was. She kept whipping and urging poor Dick the whole way to the station, quite oblivious to our assurances that there was plenty of time. The people who met us that night must have thought we were quite mad. I held on the reins, Peggy gripped the swaying side of the buggy, and Aunt Olivia bent forward, hat and hair blowing back from her set face with its strangely crimson cheeks, and plied the whip. In such a guise did we whirl through the village and over the two-mile station road.

When we drove up to the station, where the train was shunting amid the shadows, Aunt Olivia made a flying leap from the buggy and ran along the platform, with her cape streaming behind her and all her brooches and chains glittering in the lights. I tossed the reins to a boy standing near and we followed. Just under the glare of the station lamp we saw Mr. Malcolm MacPherson, grip in hand. Fortunately no one else was very near, but it would have been all the same had they been the centre of a crowd. Aunt Olivia fairly flung herself against him.

"Malcolm," she cried, "don't go—don't go—I'll marry you—I'll go anywhere—and I don't care how much mud you bring in!"

That truly Aunt Olivian touch relieved the tension of the situation a little. Mr. MacPherson put his arm about her and drew her back into the shadows.

"There, there," he soothed. "Of course I won't be going. Don't cry, Nillie-girl."

"And you'll come right back with me now?" implored Aunt Olivia, clinging to him as if she feared he would be whisked away from her yet if she let go for a moment.

"Of course, of course," he said.

Peggy got a chance home with a friend, and Aunt Olivia and Mr. Malcolm MacPherson and I drove back in the buggy. Mr. MacPherson held Aunt Olivia on his knee because there was no room, but she would have sat there, I think, had there been a dozen vacant seats. She clung to him in the most barefaced fashion, and all her former primness and reserve were swept away completely. She kissed him a dozen times or more and told him she loved him—and I did not even smile, nor did I want to. Somehow, it did not seem in the least funny to me then, nor does it now, although it doubtless will to others. There was too much real intensity of feeling in it all to leave any room for the ridiculous. So wrapped up in each other were they that I did not even feel superfluous.

I set them safely down in Aunt Olivia's yard and turned homeward, completely forgotten by the pair. But in the moonlight, which flooded the front of the house, I saw something that testified eloquently to the transformation in Aunt Olivia. It had rained that afternoon and the yard was muddy. Nevertheless, she went in at her front door and took Mr. Malcolm MacPherson in with her without even a glance at the scraper!

THE QUARANTINE AT ALEXANDER ABRAHAM'S

I REFUSED to take that class in Sunday School the first time I was asked. It was not that I objected to teaching in the Sunday School. On the contrary, I rather liked the idea; but it was the Rev. Mr. Allan who asked me, and it had always been a matter of principle with me never to do anything a man asked me to do if I could help it. I was noted for that. It saves a great deal of trouble and it simplifies everything beautifully. I had always disliked men. It must have been born in me, because, as far back as I can remember, an antipathy to men and dogs was one of my strongest characteristics. I was noted for that. My experiences through life only served to deepen it. The more I saw of men, the more I liked cats.

So, of course, when the Rev. Allan asked me if I would consent to take a class in Sunday School I said no in a fashion calculated to chasten him wholesomely. If he had sent his wife the first time, as he did the second, it would have been wiser. People generally do what Mrs. Allan asks them to do because they know it saves time.

Mrs. Allan talked smoothly for half an hour before she mentioned the Sunday School, and paid me several compliments. Mrs. Allan is famous for her tact. Tact is a faculty for meandering around to a given point instead of making a bee-

327

line. I have no tact. I am noted for that. As soon as Mrs.
Allan's conversation came in sight of the Sunday School, I,
who knew all along whither it was tending, said, straight out,

"What class do you want me to teach?"

Mrs. Allan was so surprised that she forgot to be tactful, and
answered plainly for once in her life,

"There are two classes—one of boys and one of girls—needing
a teacher. I have been teaching the girls' class, but I shall have
to give it up for a little time on account of the baby's health.
You may have your choice, Miss MacPherson."

"Then I shall take the boys," I said decidedly. I am noted
for my decision. "Since they have to grow up to be men it's
well to train them properly betimes. Nuisances they are bound
to become under any circumstances; but if they are taken in
hand young enough they may not grow up to be such nuisances
as they otherwise would and that will be some unfortunate
woman's gain."

Mrs. Allan looked dubious. I knew she had expected me to
choose the girls.

"They are a very wild set of boys," she said.

"I never knew boys who weren't," I retorted.

"I—I—think perhaps you would like the girls best," said
Mrs. Allan hesitatingly. If it had not been for one thing—which
I would never in this world have admitted to Mrs. Allan—I
might have liked the girls' class best myself. But the truth was,
Anne Shirley was in that class; and Anne Shirley was the one
living human being that I was afraid of. Not that I disliked
her. But she had such a habit of asking weird, unexpected
questions, which a Philadelphia lawyer couldn't answer. Miss
Rogerson had that class once and Anne routed her, horse, foot
and artillery. *I* wasn't going to undertake a class with a walking
interrogation point in it like that. Besides, I thought Mrs. Allan
required a slight snub. Ministers' wives are rather apt to think
they can run everything and everybody, if they are not wholesomely corrected now and again.

"It is not what *I* like best that must be considered, Mrs.
Allan," I said rebukingly. "It is what is best for those boys. I
feel that *I* shall be best for *them*."

"Oh, I've no doubt of that, Miss MacPherson," said Mrs.
Allan amiably. It was a fib for her, minister's wife though she

was. She *had* doubt. She thought I would be a dismal failure as teacher of a boys' class.

But I was not. I am not often a dismal failure when I make up my mind to do a thing. I am noted for that.

"It is wonderful what a reformation you have worked in that class, Miss MacPherson—wonderful," said the Rev. Mr. Allan some weeks later. He didn't mean to show how amazing a thing he thought it that an old maid noted for being a man hater should have managed it, but his face betrayed him.

"Where does Jimmy Spencer live?" I asked him crisply. "He came one Sunday three weeks ago and hasn't been back since. I mean to find out why."

Mr. Allan coughed.

"I believe he is hired as handy boy with Alexander Abraham Bennett, out on the White Sands road," he said.

"Then I am going out to Alexander Abraham Bennett's on the White Sands road to see why Jimmy Spencer doesn't come to Sunday School," I said firmly.

Mr. Allan's eye twinkled ever so slightly. I have always insisted that if that man were not a minister he would have a sense of humour.

"Possibly Mr. Bennett will not appreciate your kind interest! He has—ah—a singular aversion to your sex, I understand. No woman has ever been known to get inside of Mr. Bennett's house since his sister died twenty years ago."

"Oh, he is the one, is he?" I said, remembering. "He is the woman hater who threatens that if a woman comes into his yard he'll chase her out with a pitchfork. Well, he will not chase *me* out!"

Mr. Allan gave a chuckle—a ministerial chuckle, but still a chuckle. It irritated me slightly, because it seemed to imply that he thought Alexander Abraham Bennett would be one too many for me. But I did not show Mr. Allan that he annoyed me. It is always a great mistake to let a man see that he can vex you.

The next afternoon I harnessed my sorrel pony to the buggy and drove down to Alexander Abraham Bennett's. As usual, I took William Adolphus with me for company. William Adolphus is my favourite among my six cats. He is black, with a white dicky and beautiful white paws. He sat up on the seat beside me and looked far more like a gentleman than many a man I've seen in a similar position.

Alexander Abraham's place was about three miles along the White Sands road. I knew the house as soon as I came to it by its neglected appearance. It needed paint badly; the blinds were crooked and torn; weeds grew up to the very door. Plainly, there was no woman about *that* place. Still, it was a nice house, and the barns were splendid. My father always said that when a man's barns were bigger than his house it was a sign that his income exceeded his expenditure. So it was all right that they should be bigger; but it was all wrong that they should be trimmer and better painted. Still, thought I, what else could you expect of a woman hater?

"But Alexander Abraham evidently knows how to run a farm, even if he is a woman hater," I remarked to William Adolphus as I got out and tied the pony to the railing.

I had driven up to the house from the back way and now I was opposite a side door opening on the veranda. I thought I might as well go to it, so I tucked William Adolphus under my arm and marched up the path. Just as I was half way up a dog swooped around the front corner and made straight for me. He was the ugliest dog I had ever seen; and he didn't even bark—just came silently and speedily on, with a business-like eye.

I never stop to argue matters with a dog that doesn't bark. I know when discretion is the better part of valour. Firmly clasping William Adolphus, I ran—not to the door, because the dog was between me and it, but to a big, low-branching cherry tree at the back corner of the house. I reached it in time and no more. First thrusting William Adolphus on to a limb above my head, I scrambled up into that blessed tree without stopping to think how it might look to Alexander Abraham if he happened to be watching.

My time for reflection came when I found myself perched half way up the tree with William Adolphus beside me. William Adolphus was quite calm and unruffled. I can hardly say with truthfulness that I was. On the contrary, I admit that I felt considerably upset.

The dog was sitting on his haunches on the ground below, watching us, and it was quite plain to be seen, from his leisurely manner, that it was not his busy day. He bared his teeth and growled when he caught my eye.

"You *look* like a woman hater's dog," I told him. I meant it for an insult; but the beast took it for a compliment.

Then I set myself to solving the question, "How am I to get out of this predicament?"

It did not seem easy to solve it.

"Shall I scream, William Adolphus?" I demanded of that intelligent animal. William Adolphus shook his head. This is a fact. And I agreed with him.

"No, I shall not scream, William Adolphus," I said. "There is probably no one to hear me except Alexander Abraham, and I have my painful doubts about his tender mercies. Now, it is impossible to go down. Is it, then, William Adolphus, possible to go up?"

I looked up. Just above my head was an open window with a tolerably stout branch extending right across it.

"Shall we try that way, William Adolphus?" I asked.

William Adolphus, wasting no words, began to climb the tree. I followed his example. The dog ran in circles about the tree and looked things not lawful to be uttered. It probably would have been a relief to him to bark if it hadn't been so against his principles.

I got in by the window easily enough, and found myself in a bedroom the like of which for disorder and dust and general awfulness I had never seen in all my life. But I did not pause to take in details. With William Adolphus under my arm I marched downstairs, fervently hoping I should meet no one on the way.

I did not. The hall below was empty and dusty. I opened the first door I came to and walked boldly in. A man was sitting by the window, looking moodily out. I should have known him for Alexander Abraham anywhere. He had just the same uncared-for, ragged appearance that the house had; and yet, like the house, it seemed that he would not be bad looking if he were trimmed up a little. His hair looked as if it had never been combed, and his whiskers were wild in the extreme.

He looked at me with blank amazement in his countenance.

"Where is Jimmy Spencer?" I demanded. "I have come to see him."

"How did he ever let you in?" asked the man, staring at me.

"He didn't let me in," I retorted. "He chased me all over the lawn, and I only saved myself from being torn piecemeal by scrambling up a tree. You ought to be prosecuted for keeping such a dog! Where is Jimmy?"

Instead of answering Alexander Abraham began to laugh in a most unpleasant fashion.

"Trust a woman for getting into a man's house if she had made up her mind to," he said disagreeably.

Seeing that it was his intention to vex me I remained cool and collected.

"Oh, I wasn't particular about getting into your house, Mr. Bennett," I said calmly. "I had but little choice in the matter. It was get in lest a worse fate befall me. It was not you or your house I wanted to see—although I admit that it is worth seeing if a person is anxious to find out how dirty a place *can* be. It was Jimmy. For the third and last time—where is Jimmy?"

"Jimmy is not here," said Mr. Bennett gruffly—but not quite so assuredly. "He left last week and hired with a man over at Newbridge."

"In that case," I said, picking up William Adolphus, who had been exploring the room with a disdainful air, "I won't disturb you any longer. I shall go."

"Yes, I think it would be the wisest thing," said Alexander Abraham—not disagreeably this time, but reflectively, as if there was some doubt about the matter. "I'll let you out by the back door. Then the—ahem!—the dog will not interfere with you. Please go away quietly and quickly."

I wondered if Alexander Abraham thought I would go away with a whoop. But I said nothing, thinking this the most dignified course of conduct, and I followed him out to the kitchen as quickly and quietly as he could have wished. Such a kitchen!

Alexander Abraham opened the door—which was locked—just as a buggy containing two men drove into the yard.

"Too late!" he exclaimed in a tragic tone. I understood that something dreadful must have happened, but I did not care, since, as I fondly supposed, it did not concern me. I pushed out past Alexander Abraham—who was looking as guilty as if he had been caught burglarizing—and came face to face with the man who had sprung from the buggy. It was old Dr. Blair, from Carmody, and he was looking at me as if he had found me shoplifting.

"My dear Peter," he said gravely, "I am *very* sorry to see you here—very sorry indeed."

I admit that this exasperated me. Besides, no man on earth, not even my old family doctor, has any right to "My dear Peter" me!

"There is no loud call for sorrow, doctor," I said loftily. "If a woman, forty-eight years of age, a member of the Presbyterian church in good and regular standing, cannot call upon one of her Sunday School scholars without wrecking all the proprieties, how old must she be before she can?"

The doctor did not answer my question. Instead, he looked reproachfully at Alexander Abraham.

"Is this how you keep your word, Mr. Bennett?" he said. "I thought that you promised me that you would not let anyone into the house."

"I didn't let her in," growled Mr. Bennett. "Good heavens, man, she climbed in at an upstairs window, despite the presence on my grounds of a policeman and a dog! What is to be done with a woman like that?"

"I do not understand what all this means," I said, addressing myself to the doctor and ignoring Alexander Abraham entirely, "but if my presence here is so extremely inconvenient to all concerned you can soon be relieved of it. I am going at once."

"I am very sorry, my dear Peter," said the doctor impressively, "but that is just what I cannot allow you to do. This house is under quarantine for smallpox. You will have to stay here."

Smallpox! For the first and last time in my life I openly lost my temper with a man. I wheeled furiously upon Alexander Abraham.

"Why didn't you tell me?" I cried.

"Tell you!" he said, glaring at me. "When I first saw you it was too late to tell you. I thought the kindest thing I could do was to hold my tongue and let you get away in happy ignorance. This will teach you to take a man's house by storm, madam!"

"Now, now, don't quarrel, my good people." interposed the doctor seriously—but I saw a twinkle in his eye. "You'll have to spend some time together under the same roof and you won't improve the situation by disagreeing. You see, Peter, it was this way. Mr. Bennett was in town yesterday—where, as you are aware, there is a bad outbreak of smallpox—and took dinner in a boarding-house where one of the maids was ill. Last night she developed unmistakable symptoms of smallpox. The Board of Health at once got after all the people who were in the house yesterday, so far as they could locate them, and put them under quarantine. I came down here this morning and explained the matter to Mr. Bennett. I brought Jeremiah Jeffries to guard the front of the house and Mr. Bennett gave me his word of honour that he would not let anyone in by the back way while I went to get another policeman and make all the necessary arrangements. I have brought Thomas Wright and have secured the services of another man to attend to Mr. Bennett's barn work and bring provisions to the house. Jacob Green and Cleophas Lee will watch at night. I don't think there is much danger of Mr. Bennett's taking the smallpox, but until we are sure you must remain here, Peter."

While listening to the doctor I had been thinking. It was the most distressing predicament I had ever got into in my life, but there was no sense in making it worse.

"Very well, doctor," I said calmly. "Yes, I was vaccinated a month ago, when the news of the smallpox first came. When you go back through Avonlea kindly go to Sarah Pye and ask her to live in my house during my absence and look after things, especially the cats. Tell her to give them new milk twice a day and a square inch of butter apiece once a week. Get her to put my two dark print wrappers, some aprons, and some changes of underclothing in my third best valise and have it sent down to me. My pony is tied out there to the fence. Please take him home. That is all, I think."

"No, it isn't all," said Alexander Abraham grumpily. "Send that cat home, too. I won't have a cat around the place—I'd rather have the smallpox."

I looked Alexander Abraham over gradually, in a way I have, beginning at his feet and travelling up to his head. I took my time over it; and then I said, very quietly,

"You may have both. Anyway, you'll have to have William

Adolphus. He is under quarantine as well as you and I. Do you suppose I am going to have my cat ranging at large through Avonlea, scattering smallpox germs among innocent people? I'll have to put up with that dog of yours. You will have to endure William Adolphus."

Alexander Abraham groaned, but I could see that the way I had looked him over had chastened him considerably.

The doctor drove away, and I went into the house, not choosing to linger outside and be grinned at by Thomas Wright. I hung my coat up in the hall and laid my bonnet carefully on the sitting-room table, having first dusted a clean place for it with my handkerchief. I longed to fall upon that house at once and clean it up, but I had to wait until the doctor came back with my wrapper. I could not clean house in my new suit and a silk shirtwaist.

Alexander Abraham was sitting on a chair looking at me. Presently he said,

"I am *not* curious—but will you kindly tell me why the doctor called you Peter?"

"Because that is my name, I suppose," I answered, shaking up a cushion for William Adolphus and thereby disturbing the dust of years.

Alexander Abraham coughed gently.

"Isn't that—ahem!—rather a peculiar name for a woman?"

"It is," I said, wondering how much soap, if any, there was in the house.

"I am *not* curious," said Alexander Abraham, "but would you mind telling me how you came to be called Peter?"

"If I had been a boy my parents intended to call me Peter in honour of a rich uncle. When I—fortunately—turned out to be a girl my mother insisted that I should be called Angelina. They gave me both names and called me Angelina, but as soon as I grew old enough I decided to be called Peter. It was bad enough, but not so bad as Angelina."

"I should say it was more appropriate," said Alexander Abraham, intending, as I perceived, to be disagreeable.

"Precisely," I agreed calmly. "My last name is MacPherson, and I live in Avonlea. As you are *not* curious, that will be all the information you will need about me."

"Oh!" Alexander Abraham looked as if a light had broken in on him. "I've heard of you. You—ah—pretend to dislike men."

Pretend! Goodness only knows what would have happened to Alexander Abraham just then if a diversion had not taken place. But the door opened and a dog came in—*the* dog. I suppose he had got tired waiting under the cherry tree for William Adolphus and me to come down. He was even uglier indoors than out.

"Oh, Mr. Riley, Mr. Riley, see what you have let me in for," said Alexander Abraham reproachfully.

But Mr. Riley—since that was the brute's name—paid no attention to Alexander Abraham. He had caught sight of William Adolphus curled up on the cushion, and he started across the room to investigate him. William Adolphus sat up and began to take notice.

"Call off that dog," I said warningly to Alexander Abraham.

"Call him off yourself," he retorted. "Since you've brought that cat here you can protect him."

"Oh, it wasn't for William Adolphus' sake I spoke," I said pleasantly. "William Adolphus can protect himself."

William Adolphus could and did. He humped his back, flattened his ears, swore once, and then made a flying leap for Mr. Riley. William Adolphus landed squarely on Mr. Riley's brindled back and promptly took fast hold, spitting and clawing and caterwauling.

You never saw a more astonished dog than Mr. Riley. With a yell of terror he bolted out to the kitchen, out of the kitchen into the hall, through the hall into the room, and so into the kitchen and round again. With each circuit he went faster and faster, until he looked like a brindled streak with a dash of black and white on top. Such a racket and commotion I never heard, and I laughed until the tears came into my eyes. Mr. Riley flew around and around, and William Adolphus held on grimly and clawed. Alexander Abraham turned purple with rage.

"Woman, call off that infernal cat before he kills my dog," he shouted above the din of yelps and yowls.

"Oh, he won't kill him," I said reassuringly, "and he's going too fast to hear me if I did call him. If you can stop the dog,

Mr. Bennett, I'll guarantee to make William Adolphus listen to reason, but there's no use trying to argue with a lightning flash."

Alexander Abraham made a frantic lunge at the brindled streak as it whirled past him, with the result that he overbalanced himself and went sprawling on the floor with a crash. I ran to help him up, which only seemed to enrage him further.

"Woman," he spluttered viciously, "I wish you and your fiend of a cat were in—in—"

"In Avonlea," I finished quickly, to save Alexander Abraham from committing profanity. "So do I, Mr. Bennett, with all my heart. But since we are not, let us make the best of it like sensible people. And in future you will kindly remember that my name is Miss MacPherson, *not* Woman!"

With this the end came and I was thankful, for the noise those two animals made was so terrific that I expected the policeman would be rushing in, smallpox or no smallpox, to see if Alexander Abraham and I were trying to murder each other. Mr. Riley suddenly veered in his mad career and bolted into a dark corner between the stove and the wood-box. William Adolphus let go just in time.

There never was any more trouble with Mr. Riley after that. A meeker, more thoroughly chastened dog you could not find. William Adolphus had the best of it and he kept it.

Seeing that things had calmed down and that it was five o'clock I decided to get tea. I told Alexander Abraham that I would prepare it, if he would show me where the eatables were.

"You needn't mind," said Alexander Abraham. "I've been in the habit of getting my own tea for twenty years."

"I daresay. But you haven't been in the habit of getting mine," I said firmly. "I wouldn't eat anything you cooked if I starved to death. If you want some occupation you'd better get some salve and anoint the scratches on that poor dog's back."

Alexander Abraham said something that I prudently did not hear. Seeing that he had no information to hand out I went on an exploring expedition into the pantry. The place was awful beyond description, and for the first time a vague sentiment of pity for Alexander Abraham glimmered in my breast. When a man had to live in such surroundings the wonder was, not that he hated women, but that he didn't hate the whole human race.

But I got up a supper somehow. I am noted for getting up suppers. The bread was from the Carmody bakery and I made good tea and excellent toast; besides, I found a can of peaches in the pantry which, as they were bought, I wasn't afraid to eat.

That tea and toast mellowed Alexander Abraham in spite of himself. He ate the last crust, and didn't growl when I gave William Adolphus all the cream that was left. Mr. Riley did not seem to want anything. He had no appetite.

By this time the doctor's boy had arrived with my valise. Alexander Abraham gave me quite civilly to understand that there was a spare room across the hall and that I might take possession of it. I went to it and put on a wrapper. There was a set of fine furniture in the room, and a comfortable bed. But the dust! William Adolphus had followed me in and his paws left marks everywhere he walked.

"Now," I said briskly, returning to the kitchen, "I'm going to clean up and I shall begin with this kitchen. You'd better betake yourself to the sitting-room, Mr. Bennett, so as to be out of the way."

Alexander Abraham glared at me.

"I'm not going to have my house meddled with," he snapped. "It suits me. If you don't like it you can leave it."

"No, I can't. That is just the trouble," I said pleasantly. "If I could leave it I shouldn't be here for a minute. Since I can't, it simply has to be cleaned. I can tolerate men and dogs when I am compelled to, but I cannot and will not tolerate dirt and disorder. Go into the sitting-room."

Alexander Abraham went. As he closed the door, I heard him say, in capitals, "WHAT AN AWFUL WOMAN!"

I cleaned that kitchen and the pantry adjoining. It was ten o'clock when I got through, and Alexander Abraham had gone to bed without deigning further speech. I locked Mr. Riley in one room and William Adolphus in another and went to bed, too. I had never felt so dead tired in my life before. It had been a hard day.

But I got up bright and early the next morning and got a tiptop breakfast, which Alexander Abraham condescended to eat. When the provision man came into the yard I called to him from the window to bring me a box of soap in the afternoon, and then I tackled the sitting-room.

It took me the best part of a week to get that house in order, but I did it thoroughly. I am noted for doing things thoroughly. At the end of the time it was clean from garret to cellar. Alexander Abraham made no comments on my operations, though he groaned loud and often, and said caustic things to poor Mr. Riley, who hadn't the spirit to answer back after his drubbing by William Adolphus. I made allowances for Alexander Abraham because his vaccination had taken and his arm was real sore; and I cooked elegant meals, not having much else to do, once I had got things scoured up. The house was full of provisions—Alexander Abraham wasn't mean about such things, I will say that for him. Altogether, I was more comfortable than I had expected to be. When Alexander Abraham wouldn't talk I let him alone; and when he would I just said as sarcastic things as he did, only I said them smiling and pleasant. I could see he had a wholesome awe of me. But now and then he seemed to forget his disposition and talked like a human being. We had one or two real interesting conversations. Alexander Abraham was an intelligent man, though he had got terribly warped. I told him once I thought he must have been nice when he was a boy.

One day he astonished me by appearing at the dinner table with his hair brushed and a white collar on. We had a tiptop dinner that day, and I had made a pudding that was far too good for a woman hater. When Alexander Abraham had disposed of two large platefuls of it, he sighed and said,

"You can certainly cook. It's a pity you are such a detestable crank in other respects."

"It's kind of convenient being a crank," I said. "People are careful how they meddle with you. Haven't you found that out in your own experience?"

"I am *not* a crank," growled Alexander Abraham resentfully. "All I ask is to be let alone."

"That's the very crankiest kind of a crank," I said. "A person who wants to be let alone flies in the face of Providence, who decreed that folks for their own good were not to be let alone. But cheer up, Mr. Bennett. The quarantine will be up on

Tuesday and then you'll certainly be let alone for the rest of your natural life, as far as William Adolphus and I are concerned. You may then return to your wallowing in the mire and be as dirty and comfortable as of yore."

Alexander Abraham growled again. The prospect didn't seem to cheer him up as much as I should have expected. Then he did an amazing thing. He poured some cream into a saucer and set it down before William Adolphus. William Adolphus lapped it up, keeping one eye on Alexander Abraham lest the latter should change his mind. Not to be outdone, I handed Mr. Riley a bone.

Neither Alexander Abraham nor I had worried much about the smallpox. We didn't believe he would take it, for he hadn't even seen the girl who was sick. But the very next morning I heard him calling me from the upstairs landing.

"Miss MacPherson," he said in a voice so uncommonly mild that it gave me an uncanny feeling, "what are the symptoms of smallpox?"

"Chills and flushes, pain in the limbs and back, nausea and vomiting," I answered promptly, for I had been reading them up in a patent medicine almanac.

"I've got them all," said Alexander Abraham hollowly.

I didn't feel as much scared as I should have expected. After enduring a woman hater and a brindled dog and the early disorder of that house—and coming off best with all three— smallpox seemed rather insignificant. I went to the window and called to Thomas Wright to send for the doctor.

The doctor came down from Alexander Abraham's room looking grave.

"It's impossible to pronounce on the disease yet," he said. "There is no certainty until the eruption appears. But, of course, there is every likelihood that it is the smallpox. It is very unfortunate. I am afraid that it will be difficult to get a nurse. All the nurses in town who will take smallpox cases are overbusy now, for the epidemic is still raging there. However, I'll go into town tonight and do my best. Meanwhile, as Mr. Bennett does not require any attendance at present, you must not go near him, Peter."

I wasn't going to take orders from any man, and as soon as the doctor had gone I marched straight up to Alexander Abraham's room with some dinner for him on a tray. There was a lemon cream I thought he could eat even if he had the smallpox.

"You shouldn't come near me," he growled. "You are risking your life."

"I am not going to see a fellow creature starve to death, even if he is a man," I retorted.

"The worst of it all," groaned Alexander Abraham, between mouthfuls of lemon cream, "is that the doctor says I've got to have a nurse. I've got so kind of used to you being in the house that I don't mind you, but the thought of another woman coming here is too much. Did you give my poor dog anything to eat?"

"He has had a better dinner than many a Christian," I said severely.

Alexander Abraham need not have worried about another woman coming in. The doctor came back that night with care on his brow.

"I don't know what is to be done," he said. "I can't get a soul to come here."

"*I* shall nurse Mr. Bennett," I said with dignity. "It is my duty and I never shirk my duty. I am noted for that. He is a man, and he has smallpox, and he keeps a vile dog; but I am not going to see him die for lack of care for all that."

"You're a good soul, Peter," said the doctor, looking relieved, manlike, as soon as he found a woman to shoulder the responsibility.

I nursed Alexander Abraham through the smallpox, and I didn't mind it much. He was much more amiable sick than well, and he had the disease in a very mild form. Below stairs I reigned supreme and Mr. Riley and William Adolphus lay down together like the lion and the lamb. I fed Mr. Riley regularly, and once, seeing him looking lonesome, I patted him gingerly. It was nicer than I thought it would be. Mr. Riley lifted his head and looked at me with an expression in his eyes which cured me of wondering why on earth Alexander Abraham was so fond of the beast.

When Alexander Abraham was able to sit up he began to make up for the time he'd lost being pleasant. Anything more sarcastic than that man in his convalescence you couldn't imagine. I just laughed at him, having found out that that could be depended on to irritate him. To irritate him still further I cleaned the house all over again. But what vexed him most of all was that Mr. Riley took to following me about and wagging what he had of a tail at me.

"It wasn't enough that you should come into my peaceful home and turn it upside down, but you have to alienate the affections of my dog," complained Alexander Abraham.

"He'll get fond of you again when I go home," I said comfortingly. "Dogs aren't very particular that way. What they want is bones. Cats now, they love disinterestedly. William Adolphus has never swerved in his allegiance to me, although you do give him cream in the pantry on the sly."

Alexander Abraham looked foolish. He hadn't thought I knew that.

I didn't take the smallpox and in another week the doctor came out and sent the policeman home. I was disinfected and William Adolphus was fumigated, and then we were free to go.

"Goodbye, Mr. Bennett," I said, offering to shake hands in a forgiving spirit. "I've no doubt that you are glad to be rid of me, but you are no gladder than I am to go. I suppose this house will be dirtier than ever in a month's time, and Mr. Riley will have discarded the little polish his manners have taken on. Reformation with men and dogs never goes very deep."

With this Parthian shaft I walked out of the house, supposing that I had seen the last of it and Alexander Abraham.

I was glad to get back home, of course; but it did seem queer and lonesome. The cats hardly knew me, and William Adolphus roamed about forlornly and appeared to feel like an exile. I didn't take as much pleasure in cooking as usual, for it seemed kind of foolish to be fussing over oneself. The sight of a bone made me think of poor Mr. Riley. The neighbours avoided me pointedly, for they couldn't get rid of the fear that I might erupt into smallpox at any moment. My Sunday School class had been given to another woman, and altogether I felt as if I didn't belong anywhere.

I had existed like this for a fortnight when Alexander Abraham suddenly appeared. He walked in one evening at dusk, but at first sight I didn't know him he was so spruced and barbered up. But William Adolphus knew him. Will you believe it, William Adolphus, my own William Adolphus, rubbed up against that man's trouser leg with an undisguised purr of satisfaction.

"I had to come, Angelina," said Alexander Abraham. "I couldn't stand it any longer."

"My name is Peter," I said coldly, although I was feeling ridiculously glad about something.

"It isn't," said Alexander Abraham stubbornly. "It is Angelina for me, and always will be. I shall never call you Peter. Angelina just suits you exactly; and Angelina Bennett would suit you still better. You must come back, Angelina. Mr. Riley is moping for you, and I can't get along without somebody to appreciate my sarcasms, now that you have accustomed me to the luxury."

"What about the other five cats?" I demanded.

Alexander Abraham sighed.

"I suppose they'll have to come too," he sighed, "though no doubt they'll chase poor Mr. Riley clean off the premises. But I can live without him, and I can't without you. How soon can you be ready to marry me?"

"I haven't said that I was going to marry you at all, have I?" I said tartly, just to be consistent. For I wasn't feeling tart.

"No, but you will, won't you?" said Alexander Abraham anxiously. "Because if you won't, I wish you'd let me die of the smallpox. Do, dear Angelina."

To think that a man should dare to call me his "dear Angelina!" And to think that I shouldn't mind!

"Where I go, William Adolphus goes," I said, "but I shall give away the other five cats for—for the sake of Mr. Riley."

PA SLOANE'S PURCHASE

"I GUESS the molasses is getting low, ain't it?" said Pa Sloane insinuatingly. "S'pose I'd better drive up to Carmody this afternoon and get some more."

"There's a good half-gallon of molasses in the jug yet," said Ma Sloane ruthlessly.

"That so? Well, I noticed the kerosene demijohn wasn't very hefty the last time I filled the can. Reckon it needs replenishing."

"We have kerosene enough to do for a fortnight yet." Ma continued to eat her dinner with an impassive face, but a twinkle made itself apparent in her eye. Lest Pa should see it, and feel encouraged thereby, she looked immovably at her plate.

Pa Sloane sighed. His invention was giving out.

"Didn't I hear you say day before yesterday that you were out of nutmegs?" he queried, after a few moments' severe reflection.

"I got a supply of them from the egg-pedlar yesterday," responded Ma, by a great effort preventing the twinkle from spreading over her entire face. She wondered if this third failure would squelch Pa. But Pa was not to be squelched.

"Well, anyway," he said, brightening up under the influence of a sudden saving inspiration, "I'll have to go up to get the sorrel mare shod. So, if you've any little errands you want done at the store, Ma, just make a memo of them while I hitch up."

The matter of shoeing the sorrel mare was beyond Ma's province, although she had her own suspicions about the sorrel mare's need of shoes.

"Why can't you give up beating about the bush, Pa?" she demanded, with contemptuous pity. "You might as well own up what's taking you to Carmody. *I* can see through your design. You want to get away to the Garland auction. That is what is troubling you, Pa Sloane."

"I dunno but what I might step over, seeing it's so handy. But the sorrel mare railly does need shoeing, Ma," protested Pa.

"There's always something needing to be done if it's convenient," retorted Ma. "Your mania for auctions will be the ruin of you yet, Pa. A man of fifty-five ought to have grown out of such a hankering. But the older you get the worse you get. Anyway, if *I* wanted to go to auctions I'd select them as was something like, and not waste my time on little one-horse affairs like this of Garland's."

"One might pick up something real cheap at Garland's," said Pa defensively.

"Well, you are not going to pick up anything, cheap or otherwise, Pa Sloane, because I'm going with you to see that you don't. I know I can't stop you from going. I might as well try to stop the wind from blowing. But I shall go, too, out of self-defence. This house is so full now of old clutter and truck that you've brought home from auctions that I feel as if I was made up out of pieces and left overs."

Pa Sloane sighed again. It was not exhilarating to attend an auction with Ma. She would never let him bid on anything. But he realized that Ma's mind was made up beyond the power of mortal man's persuasion to alter it; so he went out to hitch up.

Pa Sloane's dissipation was going to auctions and buying things that nobody else would buy. Ma Sloane's patient endeavours of over thirty years had been able to effect only a partial reform. Sometimes Pa heroically refrained from going to an auction for six months at a time; then he would break out worse than ever, go to all that took place for miles around, and come home with a wagonful of misfits. His last exploit had been to bid in an old dasher churn for five dollars—the boys "ran things up" on Pa Sloane for the fun of it—and bring it home to outraged Ma, who had made her butter for fifteen years in the very latest, most up-to-date barrel churn. To add insult to injury this was the second dasher churn Pa had bought at auction. That settled it. Ma decreed that henceforth she would chaperon Pa when he went to auctions.

But this was the day of Pa's good angel. When he drove up to the door where Ma was waiting, a breathless, hatless imp of ten flew into the yard, and hurled himself between Ma and the wagon-step.

"Oh, Mrs. Sloane, won't you come over to our house at once?" he gasped. "The baby, he's got colic, and ma's just wild, and he's all black in the face."

Ma went, feeling that the stars in their courses fought against a woman who was trying to do her duty by her husband. But first she admonished Pa.

"I shall have to let you go alone. But I charge you, Pa, not to bid on anything—on *anything,* do you hear?"

Pa heard and promised to heed, with every intention of keeping his promise. Then he drove away joyfully. On any other occasion Ma would have been a welcome companion. But she certainly spoiled the flavour of an auction.

When Pa arrived at the Carmody store, he saw that the little yard of the Garland place below the hill was already full of people. The auction had evidently begun; so, not to miss any more of it, Pa hurried down. The sorrel mare could wait for her shoes until afterwards.

Ma had been within bounds when she called the Garland auction a "one-horse affair." It certainly was very paltry, especially when compared to the big Donaldson auction of a month ago, which Pa still lived over in happy dreams.

Horace Garland and his wife had been poor. When they died within six weeks of each other, one of consumption and one of pneumonia, they left nothing but debts and a little furniture. The house had been a rented one.

The bidding on the various poor articles of household gear put up for sale was not brisk, but had an element of resigned determination. Carmody people knew that these things had to be sold to pay the debts, and they could not be sold unless they were bought. Still, it was a very tame affair.

A woman came out of the house carrying a baby of about eighteen months in her arms, and sat down on the bench beneath the window.

"There's Marthy Blair with the Garland baby," said Robert Lawson to Pa. "I'd like to know what's to become of that poor young one!"

"Ain't there any of the father's or mother's folks to take him?" asked Pa.

"No. Horace had no relatives that anybody ever heard of. Mrs. Horace had a brother; but he went to Manitoba years ago, and nobody knows where he is now. Somebody'll have to take the baby and nobody seems anxious to. I've got eight myself, or I'd think about it. He's a fine little chap."

Pa, with Ma's parting admonition ringing in his ears, did not bid on anything, although it will never be known how great was the heroic self-restraint he put on himself, until just at the last, when he did bid on a collection of flower-pots, thinking he might indulge himself to that small extent. But Josiah Sloane had been commissioned by his wife to bring those flower-pots home to her; so Pa lost them.

"There, that's all," said the auctioneer, wiping his face, for the day was very warm for October.

"There's nothing more unless we sell the baby."

A laugh went through the crowd. The sale had been a dull affair, and they were ready for some fun. Someone called out, "Put him up, Jacob." The joke found favour and the call was repeated hilariously.

Jacob Blair took little Teddy Garland out of Martha's arms and stood him up on the table by the door, steadying the small chap with one big brown hand. The baby had a mop of yellow curls, a pink and white face, and big blue eyes. He laughed out at the men before him and waved his hands in delight. Pa Sloane thought he had never seen so pretty a baby.

"Here's a baby for sale," shouted the auctioneer. "A genuine article, pretty near as good as brand-new. A real live baby, warranted to walk and talk a little. Who bids? A dollar? Did I hear anyone mean enough to bid a dollar? No, sir, babies don't come as cheap as that, especially the curly-headed brand."

The crowd laughed again. Pa Sloane, by way of keeping on the joke, cried, "Four dollars!"

Everybody looked at him. The impression flashed through the crowd that Pa was in earnest, and meant thus to signify his intention of giving the baby a home. He was well-to-do, and his only son was grown up and married.

"Six," cried out John Clarke from the other side of the yard. John Clarke lived at White Sands and he and his wife were childless.

That bid of John Clarke's was Pa's undoing. Pa Sloane could not have an enemy; but a rival he had, and that rival was John Clarke. Everywhere at auctions John Clarke was wont to bid against Pa. At the last auction he had outbid Pa in everything, not having the fear of his wife before his eyes. Pa's fighting blood was up in a moment; he forgot Ma Sloane; he forgot what he was bidding for; he forgot everything except a determination that John Clarke should not be victor again.

"Ten," he called shrilly.

"Fifteen," shouted Clarke.

"Twenty," vociferated Pa.

"Twenty-five," bellowed Clarke.

"Thirty," shrieked Pa. He nearly burst a blood-vessel in his shrieking, but he had won. Clarke turned off with a laugh and a shrug, and the baby was knocked down to Pa Sloane by the auctioneer, who had meanwhile been keeping the crowd in roars of laughter by a quick fire of witticisms. There had not been such fun at an auction in Carmody for many a long day.

Pa Sloane came, or was pushed, forward. The baby was put into his arms; he realized that he was expected to keep it, and he was too dazed to refuse; besides, his heart went out to the child.

The auctioneer looked doubtfully at the money which Pa laid mutely down.

"I s'pose that part was only a joke," he said.

"Not a bit of it," said Robert Lawson. "All the money won't be too much to pay the debts. There's a doctor's bill, and this will just about pay it."

Pa Sloane drove back home, with the sorrel mare still unshod, the baby, and the baby's meagre bundle of clothes. The baby did not trouble him much; it had become well used to strangers in the past two months, and promptly fell asleep on his arm; but Pa Sloane did not enjoy that drive; at the end of it he mentally saw Ma Sloane.

Ma was there, too, waiting for him on the back door-step as he drove into the yard at sunset. Her face, when she saw the baby, expressed the last degree of amazement.

"Pa Sloane," she demanded, "whose is that young one, and where did you get it?"

"I—I—bought it at the auction, Ma," said Pa feebly. Then he waited for the explosion. None came. This last exploit of Pa's was too much for Ma.

With a gasp she snatched the baby from Pa's arms, and ordered him to go out and put the mare in. When Pa returned to the kitchen Ma had set the baby on the sofa, fenced him around with chairs so that he couldn't fall off and given him a molasses cooky.

"Now, Pa Sloane, you can explain," she said.

Pa explained. Ma listened in grim silence until he had finished. Then she said sternly:

"Do you reckon we're going to keep this baby?"

"I—I—dunno," said Pa. And he didn't.

"Well, we're *not*. I brought up one boy and that's enough. I don't calculate to be pestered with any more. I never was much struck on children *as* children, anyhow. You say that Mary Garland had a brother out in Manitoba? Well, we shall just write to him and tell him he's got to look out for his nephew."

"But how can you do that, Ma, when nobody knows his address?" objected Pa, with a wistful look at that delicious, laughing baby.

"I'll find out his address if I have to advertise in the papers for him," retorted Ma. "As for you, Pa Sloane, you're not fit to be out of a lunatic asylum. The next auction you'll be buying a wife, I s'pose?"

Pa, quite crushed by Ma's sarcasm, pulled his chair in to supper. Ma picked up the baby and sat down at the head of the table. Little Teddy laughed and pinched her face—Ma's face! Ma looked very grim, but she fed him his supper as skillfully as if it had not been thirty years since she had done such a thing. But then, the woman who once learns the mother knack never forgets it.

After tea Ma despatched Pa over to William Alexander's to borrow a high chair. When Pa returned in the twilight, the baby was fenced in on the sofa again, and Ma was stepping briskly about the garret. She was bringing down the little cot bed her own boy had once occupied, and setting it up in their room for Teddy. Then she undressed the baby and rocked him to sleep, crooning an old lullaby over him. Pa Sloane sat quietly and listened, with very sweet memories of the long ago, when he and Ma had been young and proud, and the bewhiskered William Alexander had been a curly-headed little fellow like this one.

Ma was not driven to advertising for Mrs. Garland's brother. That personage saw the notice of his sister's death in a home paper and wrote to the Carmody postmaster for full information. The letter was referred to Ma and Ma answered it.

She wrote that they had taken in the baby, pending further arrangements, but had no intention of keeping it; and she calmly demanded of its uncle what was to be done with it. Then she sealed and addressed the letter with an unfaltering hand; but, when it was done, she looked across the table at Pa Sloane, who was sitting in the armchair with the baby on his knee. They were having a royal good time together. Pa had always been dreadfully foolish about babies. He looked ten years younger. Ma's keen eyes softened a little as she watched them.

A prompt answer came to her letter. Teddy's uncle wrote that he had six children of his own, but was nevertheless willing and glad to give his little nephew a home. But he could not come after him. Josiah Spencer, of White Sands, was going out to Manitoba in the spring. If Mr. and Mrs. Sloane could only keep the baby till then he could be sent out with the Spencers. Perhaps they would see a chance sooner.

"There'll be no chance sooner," said Pa Sloane in a tone of satisfaction.

"No, worse luck!" retorted Ma crisply.

The winter passed by. Little Teddy grew and throve, and Pa

Sloane worshipped him. Ma was very good to him, too, and
Teddy was just as fond of her as of Pa.

Nevertheless, as the spring drew near, Pa became depressed.
Sometimes he sighed heavily, especially when he heard casual
references to the Josiah Spencer emigration.

One warm afternoon in early May Josiah Spencer arrived.
He found Ma knitting placidly in the kitchen, while Pa nodded
over his newspaper and the baby played with the cat on the
floor.

"Good afternoon, Mrs. Sloane," said Josiah with a flourish.
"I just dropped in to see about this young man here. We are
going to leave next Wednesday; so you'd better send him down
to our place Monday or Tuesday, so that he can get used to
us, and—

"Oh, Ma," began Pa, rising imploringly to his feet.

Ma transfixed him with her eye.

"Sit down, Pa," she commanded.

Unhappy Pa sat.

Then Ma glared at the smiling Josiah, who instantly felt as
guilty as if he had been caught stealing sheep red-handed.

"We are much obliged to you, Mr. Spencer," said Ma icily,
"but this baby is *ours*. We bought him, and we paid for him.
A bargain is a bargain. When I pay cash down for babies I
propose to get my money's worth. We are going to keep this
baby in spite of any number of uncles in Manitoba. Have I
made this sufficiently clear to your understanding, Mr. Spencer?"

"Certainly, certainly," stammered the unfortunate man, feeling guiltier than ever, "but I thought you didn't want him—I
thought you'd written to his uncle—I thought—"

"I really wouldn't think quite so much if I were you," said
Ma kindly. "It must be hard on you. Won't you stay and have
tea with us?"

But, no, Josiah would not stay. He was thankful to make
his escape with such rags of self-respect as remained to him.

Pa Sloane arose and came around to Ma's chair. He laid a
trembling hand on her shoulder.

"Ma, you're a good woman," he said softly.

"Go 'long, Pa," said Ma.

THE COURTING OF PRISSY STRONG

I WASN'T able to go to prayer meeting that evening because I had neuralgia in my face; but Thomas went, and the minute he came home I knew by the twinkle in his eye that he had some news.

"Who do you s'pose Stephen Clark went home with from meeting tonight?" he said, chuckling.

"Jane Miranda Blair," I said promptly. Stephen Clark's wife had been dead for two years and he hadn't taken much notice of anybody, so far as was known. But Carmody had Jane Miranda all ready for him, and really I don't know why she didn't suit him, except for the reason that a man never does what he is expected to do when it comes to marrying.

Thomas chuckled again.

"Wrong. He stepped up to Prissy Strong and walked off with her. Cold soup warmed over."

"Prissy Strong!" I just held up my hands. Then I laughed. "He needn't try for Prissy," I said. "Emmeline nipped that in the bud twenty years ago, and she'll do it again."

"Em'line is an old crank," growled Thomas. He detests Emmeline Strong, and always did.

"She's that, all right," I agreed, "and that is just the reason she can turn poor Prissy any way she likes. You mark my

352

words, she'll put her foot right down on this as soon as she finds it out."

Thomas said that I was probably right. I lay awake for a long time after I went to bed that night, thinking of Prissy and Stephen. As a general rule I don't concern my head about other people's affairs, but Prissy was such a helpless creature I couldn't get her off my mind.

Twenty years ago Stephen Clark had tried to go with Prissy Strong. That was pretty soon after Prissy's father had died. She and Emmeline were living alone together. Emmeline was thirty, ten years older than Prissy, and if ever there were two sisters totally different from each other in every way, those two were Emmeline and Prissy Strong.

Emmeline took after her father; she was big and dark and homely, and she was the most domineering creature that ever stepped on shoe leather. She simply ruled poor Prissy with a rod of iron.

Prissy herself was a pretty girl—at least most people thought so. I can't honestly say I ever admired her style much myself. I like something with more vim and snap to it. Prissy was slim and pink, with soft, appealing blue eyes, and pale gold hair all clinging in baby rings around her face. She was just as meek and timid as she looked and there wasn't a bit of harm in her. I always liked Prissy, even if I didn't admire her looks as much as some people did.

Anyway, it was plain her style suited Stephen Clark. He began to drive her, and there wasn't a speck of doubt that Prissy liked him. Then Emmeline just put a stopper on the affair. It was pure cantankerousness in her. Stephen was a good match and nothing could be said against him. But Emmeline was just determined that Prissy shouldn't marry. She couldn't get married herself, and she was sore enough about it.

Of course, if Prissy had had a spark of spirit she wouldn't have given in. But she hadn't a mite; I believe she would have cut off her nose if Emmeline had ordered her to do it. She was just her mother over again. If ever a girl belied her name Prissy Strong did. There wasn't anything strong about her.

One night, when prayer meeting came out, Stephen stepped up to Prissy as usual and asked if he might see her home. Thomas and I were just behind—we weren't married ourselves then—and we heard it all. Prissy gave one scared, appealing look at Emmeline and then said, "No, thank you, not tonight."

Stephen just turned on his heel and went. He was a high-spirited fellow and I knew he would never overlook a public slight like that. If he had had as much sense as he ought to have had he would have known that Emmeline was at the bottom of it; but he didn't, and he began going to see Althea Gillis, and they were married the next year. Althea was a rather nice girl, though giddy, and I think she and Stephen were happy enough together. In real life things are often like that.

Nobody ever tried to go with Prissy again. I suppose they were afraid of Emmeline. Prissy's beauty soon faded. She was always kind of sweet looking, but her bloom went, and she got shyer and limper every year of her life. She wouldn't have dared put on her second best dress without asking Emmeline's permission. She was real fond of cats and Emmeline wouldn't let her keep one. Emmeline even cut the serial out of the religious weekly she took before she would give it to Prissy, because she didn't believe in reading novels. It used to make me furious to see it all. They were my next door neighbours after I married Thomas, and I was often in and out. Sometimes I'd feel real vexed at Prissy for giving in the way she did; but, after all, she couldn't help it—she was born that way.

And now Stephen was going to try his luck again. It certainly did seem funny.

Stephen walked home with Prissy from prayer meeting four nights before Emmeline found it out. Emmeline hadn't been going to prayer meeting all that summer because she was mad at Mr. Leonard. She had expressed her disapproval to him because he had buried old Naomi Clark at the harbour "just as if she was a Christian," and Mr. Leonard had said something to her she couldn't get over for a while. I don't know what it was, but I know that when Mr. Leonard *was* roused to rebuke anyone the person so rebuked remembered it for a spell.

All at once I knew she must have discovered about Stephen and Prissy, for Prissy stopped going to prayer meeting.

I felt real worried about it, someway, and although Thomas said for goodness' sake not to go poking my fingers into other people's pies, I felt as if I ought to do something. Stephen Clark was a good man and Prissy would have a beautiful home;

and those two little boys of Althea's needed a mother if ever boys did. Besides, I knew quite well that Prissy, in her secret soul, was hankering to be married. So was Emmeline, too— but nobody wanted to help *her* to a husband.

The upshot of my meditations was that I asked Stephen down to dinner with us from church one day. I had heard a rumour that he was going to see Lizzie Pye over at Avonlea, and I knew it was time to be stirring, if anything were to be done. If it had been Jane Miranda I don't know that I'd have bothered; but Lizzie Pye wouldn't have done for a stepmother for Althea's boys at all. She was too bad-tempered, and as mean as second skimmings besides.

Stephen came. He seemed dull and moody, and not much inclined to talk. After dinner I gave Thomas a hint. I said, "You go to bed and have your nap. I want to talk to Stephen."

Thomas shrugged his shoulders and went. He probably thought I was brewing up lots of trouble for myself, but he didn't say anything. As soon as he was out of the way I casually remarked to Stephen that I understood that he was going to take one of my neighbours away and that I couldn't be sorry, though she was an excellent neighbour and I would miss her a great deal.

"You won't have to miss her much, I reckon," said Stephen grimly. "I've been told I'm not wanted there."

I was surprised to hear Stephen come out so plump and plain about it, for I hadn't expected to get at the root of the matter so easily. Stephen wasn't the confidential kind. But it really seemed to be a relief to him to talk about it; I never saw a man feeling so sore about anything. He told me the whole story.

Prissy had written him a letter—he fished it out of his pocket and gave it to me to read. It was in Prissy's prim, pretty little writing, sure enough, and it just said that his attentions were "unwelcome," and would he be "kind enough to refrain from offering them." Not much wonder the poor man went to see Lizzie Pye!

"Stephen, I'm surprised at you for thinking that Prissy Strong wrote that letter," I said.

"It's in her handwriting," he said stubbornly.

"Of course it is. 'The hand is the hand of Esau, but the voice is the voice of Jacob,' " I said, though I wasn't sure whether the quotation was exactly appropriate. "Emmeline composed that letter and made Prissy copy it out. I know that as well as if I'd seen her do it, and you ought to have known it, too."

"If I thought that I'd show Emmeline I could get Prissy in spite of her," said Stephen savagely. "But if Prissy doesn't want me I'm not going to force my attentions on her."

Well, we talked it over a bit, and in the end I agreed to sound Prissy, and find out what she really thought about it. I didn't think it would be hard to do; and it wasn't. I went over the very next day because I saw Emmeline driving off to the store. I found Prissy alone, sewing carpet rags. Emmeline kept her constantly at that—because Prissy hated it I suppose. Prissy was crying when I went in, and in a few minutes I had the whole story.

Prissy wanted to get married—and she wanted to get married to Stephen—and Emmeline wouldn't let her.

"Prissy Strong," I said in exasperation, "you haven't the spirit of a mouse! Why on earth did you write him such a letter?"

"Why, Emmeline made me," said Prissy, as if there couldn't be any appeal from that; and I knew there couldn't—for Prissy. I also knew that if Stephen wanted to see Prissy again Emmeline must know nothing of it, and I told him so when he came down the next evening—to borrow a hoe, he said. It was a long way to come for a hoe.

"Then what am I to do?" he said. "It wouldn't be any use to write, for it would likely fall into Emmeline's hands. She won't let Prissy go anywhere alone after this, and how am I to know when the old cat is away?"

"Please don't insult cats," I said. "I'll tell you what we'll do. You can see the ventilator on our barn from your place, can't you? You'd be able to make out a flag or something tied to it, wouldn't you, through that spy-glass of yours?"

Stephen thought he could.

"Well, you take a squint at it every now and then," I said. "Just as soon as Emmeline leaves Prissy alone I'll hoist the signal."

The chance didn't come for a whole fortnight. Then, one evening, I saw Emmeline striding over the field below our house. As soon as she was out of sight I ran through the birch grove to Prissy.

"Yes, Em'line's gone to sit up with Jane Lawson tonight," said Prissy, all fluttered and trembling.

"Then you put on your muslin dress and fix your hair," I said. "I'm going home to get Thomas to tie something to that ventilator."

But do you think Thomas would do it? Not he. He said he owed something to his position as elder in the church. In the end I had to do it myself, though I don't like climbing ladders. I tied Thomas' long red woollen scarf to the ventilator, and prayed that Stephen would see it. He did, for in less than an hour he drove down our lane and put his horse in our barn. He was all spruced up, and as nervous and excited as a schoolboy. He went right over to Prissy, and I began to tuft my new comfort with a clear conscience. I shall never know why it suddenly came into my head to go up to the garret and make sure that the moths hadn't got into my box of blankets; but I always believed that it was a special interposition of Providence. I went up and happened to look out of the east window; and there I saw Emmeline Strong coming home across our pond field.

I just flew down those garret stairs and out through the birches. I burst into the Strong kitchen, where Stephen and Prissy were sitting as cozy as you please.

"Stephen, come quick! Emmeline's nearly here," I cried.

Prissy looked out of the window and wrung her hands.

"Oh, she's in the lane now," she gasped. "He can't get out of the house without her seeing him. Oh, Rosanna, what shall we do?"

I really don't know what would have become of those two people if I hadn't been in existence to find ideas for them.

"Take Stephen up to the garret and hide him there, Prissy," I said firmly, "and take him quick."

Prissy took him quick, but she had barely time to get back to the kitchen before Emmeline marched in—mad as a wet hen because somebody had been ahead of her offering to sit up with Jane Lawson, and so she lost the chance of poking and prying into things while Jane was asleep. The minute she clapped eyes on Prissy she suspected something. It wasn't any wonder, for there was Prissy, all dressed up, with flushed cheeks and shining eyes. She was all in a quiver of excitement, and looked ten years younger.

"Priscilla Strong, you've been expecting Stephen Clark here this evening!" burst out Emmeline. "You wicked, deceitful, underhanded, ungrateful creature!"

And she went on storming at Prissy, who began to cry, and looked so weak and babyish that I was frightened she would betray the whole thing.

"This is between you and Prissy, Emmeline," I struck in, "and I'm not going to interfere. But I want to get you to come over and show me how to tuft my comfort that new pattern you learned in Avonlea, and as it had better be done before dark I wish you'd come right away."

"I s'pose I'll go," said Emmeline ungraciously, "but Priscilla shall come, too, for I see that she isn't to be trusted out of my sight after this."

I hoped Stephen would see us from the garret window and make good his escape. But I didn't dare trust to chance, so when I got Emmeline safely to work on my comfort I excused myself and slipped out. Luckily my kitchen was on the off side of the house, but I was a nervous woman as I rushed across to the Strong place and dashed up Emmeline's garret stairs to Stephen. It was fortunate I had come, for he didn't know we had gone. Prissy had hidden him behind the loom and he didn't dare move for fear Emmeline would hear him on that creaky floor. He was a sight with cobwebs.

I got him down and smuggled him into our barn, and he stayed there until it was dark and the Strong girls had gone home. Emmeline began to rage at Prissy the moment they were outside my door.

Then Stephen came in and we talked things over. He and Prissy had made good use of their time, short as it had been. Prissy had promised to marry him, and all that remained was to get the ceremony performed.

"And that will be no easy matter," I warned him. "Now that Emmeline's suspicions are aroused she'll never let Prissy out of her sight until you're married to another woman, if it's years. I know Emmeline Strong. And I know Prissy. If it was any other girl in the world she'd run away, or manage it somehow, but Prissy never will. She's too much in the habit of obeying Emmeline. You'll have an obedient wife, Stephen— if you ever get her."

Stephen looked as if he thought that wouldn't be any drawback. Gossip said that Althea had been pretty bossy. I don't know. Maybe it was so.

"Can't you suggest something, Rosanna?" he implored. "You've helped us so far, and I'll never forget it."

"The only thing I can think of is for you to have the license ready, and speak to Mr. Leonard, and keep an eye on our ventilator," I said. "I'll watch here and signal whenever there's an opening."

Well, I watched and Stephen watched, and Mr. Leonard was in the plot, too. Prissy was always a favourite of his, and he would have been more than human, saint as he is, if he'd had any love for Emmeline, after the way she was always trying to brew up strife in the church.

But Emmeline was a match for us all. She never let Prissy out of her sight. Everywhere she went she toted Prissy, too. When a month had gone by I was almost in despair. Mr. Leonard had to leave for the Assembly in another week and Stephen's neighbours were beginning to talk about him. They said that a man who spent all his time hanging around the yard with a spyglass, and trusting everything to a hired boy, couldn't be altogether right in his mind.

I could hardly believe my eyes when I saw Emmeline driving away one day alone. As soon as she was out of sight I whisked over, and Anne Shirley and Diana Barry went with me.

They were visiting me that afternoon. Diana's mother was my second cousin, and, as we visited back and forth frequently, I'd often seen Diana. But I'd never seen her chum, Anne Shirley, although I'd heard enough about her to drive anyone frantic with curiosity. So when she came home from Redmond College that summer I asked Diana to take pity on me and bring her over some afternoon.

I wasn't disappointed in her. I considered her a beauty, though some people couldn't see it. She had the most magnificent red hair and the biggest, shiningest eyes I ever saw in a girl's head. As for her laugh, it made me feel young again to hear it. She and Diana both laughed enough that afternoon, for I told them, under solemn promise of secrecy, all about poor Prissy's love affair. So nothing would do them but they must go over with me.

The appearance of the house amazed me. All the shutters were closed and the door locked. I knocked and knocked, but there was no answer. Then I walked around the house to the only window that hadn't shutters—a tiny one upstairs. I knew it was the window in the closet off the room where the girls slept. I stopped under it and called Prissy. Before long Prissy came and opened it. She was so pale and woebegone looking that I pitied her with all my heart.

"Prissy, where has Emmeline gone?" I asked.

"Down to Avonlea to see the Roger Pyes. They're sick with measles, and Emmeline couldn't take me because I've never had the measles."

Poor Prissy! She had never had anything a body ought to have.

"Then you just come and unfasten a shutter, and come right over to my house," I said exultantly. "We'll have Stephen and the minister here in no time."

"I can't—Em'line has locked me in here," said Prissy woefully.

I was posed. No living mortal bigger than a baby could have got in or out of that closet window.

"Well," I said finally, "I'll put the signal up for Stephen anyhow, and we'll see what can be done when he gets here."

I didn't know how I was ever to get the signal up on that ventilator, for it was one of the days I take dizzy spells; and if I took one up on the ladder there'd probably be a funeral instead of a wedding. But Anne Shirley said she'd put it up for me, and she did. I had never seen that girl before, and I've never seen her since, but it's my opinion that there wasn't much she couldn't do if she made up her mind to do it.

Stephen wasn't long in getting there and he brought the minister with him. Then we all, including Thomas—who was beginning to get interested in the affair in spite of himself—went over and held council of war beneath the closet window.

Thomas suggested breaking in doors and carrying Prissy off boldly, but I could see that Mr. Leonard looked very dubious over that, and even Stephen said he thought it could only be done as a last resort. I agreed with him. I knew Emmeline Strong would bring an action against him for housebreaking as likely as not. She'd be so furious she'd stick at nothing if we gave her any excuse. Then Anne Shirley, who couldn't have been more excited if she was getting married herself, came to the rescue again.

"Couldn't you put a ladder up to the closet window," she said, "and Mr. Clark can go up it and they can be married there. Can't they, Mr. Leonard?"

Mr. Leonard agreed that they could. He was always the most saintly-looking man, but I know I saw a twinkle in his eye.

"Thomas, go over and bring our little ladder over here," I said.

Thomas forgot he was an elder, and he brought the ladder as quick as it was possible for a fat man to do it. After all it was too short to reach the window, but there was no time to go for another. Stephen went up to the top of it, and he reached up and Prissy reached down, and they could just barely clasp hands so. I shall never forget the look of Prissy. The window was so small she could only get her head and one arm out of it. Besides, she was almost frightened to death.

Mr. Leonard stood at the foot of the ladder and married them. As a rule, he makes a very long and solemn thing of the marriage ceremony, but this time he cut out everything that wasn't absolutely necessary; and it was well that he did, for just as he pronounced them man and wife Emmeline drove into the lane.

She knew perfectly well what had happened when she saw the minister with his blue book in his hand. Never a word said she. She marched to the front door, unlocked it and strode upstairs. I've always been convinced it was a mercy that closet window was so small, or I believe that she would have thrown Prissy out of it. As it was, she walked her downstairs by the arm and actually flung her at Stephen.

"There, take your wife," she said, "and I'll pack up every stitch she owns and send it after her; and I never want to see her or you again as long as I live."

Then she turned to me and Thomas.

"As for you that have aided and abetted that weak-minded

fool in this, take yourselves out of my yard and never darken my door again."

"Goodness, who wants to, you old spitfire?" said Thomas.

It wasn't just the thing for him to say, perhaps, but we are all human, even elders.

The girls didn't escape. Emmeline looked daggers at them.

"This will be something for you to carry back to Avonlea," she said. "You gossips down there will have enough to talk about for a spell. That's all you ever go out of Avonlea for—just to fetch and carry tales."

Finally she finished up with the minister.

"I'm going to the Baptist church in Spencervale after this," she said. Her tone and look said a hundred other things. She whirled into the house and slammed the door.

Mr. Leonard looked around on us with a pitying smile as Stephen put poor, half-fainting Prissy into the buggy.

"I am very sorry," he said in that gentle, saintly way of his, "for the Baptists."

THE MIRACLE AT CARMODY

SALOME LOOKED out of the kitchen window, and a pucker of distress appeared on her smooth forehead.

"Dear, dear, what has Lionel Hezekiah been doing now?" she murmured anxiously.

Involuntarily she reached out for her crutch; but it was a little beyond her reach, having fallen on the floor, and without it Salome could not move a step.

"Well, anyway, Judith is bringing him in as fast as she can," she reflected. "He must have been up to something terrible this time; for she looks very cross, and she never walks like that unless she is angry clear through. Dear me, I am sometimes tempted to think that Judith and I made a mistake in adopting the child. I suppose two old maids don't know much about bringing up a boy properly. But he is *not* a bad child, and it really seems to me that there must be some way of making him behave better if we only knew what it was."

Salome's monologue was cut short by the entrance of her sister Judith, holding Lionel Hezekiah by his chubby wrist with a determined grip.

Judith Marsh was ten years older than Salome, and the two women were as different in appearance as night and day. Salome, in spite of her thirty-five years, looked almost girlish.

She was small and pink and flower-like, with little rings of pale golden hair clustering all over her head in a most unspinster-like fashion, and her eyes were big and blue, and mild as a dove's. Her face was perhaps a weak one, but it was very sweet and appealing.

Judith Marsh was tall and dark, with a plain, tragic face and iron-gray hair. Her eyes were black and sombre, and every feature bespoke unyielding will and determination. Just now she looked, as Salome had said, "angry clear through," and the baleful glances she cast on the small mortal she held would have withered a more hardened criminal than six happy-go-lucky years had made of Lionel Hezekiah.

Lionel Hezekiah, whatever his shortcomings, did not look bad. Indeed, he was as engaging an urchin as ever beamed out on a jolly good world through a pair of big, velvet-brown eyes. He was chubby and firm-limbed, with a mop of beautiful golden curls, which were the despair of his heart and the pride and joy of Salome's; and his round face was usually a lurking-place for dimples and smiles and sunshine.

But just now Lionel Hezekiah was under a blight; he had been caught red-handed in guilt, and was feeling much ashamed of himself. He hung his head and squirmed his toes under the mournful reproach in Salome's eyes. When Salome looked at him like that, Lionel Hezekiah always felt that he was paying more for his fun than it was worth.

"What do you suppose I caught him doing this time?" demanded Judith.

"I—I don't know," faltered Salome.

"Firing—at—a—mark—on—the—henhouse—door—with—new-laid—eggs," said Judith with measured distinctness. "He has broken every egg that was laid today except three. And as for the state of that henhouse door—"

Judith paused, with an indignant gesture meant to convey that the state of the henhouse door must be left to Salome's imagination, since the English language was not capable of depicting it.

"O Lionel Hezekiah, why will you do such things?" said Salome miserably.

"I—didn't know it was wrong," said Lionel Hezekiah, bursting into prompt tears. "I—I thought it would be bully fun. Seems 's if everything what's fun 's wrong."

Salome's heart was not proof against tears, as Lionel Hezekiah very well knew. She put her arm about the sobbing culprit, and drew him to her side.

"He didn't know it was wrong," she said defiantly to Judith.

"He's got to be taught, then," was Judith's retort. "No, you needn't try to beg him off, Salome. He shall go right to bed without any supper, and stay there till tomorrow morning."

"Oh! not without his supper," entreated Salome. "You—you won't improve the child's morals by injuring his stomach, Judith."

"Without his supper, I say," repeated Judith inexorably. "Lionel Hezekiah, go up-stairs to the south room, and go to bed at once."

Lionel Hezekiah went up-stairs, and went to bed at once. He was never sulky or disobedient. Salome listened to him as he stumped patiently up-stairs with a sob at every step, and her own eyes filled with tears.

"Now don't for pity's sake go crying, Salome," said Judith irritably. "I think I've let him off very easily. He is enough to try the patience of a saint, and I never was that," she added with entire truth.

"But he isn't bad," pleaded Salome. "You know he never does anything the second time after he has been told it was wrong, never."

"What good does that do when he is certain to do something new and twice as bad? I never saw anything like him for originating ideas of mischief. Just look at what he has done in the past fortnight—in one fortnight, Salome. He brought in a live snake, and nearly frightened you into fits; he drank up a bottle of liniment, and almost poisoned himself; he took three toads to bed with him; he climbed into the henhouse loft, and fell through on a hen and killed her; he painted his face all over with your water-colours; and now comes *this* exploit. And eggs at twenty-eight cents a dozen! I tell you, Salome, Lionel Hezekiah is an expensive luxury."

"But we couldn't do without him," protested Salome.

"*I* could. But as you can't, or think you can't, we'll have to keep him, I suppose. But the only way to secure any peace of mind for ourselves, as far as I can see, is to tether him in the yard, and hire somebody to watch him."

"There must be some way of managing him," said Salome desperately. She thought Judith was in earnest about the tethering. Judith was generally so terribly in earnest in all she said. "Perhaps it is because he has no other employment that he invents so many unheard-of things. If he had anything to occupy himself with—perhaps if we sent him to school—"

"He's too young to go to school. Father always said that no child should go to school until it was seven, and I don't mean Lionel Hezekiah shall. Well, I'm going to take a pail of hot water and a brush, and see what I can do to that henhouse door. I've got my afternoon's work cut out for me."

Judith stood Salome's crutch up beside her, and departed to purify the henhouse door. As soon as she was safely out of the way, Salome took her crutch, and limped slowly and painfully to the foot of the stairs. She could not go up and comfort Lionel Hezekiah as she yearned to do, which was the reason Judith had sent him up-stairs. Salome had not been up-stairs for fifteen years. Neither did she dare to call him out on the landing, lest Judith return. Besides, of course he must be punished; he had been very naughty.

"But I wish I could smuggle a bit of supper up to him," she mused, sitting down on the lowest step and listening. "I don't hear a sound. I suppose he has cried himself to sleep, poor, dear baby. He certainly is dreadfully mischievous; but it seems to me that it shows an investigating turn of mind, and if it could only be directed into the proper channels—I wish Judith would let me have a talk with Mr. Leonard about Lionel Hezekiah. I wish Judith didn't hate ministers so. I don't mind so much her not letting me go to church, because I'm so lame that it would be painful anyhow; but I'd like to talk with Mr. Leonard now and then about some things. I can never believe that Judith and father were right; I am sure they were not. There is a God, and I'm afraid it's terribly wicked not to go to church. But there, nothing short of a miracle would convince Judith; so there is no use in thinking about it. Yes, Lionel Hezekiah must have gone to sleep."

Salome pictured him so, with his long, curling lashes brushing his rosy, tear-stained cheek and his chubby fists clasped tightly over his breast as was his habit; her heart grew warm and thrilling with the maternity the picture provoked.

A year previously Lionel Hezekiah's parents, Abner and Martha Smith, had died, leaving a houseful of children and very little else. The children were adopted into various Carmody families, and Salome Marsh had amazed Judith by asking to be allowed to take the five-year-old "baby." At first Judith had laughed at the idea; but, when she found that Salome was in earnest, she yielded. Judith always gave Salome her own way except on one point.

"If you want the child, I suppose you must have him," she said finally. "I wish he had a civilized name, though. Hezekiah is bad, and Lionel is worse; but the two in combination, and tacked on to Smith at that, is something that only Martha Smith could have invented. Her judgment was the same clear through, from selecting husbands to names."

So Lionel Hezekiah came into Judith's home and Salome's heart. The latter was permitted to love him all she pleased, but Judith overlooked his training with a critical eye. Possibly it was just as well, for Salome might otherwise have ruined him with indulgence. Salome, who always adopted Judith's opinions, no matter how ill they fitted her, deferred to the former's decrees meekly, and suffered far more than Lionel Hezekiah when he was punished.

She sat on the stairs until she fell asleep herself, her head pillowed on her arm. Judith found her there when she came in, severe and triumphant, from her bout with the henhouse door. Her face softened into marvellous tenderness as she looked at Salome.

"She's nothing but a child herself in spite of her age," she thought pityingly. "A child that's had her whole life thwarted and spoiled through no fault of her own. And yet folks say there is a God who is kind and good! If there is a God, He is a cruel, jealous tyrant, and I hate Him!"

Judith's eyes were bitter and vindictive. She thought she had many grievances against the great Power that rules the universe, but the most intense was Salome's helplessness—Salome, who fifteen years before had been the brightest, happiest of maidens, light of heart and foot, bubbling over with harmless, sparkling mirth and life. If Salome could only walk like other women, Judith told herself that she would not hate that great tyrannical Power.

Lionel Hezekiah was subdued and angelic for four days after that affair of the henhouse door. Then he broke out in a new place. One afternoon he came in sobbing, with his golden curls full of burrs. Judith was not in, but Salome dropped her crochet-work and gazed at him in dismay.

"Oh, Lionel Hezekiah, what have you gone and done now?"

"I—I just stuck the burrs in 'cause I was playing I was a heathen chief," sobbed Lionel Hezekiah. "It was great fun while it lasted; but, when I tried to take them out, it hurt awful."

Neither Salome nor Lionel Hezekiah ever forgot the harrow-ing hour that followed. With the aid of comb and scissors Salome eventually got the burrs out of Lionel Hezekiah's crop of curls. It would be impossible to decide which of them suffered more in the process. Salome cried as hard as Lionel Hezekiah did, and every snip of the scissors or tug at the silken floss cut into her heart. She was almost exhausted when the performance was over; but she took the tired Lionel Hezekiah on her knee, and laid her wet cheek against his shining head.

"Oh, Lionel Hezekiah, what does make you get into mischief so constantly?" she sighed.

Lionel Hezekiah frowned reflectively.

"I don't know," he finally announced, "unless it's because you don't send me to Sunday school."

Salome started as if an electric shock had passed through her frail body.

"Why, Lionel Hezekiah," she stammered, "what put such an idea into your head?"

"Well, all the other boys go," said Lionel Hezekiah defiantly; "and they're all better'n me; so I guess that must be the reason. Teddy Markham says that all little boys should go to Sunday school, and that if they don't they're sure to go to the bad place. I don't see how you can 'spect me to behave well when you won't send me to Sunday school."

"Would you like to go?" asked Salome almost in a whisper.

"I'd like it bully," said Lionel Hezekiah frankly and succinctly.

"Oh, don't use such dreadful words," sighed Salome helplessly. "I'll see what can be done. Perhaps you can go. I'll ask your Aunt Judith."

"Oh, Aunt Judith won't let me go," said Lionel Hezekiah despondingly. "Aunt Judith doesn't believe there is any God or any bad place. Teddy Markham says she doesn't. He says she's an awful wicked woman 'cause she never goes to church. So you must be wicked too, Aunt Salome, 'cause you never go. Why don't you?"

"Your—your Aunt Judith won't let me go," faltered Salome, more perplexed than she had ever been before in her life.

"Well, it doesn't seem to me that you have much fun on Sundays," remarked Lionel Hezekiah ponderingly. "I'd have more if I was you. But I s'pose you can't 'cause you're ladies. I'm glad I'm a man. Look at Abel Blair, what splendid times he has on Sundays. He never goes to church, but he goes fishing, and has cock-fights, and gets drunk. When I grow up, I'm going to do that on Sundays too, since I won't be going to church. I don't want to go to church, but I'd like to go to Sunday school."

Salome listened in agony. Every word of Lionel Hezekiah's stung her conscience unbearably. So this was the result of her weak yielding to Judith; this innocent child looked upon her as a wicked woman, and, worse still, regarded old, depraved Abel Blair as a model to be imitated. Oh! was it too late to undo the evil? When Judith returned, Salome blurted out the whole story. "Lionel Hezekiah must go to Sunday school," she concluded appealingly.

Judith's face hardened until it was as if cut in stone.

"No, he shall not," she said stubbornly. "No one living in my household shall ever go to church or Sunday school. I gave in to you when you wanted to teach him to say his prayers, though I knew it was only foolish superstition, but I sha'n't yield another inch. You know exactly how I feel on this subject, Salome; I believe just as father did. You know he hated churches and churchgoing. And was there ever a better, kinder, more lovable man?"

"Mother believed in God; mother always went to church," pleaded Salome.

"Mother was weak and superstitious, just as you are," retorted

Judith inflexibly. "I tell you, Salome, I don't believe there is a God. But, if there is, He is cruel and unjust, and I hate Him."

"Judith!" gasped Salome, aghast at the impiety. She half expected to see her sister struck dead at her feet.

"Don't 'Judith' me!" said Judith passionately in the strange anger that any discussion of the subject always roused in her. "I mean every word I say. Before you got lame I didn't feel much about it one way or another; I'd just as soon have gone with mother as with father. But, when you were struck down like that, I knew father was right."

For a moment Salome quailed. She felt that she could not, dare not, stand out against Judith. For her own sake she could not have done so, but the thought of Lionel Hezekiah nerved her to desperation. She struck her thin, bleached little hands wildly together.

"Judith, I'm going to church tomorrow," she cried. "I tell you I am; I won't set Lionel Hezekiah a bad example one day longer. I'll not take him; I won't go against you in that, for it is your bounty feeds and clothes him; but I'm going myself."

"If you do, Salome Marsh, I'll never forgive you," said Judith, her harsh face dark with anger; and then, not trusting herself to discuss the subject any longer, she went out.

Salome dissolved into her ready tears, and cried most of the night. But her resolution did not fail. Go to church she would, for that dear baby's sake.

Judith would not speak to her at breakfast, and this almost broke Salome's heart; but she dared not yield. After breakfast she limped painfully into her room, and still more painfully dressed herself. When she was ready, she took a little old worn Bible out of her box. It had been her mother's, and Salome read a chapter in it every night, although she never dared to let Judith see her doing it.

When she limped out into the kitchen, Judith looked up with a hard face. A flame of sullen anger glowed in her dark eyes, and she went into the sitting-room and shut the door, as if by that act she were shutting her sister for evermore out of her heart and life. Salome, strung up to the last pitch of nervous tension, felt intuitively the significance of that closed door. For a moment she wavered—oh, she could not go against Judith!

She was all but turning back to her room when Lionel Hezekiah came running in, and paused to look at her admiringly.

"You look just bully, Aunt Salome," he said. "Where are you going?"

"Don't use that word, Lionel Hezekiah," pleaded Salome. "I'm going to church."

"Take me with you," said Lionel Hezekiah promptly. Salome shook her head.

"I can't, dear. Your Aunt Judith wouldn't like it. Perhaps she will let you go after a while. Now do be a good boy while I am away, won't you? Don't do any naughty things."

"I won't do them if I know they're naughty," conceded Lionel Hezekiah. "But that's just the trouble; I don't know what's naughty and what ain't. Prob'ly if I went to Sunday school I'd find out."

Salome limped out of the yard and down the lane bordered by its asters and goldenrod. Fortunately the church was just outside the lane, across the main road; but Salome found it hard to cover even that short distance. She felt almost exhausted when she reached the church and toiled painfully up the aisle to her mother's old pew. She laid her crutch on the seat, and sank into the corner by the window with a sigh of relief.

She had elected to come early so that she might get there before the rest of the people. The church was as yet empty, save for a class of Sunday school children and their teacher in a remote corner, who paused midway in their lesson to stare with amazement at the astonishing sight of Salome Marsh limping into church.

The big building, shadowy from the great elms around it, was very still. A faint murmur came from the closed room behind the pulpit where the rest of the Sunday school was assembled. In front of the pulpit was a stand bearing tall white geraniums in luxuriant blossom. The light fell through the stained-glass window in a soft tangle of hues upon the floor. Salome felt a sense of peace and happiness fill her heart. Even Judith's anger lost its importance. She leaned her head against the window-sill, and gave herself up to the flood of tender old recollections that swept over her.

Memory went back to the years of her childhood when she had sat in this pew every Sunday with her mother. Judith had

come then, too, always seeming grown up to Salome by reason
of her ten years' seniority. Her tall, dark, reserved father never
came. Salome knew that the Carmody people called him an
infidel, and looked upon him as a very wicked man. But he
had not been wicked; he had been good and kind in his own
odd way.

The gentle little mother had died when Salome was ten years
old, but so loving and tender was Judith's care that the child
did not miss anything out of her life. Judith Marsh loved her
little sister with an intensity that was maternal. She herself was
a plain, repellent girl, liked by few, sought after by no man;
but she was determined that Salome should have everything
that she had missed—admiration, friendship, love. She would
have a vicarious youth in Salome's.

All went according to Judith's planning until Salome was
eighteen, and then trouble after trouble came. Their father,
whom Judith had understood and passionately loved, died;
Salome's young lover was killed in a railroad accident; and
finally Salome herself developed symptoms of the hip-disease
which, springing from a trifling injury, eventually left her a
cripple. Everything possible was done for her. Judith, falling
heir to a snug little fortune by the death of the old aunt for
whom she was named, spared nothing to obtain the best medical
skill, and in vain. One and all, the great doctors failed.

Judith had borne her father's death bravely enough in spite
of her agony of grief; she had watched her sister pining and
fading with the pain of her broken heart without growing bitter;
but when she knew at last that Salome would never walk again
save as she hobbled painfully about on her crutch, the smouldering revolt in her soul broke its bounds, and overflowed her
nature in a passionate rebellion against the Being who had sent,
or had failed to prevent, these calamities. She did not rave or
denounce wildly; that was not Judith's way; but she never went
to church again, and it soon became an accepted fact in
Carmody that Judith Marsh was as rank an infidel as her father
had been before her; nay, worse, since she would not even
allow Salome to go to church, and shut the door in the minister's
face when he went to see her.

"I should have stood out against her for conscience' sake,"
reflected Salome in her pew self-reproachfully. "But, O dear,

I'm afraid she'll never forgive me, and how can I live if she doesn't? But I must endure it for Lionel Hezekiah's sake; my weakness has perhaps done him great harm already. They say that what a child learns in the first seven years never leaves him; so Lionel Hezekiah has only another year to get set right about these things. Oh, if I've left it till too late!"

When the people began to come in, Salome felt painfully the curious glances directed at her. Look where she would, she met them, unless she looked out of the window; so out of the window she did look unswervingly, her delicate little face burning crimson with self-consciousness. She could see her home and its back yard plainly, with Lionel Hezekiah making mud-pies joyfully in the corner. Presently she saw Judith come out of the house and stride away to the pine wood behind it. Judith always betook herself to the pines in time of mental stress and strain.

Salome could see the sunlight shining on Lionel Hezekiah's bare head as he mixed his pies. In the pleasure of watching him she forgot where she was and the curious eyes turned on her.

Suddenly Lionel Hezekiah ceased concocting pies, and betook himself to the corner of the summer kitchen, where he proceeded to climb up to the top of the storm-fence and from there to mount the sloping kitchen roof. Salome clasped her hands in agony. What if the child should fall? Oh! why had Judith gone away and left him alone? What if—what if—and then, while her brain with lightning-like rapidity pictured forth a dozen possible catastrophes, something really did happen. Lionel Hezekiah slipped, sprawled wildly, slid down, and fell off the roof, in a bewildering whirl of arms and legs, plump into the big rain-water hogshead under the spout, which was generally full to the brim with rain-water, a hogshead big and deep enough to swallow up half a dozen small boys who went climbing kitchen roofs on a Sunday.

Then something took place that is talked of in Carmody to this day, and even fiercely wrangled over, so many and conflicting are the opinions on the subject. Salome Marsh, who had not walked a step without assistance for fifteen years, suddenly sprang to her feet with a shriek, ran down the aisle, and out of the door!

Every man, woman, and child in the Carmody church followed her, even to the minister, who had just announced his text. When they got out, Salome was already half-way up her lane, running wildly. In her heart was room for but one agonized thought. Would Lionel Hezekiah be drowned before she reached him?

She opened the gate of the yard, and panted across it just as a tall, grim-faced woman came around the corner of the house and stood rooted to the ground in astonishment at the sight that met her eyes.

But Salome saw nobody. She flung herself against the hogshead, and looked in, sick with terror at what she might see. What she did see was Lionel Hezekiah sitting on the bottom of the hogshead in water that came only to his waist. He was looking rather dazed and bewildered, but was apparently quite uninjured.

The yard was full of people, but nobody had as yet said a word; awe and wonder held everybody in spellbound silence. Judith was the first to speak. She pushed through the crowd to Salome. Her face was blanched to a deadly whiteness; and her eyes, as Mrs. William Blair afterwards declared, were enough to give a body the creeps.

"Salome," she said in a high, shrill, unnatural voice, "where is your crutch?"

Salome came to herself at the question. For the first time she realized that she had walked, nay, run, all that distance from the church alone and unaided. She turned pale, swayed, and would have fallen if Judith had not caught her.

Old Dr. Blair came forward briskly.

"Carry her in," he said, "and don't all of you come crowding in, either. She wants quiet and rest for a spell."

Most of the people obediently returned to the church, their suddenly loosened tongues clattering in voluble excitement. A few women assisted Judith to carry Salome in and lay her on the kitchen lounge, followed by the doctor and the dripping Lionel Hezekiah, whom the minister had lifted out of the hogshead and to whom nobody now paid the slightest attention.

Salome faltered out her story, and her hearers listened with varying emotions.

"It's a miracle," said Sam Lawson in an awed voice.

Dr. Blair shrugged his shoulders.

"There is no miracle about it," he said bluntly.

"It's all perfectly natural. The disease in the hip has evidently been quite well for a long time; Nature does sometimes work cures like that when she is let alone. The trouble was that the muscles were paralyzed by long disuse. That paralysis was overcome by the force of a strong and instinctive effort. Salome, get up and walk across the kitchen."

Salome obeyed. She walked across the kitchen and back, slowly, stiffly, falteringly, now that the stimulus of frantic fear was spent; but still she walked. The doctor nodded his satisfaction.

"Keep that up every day. Walk as much as you can without tiring yourself, and you'll soon be as spry as ever. No more need of crutches for you, but there's no miracle in the case."

Judith Marsh turned to him. She had not spoken a word since her question concerning Salome's crutch. Now she said passionately:

"It *was* a miracle. God has worked it to prove His existence to me, and I accept the proof."

The old doctor shrugged his shoulders again. Being a wise man, he knew when to hold his tongue.

"Well, put Salome to bed, and let her sleep the rest of the day. She's worn out. And for pity's sake let someone take that poor child and put some dry clothes on him before he catches his death of cold."

That evening, as Salome Marsh lay in her bed in a glory of sunset light, her heart filled with unutterable gratitude and happiness, Judith came into the room. She wore her best hat and dress, and she held Lionel Hezekiah by the hand. Lionel Hezekiah's beaming face was scrubbed clean, and his curls fell in beautiful sleekness over the lace collar of his velvet suit.

"How do you feel now, Salome?" asked Judith gently.

"Better. I've had a lovely sleep. But where are you going, Judith?"

"I am going to church," said Judith firmly, "and I am going to take Lionel Hezekiah with me."

THE END OF A QUARREL

NANCY ROGERSON sat down on Louisa Shaw's front doorstep and looked about her, drawing a long breath of delight that seemed tinged with pain. Everything was very much the same; the square garden was as square as ever, and as disorderly, with the same old charming hodge-podge of fruit and flowers, and gooseberry bushes and tiger lilies, a gnarled old apple tree sticking up here and there, and a thick cherry copse at the foot. Behind was a row of pointed firs, coming out darkly against the swimming pink sunset sky, not looking a day older than they had looked twenty years ago, when Nancy had been a young girl walking and dreaming in their shadows. The old willow to the left was as big and sweeping and, Nancy thought with a little shudder, probably as caterpillary, as ever. Nancy had learned many things in her twenty years of exile from Avonlea, but she had never learned to conquer her dread of caterpillars.

"Nothing is much changed, Louisa," she said, propping her chin on her plump white hands, and sniffing at the delectable odour of the bruised mint upon which Louisa was trampling. "I'm glad; I was afraid to come back for fear you would have improved the old garden out of existence, or else into some prim, orderly lawn which would have been worse. It's as magnificently untidy as ever, and the fence still wobbles. It *can't* be the same fence, but it looks exactly like it. No, nothing is much changed. Thank you, Louisa."

Louisa had not the faintest idea what Nancy was thanking her for, but then she had never been able to fathom Nancy, much as she had always liked her in the old girlhood days that now seemed much further away to Louisa than they did to Nancy. Louisa was separated from them by the fulness of wifehood and motherhood, while Nancy looked back only over the narrow gap that empty years make.

"You haven't changed much yourself, Nancy," she said, looking admiringly at Nancy's trim figure, in the nurse's uniform she had donned to show Louisa what it was like, her firm, pink-and white face and the glossy waves of her golden brown hair. "You've held your own wonderfully well."

"Haven't I?" said Nancy complacently. "Modern methods of massage and cold cream have kept away the crowsfeet, and fortunately I had the Rogerson complexion to start with. You wouldn't think I was really thirty-eight, would you? Thirty-eight! Twenty years ago I thought anybody who was thirty-eight was a perfect female Methuselah. And now I feel so horribly, ridiculously young, Louisa. Every morning when I get up I have to say solemnly to myself three times, 'You're an old maid, Nancy Rogerson,' to tone myself down to anything like a becoming attitude for the day."

"I guess you don't mind being an old maid much," said Louisa, shrugging her shoulders. She would not have been an old maid herself for anything; yet she inconsistently envied Nancy her freedom, her wide life in the world, her unlined brow, and care-free lightness of spirit.

"Oh, but I do mind," said Nancy frankly. "I hate being an old maid."

"Why don't you get married, then?" asked Louisa, paying an unconscious tribute to Nancy's perennial chance by her use of the present tense.

Nancy shook her head.

"No, that wouldn't suit me either. I don't want to be married. Do you remember that story Anne Shirley used to tell long ago of the pupil who wanted to be a widow because 'if you were married your husband bossed you and if you weren't married people called you an old maid?' Well, that is precisely my opinion. I'd like to be a widow. Then I'd have the freedom of the unmarried, with the kudos of the married. I could eat my cake and have it, too. Oh, to be a widow!"

"Nancy!" said Louisa in a shocked tone.

Nancy laughed, a mellow gurgle that rippled through the garden like a brook.

"Oh, Louisa, I can shock you yet. That was just how you used to say 'Nancy' long ago, as if I'd broken all the commandments at once."

"You do say such queer things," protested Louisa, "and half the time I don't know what you mean."

"Bless you, dear coz., half the time I don't myself. Perhaps the joy of coming back to the old spot has slightly turned my brain. I've found my lost girlhood here. I'm *not* thirty-eight in this garden—it is a flat impossibility. I'm sweet eighteen, with a waist line two inches smaller. Look, the sun is just setting. I see he has still his old trick of throwing his last beams over the Wright farmhouse. By the way, Louisa, is Peter Wright still living there?"

"Yes." Louisa threw a suddenly interested glance at the apparently placid Nancy.

"Married, I suppose, with half a dozen children?" said Nancy indifferently, pulling up some more sprigs of mint and pinning them on her breast. Perhaps the exertion of leaning over to do it flushed her face. There was more than the Rogerson colour in it, anyhow, and Louisa, slow though her mental processes might be in some respects, thought she understood the meaning of a blush as well as the next one. All the instinct of the matchmaker flamed up in her.

"Indeed he isn't," she said promptly. "Peter Wright has never married. He has been faithful to your memory, Nancy."

"Ugh! You make me feel as if I were buried up there in the Avonlea cemetery and had a monument over me with a weeping willow carved on it," shivered Nancy. "When it is said that a man has been faithful to a woman's memory it generally means that he couldn't get anyone else to take him."

"That isn't the case with Peter," protested Louisa. "He is a good match, and many a woman would have been glad to take him, and would yet. He's only forty-three. But he's never taken the slightest interest in anyone since you threw him over, Nancy."

"But I didn't. He threw me over," said Nancy, plaintively, looking afar over the low-lying fields and a feathery young spruce valley to the white buildings of the Wright farm, glowing rosily in the sunset light when all the rest of Avonlea was scarfing itself in shadows. There was laughter in her eyes. Louisa could not pierce beneath that laughter to find if there were anything under it.

"Fudge!" said Louisa. "What on earth did you and Peter quarrel about?" she added, curiously.

"I've often wondered," parried Nancy.

"And you've never seen him since?" reflected Louisa.

"No. Has he changed much?"

"Well, some. He is gray and kind of tired-looking. But it isn't to be wondered at—living the life he does. He hasn't had a housekeeper for two years—not since his old aunt died. He just lives there alone and cooks his own meals. I've never been in the house, but folks say the disorder is something awful."

"Yes, I shouldn't think Peter was cut out for a tidy house-keeper," said Nancy lightly, dragging up more mint. "Just think, Louisa, if it hadn't been for that old quarrel I might be Mrs. Peter Wright at this very moment, mother to the aforesaid supposed half dozen, and vexing my soul over Peter's meals and socks and cows."

"I guess you are better off as you are," said Louisa.

"Oh, I don't know," Nancy looked up at the white house on the hill again. "I have an awfully good time out of life, but it doesn't seem to satisfy, somehow. To be candid—and oh, Louisa, candour is a rare thing among women when it comes to talking of the men—I believe I'd rather be cooking Peter's meals and dusting his house. I wouldn't mind his bad grammar now. I've learned one or two valuable little things out yonder, and one is that it doesn't matter if a man's grammar is askew, so long as he doesn't swear at you. By the way, is Peter as ungrammatical as ever?"

"I—I don't know," said Louisa helplessly. "I never knew he *was* ungrammatical."

"Does he still say, 'I seen,' and 'them things'?" demanded Nancy.

"I never noticed," confessed Louisa.

"Enviable Louisa! Would that I had been born with that blessed faculty of never noticing! It stands a woman in better stead than beauty or brains. *I* used to notice Peter's mistakes. When he said 'I seen' it jarred on me in my salad days. I tried, oh, so tactfully, to reform him in that respect. Peter didn't like being reformed—the Wrights always had a fairly good opinion of themselves, you know. It was really over a question of syntax we quarrelled. Peter told me I'd have to take him as he was, grammar and all, or go without him. I went without him— and ever since I've been wondering if I were really sorry, or if it were merely a pleasantly sentimental regret I was hugging to my heart. I daresay it's the latter. Now, Louisa, I see the beginning of the plot far down in those placid eyes of yours. Strangle it at birth, dear Louisa. There is no use in your trying to make up a match between Peter and me now—no, nor in slyly inviting him up here to tea some evening, as you are even this moment thinking of doing.

"Well, I must go and milk the cows," gasped Louisa, rather glad to make her escape. Nancy's power of thought-reading struck her as uncanny. She felt afraid to remain with her cousin any longer, lest Nancy should drag to light all the secrets of her being.

Nancy sat long on the steps after Louisa had gone—sat until the night came down, darkly and sweetly, over the garden, and the stars twinkled out above the firs. This had been her home in girlhood. Here she had lived and kept house for her father. When he died, Curtis Shaw, newly married to her cousin Louisa, bought the farm from her and moved in. Nancy stayed on with them, expecting soon to go to a home of her own. She and Peter Wright were engaged.

Then came their mysterious quarrel, concerning the cause of which kith and kin on both sides were left in annoying ignorance. Of the results they were not ignorant. Nancy promptly packed up and left Avonlea seven hundred miles behind her. She went to a hospital in Montreal and studied nursing. In the twenty years that had followed she had never even revisited Avonlea. Her sudden descent on it this summer was a whim born of a moment's homesick longing for this same old garden.

She had not thought about Peter. In very truth, she had thought little about Peter for the last fifteen years. She supposed that she had forgotten him. But now, sitting on the old doorstep, where she had often sat in her courting days, with Peter lounging on a broad stone at her feet, something tugged at her heartstrings. She looked over the valley to the light in the kitchen of the Wright farmhouse, and pictured Peter sitting there, lonely and uncared for, with naught but the cold comfort of his own providing.

"Well, he should have got married," she said snappishly. "I am not going to worry because he is a lonely old bachelor when all these years I have supposed him a comfy Benedict. Why doesn't he hire him a housekeeper, at least? He can afford it; the place looks prosperous. Ugh! I've a fat bank account, and I've seen almost everything in the world worth seeing; but I've got several carefully hidden gray hairs and a horrible conviction that grammar isn't one of the essential things in life after all. Well, I'm not going to moon out here in the dew any longer. I'm going in to read the smartest, frilliest, frothiest society novel in my trunk."

In the week that followed Nancy enjoyed herself after her own fashion. She read and swung in the garden, having a hammock hung under the firs. She went far afield, in rambles to woods and lonely uplands.

"I like it much better than meeting people," she said, when Louisa suggested going to see this one and that one, "especially the Avonlea people. All my old chums are gone, or hopelessly married and changed, and the young set who have come up know not Joseph, and make me feel uncomfortably middle-aged. It's far worse to feel middle-aged than old, you know. Away there in the woods I feel as eternally young as Nature herself. And oh, it's so nice not having to fuss with thermometers and temperatures and other people's whims. Let me indulge my own whims, Louisa dear, and punish me with a cold bite when I come in late for meals. I'm not even going to church again. It was horrible there yesterday. The church is so offensively spick-and-span brand new and modern."

"It's thought to be the prettiest church in these parts," protested Louisa, a little sorely.

"Churches shouldn't be pretty—they should be at least fifty years old and mellowed into beauty. New churches are an abomination."

"Did you see Peter Wright in church?" asked Louisa. She had been bursting to ask it.

Nancy nodded.

"Verily, yes. He sat right across from me in the corner pew. I didn't think him painfully changed. Iron-gray hair becomes him. But I was horribly disappointed in myself. I had expected to feel at least a romantic thrill, but all I felt was a comfortable interest, such as I might have taken in any old friend. Do my utmost, Louisa, I couldn't compass a thrill."

"Did he come to speak to you?" asked Louisa, who hadn't any idea what Nancy meant by her thrills.

"Alas, no. It wasn't my fault. I stood at the door outside with the most amiable expression I could assume, but Peter merely sauntered away without a glance in my direction. It would be some comfort to my vanity if I could believe it was on account of rankling spite or pride. But the honest truth, dear Weezy, is that it looked to me exactly as if he never thought of it. He was more interested in talking about the hay crop with Oliver Sloane—who, by the way, is more Oliver Sloaneish than ever."

"If you feel as you said you did the other night, why didn't you go and speak to him?" Louisa wanted to know.

"But I don't feel that way now. That was just a mood. You don't know anything about moods, dearie. You don't know what it is to yearn desperately one hour for something you wouldn't take if it were offered you the next."

"But that is foolishness," protested Louisa.

"To be sure it is—rank foolishness. But oh, it is so delightful to be foolish after being compelled to be unbrokenly sensible for twenty years. Well, I'm going picking strawberries this afternoon, Lou. Don't wait tea for me. I probably won't be back till dark. I've only four more days to stay and I want to make the most of them."

Nancy wandered far and wide in her rambles that afternoon. When she had filled her jug she still roamed about with delicious aimlessness. Once she found herself in a wood lane skirting a field where in a man was mowing hay. The man was

Peter Wright. Nancy walked faster when she discovered this, with never a roving glance, and presently the green, ferny depths of the maple woods swallowed her up.

From old recollections she knew that she was on Peter Morrison's land, and calculated that if she kept straight on she would come out where the old Morrison house used to be. Her calculations proved correct, with a trifling variation. She came out fifty yards south of the old deserted Morrison house, and found herself in the yard of the Wright farm!

Passing the house—the house where she had once dreamed of reigning as mistress—Nancy's curiosity overcame her. The place was not in view of any other near house. She deliberately went up to it intending—low be it spoken—to peep in at the kitchen window. But, seeing the door wide open, she went to it instead and halted on the step, looking about her keenly.

The kitchen was certainly pitiful in its disorder. The floor had apparently not been swept for a fortnight. On the bare deal table were the remnants of Peter's dinner, a meal that could not have been very tempting at its best.

"What a miserable place for a human being to live in!" groaned Nancy. "Look at the ashes on that stove! And that table! Is it any wonder that Peter has got gray? He'll work hard haymaking all the afternoon—and then come home to *this!*"

An idea suddenly darted into Nancy's brain. At first she looked aghast. Then she laughed and glanced at her watch.

"I'll do it—just for fun and a little pity. It's half-past two and Peter won't be home till four at the earliest. I'll have a good hour to do it in, and still make my escape in good time. Nobody will ever know; nobody can see me here."

Nancy went in, threw off her hat and seized a broom. The first thing she did was to give the kitchen a thorough sweeping. Then she kindled a fire, put a kettle full of water on to heat, and attacked the dishes. From the number of them she rightly concluded that Peter hadn't washed any for at least a week.

"I suppose he just uses the clean ones as long as they hold out, and then has a grand wash-up," she laughed. "I wonder where he keeps his dishtowels, if he has any."

Evidently Peter hadn't any. At least, Nancy couldn't find any. She marched boldly into the dusty sitting-room and explored the drawers of an old-fashioned sideboard, confiscating a towel she found there. As she worked she hummed a song; her steps were light and her eyes bright with excitement. Nancy was enjoying herself thoroughly, there was no doubt of that. The spice of mischief in the adventure pleased her mightily.

The dishes washed, she hunted up a clean, but yellow and evidently long unused tablecloth out of the sideboard, and proceeded to set the table and get Peter's tea. She found bread and butter in the pantry, a trip to the cellar furnished a pitcher of cream, and Nancy recklessly heaped the contents of her strawberry jug on Peter's plate. The tea was made and set back to keep warm. And, as a finishing touch, Nancy ravaged the old neglected garden and set a huge bowl of crimson roses in the centre of the table.

"Now I must go," she said aloud. "Wouldn't it be fun to see Peter's face when he comes in though? Ha-hum! I've enjoyed doing this—but why? Nancy Rogerson, don't be asking yourself conundrums. Put on your hat and proceed homeward, constructing on your way some reliable fib to account to Louisa for the absence of your strawberries."

Nancy paused a moment and looked around wistfully. She had made the place look cheery and neat and homelike. She felt that queer tugging at her heartstrings again. Suppose she belonged here and was waiting for Peter to come home to tea. Suppose—Nancy whirled around with a sudden horrible prescience of what she was going to see! Peter Wright was standing in the doorway.

Nancy's face went crimson. For the first time in her life she had not a word to say for herself. Peter looked at her and then at the table, with its fruit and flowers.

"Thank you," he said politely.

Nancy recovered herself. With a shamefaced laugh she held out her hand.

"Don't have me arrested for trespass, Peter. I came and looked in at your kitchen out of impertinent curiosity, and just for fun I thought I'd come in and get your tea. I thought you'd be so surprised—and I meant to go before you came home, of course."

"I wouldn't have been surprised," said Peter, shaking hands. "I saw you go past the field and I tied the horses and followed you down through the woods. I've been sitting on the fence back yonder, watching your comings and goings."

"Why didn't you come and speak to me at church yesterday, Peter?" demanded Nancy, boldly.

"I was afraid I would say something ungrammatical," answered Peter drily.

The crimson flamed over Nancy's face again. She pulled her hand away.

"That's cruel of you, Peter."

Peter suddenly laughed. There was a note of boyishness in the laughter.

"So it is," he said, "but I had to get rid of the accumulated malice and spite of twenty years somehow. It's all gone now, and I'll be as amiable as I know how. But since you have gone to the trouble of getting my supper for me, Nancy, you must stay and help me eat it. Them strawberries look good. I haven't had any this summer—been too busy to pick them."

Nancy stayed. She sat at the head of Peter's table and poured his tea for him. She talked to him wittily of the Avonlea people and the changes in their old set. Peter followed her lead with an apparent absence of self-consciousness, eating his supper like a man whose heart and mind were alike on good terms with him. Nancy felt wretched—and, at the same time, ridiculously happy. It seemed the most grotesque thing in the world that she should be presiding there at Peter's table, and yet the most natural. There were moments when she felt like crying—other moments when her laughter was as ready and spontaneous as a girl's. Sentiment and humour had always waged an equal contest in Nancy's nature.

When Peter had finished his strawberries he folded his arms on the table and looked admiringly at Nancy.

"You look well at the head of a table, Nancy," he said critically. "How is it that you haven't been presiding at one of your own long before this? I thought you'd meet with lots of men out in the world that you'd like—men who talked good grammar."

"Peter, don't!" said Nancy, wincing. "I was a goose."

"No, you were quite right. I was a tetchy fool. If I'd had any sense I'd have felt thankful you thought enough of me to want to improve me, and I'd have tried to kerrect my mistakes instead of getting mad. It's too late now, I suppose."

"Too late for what?" said Nancy, plucking up heart of grace at something in Peter's tone and look.

"For—kerrecting mistakes."

"Grammatical ones?"

"Not exactly. I guess them mistakes are past kerrecting in an old fellow like me. Worse mistakes, Nancy. I wonder what you would say if I asked you to forgive me, and have me after all."

"I'd snap you up before you'd have time to change your mind," said Nancy brazenly. She tried to look Peter in the face, but her blue eyes, where tears and mirth were blending, faltered down before his gray ones.

Peter stood up, knocking over his chair, and strode around the table to her.

"Nancy, my girl!" he said.

Further Chronicles of Avonlea

AUNT CYNTHIA'S PERSIAN CAT

MAX ALWAYS blesses the animal when it is referred to; and I don't deny that things have worked together for good after all. But when I think of the anguish of mind which Ismay and I underwent on account of that abominable cat, it is not a blessing that arises uppermost in my thoughts.

I never was fond of cats, although I admit they are well enough in their place, and I can worry along comfortably with a nice, matronly old tabby who can take care of herself and be of some use in the world. As for Ismay, she hates cats and always did.

But Aunt Cynthia, who adored them, never could bring herself to understand that any one could possibly dislike them. She firmly believed that Ismay and I really liked cats deep down in our hearts, but that, owing to some perverse twist in our moral natures, we would not own up to it, but willfully persisted in declaring we didn't.

Of all cats I loathed that white Persian cat of Aunt Cynthia's. And, indeed, as we always suspected and finally proved, Aunt herself looked upon the creature with more pride than affection. She would have taken ten times the comfort in a good, common puss that she did in that spoiled beauty. But a Persian cat with a recorded pedigree and a market value of one hundred dollars tickled Aunt Cynthia's pride of possession to such an extent that she deluded herself into believing that the animal was really the apple of her eye.

It had been presented to her when a kitten by a missionary nephew who had brought it all the way home from Persia; and for the next three years Aunt Cynthia's household existed to wait on that cat, hand and foot. It was snow-white, with a bluish-gray spot on the tip of its tail; and it was blue-eyed and deaf and delicate. Aunt Cynthia was always worrying lest it should take cold and die. Ismay and I used to wish that it would—we were so tired of hearing about it and its whims. But we did not say so to Aunt Cynthia. She would probably never have spoken to us again and there was no wisdom in offending Aunt Cynthia. When you have an unencumbered aunt, with a fat bank account, it is just as well to keep on good terms with her, if you can. Besides, we really liked Aunt Cynthia very much—at times. Aunt Cynthia was one of those rather exasperating people who nag at and find fault with you until you think you are justified in hating them, and who then turn round and do something so really nice and kind for you that you feel as if you were compelled to love them dutifully instead.

So we listened meekly when she discoursed on Fatima—the cat's name was Fatima—and, if it was wicked of us to wish for the latter's decease, we were well punished for it later on.

One day, in November, Aunt Cynthia came sailing out to Spencervale. She really came in a phaeton, drawn by a fat gray pony, but somehow Aunt Cynthia always gave you the impression of a full rigged ship coming gallantly on before a favorable wind.

That was a Jonah day for us all through. Everything had gone wrong. Ismay had spilled grease on her velvet coat, and the fit of the new blouse I was making was hopelessly askew, and the kitchen stove smoked and the bread was sour. Moreover, Huldah Jane Keyson, our tried and trusty old family nurse and cook and general "boss," had what she called the "realagy" in her shoulder; and, though Huldah Jane is as good an old creature as ever lived, when she has the "realagy" other people who are in the house want to get out of it and, if they can't, feel about as comfortable as St. Lawrence on his gridiron.

And on the top of this came Aunt Cynthia's call and request.

"Dear me," said Aunt Cynthia, sniffing, "don't I smell smoke? You girls must manage your range very badly. Mine never smokes. But it is no more than one might expect when two girls try to keep house without a man about the place."

"We get along very well without a man about the place," I said loftily. Max hadn't been in for four whole days and, though nobody wanted to see him particularly, I couldn't help wondering why. "Men are nuisances."

"I dare say you would like to pretend you think so," said Aunt Cynthia, aggravatingly. "But no woman ever does really think so, you know. I imagine that pretty Anne Shirley, who is visiting Ella Kimball, doesn't. I saw her and Dr. Irving out walking this afternoon, looking very well satisfied with themselves. If you dilly-dally much longer, Sue, you will let Max slip through your fingers yet."

That was a tactful thing to say to *me*, who had refused Max Irving so often that I had lost count. I was furious, and so I smiled most sweetly on my maddening aunt.

"Dear Aunt, how amusing of you," I said, smoothly. "You talk as if I wanted Max."

"So you do," said Aunt Cynthia.

"If so, why should I have refused him time and again?" I asked, smilingly. Right well Aunt Cynthia knew I had. Max always told her.

"Goodness alone knows why," said Aunt Cynthia, "but you may do it once too often and find yourself taken at your word. There is something very fascinating about this Anne Shirley."

"Indeed there is," I assented. "She has the loveliest eyes I ever saw. She would be just the wife for Max, and I hope he will marry her."

"Humph," said Aunt Cynthia. "Well, I won't entice you into telling any more fibs. And I didn't drive out here today in all this wind to talk sense into you concerning Max. I'm going to Halifax for two months and I want you to take charge of Fatima for me, while I am away."

"Fatima!" I exclaimed.

"Yes. I don't dare to trust her with the servants. Mind you always warm her milk before you give it to her, and don't on any account let her run out of doors."

I looked at Ismay and Ismay looked at me. We knew we were in for it. To refuse would mortally offend Aunt Cynthia. Besides, if I betrayed any unwillingness, Aunt Cynthia would be sure to put it down to grumpiness over what she had said about Max, and rub it in for years. But I ventured to ask, "What if anything happens to her while you are away?"

"It is to prevent that, I'm leaving her with you," said Aunt Cynthia. "You simply must not let anything happen to her. It will do you good to have a little responsibility. And you will have a chance to find out what an adorable creature Fatima really is. Well, that is all settled. I'll send Fatima out tomorrow."

"You can take care of that horrid Fatima beast yourself," said Ismay, when the door closed behind Aunt Cynthia. "I won't touch her with a yardstick. You had no business to say we'd take her."

"Did I say we would take her?" I demanded, crossly. "Aunt Cynthia took our consent for granted. And you know, as well as I do, we couldn't have refused. So what is the use of being grouchy?"

"If anything happens to her Aunt Cynthia will hold us responsible," said Ismay darkly.

"Do you think Anne Shirley is really engaged to Gilbert Blythe?" I asked curiously.

"I've heard that she was," said Ismay, absently. "Does she eat anything but milk? Will it do to give her mice?"

"Oh, I guess so. But do you think Max has really fallen in love with her?"

"I dare say. What a relief it will be for you if he has."

"Oh, of course," I said, frostily. "Anne Shirley or Anne Anybody Else, is perfectly welcome to Max if she wants him. I certainly do not. Ismay Meade, if that stove doesn't stop smoking I shall fly into bits. This is a detestable day. I hate that creature!"

"Oh, you shouldn't talk like that, when you don't even know her," protested Ismay. "Every one says Anne Shirley is lovely—"

"I was talking about Fatima," I cried in a rage.

"Oh!" said Ismay.

Ismay is stupid at times. I thought the way she said "Oh" was inexcusably stupid.

Fatima arrived the next day. Max brought her out in a covered basket, lined with padded crimson satin. Max likes cats and Aunt Cynthia. He explained how we were to treat Fatima and when Ismay had gone out of the room—Ismay always went out of the room when she knew I particularly wanted her to remain—he proposed to me again. Of course I said no, as usual, but I was rather pleased. Max had been proposing to me about every two months for two years. Sometimes, as in this case, he went three months, and then I always wondered why. I concluded that he could not be really interested in Anne Shirley, and I was relieved. I didn't want to marry Max but it was pleasant and convenient to have him around, and we would miss him dreadfully if any other girl snapped him up. He was so useful and always willing to do anything for us—nail a shingle on the roof, drive us to town, put down carpets—in short, a very present help in all our troubles.

So I just beamed on him when I said no. Max began counting on his fingers. When he got as far as eight he shook his head and began over again.

"What is it?" I asked.

"I'm trying to count up how many times I have proposed to you," he said. "But I can't remember whether I asked you to marry me that day we dug up the garden or not. If I did it makes—"

"No, you didn't," I interrupted.

"Well, that makes it eleven," said Max reflectively. "Pretty near the limit, isn't it? My manly pride will not allow me to propose to the same girl more than twelve times. So the next time will be the last, Sue darling."

"Oh," I said, a trifle flatly. I forgot to resent his calling me darling. I wondered if things wouldn't be rather dull when Max gave up proposing to me. It was the only excitement I had. But of course it would be best—and he couldn't go on at it forever, so, by the way of gracefully dismissing the subject, I asked him what Miss Shirley was like.

"Very sweet girl," said Max. "You know I always admired those gray-eyed girls with that splendid Titian hair."

I am dark, with brown eyes. Just then I detested Max. I got up and said I was going to get some milk for Fatima.

I found Ismay in a rage in the kitchen. She had been up in

the garret, and a mouse had run across her foot. Mice always
get on Ismay's nerves.

"We need a cat badly enough," she fumed, "but not a useless,
pampered thing, like Fatima. That garret is literally swarming
with mice. You'll not catch me going up there again."

Fatima did not prove such a nuisance as we had feared.
Huldah Jane liked her, and Ismay, in spite of her declaration
that she would have nothing to do with her, looked after her
comfort scrupulously. She even used to get up in the middle
of the night and go out to see if Fatima was warm. Max came
in every day and, being around, gave us good advice.

Then one day, about three weeks after Aunt Cynthia's departure, Fatima disappeared—just simply disappeared as if she
had been dissolved into thin air. We left her one afternoon,
curled up asleep in her basket by the fire, under Huldah Jane's
eye, while we went out to make a call. When we came home
Fatima was gone.

Huldah Jane wept and was as one whom the gods had made
mad. She vowed that she had never let Fatima out of her sight
the whole time, save once for three minutes when she ran up
to the garret for some summer savory. When she came back
the kitchen door had blown open and Fatima had vanished.

Ismay and I were frantic. We ran about the garden and
through the out-houses, and the woods behind the house, like
wild creatures, calling Fatima, but in vain. Then Ismay sat
down on the front doorsteps and cried.

"She has got out and she'll catch her death of cold and Aunt
Cynthia will never forgive us."

"I'm going for Max," I declared. So I did, through the spruce
woods and over the field as fast as my feet could carry me,
thanking my stars that there was a Max to go to in such a
predicament.

Max came over and we had another search, but without
result. Days passed, but we did not find Fatima. I would
certainly have gone crazy had it not been for Max. He was
worth his weight in gold during the awful week that followed.
We did not dare advertise, lest Aunt Cynthia should see it; but
we inquired far and wide for a white Persian cat with a blue
spot on its tail, and offered a reward for it; but nobody had
seen it, although people kept coming to the house, night and

day, with every kind of a cat in baskets, wanting to know if it was the one we had lost.

"We shall never see Fatima again," I said hopelessly to Max and Ismay one afternoon. I had just turned away an old woman with a big, yellow tommy which she insisted must be ours— "cause it kem to our place, mem, a-yowling fearful, mem, and it don't belong to nobody not down Grafton way, mem."

"I'm afraid you won't," said Max. "She must have perished from exposure long ere this."

"Aunt Cynthia will never forgive us," said Ismay, dismally. "I had a presentiment of trouble the moment that cat came to this house."

We had never heard of this presentiment before, but Ismay is good at having presentiments—after things happen.

"What shall we do?" I demanded, helplessly. "Max, can't you find some way out of this scrape for us?"

"Advertise in the Charlottetown papers for a white Persian cat," suggested Max. "Some one may have one for sale. If so, you must buy it, and palm it off on your good Aunt as Fatima. She's very short-sighted, so it will be quite possible."

"But Fatima has a blue spot on her tail," I said.

"You must advertise for a cat with a blue spot on its tail," said Max.

"It will cost a pretty penny," said Ismay dolefully. "Fatima was valued at one hundred dollars."

"We must take the money we have been saving for our new furs," I said, sorrowfully. "There is no other way out of it. It will cost us a good deal more if we lose Aunt Cynthia's favour. She is quite capable of believing that we have made away with Fatima deliberately and with malice aforethought."

So we advertised. Max went to town and had the notice inserted in the most important daily. We asked any one who had a white Persian cat, with a blue spot on the tip of its tail, to dispose of, to communicate with M.I., care of the *Enterprise*.

We really did not have much hope that anything would come of it, so we were surprised and delighted over the letter Max brought home from town four days later. It was a type-written screed from Halifax stating that the writer had for sale a white Persian cat answering to our description. The price was a hundred and ten dollars and, if M.I. cared to go to Halifax and inspect the animal, it would be found at 110 Hollis Street, by inquiring for "Persian."

"Temper your joy, my friends," said Ismay, gloomily. "The cat may not suit. The blue spot may be too big or too small or not in the right place. I consistently refuse to believe that any good thing can come out of this deplorable affair."

Just at this moment there was a knock at the door and I hurried out. The postmaster's boy was there with a telegram. I tore it open, glanced at it, and dashed back into the room.

"What is it now?" cried Ismay, beholding my face.

I held out the telegram. It was from Aunt Cynthia. She had wired us to send Fatima to Halifax by express immediately.

For the first time Max did not seem ready to rush into the breach with a suggestion. It was I who spoke first.

"Max," I said, imploringly, "you'll see us through this, won't you? Neither Ismay nor I can rush off to Halifax at once. You must go tomorrow morning. Go right to 110 Hollis Street and ask for 'Persian.' If the cat looks enough like Fatima, buy it and take it to Aunt Cynthia. If it doesn't—but it must! You'll go, won't you?"

"That depends," said Max.

I stared at him. This was so unlike Max.

"You are sending me on a nasty errand," he said, coolly. "How do I know that Aunt Cynthia will be deceived after all, even if she be short-sighted. Buying a cat in a joke is a huge risk. And if she should see through the scheme I shall be in a pretty mess."

"Oh, Max," I said, on the verge of tears.

"Of course," said Max, looking meditatively into the fire, "if I were really one of the family, or had any reasonable prospect of being so, I would not mind so much. It would be all in the day's work then. But as it is—"

Ismay got up and went out of the room.

"Oh, Max, please," I said.

"Will you marry me, Sue?" demanded Max sternly. "If you will agree, I'll go to Halifax and beard the lion in his den unflinchingly. If necessary, I will take a black street cat to Aunt Cynthia, and swear that it is Fatima. I'll get you out of the scrape, if I have to prove that you never had Fatima, that she is safe in your possession at the present time, and that there

never was such an animal as Fatima anyhow. I'll do anything,
say anything—but it must be for my future wife."

"Will nothing else content you?" I said helplessly.

"Nothing."

I thought hard. Of course Max was acting abominably—
but—but—he was really a dear fellow—and this was the twelfth
time—and there was Anne Shirley! I knew in my secret soul
that life would be a dreadfully dismal thing if Max were not
around somewhere. Besides, I would have married him long
ago had not Aunt Cynthia thrown us so pointedly at each
other's heads ever since he came to Spencervale.

"Very well," I said crossly.

Max left for Halifax in the morning. Next day we got a wire
saying it was all right. The evening of the following day he
was back in Spencervale. Ismay and I put him in a chair and
glared at him impatiently.

Max began to laugh and laughed until he turned blue.

"I am glad it is so amusing," said Ismay severely.

"If Sue and I could see the joke it might be more so."

"Dear little girls, have patience with me," implored Max. "If
you knew what it cost me to keep a straight face in Halifax
you would forgive me for breaking out now."

"We forgive you—but for pity's sake tell us all about it," I
cried.

"Well, as soon as I arrived in Halifax I hurried to 110 Hollis
Street, but—see here! Didn't you tell me your Aunt's address
was 10 Pleasant Street?"

"So it is."

" 'T isn't. You look at the address on a telegram next time
you get one. She went a week ago to visit another friend who
lives at 110 Hollis."

"Max!"

"It's a fact. I rang the bell, and was just going to ask the
maid for 'Persian' when your Aunt Cynthia herself came through
the hall and pounced on me.

" 'Max,' she said, 'have you brought Fatima?'

" 'No,' I answered, trying to adjust my wits to this new
development as she towed me into the library. 'No, I—I—just
came to Halifax on a little matter of business.'

" 'Dear me,' said Aunt Cynthia, crossly, 'I don't know what

those girls mean. I wired them to send Fatima at once. And she has not come yet and I am expecting a call every minute from some one who wants to buy her.'

" 'Oh!' I murmured, mining deeper every minute.

" 'Yes,' went on your aunt, 'there is an advertisement in the Charlotteville *Enterprise* for a Persian cat, and I answered it. Fatima is really quite a charge, you know—and so apt to die and be a dead loss'—did your aunt mean a pun, girls?—'and so, although I am considerably attached to her, I have decided to part with her.'

"By this time I had got my second wind, and I promptly decided that a judicious mixture of the truth was the thing required.

" 'Well, of all the curious coincidences,' I exclaimed. 'Why, Miss Ridley, it was I who advertised for a Persian cat—on Sue's behalf. She and Ismay have decided that they want a cat like Fatima for themselves.'

"You should have seen how she beamed. She said she knew you always really liked cats, only you would never own up to it. We clinched the dicker then and there. I passed her over your hundred and ten dollars—she took the money without turning a hair—and now you are the joint owners of Fatima. Good luck to your bargain!"

"Mean old thing," sniffed Ismay. She meant Aunt Cynthia, and, remembering our shabby furs, I didn't disagree with her.

"But there is no Fatima," I said, dubiously. "How shall we account for her when Aunt Cynthia comes home?"

"Well, your aunt isn't coming home for a month yet. When she comes you will have to tell her that the cat—is lost—but you needn't say *when* it happened. As for the rest, Fatima is your property now, so Aunt Cynthia can't grumble. But she will have a poorer opinion than ever of your fitness to run a house alone."

When Max left I went to the window to watch him down the path. He was really a handsome fellow, and I was proud of him. At the gate he turned to wave me goodby, and, as he did, he glanced upward. Even at that distance I saw the look of amazement on his face. Then he came bolting back.

"Ismay, the house is on fire!" I shrieked, as I flew to the door.

"Sue," cried Max, "I saw Fatima, or her ghost, at the garret window a moment ago!"

"Nonsense!" I cried. But Ismay was already half way up the stairs and we followed. Straight to the garret we rushed. There sat Fatima, sleek and complacent, sunning herself in the window.

Max laughed until the rafters rang.

"She can't have been up here all this time," I protested, half tearfully. "We would have heard her meowing."

"But you didn't," said Max.

"She would have died of the cold," declared Ismay.

"But she hasn't," said Max.

"Or starved," I cried.

"The place is alive with mice," said Max. "No, girls, there is no doubt the cat has been here the whole fortnight. She must have followed Huldah Jane up here, unobserved, that day. It's a wonder you didn't hear her crying—if she did cry. But perhaps she didn't, and, of course, you sleep downstairs. To think you never thought of looking here for her!"

"It has cost us over a hundred dollars," said Ismay, with a malevolent glance at the sleek Fatima.

"It has cost me more than that," I said, as I turned to the stairway.

Max held me back for an instant, while Ismay and Fatima pattered down.

"Do you think it has cost too much, Sue?" he whispered.

I looked at him sideways. He was really a dear. Niceness fairly exhaled from him.

"No-o-o," I said, "but when we are married you will have to take care of Fatima, I won't."

"Dear Fatima," said Max gratefully.

THE MATERIALIZING OF CECIL

IT HAD never worried me in the least that I wasn't married, although everybody in Avonlea pitied old maids; but it *did* worry me, and I frankly confess it, that I had never had a chance to be. Even Nancy, my old nurse and servant, knew that, and pitied me for it. Nancy is an old maid herself, but she has had two proposals. She did not accept either of them because one was a widower with seven children, and the other a very shiftless, good-for-nothing fellow; but, if anybody twitted Nancy on her single condition, she could point triumphantly to those two as evidence that "she could an she would." If I had not lived all my life in Avonlea I might have had the benefit of the doubt; but I had, and everybody knew everything about me—or thought they did.

I had really often wondered why nobody had ever fallen in love with me. I was not at all homely; indeed, years ago, George Adoniram Maybrick had written a poem addressed to me, in which he praised my beauty quite extravagantly; that didn't mean anything because George Adoniram wrote poetry to all the good-looking girls and never went with anybody but Flora King, who was cross-eyed and red-haired, but it proves that it was not my appearance that put me out of the running. Neither was it the fact that I wrote poetry myself—although not of

George Adoniram's kind—because nobody ever knew that. When I felt it coming on I shut myself up in my room and wrote it out in a little blank book I kept locked up. It is nearly full now, because I have been writing poetry all my life. It is the only thing I have ever been able to keep a secret from Nancy. Nancy, in any case, has not a very high opinion of my ability to take care of myself; but I tremble to imagine what she would think if she ever found out about that little book. I am convinced she would send for the doctor post-haste and insist on mustard plasters while waiting for him.

Nevertheless, I kept on at it, and what with my flowers and my cats and my magazines and my little book, I was really very happy and contented. But it *did* sting that Adella Gilbert, across the road, who has a drunken husband, should pity "poor Charlotte" because nobody had ever wanted her. Poor Charlotte indeed! If I had thrown myself at a man's head the way Adella Gilbert did at—but there, there, I must refrain from such thoughts. I must not be uncharitable.

The Sewing Circle met at Mary Gillespie's on my fortieth birthday. I have given up talking about my birthdays, although that little scheme is not much good in Avonlea where everybody knows your age—or if they make a mistake it is never on the side of youth. But Nancy, who grew accustomed to celebrating my birthdays when I was a little girl, never gets over the habit, and I don't try to cure her, because, after all, it's nice to have some one make a fuss over you. She brought me up my breakfast before I got up out of bed—a concession to my laziness that Nancy would scorn to make on any other day of the year. She had cooked everything I liked best, and had decorated the tray with roses from the garden and ferns from the woods behind the house. I enjoyed every bit of that breakfast, and then I got up and dressed, putting on my second best muslin gown. I would have put on my really best if I had not had the fear of Nancy before my eyes; but I knew she would never condone *that,* even on a birthday. I watered my flowers and fed my cats, and then I locked myself up and wrote a poem on June. I had given up writing birthday odes after I was thirty.

In the afternoon I went to the Sewing Circle. When I was ready for it I looked in my glass and wondered if I could really be forty. I was quite sure I didn't look it. My hair was brown and wavy, my cheeks were pink, and the lines could hardly be seen at all, though possibly that was because of the dim light. I always have my mirror hung in the darkest corner of my room. Nancy cannot imagine why. I know the lines are there, of course; but when they don't show very plain I forget that they are there.

We had a large Sewing Circle, young and old alike attending. I really cannot say I ever enjoyed the meetings—at least not up to that time—although I went religiously because I thought it my duty to go. The married women talked so much of their husbands and children, and of course I had to be quiet on those topics; and the young girls talked in corner groups about their beaux, and stopped it when I joined them, as if they felt sure that an old maid who had never had a beau couldn't understand at all. As for the other old maids, they talked gossip about every one, and I did not like that either. I knew the minute my back was turned they would fasten into me and hint that I used hair-dye and declare it was perfectly ridiculous for a woman of *fifty* to wear a pink muslin dress with lace-trimmed frills.

There was a full attendance that day, for we were getting ready for a sale of fancy work in aid of parsonage repairs. The young girls were merrier and noisier than usual. Wilhelmina Mercer was there, and she kept them going. The Mercers were quite new to Avonlea, having come here only two months previously.

I was sitting by the window and Wilhelmina Mercer, Maggie Henderson, Susette Cross and Georgie Hall were in a little group just before me. I wasn't listening to their chatter at all, but presently Georgie exclaimed teasingly:

"Miss Charlotte is laughing at us. I suppose she thinks we are awfully silly to be talking about beaux."

The truth was that I was simply smiling over some very pretty thoughts that had come to me about the roses which were climbing over Mary Gillespie's sill. I meant to inscribe them in the little blank book when I went home. Georgie's speech brought me back to harsh realities with a jolt. It hurt me, as such speeches always did.

"Didn't you ever have a beau, Miss Holmes?" said Wilhelmina laughingly.

Just as it happened, a silence had fallen over the room for a moment, and everybody in it heard Wilhelmina's question.

I really do not know what got into me and possessed me. I have never been able to account for what I said and did, because I am naturally a truthful person and hate all deceit. It seemed to me that I simply could not say "No" to Wilhelmina before that whole roomful of women. It was *too* humiliating. I suppose all the prickles and stings and slurs I had endured for fifteen years on account of never having had a lover had what the new doctor calls "a cumulative effect" and came to a head then and there.

"Yes, I had one once, my dear," I said calmly.

For once in my life I made a sensation. Every woman in that room stopped sewing and stared at me. Most of them, I saw, didn't believe me, but Wilhelmina did. Her pretty face lighted up with interest.

"Oh, won't you tell us about him, Miss Holmes?" she coaxed, "and why you didn't marry him?"

"That is right, Miss Mercer," said Josephine Cameron, with a nasty little laugh. "Make her tell. We're all interested. It's news to us that Charlotte ever had a beau."

If Josephine had not said that, I might not have gone on. But she did say it, and, moreover, I caught Mary Gillespie and Adella Gilbert exchanging significant smiles. That settled it, and made me quite reckless. "In for a penny, in for a pound," thought I, and I said with a pensive smile:

"Nobody here knew anything about him, and it was all long, long ago."

"What was his name?" asked Wilhelmina.

"Cecil Fenwick," I answered promptly. Cecil had always been my favorite name for a man; it figured quite frequently in the blank book. As for the Fenwick part of it, I had a bit of newspaper in my hand, measuring a hem, with "Try Fenwick's Porous Plasters" printed across it, and I simply joined the two in sudden and irrevocable matrimony.

"Where did you meet him?" asked Georgie.

I hastily reviewed my past. There was only one place to locate Cecil Fenwick. The only time I had ever been far enough away from Avonlea in my life was when I was eighteen and had gone to visit an aunt in New Brunswick.

"In Blakely, New Brunswick," I said, almost believing that I had when I saw how they all took it in unsuspectingly. "I was just eighteen and he was twenty-three."

"What did he look like?" Susette wanted to know.

"Oh, he was very handsome." I proceeded glibly to sketch my ideal. To tell the dreadful truth, I was enjoying myself; I could see respect dawning in those girls' eyes, and I knew that I had forever thrown off my reproach. Henceforth I should be a woman with a romantic past, faithful to the one love of her life—a very, very different thing from an old maid who had never had a lover.

"He was tall and dark, with lovely, curly black hair and brilliant, piercing eyes. He had a splendid chin, and a fine nose, and the most fascinating smile!"

"What was he?" asked Maggie.

"A young lawyer," I said, my choice of profession decided by an enlarged crayon portrait of Mary Gillespie's deceased brother on an easel before me. He had been a lawyer.

"Why didn't you marry him?" demanded Susette.

"We quarreled," I answered sadly. "A terribly bitter quarrel. Oh, we were both so young and so foolish. It was my fault. I vexed Cecil by flirting with another man"—wasn't I coming on!—"and he was jealous and angry. He went out West and never came back. I have never seen him since, and I do not even know if he is alive. But—but—I could never care for any other man."

"Oh, how interesting!" sighed Wilhelmina. "I do so love sad love stories. But perhaps he will come back some day yet, Miss Holmes."

"Oh, no, never now," I said, shaking my head. "He has forgotten all about me, I dare say. Or if he hasn't, he has never forgiven me."

Mary Gillespie's Susan Jane announced tea at this moment, and I was thankful, for my imagination was giving out, and I didn't know what question those girls would ask next. But I felt already a change in the mental atmosphere surrounding me, and all through supper I was thrilled with a secret exultation. Repentant? Ashamed? Not a bit of it! I'd have done the same thing over again, and all I felt sorry for was that I hadn't done it long ago.

When I got home that night Nancy looked at me wonderingly and said:

"You look like a girl, tonight, Miss Charlotte."

"I feel like one," I said laughing; and I ran to my room and did what I had never done before—wrote a second poem in the same day. I had to have some outlet for my feelings. I called it "In Summer Days of Long Ago," and I worked Mary Gillespie's roses and Cecil Fenwick's eyes into it, and made it so sad and reminiscent and minor-musicky that I felt perfectly happy.

For the next two months all went well and merrily. Nobody ever said anything more to me about Cecil Fenwick, but the girls all chattered freely to me of their little love affairs, and I became a sort of general confidant for them. It just warmed up the cockles of my heart, and I began to enjoy the Sewing Circle famously. I got a lot of pretty new dresses and the dearest hat, and I went everywhere I was asked and had a good time.

But there is one thing you can be perfectly sure of. If you do wrong you are going to be punished for it sometime, somehow and somewhere. My punishment was delayed for two months, and then it descended on my head and I was crushed to the very dust.

Another new family besides the Mercers had come to Avonlea in the spring—the Maxwells. There were just Mr. and Mrs. Maxwell; they were a middle-aged couple and very well off. Mr. Maxwell had bought the lumber mills, and they lived up at the old Spencer place which had always been "the" place of Avonlea. They lived quietly, and Mrs. Maxwell hardly ever went anywhere because she was delicate. She was out when I called and I was out when she returned my call, so that I had never met her.

It was the Sewing Circle day again—at Sarah Gardiner's this time. I was late; everybody else was there when I arrived, and the minute I entered the room I knew something had happened, although I couldn't imagine what. Everybody looked at me in the strangest way. Of course, Wilhelmina Mercer was the first to set her tongue going.

"Oh, Miss Holmes, have you seen him yet?" she exclaimed.

"Seen whom?" I said non-excitedly, getting out my thimble and patterns.

"Why, Cecil Fenwick. He's here—in Avonlea—visiting his sister, Mrs. Maxwell."

I suppose I did what they expected me to do. I dropped everything I held, and Josephine Cameron said afterwards that Charlotte Holmes would never be paler when she was in her coffin. If they had just known why I turned so pale!

"It's impossible!" I said blankly.

"It's really true," said Wilhelmina, delighted at this development, as she supposed it, of my romance. "I was up to see Mrs. Maxwell last night, and I met him."

"It—can't be—the same—Cecil Fenwick," I said faintly, because I had to say something.

"Oh, yes, it is. He belongs in Blakely, New Brunswick, and he's a lawyer, and he's been out West twenty-two years. He's oh! so handsome, and just as you described him, except that his hair is quite gray. He has never married—I asked Mrs. Maxwell—so you see he has never forgotten you, Miss Holmes. And, oh, I believe everything is going to come out all right."

I couldn't exactly share her cheerful belief. Everything seemed to me to be coming out most horribly wrong. I was so mixed up I didn't know what to do or say. I felt as if I were in a bad dream—it *must* be a dream—there couldn't really be a Cecil Fenwick! My feelings were simply indescribable. Fortunately every one put my agitation down to quite a different cause, and they very kindly left me alone to recover myself. I shall never forget that awful afternoon. Right after tea I excused myself and went home as fast as I could go. There I shut myself up in my room, but *not* to write poetry in my blank book. No, indeed! I felt in no poetical mood.

I tried to look the facts squarely in the face. There was a Cecil Fenwick, extraordinary as the coincidence was, and he was here in Avonlea. All my friends—and foes—believed that he was the estranged lover of my youth. If he stayed long in Avonlea, one of two things was bound to happen. He would hear the story I had told about him and deny it, and I would be held up to shame and derision for the rest of my natural life; or else he would simply go away in ignorance, and everybody would suppose he had forgotten me and would pity me maddeningly. The latter possibility was bad enough, but it wasn't to be compared to the former; and, oh, how I prayed—yes, I *did* pray about it—that he would go right away. But Providence had other views for me.

Cecil Fenwick didn't go away. He stayed right on in Avonlea, and the Maxwells blossomed out socially in his honor and tried to give him a good time. Mrs. Maxwell gave a party for him. I got a card—but you may be very sure I didn't go, although Nancy thought I was crazy not to. Then everyone else gave parties in honor of Mr. Fenwick and I was invited and never went. Wilhelmina Mercer came and pleaded and scolded and told me if I avoided Mr. Fenwick like that he would think I still cherished bitterness against him, and he wouldn't make any advances towards a reconciliation. Wilhelmina means well, but she hasn't a great deal of sense.

Cecil Fenwick seemed to be a great favorite with everybody, young and old. He was very rich, too, and Wilhelmina declared that half the girls were after him.

"If it wasn't for you, Miss Holmes, I believe I'd have a try for him myself, in spite of his gray hair and quick temper—for Mrs. Maxwell says he has a pretty quick temper, but it's all over in a minute," said Wilhelmina, half in jest and wholly in earnest.

As for me, I gave up going out at all, even to church. I fretted and pined and lost my appetite and never wrote a line in my blank book. Nancy was half frantic and insisted on dosing me with her favorite patent pills. I took them meekly, because it is a waste of time and energy to oppose Nancy, but, of course, they didn't do me any good. My trouble was too deep-seated for pills to cure. If ever a woman was punished for telling a lie I was that woman. I stopped my subscription to the *Weekly Advocate* because it still carried that wretched porous plaster advertisement, and I couldn't bear to see it. If it hadn't been for that I would never have thought of Fenwick for a name, and all this trouble would have been averted.

One evening, when I was moping in my room, Nancy came up.

"There's a gentleman in the parlor asking for you, Miss Charlotte."

My heart just gave one horrible bounce.

"What—sort of a gentleman, Nancy?" I faltered.

"I think it's that Fenwick man that there's been such a time

about," said Nancy, who didn't know anything about my imaginary escapades, "and he looks to be mad clean through about
something, for such a scowl I never seen."

"Tell him I'll be down directly, Nancy," I said quite calmly.

As soon as Nancy had clumped downstairs again I put on
my lace fichu and put two hankies in my belt, for I thought
I'd probably need more than one. Then I hunted up an old
Advocate for proof, and down I went to the parlor. I know
exactly how a criminal feels going to execution, and I've been
opposed to capital punishment ever since.

I opened the parlor door and went in, carefully closing it
behind me, for Nancy has a deplorable habit of listening in
the hall. Then my legs gave out completely, and I couldn't
have walked another step to save my life. I just stood there,
my hand on the knob, trembling like a leaf.

A man was standing by the south window looking out; he
wheeled around as I went in, and, as Nancy said, he had a
scowl on and looked angry clear through. He was very handsome, and his gray hair gave him such a distinguished look. I
recalled this afterward, but just at the moment you may be
quite sure I wasn't thinking about it at all.

Then all at once a strange thing happened. The scowl went
right off his face and the anger out of his eyes. He looked
astonished, and then foolish. I saw the color creeping up into
his cheeks. As for me, I still stood there staring at him, not
able to say a single word.

"Miss Holmes, I presume." he said at last, in a deep, thrilling
voice. "I—I—oh, confound it! I have called—I heard some
foolish stories and I came here in a rage. I've been a fool—I
know now they weren't true. Just excuse me and I'll go away
and kick myself."

"No," I said, finding my voice with a gasp, "you mustn't
go until you've heard the truth. It's dreadful enough, but not
as dreadful as you might otherwise think. Those—those stories—
I have a confession to make. I did tell them, but I didn't know
there was such a person as Cecil Fenwick in existence."

He looked puzzled, as well he might. Then he smiled, took
my hand and led me away from the door—to the knob of
which I was still holding with all my might—to the sofa.

"Let's sit down and talk it over 'comfy,' " he said.

I just confessed the whole shameful business. It was terribly humiliating, but it served me right. I told him how people were always twitting me for never having had a beau, and how I had told them I had; and then I showed him the porous plaster advertisement.

He heard me right through without a word, and then he threw back his big, curly, gray head and laughed.

"This clears up a great many mysterious hints I've been receiving ever since I came to Avonlea," he said, "and finally a Mrs. Gilbert came to my sister this afternoon with a long farrago of nonsense about the love affair I had once had with some Charlotte Holmes here. She declared you had told her about it yourself. I confess I flamed up. I'm a peppery chap, and I thought—I thought—oh, confound it, it might as well out: I thought you were some lank old maid who was amusing herself telling ridiculous stories about me. When you came into the room I knew that, whoever was to blame, you were not."

"But I was," I said ruefully. "It wasn't right of me to tell such a story—and it was very silly, too. But who would ever have supposed that there could be a real Cecil Fenwick who had lived in Blakely? I never heard of such a coincidence."

"It's more than a coincidence," said Mr. Fenwick decidedly. "It's predestination; that is what it is. And now let's forget it and talk of something else."

We talked of something else—or at least Mr. Fenwick did, for I was too ashamed to say much—so long that Nancy got restive and clumped through the hall every five minutes; but Mr. Fenwick never took the hint. When he finally went away he asked if he might come again.

"It's time we made up that old quarrel, you know," he said, laughing.

And I, an old maid of forty, caught myself blushing like a girl. But I felt like a girl, for it was such a relief to have that explanation all over. I couldn't even feel angry with Adella Gilbert. She was always a mischief maker, and when a woman is born that way she is more to be pitied than blamed. I wrote a poem in the blank book before I went to sleep; I hadn't written anything for a month, and it was lovely to be at it once more.

Mr. Fenwick did come again—the very next evening, but

one. And he came so often after that that even Nancy got resigned to him. One day I had to tell her something. I shrank from doing it, for I feared it would make her feel badly.

"Oh, I've been expecting to hear it," she said grimly. "I felt the minute that man came into the house he brought trouble with him. Well, Miss Charlotte, I wish you happiness. I don't know how the climate of California will agree with me, but I suppose I'll have to put up with it."

"But, Nancy," I said, "I can't expect you to go away out there with me. It's too much to ask of you."

"And where else would I be going?" demanded Nancy in genuine astonishment. "How under the canopy could you keep house without me? I'm not going to trust you to the mercies of a yellow Chinee with a pig-tail. Where you go I go, Miss Charlotte, and there's an end of it."

I was very glad, for I hated to think of parting with Nancy even to go with Cecil. As for the blank book, I haven't told my husband about it yet, but I mean to some day. And I've subscribed for the *Weekly Advocate* again.

HER FATHER'S DAUGHTER

"WE MUST invite your Aunt Jane, of course," said Mrs. Spencer.

Rachel made a protesting movement with her large, white, shapely hands—hands which were so different from the thin, dark, twisted ones folded on the table opposite her. The difference was not caused by hard work or the lack of it; Rachel had worked hard all her life. It was a difference inherent in temperament. The Spencers, no matter what they did, or how hard they labored, all had plump, smooth, white hands, with firm, supple fingers; the Chiswicks, even those who toiled not, neither did they spin, had hard, knotted, twisted ones. Moreover the contrast went deeper than externals, and twined itself with the innermost fibers of life, and thought, and action.

"I don't see why we must invite Aunt Jane," said Rachel, with as much impatience as her soft, throaty voice could express. "Aunt Jane doesn't like me, and I don't like Aunt Jane."

"I'm sure I don't see why you don't like her," said Mrs. Spencer. "It's ungrateful of you. She has always been very kind to you."

"She has always been very kind with one hand," smiled Rachel. "I remember the first time I ever saw Aunt Jane. I was six years old. She held out to me a small velvet pincushion with beads on it. And then, because I did not, in my shyness,

411

thank her quite as promptly as I should have done, she rapped my head with her bethimbled finger to 'teach me better manners.' It hurt horribly—I've always had a tender head. And that has been Aunt Jane's way ever since. When I grew too big for the thimble treatment she used her tongue instead—and that hurt worse. And you know, mother, how she used to talk about my engagement. She is able to spoil the whole atmosphere if she happens to come in a bad humor. I don't want her."

"She must be invited. People would talk so if she wasn't."

"I don't see why they should. She's only my great-aunt by marriage. I wouldn't mind in the least if people did talk. They'll talk anyway—you know that, mother."

"Oh, we must have her," said Mrs. Spencer, with the indifferent finality that marked all her words and decisions—a finality against which it was seldom of any avail to struggle. People, who knew, rarely attempted it; strangers occasionally did, misled by the deceit of appearances.

Isabella Spencer was a wisp of a woman, with a pale, pretty face, uncertainly-colored, long-lashed, grayish eyes, and great masses of dull, soft, silky, brown hair. She had delicate aquiline features and a small, babyish, red mouth. She looked as if a breath would sway her. The truth was that a tornado would hardly have caused her to swerve an inch from her chosen path.

For a moment Rachel looked rebellious; then she yielded, as she generally did in all differences of opinion with her mother. It was not worth while to quarrel over the comparatively unimportant matter of Aunt Jane's invitation. A quarrel might be inevitable later on; Rachel wanted to save all her resources for that. She gave her shoulders a shrug, and wrote Aunt Jane's name down on the wedding list in her large, somewhat untidy handwriting—a handwriting which always seemed to irritate her mother. Rachel never could understand this irritation. She could never guess that it was because her writing looked so much like that in a certain packet of faded letters which Mrs. Spencer kept at the bottom of an old horsehair trunk in her bedroom. They were postmarked from seaports all over the world. Mrs. Spencer never read them or looked at them; but she remembered every dash and curve of the handwriting.

Isabella Spencer had overcome many things in her life by

the sheer force and persistency of her will. But she could not get the better of heredity. Rachel was her father's daughter at all points, and Isabella Spencer escaped hating her for it only by loving her the more fiercely because of it. Even so, there were many times when she had to avert her eyes from Rachel's face because of the pang of the more subtle remembrances; and never, since her child was born, could Isabella Spencer bear to gaze on that child's face in sleep.

Rachel was to be married to Frank Bell in a fortnight's time. Mrs. Spencer was pleased with the match. She was very fond of Frank, and his farm was so near to her own that she would not lose Rachel altogether. Rachel fondly believed that her mother would not lose her at all; but Isabella Spencer, wiser by olden experience, knew what her daughter's marriage must mean to her, and steeled her heart to bear it with what fortitude she might.

They were in the sitting-room, deciding on the wedding guests and other details. The September sunshine was coming in through the waving boughs of the apple tree that grew close up to the low window. The glints wavered over Rachel's face, as white as a wood lily, with only a faint dream of rose in the cheeks. She wore her sleek, golden hair in a quaint arch around it. Her forehead was very broad and white. She was fresh and young and hopeful. The mother's heart contracted in a spasm of pain as she looked at her. How like the girl was to—to— to the Spencers! Those easy, curving outlines, those large, mirthful blue eyes, that finely molded chin! Isabella Spencer shut her lips firmly, and crushed down some unbidden, unwelcome memories.

"There will be about sixty guests, all told," she said, as if she were thinking of nothing else. "We must move the furniture all out of this room and set the supper-table here. The dining-room is too small. We must borrow Mrs. Bell's forks and spoons. She offered to lend them. I'd never have been willing to ask her. The damask table cloths with the ribbon pattern must be bleached tomorrow. Nobody else in Avonlea has such tablecloths. And we'll put the little dining-room table on the hall landing, upstairs, for the presents."

Rachel was not thinking about the presents, or the housewifely details of the wedding. Her breath was coming quicker, and the faint blush on her smooth cheeks had deepened to crimson. She knew that a critical moment was approaching. With a steady hand she wrote the last name on her list and drew a line under it.

"Well, have you finished?" asked her mother impatiently. "Hand it here and let me look over it to make sure that you haven't left anybody out that should be in."

Rachel passed the paper across the table in silence. The room seemed to her to have grown very still. She could hear the flies buzzing on the panes, the soft purr of the wind about the low eaves and through the apple boughs, the jerky beating of her own heart. She felt frightened and nervous, but resolute.

Mrs. Spencer glanced down the list, murmuring the names aloud and nodding approval at each. But when she came to the last name, she did not utter it. She cast a black glance at Rachel, and a spark leaped up in the depths of her pale eyes. On her face were anger, amazement, incredulity, the last predominating.

The final name on the list of wedding guests was the name of David Spencer. David Spencer lived alone in a little cottage down at the Cove. He was a combination of sailor and fisherman. He was also Isabella Spencer's husband and Rachel's father.

"Rachel Spencer, have you taken leave of your senses? What do you mean by such nonsense as this?"

"I simply mean that I am going to invite my father to my wedding," answered Rachel quietly.

"Not in my house," cried Mrs. Spencer, her lips as white as if her fiery tone had scathed them.

Rachel leaned forward, folded her large, capable hands deliberately on the table, and gazed unflinchingly into her mother's bitter face. Her fright and nervousness were gone. Now that the conflict was actually on she found herself rather enjoying it. She wondered a little at herself, and thought that she must be wicked. She was not given to self-analysis, or she might have concluded that it was the sudden assertion of her own personality, so long dominated by her mother's, which she was finding so agreeable.

"Then there will be no wedding, mother," she said. "Frank and I will simply go to the manse, be married, and go home.

If I cannot invite my father to see me married, no one else shall be invited."

Her lips narrowed tightly. For the first time in her life Isabella Spencer saw a reflection of herself looking back at her from her daughter's face—a strange, indefinable resemblance that was more of soul and spirit than of flesh and blood. In spite of her anger her heart thrilled to it. As never before, she realized that this girl was her own and her husband's child, a living bond between them wherein their conflicting natures mingled and were reconciled. She realized too, that Rachel, so long sweetly meek and obedient, meant to have her own way in this case—and would have it.

"I must say that I can't see why you are so set on having your father see you married," she said with a bitter sneer. "*He* has never remembered that he is your father. He cares nothing about you—never did care."

Rachel took no notice of this taunt. It had no power to hurt her, its venom being neutralized by a secret knowledge of her own in which her mother had no share.

"Either I shall invite my father to my wedding, or I shall not have a wedding," she repeated steadily, adopting her mother's own effective tactics of repetition undistracted by argument.

"Invite him then," snapped Mrs. Spencer, with the ungraceful anger of a woman, long accustomed to having her own way, compelled for once to yield. "It'll be like chips in porridge anyhow—neither good nor harm. He won't come."

Rachel made no response. Now that the battle was over, and the victory won, she found herself tremulously on the verge of tears. She rose quickly and went upstairs to her own room, a dim little place shadowed by the white birches growing thickly outside—a virginal room, where everything bespoke the maiden. She lay down on the blue and white patchwork quilt on her little bed, and cried softly and bitterly.

Her heart, at this crisis in her life, yearned for her father, who was almost a stranger to her. She knew that her mother had probably spoken the truth when she said that he would not come. Rachel felt that her marriage vows would be lacking in some indefinable sacredness if her father were not by to hear them spoken.

Twenty-five years before this, David Spencer and Isabella

Chiswick had been married. Spiteful people said there could be no doubt that Isabella had married David for love, since he had neither lands nor money to tempt her into a match of bargain and sale. David was a handsome fellow, with the blood of a seafaring race in his veins.

He had been a sailor, like his father and grandfather before him; but, when he married Isabella, she induced him to give up the sea and settle down with her on a snug farm her father had left her. Isabella liked farming, and loved her fertile acres and opulent orchards. She abhorred the sea and all that pertained to it, less from any dread of its dangers than from an inbred conviction that sailors were "low" in the social scale— a species of necessary vagabonds. In her eyes there was a taint of disgrace in such a calling. David must be transformed into a respectable, home-abiding tiller of broad lands.

For five years all went well enough. If, at times, David's longing for the sea troubled him, he stifled it, and listened not to its luring voice. He and Isabella were very happy; the only drawback to their happiness lay in the regretted fact that they were childless.

Then, in the sixth year, came a crisis and a change. Captain Barrett, an old crony of David's, wanted him to go with him on a voyage as mate. At the suggestion all David's long-repressed craving for the wide blue wastes of the ocean, and the wind whistling through the spars with the salt foam in its breath, broke forth with a passion all the more intense for that very repression. He must go on that voyage with James Barrett— he *must!* That over, he would be contented again; but go he must. His soul struggled within him like a fettered thing.

Isabella opposed the scheme vehemently and unwisely, with mordant sarcasm and unjust reproaches. The latent obstinacy of David's character came to the support of his longing—a longing which Isabella, with five generations of land-loving ancestry behind her, could not understand at all.

He was determined to go, and he told Isabella so.

"I'm sick of plowing and milking cows," he said hotly.

"You mean that you are sick of a respectable life," sneered Isabella.

"Perhaps," said David, with a contemptuous shrug of his shoulders. "Anyway, I'm going."

"If you go on this voyage, David Spencer, you need never come back here," said Isabella resolutely.

David had gone; he did not believe that she meant it. Isabella believed that he did not care whether she meant it or not. David Spencer left behind him a woman, calm outwardly, inwardly a seething volcano of anger, wounded pride, and thwarted will.

He found precisely the same woman when he came home, tanned, joyous, tamed for a while of his *wanderlust*, ready, with something of real affection, to go back to the farm fields and the stock-yard.

Isabella met him at the door, smileless, cold-eyed, set-lipped.

"What do you want here?" she said, in the tone she was accustomed to use to tramps and Syrian peddlers.

"Want!" David's surprise left him at a loss for words. "Want! Why, I—I—want my wife. I've come home."

"This is not your home. I'm no wife of yours. You made your choice when you went away," Isabella had replied. Then she had gone in, shut the door, and locked it in his face.

David had stood there for a few minutes like a man stunned. Then he had turned and walked away up the lane under the birches. He said nothing—then or at any other time. From that day no reference to his wife or her concerns ever crossed his lips.

He went directly to the harbor, and shipped with Captain Barrett for another voyage. When he came back from that in a month's time, he bought a small house and had it hauled to the "Cove," a lonely inlet from which no other human habitation was visible. Between his sea voyages he lived there the life of a recluse; fishing and playing his violin were his only employments. He went nowhere and encouraged no visitors.

Isabella Spencer also had adopted the tactics of silence. When the scandalized Chiswicks, Aunt Jane at their head, tried to patch up the matter with argument and entreaty, Isabella met them stonily, seeming not to hear what they said, and making no response. She worsted them totally. As Aunt Jane said in disgust, "What can you do with a woman who won't even *talk?*"

Five months after David Spencer had been turned from his wife's door, Rachel was born. Perhaps, if David had come to them then, with due penitence and humility, Isabella's heart, softened by the pain and joy of her long and ardently desired motherhood might have cast out the rankling venom of resentment that had poisoned it and taken him back into it. But David had not come; he gave no sign of knowing or caring that his once longed-for child had been born.

When Isabella was able to be about again, her pale face was harder than ever; and, had there been about her any one discerning enough to notice it, there was a subtle change in her bearing and manner. A certain nervous expectancy, a fluttering restlessness was gone. Isabella had ceased to hope secretly that her husband would yet come back. She had in her secret soul thought he would; and she had meant to forgive him when she had humbled him sufficiently, and when he had abased himself as she considered he should. But now she knew that he did not mean to sue for her forgiveness; and the hate that sprang out of her old love was a rank and speedy and persistent growth.

Rachel, from her earliest recollection, had been vaguely conscious of a difference between her own life and the lives of her playmates. For a long time it puzzled her childish brain. Finally, she reasoned it out that the difference consisted in the fact that they had fathers and she, Rachel Spencer, had none—not even one in the graveyard, as Carrie Bell and Lilian Boulter had. Why was this? Rachel went straight to her mother, put one little dimpled hand on Isabella Spencer's knee, looked up with great searching blue eyes, and said gravely,

"Mother, why haven't I got a father like the other little girls?"

Isabella Spencer laid aside her work, took the seven year old child on her lap, and told her the whole story in a few direct and bitter words that imprinted themselves indelibly on Rachel's remembrance. She understood clearly and hopelessly that she could never have a father—that, in this respect, she must always be unlike other people.

"Your father cares nothing for you," said Isabella Spencer in conclusion. "He never did care. You must never speak of him to anybody again."

Rachel slipped silently from her mother's knee and ran out to the Springtime garden with a full heart. There she cried passionately over her mother's last words. It seemed to her a terrible thing that her father should not love her, and a cruel thing that she must never talk of him.

Oddly enough, Rachel's sympathies were all with her father, in as far as she could understand the old quarrel. She did not dream of disobeying her mother and she did not disobey her. Never again did the child speak of her father; but Isabella had not forbidden her to think of him, and thenceforth Rachel thought of him very constantly—so constantly that, in some strange way, he seemed to become an unguessed-of part of her inner life—the unseen, ever-present companion in all her experiences.

She was an imaginative child, and in fancy she made the acquaintance of her father. She had never seen him, but he was more real to her than most of the people she had seen. He played and talked with her as her mother never did; he walked with her in the orchard and field and garden; he sat by her pillow in the twilight; to him she whispered secrets she told to none other.

Once her mother asked her impatiently why she talked so much to herself.

"I am not talking to myself. I am talking to a very dear friend of mine," Rachel answered gravely.

"Silly child," laughed her mother, half tolerantly, half disapprovingly.

Two years later something wonderful had happened to Rachel. One summer afternoon she had gone to the harbor with several of her little playmates. Such a jaunt was a rare treat to the child, for Isabella Spencer seldom allowed her to go from home with anybody but herself. And Isabella was not an entertaining companion. Rachel never particularly enjoyed an outing with her mother.

The children wandered far along the shore; at last they came to a place Rachel had never seen before. It was a shallow cove where the waters purred on the yellow sands. Beyond it, the sea was laughing and flashing and preening and alluring, like a beautiful, coquettish woman. Outside, the wind was boisterous and rollicking; here, it was reverent and gentle. A white boat was hauled up on the skids, and there was a queer little house close down to the sands, like a big shell tossed up by the waves. Rachel looked on it all with secret delight; she, too, loved the lonely places of sea and shore, as her father had done. She wanted to linger awhile in this dear spot and revel in it.

"I'm tired, girls," she announced. "I'm going to stay here and rest for a spell. I don't want to go to Gull Point. You go on yourselves; I'll wait for you here."

"All alone?" said Carrie Bell, wonderingly.

"I'm not so afraid of being alone as some people are," said Rachel, with dignity.

The other girls went on, leaving Rachel sitting on the skids, in the shadow of the big white boat. She sat there for a time dreaming happily, with her blue eyes on the far, pearly horizon, and her golden head leaning against the boat.

Suddenly she heard a step behind her. When she turned her head a man was standing beside her, looking down at her with big, merry, blue eyes. Rachel was quite sure that she had never seen him before; yet those eyes seemed to her to have a strangely familiar look. She liked him. She felt no shyness nor timidity, such as usually afflicted her in the presence of strangers.

He was a tall, stout man, dressed in a rough fishing suit, and wearing an oilskin cap on his head. His hair was very thick and curly and fair; his cheeks were tanned and red; his teeth, when he smiled, were very even and white. Rachel thought he must be quite old, because there was a good deal of gray mixed with his fair hair.

"Are you watching for the mermaids?" he said.

Rachel nodded gravely. From any one else she would have scrupulously hidden such a thought.

"Yes, I am," she said. "Mother says there is no such thing as a mermaid, but I like to think there is. Have you ever seen one?"

The big man sat down on a bleached log of driftwood and smiled at her.

"No, I'm sorry to say that I haven't. But I have seen many other very wonderful things. I might tell you about some of them, if you would come over here and sit by me."

Rachel went unhesitatingly. When she reached him he pulled her down on his knee, and she liked it.

"What a nice little craft you are," he said. "Do you suppose, now, that you could give me a kiss?"

As a rule Rachel hated kissing. She could seldom be prevailed upon to kiss even her uncles—who knew it and liked to tease her for kisses until they aggravated her so terribly that she told them she couldn't bear men. But now she promptly put her arms about this strange man's neck and gave him a hearty smack.

"I like you," she said frankly.

She felt his arms tighten suddenly about her. The blue eyes looking into hers grew misty and very tender. Then, all at once, Rachel knew who he was. He was her father. She did not say anything, but she laid her curly head down on his shoulder and felt a great happiness, as of one who had come into some longed-for haven.

If David Spencer realized that she understood he said nothing. Instead, he began to tell her fascinating stories of far lands he had visited, and strange things he had seen. Rachel listened entranced, as if she were hearkening to a fairy tale. Yes, he was just as she had dreamed him. She had always been sure he could tell beautiful stories.

"Come up to the house and I'll show you some pretty things," he said finally.

Then followed a wonderful hour. The little low-ceilinged room, with its square window, into which he took her, was filled with the flotsam and jetsam of his roving life—things beautiful and odd and strange beyond all telling. The things that pleased Rachel most were two huge shells on the chimney piece—pale pink shells with big crimson and purple spots.

"Oh, I didn't know there could be such pretty things in the world," she exclaimed.

"If you would like," began the big man; then he paused for a moment. "I'll show you something prettier still."

Rachel felt vaguely that he meant to say something else when he began; but she forgot to wonder what it was when she saw what he brought out of a little corner cupboard. It was a teapot of some fine, glistening purple ware, coiled over by golden dragons with gilded claws and scales. The lid looked like a beautiful golden flower and the handle was a coil of a dragon's tail. Rachel sat and looked at it rapt-eyed.

"That's the only thing of any value I have in the world—now," he said.

Rachel knew there was something very sad in his eyes and

voice. She longed to kiss him again and comfort him. But suddenly he began to laugh, and then he rummaged out some goodies for her to eat, sweetmeats more delicious than she had ever imagined. While she nibbled them he took down an old violin and played music that made her want to dance and sing. Rachel was perfectly happy. She wished she might stay forever in that low, dim room with all its treasures.

"I see your little friends coming around the point," he said, finally. "I suppose you must go. Put the rest of the goodies in your pocket."

He took her up in his arms and held her tightly against his breast for a single moment. She felt him kissing her hair.

"There, run along, little girl. Goodbye," he said gently.

"Why don't you ask me to come and see you again?" cried Rachel, half in tears. "I'm coming *anyhow*."

"If you can come, *come*," he said. "If you don't come, I shall know it is because you can't—and that is much to know. I'm very, very, *very* glad, little woman, that you have come once."

Rachel was sitting demurely on the skids when her companions came back. They had not seen her leaving the house, and she said not a word to them of her experiences. She only smiled mysteriously when they asked her if she had been lonesome.

That night, for the first time, she mentioned her father's name in her prayers. She never forgot to do so afterwards. She always said "bless mother—and father," with an instinctive pause between the two names—a pause which indicated new realization of the tragedy which had sundered them. And the tone in which she said "father" was softer and more tender than the one which voiced "mother."

Rachel never visited the Cove again. Isabella Spencer discovered that the children had been there, and, although she knew nothing of Rachel's interview with her father, she told the child that she must never again go to that part of the shore.

Rachel shed many a bitter tear in secret over this command; but she obeyed it. Thenceforth there had been no communication between her and her father, save the unworded messages of soul to soul across whatever may divide them.

David Spencer's invitation to his daughter's wedding was sent with the others, and the remaining days of Rachel's maidenhood slipped away in a whirl of preparation and excitement in which her mother reveled, but which was distasteful to the girl.

The wedding day came at last, breaking softly and fairly over the great sea in a sheen of silver and pearl and rose, a September day, as mild and beautiful as June.

The ceremony was to be performed at eight o'clock in the evening. At seven Rachel stood in her room, fully dressed and alone. She had no bridesmaid, and she had asked her cousins to leave her to herself in this last solemn hour of girlhood. She looked very fair and sweet in the sunset-light that showered through the birches. Her wedding gown was a fine, sheer organdie, simply and daintily made. In the loose waves of her bright hair she wore her bridegroom's flowers, roses as white as a virgin's dream. She was very happy; but her happiness was faintly threaded with the sorrow inseparable from all change.

Presently her mother came in, carrying a small basket.

"Here is something for you, Rachel. One of the boys from the harbor brought it up. He was bound to give it into your own hands—said that was his orders. I just took it and sent him to the right-about—told him I'd give it to you at once, and that that was all that was necessary."

She spoke coldly. She knew quite well who had sent the basket, and she resented it; but her resentment was not quite strong enough to overcome her curiosity. She stood silently by while Rachel unpacked the basket.

Rachel's hands trembled as she took off the cover. Two huge pink-spotted shells came first. How well she remembered them! Beneath them, carefully wrapped up in a square of foreign-looking, strangely scented silk, was the dragon teapot. She held it in her hands and gazed at it with tears gathering thickly in her eyes.

"Your father sent that," said Isabella Spencer with an odd sound in her voice. "I remember it well. It was among the things I packed up and sent after him. His father had brought it home from China fifty years ago, and he prized it beyond anything. They used to say it was worth a lot of money."

"Mother, please leave me alone for a little while," said Rachel, imploringly. She had caught sight of a little note at the bottom of the basket, and she felt that she could not read it under her mother's eyes.

Mrs. Spencer went out with unaccustomed acquiescence, and Rachel went quickly to the window, where she read her letter by the fading gleams of twilight. It was very brief, and the writing was that of a man who holds a pen but seldom.

"My dear little girl," it ran, "I'm sorry I can't go to your wedding. It was like you to ask me—for I know it was your doing. I wish I could see you married, but I can't go to the house I was turned out of. I hope you will be very happy. I am sending you the shells and teapot you liked so much. Do you remember that day we had such a good time? I would liked to have seen you again before you were married, but it can't be.

"Your loving father,
"DAVID SPENCER."

Rachel resolutely blinked away the tears that filled her eyes. A fierce desire for her father sprang up in her heart—an insistent hunger that would not be denied. She *must* see her father; she *must* have his blessing on her new life. A sudden determination took possession of her whole being—a determination that swept aside all conventionalities and objections as if they had not been.

It was now almost dark. The guests would not be coming for half an hour yet. It was only fifteen minutes' walk over the hill to the Cove. Hastily Rachel shrouded herself in her new raincoat, and drew a dark, protecting hood over her gay head. She opened her door and slipped noiselessly down-stairs. Mrs. Spencer and her assistants were all busy in the back part of the house. In a moment Rachel was out in the dewy garden. She would go straight over the fields. Nobody would see her.

It was quite dark when she reached the Cove. In the crystal cup of the sky over her the stars were blinking. Flying flakes of foam were scurrying over the sand like elfin things. A soft little wind was crooning about the eaves of the little gray house where David Spencer was sitting, alone in the twilight, his violin on his knee. He had been trying to play, but could not. His heart yearned after his daughter—yes, and after a long-estranged bride of his youth. His love of the sea was sated forever; his love for wife and child still cried for its own under all his old anger and stubbornness.

The door opened suddenly and the very Rachel of whom he

was dreaming came suddenly in, flinging off her wraps and standing forth in her young beauty and bridal adornments, a splendid creature, almost lighting up the gloom with her radiance.

"Father," she cried, brokenly, and her father's eager arms closed around her.

Back in the house she had left, the guests were coming to the wedding. There were jests and laughter and friendly greeting. The bridegroom came, too, a slim, dark-eyed lad who tiptoed bashfully upstairs to the spare room, from which he presently emerged to confront Mrs. Spencer on the landing.

"I want to see Rachel before we go down," he said, blushing.

Mrs. Spencer deposited a wedding present of linen on the table which was already laden with gifts, opened the door of Rachel's room, and called her. There was no reply; the room was dark and still. In sudden alarm, Isabella Spencer snatched the lamp from the hall table and held it up. The little white room was empty. No blushing, white-clad bride tenanted it. But David Spencer's letter was lying on the stand. She caught it up and read it.

"Rachel is gone," she gasped. A flash of intuition had revealed to her where and why the girl had gone.

"Gone!" echoed Frank, his face blanching. His pallid dismay recalled Mrs. Spencer to herself. She gave a bitter, ugly little laugh.

"Oh, you needn't look so scared, Frank. She hasn't run away from you. Hush; come in here—shut the door. Nobody must know of this. Nice gossip it would make! That little fool has gone to the Cove to see her—her father. I know she has. It's just like what she would do. He sent her those presents—look— and this letter. Read it. She has gone to coax him to come and see her married. She was crazy about it. And the minister is here and it is half-past seven. She'll ruin her dress and shoes in the dust and dew. And what if some one has seen her! Was there ever such a little fool?"

Frank's presence of mind had returned to him. He knew all about Rachel and her father. She had told him everything.

"I'll go after her," he said gently. "Get me my hat and coat. I'll slip down the back stairs and over to the Cove."

"You must get out of the pantry window, then," said Mrs.

Spencer firmly, mingling comedy and tragedy after her characteristic fashion. "The kitchen is full of women. I won't have this known and talked about if it can possibly be helped."

The bridegroom, wise beyond his years in the knowledge that it was well to yield to women in little things, crawled obediently out of the pantry window and darted through the birch wood. Mrs. Spencer had stood quakingly on guard until he had disappeared.

So Rachel had gone to her father! Like had broken the fetters of years and fled to like.

"It isn't much use fighting against nature, I guess," she thought grimly. "I'm beat. He must have thought something of her, after all, when he sent her that teapot and letter. And what does he mean about the 'day they had such a good time'? Well, it just means that she's been to see him before, sometime, I suppose, and kept me in ignorance of it all."

Mrs. Spencer shut down the pantry window with a vicious thud.

"If only she'll come quietly back with Frank in time to prevent gossip I'll forgive her," she said, as she turned to the kitchen.

Rachel was sitting on her father's knee, with both her white arms around his neck, when Frank came in. She sprang up, her face flushed and appealing, her eyes bright and dewy with tears. Frank thought he had never seen her look so lovely.

"Oh, Frank, is it very late? Oh, are you angry?" she exclaimed timidly.

"No, no, dear. Of course I'm not angry. But don't you think you'd better come back now? It's nearly eight and everybody is waiting."

"I've been trying to coax father to come up and see me married," said Rachel. "Help me, Frank."

"You'd better come, sir," said Frank heartily, "I'd like it as much as Rachel would."

David Spencer shook his head stubbornly.

"No, I can't go to that house. I was locked out of it. Never mind me. I've had my happiness in this half hour with my little girl. I'd like to see her married, but it isn't to be."

"Yes, it is to be—it shall be," said Rachel resolutely. "You *shall* see me married. Frank, I'm going to be married here in my father's house! That is the right place for a girl to be married. Go back and tell the guests so, and bring them all down."

Frank looked rather dismayed. David Spencer said deprecatingly: "Little girl, don't you think it would be—"

"I'm going to have my own way in this," said Rachel, with a sort of tender finality. "Go, Frank. I'll obey you all my life after, but you must do this for me. Try to understand," she added beseechingly.

"Oh, I understand," Frank reassured her. "Besides, I think you are right. But I was thinking of your mother. She won't come."

"Then you tell her that if she doesn't come I shan't be married at all," said Rachel. She was betraying unsuspected ability to manage people. She knew that ultimatum would urge Frank to his best endeavors.

Frank, much to Mrs. Spencer's dismay, marched boldly in at the front door upon his return. She pounced on him and whisked him out of sight into the supper room.

"Where's Rachel? What made you come that way? Everybody saw you!"

"It makes no difference. They will all have to know, anyway. Rachel says she is going to be married from her father's house, or not at all. I've come back to tell you so."

Isabella's face turned crimson.

"Rachel has gone crazy. I wash my hands of this affair. Do as you please. Take the guests—the supper, too, if you can carry it."

"We'll all come back here for supper," said Frank, ignoring the sarcasm. "Come, Mrs. Spencer, let's make the best of it."

"Do you suppose that *I* am going to David Spencer's house?" said Isabella Spencer violently.

"Oh, you *must* come, Mrs. Spencer," cried poor Frank desperately. He began to fear that he would lose his bride past all finding in this maze of triple stubbornness. "Rachel says she won't be married at all if you don't go, too. Think what a talk it will make. You know she will keep her word."

Isabella Spencer knew it. Amid all the conflict of anger and revolt in her soul was a strong desire not to make a worse scandal than must of necessity be made. The desire subdued and tamed her, as nothing else could have done.

"I will go, since I have to," she said icily. "What can't be cured must be endured. Go and tell them."

Five minutes later the sixty wedding guests were all walking over the fields to the Cove, with the minister and the bridegroom in the front of the procession. They were too amazed even to talk about the strange happening. Isabella Spencer walked behind, fiercely alone.

They all crowded into the little room of the house at the Cove, and a solemn hush fell over it, broken only by the purr of the sea-wind around it and the croon of the waves on the shore. David Spencer gave his daughter away; but, when the ceremony was concluded, Isabella was the first to take the girl in her arms. She clasped her and kissed her, with tears streaming down her pale face, all her nature melted in a mother's tenderness.

"Rachel, Rachel! My child, I hope and pray that you may be happy," she said brokenly.

In the surge of the suddenly merry crowd of well-wishers around the bride and groom, Isabella was pushed back into a shadowy corner behind a heap of sails and ropes. Looking up, she found herself crushed against David Spencer. For the first time in twenty years the eyes of husband and wife met. A strange thrill shot to Isabella's heart; she felt herself trembling.

"Isabella." It was David's voice in her ear—a voice full of tenderness and pleading—the voice of the young wooer of her girlhood—"Is it too late to ask you to forgive me? I've been a stubborn fool—but there hasn't been an hour in all these years that I haven't thought about you and our baby and longed for you."

Isabella Spencer had hated this man; yet her hate had been but a parasite growth on a nobler stem, with no abiding roots of its own. It withered under his words, and lo, there was the old love, fair and strong and beautiful as ever.

"Oh—David—I—was—all—to—blame," she murmured brokenly.

Further words were lost on her husband's lips.

When the hubbub of handshaking and congratulations had subsided, Isabella Spencer stepped out before the company. She looked almost girlish and bridal herself, with her flushed cheeks and bright eyes.

"Let's go back now and have supper, and be sensible," she said crisply. "Rachel, your father is coming, too. He is coming to *stay*"—with a defiant glance around the circle. "Come, everybody."

They went back with laughter and raillery over the quiet autumn fields, faintly silvered now by the moon that was rising over the hills. The young bride and groom lagged behind; they were very happy, but they were not so happy, after all, as the old bride and groom who walked swiftly in front. Isabella's hand was in her husband's and sometimes she could not see the moonlit hills for a mist of glorified tears.

"David," she whispered, as he helped her over the fence, "how can you ever forgive me?"

"There's nothing to forgive," he said. "We're only just married. Who ever heard of a bridegroom talking of forgiveness? Everything is beginning over new for us, my girl."

JANE'S BABY

MISS ROSETTA ELLIS, with her front hair in curl-papers, and her back hair bound with a checked apron, was out in her breezy side yard under the firs, shaking her parlor rugs, when Mr. Nathan Patterson drove in. Miss Rosetta had seen him coming down the long red hill, but she had not supposed he would be calling at that time of the morning. So she had not run. Miss Rosetta always ran if anybody called and her front hair was in curl-papers; and, though the errand of the said caller might be life or death, he or she had to wait until Miss Rosetta had taken her hair out. Everybody in Avonlea knew this, because everybody in Avonlea knew everything about everybody else.

But Mr. Patterson had wheeled into the lane so quickly and unexpectedly that Miss Rosetta had had no time to run; so, twitching off the checked apron, she stood her ground as calmly as might be under the disagreeable consciousness of curl-papers.

"Good morning, Miss Ellis," said Mr. Patterson, so somberly that Miss Rosetta instantly felt that he was the bearer of bad news. Usually Mr. Patterson's face was as broad and beaming as a harvest moon. Now his expression was very melancholy and his voice positively sepulchral.

"Good morning," returned Miss Rosetta, crisply and cheer-

430

fully. She, at any rate, would not go into eclipse until she knew the reason therefor. "It is a fine day."

"A very fine day," assented Mr. Patterson, solemnly. "I have just come from the Wheeler place, Miss Ellis, and I regret to say—"

"Charlotte is sick!" cried Miss Rosetta, rapidly. "Charlotte has got another spell with her heart! I knew it! I've been expecting to hear it! Any woman that drives about the country as much as she does is liable to heart disease at any moment. *I* never go outside of my gate but I meet her gadding off somewhere. Goodness knows who looks after her place. I shouldn't like to trust as much to a hired man as she does. Well, it is very kind of you, Mr. Patterson, to put yourself out to the extent of calling in to tell me that Charlotte is sick, but I don't really see why you should take so much trouble—I really don't. It doesn't matter to me whether Charlotte is sick or whether she isn't. *You* know that perfectly well, Mr. Patterson, if anybody does. When Charlotte went and got married, on the sly, to that good-for-nothing Jacob Wheeler—"

"Mrs. Wheeler is quite well," interrupted Mr. Patterson desperately. "Quite well. Nothing at all the matter with her, in fact. I only—"

"Then what do you mean by coming here and telling me she wasn't, and frightening me half to death?" demanded Miss Rosetta, indignantly. "My own heart isn't very strong—it runs in our family—and my doctor warned me to avoid all shocks and excitement. I don't want to be excited, Mr. Patterson. I won't be excited, not even if Charlotte has another spell. It's perfectly useless for you to try to excite me, Mr. Patterson."

"Bless the woman, I'm not trying to excite anybody!" declared Mr. Patterson in exasperation. "I merely called to tell you—"

"To tell me *what?*" said Miss Rosetta. "How much longer do you mean to keep me in suspense, Mr. Patterson. No doubt you have abundance of spare time, but—I—have *not.*"

"—that your sister, Mrs. Wheeler, has had a letter from a cousin of yours, and she's in Charlottetown. Mrs. Roberts, I think her name is—"

"Jane Roberts," broke in Miss Rosetta. "Jane Ellis she was, before she was married. What was she writing to Charlotte about? Not that I want to know, of course. I'm not interested in Charlotte's correspondence, goodness knows. But if Jane had anything in particular to write about she should have written to *me*. I am the oldest. Charlotte had no business to get a letter from Jane Roberts without consulting me. It's just like her underhanded ways. She got married the same way. Never said a word to me about it, but just sneaked off with that unprincipled Jacob Wheeler—"

"Mrs. Roberts is very ill. I understand," persisted Mr. Patterson, nobly resolved to do what he had come to do, "dying, in fact, and—"

"Jane ill! Jane dying!" exclaimed Miss Rosetta. "Why, she was the healthiest girl I ever knew! But then I've never seen her, nor heard from her, since she got married fifteen years ago. I dare say her husband was a brute and neglected her, and she's pined away by slow degrees. I've no faith in husbands. Look at Charlotte! Everybody knows how Jacob Wheeler used her. To be sure, she deserved it, but—"

"Mrs. Roberts' husband is dead," said Mr. Patterson. "Died about two months ago, I understand, and she has a little baby six months old, and she thought perhaps Mrs. Wheeler would take it for old times' sake—"

"Did Charlotte ask you to call and tell me this?" demanded Miss Rosetta eagerly.

"No; she just told me what was in the letter. She didn't mention you; but I thought, perhaps, you ought to be told—"

"I knew it," said Miss Rosetta in a tone of bitter assurance. "I could have told you so. Charlotte wouldn't even let me know that Jane was ill. Charlotte would be afraid I would want to get the baby, seeing that Jane and I were such intimate friends long ago. And who has a better right to it than me, I should like to know? Ain't I the oldest? And haven't I had experience in bringing up babies? Charlotte needn't think she is going to run the affairs of our family just because she happened to get married. Jacob Wheeler—"

"I must be going," said Mr. Patterson, gathering up his reins thankfully.

"I am much obliged to you for coming to tell me about Jane," said Miss Rosetta, "even though you have wasted a lot of precious time getting it out. If it hadn't been for you I suppose I should never have known it at all. As it is, I shall start for town just as soon as I can get ready."

"You'll have to hurry if you want to get ahead of Mrs. Wheeler," advised Mr. Patterson. "She's packing her trunk and going on the morning train."

"I'll pack a valise and go on the afternoon train," retorted Miss Rosetta triumphantly. "I'll show Charlotte she isn't running the Ellis affairs. She married out of them into the Wheelers. She can attend to them. Jacob Wheeler was the most—"

But Mr. Patterson had driven away. He felt that he had done his duty in the face of fearful odds, and he did not want to hear anything more about Jacob Wheeler.

Rosetta Ellis and Charlotte Wheeler had not exchanged a word for ten years. Before that time they had been devoted to each other, living together in the little Ellis cottage on the White Sands road, as they had done ever since their parents' death. The trouble began when Jacob Wheeler had commenced to pay attention to Charlotte, the younger and prettier of two women who had both ceased to be either very young or very pretty. Rosetta had been bitterly opposed to the match from the first. She vowed she had no use for Jacob Wheeler. There were not lacking malicious people to hint that this was because the aforesaid Jacob Wheeler had selected the wrong sister upon whom to bestow his affections. Be that as it might, Miss Rosetta certainly continued to render the course of Jacob Wheeler's true love exceedingly rough and tumultuous. The end of it was that Charlotte had gone quietly away one morning and married Jacob Wheeler without Miss Rosetta's knowing anything about it. Miss Rosetta had never forgiven her for it, and Charlotte had never forgiven the things Rosetta had said to her when she and Jacob returned to the Ellis cottage. Since then the sisters had been avowed and open foes, the only difference being that Miss Rosetta aired her grievances publicly, in season and out of season, while Charlotte was never heard to mention Rosetta's name. Even the death of Jacob Wheeler, five years after the marriage, had not healed the breach.

Miss Rosetta took out her curl-papers, packed her valise, and caught the late afternoon train for Charlottetown, as she had threatened. All the way there she sat rigidly upright in her seat and held imaginary dialogues with Charlotte in her mind, running something like this on her part:—

"No, Charlotte Wheeler, you are not going to have Jane's baby, and you're very much mistaken if you think so. Oh, all right—we'll see! You don't know anything about babies, even if you are married. I do. Didn't I take William Ellis's baby, when his wife died? Tell me that, Charlotte Wheeler! And didn't the little thing thrive with me, and grow strong and healthy? Yes, even you have to admit that it did, Charlotte Wheeler. And yet you have the presumption to think that you ought to have Jane's baby! Yes, it is presumption, Charlotte Wheeler. And when William Ellis got married again, and took the baby, didn't the child cling to me and cry as if I was its real mother? You know it did, Charlotte Wheeler. I'm going to get and keep Jane's baby in spite of you, Charlotte Wheeler, and I'd like to see you try to prevent me—you that went and got married and never so much as let your own sister know of it! If I had got married in such a fashion, Charlotte Wheeler, I'd be ashamed to look anybody in the face for the rest of my natural life!"

Miss Rosetta was so interested in thus laying down the law to Charlotte, and in planning out the future life of Jane's baby, that she didn't find the journey to Charlottetown so long or tedious as might have been expected, considering her haste. She soon found her way to the house where her cousin lived. There, to her dismay and real sorrow, she learned that Mrs. Roberts had died at four o'clock that afternoon.

"She seemed dreadful anxious to live until she heard from some of her folks out in Avonlea," said the woman who gave Miss Rosetta the information. "She had written to them about her little girl. She was my sister-in-law, and she lived with me ever since her husband died. I've done my best for her; but I've a big family of my own and I can't see how I'm to keep the child. Poor Jane looked and longed for some one to come from Avonlea, but she couldn't hold out. A patient, suffering creature she was!"

"I'm her cousin," said Miss Rosetta, wiping her eyes, "and I have come for the baby. I'll take it home with me after the funeral; and, if you please, Mrs. Gordon, let me see it right away, so it can get accustomed to me. Poor Jane! I wish I could have got here in time to see her, she and I were such friends long ago. We were far more intimate and confidential than ever her and Charlotte was. Charlotte knows that, too!"

The vim with which Miss Rosetta snapped this out rather amazed Mrs. Gordon, who couldn't understand it at all. But she took Miss Rosetta up-stairs to the room where the baby was sleeping.

"Oh, the little darling," cried Miss Rosetta, all her old maidishness and oddity falling away from her like a garment, and all her innate and denied motherhood shining out in her face like a transforming illumination. "Oh, the sweet, dear, pretty little thing!"

The baby was a darling—a six-months' old beauty with little golden ringlets curling and glistening all over its tiny head. As Miss Rosetta hung over it, it opened its eyes and then held out its tiny hands to her with a gurgle of confidence.

"Oh, you sweetest!" said Miss Rosetta rapturously, gathering it up in her arms. "You belong to me, darling—never, never, to that under-handed Charlotte! What is its name, Mrs. Gordon?"

"It wasn't named," said Mrs. Gordon. "Guess you'll have to name it yourself, Miss Ellis."

"Camilla Jane," said Miss Rosetta without a moment's hesitation. "Jane after its mother, of course; and I have always thought Camilla the prettiest name in the world. Charlotte would be sure to give it some perfectly heathenish name. I wouldn't put it past her calling the poor innocent Mehitable."

Miss Rosetta decided to stay in Charlottetown until after the funeral. That night she lay with the baby on her arm, listening with joy to its soft little breathing. She did not sleep or wish to sleep. Her waking fancies were more alluring than any visions of dreamland. Moreover, she gave a spice to them by occasionally snapping some vicious sentences out loud at Charlotte.

Miss Rosetta fully expected Charlotte along on the following morning and girded herself for the fray; but no Charlotte appeared. Night came; no Charlotte. Another morning and no Charlotte. Miss Rosetta was hopelessly puzzled. What had happened? Dear, dear, had Charlotte taken a bad heart spell, on hearing that she, Rosetta, had stolen a march on her to Charlottetown? It was quite likely. You never knew what to expect of a woman who had married Jacob Wheeler!

The truth was, that the very evening Miss Rosetta had left

Avonlea Mrs. Jacob Wheeler's hired man had broken his leg and had had to be conveyed to his distant home on a feather bed in an express wagon. Mrs. Wheeler could not leave home until she had obtained another hired man. Consequently it was the evening after the funeral when Mrs. Wheeler whisked up the steps of the Gordon house and met Miss Rosetta coming out with a big white bundle in her arms.

The eyes of the two women met defiantly. Miss Rosetta's face wore an air of triumph, chastened by a remembrance of the funeral that afternoon. Mrs. Wheeler's face, except for eyes, was as expressionless as it usually was. Unlike the tall, fair, fat Miss Rosetta, Mrs. Wheeler was small and dark and thin, with an eager, careworn face.

"How is Jane?" she said abruptly, breaking the silence of ten years in saying it.

"Jane is dead and buried, poor thing," said Miss Rosetta calmly. "I am taking her baby, little Camilla Jane, home with me."

"The baby belongs to me," cried Mrs. Wheeler passionately. "Jane wrote to me about her. Jane meant that I should have her. I've come for her."

"You'll go back without her, then," said Miss Rosetta, serene in the possession that is nine points of the law. "The child is mine, and she is going to stay mine. You can make up your mind to that, Charlotte Wheeler. A woman who eloped to get married isn't fit to be trusted with a baby, anyhow. Jacob Wheeler—"

But Mrs. Wheeler had rushed past into the house. Miss Rosetta composedly stepped into the cab and drove to the station. She fairly bridled with triumph; and underneath the triumph ran a queer undercurrent of satisfaction over the fact that Charlotte had spoken to her at last. Miss Rosetta would not look at this satisfaction, or give it a name, but it was there.

Miss Rosetta arrived safely back in Avonlea with Camilla Jane and within ten hours everybody in the settlement knew the whole story, and every woman who could stand on her feet had been up to the Ellis cottage to see the baby. Mrs. Wheeler arrived home twenty-four hours later, and silently betook herself to her farm. When her Avonlea neighbors sympathized with her in her disappointment, she said nothing, but looked all the more darkly determined. Also, a week later, Mr. William J. Blair, the Carmody storekeeper, had an odd tale to tell. Mrs. Wheeler had come to the store and bought a lot of fine flannel and muslin and valenciennes. Now, what in the name of time, did Mrs. Wheeler want with such stuff? Mr. William J. Blair couldn't make head or tail of it, and it worried him. Mr. Blair was so accustomed to know what everybody bought anything for that such a mystery quite upset him.

Miss Rosetta had exulted in the possession of little Camilla Jane for a month, and had been so happy that she had almost given up inveighing against Charlotte. Her conversation, instead of tending always to Jacob Wheeler now ran Camilla Janeward; and this, folks thought, was an improvement.

One afternoon, Miss Rosetta, leaving Camilla Jane snugly sleeping in her cradle in the kitchen, had slipped down to the bottom of the garden to pick her currants. The house was hidden from her sight by the copse of cherry trees, but she had left the kitchen window open, so that she could hear the baby if it awakened and cried. Miss Rosetta sang happily as she picked her currants. For the first time since Charlotte had married Jacob Wheeler Miss Rosetta felt really happy—so happy that there was no room in her heart for bitterness. In fancy she looked forward to the coming years, and saw Camilla Jane growing up into girlhood, fair and lovable.

"She'll be a beauty," reflected Miss Rosetta complacently. "Jane was a handsome girl. She shall always be dressed as nice as I can manage it, and I'll get her an organ, and have her take painting and music lessons. Parties, too! I'll give her a real coming-out party when she's eighteen and the very prettiest dress that's to be had. Dear me, I can hardly wait for her to grow up, though she's sweet enough now to make one wish she could stay a baby forever."

When Miss Rosetta returned to the kitchen, her eyes fell on an empty cradle. Camilla Jane was gone!

Miss Rosetta promptly screamed. She understood at a glance what had happened. Six months' old babies do not get out of their cradles and disappear through closed doors without any assistance.

"Charlotte has been here," gasped Miss Rosetta. "Charlotte

has stolen Camilla Jane! I might have expected it. I might have
known when I heard that story about her buying muslin and
flannel. It's just like Charlotte to do such an underhand trick.
But I'll go after her! I'll show her! She'll find out she has got
Rosetta Ellis to deal with and no Wheeler!"

Like a frantic creature and wholly forgetting that her hair
was in curl-papers, Miss Rosetta hurried up the hill and down
the shore road to the Wheeler Farm—a place she had never
visited in her life before.

The wind was off-shore and only broke the bay's surface into
long silvery ripples, and sent sheeny shadows flying out across
it from every point and headland, like transparent wings.

The little gray house, so close to the purring waves that in
storms their spray splashed over its very doorstep, seemed
deserted. Miss Rosetta pounded lustily on the front door. This
producing no result, she marched around to the back door and
knocked. No answer. Miss Rosetta tried the door. It was locked.

"Guilty conscience," sniffed Miss Rosetta. "Well, I shall stay
here until I see that perfidious Charlotte, if I have to camp in
the yard all night."

Miss Rosetta was quite capable of doing this, but she was
spared the necessity; walking boldly up to the kitchen window,
and peering through it, she felt her heart swell with anger as
she beheld Charlotte sitting calmly by the table with Camilla
Jane on her knee. Beside her was a befrilled and bemuslined
cradle, and on a chair lay the garments in which Miss Rosetta
had dressed the baby. It was clad in an entirely new outfit,
and seemed quite at home with its new possessor. It was laughing
and cooing, and making little dabs at her with its dimpled
hands.

"Charlotte Wheeler," cried Miss Rosetta, rapping sharply on
the window-pane. "I've come for that child! Bring her out to
me at once—at once, I say! How dare you come to my house
and steal a baby? You're no better than a common burglar.
Give me Camilla Jane, I say!"

Charlotte came over to the window with the baby in her
arms and triumph glittering in her eyes.

"There is no such child as Camilla Jane here," she said.
"This is Barbara Jane. She belongs to me."

With that Mrs. Wheeler pulled down the shade.

Miss Rosetta had to go home. There was nothing else for her to do. On her way she met Mr. Patterson and told him in full the story of her wrongs. It was all over Avonlea by night, and created quite a sensation. Avonlea had not had such a toothsome bit of gossip for a long time.

Mrs. Wheeler exulted in the possession of Barbara Jane for six weeks, during which Miss Rosetta broke her heart with loneliness and longing, and meditated futile plots for the recovery of the baby. It was hopeless to think of stealing it back or she would have tried to. The hired man at the Wheeler place reported that Mrs. Wheeler never left it night or day for a single moment. She even carried it with her when she went to milk the cows.

"But my turn will come," said Miss Rosetta grimly. "Camilla Jane is mine, and if she was called Barbara for a century it wouldn't alter that fact. Barbara, indeed! Why not have called her Methusaleh and have done with it?"

One afternoon in October, when Miss Rosetta was picking her apples and thinking drearily about lost Camilla Jane, a woman came running breathlessly down the hill and into the yard. Miss Rosetta gave an exclamation of amazement, and dropped her basket of apples. Of all incredible things! The woman was Charlotte—Charlotte who had never set foot on the grounds of the Ellis cottage since her marriage ten years ago, Charlotte, bare-headed, wild-eyed, distraught, wringing her hands and sobbing.

Miss Rosetta flew to meet her.

"You've scalded Camilla Jane to death!" she exclaimed. "I always knew you would—always expected it!"

"Oh, for heaven's sake, come quick, Rosetta!" gasped Charlotte. "Barbara Jane is in convulsions and I don't know what to do. The hired man has gone for the doctor. You were the nearest, so I came to you. Jenny White was there when they came on, so I left her and ran. Oh, Rosetta, come, come, if you have a spark of humanity in you! You know what to do for convulsions—you saved the Ellis baby when it had them. Oh, come and save Barbara Jane!"

"You mean Camilla Jane, I presume?" said Miss Rosetta firmly, in spite of her agitation.

For a second Charlotte Wheeler hesitated. Then she said

passionately: "Yes, yes, Camilla Jane—any name you like! Only come."

Miss Rosetta went, and not a moment too soon, either. The doctor lived eight miles away and the baby was very bad. The two women and Jenny White worked over her for hours. It was not until dark, when the baby was sleeping soundly and the doctor had gone, after telling Miss Rosetta that she had saved the child's life, that a realization of the situation came home to them.

"Well," said Miss Rosetta, dropping into an armchair with a long sigh of weariness, "I guess you'll admit now, Charlotte Wheeler, that you are hardly a fit person to have charge of a baby, even if you had to go and steal it from me. I should think your conscience would reproach you—that is, if any woman who would marry Jacob Wheeler in such an underhanded fashion has a—"

"I—I wanted the baby," sobbed Charlotte, tremulously. "I was so lonely here. I didn't think it was any harm to take her, because Jane gave her to me in her letter. But you have saved her life, Rosetta, and you—you can have her back, although it will break my heart to give her up. But, oh, Rosetta, won't you let me come and see her sometimes? I love her so I can't bear to give her up entirely."

"Charlotte," said Miss Rosetta firmly, "the most sensible thing for you to do is just to come back with the baby. You are worried to death trying to run this farm with the debt Jacob Wheeler left on it for you. Sell it, and come home with me. And we'll both have the baby then."

"Oh, Rosetta, I'd love to," faltered Charlotte. "I've—I've wanted to be good friends with you again so much. But I thought you were so hard and bitter you'd never make up."

"Maybe I've talked too much," conceded Miss Rosetta, "but you ought to know me well enough to know I didn't mean a word of it. It was your never saying anything, no matter what I said, that riled me up so bad. Let bygones be bygones, and come home, Charlotte."

"I will," said Charlotte resolutely, wiping away her tears. "I'm sick of living here and putting up with hired men. I'll be real glad to go home, Rosetta, and that's the truth. I've had a hard enough time. I s'pose you'll say I deserved it; but I was fond of Jacob, and—"

"Of course, of course. Why shouldn't you be?" said Miss Rosetta briskly. "I'm sure Jacob Wheeler was a good enough soul, if he was a little slack-twisted. I'd like to hear anybody say a word against him in my presence. Look at that blessed child, Charlotte. Isn't she the sweetest thing? I'm desperate glad you are coming back home, Charlotte. I've never been able to put up a decent mess of mustard pickles since you went away, and you were always such a hand with them! We'll be real snug and cozy again—you and me and little Camilla Barbara Jane."

THE DREAM-CHILD

A MAN'S heart—aye, and a woman's, too—should be light in the spring. The spirit of resurrection is abroad, calling the life of the world out of its wintry grave, knocking with radiant fingers at the gates of its tomb. It stirs in human hearts, and makes them glad with the old primal gladness they felt in childhood. It quickens human souls, and brings them, if so they will, so close to God that they may clasp hands with Him. It is a time of wonder and renewed life, and a great outward and inward rapture, as of a young angel softly clapping his hands for creation's joy. At least, so it should be; and so it always had been with me until the spring when the dream-child first came into our lives.

That year I hated the spring—I, who had always loved it so. As boy I had loved it, and as man. All the happiness that had ever been mine, and it was much, had come to blossom in the springtime. It was in the spring that Josephine and I had first loved each other, or, at least, had first come into the full knowledge that we loved. I think that we must have loved each other all our lives, and that each succeeding spring was a word in the revelation of that love, not to be understood until, in the fullness of time, the whole sentence was written out in that most beautiful of all beautiful springs.

How beautiful it was! And how beautiful she was! I suppose every lover thinks that of his lass; otherwise he is a poor sort of lover. But it was not only my eyes of love that made my dear lovely. She was slim and lithe as a young, white-stemmed birch tree; her hair was like a soft, dusky cloud; and her eyes were as blue as Avonlea Harbor on a fair twilight, when all the sky is abloom over it. She had dark lashes, and a little red mouth that quivered when she was very sad or very happy, or when she loved very much—quivered like a crimson rose too rudely shaken by the wind. At such times what was a man to do save kiss it?

The next spring we were married, and I brought her home to my gray old homestead on the gray old harbor shore. A lonely place for a young bride, said Avonlea people. Nay, it was not so. She was happy here, even in my absences. She loved the great, restless harbor and the vast, misty sea beyond; she loved the tides, keeping their world-old tryst with the shore, and the gulls, and the croon of the waves, and the call of the winds in the fir woods at noon and even; she loved the moonrises and the sunsets, and the clear, calm nights when the stars seemed to have fallen into the water and to be a little dizzy from such a fall. She loved these things, even as I did. No, she was never lonely here then.

The third spring came, and our boy was born. We thought we had been happy before; now we knew that we had only dreamed a pleasant dream of happiness, and had awakened to this exquisite reality. We thought we had loved each other before; now, as I looked into my wife's pale face, blanched with its baptism of pain, and met the uplifted gaze of her blue eyes, aglow with the holy passion of motherhood, I knew we had only imagined what love might be. The imagination had been sweet, as the thought of the rose is sweet before the bud is open; but as the rose to the thought, so was love to the imagination of it.

"All my thoughts are poetry since baby came," my wife said once, rapturously.

Our boy lived for twenty months. He was a sturdy, toddling rogue, so full of life and laughter and mischief that, when he died, one day, after the illness of an hour, it seemed a most absurd thing that he should be dead—a thing I could have laughed at, until belief forced itself into my soul like a burning, searing iron.

I think I grieved over my little son's death as deeply and sincerely as ever man did, or could. But the heart of the father is not as the heart of the mother. Time brought no healing to Josephine; she fretted and pined; her cheeks lost their pretty oval, and her red mouth grew pale and drooping.

I hoped that spring might work its miracle upon her. When the buds swelled, and the old earth grew green in the sun, and the gulls came back to the gray harbor, whose very grayness grew golden and mellow, I thought I should see her smile again. But, when the spring came, came the dream-child, and the fear that was to be my companion, at bed and board, from sunsetting to sunsetting.

One night I wakened from sleep, realizing in the moment of awakening that I was alone. I listened to hear whether my wife were moving about the house. I heard nothing but the little splash of waves on the shore below and the low moan of the distant ocean.

I rose and searched the house. She was not in it. I did not know where to seek her; but, at a venture, I started along the shore.

It was pale, fainting moonlight. The harbor looked like a phantom harbor, and the night was as still and cold and calm as the face of a dead man. At last I saw my wife coming to me along the shore. When I saw her, I knew what I had feared and how great my fear had been.

As she drew near, I saw that she had been crying; her face was stained with tears, and her dark hair hung loose over her shoulders in little, glossy ringlets like a child's. She seemed to be very tired, and at intervals she wrung her small hands together.

She showed no surprise when she met me, but only held out her hands to me as if glad to see me.

"I followed him—but I could not overtake him," she said with a sob. "I did my best—I hurried so; but he was always a little way ahead. And then I lost him—and so I came back. But I did my best—indeed I did. And oh, I am so tired!"

"Josie, dearest, what do you mean, and where have you

been?" I said, drawing her close to me. "Why did you go out so—alone in the night?"

She looked at me wonderingly.

"How could I help it, David? He called me. I had to go."

"Who called you?"

"The child," she answered in a whisper. "Our child, David— our pretty boy. I awakened in the darkness and heard him calling to me down on the shore. Such a sad, little wailing cry, David, as if he were cold and lonely and wanted his mother. I hurried out to him, but I could not find him. I could only hear the call, and I followed it on and on, far down the shore. Oh, I tried so hard to overtake it, but I could not. Once I saw a little white hand beckoning to me far ahead in the moonlight. But still I could not go fast enough. And then the cry ceased, and I was there all alone on that terrible, cold, gray shore. I was so tired and I came home. But I wish I could have found him. Perhaps he does not know that I tried to. Perhaps he thinks his mother never listened to his call. Oh, I would not have him think that."

"You have had a bad dream, dear," I said. I tried to say it naturally; but it is hard for a man to speak naturally when he feels a mortal dread striking into his very vitals with its deadly chill.

"It was no dream," she answered reproachfully. "I tell you I heard him calling me—me, his mother. What could I do but go to him? You cannot understand—you are only his father. It was not you who gave him birth. It was not you who paid the price of his dear life in pain. He would not call to you— he wanted his mother."

I got her back to the house and to her bed, whither she went obediently enough, and soon fell into the sleep of exhaustion. But there was no more sleep for me that night. I kept a grim vigil with dread.

When I had married Josephine, one of those officious relatives that are apt to buzz about a man's marriage told me that her grandmother had been insane all the latter part of her life. She had grieved over the death of a favorite child until she lost her mind, and, as the first indication of it, she had sought by nights a white dream-child which always called her, so she said, and led her afar with a little, pale, beckoning hand.

I had smiled at the story then. What had that grim old bygone to do with springtime and love and Josephine? But it came back to me now, hand in hand with my fear. Was this fate coming on my dear wife? It was too horrible for belief. She was so young, so fair, so sweet, this girl-wife of mine. It had been only a bad dream, with a frightened, bewildered waking. So I tried to comfort myself.

When she awakened in the morning she did not speak of what had happened and I did not dare to. She seemed more cheerful that day than she had been, and went about her household duties briskly and skillfully. My fear lifted. I was sure now that she had only dreamed. And I was confirmed in my hopeful belief when two nights had passed away uneventfully.

Then, on the third night, the dream-child called to her again. I wakened from a troubled doze to find her dressing herself with feverish haste.

"He is calling me," she cried. "Oh, don't you hear him? Can't you hear him? Listen—listen—the little, lonely cry! Yes, yes, my precious, mother is coming. Wait for me. Mother is coming to her pretty boy!"

I caught her hand and let her lead me where she would. Hand in hand we followed the dream-child down the harbor shore in that ghostly, clouded moonlight. Ever, she said, the little cry sounded before her. She entreated the dream-child to wait for her; she cried and implored and uttered tender mother-talk. But, at last, she ceased to hear the cry; and then, weeping, wearied, she let me lead her home again.

What a horror brooded over that spring—that so beautiful spring! It was a time of wonder and marvel; of the soft touch of silver rain on greening fields; of the incredible delicacy of young leaves; of blossom on the land and blossom in the sunset. The whole world bloomed in a flush and tremor of maiden loveliness, instinct with all the evasive, fleeting charm of spring and girlhood and young morning. And almost every night of this wonderful time the dream-child called his mother, and we roved the gray shore in quest of him.

In the day she was herself; but, when the night fell, she was restless and uneasy until she heard the call. Then follow it she would, even through storm and darkness. It was then, she said, that the cry sounded loudest and nearest, as if her pretty boy were frightened by the tempest. What wild, terrible rovings we had, she straining forward, eager to overtake the dream-child; I, sick at heart, following, guiding, protecting, as best I could; then afterwards leading her gently home, heart-broken because she could not reach the child.

I bore my burden in secret, determining that gossip should not busy itself with my wife's condition so long as I could keep it from becoming known. We had no near relatives—none with any right to share any trouble—and whoso accepteth human love must bind it to his soul with pain.

I thought, however, that I should have medical advice, and I took our old doctor into my confidence. He looked grave when he heard my story. I did not like his expression nor his few guarded remarks. He said he thought human aid would avail little; she might come all right in time; humor her, as far as possible, watch over her, protect her. He needed not to tell me *that*.

The spring went out and summer came in—and the horror deepened and darkened. I knew that suspicions were being whispered from lip to lip. We had been seen on our nightly quests. Men and women began to look at us pityingly when we went abroad.

One day, on a dull, drowsy afternoon, the dream-child called. I knew then that the end was near; the end had been near in the old grandmother's case sixty years before when the dream-child called in the day. The doctor looked graver than ever when I told him, and said that the time had come when I must have help in my task. I could not watch by day and night. Unless I had assistance I would break down.

I did not think that I should. Love is stronger than that. And on one thing I was determined—they should never take my wife from me. No restraint sterner than a husband's loving hand should ever be put upon her, my pretty, piteous darling.

I never spoke of the dream-child to her. The doctor advised against it. It would, he said, only serve to deepen the delusion. When he hinted at an asylum I gave him a look that would have been a fierce word for another man. He never spoke of it again.

One night in August there was a dull, murky sunset after a dead, breathless day of heat, with not a wind stirring. The sea was not blue as a sea should be, but pink—all pink—a ghastly, staring, painted pink. I lingered on the harbor shore below the house until dark. The evening bells were ringing faintly and mournfully in a church across the harbor. Behind me, in the kitchen, I heard my wife singing. Sometimes now her spirits were fitfully high, and then she would sing the old songs of her girlhood. But even in her singing was something strange, as if a wailing, unearthly cry rang through it. Nothing about her was sadder than that strange singing.

When I went back to the house the rain was beginning to fall; but there was no wind or sound in the air—only that dismal stillness, as if the world were holding its breath in expectation of a calamity.

Josie was standing by the window, looking out and listening. I tried to induce her to go to bed, but she only shook her head.

"I might fall asleep and not hear him when he called," she said. "I am always afraid to sleep, now, for fear he should call and his mother fail to hear him."

Knowing it was of no use to entreat, I sat down by the table and tried to read. Three hours passed on. When the clock struck midnight she started up, with the wild light in her sunken blue eyes.

"He is calling," she cried, "calling out there in the storm. Yes, yes, sweet, I am coming!"

She opened the door and fled down the path to the shore. I snatched a lantern from the wall, lighted it, and followed. It was the blackest night I was ever out in, dark with the very darkness of death. The rain fell thickly and heavily. I overtook Josie, caught her hand, and stumbled along in her wake, for she went with the speed and recklessness of a distraught woman. We moved in the little flitting circle of light shed by the lantern. All around us and above us was a horrible, voiceless darkness, held, as it were, at bay by the friendly light.

"If I could only overtake him once," moaned Josie. "If I could just kiss him once, and hold him close against my aching heart. This pain, that never leaves me, would leave me then. Oh, my pretty boy, wait for mother! I am coming to you.

Listen, David; he cries—he cries so pitifully; listen! Can't you hear it?"

I *did* hear it! Clear and distinct, out of the deadly still darkness before us, came a faint, wailing cry. What was it? Was I, too, going mad, or *was* there something out there—something that cried and moaned—longing for human love, yet ever retreating from human footsteps? I am not a superstitious man; but my nerve had been shaken by my long trial, and I was weaker than I thought. Terror took possession of me—terror unnameable. I trembled in every limb; clammy perspiration oozed from my forehead; I was possessed by a wild impulse to turn and flee—anywhere, away from that unearthly cry. But Josephine's cold hand gripped mine firmly, and led me on. That strange cry still rang in my ears. But it did not recede; it sounded clearer and stronger; it was a wail, but a loud, insistent wail; it was nearer—nearer; it was in the darkness just beyond us.

Then we came to it; a little dory had been beached on the pebbles and left there by the receding tide. There was a child in it—a boy, of perhaps two years old, who crouched in the bottom of the dory in water to his waist, his big, blue eyes wild and wide with terror, his face white and tear-stained. He wailed again when he saw us, and held out his little hands.

My horror fell away from me like a discarded garment. *This* child was living. How he had come there, whence and why, I did not know and, in my state of mind, did not question. It was no cry of parted spirit I had heard—that was enough for me.

"Oh, the poor darling!" cried my wife.

She stooped over the dory and lifted the baby in her arms. His long, fair curls fell on her shoulder; she laid her face against his and wrapped her shawl around him.

"Let me carry him, dear," I said. "He is very wet, and too heavy for you."

"No, no, I must carry him. My arms have been so empty—they are full now. Oh, David, the pain at my heart has gone. He has come to me to take the place of my own. God has sent him to me out of the sea. He is wet and cold and tired. Hush, sweet one, we will go home."

Silently I followed her home. The wind was rising, coming

in sudden, angry gusts; the storm was at hand, but we reached shelter before it broke. Just as I shut our door behind us it smote the house with the roar of a baffled beast. I thanked God that we were not out in it, following the dream-child.

"You are very wet, Josie," I said. "Go and put on dry clothes at once."

"The child must be looked to first," she said firmly. "See how chilled and exhausted he is, the pretty dear. Light a fire quickly, David, while I get dry things for him."

I let her have her way. She brought out the clothes our own child had worn and dressed the waif in them, rubbing his chilled limbs, brushing his wet hair, laughing over him, mothering him. She seemed like her old self.

For my own part, I was bewildered. All the questions I had not asked before came crowding to my mind now. Whose child was this? Whence had he come? What was the meaning of it all?

He was a pretty baby, fair and plump and rosy. When he was dried and fed, he fell asleep in Josie's arms. She hung over him in a passion of delight. It was with difficulty I persuaded her to leave him long enough to change her wet clothes. She never asked whose he might be or from where he might have come. He had been sent to her from the sea; the dream-child had led her to him; that was what she believed, and I dared not throw any doubt on that belief. She slept that night with the baby on her arm, and in her sleep her face was the face of a girl in her youth, untroubled and unworn.

I expected that the morrow would bring some one seeking the baby. I had come to the conclusion that he must belong to the "Cove" across the harbor, where the fishing hamlet was; and all day, while Josie laughed and played with him, I waited and listened for the footsteps of those who would come seeking him. But they did not come. Day after day passed, and still they did not come.

I was in a maze of perplexity. What should I do? I shrank from the thought of the boy being taken away from us. Since we had found him the dream-child never had called. My wife seemed to have turned back from the dark borderland, where her feet had strayed, to walk again with me in our own homely paths. Day and night she was her old, bright self, happy and serene in the new motherhood that had come to her. The only thing strange in her was her calm acceptance of the event. She never wondered who or whose the child might be—never seemed to fear that he would be taken from her; and she gave him our dream-child's name.

At last, when a full week had passed, I went, in my bewilderment, to our old doctor.

"A most extraordinary thing," he said thoughtfully. "The child, as you say, must belong to the Spruce Cove people. Yet it is an almost unbelievable thing that there has been no search or inquiry after him. Probably there is some simple explanation of the mystery, however. I advise you to go over to the Cove and inquire. When you find the parents or guardians of the child, ask them to allow you to keep it for a time. It may prove your wife's salvation. I have known such cases. Evidently on that night the crisis of her mental disorder was reached. A little thing might have sufficed to turn her feet either way— back to reason and sanity, or into deeper darkness. It is my belief that the former has occurred, and that, if she is left in undisturbed possession of this child for a time, she will recover completely."

I drove around the harbor that day with a lighter heart than I had hoped ever to possess again. When I reached Spruce Cove the first person I met was old Abel Blair. I asked him if any child were missing from the Cove or along shore. He looked at me in surprise, shook his head, and said he had not heard of any. I told him as much of the tale as was necessary, leaving him to think that my wife and I had found the dory and its small passenger during an ordinary walk along the shore.

"A green dory!" he exclaimed. "Ben Forbes' old green dory has been missing for a week, but it was so rotten and leaky he didn't bother looking for it. But this child, sir—it beats me. What might he be like?"

I described the child as closely as possible.

"That fits little Harry Martin to a hair," said old Abel, perplexedly, "but, sir, it can't be. Or, if it is, there's been foul work somewhere. James Martin's wife died last winter, sir, and he died the next month. They left a baby and not much else. There weren't nobody to take the child but Jim's half-sister, Maggie Fleming. She lived here at the Cove, and, I'm sorry to say, sir, she hadn't too good a name. She didn't want to be bothered with the baby, and folks say she neglected him scandalous. Well, last spring she begun talking of going away to the States. She said a friend of hers had got her a good place in Boston, and she was going to go and take little Harry. We supposed it was all right. Last Saturday she went, sir. She was going to walk to the station, and the last seen of her she was trudging along the road, carrying the baby. It hasn't been thought of since. But, sir, d'ye suppose she set that innocent child adrift in that old leaky dory to send him to his death? I knew Maggie was no better than she should be, but I can't believe she was as bad as that."

"You must come over with me and see if you can identify the child," I said. "If he is Harry Martin I shall keep him. My wife has been very lonely since our baby died, and she has taken a fancy to this little chap."

When we reached my home old Abel recognized the child as Harry Martin.

He is with us still. His baby hands led my dear wife back to health and happiness. Other children have come to us, she loves them all dearly; but the boy who bears her dead son's name is to her—aye, and to me—as dear as if she had given him birth. He came from the sea, and at his coming the ghostly dream-child fled, nevermore to lure my wife away from me with its exciting cry. Therefore I look upon him and love him as my first-born.

THE BROTHER WHO FAILED

THE MONROE family were holding a Christmas reunion at the old Prince Edward Island homestead at White Sands. It was the first time they had all been together under one roof since the death of their mother, thirty years before. The idea of this Christmas reunion had originated with Edith Monroe the preceding spring, during her tedious convalescence from a bad attack of pneumonia among strangers in an American city, where she had not been able to fill her concert engagements, and had more spare time in which to feel the tug of old ties and the homesick longing for her own people than she had had for years. As a result, when she recovered, she wrote to her second brother, James Monroe, who lived on the homestead; and the consequence was this gathering of the Monroes under the old roof-tree. Ralph Monroe for once laid aside the cares of his railroads, and the deceitfulness of his millions, in Toronto and took the long-promised, long-deferred trip to the homeland. Malcolm Monroe journeyed from the far western university of which he was president. Edith came, flushed with the triumph of her latest and most successful concert tour. Mrs. Woodburn, who had been Margaret Monroe, came from the Nova Scotia town where she lived a busy, happy life as the wife of a rising young lawyer. James, prosperous and hearty, greeted them

453

warmly at the old homestead whose fertile acres had well repaid his skillful management.

They were a merry party, casting aside their cares and years, and harking back to joyous boyhood and girlhood once more. James had a family of rosy lads and lasses; Margaret brought her two blue-eyed little girls; Ralph's dark, clever-looking son accompanied him, and Malcolm brought his, a young man with a resolute face, in which there was less of boyishness than in his father's, and the eye of a keen, perhaps a hard bargainer. The two cousins were the same age to a day, and it was a family joke among the Monroes that the stork must have mixed the babies, since Ralph's son was like Malcolm in face and brain, while Malcolm's boy was a second edition of his Uncle Ralph.

To crown all, Aunt Isabel came, too—a talkative, clever, shrewd old lady, as young at eighty-five as she had been at thirty, thinking the Monroe stock the best in the world, and beamingly proud of her nephews and nieces, who had gone out from this humble, little farm to destinies of such brilliance and influence in the world beyond.

I have forgotten Robert. Robert Monroe was apt to be forgotten. Although he was the oldest of the family, White Sands people, in naming over the various members of the Monroe family, would add, "and Robert," in a tone of surprise over the remembrance of his existence.

He lived on a poor, sandy little farm down by the shore, but he had come up to James' place on the evening when the guests arrived; they had all greeted him warmly and joyously, and then did not think about him again in their laughter and conversation. Robert sat back in a corner and listened with a smile, but he never spoke. Afterwards he had slipped noiselessly away and gone home, and nobody noticed his going. They were all gayly busy recalling what had happened in the old times and telling what had happened in the new.

Edith recounted the successes of her concert tours; Malcolm expatiated proudly on his plans for developing his beloved college; Ralph described the country through which his new railroad ran, and the difficulties he had had to overcome in connection with it. James, aside, discussed his orchard and his crops with Margaret, who had not been long enough away from the farm to lose touch with its interests. Aunt Isabel knitted and smiled complacently on all, talking now with one, now with the other, secretly quite proud of herself that she, an old woman of eighty-five, who had seldom been out of White Sands in her life, could discuss high finance with Ralph, and higher education with Malcolm, and hold her own with James in an argument on drainage.

The White Sands school teacher, an arch-eyed, red-mouthed bit of a girl—a Bell from Avonlea—who boarded with the James Monroes, amused herself with the boys. All were enjoying themselves hugely, so it is not to be wondered at that they did not miss Robert, who had gone home early because his old housekeeper was nervous if left alone at night.

He came again the next afternoon. From James, in the barnyard, he learned that Malcolm and Ralph had driven to the harbor, that Margaret and Mrs. James had gone to call on friends in Avonlea, and that Edith was walking somewhere in the woods on the hill. There was nobody in the house except Aunt Isabel and the teacher.

"You'd better wait and stay the evening," said James indifferently. "They'll all be back soon."

Robert went across the yard and sat down on the rustic bench in the angle of the front porch. It was a fine December evening, as mild as autumn; there had been no snow, and the long fields, sloping down from the homestead, were brown and mellow. A weird, dreamy stillness had fallen upon the purple earth, the windless woods, the rain of the valleys, the sere meadows. Nature seemed to have folded satisfied hands to rest, knowing that her long, wintry slumber was coming upon her. Out to sea, a dull, red sunset faded out into somber clouds, and the ceaseless voice of many waters came up from the tawny shore.

Robert rested his chin on his hand and looked across the vales and hills, where the feathery gray of leafless hardwoods was mingled with the sturdy, unfailing green of the conebearers. He was a tall, bent man, with thin, gray hair, a lined face, and deeply-set, gentle, brown eyes—the eyes of one who, looking through pain, sees rapture beyond.

He felt very happy. He loved his family clannishly, and he was rejoiced that they were all again near to him. He was proud of their success and fame. He was glad that James had prospered so well of late years. There was no canker of envy or discontent in his soul.

He heard absently indistinct voices at the open hall window above the porch, where Aunt Isabel was talking to Kathleen Bell. Presently Aunt Isabel moved nearer to the window, and her words came down to Robert with startling clearness.

"Yes, I can assure you, Miss Bell, that I'm real proud of my nephews and nieces. They're a smart family. They've almost all done well, and they hadn't any of them much to begin with. Ralph had absolutely nothing and today he is a millionaire. Their father met with so many losses, what with his ill-health and the bank failing, that he couldn't help them any. But they've all succeeded, except poor Robert—and I must admit that he's a total failure."

"Oh, no, no," said the little teacher deprecatingly.

"A total failure!" Aunt Isabel repeated her words emphatically. She was not going to be contradicted by anybody, least of all a Bell from Avonlea. "He has been a failure since the time he was born. He is the first Monroe to disgrace the old stock that way. I'm sure his brothers and sisters must be dreadfully ashamed of him. He has lived sixty years and he hasn't done a thing worth while. He can't even make his farm pay. If he's kept out of debt it's as much as he's ever managed to do."

"Some men can't even do that," murmured the little school teacher. She was really so much in awe of this imperious, clever old Aunt Isabel that it was positive heroism on her part to venture even this faint protest.

"More is expected of a Monroe," said Aunt Isabel majestically. "Robert Monroe is a failure, and that is the only name for him."

Robert Monroe stood up below the window in a dizzy, uncertain fashion. Aunt Isabel had been speaking of him! He, Robert, was a failure, a disgrace to his blood, of whom his nearest and dearest were ashamed! Yes, it was true; he had never realized it before; he had known that he could never win power or accumulate riches, but he had not thought that mattered much. Now, through Aunt Isabel's scornful eyes, he saw himself as the world saw him—as his brothers and sisters must see him. *There* lay the sting. What the world thought of him did not matter; but that his own should think him a failure and disgrace was agony. He moaned as he started to walk across the yard, only anxious to hide his pain and shame away from all human sight, and in his eyes was the look of a gentle animal which had been stricken by a cruel and unexpected blow.

Edith Monroe, who, unaware of Robert's proximity, had been standing at the other side of the porch, saw that look, as he hurried past her, unseeing. A moment before her dark eyes had been flashing with anger at Aunt Isabel's words; now the anger was drowned in a sudden rush of tears.

She took a quick step after Robert, but checked the impulse. Not then—and not by her alone—could that deadly hurt be healed. Nay, more, Robert must never suspect that she knew of any hurt. She stood and watched him through her tears as he went away across the low-lying shore fields to hide his broken heart under his own humble roof. She yearned to hurry after him and comfort him, but she knew that comfort was not what Robert needed now. Justice, and justice only, could pluck out the sting, which otherwise must rankle to the death.

Ralph and Malcolm were driving into the yard. Edith went over to them.

"Boys," she said resolutely, "I want to have a talk with you."

The Christmas dinner at the old homestead was a merry one. Mrs. James spread a feast that was fit for the halls of Lucullus. Laughter, jest, and repartee flew from lip to lip. Nobody appeared to notice that Robert ate little, said nothing, and sat with his form shrinking in his shabby "best" suit, his gray head bent even lower than usual, as if desirous of avoiding all observation. When the others spoke to him he answered deprecatingly, and shrank still further into himself.

Finally all had eaten all they could, and the remainder of the plum pudding was carried out. Robert gave a low sigh of relief. It was almost over. Soon he would be able to escape and hide himself and his shame away from the mirthful eyes of these men and women who had earned the right to laugh at the world in which their success gave them power and influence. He—he—only—was a failure.

He wondered impatiently why Mrs. James did not rise. Mrs. James merely leaned comfortably back in her chair, with the righteous expression of one who has done her duty by her fellow creatures' palates, and looked at Malcolm.

Malcolm rose in his place. Silence fell on the company; everybody looked suddenly alert and expectant, except Robert. He still sat with bowed head, wrapped in his own bitterness.

"I have been told that I must lead off," said Malcolm, "because I am supposed to possess the gift of gab. But, if I do, I am not going to use it for any rhetorical effect today. Simple, earnest words must express the deepest feelings of the heart in doing justice to its own. Brothers and sisters, we meet today under our own roof-tree, surrounded by the benedictions of the past years. Perhaps invisible guests are here—the spirits of those who founded this home and whose work on earth has long been finished. It is not amiss to hope that this is so and our family circle made indeed complete. To each one of us who are here in visible bodily presence some measure of success has fallen; but only one of us has been supremely successful in the only things that really count—the things that count for eternity as well as time—sympathy and unselfishness and self-sacrifice.

"I shall tell you my own story for the benefit of those who have not heard it. When I was a lad of sixteen I started to work out my own education. Some of you will remember that old Mr. Blair of Avonlea offered me a place in his store for the summer, at wages which would go far towards paying my expenses at the county academy the next winter. I went to work, eager and hopeful. All summer I tried to do my faithful best for my employer. In September the blow fell. A sum of money was missing from Mr. Blair's till. I was suspected and discharged in disgrace. All my neighbors believed me guilty; even some of my own family looked upon me with suspicion— nor could I blame them, for the circumstantial evidence was strongly against me."

Ralph and James looked ashamed; Edith and Margaret, who had not been born at the time referred to, lifted their faces innocently. Robert did not move or glance up. He hardly seemed to be listening.

"I was crushed in an agony of shame and despair," continued

Malcolm. "I believed my career was ruined. I was bent on casting all my ambitions behind me, and going west to some place where nobody knew me or my disgrace. But there was one person who believed in my innocence, who said to me, 'You shall not give up—you shall not behave as if you were guilty. You are innocent, and in time your innocence will be proved. Meanwhile show yourself a man. You have nearly enough money to pay your way next winter at the Academy. I have a little I can give to help you out. Don't give in—never give in when you have done no wrong.'

"I listened and took his advice. I went to the Academy. My story was there as soon as I was, and I found myself sneered at and shunned. Many a time I would have given up in despair, had it not been for the encouragement of my counselor. He furnished the backbone for me. I was determined that his belief in me should be justified. I studied hard and came out at the head of my class. Then there seemed to be no chance of my earning any more money that summer. But a farmer at New-bridge, who cared nothing about the character of his help, if he could get the work out of them, offered to hire me. The prospect was distasteful but, urged by the man who believed in me, I took the place and endured the hardships. Another winter of lonely work passed at the Academy. I won the Farrell Scholarship the last year it was offered, and that meant an Arts course for me. I went to Redmond College. My story was not openly known there, but something of it got abroad, enough to taint my life there also with its suspicion. But the year I graduated, Mr. Blair's nephew, who, as you know, was the real culprit, confessed his guilt, and I was cleared before the world. Since then my career has been what is called a brilliant one. But,"—Malcolm turned and laid his hand on Robert's thin shoulder—"all my success I owe to my brother Robert. It is his success—not mine—and here today, since we have agreed to say what is too often left to be said over a coffin lid, I thank him for all he did for me, and tell him that there is nothing I am more proud of and thankful for than such a brother."

Robert had looked up at last, amazed, bewildered, incredulous. His face crimsoned as Malcolm sat down. But now Ralph was getting up.

"I am no orator as Malcolm is," he quoted gayly, "but I've

got a story to tell, too, which only one of you knows. Forty years ago, when I started in life as a business man, money wasn't so plentiful with me as it may be today. And I needed it badly. A chance came my way to make a pile of it. It wasn't a clean chance. It was a dirty chance. It looked square on the surface; but, underneath, it meant trickery and roguery. I hadn't enough perception to see that, though—I was fool enough to think it was all right. I told Robert what I meant to do. And Robert saw clear through the outward sham to the real, hideous thing underneath. He showed me what it meant and he gave me a preachment about a few Monroe Traditions of truth and honor. I saw what I had been about to do as he saw it—as all good men and true must see it. And I vowed then and there that I'd never go into anything that I wasn't sure was fair and square and clean through and through. I've kept that vow. I am a rich man, and not a dollar of my money is 'tainted' money. But I didn't make it. Robert really made every cent of my money. If it hadn't been for him I'd have been a poor man today, or behind prison bars, as are the other men who went into that deal when I backed out. I've got a son here. I hope he'll be as clever as his Uncle Malcolm; but I hope, still more earnestly, that he'll be as good and honorable a man as his Uncle Robert."

By this time Robert's head was bent again, and his face buried in his hands.

"My turn next," said James. "I haven't much to say—only this. After mother died I took typhoid fever. Here I was with no one to wait on me. Robert came and nursed me. He was the most faithful, tender, gentle nurse ever a man had. The doctor said Robert saved my life. I don't suppose any of the rest of us here can say we have saved a life."

Edith wiped away her tears and sprang up impulsively.

"Years ago," she said, "there was a poor, ambitious girl who had a voice. She wanted a musical education and her only apparent chance of obtaining it was to get a teacher's certificate and earn money enough to have her voice trained. She studied hard, but her brains, in mathematics at least, weren't as good as her voice, and the time was short. She failed. She was lost in disappointment and despair, for that was the last year in which it was possible to obtain a teacher's certificate without attending Queen's Academy, and she could not afford that. Then her oldest brother came to her and told her he could spare enough money to send her to the conservatory of music in Halifax for a year. He made her take it. She never knew till long afterwards that he had sold the beautiful horse which he loved like a human creature, to get the money. She went to the Halifax conservatory. She won a musical scholarship. She has had a happy life and a successful career. And she owes it all to her brother Robert—"

But Edith could go no further. Her voice failed her and she sat down in tears. Margaret did not try to stand up.

"I was only five when my mother died," she sobbed. "Robert was both father and mother to me. Never had child or girl so wise and loving a guardian as he was to me. I have never forgotten the lessons he taught me. Whatever there is of good in my life or character I owe to him. I was often headstrong and willful, but he never lost patience with me. I owe everything to Robert."

Suddenly the little teacher rose with wet eyes and crimson cheeks.

"I have something to say, too," she said resolutely. "You have spoken for yourselves. I speak for the people of White Sands. There is a man in this settlement whom everybody loves. I shall tell you some of the things he has done.

"Last fall, in an October storm, the harbor lighthouse flew a flag of distress. Only one man was brave enough to face the danger of sailing to the lighthouse to find out what the trouble was. That was Robert Monroe. He found the keeper alone with a broken leg; and he sailed back and made—yes, *made* the unwilling and terrified doctor go with him to the lighthouse. I saw him when he told the doctor he must go; and I tell you that no man living could have set his will against Robert Monroe's at that moment.

"Four years ago old Sarah Cooper was to be taken to the poorhouse. She was broken-hearted. One man took the poor, bed-ridden, fretful old creature into his home, paid for medical attendance, and waited on her himself, when his housekeeper couldn't endure her tantrums and temper. Sarah Cooper died two years afterwards, and her latest breath was a benediction on Robert Monroe—the best man God ever made.

"Eight years ago Jack Blewett wanted a place. Nobody would hire him, because his father was in the penitentiary, and some people thought Jack ought to be there, too. Robert Monroe hired him—and helped him, and kept him straight, and got him started right—and Jack Blewett is a hard-working, respected young man today, with every prospect of a useful and honorable life. There is hardly a man, woman, or child in White Sands who doesn't owe something to Robert Monroe!"

As Kathleen Bell sat down, Malcolm sprang up and held out his hands.

"Every one of us stand up and sing Auld Lang Syne," he cried.

Everybody stood up and joined hands, but one did not sing. Robert Monroe stood erect, with a great radiance on his face and in his eyes. His reproach had been taken away; he was crowned among his kindred with the beauty and blessing of sacred yesterdays.

When the singing ceased Malcolm's stern-faced son reached over and shook Robert's hands.

"Uncle Rob," he said heartily, "I hope that when I'm sixty I'll be as successful a man as you."

"I guess," said Aunt Isabel, aside to the little school teacher, as she wiped the tears from her keen old eyes, "that there's a kind of failure that's the best success."

THE RETURN OF HESTER

JUST AT dusk, that evening, I had gone upstairs and put on my muslin gown. I had been busy all day attending to the strawberry preserving—for Mary Sloane could not be trusted with that—and I was a little tired, and thought it was hardly worth while to change my dress, especially since there was nobody to see or care, since Hester was gone. Mary Sloane did not count.

But I did it because Hester would have cared if she had been here. She always liked to see me neat and dainty. So, although I was tired and sick at heart, I put on my pale blue muslin and dressed my hair.

At first I did my hair up in a way I had always liked; but had seldom worn, because Hester had disapproved of it. It became me; but I suddenly felt as if it were disloyal to her, so I took the puffs down again and arranged my hair in the plain, old-fashioned way she had liked. My hair, though it had a good many gray threads in it, was thick and long and brown still; but that did not matter—nothing mattered since Hester was dead and I had sent Hugh Blair away for the second time.

The Newbridge people all wondered why I had not put on mourning for Hester. I did not tell them it was because Hester had asked me not to. Hester had never approved of mourning;

463

she said that if the heart did not mourn crape would not mend matters; and if it did there was no need of the external trappings of woe. She told me calmly, the night before she died, to go on wearing my pretty dresses just as I had always worn them, and to make no difference in my outward life because of her going.

"I know there will be a difference in your inward life," she said wistfully.

And oh, there was! But sometimes I wondered uneasily, feeling almost conscience-stricken, whether it were *wholly* because Hester had left me—whether it were not partly because, for a second time, I had shut the door of my heart in the face of love at her bidding.

When I had dressed I went downstairs to the front door, and sat on the sandstone steps under the arch of the Virginia creeper. I was all alone, for Mary Sloane had gone to Avonlea.

It was a beautiful night; the full moon was just rising over the wooded hills, and her light fell through the poplars into the garden before me. Through an open corner on the western side I saw the sky all silvery blue in the afterlight. The garden was very beautiful just then, for it was the time of the roses, and ours were all out—so many of them—great pink, and red, and white, and yellow roses.

Hester had loved roses and could never have enough of them. Her favorite bush was growing by the steps, all gloried over with blossoms—white, with pale pink hearts. I gathered a cluster and pinned it loosely on my breast. But my eyes filled as I did so—I felt so very, very desolate.

I was all alone, and it was bitter. The roses, much as I loved them, could not give me sufficient companionship. I wanted the clasp of a human hand, and the love-light in human eyes. And then I fell to thinking of Hugh, although I tried not to.

I had always lived alone with Hester. I did not remember our parents, who had died in my babyhood. Hester was fifteen years older than I, and she had always seemed more like a mother than a sister. She had been very good to me and had never denied me anything I wanted, save the one thing that mattered.

I was twenty-five before I ever had a lover. This was not, I think, because I was more unattractive than other women. The

Merediths had always been the "big" family of Newbridge. The rest of the people looked up to us, because we were the grand-daughters of old Squire Meredith. The Newbridge young men would have thought it no use to try to woo a Meredith.

I had not a great deal of family pride, as perhaps I should be ashamed to confess. I found our exalted position very lonely, and cared more for the simple joys of friendship and companionship which other girls had. But Hester possessed it in a double measure; she never allowed me to associate on a level of equality with the young people of Newbridge. We must be very nice and kind and affable to them—*noblesse oblige,* as it were—but we must never forget that we were Merediths.

When I was twenty-five, Hugh Blair came to Newbridge, having bought a farm near the village. He was a stranger, from Lower Carmody, and so was not imbued with any preconceptions of Meredith superiority. In his eyes I was just a girl like others—a girl to be wooed and won by any man of clean life and honest heart. I met him at a little Sunday-School picnic over at Avonlea, which I attended because of my class. I thought him very handsome and manly. He talked to me a great deal, and at last he drove me home. The next Sunday evening he walked up from church with me.

Hester was away, or, of course, this would never have happened. She had gone for a month's visit to distant friends.

In that month I lived a lifetime. Hugh Blair courted me as the other girls in Newbridge were courted. He took me out driving and came to see me in the evenings, which we spent for the most part in the garden. I did not like the stately gloom and formality of our old Meredith parlor, and Hugh never seemed to feel at ease there. His broad shoulders and hearty laughter were oddly out of place among our faded, old-maidish furnishings.

Mary Sloane was very much pleased at Hugh's visit. She had always resented the fact that I had never had a "beau," seeming to think it reflected some slight or disparagement upon me. She did all she could to encourage him.

But when Hester returned and found out about Hugh she was very angry—and grieved, which hurt me far more. She told me that I had forgotten myself and that Hugh's visits must cease.

I had never been afraid of Hester before, but I was afraid of her then. I yielded. Perhaps it was very weak of me, but then I was always weak. I think that was why Hugh's strength had appealed so to me. I needed love and protection. Hester, strong and self-sufficient, had never felt such a need. She could not understand. Oh, how contemptuous she was.

I told Hugh timidly that Hester did not approve of our friendship and that it must end. He took it quietly enough, and went away. I thought he did not care much, and the thought selfishly made my own heartache worse. I was very unhappy for a long time, but I tried not to let Hester see it, and I don't think she did. She was not very discerning in some things.

After a time I got over it; that is, the heartache ceased to ache all the time. But things were never quite the same again. Life always seemed rather dreary and empty, in spite of Hester and my roses and my Sunday-School.

I supposed that Hugh Blair would find him a wife elsewhere, but he did not. The years went by and we never met, although I saw him often at church. At such times Hester always watched me very closely, but there was no need of her to do so. Hugh made no attempt to meet me, or speak with me, and I would not have permitted it if he had. But my heart always yearned after him. I was selfishly glad he had not married, because if he had I could not have thought and dreamed of him—it would have been wrong. Perhaps, as it was, it was foolish; but it seemed to me that I must have something, if only foolish dreams, to fill my life.

At first there was only pain in the thought of him, but afterwards a faint, misty little pleasure crept in, like a mirage from a land of lost delight.

Ten years slipped away thus. And then Hester died. Her illness was sudden and short; but, before she died, she asked me to promise that I would never marry Hugh Blair.

She had not mentioned his name for years. I thought she had forgotten all about him.

"Oh, dear sister, is there any need of such a promise?" I asked, weeping. "Hugh Blair does not want to marry me now. He never will again."

"He has never married—he has not forgotten you," she said

fiercely. "I could not rest in my grave if I thought you would disgrace your family by marrying beneath you. Promise me, Margaret."

I promised. I would have promised anything in my power to make her dying pillow easier. Besides, what did it matter? I was sure that Hugh would never think of me again.

She smiled when she heard me, and pressed my hand.

"Good little sister—that is right. You were always a good girl, Margaret—good and obedient, though a little sentimental and foolish in some ways. You are like our mother—she was always weak and loving. I took after the Merediths."

She did, indeed. Even in her coffin her dark, handsome features preserved their expression of pride and determination. Somehow, that last look of her dead face remained in my memory, blotting out the real affection and gentleness which her living face had almost always shown me. This distressed me, but I could not help it. I wished to think of her as kind and loving, but I could remember only the pride and coldness with which she had crushed out my new-born happiness. Yet I felt no anger or resentment towards her for what she had done. I knew she had meant it for the best—my best. It was only that she was mistaken.

And then, a month after she had died, Hugh Blair came to me and asked me to be his wife. He said he had always loved me, and could never love any other woman.

All my old love for him reawakened. I wanted to say yes— to feel his strong arms about me, and the warmth of his love enfolding and guarding me. In my weakness I yearned for his strength.

But there was my promise to Hester—that promise given by her deathbed. I could not break it, and I told him so. It was the hardest thing I had ever done.

He did not go away quietly this time. He pleaded and reasoned and reproached. Every word of his hurt me like a knife-thrust. But I could not break my promise to the dead. If Hester had been living I would have braved her wrath and her estrangement and gone to him. But she was dead and I could not do it.

Finally he went away in grief and anger. That was three weeks ago—and now I sat alone in the moonlit rose-garden and wept for him. But after a time my tears dried and a very strange feeling came over me. I felt calm and happy, as if some wonderful love and tenderness were very near me.

And now comes the strange part of my story—the part which will not, I suppose, be believed. If it were not for one thing I think I should hardly believe it myself. I should feel tempted to think I had dreamed it. But because of that one thing I know it was real. The night was very calm and still. Not a breath of wind stirred. The moonshine was the brightest I had ever seen. In the middle of the garden, where the shadow of the poplars did not fall, it was almost as bright as day. One could have read fine print. There was still a little rose glow in the west, and over the airy boughs of the tall poplars one or two large, bright stars were shining. The air was sweet with a hush of dreams, and the world was so lovely that I held my breath over its beauty.

Then, all at once, down at the far end of the garden, I saw a woman walking. I thought at first that it must be Mary Sloane; but, as she crossed a moonlit path, I saw it was not our old servant's stout, homely figure. This woman was tall and erect.

Although no suspicion of the truth came to me, something about her reminded me of Hester. Even so had Hester liked to wander about the garden in the twilight. I had seen her thus a thousand times.

I wondered who the woman could be. Some neighbor, of course. But what a strange way for her to come! She walked up the garden slowly in the poplar shade. Now and then she stooped, as if to caress a flower, but she plucked none. Half way up she came out into the moonlight and walked across the plot of grass in the center of the garden. My heart gave a great throb and I stood up. She was quite near to me now— and I saw that it was Hester.

I can hardly say just what my feelings were at this moment. I know that I was not surprised. I was frightened and yet I was not frightened. Something in me shrank back in a sickening terror; but *I,* the real I, was not frightened. I knew that this was my sister, and that there could be no reason why I should be frightened of her, because she loved me still, as she had always done. Further than this I was not conscious of any coherent thought, either of wonder or attempt at reasoning.

Hester paused when she came to within a few steps of me. In the moonlight I saw her face quite plainly. It wore an expression I had never before seen on it—a humble, wistful, tender look. Often in life Hester had looked lovingly, even tenderly, upon me; but always, as it were, through a mask of pride and sternness. This was gone now, and I felt nearer to her than ever before. I knew suddenly that she understood me. And then the half-conscious awe and terror some part of me had felt vanished, and I only realized that Hester was here, and that there was no terrible gulf of change between us.

Hester beckoned to me and said,

"Come."

I stood up and followed her out of the garden. We walked side by side down our lane, under the willows and out to the road, which lay long and still in that bright, calm moonshine. I felt as if I were in a dream, moving at the bidding of a will not my own, which I could not have disputed even if I had wished to do so. But I did not wish it; I had only the feeling of a strange, boundless content.

We went down the road between the growths of young fir that bordered it. I smelled their balsam as we passed, and noticed how clearly and darkly their pointed tops came out against the sky. I heard the tread of my own feet on little twigs and plants in our way, and the trail of my dress over the grass; but Hester moved noiselessly.

Then we went through the Avenue—that stretch of road under the apple trees that Anne Shirley, over at Avonlea, calls "The White Way of Delight." It was almost dark here; and yet I could see Hester's face just as plainly as if the moon were shining on it; and whenever I looked at her she was always looking at me with that strangely gentle smile on her lips.

Just as we passed out of the Avenue, James Trent overtook us, driving. It seems to me that our feelings at a given moment are seldom what we would expect them to be. I simply felt annoyed that James Trent, the most notorious gossip in New-bridge, should have seen me walking with Hester. In a flash I anticipated all the annoyance of it; he would talk of the matter far and wide.

But James Trent merely nodded and called out,

"Howdy, Miss Margaret. Taking a moonlight stroll by yourself? Lovely night, ain't it?"

Just then his horse suddenly swerved, as if startled, and broke into a gallop. They whirled around the curve of the road in an instant. I felt relieved, but puzzled. *James Trent had not seen Hester.*

Down over the hill was Hugh Blair's place. When we came to it, Hester turned in at the gate. Then, for the first time, I understood why she had come back, and a blinding flash of joy broke over my soul. I stopped and looked at her. Her deep eyes gazed into mine, but she did not speak.

We went on. Hugh's house lay before us in the moonlight, grown over by a tangle of vines. His garden was on our right, a quaint spot, full of old-fashioned flowers growing in a sort of disorderly sweetness. I trod on a bed of mint, and the spice of it floated up to me like the incense of some strange, sacred, solemn ceremonial. I felt unspeakably happy and blessed.

When we came to the door Hester said,

"Knock, Margaret."

I rapped gently. In a moment Hugh opened it. Then that happened by which, in after days, I was to know that this strange thing was no dream or fancy of mine. Hugh looked not at me, but past me.

"Hester!" he exclaimed, with human fear and horror in his voice.

He leaned against the door-post, the big, strong fellow, trembling from head to foot.

"I have learned," said Hester, "that nothing matters in all God's universe, except love. There is no pride where I have been and no false ideals."

Hugh and I looked into each other's eyes, wondering, and then we knew that we were alone.

THE LITTLE BROWN BOOK OF MISS EMILY

THE FIRST summer Mr. Irving and Miss Lavendar—Diana and I could never call her anything else, even after she was married—were at Echo Lodge after their marriage, both Diana and I spent a great deal of time with them. We became acquainted with many of the Grafton people whom we had not known before, and, among others, the family of Mr. Mack Leith. We often went up to the Leiths in the evening to play croquet. Millie and Margaret Leith were very nice girls, and the boys were nice, too. Indeed, we liked every one in the family, except poor old Miss Emily Leith. We tried hard enough to like her, because she seemed to like Diana and me very much, and always wanted to sit with us and talk to us, when we would much rather have been somewhere else. We often felt a good deal of impatience at these times, but I am very glad to think now that we never showed it.

In a way, we felt sorry for Miss Emily. She was Mr. Leith's old-maid sister and she was not of much importance in the household. But, though we felt sorry for her, we couldn't like her. She really was fussy and meddlesome; she liked to poke a finger into every one's pie, and she was not at all tactful. Then, too, she had a sarcastic tongue, and seemed to feel bitter towards all the young folks and their love affairs. Diana and

471

I thought this was because she had never had a lover of her own.

Somehow, it seemed impossible to think of lovers in connection with Miss Emily. She was short and stout and pudgy, with a face so round and fat and red that it seemed quite featureless; and her hair was scanty and gray. She walked with a waddle, just like Mrs. Rachel Lynde, and she was always rather short of breath. It was hard to believe Miss Emily had ever been young; yet old Mr. Murray, who lived next door to the Leiths, not only expected us to believe it, but assured us that she had been very pretty.

"That, at least, is impossible," said Diana to me.

And then, one day, Miss Emily died. I'm afraid no one was very sorry. It seems to me a most dreadful thing to go out of the world and leave not one person behind to be sorry because you have gone. Miss Emily was dead and buried before Diana and I heard of it at all. The first I knew of it was when I came home from Orchard Slope one day and found a queer, shabby little black horsehair trunk, all studded with brass nails, on the floor of my room at Green Gables. Marilla told me that Jack Leith had brought it over, and said that it had belonged to Miss Emily and that, when she was dying, she asked them to send it to me.

"But what is in it? And what am I to do with it?" I asked in bewilderment.

"There was nothing said about what you were to do with it. Jack said they didn't know what was in it, and hadn't looked into it, seeing that it was your property. It seems a rather queer proceeding—but you're always getting mixed up in queer proceedings, Anne. As for what is in it, the easiest way to find out, I reckon, is to open it and see. The key is tied to it. Jack said Miss Emily said she wanted you to have it because she loved you and saw her lost youth in you. I guess she was a bit delirious at the last and wandered a good deal. She said she wanted you 'to understand her.' "

I ran over to Orchard Slope and asked Diana to come over and examine the trunk with me. I hadn't received any instructions about keeping its contents secret and I knew Miss Emily wouldn't mind Diana knowing about them, whatever they were.

It was a cool, gray afternoon and we got back to Green Gables just as the rain was beginning to fall. When we went up to my room the wind was rising and whistling through the boughs of the big old Snow Queen outside of my window. Diana was excited, and, I really believe, a little bit frightened.

We opened the old trunk. It was very small, and there was nothing in it but a big cardboard box. The box was tied up and the knots sealed with wax. We lifted it out and untied it. I touched Diana's fingers as we did it, and both of us exclaimed at once, "How cold your hand is!"

In the box was a quaint, pretty, old-fashioned gown, not at all faded, made of blue muslin, with a little darker blue flower in it. Under it we found a sash, a yellowed feather fan, and an envelope full of withered flowers. At the bottom of the box was a little brown book.

It was small and thin, like a girl's exercise book, with leaves that had once been blue and pink, but were now quite faded, and stained in places. On the fly leaf was written, in a very delicate hand, "Emily Margaret Leith," and the same writing covered the first few pages of the book. The rest were not written on at all. We sat there on the floor, Diana and I, and read the little book together, while the rain thudded against the window panes.

June 19, 18—

I came today to spend a while with Aunt Margaret in Charlottetown. It is so pretty here, where she lives—and ever so much nicer than on the farm at home. I have no cows to milk here or pigs to feed. Aunt Margaret has given me such a lovely blue muslin dress, and I am to have it made to wear at a garden party out at Brighton next week. I never had a muslin dress before—nothing but ugly prints and dark woolens. I wish we were rich, like Aunt Margaret. Aunt Margaret laughed when I said this, and declared she would give all her wealth for my youth and beauty and light-heartedness. I am only eighteen and I know I am very merry but I wonder if I am really pretty. It seems to me that I am when I look in Aunt Margaret's beautiful mirrors. They make me look very different from the old cracked one in my room at home which always twisted my face and turned me green. But Aunt Margaret spoiled her compliment by telling me I look exactly as she did at my age. If I thought I'd ever look as Aunt Margaret does now, I don't know what I'd do. She is so fat and red.

June 29.

Last week I went to the garden party and I met a young man called Paul Osborne. He is a young artist from Montreal who is boarding over at Heppoch. He is the handsomest man I have ever seen—very tall and slender, with dreamy, dark eyes and a pale, clever face. I have not been able to keep from thinking about him ever since, and today he came over here and asked if he could paint me. I felt very much flattered and so pleased when Aunt Margaret gave him permission. He says he wants to paint me as "Spring," standing under the poplars where a fine rain of sunshine falls through. I am o wear my blue muslin gown and a wreath of flowers on my hair. He says I have such beautiful hair. He has never seen any of such a real pale gold. Somehow it seems prettier than ever to me since he praised it.

I had a letter from home today. Ma says the blue hen stole her nest and came off with fourteen chickens, and that pa has sold the little spotted calf. Somehow those things don't interest me like they once did.

July 9.

The picture is coming on very well, Mr. Osborne says. I know he is making me look far too pretty in it, although he persists in saying he can't do me justice. He is going to send it to some great exhibition when finished, but he says he will make a little water-color copy for me.

He comes over every day to paint and we talk a great deal and he reads me lovely things out of his books. I don't understand them all, but I try to, and he explains them so nicely and is so patient with my stupidity. And he says any one with my eyes and hair and coloring does not need to be clever. He says I have the sweetest, merriest laugh in the world. But I will not write down all the compliments he has paid me. I dare say he does not mean them at all.

In the evening we stroll among the spruces or sit on the bench under the acacia tree. Sometimes we don't talk at all, but I never find the time long. Indeed, the minutes just seem to fly—and then the moon will come up, round and red, over the harbor and Mr. Osborne will sigh and say he supposes it is time for him to go.

July 24.

I am so happy. I am frightened at my happiness. Oh, I didn't think life could ever be so beautiful for me as it is!

Paul loves me! He told me so tonight as we walked by the harbor and watched the sunset, and he asked me to be his wife. I have cared for him ever since I met him, but I am afraid I am not clever and well-educated enough for a wife for Paul. Because, of course, I'm only an ignorant little country girl and have lived all my life on a farm. Why, my hands are quite rough yet from the work I've done. But Paul just laughed when I said so, and took my hands and kissed them. Then he looked into my eyes and laughed again, because I couldn't hide from him how much I loved him.

We are to be married next spring and Paul says he will take me to Europe. That will be very nice, but nothing matters so long as I am with him.

Paul's people are very wealthy and his mother and sisters are very fashionable. I am frightened of them, but I did not tell Paul so because I think it would hurt him and oh, I wouldn't do that for the world.

There is nothing I wouldn't suffer if it would do him any good. I never thought any one could feel so. I used to think if I loved anybody I would want him to do everything for me and wait on me as if I were a princess. But that is not the way at all. Love makes you very humble and you want to do everything yourself for the one you love.

August 10.

Paul went home today. Oh, it is so terrible! I don't know how I can bear to live even for a little while without him. But this is silly of me, because I know he has to go and he will write often and come to me often. But, still, it is so lonesome. I didn't cry when he left me because I wanted him to remember me smiling in the way he liked best, but I have been crying ever since and I can't stop, no matter how hard I try. We have had such a beautiful fortnight. Every day seemed dearer and happier than the last, and now it is ended and I feel as if it could never be the same again. Oh, I am very foolish—but I love him so dearly and if I were to lose his love I know I would die.

August 17.

I think my heart is dead. But no, it can't be, for it aches too much.

Paul's mother came here to see me today. She was not angry or disagreeable. I wouldn't have been so frightened of her if she had been. As it was, I felt that I couldn't say a word. She is very beautiful and stately and wonderful, with a low, cold voice and proud, dark eyes. Her face is like Paul's but without the lovableness of his.

She talked to me for a long time and she said terrible things— terrible, because I knew they were all true. I seemed to see everything through her eyes. She said that Paul was infatuated with my youth and beauty but that it would not last and what else had I to give him? She said Paul must marry a woman of his own class, who could do honor to his fame and position. She said that he was very talented and had a great career before him, but that if he married me it would ruin his life.

I saw it all, just as she explained it out, and I told her at last that I would not marry Paul, and she might tell him so. But she smiled and said I must tell him myself, because he would not believe any one else. I could have begged her to spare me that, but I knew it would be of no use. I do not think she has any pity or mercy for any one. Besides, what she said was quite true.

When she thanked me for being so *reasonable* I told her I was not doing it to please her, but for Paul's sake, because I would not spoil his life, and that I would always hate her. She smiled again and went away.

Oh, how can I bear it? I did not know any one could suffer like this!

August 18.

I have done it. I wrote to Paul today. I knew I must tell him by letter, because I could never make him believe it face to face. I was afraid I could not even do it by letter. I suppose a clever woman easily could, but I am so stupid. I wrote a great many letters and tore them up, because I felt sure they wouldn't convince Paul. At last I got one that I thought would do. I knew I must make it seem as if I were very frivolous and heartless, or he would never believe. I spelled some words wrong and put in some mistakes of grammar on purpose. I told him I had just been flirting with him, and that I had another fellow at home I liked better. I said *fellow* because I knew it would disgust him. I said that it was only because he was rich that I was tempted to marry him.

I thought my heart would break while I was writing those dreadful falsehoods. But it was for his sake, because I must not spoil his life. His mother told me I would be a millstone around his neck. I love Paul so much that I would do anything rather than be that. It would be easy to die for him, but I don't see how I can go on living. I think my letter will convince Paul.

I suppose it convinced Paul, because there was no further entry in the little brown book. When we had finished it the tears were running down both our faces.

"Oh, poor, dear Miss Emily," sobbed Diana. "I'm so sorry I ever thought her funny and meddlesome."

"She was good and strong and brave," I said. "I could never have been as unselfish as she was."

And I thought of Whittier's lines,

> The outward, wayward life we see
> The hidden springs we may not know.

At the back of the little brown book we found a faded water-color sketch of a young girl—such a slim, pretty little thing, with big blue eyes and lovely, long, rippling, golden hair. Paul Osborne's name was written in faded ink across the corner.

We put everything back in the box. Then we sat for a long time by my window in silence and thought of many things, until the rainy twilight came down and blotted out the world.

SARA'S WAY

THE WARM June sunshine was coming down through the trees, white with the virginal bloom of apple-blossoms, and through the shining panes, making a tremulous mosaic upon Mrs. Eben Andrews' spotless kitchen floor. Through the open door, a wind, fragrant from long wanderings over orchards and clover meadows, drifted in, and, from the window, Mrs. Eben and her guest could look down over a long, misty valley sloping to a sparkling sea.

Mrs. Jonas Andrews was spending the afternoon with her sister-in-law. She was a big, sonsy woman, with full-blown peony cheeks and large, dreamy, brown eyes. When she had been a slim, pink-and-white girl those eyes had been very romantic. Now they were so out of keeping with the rest of her appearance as to be ludicrous.

Mrs. Eben, sitting at the other end of the small tea-table that was drawn up against the window, was a thin little woman, with a very sharp nose and light, faded blue eyes. She looked like a woman whose opinions were always very decided and warranted to wear.

"How does Sara like teaching at Newbridge?" asked Mrs. Jonas, helping herself a second time to Mrs. Eben's matchless black fruit cake, and thereby bestowing a subtle compliment

478

which Mrs. Eben did not fail to appreciate.

"Well, I guess she likes it pretty well—better than down at White Sands, anyway," answered Mrs. Eben. "Yes, I may say it suits her. Of course it's a long walk there and back. I think it would have been wiser for her to keep on boarding at Morrison's, as she did all winter, but Sara is bound to be home all she can. And I must say the walk seems to agree with her."

"I was down to see Jonas' aunt at Newbridge last night," said Mrs. Jonas, "and she said she'd heard that Sara had made up her mind to take Lige Baxter at last, and that they were to be married in the fall. She asked me if it was true. I said I didn't know, but I hoped to mercy it was. Now, is it, Louisa?"

"Not a word of it," said Mrs. Eben sorrowfully. "Sara hasn't any more notion of taking Lige than ever she had. I'm sure it's not *my* fault. I've talked and argued till I'm tired. I declare to you, Amelia, I am terribly disappointed. I'd set my heart on Sara's marrying Lige—and now to think she won't!"

"She is a very foolish girl," said Mrs. Jonas, judicially. "If Lige Baxter isn't good enough for her, who is?"

"And he's so well off," said Mrs. Eben, "and does such a good business, and is well spoken of by every one. And that lovely new house of his at Newbridge, with bay windows and hardwood floors! I've dreamed and dreamed of seeing Sara there as mistress."

"Maybe you'll see her there yet," said Mrs. Jonas, who always took a hopeful view of everything, even of Sara's contrariness. But she felt discouraged, too. Well, she had done her best.

If Lige Baxter's broth was spoiled it was not for lack of cooks. Every Andrews in Avonlea had been trying for two years to bring about a match between him and Sara, and Mrs. Jonas had borne her part valiantly.

Mrs. Eben's despondent reply was cut short by the appearance of Sara herself. The girl stood for a moment in the doorway and looked with a faintly amused air at her aunts. She knew quite well that they had been discussing her, for Mrs. Jonas, who carried her conscience in her face, looked guilty, and Mrs. Eben had not been able wholly to banish her aggrieved expression.

Sara put away her books, kissed Mrs. Jonas' rosy cheek, and sat down at the table. Mrs. Eben brought her some fresh tea, some hot rolls, and a little jelly-pot of the apricot preserves Sara liked, and she cut some more fruit cake for her in moist plummy slices. She might be out of patience with Sara's "contrariness," but she spoiled and petted her for all that, for the girl was the very core of her childless heart.

Sara Andrews was not, strictly speaking, pretty; but there was that about her which made people look at her twice. She was very dark, with a rich, dusky sort of darkness, her deep eyes were velvety brown, and her lips and cheeks were crimson.

She ate her rolls and preserves with a healthy appetite, sharpened by her long walk from Newbridge, and told amusing little stories of her day's work that made the two older women shake with laughter, and exchange shy glances of pride over her cleverness.

When tea was over she poured the remaining contents of the cream jug into a saucer.

"I must feed my pussy," she said as she left the room.

"That girl beats me," said Mrs. Eben with a sigh of perplexity. "You know that black cat we've had for two years? Eben and I have always made a lot of him, but Sara seemed to have a dislike to him. Never a peaceful nap under the stove could he have when Sara was home—out he must go. Well, a little spell ago he got his leg broke accidentally and we thought he'd have to be killed. But Sara wouldn't hear of it. She got splints and set his leg just as knacky, and bandaged it up, and she has tended him like a sick baby ever since. He's just about well now, and he lives in clover, that cat does. It's just her way. There's them sick chickens she's been doctoring for a week, giving them pills and things!

"And she thinks more of that wretched-looking calf that got poisoned with paris green than of all the other stock on the place."

As the summer wore away Mrs. Eben tried to reconcile herself to the destruction of her air castles. But she scolded Sara considerably.

"Sara, why don't you like Lige? I'm sure he is a model young man."

"I don't like model young men," answered Sara impatiently. "And I really think I hate Lige Baxter. He has always been held up to me as such a paragon. I'm tired of hearing about all his perfections. I know them all off by heart. He doesn't drink, he doesn't smoke, he doesn't steal, he doesn't tell fibs, he never loses his temper, he doesn't swear, and he goes to church regularly. Such a faultless creature as that would certainly get on my nerves. No, no, you'll have to pick out another mistress for your new house at the Bridge, Aunt Louisa."

When the apple trees, that had been pink and white in June, were russet and bronze in October, Mrs. Eben had a quilting. The quilt was of the "Rising Star" pattern, which was considered in Avonlea to be very handsome. Mrs. Eben had intended it for part of Sara's "setting out," and, while she sewed the red-and-white diamonds together, she had regaled her fancy by imagining she saw it spread out on the spare-room bed of the house at Newbridge, with herself laying her bonnet and shawl on it when she went to see Sara. Those bright visions had faded with the apple blossoms, and Mrs. Eben hardly had the heart to finish the quilt at all.

The quilting came off on Saturday afternoon, when Sara could be home from school. All Mrs. Eben's particular friends were ranged around the quilt, and tongues and fingers flew. Sara flitted about, helping her aunt with the supper preparations. She was in the room, getting the custard dishes out of the cupboard, when Mrs. George Pye arrived.

Mrs. George had a genius for being late. She was later than usual today, and she looked excited. Every woman around the "Rising Star" felt that Mrs. George had some news worth listening to, and there was an expectant silence while she pulled out her chair and settled herself at the quilt.

She was a tall, thin woman, with a long pale face and liquid green eyes. As she looked around the circle she had the air of a cat daintily licking its chops over some titbit.

"I suppose," she said, "that you have heard the news?"

She knew perfectly well that they had not. Every other woman at the frame stopped quilting. Mrs. Eben came to the door with a pan of puffy, smoking-hot soda biscuits in her hand. Sara stopped counting her custard dishes, and turned her ripely-colored face over her shoulder. Even the black cat, at her feet, ceased preening his fur. Mrs. George felt that the undivided attention of her audience was hers.

"Baxter Brothers have failed," she said, her green eyes shooting out flashes of light. "Failed *disgracefully!*"

She paused for a moment; but, since her hearers were as yet speechless from surprise, she went on.

"George came home from Newbridge, just before I left, with the news. You could have knocked me down with a feather. I should have thought that firm was as steady as the rock of Gibraltar! But they're ruined—absolutely ruined. Louisa, dear, can you find me a good needle?"

"Louisa, dear," had set her biscuits down with a sharp thud, reckless of results. A sharp, metallic tinkle sounded at the closet where Sara had struck the edge of her tray against a shelf. The sound seemed to loosen the paralyzed tongues, and everybody began talking and exclaiming at once. Clear and shrill above the confusion rose Mrs. George Pye's voice.

"Yes, indeed, you may well say so. It *is* disgraceful. And to think how everybody trusted them! George will lose considerable by the crash, and so will a good many folks. Everything will have to go—Peter Baxter's farm and Lige's grand new house. Mrs. Peter won't carry her head so high after this, I'll be bound. George saw Lige at the Bridge, and he said he looked dreadful cut up and ashamed."

"Who, or what's to blame for the failure?" asked Mrs. Rachel Lynde sharply. She did not like Mrs. George Pye.

"There are a dozen different stories on the go," was the reply. "As far as George could make out, Peter Baxter has been speculating with other folks' money, and this is the result. Everybody always suspected that Peter was crooked; but you'd have thought that Lige would have kept him straight. *He* had always such a reputation for saintliness."

"I don't suppose Lige knew anything about it," said Mrs. Rachel indignantly.

"Well, he'd ought to, then. If he isn't a knave he's a fool," said Mrs. Harmon Andrews, who had formerly been among his warmest partisans. "He should have kept watch on Peter and found out how the business was being run. Well, Sara, you were the level-headest of us all—I'll admit that now. A nice mess it would be if you were married or engaged to Lige, and him left without a cent—even if he can clear his character!"

"There is a good deal of talk about Peter, and swindling,

and a lawsuit," said Mrs. George Pye, quilting industriously. "Most of the Newbridge folks think it's all Peter's fault, and that Lige isn't to blame. But you can't tell. I dare say Lige is as deep in the mire as Peter. He was always a little too good to be wholesome, *I* thought."

There was a clink of glass at the cupboard, as Sara set the tray down. She came forward and stood behind Mrs. Rachel Lynde's chair, resting her shapely hands on that lady's broad shoulders. Her face was very pale, but her flashing eyes sought and faced defiantly Mrs. George Pye's cat-like orbs. Her voice quivered with passion and contempt.

"You'll all have a fling at Lige Baxter, now that he's down. You couldn't say enough in his praise, once. I'll not stand by and hear it hinted that Lige Baxter is a swindler. You all know perfectly well that Lige is as honest as the day, if he *is* so unfortunate as to have an unprincipled brother. You, Mrs. Pye, know it better than any one, yet you come here and run him down the minute he's in trouble. If there's another word said here against Lige Baxter I'll leave the room and the house till you're gone, every one of you."

She flashed a glance around the quilt that cowed the gossips. Even Mrs. George Pye's eyes flickered and waned and quailed. Nothing more was said until Sara had picked up her glasses and marched from the room. Even then they dared not speak above a whisper. Mrs. Pye, alone, smarting from her snub, ventured to ejaculate, "Pity save us!" as Sara slammed the door.

For the next fortnight gossip and rumor held high carnival in Avonlea and Newbridge, and Mrs. Eben grew to dread the sight of a visitor.

"They're bound to talk about the Baxter failure and criticize Lige," she deplored to Mrs. Jonas. "And it riles Sara up so terrible. She used to declare that she hated Lige, and now she won't listen to a word against him. Not that I say any, myself. I'm sorry for him, and I believe he's done his best. But I can't stop other people from talking."

One evening Harmon Andrews came in with a fresh budget of news.

"The Baxter business is pretty near wound up at last," he said, as he lighted his pipe. "Peter has got his lawsuits settled

and has hushed up the talk about swindling, somehow. Trust
him for slipping out of a scrape clean and clever. He don't
seem to worry any, but Lige looks like a walking skeleton.
Some folks pity him, but I say he should have kept the run
of things better and not have trusted everything to Peter. I hear
he's going out West in the Spring, to take up land in Alberta
and try his hand at farming. Best thing he can do, I guess.
Folks hereabouts have had enough of the Baxter breed. Newbridge will be well rid of them."

Sara, who had been sitting in the dark corner by the stove,
suddenly stood up, letting the black cat slip from her lap to
the floor. Mrs. Eben glanced at her apprehensively, for she was
afraid the girl was going to break out into a tirade against the
complacent Harmon.

But Sara only walked fiercely out of the kitchen, with a
sound as if she were struggling for breath. In the hall she
snatched a scarf from the wall, flung open the front door, and
rushed down the lane in the chill, pure air of the autumn
twilight. Her heart was throbbing with the pity she always felt
for bruised and baited creatures.

On and on she went heedlessly, intent only on walking away
her pain, over gray, brooding fields and winding slopes, and
along the skirts of ruinous, dusky pine woods, curtained with
fine spun purple gloom. Her dress brushed against the brittle
grasses and sere ferns, and the moist night wind, loosed from
wild places far away, blew her hair about her face.

At last she came to a little rustic gate, leading into a shadowy
wood-lane. The gate was bound with willow withes, and, as
Sara fumbled vainly at them with her chilled hands, a man's
firm step came up behind her, and Lige Baxter's hand closed
over her's.

"Oh, Lige!" she said, with something like a sob.

He opened the gate and drew her through. She left her hand
in his, as they walked through the lane where lissome boughs
of young saplings flicked against their heads, and the air was
wildly sweet with the woodsy odors.

"It's a long while since I've seen you, Lige," Sara said at
last.

Lige looked wistfully down at her through the gloom.

"Yes, it seems very long to me, Sara. But I didn't think

you'd care to see me, after what you said last spring. And you know things have been going against me. People have said hard things. I've been unfortunate, Sara, and may be too easy-going, but I've been honest. Don't believe folks if they tell you I wasn't."

"Indeed, I never did—not for a minute!" fired Sara.

"I'm glad of that. I'm going away, later on. I felt bad enough when you refused to marry me, Sara; but it's well that you didn't. I'm man enough to be thankful my troubles don't fall on you."

Sara stopped and turned to him. Beyond them the lane opened into a field and a clear lake of crocus sky cast a dim light into the shadow where they stood. Above it was a new moon, like a gleaming silver scimitar. Sara saw it was over her left shoulder, and she saw Lige's face above her, tender and troubled.

"Lige," she said softly, "do you love me still?"

"You know I do," said Lige sadly.

That was all Sara wanted. With a quick movement she nestled into his arms, and laid her warm, tear-wet cheek against his cold one.

When the amazing rumor that Sara was going to marry Lige Baxter, and go out West with him, circulated through the Andrews clan, hands were lifted and heads were shaken. Mrs. Jonas puffed and panted up the hill to learn if it were true. She found Mrs. Eben stitching for dear life on an "Irish Chain" quilt, while Sara was sewing the diamonds on another "Rising Star" with a martyr-like expression on her face. Sara hated patchwork above everything else, but Mrs. Eben was mistress up to a certain point.

"You'll have to make that quilt, Sara Andrews. If you're going to live out on those prairies, you'll need piles of quilts, and you shall have them if I sew my fingers to the bone. But you'll have to help make them."

And Sara had to.

When Mrs. Jonas came, Mrs. Eben sent Sara off to the post-office to get her out of the way.

"I suppose it's true, this time?" said Mrs. Jonas.

"Yes, indeed," said Mrs. Eben briskly. "Sara is set on it. There is no use trying to move her—you know that—so I've just concluded to make the best of it. I'm no turn-coat. Lige

Baxter is Lige Baxter still, neither more nor less. I've always said he was a fine young man, and I say so still. After all, he and Sara won't be any poorer than Eben and I were when we started out."

Mrs. Jonas heaved a sigh of relief.

"I'm real glad you take that view of it, Louisa. I'm not displeased, either, although Mrs. Harmon would take my head off if she heard me say so. I always liked Lige. But I must say I'm amazed, too, after the way Sara used to rail at him."

"Well we might have expected it," said Mrs. Eben sagely. "It was always Sara's way. When any creature got sick or unfortunate she seemed to take it right into her heart. So you may say Lige Baxter's failure was a success after all."

THE SON OF HIS MOTHER

THYRA CAREWE was waiting for Chester to come home. She sat by the west window of the kitchen, looking out into the gathering of the shadows with the expectant immovability that characterized her. She never twitched or fidgeted. Into whatever she did she put the whole force of her nature. If it was sitting still, she sat still.

"A stone image would be twitchedly beside Thyra," said Mrs. Cynthia White, her neighbor across the lane. "It gets on my nerves, the way she sits at that window sometimes, with no more motion than a statue and her great eyes burning down the lane. When I read the commandment, 'Thou shalt have no other gods before me,' I declare I always think of Thyra. She worships that son of hers far ahead of her Creator. She'll be punished for it yet."

Mrs. White was watching Thyra now, knitting furiously, as she watched, in order to lose no time. Thyra's hands were folded idly in her lap. She had not moved a muscle since she sat down. Mrs. White complained that it gave her the weeps.

"It doesn't seem natural to see a woman sit so still," she said. "Sometimes the thought comes to me, 'what if she's had a stroke, like her old Uncle Horatio, and is sitting there stone dead!'"

487

The evening was cold and autumnal. There was a fiery red spot out at sea, where the sun had set, and, above it, over a chill, clear, saffron sky, were reefs of purple-black clouds. The river, below the Carewe homestead, was livid. Beyond it, the sea was dark and brooding. It was an evening to make most people shiver and forebode an early winter; but Thyra loved it, as she loved all stern, harshly beautiful things. She would not light a lamp because it would blot out the savage grandeur of sea and sky. It was better to wait in the darkness until Chester came home.

He was late tonight. She thought he had been detained over-time at the harbor, but she was not anxious. He would come straight home to her as soon as his business was completed—of that she felt sure. Her thoughts went out along the bleak harbor road to meet him. She could see him plainly, coming with his free stride through the sandy hollows and over the windy hills, in the harsh, cold light of that forbidding sunset, strong and handsome in his comely youth, with her own deeply cleft chin and his father's dark gray, straightforward eyes. No other woman in Avonlea had a son like hers—her only one. In his brief absences she yearned after him with a maternal passion that had in it something of physical pain, so intense was it. She thought of Cynthia White, knitting across the road, with contemptuous pity. That woman had no son—nothing but pale-faced girls. Thyra had never wanted a daughter, but she pitied and despised all sonless women.

Chester's dog whined suddenly and piercingly on the doorstep outside. He was tired of the cold stone and wanted his warm corner behind the stove. Thyra smiled grimly when she heard him. She had no intention of letting him in. She said she had always disliked dogs, but the truth, although she would not glance at it, was that she hated the animal because Chester loved him. She could not share his love with even a dumb brute. She loved no living creature in the world but her son, and fiercely demanded a like concentrated affection from him. Hence it pleased her to hear his dog whine.

It was now quite dark; the stars had begun to shine out over the shorn harvest fields, and Chester had not come. Across the lane Cynthia White had pulled down her blind, in despair of out-watching Thyra, and had lighted a lamp. Lively shadows of little girl-shapes passed and repassed on the pale oblong of light. They made Thyra conscious of her exceeding loneliness. She had just decided that she would walk down the lane and wait for Chester on the bridge, when a thunderous knock came at the east kitchen door.

She recognized August Vorst's knock and lighted a lamp in no great haste, for she did not like him. He was a gossip and Thyra hated gossip, in man or woman. But August was privileged.

She carried the lamp in her hand, when she went to the door, and its upward-striking light gave her face a ghastly appearance. She did not mean to ask August in, but he pushed past her cheerfully, not waiting to be invited. He was a midget of a man, lame of foot and hunched of back, with a white, boyish face, despite his middle age and deep-set, malicious black eyes.

He pulled a crumpled newspaper from his pocket and handed it to Thyra. He was the unofficial mailcarrier of Avonlea. Most of the people gave him a trifle for bringing their letters and papers from the office. He earned small sums in various other ways, and so contrived to keep the life in his stunted body. There was always venom in August's gossip. It was said that he made more mischief in Avonlea in a day than was made otherwise in a year, but people tolerated him by reason of his infirmity. To be sure, it was the tolerance they gave to inferior creatures, and August felt this. Perhaps it accounted for a good deal of his malignity. He hated most those who were kindest to him, and, of these, Thyra Carewe above all. He hated Chester, too, as he hated strong, shapely creatures. His time had come at last to wound them both, and his exultation shone through his crooked body and pinched features like an illuminating lamp. Thyra perceived it and vaguely felt something antagonistic in it. She pointed to the rocking-chair, as she might have pointed out a mat to a dog.

August crawled into it and smiled. He was going to make her writhe presently, this woman who looked down upon him as some venomous creeping thing she disdained to crush with her foot.

"Did you see anything of Chester on the road?" asked Thyra, giving August the very opening he desired. "He went to the harbor after tea to see Joe Raymond about the loan of his boat, but it's past the time he should be back. I can't think what keeps the boy."

"Just what keeps most men—leaving out creatures like me—at some time or other in their lives. A girl—a pretty girl, Thyra. It pleases me to look at her. Even a hunchback can use his eyes, eh? Oh, she's a rare one!"

"What is the man talking about?" said Thyra wonderingly.

"Damaris Garland, to be sure. Chester's down at Tom Blair's now, talking to her—and looking more than his tongue says, too, of that you may be sure. Well, well, we were all young once, Thyra—all young once, even crooked little August Vorst. Eh, now?"

"What do you mean?" said Thyra.

She had sat down in a chair before him, with her hands folded in her lap. Her face, always pale, had not changed; but her lips were curiously white. August Vorst saw this and it pleased him. Also, her eyes were worth looking at, if you liked to hurt people—and that was the only pleasure August took in life. He would drink this delightful cup of revenge for her long years of disdainful kindness—Ah, he would drink it slowly to prolong its sweetness. Sip by sip—he rubbed his long, thin, white hands together—sip by sip, tasting each mouthful.

"Eh, now? You know well enough, Thyra."

"I know nothing of what you would be at, August Vorst. You speak of my son and Damaris—was that the name?—Damaris Garland as if they were something to each other. I ask you what you mean by it?"

"Tut, tut, Thyra, nothing very terrible. There's no need to look like that about it. Young men will be young men to the end of time, and there's no harm in Chester's liking to look at a lass, eh, now? Or in talking to her either? The little baggage, with the red lips of her! She and Chester will make a pretty pair. He's not so ill-looking for a man, Thyra."

"I am not a very patient woman, August," said Thyra coldly. "I have asked you what you mean, and I want a straight answer. Is Chester down at Tom Blair's while I have been sitting here, alone, waiting for him?"

August nodded. He saw that it would not be wise to trifle longer with Thyra.

"That he is. I was there before I came here. He and Damaris were sitting in a corner by themselves, and very well-satisfied they seemed to be with each other. Tut, tut, Thyra, don't take the news so. I thought you knew. It's no secret that Chester has been going after Damaris ever since she came here. But what then? You can't tie him to your apron strings forever, woman. He'll be finding a mate for himself, as he should. Seeing that he's straight and well-shaped, no doubt Damaris will look with favor on him. Old Martha Blair declares the girl loves him better than her eyes."

Thyra made a sound like a strangled moan in the middle of August's speech. She heard the rest of it inmovably. When it came to an end she stood up and looked down upon him in a way that silenced him.

"You've told the news you came to tell, and gloated over it, and now get you gone," she said slowly.

"Now, Thyra," he began, but she interrupted him threateningly.

"Get you gone, I say! And you need not bring my mail here any longer. I want no more of your misshapen body and lying tongue!"

August went, but at the door he turned for a parting stab.

"My tongue is not a lying one, Mrs. Carewe. I've told you the truth, as all Avonlea knows it. Chester is mad about Damaris Garland. It's no wonder I thought you knew what all the settlement can see. But you're such a jealous, odd body, I suppose the boy hid it from you for fear you'd go into a tantrum. As for me, I'll not forget that you've turned me from your door because I chanced to bring you news you'd no fancy for."

Thyra did not answer him. When the door closed behind him she locked it and blew out the light. Then she threw herself face downward on the sofa and burst into wild tears. Her very soul ached. She wept as tempestuously and unreasoningly as youth weeps, although she was not young. It seemed as if she was afraid to stop weeping lest she should go mad thinking. But, after a time, tears failed her, and she began bitterly to go over, word by word, what August Vorst had said.

That her son should ever cast eyes of love on any girl was something Thyra had never thought about. She would not believe it possible that he should love any one but herself, who loved him so much. And now the possibility invaded her mind as subtly and coldly and remorselessly as a sea-fog stealing landward.

Chester had been born to her at an age when most women are letting their children slip from them into the world, with some natural tears and heartaches, but content to let them go, after enjoying their sweetest years. Thyra's late-come motherhood was all the more intense and passionate because of its very lateness. She had been very ill when her son was born, and had lain helpless for long weeks, during which other women had tended her baby for her. She had never been able to forgive them for this.

Her husband had died before Chester was a year old. She had laid their son in his dying arms and received him back again with a last benediction. To Thyra that moment had something of a sacrament in it. It was as if the child had been doubly given to her, with a right to him solely that nothing could take away or transcend.

Marrying! She had never thought of it in connection with him. He did not come of a marrying race. His father had been sixty when he had married her, Thyra Lincoln, likewise well on in life. Few of the Lincolns or Carewes had married young, many not at all. And, to her, Chester was her baby still. He belonged solely to her.

And now another woman had dared to look upon him with eyes of love. Damaris Garland! Thyra now remembered seeing her. She was a new-comer in Avonlea, having come to live with her uncle and aunt after the death of her mother. Thyra had met her on the bridge one day a month previously. Yes, a man might think she was pretty—a low-browed girl, with a wave of reddish-gold hair, and crimson lips blossoming out against the strange, milk-whiteness of her skin. Her eyes, too— Thyra recalled them—hazel in tint, deep, and laughter-brimmed.

The girl had gone past her with a smile that brought out many dimples. There was a certain insolent quality in her beauty, as if it flaunted itself somewhat too defiantly in the beholder's eye. Thyra had turned and looked after the lithe, young creature, wondering who she might be.

And tonight, while she, his mother, waited for him in darkness and loneliness, he was down at Blairs', talking to this girl! He loved her; and it was past doubt that she loved him. The thought was more bitter than death to Thyra. That she should dare! Her anger was all against the girl. She had laid a snare to get Chester and he, like a fool, was entangled in it, thinking, man-fashion, only of her great eyes and red lips. Thyra thought savagely of Damaris' beauty.

"She shall not have him," she said, with slow emphasis. "I will never give him up to any other woman, and, least of all, to her. She would leave me no place in his heart at all—me, his mother, who almost died to give him life. He belongs to me! Let her look for the son of some other woman—some woman who has many sons. She shall not have my only one!"

She got up, wrapped a shawl about her head, and went out into the darkly golden evening. The clouds had cleared away, and the moon was shining. The air was chill, with a bell-like clearness. The alders by the river rustled eerily as she walked by them and out upon the bridge. Here she paced up and down, peering with troubled eyes along the road beyond, or leaning over the rail, looking at the sparkling silver ribbon of moonlight that garlanded the waters. Late travelers passed her, and wondered at her presence and mien. Carl White saw her, and told his wife about her when he got home.

"Striding to and fro over the bridge like mad! At first I thought it was old, crazy May Blair. What do you suppose she was doing down there at this hour of the night?"

"Watching for Ches, no doubt," said Cynthia. "He ain't home yet. Likely he's snug at Blairs'. I do wonder if Thyra suspicions that he goes after Damaris. I've never dared to hint it to her. She'd be as liable to fly at me, tooth and claw, as not."

"Well, she picks out a precious queer night for moon-gazing," said Carl, who was a jolly soul and took life as he found it. "It's bitter cold—there'll be a hard frost. It's a pity she can't get it grained into her that the boy is grown up and must have his fling like other lads. She'll go out of her mind yet, like her old grandmother Lincoln, if she doesn't ease up. I've a notion to go down to the bridge and reason a bit with her."

"Indeed, and you'll do no such thing!" cried Cynthia. "Thyra Carewe is best left alone, if she is in a tantrum. She's like no other woman in Avonlea—or out of it. I'd as soon meddle with a tiger as her, if she's rampaging about Chester. I don't envy Damaris Garland her life if she goes in there. Thyra'd sooner strangle her than not, I guess."

"You women are all terrible hard on Thyra," said Carl, good-naturedly. He had been in love with Thyra, himself, long ago, and he still liked her in a friendly fashion. He always stood up for her when the Avonlea women ran her down. He felt troubled about her all night, recalling her as she paced the bridge. He wished he had gone back, in spite of Cynthia.

When Chester came home he met his mother on the bridge. In the faint, yet penetrating, moonlight they looked curiously alike, but Chester had the milder face. He was very handsome. Even in the seething of her pain and jealousy Thyra yearned over his beauty. She would have liked to put up her hands and caress his face, but her voice was very hard when she asked him where he had been so late.

"I called in at Tom Blair's on my way home from the harbor," he answered, trying to walk on. But she held him back by his arm.

"Did you go there to see Damaris?" she demanded fiercely.

Chester was uncomfortable. Much as he loved his mother, he felt, and always had felt, an awe of her and an impatient dislike of her dramatic ways of speaking and acting. He reflected, resentfully, that no other young man in Avonlea, who had been paying a friendly call, would be met by his mother at midnight and held up in such tragic fashion to account for himself. He tried vainly to loosen her hold upon his arm, but he understood quite well that he must give her an answer. Being strictly straightforward by nature and upbringing, he told the truth, albeit with more anger in his tone than he had ever shown to his mother before.

"Yes," he said shortly.

Thyra released his arm, and struck her hands together with a sharp cry. There was a savage note in it. She could have slain Damaris Garland at that moment.

"Don't go on so, mother," said Chester, impatiently. "Come in out of the cold. It isn't fit for you to be here. Who has been tampering with you? What if I did go to see Damaris?"

"Oh—oh—oh!" cried Thyra. "I was waiting for you—alone— and you were thinking only of her! Chester, answer me—do you love her?"

The blood rolled rapidly over the boy's face. He muttered something and tried to pass on, but she caught him again. He forced himself to speak gently.

"What if I do, mother? It wouldn't be such a dreadful thing, would it?"

"And me? And me?" cried Thyra. "What am I to you, then?"

"You are my mother. I wouldn't love you any the less because I cared for another, too."

"I won't have you love another," she cried. "I want all your love—all! What's that baby-face to you, compared to your mother? I have the best right to you. I won't give you up."

Chester realized that there was no arguing with such a mood. He walked on, resolved to set the matter aside until she might be more reasonable. But Thyra would not have it so. She followed on after him, under the alders that crowded over the lane.

"Promise me that you'll not go there again," she entreated. "Promise me that you'll give her up."

"I can't promise such a thing," he cried angrily.

His anger hurt her worse than a blow, but she did not flinch.

"You're not engaged to her?" she cried out.

"Now, mother, be quiet. All the settlement will hear you. Why do you object to Damaris? You don't know how sweet she is. When you do know her—"

"I will never know her!" cried Thyra furiously. "And she shall not have you! She shall not, Chester!"

He made no answer. She suddenly broke into tears and loud sobs. Touched with remorse, he stopped and put his arms about her.

"Mother, mother, don't! I can't bear to see you cry so. But, indeed, you are unreasonable. Didn't you ever think the time would come when I would want to marry, like other men?"

"No, no! And I will not have it—I cannot bear it, Chester. You must promise not to go to see her again. I won't go into the house this night until you do. I'll stay out here in the bitter cold until you promise to put her out of your thoughts."

"That's beyond my power, mother. Oh, mother, you're making it hard for me. Come in, come in! You're shivering with cold now. You'll be sick."

"Not a step will I stir till you promise. Say you won't go to see that girl any more, and there's nothing I won't do for you. But, if you put her before me, I'll not go in—I never will go in."

With most women this would have been an empty threat; but it was not so with Thyra, and Chester knew it. He knew she would keep her word. And he feared more than that. In this frenzy of hers what might she not do? She came of a strange breed, as had been said disapprovingly when Luke Carewe married her. There was a strain of insanity in the Lincolns. A Lincoln woman had drowned herself once. Chester thought of the river, and grew sick with fright. For a moment even his passion for Damaris weakened before the older tie.

"Mother, calm yourself. Oh, surely there's no need of all this! Let us wait until tomorrow, and talk it over then. I'll hear all you have to say. Come in, dear."

Thyra loosened her arms from about him, and stepped back into a moon-lit space. Looking at him tragically, she extended her arms and spoke slowly and solemnly.

"Chester, choose between us. If you choose her, I shall go from you tonight, and you will never see me again!"

"Mother!"

"Choose!" she reiterated, fiercely.

He felt her long ascendancy. Its influence was not to be shaken off in a moment. In all his life he had never disobeyed her. Besides, with it all, he loved her more deeply and under-standingly than most sons love their mothers. He realized that, since she would have it so, his choice was already made—or, rather that he had no choice.

"Have your way," he said sullenly.

She ran to him and caught him to her heart. In the reaction of her feeling she was half laughing, half crying. All was well again—all would be well; she never doubted this, for she knew he would keep his ungracious promise sacredly.

"Oh, my son, my son," she murmured, "you'd have sent me to my death if you had chosen otherwise. But now you are mine again!"

She did not heed that he was sullen—that he resented her

unjustice with all her own intensity. She did not heed his silence as they went into the house together. Strangely enough, she slept well and soundly that night. Not until many days had passed did she understand that, though Chester might keep his promise in the letter, it was beyond his power to keep it in the spirit. She had taken him from Damaris Garland; but she had not won him back to herself. He could never be wholly her son again. There was a barrier between them which not all her passionate love could break down. Chester was gravely kind to her, for it was not in his nature to remain sullen long, or visit his own unhappiness upon another's head; besides, he understood her exacting affection, even in its injustice, and it has been well-said that to understand is to forgive. But he avoided her, and she knew it. The flame of her anger burned bitterly towards Damaris.

"He thinks of her all the time," she moaned to herself. "He'll come to hate me yet, I fear, because it's I who made him give her up. But I'd rather even that than share him with another woman. Oh, my son, my son!"

She knew that Damaris was suffering, too. The girl's wan face told that when she met her. But this pleased Thyra. It eased the ache in her bitter heart to know that pain was gnawing at Damaris' also.

Chester was absent from home very often now. He spent much of his spare time at the harbor, consorting with Joe Raymond and others of that ilk, who were but sorry associates for him, Avonlea people thought.

In late November he and Joe started for a trip down the coast in the latter's boat. Thyra protested against it, but Chester laughed at her alarm.

Thyra saw him go with a heart sick from fear. She hated the sea, and was afraid of it at any time; but, most of all, in this treacherous month, with its sudden, wild gales.

Chester had been fond of the sea from boyhood. She had always tried to stifle this fondness and break off his associations with the harbor fishermen, who liked to lure the high-spirited boy out with them on fishing expeditions. But her power over him was gone now.

After Chester's departure she was restless and miserable, wandering from window to window to scan the dour, unsmiling sky. Carl White, dropping in to pay a call, was alarmed when he heard that Chester had gone with Joe, and had not tact enough to conceal his alarm from Thyra.

" 'T isn't safe this time of year," he said. "Folks expect no better from that reckless, harum-scarum Joe Raymond. He'll drown himself some day, there's nothing surer. This mad freak of starting off down the shore in November is just of a piece with his usual performances. But you shouldn't have let Chester go, Thyra."

"I couldn't prevent him. Say what I could, he would go. He laughed when I spoke of danger. Oh, he's changed from what he was! I know who has wrought the change, and I hate her for it!"

Carl shrugged his fat shoulders. He knew quite well that Thyra was at the bottom of the sudden coldness between Chester Carewe and Damaris Garland, about which Avonlea gossip was busying itself. He pitied Thyra, too. She had aged rapidly the past month.

"You're too hard on Chester, Thyra. He's out of leading-strings now, or should be. You must just let me take an old friend's privilege, and tell you that you're taking the wrong way with him. You're too jealous and exacting, Thyra."

"You don't know anything about it. You have never had a son," said Thyra, cruelly enough, for she knew that Carl's sonlessness was a rankling thorn in his mind. "You don't know what it is to pour out your love on one human being, and have it flung back in your face!"

Carl could not cope with Thyra's moods. He had never understood her, even in youth. Now he went home, still shrugging his shoulders, and thinking that it was a good thing Thyra had not looked on him with favor in the old days. Cynthia was much easier to get along with.

More than Thyra looked anxiously to sea and sky that night in Avonlea. Damaris Garland listened to the smothered roar of the Atlantic in the murky northeast with a prescience of coming disaster. Friendly longshoremen shook their heads and said that Ches and Joe would better have kept to good, dry land.

"It's sorry work joking with a November gale," said Abel Blair. He was an old man and, in his life, had seen some sad things along the shore.

Thyra could not sleep that night. When the gale came shrieking up the river, and struck the house, she got out of bed and dressed herself. The wind screamed like a ravening beast at her window. All night she wandered to and fro in the house, going from room to room, now wringing her hands with loud outcries, now praying below her breath with white lips, now listening in dumb misery to the fury of the storm.

The wind raged all the next day; but spent itself in the following night, and the second morning was calm and fair. The eastern sky was a great arc of crystal, smitten through with auroral crimsonings. Thyra, looking from her kitchen window, saw a group of men on the bridge. They were talking to Carl White, with looks and gestures directed towards the Carewe house.

She went out and down to them. None of these who saw her white, rigid face that day ever forgot the sight.

"You have news for me," she said.

They looked at each other, each man mutely imploring his neighbor to speak.

"You need not fear to tell me," said Thyra calmly. "I know what you have come to say. My son is drowned."

"We don't know *that,* Mrs. Carewe," said Abel Blair quickly. "We haven't got the worst to tell you—there's hope yet. But Joe Raymond's boat was found last night, stranded, bottom up, on the Blue Point sand shore, forty miles down the coast."

"Don't look like that, Thyra," said Carl White pityingly. "They may have escaped—they may have been picked up."

Thyra looked at him with dull eyes.

"You know they have not. Not one of you has any hope. I have no son. The sea has taken him from me—my bonny baby!"

She turned and went back to her desolate home. None dared to follow her. Carl White went home and sent his wife over to her.

Cynthia found Thyra sitting in her accustomed chair. Her hands lay, palms upward, on her lap. Her eyes were dry and burning. She met Cynthia's compassionate look with a fearful smile.

"Long ago, Cynthia White," she said slowly, "you were vexed with me one day, and you told me that God would punish me yet, because I made an idol of my son, and set it up in

His place. Do you remember? Your word was a true one. God saw that I loved Chester too much, and He meant to take him from me. I thwarted one way when I made him give up Damaris. But one can't fight against the Almighty. It was decreed that I must lose him—if not in one way, then in another. He has been taken from me utterly. I shall not even have his grave to tend, Cynthia."

"As near to a mad woman as anything you ever saw, with her awful eyes," Cynthia told Carl, afterwards. But she did not say so there. Although she was a shallow, commonplace soul, she had her share of womanly sympathy, and her own life had not been free from suffering. It taught her the right thing to do now. She sat down by the stricken creature and put her arms about her, while she gathered the cold hands in her own warm clasp. The tears filled her big blue eyes and her voice trembled as she said:

"Thyra, I'm sorry for you. I—I—lost a child once—my little first-born. And Chester was a dear, good lad."

For a moment Thyra strained her small, tense body away from Cynthia's embrace. Then she shuddered and cried out. The tears came, and she wept her agony out on the other woman's breast.

As the ill news spread, other Avonlea women kept dropping in all through the day to condole with Thyra. Many of them came in real sympathy, but some out of mere curiosity to see how she took it. Thyra knew this, but she did not resent it, as she would once have done. She listened very quietly to all the halting efforts at consolation, and the little platitudes with which they strove to cover the nakedness of bereavement.

When darkness came Cynthia said she must go home, but would send one of her girls over for the night.

"You won't feel like staying alone," she said.

Thyra looked up steadily.

"No. But I want you to send for Damaris Garland."

"Damaris Garland!" Cynthia repeated the name as if disbelieving her own ears. There was never any knowing what whim Thyra might take, but Cynthia had not expected this.

"Yes. Tell her I want her—tell her she must come. She must hate me bitterly; but I am punished enough to satisfy even her hate. Tell her to come to me for Chester's sake."

Cynthia did as she was bid, she sent her daughter, Jeanette, for Damaris. Then she waited. No matter what duties were calling for her at home she must see the interview between Thyra and Damaris. Her curiosity would be the last thing to fail Cynthia White. She had done very well all day; but it would be asking too much of her to expect that she would consider the meeting of these two women sacred from her eyes.

She half believed that Damaris would refuse to come. But Damaris came. Jeanette brought her in amid the fiery glow of a November sunset. Thyra stood up, and for a moment they looked at each other.

The insolence of Damaris' beauty was gone. Her eyes were dull and heavy with weeping, her lips were pale, and her face had lost its laughter and dimples. Only her hair, escaping from the shawl she had cast around it, gushed forth in warm splendor in the sunset light, and framed her wan face like the aureole of a Madonna. Thyra looked upon her with a shock of remorse. This was not the radiant creature she had met on the bridge that summer afternoon. This—this—was *her* work. She held out her arms.

"Oh, Damaris, forgive me. We both loved him—that must be a bond between us for life."

Damaris came forward and threw her arms about the older woman, lifting her face. As their lips met even Cynthia White realized that she had no business there. She vented the irritation of her embarrassment on the innocent Jeanette.

"Come away," she whispered crossly. "Can't you see we're not wanted here?"

She drew Jeanette out, leaving Thyra rocking Damaris in her arms, and crooning over her like a mother over her child.

When December had grown old Damaris was still with Thyra. It was understood that she was to remain there for the winter, at least. Thyra could not bear her to be out of her sight. They talked constantly about Chester; Thyra confessed all her anger and hatred. Damaris had forgiven her; but Thyra could never forgive herself. She was greatly changed, and had grown very gentle and tender. She even sent for August Vorst and begged him to pardon her for the way she had spoken to him.

Winter came late that year, and the season was a very open one. There was no snow on the ground and, a month after

Joe Raymond's boat had been cast up on the Blue Point sand shore, Thyra, wandering about in her garden, found some pansies blooming under their tangled leaves. She was picking them for Damaris when she heard a buggy rumble over the bridge and drive up the White lane, hidden from her sight by the alders and firs. A few minutes later Carl and Cynthia came hastily across their yard under the huge balm-of-gileads. Carl's face was flushed, and his big body quivered with excitement. Cynthia ran behind him, with tears rolling down her face.

Thyra felt herself growing sick with fear. Had anything happened to Damaris? A glimpse of the girl, sewing by an upper window of the house, reassured her.

"Oh, Thyra, Thyra!" gasped Cynthia.

"Can you stand some good news, Thyra?" asked Carl, in a trembling voice. "Very, very good news!"

Thyra looked wildly from one to the other.

"There's but one thing you would dare to call good news to me," she cried. "Is it about—about—"

"Chester! Yes, it's about Chester! Thyra, he is alive—he's safe—he and Joe, both of them, thank God! Cynthia, catch her!"

"No, I am not going to faint," said Thyra, steadying herself by Cynthia's shoulder. "My son alive! How did you hear? How did it happen? Where has he been?"

"I heard it down at the harbor, Thyra. Mike McCready's vessel, the *Nora Lee,* was just in from the Magdalens. Ches and Joe got capsized the night of the storm, but they hung on to their boat somehow, and at daybreak they were picked up by the *Nora Lee,* bound for Quebec. But she was damaged by the storm and blown clear out of her course. Had to put into the Magdalens for repairs, and has been there ever since. The cable to the islands was out of order, and no vessels call there this time of year for mails. If it hadn't been an extra open season the *Nora Lee* wouldn't have got away, but would have had to stay there till spring. You never saw such rejoicing as there was this morning at the harbor, when the *Nora Lee* came in, flying flags at the mast head."

"And Chester—where is he?" demanded Thyra.

Carl and Cynthia looked at each other.

"Well, Thyra," said the latter, "the fact is, he's over there in our yard this blessed minute. Carl brought him home from the harbor, but I wouldn't let him come over until we had prepared you for it. He's waiting for you there."

Thyra made a quick step in the direction of the gate. Then she turned, with a little of the glow dying out of her face.

"No, there's one has a better right to go to him first. I can atone to him—thank God, I can atone to him!"

She went into the house and called Damaris. As the girl came down the stairs Thyra held out her hands with a wonderful light of joy and renunciation on her face.

"Damaris," she said, "Chester has come back to us—the sea has given him back to us. He is over at Carl White's house. Go to him, my daughter, and bring him to me!"

THE EDUCATION OF BETTY

WHEN SARA CURRIE married Jack Churchill I was broken-hearted . . . or believed myself to be so, which, in a boy of twenty-two, amounts to pretty much the same thing. Not that I took the world into my confidence; that was never the Douglas way, and I held myself in honor bound to live up to the family traditions. I thought, then, that nobody but Sara knew; but I dare say, now, that Jack knew it also, for I don't think Sara could have helped telling him. If he did know, however, he did not let me see that he did, and never insulted me by any implied sympathy; on the contrary, he asked me to be his best man. Jack was always a thoroughbred.

I was best man. Jack and I had always been bosom friends, and, although I had lost my sweetheart, I did not intend to lose my friend into the bargain. Sara had made a wise choice, for Jack was twice the man I was; he had had to work for his living, which perhaps accounts for it.

So I danced at Sara's wedding as if my heart were as light as my heels; but, after she and Jack had settled down at Glenby I closed The Maples and went abroad . . . being, as I have hinted, one of those unfortunate mortals who need consult nothing but their own whims in the matter of time and money. I stayed away for ten years, during which The Maples was given

504

over to moth and rust, while I enjoyed life elsewhere. I did enjoy it hugely, but always under protest, for I felt that a broken-hearted man ought not to enjoy himself as I did. It jarred on my sense of fitness, and I tried to moderate my zest, and think more of the past than I did. It was no use; the present insisted on being intrusive and pleasant; as for the future . . . well, there was no future.

Then Jack Churchill, poor fellow, died. A year after his death, I went home and again asked Sara to marry me, as in duty bound. Sara again declined, alleging that her heart was buried in Jack's grave, or words to that effect. I found that it did not much matter . . . of course, at thirty-two one does not take these things to heart as at twenty-two. I had enough to occupy me in getting The Maples into working order, and beginning to educate Betty.

Betty was Sara's ten-year-old daughter, and she had been thoroughly spoiled. That is to say, she had been allowed her own way in everything and, having inherited her father's outdoor tastes, had simply run wild. She was a thorough tomboy, a thin, scrawny little thing without a trace of Sara's beauty. Betty took after her father's dark, tall race and, on the occasion of my first introduction to her, seemed to be all legs and neck. There were points about her, though, which I considered promising. She had fine, almond-shaped, hazel eyes, the smallest and most shapely hands and feet I ever saw, and two enormous braids of thick, nut-brown hair.

For Jack's sake I decided to bring his daughter up properly. Sara couldn't do it, and didn't try. I saw that, if somebody didn't take Betty in hand, wisely and firmly, she would certainly be ruined. There seemed to be nobody except myself at all interested in the matter, so I determined to see what an old bachelor could do as regards bringing up a girl in the way she should go. I might have been her father; as it was, her father had been my best friend. Who had a better right to watch over his daughter? I determined to be a father to Betty, and do all for her that the most devoted parent could do. It was, self-evidently, my duty.

I told Sara I was going to take Betty in hand. Sara sighed one of the plaintive little sighs which I had once thought so charming, but now, to my surprise, found faintly irritating, and said that she would be very much obliged if I would.

"I feel that I am not able to cope with the problem of Betty's education, Stephen," she admitted. "Betty is a strange child . . . all Churchill. Her poor father indulged her in everything, and she has a will of her own, I assure you. I have really no control over her, whatever. She does as she pleases, and is ruining her complexion by running and galloping out of doors the whole time. Not that she had much complexion to start with. The Churchills never had, you know." . . . Sara cast a complacent glance at her delicately tinted reflection in the mirror. . . . "I tried to make Betty wear a sunbonnet this summer, but I might as well have talked to the wind."

A vision of Betty in a sunbonnet presented itself to my mind, and afforded me so much amusement that I was grateful to Sara for having furnished it. I rewarded her with a compliment.

"It is to be regretted that Betty has not inherited her mother's charming color," I said, "but we must do the best we can for her under her limitations. She may have improved vastly by the time she has grown up. And, at least, we must make a lady of her; she is a most alarming tomboy at present, but there is good material to work upon . . . there must be, in the Churchill and Currie blend. But even the best material may be spoiled by unwise handling. I think I can promise you that I will not spoil it. I feel that Betty is my vocation; and I shall set myself up as a rival of Wordsworth's 'nature,' of whose methods I have always had a decided distrust, in spite of his insidious verses."

Sara did not understand me in the least; but, then, she did not pretend to.

"I confide Betty's education entirely to you, Stephen," she said, with another plaintive sigh. "I feel sure I could not put it into better hands. You have always been a person who could be thoroughly depended on."

Well, that was something by way of reward for a life-long devotion. I felt that I was satisfied with my position as unofficial adviser-in-chief to Sara and self-appointed guardian of Betty. I also felt that, for the furtherance of the cause I had taken to heart, it was a good thing that Sara had again refused to marry me. I had a sixth sense which informed me that a staid old family friend might succeed with Betty where a stepfather would have signally failed. Betty's loyalty to her father's memory was passionate and vehement; she would view his supplanter with resentment and distrust; but his old familiar comrade was a person to be taken to her heart.

Fortunately for the success of my enterprise, Betty liked me. She told me this with the same engaging candor she would have used in informing me that she hated me, if she had happened to take a bias in that direction, saying frankly:

"You are one of the very nicest old folks I know, Stephen. Yes, you are a ripping good fellow!"

This made my task a comparatively easy one; I sometimes shudder to think what it might have been if Betty had not thought I was a "ripping good fellow." I should have stuck to it, because that is my way; but Betty would have made my life a misery to me. She had startling capacities for tormenting people when she chose to exert them; I certainly should not have liked to be numbered among Betty's foes.

I rode over to Glenby the next morning after my paternal interview with Sara, intending to have a frank talk with Betty and lay the foundations of a good understanding on both sides. Betty was a sharp child, with a disconcerting knack of seeing straight through grindstones; she would certainly perceive and probably resent any underhand management. I thought it best to tell her plainly that I was going to look after her.

When, however, I had encountered Betty, tearing madly down the beech avenue with a couple of dogs, her loosened hair streaming behind her like a banner of independence, and had lifted her, hatless and breathless, up before me on my mare, I found that Sara had saved me the trouble of an explanation.

"Mother says you are going to take charge of my education, Stephen," said Betty, as soon as she could speak. "I'm glad, because I think that, for an old person, you have a good deal of sense. I suppose my education has to be seen to, some time or other, and I'd rather you'd do it than anybody else I know."

"Thank you, Betty," I said gravely. "I hope I shall deserve your good opinion of my sense. I shall expect you to do as I tell you, and be guided by my advice in everything."

"Yes, I will," said Betty, "because I'm sure you won't tell

me to do anything I'd really hate to do. You won't shut me up in a room and make me sew, will you? Because I won't do it."

I assured her I would not.

"Nor send me to a boarding-school," pursued Betty. "Mother's always threatening to send me to one. I suppose she would have done it before this, only she knew I'd run away. You won't send me to a boarding-school, will you, Stephen? Because I won't go."

"No," I said obligingly, "I won't. I should never dream of cooping a wild little thing, like you, up in a boarding-school. You'd fret your heart out like a caged skylark."

"I know you and I are going to get along together splendidly, Stephen," said Betty, rubbing her brown cheek chummily against my shoulder. "You are so good at understanding. Very few people are. Even dad darling didn't understand. He let me do just as I wanted to, just because I wanted to, not because he really understood that I couldn't be tame and play with dolls. I hate dolls! Real live babies are jolly; but dogs and horses are ever so much nicer than dolls."

"But you must have lessons, Betty. I shall select your teachers and superintend your studies, and I shall expect you to do me credit along that line, as well as along all others."

"I'll try, honest and true, Stephen," declared Betty. And she kept her word.

At first I looked upon Betty's education as a duty; in a very short time it had become a pleasure . . . the deepest and most abiding interest of my life. As I had premised, Betty was good material, and responded to my training with gratifying plasticity. Day by day, week by week, month by month, her character and temperament unfolded naturally under my watchful eye. It was like beholding the gradual development of some rare flower in one's garden. A little checking and pruning here, a careful training of shoot and tendril there, and, lo, the reward of grace and symmetry!

Betty grew up as I would have wished Jack Churchill's girl to grow—spirited and proud, with the fine spirit and gracious pride of pure womanhood, loyal and loving, with the loyalty and love of a frank unspoiled nature; true to her heart's core, hating falsehood and sham—as crystal-clear a mirror of maidenhood as ever man looked into and saw himself reflected back in such a halo as made him ashamed of not being more worthy of it. Betty was kind enough to say that I had taught her everything she knew. But what had she not taught me? If there were a debt between us, it was on my side.

Sara was fairly well satisfied. It was not my fault that Betty was not better looking, she said. I had certainly done everything for her mind and character that could be done. Sara's manner implied that these unimportant details did not count for much, balanced against the lack of a pink-and-white skin and dimpled elbows; but she was generous enough not to blame me.

"When Betty is twenty-five," I said patiently—I had grown used to speaking patiently to Sara—"she will be a magnificent woman—far handsomer than you ever were, Sara, in your pinkest and whitest prime. Where are your eyes, my dear lady, that you can't see the promise of loveliness in Betty?"

"Betty is seventeen, and she is as lanky and brown as ever she was," sighed Sara. "When I was seventeen I was the belle of the county and had had five proposals. I don't believe the thought of a lover has ever entered Betty's head."

"I hope not," I said shortly. Somehow, I did not like the suggestion. "Betty is a child yet. For pity's sake, Sara, don't go putting nonsensical ideas into her head."

"I'm afraid I can't," mourned Sara, as if it were something to be regretted. "You have filled it too full of books and things like that. I've every confidence in your judgment, Stephen— and really you've done wonders with Betty. But don't you think you've made her rather too clever? Men don't like women who are too clever. Her poor father, now—he always said that a woman who liked books better than beaux was an unnatural creature."

I didn't believe Jack had ever said anything so foolish. Sara imagined things. But I resented the aspersion of blue-stocking-ness cast on Betty.

"When the time comes for Betty to be interested in beaux," I said severely, "she will probably give them all due attention. Just at present her head is a great deal better filled with books than with silly premature fancies and sentimentalities. I'm a critical old fellow—but I'm satisfied with Betty, Sara—perfectly satisfied."

Sara sighed.

"Oh, I dare say she is all right, Stephen. And I'm really grateful to you. I'm sure I could have done nothing at all with her. It's not your fault, of course—but I can't help wishing she were a little more like other girls."

I galloped away from Glenby in a rage. What a blessing Sara had not married me in my absurd youth! She would have driven me wild with her sighs and her obtuseness and her everlasting pink-and-whiteness. But there—there—there—gently! She was a sweet, good-hearted little woman; she had made Jack happy; and she had contrived, heaven only knew how, to bring a rare creature like Betty into the world. For that, much might be forgiven her. By the time I reached The Maples and had flung myself down in an old, kinky, comfortable chair in my library I had forgiven her and was even paying her the compliment of thinking seriously over what she had said.

Was Betty really unlike other girls? That is to say, unlike them in any respect wherein she should resemble them? I did not wish this; although I was a crusty old bachelor I approved of girls, holding them the sweetest things the good God has made. I wanted Betty to have her full complement of girlhood in all its best and highest manifestation. Was there anything lacking?

I observed Betty very closely during the next week or so, riding over to Glenby every day and riding back at night, meditating upon my observations. Eventually I concluded to do what I had never thought myself in the least likely to do. I would send Betty to a boarding-school for a year. It was necessary that she should learn how to live with other girls.

I went over to Glenby the next day and found Betty under the beeches on the lawn, just back from a canter. She was sitting on the dappled mare I had given her on her last birthday, and was laughing at the antics of her rejoicing dogs around her. I looked at her with pleasure; it gladdened me to see how much, nay, how totally a child she still was, despite her Churchill height. Her hair, under her velvet cap, still hung over her shoulders in the same thick plaits; her face had the firm leanness of early youth, but its curves were very fine and delicate. The brown skin, that worried Sara so, was flushed through with dusky color from her gallop; her long, dark eyes were filled with the beautiful unconsciousness of childhood. More than all, the soul in her was still the soul of a child. I found myself wishing that it could always remain so. But I knew it could not; the woman must blossom out some day; it was my duty to see that the flower fulfilled the promise of the bud.

When I told Betty that she must go away to a school for a year, she shrugged, frowned and consented. Betty had learned that she must consent to what I decreed, even when my decrees were opposed to her likings, as she had once fondly believed they never would be. But Betty had acquired confidence in me to the beautiful extent of acquiescing in everything I commanded.

"I'll go, of course, since you wish it, Stephen," she said. "But why do you want me to go? You must have a reason—you always have a reason for anything you do. What is it?"

"That is for you to find out, Betty," I said. "By the time you come back you will have discovered it, I think. If not, it will not have proved itself a good reason and shall be forgotten."

When Betty went away I bade her goodbye without burdening her with any useless words of advice.

"Write to me every week, and remember that you are Betty Churchill," I said.

Betty was standing on the steps above, among her dogs. She came down a step and put her arms about my neck.

"I'll remember that you are my friend and that I must live up to you," she said. "Goodbye, Stephen."

She kissed me two or three times—good, hearty smacks! did I not say she was still a child?—and stood waving her hand to me as I rode away. I looked back at the end of the avenue and saw her standing there, short-skirted and hatless, fronting the lowering sun with those fearless eyes of hers. So I looked my last on the child Betty.

That was a lonely year. My occupation was gone and I began to fear that I had outlived my usefulness. Life seemed flat, stale and unprofitable. Betty's weekly letters were all that lent it any savor. They were spicy and piquant enough. Betty was discovered to have unsuspected talents in the epistolary line. At first she was dolefully homesick, and begged me to let her come home. When I refused—it was amazingly hard to refuse—she sulked through three letters, then cheered up and began to enjoy herself. But it was nearly the end of the year when she wrote:

"I've found out why you sent me here, Stephen—and I'm glad you did."

I had to be away from home on unavoidable business the day Betty returned to Glenby. But the next afternoon I went over. I found Betty out and Sara in. The latter was beaming. Betty was so much improved, she declared delightedly. I would hardly know "the dear child."

This alarmed me terribly. What on earth had they done to Betty? I found that she had gone up to the pineland for a walk, and thither I betook myself speedily. When I saw her coming down a long, golden-brown alley I stepped behind a tree to watch her—I wished to see her, myself unseen. As she drew near I gazed at her with pride, and admiration and amazement—and, under it all, a strange, dreadful, heart-sinking, which I could not understand and which I had never in all my life experienced before—no, not even when Sara had refused me.

Betty was a woman! Not by virtue of the simple white dress that clung to her tall, slender figure, revealing lines of exquisite grace and litheness; not by virtue of the glossy masses of dark brown hair heaped high on her head and held there in wonderful shining coils; not by virtue of added softness of curve and daintiness of outline; not because of all these, but because of the dream and wonder and seeking in her eyes. She was a woman, looking, all unconscious of her quest, for love.

The understanding of the change in her came home to me with a shock that must have left me, I think, something white about the lips. I was glad. She was what I had wished her to become. But I wanted the child Betty back; this womanly Betty seemed far away from me.

I stepped out into the path and she saw me, with a brightening of her whole face. She did not rush forward and fling herself into my arms as she would have done a year ago; but she came towards me swiftly, holding out her hand. I had thought her slightly pale when I had first seen her; but now I concluded I had been mistaken, for there was a wonderful sunrise of color in her face. I took her hand—there were no kisses this time.

"Welcome home, Betty," I said.

"Oh, Stephen, it is so good to be back," she breathed, her eyes shining.

She did not say it was good to see me again, as I had hoped she would do. Indeed, after the first minute of greeting, she seemed a trifle cool and distant. We walked for an hour in the pine wood and talked. Betty was brilliant, witty, self-possessed, altogether charming. I thought her perfect and yet my heart ached. What a glorious young thing she was, in that splendid youth of hers! What a prize for some lucky man—confound the obtrusive thought! No doubt we should soon be overrun at Glenby with lovers. I should stumble over some forlorn youth at every step! Well, what of it? Betty would marry, of course. It would be my duty to see that she got a good husband, worthy of her as men go. I thought I preferred the old duty of superintending her studies. But there, it was all the same thing—merely a post-graduate course in applied knowledge. When she began to learn life's greatest lesson of love, I, the tried and true old family friend and mentor, must be on hand to see that the teacher was what I would have him be, even as I had formerly selected her instructor in French and botany. Then, and not until then, would Betty's education be complete.

I rode home very soberly. When I reached The Maples I did what I had not done for years . . . looked critically at myself in the mirror. The realization that I had grown older came home to me with a new and unpleasant force. There were marked lines on my lean face, and silver glints in the dark hair over my temples. When Betty was ten she had thought me "an old person." Now, at eighteen, she probably thought me a veritable ancient of days. Pshaw, what did it matter? And yet . . . I thought of her as I had seen her, standing under the pines, and something cold and painful laid its hand on my heart.

My premonitions as to lovers proved correct. Glenby was soon infested with them. Heaven knows where they all came from. I had not supposed there was a quarter as many young men in the whole county; but there they were. Sara was in the seventh heaven of delight. Was not Betty at last a belle? As for the proposals . . . well, Betty never counted her scalps in public; but every once in a while a visiting youth dropped out and was seen no more at Glenby. One could guess what that meant.

Betty apparently enjoyed all this. I grieve to say that she was a bit of a coquette. I tried to cure her of this serious defect, but for once I found that I had undertaken something I could not accomplish. In vain I lectured, Betty only laughed; in vain I gravely rebuked, Betty only flirted more vivaciously than before. Men might come and men might go, but Betty went on forever. I endured this sort of thing for a year and then I decided that it was time to interfere seriously. I must find a husband for Betty . . . my fatherly duty would not be fulfilled until I had . . . nor, indeed, my duty to society. She was not a safe person to have running at large.

None of the men who haunted Glenby was good enough for her. I decided that my nephew, Frank, would do very well. He was a capital young fellow, handsome, clean-souled, and whole-hearted. From a worldly point of view he was what Sara would have termed an excellent match; he had money, social standing and a rising reputation as a clever young lawyer. Yes, he should have Betty, confound him!

They had never met. I set the wheels going at once. The sooner all the fuss was over the better. I hated fuss and there was bound to be a good deal of it. But I went about the business like an accomplished matchmaker. I invited Frank to visit The Maples and, before he came, I talked much . . . but not too much . . . of him to Betty, mingling judicious praise and still more judicious blame together. Women never like a paragon. Betty heard me with more gravity than she usually accorded to my dissertations on young men. She even condescended to ask several questions about him. This I thought a good sign.

To Frank I had not said a word about Betty; when he came to The Maples I took him over to Glenby and, coming upon Betty wandering about among the beeches in the sunset, I introduced him without any warning.

He would have been more than mortal if he had not fallen in love with her upon the spot. It was not in the heart of man to resist her . . . that dainty, alluring bit of womanhood. She was all in white, with flowers in her hair, and, for a moment, I could have murdered Frank or any other man who dared to commit the sacrilege of loving her.

Then I pulled myself together and left them alone. I might have gone in and talked to Sara . . . two old folks gently reviewing their youth while the young folks courted outside . . . but I did not. I prowled about the pine wood, and tried to forget how blithe and handsome that curly-headed boy, Frank, was, and what a flash had sprung into his eyes when he had seen Betty. Well, what of it? Was not that what I had brought him there for? And was I not pleased at the success of my scheme? Certainly I was! Delighted!

Next day Frank went to Glenby without even making the poor pretense of asking me to accompany him. I spent the time of his absence overseeing the construction of a new greenhouse I was having built. I was conscientious in my supervision; but I felt no interest in it. The place was intended for roses, and roses made me think of the pale yellow ones Betty had worn at her breast one evening the week before, when, all lovers being unaccountably absent, we had wandered together under the pines and talked as in the old days before her young womanhood and my gray hairs had risen up to divide us. She had dropped a rose on the brown floor, and I had sneaked back, after I had left her in the house, to get it, before I went home. I had it now in my pocket-book. Confound it, mightn't a future uncle cherish a family affection for his prospective niece?

Frank's wooing seemed to prosper. The other young sparks, who had haunted Glenby, faded away after his advent. Betty treated him with most encouraging sweetness; Sara smiled on him; I stood in the background, like a benevolent god of the machine, and flattered myself that I pulled the strings.

At the end of a month something went wrong. Frank came home from Glenby one day in the dumps, and moped for two whole days. I rode down myself on the third. I had not gone much to Glenby that month; but, if there were trouble Bettyward, it was my duty to make smooth the rough places.

As usual, I found Betty in the pineland. I thought she looked rather pale and dull . . . fretting about Frank no doubt. She brightened up when she saw me, evidently expecting that I had come to straighten matters out; but she pretended to be haughty and indifferent.

" 'I am glad you haven't forgotten us altogether, Stephen,"

she said coolly. "You haven't been down for a week."

"I'm flattered that you noticed it," I said, sitting down on a fallen tree and looking up at her as she stood, tall and lithe, against an old pine, with her eyes averted. "I shouldn't have supposed you'd want an old fogy like myself poking about and spoiling the idyllic moments of love's young dream."

"Why do you always speak of yourself as old?" said Betty, crossly, ignoring my reference to Frank.

"Because I am old, my dear. Witness these gray hairs."

I pushed up my hat to show them the more recklessly.

Betty barely glanced at them.

"You have just enough to give you a distinguished look," she said, "and you are only forty. A man is in his prime at forty. He never has any sense until he is forty—and sometimes he doesn't seem to have any even then," she concluded impertinently.

My heart beat. Did Betty suspect? Was that last sentence meant to inform me that she was aware of my secret folly, and laughed at it?

"I came over to see what has gone wrong between you and Frank," I said gravely.

Betty bit her lips.

"Nothing," she said.

"Betty," I said reproachfully, "I brought you up . . . or endeavored to bring you up . . . to speak the truth, the whole truth, and nothing but the truth. Don't tell me I have failed. I'll give you another chance. Have you quarreled with Frank?"

"No," said that maddening Betty, "*he* quarreled with me. He went away in a temper and I do not care if he never comes back!"

I shook my head.

"This won't do, Betty. As your old family friend I still claim the right to scold you until you have a husband to do the scolding. You mustn't torment Frank. He is too fine a fellow. You must marry him, Betty."

"Must I?" said Betty, a dusky red flaming out on her cheek. She turned her eyes on me in a most disconcerting fashion. "Do *you* wish me to marry Frank, Stephen?"

Betty had a wretched habit of emphasizing pronouns in a fashion calculated to rattle anybody.

"Yes, I do wish it, because I think it will be best for you," I replied, without looking at her. "You must marry some time, Betty, and Frank is the only man I know to whom I could trust you. As your guardian, I have an interest in seeing you well and wisely settled for life. You have always taken my advice and obeyed my wishes; and you've always found my way the best, in the long run, haven't you, Betty? You won't prove rebellious now, I'm sure. You know quite well that I am advising you for your own good. Frank is a splendid young fellow, who loves you with all his heart. Marry him, Betty. Mind, I don't *command*. I have no right to do that, and you are too old to be ordered about, if I had. But I wish and advise. Isn't that enough, Betty?"

I had been looking away from her all the time I was talking, gazing determinedly down a sunlit vista of pines. Every word I said seemed to tear my heart, and come from my lips stained with lifeblood. Yes, Betty should marry Frank! But, good God, what would become of me!

Betty left her station under the pine tree, and walked around me until she got right in front of my face. I couldn't help looking at her, for if I moved my eyes she moved, too. There was nothing meek or submissive about her; her head was held high, her eyes were blazing, and her cheeks were crimson. But her words were meek enough.

"I will marry Frank if you wish it, Stephen," she said. "You are my friend. I have never crossed your wishes, and, as you say, I have never regretted being always guided by them. I will do exactly as you wish in this case also, I promise you that. But, in so solemn a question, I must be very certain what you *do* wish. There must be no doubt in my mind or heart. Look me squarely in the eyes, Stephen—as you haven't done once today, no, nor once since I came home from school—and, so looking, tell me that you wish me to marry Frank Douglas and I will do it! *Do* you, Stephen?"

I had to look her in the eyes, since nothing else would do her; and, as I did so, all the might of manhood in me rose up in hot revolt against the lie I would have told her. That unfaltering, impelling gaze of hers drew the truth from my lips in spite of myself.

"No, I don't wish you to marry Frank Douglas, a thousand

times no!" I said passionately. "I don't wish you to marry any man on earth but myself. I love you—I love you, Betty. You are dearer to me than life—dearer to me than my own happiness. It was your happiness I thought of—and so I asked you to marry Frank because I believed he would make you a happy woman. That is all!"

Betty's defiance went from her like a flame blown out. She turned away and drooped her proud head.

"It could not have made me a happy woman to marry one man, loving another," she said, in a whisper.

I got up and went over to her.

"Betty, whom do you love?" I asked, also in a whisper.

"You," she murmured meekly—oh, so meekly, my proud little girl!

"Betty," I said brokenly, "I'm old—too old for you—I'm more than twenty years your senior—I'm—"

"Oh!" Betty wheeled around on me and stamped her foot. "Don't mention your age to me again. I don't care if you're as old as Methusaleh. But I'm not going to coax you to marry me, sir! If you won't, I'll never marry anybody—I'll live and die an old maid. You can please yourself, of course!"

She turned away, half-laughing, half-crying; but I caught her in my arms and crushed her sweet lips against mine.

"Betty, I'm the happiest man in the world—and I was the most miserable when I came here."

"You deserved to be," said Betty cruelly. "I'm glad you were. Any man as stupid as you deserves to be unhappy. What do you think I felt like, loving you with all my heart, and seeing you simply throwing me at another man's head. Why, I've always loved you, Stephen; but I didn't know it until I went to that detestable school. Then I found out—and I thought that was why you had sent me. But, when I came home, you almost broke my heart. That was why I flirted so with all those poor, nice boys—I wanted to hurt you but I never thought I succeeded. You just went on being *fatherly*. Then, when you brought Frank here, I almost gave up hope; and I tried to make up my mind to marry him; I should have done it if you had insisted. But I had to have one more try for happiness first. I had just one little hope to inspire me with sufficient boldness. I saw you, that night, when you came back here and picked up my rose! I had come back, myself, to be alone and unhappy."

"It is the most wonderful thing that ever happened—that you should love me," I said.

"It's not—I couldn't help it," said Betty, nestling her brown head on my shoulder. "You taught me everything else, Stephen, so nobody but you could teach me how to love. You've made a thorough thing of educating me."

"When will you marry me, Betty?" I asked.

"As soon as I can fully forgive you for trying to make me marry somebody else," said Betty.

It was rather hard lines on Frank, when you come to think of it. But, such is the selfishness of human nature that we didn't think much about Frank. The young fellow behaved like the Douglas he was. Went a little white about the lips when I told him, wished me all the happiness, and went quietly away, "gentleman unafraid."

He has since married and is, I understand, very happy. Not as happy as I am, of course; that is impossible, because there is only one Betty in the world, and she is my wife.

IN HER SELFLESS MOOD

THE RAW wind of an early May evening was puffing in and out the curtains of the room where Naomi Holland lay dying. The air was moist and chill, but the sick woman would not have the window closed.

"I can't get my breath if you shut everything up so tight," she said. "Whatever comes, I ain't going to be smothered to death, Car'line Holland."

Outside of the window grew a cherry tree, powdered with moist buds with the promise of blossoms she would not live to see. Between its boughs she saw a crystal cup of sky over hills that were growing dim and purple. The outside air was full of sweet, wholesome springtime sounds that drifted in fitfully. There were voices and whistles in the barnyard, and now and then faint laughter. A bird alighted for a moment on a cherry bough, and twittered restlessly. Naomi knew that white mists were hovering in the silent hollows, that the maple at the gate wore a misty blossom red, and that violet stars were shining bluely on the brooklands.

The room was a small, plain one. The floor was bare, save for a couple of braided rugs, the plaster discolored, the walls dingy and glaring. There had never been much beauty in Naomi

Holland's environment, and, now that she was dying, there was even less.

At the open window a boy of about ten years was leaning out over the sill and whistling. He was tall for his age, and beautiful—the hair a rich auburn with a glistening curl in it, skin very white and warm-tinted, eyes small and of a greenish blue, with dilated pupils and long lashes. He had a weak chin, and a full, sullen mouth.

The bed was in the corner farthest from the window; on it the sick woman, in spite of the pain that was her portion continually, was lying as quiet and motionless as she had done ever since she had lain down upon it for the last time. Naomi Holland never complained; when the agony was at its worst, she shut her teeth more firmly over her bloodless lip, and her great black eyes glared at the blank wall before her in a way that gave her attendants what they called "the creeps," but no word or moan escaped her.

Between the paroxysms she kept up her keen interest in the life that went on about her. Nothing escaped her sharp, alert eyes and ears. This evening she lay spent on the crumpled pillows; she had had a bad spell in the afternoon and it had left her very weak. In the dim light her extremely long face looked corpse-like already. Her black hair lay in a heavy braid over the pillow and down the counterpane. It was all that was left of her beauty, and she took a fierce joy in it. Those long, glistening, sinuous tresses must be combed and braided every day, no matter what came.

A girl of fourteen was curled up on a chair at the head of the bed, with her head resting on the pillow. The boy at the window was her half-brother; but, between Christopher Holland and Eunice Carr, not the slightest resemblance existed.

Presently the sibilant silence was broken by a low, half-strangled sob. The sick woman, who had been watching a white evening star through the cherry boughs, turned impatiently at the sound.

"I wish you'd get over that, Eunice," she said sharply. "I don't want anyone crying over me until I'm dead; and then you'll have plenty else to do, most likely. If it wasn't for Christopher I wouldn't be anyways unwilling to die. When one has had such a life as I've had, there isn't much in death to be afraid of. Only, a body would like to go right off, and not die by inches, like this. 'Tain't fair!"

She snapped out the last sentence as if addressing some unseen, tyrannical presence; her voice, at least, had not weakened, but was as clear and incisive as ever. The boy at the window stopped whistling, and the girl silently wiped her eyes on her faded gingham apron.

Naomi drew her own hair over her lips, and kissed it.

"You'll never have hair like that, Eunice," she said. "It does seem most too pretty to bury, doesn't it? Mind you see that it is fixed nice when I'm laid out. Comb it right up on my head and braid it there."

A sound, such as might be wrung from a suffering animal, came from the girl, but at the same moment the door opened and a woman entered.

"Chris," she said sharply, "you get right off for the cows, you lazy little scamp! You knew right well you had to go for them, and here you've been idling, and me looking high and low for you. Make haste now; it's ridiculous late."

The boy pulled in his head and scowled at his aunt, but he dared not disobey, and went out slowly with a sulky mutter.

His aunt subdued a movement, that might have developed into a sound box on his ears, with a rather frightened glance at the bed. Naomi Holland was spent and dying, but her temper was still a thing to hold in dread, and her sister-in-law did not choose to rouse it by slapping Christopher. To her and her co-nurse the spasms of rage, which the sick woman sometimes had, seemed to partake of the nature of devil possession. The last one, only three days before, had been provoked by Christopher's complaint of some real or fancied ill-treatment from his aunt, and the latter had no mind to bring on another. She went over to the bed, and straightened the clothes.

"Sarah and I are going out to milk, Naomi. Eunice will stay with you. She can run for us if you feel another spell coming on."

Naomi Holland looked up at her sister-in-law with something like malicious enjoyment.

"I ain't going to have any more spells, Car'line Anne. I'm

going to die tonight. But you needn't hurry milking for that, at all. I'll take my time."

She liked to see the alarm that came over the other woman's face. It was richly worth while to scare Caroline Holland like that.

"Are you feeling any worse, Naomi?" asked the latter shakily. "If you are I'll send for Charles to go for the doctor."

"No, you won't. What good can the doctor do me? I don't want either his or Charles' permission to die. You can go and milk at your ease. I won't die till you're done—I won't deprive you of the pleasure of seeing me."

Mrs. Holland shut her lips and went out of the room with a martyr-like expression. In some ways Naomi Holland was not an exacting patient, but she took her satisfaction out in the biting, malicious speeches she never failed to make. Even on her death-bed her hostility to her sister-in-law had to find vent.

Outside, at the steps, Sarah Spencer was waiting, with the milk pails over her arm. Sarah Spencer had no fixed abiding place, but was always to be found where there was illness. Her experience, and an utter lack of nerves, made her a good nurse. She was a tall, homely woman with iron gray hair and a lined face. Beside her, the trim little Caroline Anne, with her light step and round, apple-red face, looked almost girlish.

The two women walked to the barnyard, discussing Naomi in undertones as they went. The house they had left behind grew very still.

In Naomi Holland's room the shadows were gathering. Eunice timidly bent over her mother.

"Ma, do you want the light lit?"

"No, I'm watching that star just below the big cherry bough. I'll see it set behind the hill. I've seen it there, off and on, for twelve years, and now I'm taking a goodbye look at it. I want you to keep still, too. I've got a few things to think over, and I don't want to be disturbed."

The girl lifted herself about noiselessly and locked her hands over the bed-post. Then she laid her face down on them, biting at them silently until the marks of her teeth showed white against their red roughness.

Naomi Holland did not notice her. She was looking steadfastly at the great, pearl-like sparkle in the faint-hued sky. When it finally disappeared from her vision she struck her long, thin hands together twice, and a terrible expression came over her face for a moment. But, when she spoke, her voice was quite calm.

"You can light the candle now, Eunice. Put it up on the shelf here, where it won't shine in my eyes. And then sit down on the foot of the bed where I can see you. I've got something to say to you."

Eunice obeyed her noiselessly. As the pallid light shot up, it revealed the child plainly. She was thin and ill-formed—one shoulder being slightly higher than the other. She was dark, like her mother, but her features were irregular, and her hair fell in straggling, dim locks about her face. Her eyes were a dark brown, and over one was the slanting red scar of a birth mark.

Naomi Holland looked at her with the contempt she had never made any pretense of concealing. The girl was bone of her bone and flesh of her flesh, but she had never loved her; all the mother love in her had been lavished on her son.

When Eunice had placed the candle on the shelf and drawn down the ugly blue paper blinds, shutting out the strips of violet sky where a score of glimmering points were now visible, she sat down on the foot of the bed, facing her mother.

"The door is shut, is it, Eunice?"

Eunice nodded.

"Because I don't want Car'line or anyone else peeking and harking to what I've got to say. She's out milking now, and I must make the most of the chance. Eunice, I'm going to die, and . . . "

"Ma!"

"There now, no taking on! You knew it had to come some-time soon. I haven't the strength to talk much, so I want you just to be quiet and listen. I ain't feeling any pain now, so I can think and talk pretty clear. Are you listening, Eunice?"

"Yes, ma."

"Mind you are. It's about Christopher. It hasn't been out of my mind since I laid down here. I've fought for a year to live, on his account, and it ain't any use. I must just die and leave him, and I don't know what he'll do. It's dreadful to think of."

She paused, and struck her shrunken hand sharply against the table.

"If he was bigger and could look out for himself it wouldn't be so bad. But he is only a little fellow, and Car'line hates him. You'll both have to live with her until you're grown up. She'll put on him and abuse him. He's like his father in some ways; he's got a temper and he is stubborn. He'll never get on with Car'line. Now, Eunice, I'm going to get you to promise to take my place with Christopher when I'm dead, as far as you can. You've got to; it's your duty. But I want you to promise."

"I will, ma," whispered the girl solemnly.

"You haven't much force—you never had. If you was smart, you could do a lot for him. But you'll have to do your best. I want you to promise me faithfully that you'll stand by him and protect him—that you won't let people impose on him; that you'll never desert him as long as he needs you, no matter what comes. Eunice, promise me this!"

In her excitement the sick woman raised herself up in the bed, and clutched the girl's thin arm. Her eyes were blazing and two scarlet spots glowed in her thin cheeks.

Eunice's face was white and tense. She clasped her hands as one in prayer.

"Mother, I promise it!"

Naomi relaxed her grip on the girl's arm and sank back exhausted on the pillow. A death-like look came over her face as the excitement faded.

"My mind is easier now. But if I could only have lived another year or two! And I hate Car'line—hate her! Eunice, don't you ever let her abuse my boy! If she did, or if you neglected him, I'd come back from my grave to you! As for the property, things will be pretty straight. I've seen to that. There'll be no squabbling and doing Christopher out of his rights. He's to have the farm as soon as he's old enough to work it, and he's to provide for you. And, Eunice, remember what you've promised!"

Outside, in the thickly gathering dusk, Caroline Holland and

Sarah Spencer were at the dairy, straining the milk into cream-
ers, for which Christopher was sullenly pumping water. The
house was far from the road, up to which a long red lane led;
across the field was the old Holland homestead where Caroline
lived; her unmarried sister-in-law, Electa Holland, kept house
for her while she waited on Naomi.

It was her night to go home and sleep, but Naomi's words
haunted her, although she believed they were born of pure
"cantankerousness."

"You'd better go in and look at her, Sarah," she said, as she
rinsed out the pails. "If you think I'd better stay here tonight,
I will. If the woman was like anybody else a body would know
what to do; but, if she thought she could scare us by saying
she was going to die, she'd say it."

When Sarah went in, the sick room was very quiet. In her
opinion Naomi was no worse than usual, and she told Caroline
so; but the latter felt vaguely uneasy and concluded to stay.

Naomi was as cool and defiant as customary. She made them
bring Christopher in to say goodnight and had him lifted up
on the bed to kiss her. Then she held him back and looked
at him admiringly—at the bright curls and rosy cheeks and
round, firm limbs. The boy was uncomfortable under her gaze
and squirmed hastily down. Her eyes followed him greedily, as
he went out. When the door closed behind him she groaned.
Sarah Spencer was startled. She had never heard Naomi Holland
groan since she had come to wait on her.

"Are you feeling any worse, Naomi? Is the pain coming
back?"

"No. Go and tell Car'line to give Christopher some of that
grape jelly on his bread before he goes to bed. She'll find it in
the cupboard under the stairs."

Presently the house grew very still. Caroline had dropped
asleep on the sitting-room lounge, across the hall. Sarah Spencer
nodded over her knitting by the table in the sick room. She
had told Eunice to go to bed, but the child refused. She still
sat huddled up on the foot of the bed, watching her mother's
face intently. Naomi appeared to sleep. The candle burned long,
and the wick was crowned by a little cap of fiery red that
seemed to watch Eunice like some impish goblin. The wavering
light cast grotesque shadows of Sarah Spencer's head on the

wall. The thin curtains at the window wavered to and fro, as if shaken by ghostly hands.

At midnight Naomi Holland opened her eyes. The child she had never loved was the only one to go with her to the brink of the Unseen.

"Eunice—remember!"

It was the faintest whisper. The soul, passing over the threshold of another life, strained back to its only earthly tie. A quiver passed over the long, pallid face.

A horrible scream rang through the silent house. Sarah Spencer sprang out of her doze in consternation, and gazed blankly at the shrieking child. Caroline came hurrying in with distended eyes. On the bed Naomi Holland lay dead.

In the room where she had died Naomi Holland lay in her coffin. It was dim and hushed; but, in the rest of the house, the preparations for the funeral were being hurried on. Through it all Eunice moved, calm and silent. Since her one wild spasm of screaming by her mother's death-bed she had shed no tear, given no sign of grief. Perhaps, as her mother had said, she had no time. There was Christopher to be looked after. The boy's grief was stormy and uncontrolled. He had cried until he was utterly exhausted. It was Eunice who soothed him, coaxed him to eat, kept him constantly by her. At night she took him to her own room and watched over him while he slept.

When the funeral was over the household furniture was packed away or sold. The house was locked up and the farm rented. There was nowhere for the children to go, save to their uncle's. Caroline Holland did not want them, but, having to take them, she grimly made up her mind to do what she considered her duty by them. She had five children of her own and between them and Christopher a standing feud had existed from the time he could walk.

She had never liked Naomi. Few people did. Benjamin Holland had not married until late in life, and his wife had declared war on his family at sight. She was a stranger in Avonlea—a widow, with a three-year-old child. She made few friends, as some people always asserted that she was not in her right mind.

Within a year of her second marriage Christopher was born,

and from the hour of his birth his mother had worshipped him blindly. He was her only solace. For him she toiled and pinched and saved. Benjamin Holland had not been "fore-handed" when she married him; but, when he died, six years after his marriage, he was a well-to-do man.

Naomi made no pretense of mourning for him. It was an open secret that they had quarreled like the proverbial cat and dog. Charles Holland and his wife had naturally sided with Benjamin, and Naomi fought her battles single-handed. After her husband's death, she managed to farm alone, and made it pay. When the mysterious malady which was to end her life first seized on her she fought against it with all the strength and stubbornness of her strong and stubborn nature. Her will won for her an added year of life, and then she had to yield. She tasted all the bitterness of death the day on which she lay down on her bed, and saw her enemy come in to rule her house.

But Caroline Holland was not a bad or unkind woman. True, she did not love Naomi or her children; but the woman was dying and must be looked after for the sake of common humanity. Caroline thought she had done well by her sister-in-law.

When the red clay was heaped over Naomi's grave in the Avonlea burying ground, Caroline took Eunice and Christopher home with her. Christopher did not want to go; it was Eunice who reconciled him. He clung to her with an exacting affection born of loneliness and grief.

In the days that followed Caroline Holland was obliged to confess to herself that there would have been no doing anything with Christopher had it not been for Eunice. The boy was sullen and obstinate, but his sister had an unfailing influence over him.

In Charles Holland's household no one was allowed to eat the bread of idleness. His own children were all girls, and Christopher came in handy as a chore boy. He was made to work—perhaps too hard. But Eunice helped him, and did half his work for him when nobody knew. When he quarreled with his cousins, she took his part; whenever possible she took on herself the blame and punishment of his misdeeds.

Electa Holland was Charles' unmarried sister. She had kept

house for Benjamin until he married; then Naomi had bundled her out. Electa had never forgiven her for it. Her hatred passed on to Naomi's children. In a hundred petty ways she revenged herself on them. For herself, Eunice bore it patiently; but it was a different matter when it touched Christopher.

Once Electa boxed Christopher's ears. Eunice, who was knitting by the table, stood up. A resemblance to her mother, never before visible, came out in her face like a brand. She lifted her hand and slapped Electa's cheek deliberately twice, leaving a dull red mark where she struck.

"If you ever strike my brother again," she said, slowly and vindictively, "I will slap your face every time you do. You have no right to touch him."

"My patience, what a fury!" said Electa. "Naomi Holland'll never be dead as long as you're alive!"

She told Charles of the affair and Eunice was severely punished. But Electa never interfered with Christopher again.

All the discordant elements in the Holland household could not prevent the children from growing up. It was a consummation which the harassed Caroline devoutly wished. When Christopher Holland was seventeen he was a man grown—a big, strapping fellow. His childish beauty had coarsened, but he was thought handsome by many.

He took charge of his mother's farm then, and the brother and sister began their new life together in the long-unoccupied house. There were few regrets on either side when they left Charles Holland's roof. In her secret heart Eunice felt an unspeakable relief.

Christopher had been "hard to manage," as his uncle said, in the last year. He was getting into the habit of keeping late hours and doubtful company. This always provoked an explosion of wrath from Charles Holland, and the conflicts between him and his nephew were frequent and bitter.

For four years after their return home Eunice had a hard and anxious life. Christopher was idle and dissipated. Most people regarded him as a worthless fellow, and his uncle washed his hands of him utterly. Only Eunice never failed him; she never reproached or railed; she worked like a slave to keep things together. Eventually her patience prevailed. Christopher, to a great extent, reformed and worked harder. He was never unkind to Eunice, even in his rages. It was not in him to appreciate or return her devotion; but his tolerant acceptance of it was her solace.

When Eunice was twenty-eight, Edward Bell wanted to marry her. He was a plain, middle-aged widower with four children; but, as Caroline did not fail to remind her, Eunice herself was not for every market, and the former did her best to make the match. She might have succeeded had it not been for Christopher. When he, in spite of Caroline's skillful management, got an inkling of what was going on, he flew into a true Holland rage. If Eunice married and left him—he would sell the farm and go to the Devil by way of the Klondike. He could not, and would not, do without her. No arrangement suggested by Caroline availed to pacify him, and, in the end, Eunice refused to marry Edward Bell. She could not leave Christopher, she said simply, and in this she stood rock-firm. Caroline could not budge her an inch.

"You're a fool, Eunice," she said, when she was obliged to give up in despair. "It's not likely you'll ever have another chance. As for Chris, in a year or two he'll be marrying himself, and where will you be then? You'll find your nose nicely out of joint when he brings a wife in here."

The shaft went home. Eunice's lips turned white. But she said, faintly, "The house is big enough for us both, if he does."

Caroline sniffed.

"Maybe so. You'll find out. However, there's no use talking. You're as set as your mother was, and nothing would ever budge her an inch. I only hope you won't be sorry for it."

When three more years had passed Christopher began to court Victoria Pye. The affair went on for some time before either Eunice or the Hollands got wind of it. When they did there was an explosion. Between the Hollands and the Pyes, root and branch, existed a feud that dated back for three generations. That the original cause of the quarrel was totally forgotten did not matter; it was a matter of family pride that a Holland should have no dealings with a Pye.

When Christopher flew so openly in the face of this cherished hatred, there could be nothing less than consternation. Charles Holland broke through his determination to have nothing to do with Christopher, to remonstrate. Caroline went to Eunice in as much of a splutter as if Christopher had been her own brother.

Eunice did not care a row of pins for the Holland-Pye feud. Victoria was to her what any other girl, upon whom Christopher cast eyes of love, would have been—a supplanter. For the first time in her life she was torn with passionate jealousy; existence became a nightmare to her. Urged on by Caroline, and her own pain, she ventured to remonstrate with Christopher, also. She had expected a burst of rage, but he was surprisingly good-natured. He seemed even amused.

"What have you got against Victoria?" he asked, tolerantly.

Eunice had no answer ready. It was true that nothing could be said against the girl. She felt helpless and baffled. Christopher laughed at her silence.

"I guess you're a little jealous," he said. "You must have expected I would get married sometime. This house is big enough for us all. You'd better look at the matter sensibly, Eunice. Don't let Charles and Caroline put nonsense into your head. A man must marry to please himself."

Christopher was out late that night. Eunice waited up for him, as she always did. It was a chilly spring evening, reminding her of the night her mother had died. The kitchen was in spotless order, and she sat down on a stiff-backed chair by the window to wait for her brother.

She did not want a light. The moonlight fell in with faint illumination. Outside, the wind was blowing over a bed of new-sprung mint in the garden, and was suggestively fragrant. It was a very old-fashioned garden, full of perennials Naomi Holland had planted long ago. Eunice always kept it primly neat. She had been working in it that day, and felt tired.

She was all alone in the house and the loneliness filled her with a faint dread. She had tried all that day to reconcile herself to Christopher's marriage, and had partially succeeded. She told herself that she could still watch over him and care for his comfort. She would even try to love Victoria; after all, it might be pleasant to have another woman in the house. So, sitting there, she fed her hungry soul with these husks of comfort.

When she heard Christopher's step she moved about quickly to get a light. He frowned when he saw her; he had always resented her sitting up for him. He sat down by the stove and took off his boots, while Eunice got a lunch for him. After he had eaten it in silence he made no move to go to bed. A chill, premonitory fear crept over Eunice. It did not surprise her at all when Christopher finally said, abruptly, "Eunice, I've a notion to get married this spring."

Eunice clasped her hands together under the table. It was what she had been expecting. She said so, in a monotonous voice.

"We must make some arrangement for—for you, Eunice," Christopher went on, in a hurried, hesitant way, keeping his eyes riveted doggedly on his plate. "Victoria doesn't exactly like—well, she thinks it's better for young married folks to begin life by themselves, and I guess she's about right. You wouldn't find it comfortable, anyhow, having to step back to second place after being mistress here so long."

Eunice tried to speak, but only an indistinct murmur came from her bloodless lips. The sound made Christopher look up. Something in her face irritated him. He pushed back his chair impatiently.

"Now, Eunice, don't go to taking on. It won't be any use. Look at this business in a sensible way. I'm fond of you, and all that, but a man is bound to consider his wife first. I'll provide for you comfortably."

"Do you mean to say that your wife is going to turn me out?" Eunice gasped, rather than spoke, the words.

Christopher drew his reddish brows together.

"I just mean that Victoria says she won't marry me if she has to live with you. She's afraid of you. I told her you wouldn't interfere with her, but she wasn't satisfied. It's your own fault, Eunice. You've always been so queer and close that people think you're an awful crank. Victoria's young and lively, and you and she wouldn't get on at all. There isn't any question of turning you out. I'll build a little house for you somewhere, and you'll be a great deal better off there than you would be here. So don't make a fuss."

Eunice did not look as if she were going to make a fuss. She sat as if turned to stone, her hands lying palm upward in her lap. Christopher got up, hugely relieved that the dreaded explanation was over.

"Guess I'll go to bed. You'd better have gone long ago. It's all nonsense, this waiting up for me."

When he had gone Eunice drew a long, sobbing breath and looked about her like a dazed soul. All the sorrow of her life was as nothing to the desolation that assailed her now.

She rose and, with uncertain footsteps, passed out through the hall and into the room where her mother died. She had always kept it locked and undisturbed; it was arranged just as Naomi Holland had left it. Eunice tottered to the bed and sat down on it.

She recalled the promise she had made to her mother in that very room. Was the power to keep it to be wrested from her? Was she to be driven from her home and parted from the only creature she had on earth to love? And would Christopher allow it, after all her sacrifices for him? Aye, that he would! He cared more for that black-eyed, waxen-faced girl at the old Pye place than for his own kin. Eunice put her hands over her dry, burning eyes and groaned aloud.

Caroline Holland had her hour of triumph over Eunice when she heard it all. To one of her nature there was no pleasure so sweet as that of saying, "I told you so." Having said it, however, she offered Eunice a home. Electa Holland was dead, and Eunice might fill her place very acceptably, if she would.

"You can't go off and live by yourself," Caroline told her. "It's all nonsense to talk of such a thing. We will give you a home, if Christopher is going to turn you out. You were always a fool, Eunice, to pet and pamper him as you've done. This is the thanks you get for it—turned out like a dog for his fine wife's whim! I only wish your mother was alive!"

It was probably the first time Caroline had ever wished this. She had flown at Christopher like a fury about the matter, and had been rudely insulted for her pains. Christopher had told her to mind her own business.

When Caroline cooled down she made some arrangements with him, to all of which Eunice listlessly assented. She did not care what became of her. When Christopher Holland brought Victoria as mistress to the house where his mother had toiled, and suffered, and ruled with her rod of iron, Eunice was gone. In Charles Holland's household she took Electa's place—an unpaid upper servant.

Charles and Caroline were kind enough to her, and there was plenty to do. For five years her dull, colorless life went on, during which time she never crossed the threshold of the house where Victoria Holland ruled with a sway as absolute as Naomi's had been. Caroline's curiosity led her, after her first anger had cooled, to make occasional calls, the observations of which she faithfully reported to Eunice. The latter never betrayed any interest in them, save once. This was when Caroline came home full of the news that Victoria had had the room where Naomi died opened up, and showily furnished as a parlor. Then Eunice's sallow face crimsoned, and her eyes flashed, over the desecration. But no word of comment or complaint ever crossed her lips.

She knew, as everyone else knew, that the glamor soon went from Christopher Holland's married life. The marriage proved an unhappy one. Not unnaturally, although unjustly, Eunice blamed Victoria for this, and hated her more than ever for it.

Christopher seldom came to Charles' house. Possibly he felt ashamed. He had grown into a morose, silent man, at home and abroad. It was said he had gone back to his old drinking habits.

One fall Victoria Holland went to town to visit her married sister. She took their only child with her. In her absence Christopher kept house for himself.

It was a fall long remembered in Avonlea. With the dropping of the leaves, and the shortening of the dreary days, the shadow of a fear fell over the land. Charles Holland brought the fateful news home one night.

"There's smallpox in Charlottetown—five or six cases. Came in one of the vessels. There was a concert, and a sailor from one of the ships was there, and took sick the next day."

This was alarming enough. Charlottetown was not so very far away and considerable traffic went on between it and the north shore districts.

When Caroline recounted the concert story to Christopher the next morning his ruddy face turned quite pale. He opened his lips as if to speak, then closed them again. They were sitting in the kitchen; Caroline had run over to return some tea she had borrowed, and, incidentally, to see what she could of Victoria's housekeeping in her absence. Her eyes had been busy while her tongue ran on, so she did not notice the man's pallor and silence.

"How long does it take for smallpox to develop after one has been exposed to it?" he asked abruptly, when Caroline rose to go.

"Ten to fourteen days, I calc'late," was her answer. "I must see about having the girls vaccinated right off. It'll likely spread. When do you expect Victoria home?"

"When she's ready to come, whenever that will be," was the gruff response.

A week later Caroline said to Eunice, "Whatever's got Christopher? He hasn't been out anywhere for ages—just hangs round home the whole time. It's something new for him. I s'pose the place is so quiet, now Madam Victoria's away, that he can find some rest for his soul. I believe I'll run over after milking and see how he's getting on. You might as well come, too, Eunice."

Eunice shook her head. She had all her mother's obstinacy, and darken Victoria's door she would not. She went on patiently darning socks, sitting at the west window, which was her favorite position—perhaps because she could look from it across the sloping field and past the crescent curve of the maple grove to her lost home.

After milking, Caroline threw a shawl over her head and ran across the field. The house looked lonely and deserted. As she fumbled at the latch of the gate the kitchen door opened, and Christopher Holland appeared on the threshold.

"Don't come any farther," he called.

Caroline fell back in blank astonishment. Was this some more of Victoria's work?

"I ain't an agent for the smallpox," she called back viciously.

Christopher did not heed her.

"Will you go home and ask uncle if he'll go, or send for Dr. Spencer? He's the smallpox doctor. I'm sick."

Caroline felt a thrill of dismay and fear. She faltered a few steps backward.

"Sick? What's the matter with you?"

"I was in Charlottetown that night, and went to the concert. That sailor sat right beside me. I thought at the time he looked sick. It was just twelve days ago. I've felt bad all day yesterday and today. Send for the doctor. Don't come near the house, or let anyone else come near."

He went in and shut the door. Caroline stood for a few moments in an almost ludicrous panic. Then she turned and ran, as if for her life, across the field. Eunice saw her coming and met her at the door.

"Mercy on us!" gasped Caroline. "Christopher's sick and he thinks he's got the smallpox. Where's Charles?"

Eunice tottered back against the door. Her hand went up to her side in a way that had been getting very common with her of late. Even in the midst of her excitement Caroline noticed it.

"Eunice, what makes you do that every time anything startles you?" she asked sharply. "Is it anything about your heart?"

"I don't—know. A little pain—it's gone now. Did you say that Christopher has—the smallpox?"

"Well, he says so himself, and it's more than likely, considering the circumstances. I declare, I never got such a turn in my life. It's a dreadful thing. I must find Charles at once—there'll be a hundred things to do."

Eunice hardly heard her. Her mind was centered upon one idea. Christopher was ill—alone—she must go to him. It did not matter what his disease was. When Caroline came in from her breathless expedition to the barn, she found Eunice standing by the table, with her hat and shawl on, tying up a parcel.

"Eunice! Where on earth are you going?"

"Over home," said Eunice. "If Christopher is going to be ill he must be nursed, and I'm the one to do it. He ought to be seen to right away."

"Eunice Carr! Have you gone clean out of your senses? It's the smallpox—the smallpox! If he's got it he'll have to be taken to the smallpox hospital in town. You shan't stir a step to go to that house!"

"I will." Eunice faced her excited aunt quietly. The odd resemblance to her mother, which only came out in moments of great tension, was plainly visible. "He shan't go to that hospital—they never get proper attention there. You needn't try to stop me. It won't put you or your family in any danger."

Caroline fell helplessly into a chair. She felt that it would be of no use to argue with a woman so determined. She wished

Charles was there. But Charles had already gone, post-haste, for the doctor.

With a firm step, Eunice went across the field foot-path she had not trodden for so long. She felt no fear—rather a sort of elation. Christopher needed her once more; the interloper who had come between them was not there. As she walked through the frosty twilight she thought of the promise made to Naomi Holland, years ago.

Christopher saw her coming and waved her back.

"Don't come any nearer, Eunice. Didn't Caroline tell you? I'm taking smallpox."

Eunice did not pause. She went boldly through the yard and up the porch steps. He retreated before her and held the door.

"Eunice, you're crazy, girl! Go home, before it's too late."

Eunice pushed open the door resolutely and went in.

"It's too late now. I'm here, and I mean to stay and nurse you, if it's the smallpox you've got. Maybe it's not. Just now, when a person has a finger-ache, he thinks it's smallpox. Anyhow, whatever it is, you ought to be in bed and looked after. You'll catch cold. Let me get a light and have a look at you."

Christopher had sunk into a chair. His natural selfishness reasserted itself, and he made no further effort to dissuade Eunice. She got a lamp and set it on the table by him, while she scrutinized his face closely.

"You look feverish. What do you feel like? When did you take sick?"

"Yesterday afternoon. I have chills and hot spells and pains in my back. Eunice, do you think it's really smallpox? And will I die?"

He caught her hands, and looked imploringly up at her, as a child might have done. Eunice felt a wave of love and tenderness sweep warmly over her starved heart.

"Don't worry. Lots of people recover from smallpox if they're properly nursed, and you'll be that, for I'll see to it. Charles has gone for the doctor, and we'll know when he comes. You must go straight to bed."

She took off her hat and shawl, and hung them up. She felt as much at home as if she had never been away. She had got back to her kingdom, and there was none to dispute it with her. When Dr. Spencer and old Giles Blewett, who had had smallpox in his youth, came, two hours later, they found Eunice in serene charge. The house was in order and reeking with disinfectants. Victoria's fine furniture and fixings were being bundled out of the parlor. There was no bedroom downstairs, and, if Christopher was going to be ill, he must be installed there.

The doctor looked grave.

"I don't like it," he said, "but I'm not quite sure yet. If it is smallpox the eruption will probably be out by the morning. I must admit he has most of the symptoms. Will you have him taken to the hospital?"

"No," said Eunice, decisively. "I'll nurse him myself. I'm not afraid and I'm well and strong."

The doctor nodded.

"Very well. You've been vaccinated lately?"

"Yes."

"Well, nothing more can be done at present. You may as well lie down for a while and save your strength."

But Eunice could not do that. There was too much to attend to. She went out to the hall and threw up the window. Down below, at a safe distance, Charles Holland was waiting. The cold wind blew up to Eunice the odor of the disinfectants with which he had steeped himself.

"What does the doctor say?" he shouted.

"He thinks it's the smallpox. Have you sent word to Victoria?"

"Yes, Jim Blewett drove into town and told her. She'll stay with her sister till it is over. Of course it's the best thing for her to do. She's terribly frightened."

Eunice's lip curled contemptuously. To her, a wife who could desert her husband, no matter what disease he had, was an incomprehensible creature. But it was better so; she would have Christopher all to herself.

The night was long and wearisome, but the morning came all too soon for the dread certainty it brought. The doctor pronounced the case smallpox. Eunice had hoped against hope, but now, knowing the worst, she was very calm and resolute.

By noon the fateful yellow flag was flying over the house, and all arrangements had been made. Caroline was to do the necessary cooking, and Charles was to bring the food and leave it in the yard. Old Giles Blewett was to come every day and attend to the stock, as well as help Eunice with the sick man; and the long, hard fight with death began.

It was a hard fight, indeed. Christopher Holland, in the clutches of the loathsome disease, was an object from which his nearest and dearest might have been pardoned for shrinking. But Eunice never faltered; she never left her post. Sometimes she dozed in a chair by the bed, but she never lay down. Her endurance was something wonderful, her patience and tenderness almost superhuman. To and fro she went, in noiseless ministry, as the long, dreadful days wore away, with a quiet smile on her lips, and in her dark, sorrowful eyes the rapt look of a pictured saint in some dim cathedral niche. For her there was no world outside the bare room where lay the repulsive object she loved.

One day the doctor looked very grave. He had grown well-hardened to pitiful scenes in his lifetime; but he shrank from telling Eunice that her brother could not live. He had never seen such devotion as hers. It seemed brutal to tell her that it had been in vain.

But Eunice had seen it for herself. She took it very calmly, the doctor thought. And she had her reward at last—such as it was. She thought it amply sufficient.

One night Christopher Holland opened his swollen eyes as she bent over him. They were alone in the old house. It was raining outside, and the drops rattled noisily on the panes.

Christopher smiled at his sister with parched lips, and put out a feeble hand towards her.

"Eunice," he said faintly, "you've been the best sister ever a man had. I haven't treated you right; but you've stood by me to the last. Tell Victoria—tell her—to be good to you—"

His voice died away into an inarticulate murmur. Eunice Carr was alone with her dead.

They buried Christopher Holland in haste and privacy the next day. The doctor disinfected the house, and Eunice was to stay there alone until it might be safe to make other arrangements. She had not shed a tear; the doctor thought she was a rather odd person, but he had a great admiration for her. He told her she was the best nurse he had ever seen. To Eunice, praise or blame mattered nothing. Something in her life had snapped—some vital interest had departed. She wondered how she could live through the dreary, coming years.

Late that night she went into the room where her mother and brother had died. The window was open and the cold, pure air was grateful to her after the drug-laden atmosphere she had breathed so long. She knelt down by the stripped bed.

"Mother," she said aloud, "I have kept my promise."

When she tried to rise, long after, she staggered and fell across the bed, with her hand pressed on her heart. Old Giles Blewett found her there in the morning. There was a smile on her face.

THE CONSCIENCE CASE OF DAVID BELL

EBEN BELL came in with an armful of wood and banged it cheerfully down in the box behind the glowing Waterloo stove, which was coloring the heart of the little kitchen's gloom with tremulous, rose-red whirls of light.

"There, sis, that's the last chore on my list. Bob's milking. Nothing more for me to do but put on my white collar for meeting. Avonlea is more than lively since the evangelist came, ain't it, though!"

Mollie Bell nodded. She was curling her hair before the tiny mirror that hung on the whitewashed wall and distorted her round, pink-and-white face into a grotesque caricature.

"Wonder who'll stand up tonight," said Eben reflectively, sitting down on the edge of the wood-box. "There ain't many sinners left in Avonlea—only a few hardened chaps like myself."

"You shouldn't talk like that," said Mollie rebukingly. "What if father heard you?"

"Father wouldn't hear me if I shouted it in his ear," returned Eben. "He goes around, these days, like a man in a dream and a mighty bad dream at that. Father has always been a good man. What's the matter with him?"

"I don't know," said Mollie, dropping her voice. "Mother is dreadfully worried over him. And everybody is talking, Eb. It

541

just makes me squirm. Flora Jane Fletcher asked me last night why father never testified, and him one of the elders. She said the minister was perplexed about it. I felt my face getting red."

"Why didn't you tell her it was no business of hers?" said Eben angrily. "Old Flora Jane had better mind her own business."

"But all the folks are talking about it, Eb. And mother is fretting her heart out over it. Father has never acted like himself since these meetings began. He just goes there night after night, and sits like a mummy, with his head down. And almost everybody else in Avonlea has testified."

"Oh, no, there's lots haven't," said Eben. "Matthew Cuthbert never has, nor Uncle Elisha, nor any of the Whites."

"But everybody knows they don't believe in getting up and testifying, so nobody wonders when they don't. Besides," Mollie laughed—"Matthew could never get a word out in public, if he did believe in it. He'd be too shy. But," she added with a sigh, "it isn't that way with father. He believes in testimony, so people wonder why he doesn't get up. Why, even old Josiah Sloane gets up every night."

"With his whiskers sticking out every which way, and his hair ditto," interjected the graceless Eben.

"When the minister calls for testimonials and all the folks look at our pew, I feel ready to sink through the floor for shame," sighed Mollie. "If father would get up just once!"

Miriam Bell now entered the kitchen. She was ready for the meeting, to which Major Spencer was to take her. She was a tall, pale girl, with a serious face, and dark, thoughtful eyes, totally unlike Mollie. She had "come under conviction" during the meetings, and had stood up for prayer and testimony several times. The evangelist thought her very spiritual. She heard Mollie's concluding sentence and spoke reprovingly.

"You shouldn't criticize your father, Mollie. It isn't for you to judge him."

Eben had hastily slipped out. He was afraid Miriam would begin talking religion to him if he stayed. He had with difficulty escaped from an exhortation by Robert in the cow-stable. There was no peace in Avonlea for the unregenerate, he reflected. Robert and Miriam had both "come out," and Mollie was hovering on the brink.

"Dad and I are the black sheep of the family," he said, with a laugh, for which he at once felt guilty. Eben had been brought up with a strict reverence for all religious matters. On the surface he might sometimes laugh at them, but the deeps troubled him whenever he did so.

Indoors, Miriam touched her younger sister's shoulder and looked at her affectionately.

"Won't you decide tonight, Mollie?" she asked, in a voice tremulous with emotion.

Mollie crimsoned and turned her face away uncomfortably. She did not know what answer to make, and was glad that a jingle of bells outside saved her the necessity of replying.

"There's your beau, Miriam," she said, as she darted into the sitting room.

Soon after, Eben brought the family pung and his chubby red mare to the door for Mollie. He had not as yet attained to the dignity of a cutter of his own. That was for his elder brother, Robert, who presently came out in his new fur coat and drove dashingly away with bells and glitter.

"Thinks he's the people," remarked Eben, with a fraternal grin.

The rich winter twilight was purpling over the white world as they drove down the lane under the over-arching wild cherry trees that glittered with gemmy hoar-frost. The snow creaked and crisped under the runners. A shrill wind was keening in the leafless dogwoods. Over the trees the sky was a dome of silver, with a lucent star or two on the slope of the west. Earth-stars gleamed warmly out here and there, where homesteads were tucked snugly away in their orchards or groves of birch.

"The church will be jammed tonight," said Eben. "It's so fine that folks will come from near and far. Guess it'll be exciting."

"If only father would testify!" sighed Mollie, from the bottom of the pung, where she was snuggled amid furs and straw. "Miriam can say what she likes, but I do feel as if we were all disgraced. It sends a creep all over me to hear Mr. Bentley say, 'Now, isn't there one more to say a word for Jesus?' and look right over at father."

Eben flicked his mare with his whip, and she broke into a trot. The silence was filled with a faint, fairy-like melody from afar down the road where a pungful of young folks from White

Sands were singing hymns on their way to meeting.

"Look here, Mollie," said Eben awkwardly at last, "are you going to stand up for prayers tonight?"

"I—I can't as long as father acts this way," answered Mollie, in a choked voice. "I—I want to, Eb, and Mirry and Bob want me to, but I can't. I do hope that the evangelist won't come and talk to me special tonight. I always feel as if I was being pulled two different ways, when he does."

Back in the kitchen at home Mrs. Bell was waiting for her husband to bring the horse to the door. She was a slight, dark-eyed little woman, with thin, vivid-red cheeks. From out of the swathings in which she had wrapped her bonnet, her face gleamed sad and troubled. Now and then she sighed heavily.

The cat came to her from under the stove, languidly stretching himself, and yawning until all the red cavern of his mouth and throat was revealed. At the moment he had an uncanny resemblance to Elder Joseph Blewett of White Sands—Roaring Joe, the irreverent boys called him—when he grew excited and shouted. Mrs. Bell saw it—and then reproached herself for the sacrilege.

"But it's no wonder I've wicked thoughts," she said, wearily. "I'm that worried I ain't rightly myself. If he would only tell me what the trouble is, maybe I could help him. At any rate, I'd *know*. It hurts me so to see him going about, day after day, with his head hanging and that look on his face, as if he had something fearful on his conscience—him that never harmed a living soul. And then the way he groans and mutters in his sleep! He has always lived a just, upright life. He hasn't no right to go on like this, disgracing his family."

Mrs. Bell's angry sob was cut short by the sleigh at the door. Her husband poked in his bushy, iron-gray head and said, "Now, mother." He helped her into the sleigh, tucked the rugs warmly around her, and put a hot brick at her feet. His solicitude hurt her. It was all for her material comfort. It did not matter to him what mental agony she might suffer over his strange attitude. For the first time in their married life Mary Bell felt resentment against her husband.

They drove along in silence, past the snow-powdered hedges of spruce, and under the arches of the forest roadways. They were late, and a great stillness was over all the land. David

Bell never spoke. All his usual cheerful talkativeness had disappeared since the revival meetings had begun in Avonlea. From the first he had gone about as a man over whom some strange doom is impending, seemingly oblivious to all that might be said or thought of him in his own family or in the church. Mary Bell thought she would go out of her mind if her husband continued to act in this way. Her reflections were bitter and rebellious as they sped along through the glittering night of the winter's prime.

"I don't get one bit of good out of the meetings," she thought resentfully. "There ain't any peace or joy for me, not even in testifying myself, when David sits there like a stick or stone. If he'd been opposed to the revivalist coming here, like old Uncle Jerry, or if he didn't believe in public testimony, I wouldn't mind. I'd understand. But, as it is, I feel dreadful humiliated."

Revival meetings had never been held in Avonlea before. "Uncle" Jerry MacPherson, who was the supreme local authority in church matters, taking precedence of even the minister, had been uncompromisingly opposed to them. He was a stern, deeply religious Scotchman, with a horror of the emotional form of religion. As long as Uncle Jerry's spare, ascetic form and deeply-graved square-jawed face filled his accustomed corner by the northeast window of Avonlea church no revivalist might venture therein, although the majority of the congregation, including the minister, would have welcomed one warmly.

But now Uncle Jerry was sleeping peacefully under the tangled grasses and white snows of the burying ground, and, if dead people ever do turn in their graves, Uncle Jerry might well have turned in his when the revivalist came to Avonlea church, and there followed the emotional services, public testimonies, and religious excitement which the old man's sturdy soul had always abhorred.

Avonlea was a good field for an evangelist. The Rev. Geoffrey Mountain, who came to assist the Avonlea minister in revivifying the dry bones thereof, knew this and reveled in the knowledge. It was not often that such a virgin parish could be found nowadays, with scores of impressionable, unspoiled souls on which fervid oratory could play skillfully, as a master on a mighty organ, until every note in them thrilled to life and utterance. The Rev. Geoffrey Mountain was a good man; of the earth, earthy, to be sure, but with an unquestionable sincerity of belief and purpose which went far to counterbalance the sensationalism of some of his methods.

He was large and handsome, with a marvelously sweet and winning voice—a voice that could melt into irresistible tenderness, or swell into sonorous appeal and condemnation, or ring like a trumpet calling to battle.

His frequent grammatical errors, and lapses into vulgarity, counted for nothing against its charm, and the most commonplace words in the world would have borrowed much of the power of real oratory from its magic. He knew its value and used it effectively—perhaps even ostentatiously.

Geoffrey Mountain's religion and methods, like the man himself, were showy, but, of their kind, sincere, and, though the good he accomplished might not be unmixed, it was a quantity to be reckoned with.

So the Rev. Geoffrey Mountain came to Avonlea, conquering and to conquer. Night after night the church was crowded with eager listeners, who hung breathlessly on his words and wept and thrilled and exulted as he willed. Into many young souls his appeals and warnings burned their way, and each night they rose for prayer in response to his invitation. Older Christians, too, took on a new lease of intensity, and even the unregenerate and the scoffers found a certain fascination in the meetings. Threading through it all, for old and young, converted and unconverted, was an unacknowledged feeling for religious dissipation. Avonlea was a quiet place—and the revival meetings were lively.

When David and Mary Bell reached the church the services had begun, and they heard the refrain of a hallelujah hymn as they were crossing Harmon Andrews' field. David Bell left his wife at the platform and drove to the horse-shed.

Mrs. Bell unwound the scarf from her bonnet and shook the frost crystals from it. In the porch Flora Jane Fletcher and her sister, Mrs. Harmon Andrews, were talking in low whispers. Presently Flora Jane put out her lank, cashmere-gloved hand and plucked Mrs. Bell's shawl.

"Mary, is the elder going to testify tonight?" she asked, in a shrill whisper.

Mrs. Bell winced. She would have given much to be able to answer "Yes," but she had to say stiffly,

"I don't know."

Flora Jane lifted her chin.

"Well, Mrs. Bell, I only asked because every one thinks it is strange he doesn't—and an elder, of all people. It looks as if he didn't think himself a Christian, you know. Of course, we all know better, but it *looks* that way. If I was you, I'd tell him folks was talking about it. Mr. Bentley says it is hindering the full success of the meetings."

Mrs. Bell turned on her tormentor in swift anger. She might resent her husband's strange behavior herself, but nobody else should dare to criticize him to her.

"I don't think you need worry yourself about the elder, Flora Jane," she said bitingly. "Maybe 'tisn't the best Christians that do the most talking about it always. I guess, as far as living up to his profession goes, the elder will compare pretty favorably with Levi Boulter, who gets up and testifies every night, and cheats the very eye-teeth out of people in the daytime."

Levi Boulter was a middle-aged widower, with a large family, who was supposed to have cast a matrimonial eye Flora Jane-ward. The use of his name was an effective thrust on Mrs. Bell's part, and silenced Flora Jane. Too angry for speech she seized her sister's arm and hurried her into church.

But her victory could not remove from Mary Bell's soul the sting implanted there by Flora Jane's words. When her husband came up to the platform she put her hand on his snowy arm appealingly.

"Oh, David, won't you get up tonight? I do feel so dreadful bad—folks are talking so—I just feel humiliated."

David Bell hung his head like a shamed schoolboy.

"I can't, Mary," he said huskily. "'Tain't no use to pester me."

"You don't care for my feelings," said his wife bitterly. "And Mollie won't come out because you're acting so. You're keeping her back from salvation. And you're hindering the success of the revival—Mr. Bentley says so."

David Bell groaned. This sign of suffering wrung his wife's heart. With quick contrition she whispered,

"There, never mind, David. I oughtn't to have spoken to

you so. You know your duty best. Let's go in."

"Wait." His voice was imploring.

"Mary, is it true that Mollie won't come out because of me? Am I standing in my child's light?"

"I—don't—know. I guess not. Mollie's just a foolish young girl yet. Never mind—come in."

He followed her dejectedly in, and up the aisle to their pew in the center of the church. The building was warm and crowded. The pastor was reading the Bible lesson for the evening. In the choir, behind him, David Bell saw Mollie's girlish face, tinged with a troubled seriousness. His own wind-ruddy face and bushy gray eyebrows worked convulsively with his inward throes. A sigh that was almost a groan burst from him.

"I'll have to do it," he said to himself in agony.

When several more hymns had been sung, and late arrivals began to pack the aisles, the evangelist arose. His style for the evening was the tender, the pleading, the solemn. He modulated his tones to marvelous sweetness, and sent them thrillingly over the breathless pews, entangling the hearts and souls of his listeners in a mesh of subtle emotion. Many of the women began to cry softly. Fervent amens broke from some of the members. When the evangelist sat down, after a closing appeal which, in its way, was a masterpiece, an audible sigh of relieved tension passed like a wave over the audience.

After prayer the pastor made the usual request that, if any of those present wished to come out on the side of Christ, they would signify the wish by rising for a moment in their places. After a brief interval, a pale boy under the gallery rose, followed by an old man at the top of the church. A frightened, sweet-faced child of twelve got tremblingly upon her feet, and a dramatic thrill passed over the congregation when her mother suddenly stood up beside her. The evangelist's "Thank God" was hearty and insistent.

David Bell looked almost imploringly at Mollie; but she kept her seat, with downcast eyes. Over in the big square "stone pew" he saw Eben bending forward, with his elbows on his knees, gazing frowningly at the floor.

"I'm a stumbling block to them both," he thought bitterly.

A hymn was sung and prayer offered for those under conviction. Then testimonies were called for. The evangelist asked for them in tones which made it seem a personal request to every one in that building.

Many testimonies followed, each infused with the personality of the giver. Most of them were brief and stereotyped. Finally a pause ensued. The evangelist swept the pews with his kindling eyes and exclaimed, appealingly,

"Has *every* Christian in this church tonight spoken a word for his Master?"

There were many who had not testified, but every eye in the building followed the pastor's accusing glance to the Bell pew. Mollie crimsoned with shame. Mrs. Bell cowered visibly.

Although everybody looked thus at David Bell, nobody now expected him to testify. When he rose to his feet, a murmur of surprise passed over the audience, followed by a silence so complete as to be terrible. To David Bell it seemed to possess the awe of final judgment.

Twice he opened his lips, and tried vainly to speak. The third time he succeeded; but his voice sounded strangely in his own ears. He gripped the back of the pew before him with his knotty hands, and fixed his eyes unseeingly on the Christian Endeavor pledge that hung over the heads of the choir.

"Brethren and sisters," he said hoarsely, "before I can say a word of Christian testimony here tonight I've got something to confess. It's been lying hard and heavy on my conscience ever since these meetings begun. As long as I kept silence about it I couldn't get up and bear witness for Christ. Many of you have expected me to do it. Maybe I've been a stumbling block to some of you. This season of revival has brought no blessing to me because of my sin, which I repented of, but tried to conceal. There has been a spiritual darkness over me.

"Friends and neighbors, I have always been held by you as an honest man. It was the shame of having you know I was not which has kept me back from open confession and testimony. Just afore these meetings commenced I come home from town one night and found that somebody had passed a counterfeit ten-dollar bill on me. Then Satan entered into me and possessed me. When Mrs. Rachel Lynde come next day, collecting for foreign missions, I give her that ten dollar bill. She never knowed the difference, and sent it away with the rest. But I knew I'd done a mean and sinful thing. I couldn't drive it out of my thoughts. A few days afterwards I went down to Mrs. Rachel's and give her ten good dollars for the fund. I told her I had come to the conclusion I ought to give more than ten dollars, out of my abundance, to the Lord. That was a lie. Mrs. Lynde thought I was a generous man, and I felt ashamed to look her in the face. But I'd done what I could to right the wrong, and I thought it would be all right. But it wasn't. I've never known a minute's peace of mind or conscience since. I tried to cheat the Lord, and then tried to patch it up by doing something that redounded to my worldly credit. When these meetings begun, and everybody expected me to testify, I couldn't do it. It would have seemed like blasphemy. And I couldn't endure the thought of telling what I'd done, either. I argued it all out a thousand times that I hadn't done any real harm after all, but it was no use. I've been so wrapped up in my own brooding and misery that I didn't realize I was inflicting suffering on those dear to me by my conduct, and, maybe, holding some of them back from the paths of salvation. But my eyes have been opened to this tonight, and the Lord has given me strength to confess my sin and glorify His holy name."

The broken tones ceased, and David Bell sat down, wiping the great drops of perspiration from his brow. To a man of his training, and cast of thought, no ordeal could be more terrible than that through which he had just passed. But underneath the turmoil of his emotion he felt a great calm and peace, threaded with the exultation of a hard-won spiritual victory.

Over the whole church was a solemn hush. The evangelist's "amen" was not spoken with his usual unctuous fervor, but very gently and reverently. In spite of his coarse fiber, he could appreciate the nobility behind such a confession as this, and the deeps of stern suffering it sounded.

Before the last prayer the pastor paused and looked around.

"Is there yet one," he asked gently, "who wishes to be especially remembered in our concluding prayer?"

For a moment nobody moved. Then Mollie Bell stood up in the choir seat, and, down by the stove, Eben, his flushed, boyish face held high, rose sturdily to his feet in the midst of his companions.

"Thank God," whispered Mary Bell.

"Amen," said her husband, huskily.

"Let us pray," said Mr. Bentley.

ONLY A COMMON FELLOW

ON MY dearie's wedding morning I wakened early and went to her room. Long and long ago she had made me promise that I would be the one to wake her on the morning of her wedding day.

"You were the first to take me in your arms when I came into the world, Aunt Rachel," she had said, "and I want you to be the first to greet me on that wonderful day."

But that was long ago, and now my heart foreboded that there would be no need of wakening her. And there was not. She was lying there awake, very quiet, with her hand under her cheek, and her big blue eyes fixed on the window, through which a pale, dull light was creeping in—a joyless light it was, and enough to make a body shiver. I felt more like weeping than rejoicing, and my heart took to aching when I saw her there so white and patient, more like a girl who was waiting for a winding-sheet than for a bridal veil. But she smiled brave-like, when I sat down on her bed and took her hand.

"You look as if you haven't slept all night, dearie," I said.

"I didn't—not a great deal," she answered me. "But the night didn't seem long; no, it seemed too short. I was thinking of a great many things. What time is it, Aunt Rachel?"

"Five o'clock."

"Then in six hours more—"

She suddenly sat up in her bed, her great, thick rope of brown hair falling over her white shoulders, and flung her arms about me, and burst into tears on my old breast. I petted and soothed her, and said not a word; and, after a while, she stopped crying; but she still sat with her head so that I couldn't see her face.

"We didn't think it would be like this once, did we, Aunt Rachel?" she said, very softly.

"It shouldn't be like this, now," I said. I had to say it. I never could hide the thought of that marriage, and I couldn't pretend to. It was all her stepmother's doings—right well I knew that. My dearie would never have taken Mark Foster else.

"Don't let us talk of that," she said, soft and beseeching, just the same way she used to speak when she was a baby-child and wanted to coax me into something. "Let us talk about the old days—and *him.*"

"I don't see much use in talking of *him,* when you're going to marry Mark Foster today," I said.

But she put her hand on my mouth.

"It's for the last time, Aunt Rachel. After today I can never talk of him, or even think of him. It's four years since he went away. Do you remember how he looked, Aunt Rachel?"

"I mind well enough, I reckon," I said, kind of curt-like. And I did. Owen Blair hadn't a face a body could forget—that long face of his with its clean color and its eyes made to look love into a woman's. When I thought of Mark Foster's sallow skin and lank jaws I felt sick-like. Not that Mark was ugly—he was just a common-looking fellow.

"He was so handsome, wasn't he, Aunt Rachel?" my dearie went on, in that patient voice of hers. "So tall and strong and handsome. I wish we hadn't parted in anger. It was so foolish of us to quarrel. But it would have been all right if he had lived to come back. I know it would have been all right. I know he didn't carry any bitterness against me to his death. I thought once, Aunt Rachel, that I would go through life true to him, and then, over on the other side, I'd meet him just as before, all his and his only. But it isn't to be."

"Thanks to your stepma's wheedling and Mark Foster's scheming," said I.

"No, Mark didn't scheme," she said patiently. "Don't be unjust to Mark, Aunt Rachel. He has been very good and kind."

"He's as stupid as an owlet and as stubborn as Solomon's mule," I said, for I *would* say it. "He's just a common fellow, and yet he thinks he's good enough for my beauty."

"Don't talk about Mark," she pleaded again. "I mean to be a good, faithful wife to him. But I'm my own woman yet— *yet*—for just a few more sweet hours, and I want to give them to *him*. The last hours of my maidenhood—they must belong to *him.*"

So she talked of him, me sitting there and holding her, with her lovely hair hanging down over my arm, and my heart aching so for her that it hurt bitter. She didn't feel as bad as I did, because she'd made up her mind what to do and was resigned. She was going to marry Mark Foster, but her heart was in France, in that grave nobody knew of, where the Huns had buried Owen Blair—if they had buried him at all. And she went over all they had been to each other, since they were mites of babies, going to school together and meaning, even then, to be married when they grew up; and the first words of love he'd said to her, and what she'd dreamed and hoped for. The only thing she didn't bring up was the time he thrashed Mark Foster for bringing her apples. She never mentioned Mark's name; it was all Owen—Owen—and how he looked, and what might have been, if he hadn't gone off to the awful war and got shot. And there was me, holding her and listening to it all, and her stepma sleeping sound and triumphant in the next room.

When she had talked it all out she lay down on her pillow again. I got up and went downstairs to light the fire. I felt terrible old and tired. My feet seemed to drag, and the tears kept coming to my eyes, though I tried to keep them away, for well I knew it was a bad omen to be weeping on a wedding day.

Before long Isabella Clark came down; bright and pleased-looking enough, *she* was. I'd never liked Isabella, from the day

Phillippa's father brought her here; and I liked her less than ever this morning. She was one of your sly, deep women, always smiling smooth, and scheming underneath it. I'll say it for her, though, she had been good to Phillippa; but it was her doing that my dearie was to marry Mark Foster that day.

"Up betimes, Rachel," she said, smiling and speaking me fair, as she always did, and hating me in her heart, as I well knew. "That is right, for we'll have plenty to do today. A wedding makes lots of work."

"Not this sort of a wedding," I said, sour-like. "I don't call it a wedding when two people get married and sneak off as if they were ashamed of it—as well they might be in this case."

"It was Phillippa's own wish that all should be very quiet," said Isabella, as smooth as cream. "You know I'd have given her a big wedding, if she'd wanted it."

"Oh, it's better quiet," I said. "The fewer to see Phillippa marry a man like Mark Foster the better."

"Mark Foster is a good man, Rachel."

"No good man would be content to buy a girl as he's bought Phillippa," I said, determined to give it in to her. "He's a common fellow, not fit for my dearie to wipe her feet on. It's well that her mother didn't live to see this day; but this day would never have come, if she'd lived."

"I dare say Phillippa's mother would have remembered that Mark Foster is very well off, quite as readily as worse people," said Isabella, a little spitefully.

I liked her better when she was spiteful than when she was smooth. I didn't feel so scared of her then.

The marriage was to be at eleven o'clock, and, at nine, I went up to help Phillippa dress. She was no fussy bride, caring much what she looked like. If Owen had been the bridegroom it would have been different. Nothing would have pleased her then; but now it was only just "That will do very well, Aunt Rachel," without even glancing at it.

Still, nothing could prevent her from looking lovely when she was dressed. My dearie would have been a beauty in a beggarmaid's rags. In her white dress and veil she was as fair as a queen. And she was as good as she was pretty. It was the right sort of goodness, too, with just enough spice of original sin in it to keep it from spoiling by reason of over-sweetness.

Then she sent me out.

"I want to be alone my last hour," she said. "Kiss me, Aunt Rachel—*Mother* Rachel."

When I'd gone down, crying like the old fool I was, I heard a rap at the door. My first thought was to go out and send Isabella to it, for I supposed it was Mark Foster, come ahead of time, and small stomach I had for seeing him. I fall trembling, even yet, when I think, "What if I had sent Isabella to that door?"

But go I did, and opened it, defiant-like, kind of hoping it was Mark Foster to see the tears on my face. I opened it— and staggered back like I'd got a blow.

"Owen! Lord ha' mercy on us! Owen!" I said, just like that, going cold all over, for it's the truth that I thought it was his spirit come back to forbid that unholy marriage.

But he sprang right in, and caught my wrinkled old hands in a grasp that was of flesh and blood.

"Aunt Rachel, I'm not too late?" he said, savage-like. "Tell me I'm in time."

I looked up at him, standing over me there, tall and handsome, no change in him except he was so brown and had a little white scar on his forehead; and, though I couldn't understand it all, being all bewildered-like, I felt a great deep thankfulness.

"No, you're not too late," I said.

"Thank God," said he, under his breath. And then he pulled me into the parlor and shut the door.

"They told me at the station that Phillippa was to be married to Mark Foster today. I couldn't believe it, but I came here as fast as horse-flesh could bring me. Aunt Rachel, it can't be true! She can't care for Mark Foster, even if she had forgotten me!"

"It's true enough that she is to marry Mark," I said, half-laughing, half-crying, "but she doesn't care for him. Every beat of her heart is for you. It's all her stepma's doings. Mark has got a mortgage on the place, and he told Isabella Clark that, if Phillippa would marry him, he'd burn the mortgage, and, if she wouldn't, he'd foreclose. Phillippa is sacrificing herself to save her stepma for her dead father's sake. It's all your fault," I cried, getting over my bewilderment. "We thought you were dead. Why didn't you come home when you were alive? Why didn't you write?"

"I *did* write, after I got out of the hospital, several times," he said, "and never a word in answer, Aunt Rachel. What was I to think when Phillippa wouldn't answer my letters?"

"She never got one," I cried. "She wept her sweet eyes out over you. *Somebody* must have got those letters."

And I knew then, and I know now, though never a shadow of proof have I, that Isabella Clark had got them—and kept them. That woman would stick at nothing.

"Well, we'll sift that matter some other time," said Owen impatiently. "There are other things to think of now. I must see Phillippa."

"I'll manage it for you," I said eagerly; but, just as I spoke, the door opened and Isabella and Mark came in. Never shall I forget the look on Isabella's face. I almost felt sorry for her. She turned sickly yellow and her eyes went wild; they were looking at the downfall of all her schemes and hopes. I didn't look at Mark Foster, at first, and when I did, there wasn't anything to see. His face was just as sallow and wooden as ever; he looked undersized and common beside Owen. Nobody'd ever have picked him out for a bridegroom.

Owen spoke first.

"I want to see Phillippa," he said, as if it were but yesterday that he had gone away.

All Isabella's smoothness and policy had dropped away from her, and the real woman stood there, plotting and unscrupulous, as I'd always known her.

"You can't see her," she said desperate-like. "She doesn't want to see you. You went and left her and never wrote, and she knew you weren't worth fretting over, and she has learned to care for a better man."

"I *did* write and I think you know that better than most folks," said Owen, trying hard to speak quiet. "As for the rest, I'm not going to discuss it with you. When I hear from Phillippa's own lips that she cares for another man I'll believe it—and not before."

"You'll never hear it from her lips," said I.

Isabella gave me a venomous look.

"You'll not see Phillippa until she is a better man's wife," she said stubbornly, "and I order you to leave my house, Owen Blair."

"No!"

It was Mark Foster who spoke. He hadn't said a word; but he came forward now, and stood before Owen. Such a difference as there was between them! But he looked Owen right in the face, quiet-like, and Owen glared back in fury.

"Will it satisfy you, Owen, if Phillippa comes down here and chooses between us?"

"Yes, it will," said Owen.

Mark Foster turned to me.

"Go and bring her down," said he.

Isabella, judging Phillippa by herself, gave a little moan of despair, and Owen, blinded by love and hope, thought his cause was won. But I knew my dearie too well to be glad, and Mark Foster did, too, and I hated him for it.

I went up to my dearie's room, all pale and shaking. When I went in she came to meet me, like a girl going to meet death.

"Is—it—time?" she said, with her hands locked tight together.

I said not a word, hoping that the unlooked-for sight of Owen would break down her resolution. I just held out my hand to her, and led her downstairs. She clung to me and her hands were as cold as snow. When I opened the parlor door I stood back, and pushed her in before me.

She just cried "Owen!" and shook so that I put my arms about her to steady her.

Owen made a step towards her, his face and eyes all aflame with his love and longing, but Mark barred his way.

"Wait till she has made her choice," he said, and then he turned to Phillippa. I couldn't see my dearie's face, but I could see Mark's, and there wasn't a spark of feeling in it. Behind it was Isabella's, all pinched and gray.

"Phillippa," said Mark, "Owen Blair has come back. He says he has never forgotten you, and that he wrote to you several times. I have told him that you have promised me, but I leave you freedom of choice. Which of us will you marry, Phillippa?"

My dearie stood straight up and the trembling left her. She stepped back, and I could see her face, white as the dead, but calm and resolved.

"I have promised to marry you, Mark, and I will keep my word," she said.

The color came back to Isabella Clark's face; but Mark's did not change.

"Phillippa," said Owen, and the pain in his voice made my old heart ache bitterer than ever, "have you ceased to love me?"

My dearie would have been more than human, if she could have resisted the pleading in his tone. She said no word, but just looked at him for a moment. We all saw the look; her whole soul, full of love for Owen, showed out in it. Then she turned and stood by Mark.

Owen said never a word. He went as white as death, and started for the door. But again Mark Foster put himself in the way.

"Wait," he said. "She has made her choice, as I knew she would; but I have yet to make mine. And I choose to marry no woman whose love belongs to another living man. Phillippa, I thought Owen Blair was dead, and I believed that, when you were my wife, I could win your love. But I love you too well to make you miserable. Go to the man you love—you are free!"

"And what is to become of me?" wailed Isabella.

"Oh, you!—I had forgotten about you," said Mark, kind of weary-like. He took a paper from his pocket, and dropped it in the grate. "There is the mortgage. That is all you care about, I think. Goodmorning."

He went out. He was only a common fellow, but, somehow, just then he looked every inch the gentleman. I would have gone after him and said something but—the look on his face— no, it was no time for my foolish old words!

Phillippa was crying, with her head on Owen's shoulder. Isabella Clark waited to see the mortgage burned up, and then she came to me in the hall, all smooth and smiling again.

"Really, it's all very romantic, isn't it? I suppose it's better as it is, all things considered. Mark behaved splendidly, didn't he? Not many men would have done as he did."

For once in my life I agreed with Isabella. But I felt like having a good cry over it all—and I had it. I was glad for my dearie's sake and Owen's; but Mark Foster had paid the price of their joy, and I knew it had beggared him of happiness for life.

TANNIS OF THE FLATS

FEW PEOPLE in Avonlea could understand why Elinor Blair had never married. She had been one of the most beautiful girls in our part of the Island and, as a woman of fifty, she was still very attractive. In her youth she had had ever so many beaux, as we of our generation well remembered; but, after her return from visiting her brother Tom in the Canadian North-west, more than twenty-five years ago, she had seemed to withdraw within herself, keeping all men at a safe, though friendly, distance. She had been a gay, laughing girl when she went West; she came back quiet and serious, with a shadowed look in her eyes which time could not quite succeed in blotting out.

Elinor had never talked much about her visit, except to describe the scenery and the life, which in that day was rough indeed. Not even to me, who had grown up next door to her and who had always seemed more a sister than a friend, did she speak of other than the merest commonplaces. But when Tom Blair made a flying trip back home, some ten years later, there were one or two of us to whom he related the story of Jerome Carey—a story revealing only too well the reason for Elinor's sad eyes and utter indifference to masculine attentions. I can recall almost his exact words and the inflections of his

561

voice, and I remember, too, that it seemed to me a far cry
from the tranquil, pleasant scene before us, on that lovely
summer day, to the elemental life of the Flats.

The Flats was a forlorn little trading station fifteen miles up
the river from Prince Albert, with a scanty population of half-
breeds and three white men. When Jerome Carey was sent to
take charge of the telegraph office there, he cursed his fate in
the picturesque language permissible in the far Northwest.

Not that Carey was a profane man, even as men go in the
West. He was an English gentleman, and he kept both his life
and his vocabulary pretty clean. But—the Flats!

Outside of the ragged cluster of log shacks, which comprised
the settlement, there was always a shifting fringe of teepees
where the Indians, who drifted down from the Reservation;
camped with their dogs and squaws and papooses. There are
standpoints from which Indians are interesting, but they cannot
be said to offer congenial social attractions. For three weeks
after Carey went to the Flats he was lonelier than he had ever
imagined it possible to be, even in the Great Lone Land. If it
had not been for teaching Paul Dumont the telegraphic code,
Carey believed that he would have been driven to suicide in
self-defense.

The telegraphic importance of the Flats consisted in the fact
that it was the starting point of three telegraph lines to remote
trading posts up North. Not many messages came therefrom,
but the few that did come generally amounted to something
worth while. Days and even weeks would pass without a single
one being clicked to the Flats. Carey was debarred from talking
over the wires to the Prince Albert man for the reason that
they were on officially bad terms. He blamed the latter for his
transfer to the Flats.

Carey slept in a loft over the office, and got his meals at
Joe Esquint's, across the "street." Joe Esquint's wife was a good
cook, as cooks go among the breeds, and Carey soon became
a great pet of hers. Carey had a habit of becoming a pet with
women. He had the "way" that has to be born in a man and
can never be acquired. Besides, he was as handsome as clean-
cut features, deep-set, dark-blue eyes, fair curls and six feet of
muscle could make him. Mrs. Joe Esquint thought that his

mustache was the most wonderfully beautiful thing, in its line, that she had ever seen.

Fortunately, Mrs. Joe was so old and fat and ugly that even the malicious and inveterate gossip of skulking breeds and Indians, squatting over teepee fires, could not hint at anything questionable in the relations between her and Carey. But it was a different matter with Tannis Dumont.

Tannis came home from the academy at Prince Albert early in July, when Carey had been at the Flats a month and had exhausted all the few novelties of his position. Paul Dumont had already become so expert at the code that his mistakes no longer afforded Carey any fun, and the latter was getting desperate. He had serious intentions of throwing up the business altogether, and betaking himself to an Alberta ranch, where at least one would have the excitement of roping horses. When he saw Tannis Dumont he thought he would hang on a while longer, anyway.

Tannis was the daughter of old Auguste Dumont, who kept the one small store at the Flats, lived in the one frame house that the place boasted, and was reputed to be worth an amount of money which, in half-breed eyes, was a colossal fortune. Old Auguste was black and ugly and notoriously bad-tempered. But Tannis was a beauty.

Tannis' great-grandmother had been a Cree squaw who married a French trapper. The son of this union became in due time the father of Auguste Dumont. Auguste married a woman whose mother was a French half-breed and whose father was a pure-bred Highland Scotchman. The result of this atrocious mixture was its justification—Tannis of the Flats—who looked as if all the blood of all the Howards might be running in her veins.

But, after all, the dominant current in those same veins was from the race of plain and prairie. The practiced eye detected it in the slender stateliness of carriage, in the graceful, yet voluptuous, curves of the lithe body, in the smallness and delicacy of hand and foot, in the purple sheen on straight-falling masses of blue-black hair, and, more than all else, in the long, dark eye, full and soft, yet alight with a slumbering fire. France, too, was responsible for somewhat in Tannis. It gave her a light step in place of the stealthy half-breed shuffle, it arched her red upper lip into a more tremulous bow, it lent a note of laughter to her voice and a sprightlier wit to her tongue. As for her red-headed Scotch grandfather, he had bequeathed her a somewhat whiter skin and ruddier bloom than is usually found in the breeds.

Old Auguste was mightily proud of Tannis. He sent her to school for four years in Prince Albert, bound that his girl should have the best. A High School course and considerable mingling in the social life of the town—for old Auguste was a man to be conciliated by astute politicians, since he controlled some two or three hundred half-breed votes—sent Tannis home to the Flats with a very thin, but very deceptive, veneer of culture and civilization overlying the primitive passions and ideas of her nature.

Carey saw only the beauty and the veneer. He made the mistake of thinking that Tannis was what she seemed to be— a fairly well-educated, up-to-date young woman with whom a friendly flirtation was just what it was with white womankind— the pleasant amusement of an hour or season. It was a mistake— a very big mistake. Tannis understood something of piano playing, something less of grammar and Latin, and something less still of social prevarications. But she understood absolutely nothing of flirtation. You can never get an Indian to see the sense of Platonics.

Carey found the Flats quite tolerable after the homecoming of Tannis. He soon fell into the habit of dropping into the Dumont house to spend the evening, talking with Tannis in the parlor—which apartment was amazingly well done for a place like the Flats—Tannis had not studied Prince Albert parlors four years for nothing—or playing violin and piano duets with her. When music and conversation palled, they went for long gallops over the prairies together. Tannis rode to perfection, and managed her bad-tempered brute of a pony with a skill and grace that made Carey applaud her. She was glorious on horseback.

Sometimes he grew tired of the prairies and then he and Tannis paddled themselves over the river in Nitchie Joe's dugout, and landed on the old trail that struck straight into the wooded belt of the Saskatchewan valley, leading north to trading posts on the frontier of civilization. There they rambled under huge pines, hoary with the age of centuries, and Carey talked to Tannis about England and quoted poetry to her. Tannis liked poetry; she had studied it at school, and understood it fairly well. But once she told Carey that she thought it a long, round-about way of saying what you could say just as well in about a dozen plain words. Carey laughed. He liked to evoke those little speeches of hers. They sounded very clever, dropping from such arched, ripely-tinted lips.

If you had told Carey that he was playing with fire he would have laughed at you. In the first place he was not in the slightest degree in love with Tannis—he merely admired and liked her. In the second place, it never occurred to him that Tannis might be in love with him. Why, he had never attempted any love-making with her! And, above all, he was obsessed with that aforesaid fatal idea that Tannis was like the women he had associated with all his life, in reality as well as in appearance. He did not know enough of the racial characteristics to understand.

But, if Carey thought that his relationship with Tannis was that of friendship merely, he was the only one at the Flats who did think so. All the half-breeds and quarter-breeds and any-fractional breeds there believed that he meant to marry Tannis. There would have been nothing surprising to them in that. They did not know that Carey's second cousin was a baronet, and they would not have understood that it need make any difference, if they had. They thought that rich old Auguste's heiress, who had been to school for four years in Prince Albert, was a catch for anybody.

Old Auguste himself shrugged his shoulders over it and was well-pleased enough. An Englishman was a prize by way of a husband for a half-breed girl, even if he were only a telegraph operator. Young Paul Dumont worshipped Carey, and the half-Scotch mother, who might have understood, was dead. In all the Flats there were but two people who disapproved of the match they thought an assured thing. One of these was the little priest, Father Gabriel. He liked Tannis, and he liked Carey; but he shook his head dubiously when he heard the gossip of the shacks and teepees. Religions might mingle, but the different bloods—ah, it was not the right thing! Tannis was a good girl, and a beautiful one; but she was no fit mate for the fair, thorough-bred Englishman. Father Gabriel wished fervently that Jerome Carey might soon be transferred elsewhere. He even went to Prince Albert and did a little wire-pulling on his own account, but nothing came of it. He was on the wrong side of politics.

The other malcontent was Lazarre Mérimée, a lazy, besotted French half-breed, who was, after his fashion, in love with Tannis. He could never have got her, and he knew it—old Auguste and young Paul would have incontinently riddled him with bullets had he ventured near the house as a suitor,—but he hated Carey none the less, and watched for a chance to do him an ill-turn. There is no worse enemy in all the world than a half-breed. Your true Indian is bad enough, but his diluted descendant is ten times worse.

As for Tannis, she loved Carey with all her heart, and that was all there was about it.

If Elinor Blair had never gone to Prince Albert there is no knowing what might have happened, after all. Carey, so powerful in propinquity, might even have ended by learning to love Tannis and marrying her, to his own worldly undoing. But Elinor did go to Prince Albert, and her going ended all things for Tannis of the Flats.

Carey met her one evening in September, when he had ridden into town to attend a dance, leaving Paul Dumont in charge of the telegraph office. Elinor had just arrived in Prince Albert on a visit to Tom, to which she had been looking forward during the five years since he had married and moved out West from Avonlea. As I have already said, she was very beautiful at that time, and Carey fell in love with her at the first moment of their meeting.

During the next three weeks he went to town nine times and called at Dumonts' only once. There were no more rides and walks with Tannis. This was not intentional neglect on his part. He had simply forgotten all about her. The breeds surmised a lover's quarrel, but Tannis understood. There was another woman back there in town.

It would be quite impossible to put on paper any adequate idea of her emotions at this stage. One night, she followed Carey when he went to Prince Albert, riding out of earshot, behind him on her plains pony, but keeping him in sight. Lazarre, in a fit of jealousy, had followed Tannis, spying on her until she started back to the Flats. After that he watched both Carey and Tannis incessantly, and months later had told Tom all he had learned through his low sneaking.

Tannis trailed Carey to the Blair house, on the bluffs above the town, and saw him tie his horse at the gate and enter. She, too, tied her pony to a poplar, lower down, and then crept stealthily through the willows at the side of the house until she was close to the windows. Through one of them she could see Carey and Elinor. The half-breed girl crouched down in the shadow and glared at her rival. She saw the pretty, fair-tinted face, the fluffy coronal of golden hair, the blue, laughing eyes of the woman whom Jerome Carey loved, and she realized very plainly that there was nothing left to hope for. She, Tannis of the Flats, could never compete with that other. It was well to know so much, at least.

After a time, she crept softly away, loosed her pony, and lashed him mercilessly with her whip through the streets of the town and out the long, dusty river trail. A man turned and looked after her as she tore past a brightly lighted store on Water Street.

"That was Tannis of the Flats," he said to a companion. "She was in town last winter, going to school—a beauty and a bit of a devil, like all those breed girls. What in thunder is she riding like that for?"

One day, a fortnight later, Carey went over the river alone for a ramble up the northern trail, and an undisturbed dream of Elinor. When he came back Tannis was standing at the canoe landing, under a pine tree, in a rain of finely sifted sunlight. She was waiting for him and she said, without any preface:

"Mr. Carey, why do you never come to see me, now?"

Carey flushed like any girl. Her tone and look made him feel very uncomfortable. He remembered, self-reproachfully, that he must have seemed very neglectful, and he stammered something about having been busy.

"Not very busy," said Tannis, with her terrible directness. "It is not that. It is because you are going to Prince Albert to see a white woman!"

Even in his embarrassment Carey noted that this was the first time he had ever heard Tannis use the expression, "a white woman," or any other that would indicate her sense of a difference between herself and the dominant race. He understood, at the same moment, that this girl was not to be trifled with—that she would have the truth out of him, first or last. But he felt indescribably foolish.

"I suppose so," he answered lamely.

"And what about me?" asked Tannis.

When you come to think of it, this was an embarrassing question, especially for Carey, who had believed that Tannis understood the game, and played it for its own sake, as he did.

"I don't understand you, Tannis," he said hurriedly.

"You have made me love you," said Tannis.

The words sound flat enough on paper. They did not sound flat to Tom, as repeated by Lazarre, and they sounded anything but flat to Carey, hurled at him as they were by a woman trembling with all the passions of her savage ancestry. Tannis had justified her criticism of poetry. She had said her half-dozen words, instinct with all the despair and pain and wild appeal that all the poetry in the world had ever expressed.

They made Carey feel like a scoundrel. All at once he realized how impossible it would be to explain matters to Tannis, and that he would make a still bigger fool of himself, if he tried.

"I am very sorry," he stammered, like a whipped schoolboy.

"It is no matter," interrupted Tannis violently. "What difference does it make about me—a half-breed girl? We breed girls are only born to amuse the white men. That is so—is it not? Then, when they are tired of us, they push us aside and go back to their own kind. Oh, it is very well. But I will not forget—my father and brother will not forget. They will make you sorry to some purpose!"

She turned, and stalked away to her canoe. He waited under the pines until she crossed the river; then he, too, went miserably home. What a mess he had contrived to make of things! Poor Tannis! How handsome she had looked in her fury—and how much like a squaw! The racial marks always come out plainly under the stress of emotion, as Tom noted later.

Her threat did not disturb him. If young Paul and old Auguste made things unpleasant for him, he thought himself more than a match for them. It was the thought of the suffering he had brought upon Tannis that worried him. He had not, to be sure, been a villain; but he had been a fool, and that is almost as bad, under some circumstances.

The Dumonts, however, did not trouble him. After all, Tannis' four years in Prince Albert had not been altogether wasted. She knew that white girls did not mix their male relatives up in a vendetta when a man ceased calling on them—and she had nothing else to complain of that could be put in words. After some reflection she concluded to hold her tongue. She even laughed when old Auguste asked her what was up between her and her fellow, and said she had grown tired of him. Old Auguste shrugged his shoulders resignedly. It was just as well, maybe. Those English sons-in-law sometimes gave themselves too many airs.

So Carey rode often to town and Tannis bided her time, and plotted futile schemes of revenge, and Lazarre Mérimée scowled and got drunk—and life went on at the Flats as usual, until the last week in October, when a big wind and rainstorm swept over the northland.

It was a bad night. The wires were down between the Flats and Prince Albert and all communication with the outside world was cut off. Over at Joe Esquint's the breeds were having a carouse in honor of Joe's birthday. Paul Dumont had gone over, and Carey was alone in the office, smoking lazily and dreaming of Elinor.

Suddenly, above the plash of rain and whistle of wind, he heard outcries in the street. Running to the door he was met by Mrs. Joe Esquint, who grasped him breathlessly.

"Meestair Carey—come quick! Lazarre, he kill Paul—they fight!"

Carey, with a smothered oath, rushed across the street. He had been afraid of something of the sort, and had advised Paul not to go, for those half-breed carouses almost always ended in a free fight. He burst into the kitchen at Joe Esquint's, to find a circle of mute spectators ranged around the room and Paul and Lazarre in a clinch in the center. Carey was relieved to find it was only an affair of fists. He promptly hurled himself at the combatants and dragged Paul away, while Mrs. Joe Esquint—Joe himself being dead-drunk in a corner—flung her fat arms about Lazarre and held him back.

"Stop this," said Carey sternly.

"Let me get at him," foamed Paul. "He insulted my sister. He said that you—let me get at him!"

He could not writhe free from Carey's iron grip. Lazarre, with a snarl like a wolf, sent Mrs. Joe spinning, and rushed at Paul. Carey struck out as best he could, and Lazarre went reeling back against the table. It went over with a crash and the light went out!

Mrs. Joe's shrieks might have brought the roof down. In the confusion that ensued two pistol shots rang out sharply. There was a cry, a groan, a fall——then a rush for the door. When Mrs. Joe Esquint's sister-in-law, Marie, dashed in with another lamp, Mrs. Joe was still shrieking. Paul Dumont was leaning sickly against the wall with a dangling arm, and Carey lay face downward on the floor, with blood trickling from under him.

Marie Esquint was a woman of nerve. She told Mrs. Joe to shut up, and she turned Carey over. He was conscious, but seemed dazed and could not help himself. Marie put a coat under his head, told Paul to lie down on the bench, ordered Mrs. Joe to get a bed ready, and went for the doctor. It happened that there was a doctor at the Flats that night—a Prince Albert man who had been up at the Reservation, fixing up some sick Indians, and had been stormstaid at old Auguste's on his way back.

Marie soon returned with the doctor, old Auguste, and Tannis. Carey was carried in and laid on Mrs. Esquint's bed. The doctor made a brief examination, while Mrs. Joe sat on the floor and howled at the top of her lungs. Then he shook his head.

"Shot in the back," he said briefly.

"How long?" asked Carey, understanding.

"Perhaps till morning," answered the doctor. Mrs. Joe gave a louder howl than ever at this, and Tannis came and stood by the bed. The doctor, knowing that he could do nothing for Carey, hurried into the kitchen to attend to Paul, who had a badly shattered arm, and Marie went with him.

Carey looked stupidly at Tannis.

"Send for her," he said.

Tannis smiled cruelly.

"There is no way. The wires are down, and there is no man

at the Flats who will go to town tonight," she answered.

"My God, I *must* see her before I die," burst out Carey pleadingly. "Where is Father Gabriel? *He* will go."

"The priest went to town last night and has not come back," said Tannis.

Carey groaned and shut his eyes. If Father Gabrial was away, there was indeed no one to go. Old Auguste and the doctor could not leave Paul and he knew well that no breed of them all at the Flats would turn out on such a night, even if they were not, one and all, mortally scared of being mixed up in the law and justice that would be sure to follow the affair. He must die without seeing Elinor.

Tannis looked inscrutably down on the pale face on Mrs. Joe Esquint's dirty pillows. Her immobile features gave no sign of the conflict raging within her. After a short space she turned and went out, shutting the door softly on the wounded man and Mrs. Joe, whose howls had now simmered down to whines. In the next room Paul was crying out with pain as the doctor worked on his arm, but Tannis did not go to him. Instead, she slipped out and hurried down the stormy street to old Auguste's stable. Five minutes later she was galloping down the black, wind-lashed river trail, on her way to town, to bring Elinor Blair to her lover's deathbed.

I hold that no woman ever did anything more unselfish than this deed of Tannis! For the sake of love she put under her feet the jealousy and hatred that had clamored at her heart. She held, not only revenge, but the dearer joy of watching by Carey to the last, in the hollow of her hand, and she cast both away that the man she loved might draw his dying breath somewhat easier. In a white woman the deed would have been merely commendable. In Tannis of the Flats, with her ancestry and tradition, it was lofty self-sacrifice.

It was eight o'clock when Tannis left the Flats; it was ten when she drew bridle before the house on the bluff. Elinor was regaling Tom and his wife with Avonlea gossip when the maid came to the door.

"Pleas'm, there's a breed girl out on the verandah and she's asking for Miss Blair."

Elinor went out wonderingly, followed by Tom. Tannis, whip in hand, stood by the open door, with the stormy night behind her, and the warm ruby light of the hall lamp showering over her white face and the long rope of drenched hair that fell from her bare head. She looked wild enough.

"Jerome Carey was shot in a quarrel at Joe Esquint's tonight," she said. "He is dying—he wants you—I have come for you."

Elinor gave a little cry, and steadied herself on Tom's shoulder. Tom said he knew he made some exclamation of horror. He had never approved of Carey's attention to Elinor, but such news was enough to shock anybody. He was determined, however, that Elinor should not go out in such a night and to such a scene, and told Tannis so in no uncertain terms.

"I came through the storm," said Tannis contemptuously. "Cannot she do as much for him as I can?"

The good, old Island blood in Elinor's veins showed to some purpose. "Yes," she answered firmly. "No, Tom, don't object— I must go. Get my horse—and your own."

Ten minutes later three riders galloped down the bluff road and took the river trail. Fortunately the wind was at their backs and the worst of the storm was over. Still, it was a wild, black ride enough. Tom rode, cursing softly under his breath. He did not like the whole thing—Carey done to death in some low half-breed shack, this handsome, sullen girl coming as his messenger, this nightmare ride through wind and rain. It all savored too much of melodrama, even for the Northland, where people still did things in a primitive way. He heartily wished Elinor had never left Avonlea.

It was past twelve when they reached the Flats. Tannis was the only one who seemed to be able to think coherently. It was she who told Tom where to take the horses and who then led Elinor to the room where Carey was dying. The doctor was sitting by the bedside and Mrs. Joe was curled up in a corner, sniffling to herself. Tannis took her by the shoulder and turned her, none too gently, out of the room. The doctor, understanding, left at once. As Tannis shut the door she saw Elinor sink on her knees by the bed, and Carey's trembling hand go out to her head.

Tannis sat down on the floor outside of the door and wrapped herself up in a shawl Marie Esquint had dropped. In that attitude she looked exactly like a squaw, and all comers and goers, even old Auguste, who was hunting for her, thought she was one, and left her undisturbed. She watched there until dawn came whitely up over the prairies and Jerome Carey died. She knew when it happened by Elinor's cry.

Tannis sprang up and rushed in. She was too late for even a parting look.

The girl took Carey's hand in hers, and turned to the weeping Elinor with a cold dignity.

"Now go," she said. "You had him in life to the very last. He is mine now."

"There must be some arrangements made," faltered Elinor.

"My father and brother will make all arrangements, as you call them," said Tannis steadily. "He had no near relatives in the world—none at all in Canada—he told me so. You may send out a Protestant minister from town, if you like; but he will be buried here at the Flats and his grave will be mine— all mine! Go!"

And Elinor, reluctant, sorrowful, yet swayed by a will and an emotion stronger than her own, went slowly out, leaving Tannis of the Flats alone with her dead.